WHISPERS OF THE WILD

PATH OF DRAGONS

BOOK TWO

WHISPERS OF THE WILD

NICHOLAS SEARCY

Podium

Podium

THE PATH SO FAR . . .

I'm not sure why I'm writing this. Honestly, if somebody found it, they would probably think it was fiction. Or maybe the ramblings of a lunatic. Most of it sounds implausible, even to me, and I lived through it. So, yeah.

Even so, I keep reminding myself that tomorrow isn't guaranteed, and if something happens to me, I want there to be some sort of record of what happened. My family—wherever they are—deserves that much, even if they end up thinking I've lost my mind.

So, here it is—the story of how a terminally ill marine biologist managed to survive—and dare I say, thrive—in a world gone insane.

It all started when the World Tree extended its branches and touched Earth. Sounds a bit poetic, right? I guess it kind of is. But at the time, I was on a plane heading back from Hawaii to the mainland to die in peace. Cancer, and not the sort you can cure. Anyway, the idea was that I'd spend my last days with my sister and her family. You know, to make up for lost time.

Then, everything changed.

The World Tree's touch brought with it the System—a magical-upgrade-slash-apocalypse-delivery device—that rewrote the rules of reality. Suddenly, magic was a real thing. People had access to archetypes and classes that could potentially give them what amounted to superpowers. As for me, I became a Druid, and not by choice. It's hard to pick an archetype when you're in a plane crash. Still, the System did me a solid because, as it turns out, I have a knack for everything nature related. Who knew, right?

I guess it makes sense, what with my background. But still, it surprised me.

In any case, the System definitely knew what it was doing, which is probably the only reason I'm still breathing. Any other archetype, and I'd have ended up dead.

Not that survival came easy. After the plane crashed, I washed ashore only to find a bunch of mutated purple shore crabs trying—well, succeeding, really—in turning my legs into an afternoon snack. I managed to fend them off, then stumbled inland. That's when I discovered that I was utterly and completely alone.

Lots of people romanticize that kind of thing. Just a man and the wilderness, forming a spiritual connection with nature. I mean—that happened, but not until way later. In the aftermath of washing ashore, I was confronted with the very real terror that came with being so alone. No safety net. Just me and beautiful, brutal nature.

Definitely not a vacation, if you catch my drift.

But I made it work. Scavenging, hunting crabs, and fishing—it wasn't glamorous or easy, but it kept me alive. And I wasn't as alone as I thought, either. Sure, there were no people around, but there were a couple of other helpers. First, there was Nerthus—a sentient tree spirit who became a friend and something of a mentor. He guided me on the path of cultivation—a magical path that not only helped me survive, but also cured my cancer.

Take that, modern medicine.

Then there was the panther. Often silent. Usually unseen. Always terrifying. It wasn't some cuddly house cat, either. It was a sleek murder machine that, for reasons I didn't understand at the time, decided that I was worth protecting. While I focused on the mundanity of survival, it kept larger predators—like interdimensional lizard monsters—at bay.

Yeah. You heard that right. Interdimensional lizard monsters. But I won't go too deep into that. They were just one more danger I had to account for.

My relationship with the panther was simple. I ended up buying its tolerance by sharing with it whatever food I managed to acquire. It ate more than its share, but keeping my face uneaten by the aforementioned lizard monsters was worth every fish I threw its way.

For a while, things were going really well. I wasn't precisely thriving, but by that point, I didn't have to worry about where my next meal was coming from.

Things took a bad turn when I stumbled on the panther engaged in battle with a bunch of gnomes, goblins, and dwarves. Yeah—when the World Tree touched Earth, it didn't just bring magic. It brought company in the form of alien invaders. Or colonizers, maybe. Whatever word you use for them, this particular group wasn't friendly. I inexpertly fought alongside the panther, and together, we managed to win.

But the damage was done.

Being a Druid comes with a few healing spells, but I was too weak to save the panther. As it lay dying, we bonded. And when I say that, I mean I got a magical download of its deepest emotions. They amounted a single clear message.

End it.

I did, and it was one of the hardest things I'd done to that point. Mercy killing isn't a new concept. Pets are put down every day—or they were before the World Tree extended its influence onto Earth—but it's never easy. And in this case, it was even more difficult because I understood the panther on a much deeper level than I could truly handle.

Making it worse—or maybe better, I'm not entirely sure—was that the battle and killing the panther had given me a bunch of levels and access to a new class. I became an Animist, which sounds like someone that animates objects or communes with the spirits, right? Well, not according to the System. It gave me the ability to shape-shift into animals.

Look—I didn't name it. I just roll with it.

The first form I unlocked? A mist panther, eerily similar to the animal I'd just put down. It was bittersweet, to say the least. On the one hand, I couldn't help but be reminded of what I'd lost. But on the other, the transformation gave me increased attributes and all the survival skills of a wild hunting cat.

Catching food became a breeze. Navigating my island was a cinch. Even the weather couldn't touch me, courtesy of my built-in fur coat.

But power comes with responsibility, and the panther's old job—keeping the island safe—now fell to me. The island played host to dimensional rifts that acted as entry points for the Voxx—those interdimensional lizards I talked about before—and it was up to me to stop their corruptive influence. On the bright side, all the fighting that followed ended up pushing my level high enough to break into the top hundred globally.

Small victories and silver linings, I guess.

Then there was the tower. According to Nerthus, if I didn't deal with it, the island was toast. So, after getting a firsthand look at what he meant—and having to defend the island from an invasion of Voxx—I geared up and dove in.

The first level wasn't terrible—just a bunch of goblins, some improbably nice walrus people, and a magical ring that let me breathe underwater. The second level? That was a nightmare. It was entirely submerged and crawling with creatures that weren't shy about trying to turn me into lunch. Isopods the size of vans, turtles that could crush a motorcycle—you get the idea. The worst was the orca boss, who decided to literally swallow me whole.

If you've never been digested alive, I definitely do not recommend it.

In any case, I survived, and I made it to the third level. At first, I just thought it was a primordial jungle filled with dinosaurs and the Sasquatch-like monsters who hunted them. Fun stuff. My mist-panther instincts almost got the better of me, but after a while, I pulled through, finding a maze populated by velociraptors—think Jurassic Park, rather than the turkey-sized reality—made of roots, thorns, and leaves. I managed to navigate the maze, defeat the alpha raptor, then complete the tower.

That earned me a Shard of the World Tree as my reward, which Nerthus used to enhance the power of the grove.

Shortly after that, I got a quest from an unseen but insanely powerful being who needed me to rescue her daughter. Sounds noble, right? Except her daughter was a juvenile dragon, and her captor, Eason Cabbot, was a sadistic gnome berserker intent on siphoning her essence to use for his own progression. Long story short, I infiltrated the town—did I mention there was a fledgling city across the strait from my island?—killed a bunch of bad guys, and saved the dragon. When I got back to the island, Kirlissa whisked her daughter away and rewarded me with a Dragon Core, which affected me in all sorts of ways.

And I guess it put me on the Path of Dragons, but at the time, I just knew it gave me a bunch more power.

It was a good thing, too, because it wasn't long before Eason Cabbot came to my island with fifty mercenaries. I don't know if he'd tracked me or if he just thought the island held treasures that could help him, but it doesn't really matter. My reaction would have been the same regardless of their reasons for invading my island.

I annihilated them, killing all but one before sending her back to that little town across the strait with a message. Leave my island or face my wrath.

While I was doing all of this, my sister, Alyssa, was fighting her own battles. I didn't know it at the time, but as I was struggling to survive on my island, she was busy helping to establish a community of survivors on the mainland. In the end, she was betrayed by her closest friend, and during a tower run, Roman killed her.

It would take me a long time to find the truth of what happened. If I'd known, would it have changed anything? Maybe. Maybe not. But the past is unchangeable, and as I've long since discovered, dead is dead. All I can do now is keep moving forward.

Which is exactly what I did.

Whispers of the Wild

1

RECOVERY

Elijah watched Calix as she shoved one of the rowboats into the surf before she hopped aboard the small vessel and started paddling away. He didn't avert his eyes until almost twenty minutes later when the little boat—and the goblin Sorcerer it carried—disappeared behind a rolling wave. Only when she was out of sight did his shoulders finally sag in relief.

He knew that letting her go constituted a significant risk. There was every chance that, as soon as she reached Ironshore, she would gather as many fighters as she could find before leading them back to his island on a quest of vengeance. But he was also well aware of his own limitations. Certainly, if the entirety of the expedition had remained missing, they would be wary of setting foot on his island. They would also be curious, and that curiosity would eventually drive them back to the island.

Now, though, the goblin mage would tell her people precisely what had happened to her colleagues. Elijah had seen the fear in her eyes, and he suspected that she would do just about anything to avoid setting one foot on his island again. Hopefully, she would warn the other residents of Ironshore, telling them tales of brutality and death that would hopefully keep everyone away.

It was still a risky move, though, and one he hoped wouldn't come back to bite him. It wasn't that he had issues with killing the invaders. He clearly didn't. They'd come to his island with avarice in their hearts; that much was proved the moment they'd abducted and attempted to drain the young dragon, Saraalinisa.

Even so, Elijah was willing to live in peace, so long as they left him alone.

For now, though, he had other issues at hand—like cleaning up his island. He could feel every single dead body, and though he was tempted to let them rot, he chose another tactic. After all, he'd already dug a bunch of holes, hadn't he? He still needed to refill those traps—otherwise, the local wildlife might fall afoul of them—so throwing a few dead bodies into each one wouldn't really require much extra effort.

With that in mind, Elijah set off across his island and began the arduous task of gathering corpses. At first, he'd resolved to simply carry them, but the first few he'd killed had already begun to bloat, so he retreated to his Grove, gathered a few coils of homemade cordage as well as some of the old Ritualist's robes he'd intended to use to make clothes. Then, he stretched those robes between a pair of long, stout branches, tying them off before heading back to the first bodies.

The task of loading the litter was, in a word, disgusting—especially considering that he couldn't just toss them into place. Instead, he had to search the bodies first. The initial group—which was the first trio he'd ambushed the day before—had a few weapons, some clothes, and various leather goods like belts and pouches. Each subsequent group was much the same, though he also came away with a decent stash of curious coins. He'd seen their like before, but he hadn't taken the time to really examine them.

Now, he did, and he came away with a host of questions. First, each one emitted its own localized cloud of dense ethera. Second, they looked and felt like copper, though they were far lighter than they should have been. Knowing he wasn't going to figure it out anytime soon—not without Nerthus's input, at least—Elijah thrust the copper- and silver-colored coins into the largest pouch he'd looted.

Over the next couple of days, Elijah went through the bodies, one by one, and he even combed through the former campsite near the beach. He looted a ton of interesting items—tents, tools, and more cloth than he knew what to do with—but the one that excited him most was a small sewing kit he found on one of the goblins. Until then, Elijah had been forced to make do with needles of bone or crab shell, so the addition of a few good steel needles was a godsend. And he hoped it would let him sew some decent clothes.

He still wore nothing but a gnome-sized robe he'd repurposed into a makeshift kilt and tied around his waist with a bit of homemade cordage, so the sewing kit was a fantastic find, as was the rope he gathered from the campsite. However, the biggest score was when he uncovered a crate of dried meat, cheese, and bread.

Elijah stared at it in awe. For two years—or something like that—he'd been eating nothing but what he could hunt, fish, or gather. And while there was something to be said for mushrooms and wild edibles, the reality was that he'd never been a very good cook. More, even if he'd had the skill, he didn't have the spices to make any decent recipes work. So, aside from some wild onions he'd managed to grow in his garden, his cooking didn't feature much in the way of seasoning.

And that wasn't even considering the fact that, in the tower, he'd eaten his meals raw. Sometimes, that was as a panther, which somehow made it better, but he'd done so in his natural human form often enough that he would appreciate any bit of civilized food he could get.

Still, he didn't eat right away. Instead, he continued his task of burying the bodies, then took everything he'd gathered back to his Grove. It took a few trips because there was so much, and when he finally had everything in one place, he couldn't stifle an appreciative sigh.

"The Grove is secure?" came a familiar voice. Elijah looked up to see Nerthus perched on one of the steps leading up to his tree house.

"Yep. I let one go, though," he said. "I thought she might warn the others off."

"Do you think that will work?"

Elijah shrugged. "Honestly, I'm not sure. It'll probably keep them away for a while, but it's definitely not a permanent solution," he said. "If they're willing to kidnap a dragon, they won't be scared off by me. Not indefinitely."

"What do you intend to do?" Nerthus asked.

"For now? I want to eat my weight in dried meat and cheese," he answered. "Then, I'm going to keep going the same way I've been going. I don't know. I have a few projects in the back of my mind. Plus, I just want to rest for a while."

The tree spirit cocked his head to the side, then asked, "And what about when you get bored?"

Elijah shrugged. "Who says I'll get bored?"

"I do."

He sighed, then favored the tree spirit with a guilty smile. "Fine. Once I'm happy with the security of the Grove, I plan to explore a little," he said. "Branch out, you know? Maybe I can find my sister."

Nerthus said, "Hmm. Perhaps this is overstepping, but you may want to consider diplomatic relations with the settlement across the strait."

"What? Why?"

"They clearly have a Branch of the World Tree," Nerthus explained.

"I figured as much. That's how they got here, right? Through the World Tree."

"Yes, but not like you're thinking. When the World Tree touched this world, settlers were given the opportunity to come here," Nerthus said. "Some did so as representatives of larger organizations. From what you have told me, the people in Ironshore are like that. Others came to escape something in the more settled worlds. Still others came to take advantage of a virgin world and the progression that will inevitably come from taming it."

"Okay? What does that have to do with anything? I mean, don't get me wrong—it's interesting, I guess. But it doesn't really answer the question, does it?"

"Right. I was getting to that. Many of these colonizers brought Envoys with them," Nerthus went on. "The Branches they can summon are a little more advanced than the ones native to this world. So, in addition to the most basic functions, like accessing the Knowledge Base, Market, and Communications Apparatus, they will often come with the ability to detect additional settlements within a certain territory."

"I see," Elijah said. Indeed, if what Nerthus had said was true, then once he gained access to the Branch, he could use it as a guide to find the next closest settlement. Then that one could direct him to the next. And so on. Eventually, he would find Easton—or at least Seattle. At worst, he could find other people who could send him in the right direction.

It was as good of a plan to find his sister and her family as any he'd come up with. So far, the best he'd thought of was to simply roam around and search for signs of civilization, which he could readily admit was a bad plan.

The only problem was that the people of Ironshore weren't very likely to let him simply waltz into town and use their Branch. At best, they would refuse him entry. At worst, they would attack him on sight.

But then again, if there was one settlement like Ironshore around, then there were probably others, as well. And perhaps they would be more amenable to a good relationship.

Elijah shook his head and said, "I guess that's a start."

After that, Nerthus retreated into his tree, and Elijah set about the task of cataloging his new cache of supplies. Soon enough, he had everything sorted into separate piles. One pile held various weaponry—almost a dozen axes, at least as many staves, and a few swords—while another was composed of the clothing he'd stripped from the corpses. The next was a little smaller, and it contained various leather items ranging from belts and pouches to armor.

The next pile contained various bits of metallic armor. It was all valuable enough, though not to Elijah. If they'd been sized to fit him, it would have been one thing, but given that each piece was made for the much smaller dwarves, gnomes, and goblins, they were useless to him. However, he hoped that perhaps he could find some use for the metal. He was only basically familiar with blacksmithing methods, but he was willing to learn via trial and error.

The final pile had diverse odds and ends he'd found in camp. Pots and pans, cooking utensils, and various other tools were prominent.

"Aren't you a beauty," he said, holding up a large pot. For the longest time, he'd had to make do with an old, rusted, and far too small pot. But now, he was spoiled for choice, which would go a long way toward improving his quality of life.

In all, looting fifty corpses and the camp they'd built on the shore had proved extremely valuable, and Elijah couldn't help but feel a sense of optimism about life going forward. More than anything, though, he was looking forward to digging into the crate of food he'd taken.

Still, he took the time to head down to his garden, where he gathered a basket of berries and a handful of wild onions. Then, he went back to his tree house where he laid out a feast. He only took a few moments to admire the spread before he tore into with all the gusto of a man who hadn't eaten anything but poorly cooked crab, fish, and wild edibles for the past two years.

Which was to say, he quickly gorged himself.

The meal wasn't anything complicated. Generously, the contents of that crate would have been called travel rations. But still, it was better than anything Elijah had eaten in quite some time. And he enjoyed every last bite until, finally, he'd had enough. Once that was done, he stripped down, took a shower—using his homemade soap—and then went to bed.

But he didn't immediately go to sleep. Instead, he lay there for a long time, just staring at the gently glowing flowers on the ceiling. As he did, he thought back to what he'd been through for the past couple of years.

Sometimes, it was difficult to wrap his head around it all. From the moment he'd washed ashore, Elijah had struggled to survive. For the longest time, even getting enough food had been difficult, but gradually, he had adjusted. Along the way, he'd been forced to become a killer. Not only had he slain dozens of Voxx—the interdimensional lizard creatures who threatened the entire world—but he'd also slaughtered plenty of sentients as well. Goblins. Gnomes. Dwarves. He'd even fought and killed raptors that seemed like they were made of roots and moss.

More than anything, though, he had survived.

And he had protected his island. His Grove.

But now, Elijah felt like he'd turned a corner. Not just because he suddenly had a glut of supplies. That was part of it, but he'd also proved that he could stand toe-to-toe with anyone. So, with that in mind, he was running out of excuses not to venture out into the wider world, where he hoped to reunite with his sister and the rest of humanity.

It was with those thoughts enveloping his mind that he finally succumbed to a blessedly dreamless sleep.

2

A GREAT LOSS

Carmen hammered away at the hunk of steel, steadily shaping it until she finally achieved her goal—the blade of a utilitarian longsword. The result was nothing impressive, though she hoped that once she was finished, it would at least reach Crude grade so she could practice her enchanting. Either way, it would be a useful piece, if only by virtue of her skill. Even her failures were head and shoulders above what anything the other Blacksmiths in Easton could forge.

She was busy inspecting the cooling blade for any major flaws when she felt someone standing behind her. It was a trick she'd learned from her habit of constantly immersing herself in ethera; she could tell when someone was nearby, just by the way the ambient energy swirled around them. Still, she didn't turn as she said, "If you're here to put in an order, just know that I'm booked for at least three weeks solid. Longer, probably. So, I don't know when I'll be able to get to your project."

"It's not about that," came an unfamiliar voice. Carmen turned to see an older woman she didn't recognize. The newcomer carried a wicked-looking morning star strapped to her waist, but otherwise had a middle-aged, matronly look about her. The ethnicity was wrong, but still, the woman reminded Carmen of her abuela.

"Don't know you," Carmen said, crossing the smithy to a barrel full of clean water. She dipped her hands in, then splashed some of it on her face. "If you're not here to hire me, then what do you want?"

"It's the . . . uh . . . council," the woman said. "They want to see you."

"Yeah? Well, they can wait," she responded with no small degree of impatience. She'd long since grown weary of their petty bickering, and it had grown even worse since Alyssa and Roman had gone to conquer the tower. If they were self-serving before, then Carmen really didn't know a strong enough word to categorize their selfishness in Roman's absence. Hopefully, when the chief returned, he would set them straight.

Or maybe Alyssa would.

"It's important," the older woman stated.

Carmen sighed. "What's your name?"

"Verin."

"Well, Verin, do you know what I do?" she asked.

"You're a crafter."

"Right. But do you know what that really means? Every day, our hunters encounter stronger creatures. Monsters, really. Even the normal animals have gotten powerful enough to give a classer a good fight. Do you know why so many of them have survived?" she asked.

"Skill?"

Carmen chuckled. "Partially," she admitted. "But I can say with no false modesty that it's at least partly because of me. And people like me. I spend my days crafting armor and weapons so that the people who keep us safe can fight the things that, with every passing day, get a bit better at trying to kill us. So, with all due respect—I don't come running when those assholes in the council whistle for me."

She frowned. "Roman is there," she said.

"What?"

"Roman is back from the tower."

Carmen broke into a wide grin. It was the wonderful news she'd been waiting to hear, though if Alyssa hadn't come straight to find her, then that meant something had gone wrong. Had they failed in conquering the tower? Was there some other threat? Probably the latter, given the pattern since the apocalypse had started.

"Well, why didn't you lead with that, then? Come on. Let's go see what's going on."

Verin looked like she wanted to respond, but then clearly thought better of it. Not that Carmen much cared. She was already striding toward the door before she even finished her sentence. After passing through and into the street, she paused only long enough to ensure that Verin had followed. Then, once she'd locked her door—Easton was a fairly orderly place, but thievery was still a problem—she strode off through the settlement and toward the five-story government building. Once, it had been a two-story police station, but as the little settlement had grown into a proper city, the Architects and Builders had worked overtime to add more space. A good thing, too, because with a population that had climbed into the high five-digit range, it took quite a lot of people to ensure that everything ran smoothly.

Still, as Carmen joined the throng of pedestrians—they still hadn't figured out how to get any motorized form of transportation but electric cars to work, and even those had been deemed mostly useless because of how inconvenient they were—she barely noticed the city's growth. Once, it had only been a collection of ramshackle huts, but now, the structures were strong and sturdy as well as architecturally interesting. Even the streets had been paved with cobblestones, giving Easton an atmosphere that hovered between that of a modern city and something from a bygone era.

The people themselves wore an eclectic mixture of contemporary clothing from before Earth had been touched by the World Tree and the latest from the city's Tailors. There were people wearing blue jeans walking side by side with those clad in elaborate robes. Some people, it seemed, had taken the magical nature of their transformed world as an excuse to indulge some eclectic stylistic choices.

There were plenty of people wearing armor, as well. Some were Guards, as denoted by the standard-issue chain mail and sky-blue sashes of their offices, but others were the people tasked with patrolling the outskirts for threats to the city. Carmen had been on a few such hunts, so she recognized the necessity of armor, even if it was a bit mismatched, as was the case with those fighters.

Gradually, the pair of women made their way to the government building. There had been talk about renaming it, but getting the council to agree on anything was a tall order. Especially without Roman's steady hand on the tiller. Carmen didn't particularly like the man, but she could at least acknowledge that he was necessary for Easton's survival. Without his influence, most of the people within the town's walls would long since have died.

A few times, Carmen's escort tried to make conversation, but she quickly realized that it was a useless endeavor. It wasn't that Carmen was antisocial—quite the contrary—but she was too eager to see her wife to let even idle conversation slow them down.

Soon enough, Carmen found herself walking through the government building's familiar front doors. The entire first floor, which had once played host to the entire police force, had been completely remodeled into a grand lobby with the Branch of the World Tree standing at its center.

Dirk, the Envoy of the Cult of the World Tree, stood silent sentry as a line of people accessed the Branch's features. With a thought, he could ban anyone who displeased him, and in the Branch's vicinity, he wielded significant physical power. So, no one even considered stepping a single toe out of line.

Carmen gave him a nod, which he returned. Once, he'd been a fairly timid man, but the power had gone to his head. Now, he had cultivated an inflated sense of self-importance that was perfectly characterized by his elaborate robes and haughty demeanor. Fortunately, Carmen rarely had reason to rub shoulders with the likes of him, so his faults were easily ignored.

After crossing through the lobby, Carmen and her morning-star-wielding escort approached the stairs that would lead them to the council chambers on the top floor. There, she hoped to be reunited with her triumphant wife. Still, even with her excitement distracting her, Carmen couldn't help but be mildly distracted by the questions circling her mind. The most prominent of which concerned why Alyssa hadn't come to fetch Carmen herself.

But she didn't have to suffer such questions for much longer before, at last, they reached the pair of carved, wooden double doors that would lead to the chambers. Surprisingly, Verin didn't hesitate before pushing them open and stepping inside. Carmen followed.

"Carmen," said Roman, pushing himself to his feet. He'd been sitting at the head of a polished oak table, so he was still more than a dozen feet away. "Sit. There's much we need to discuss."

"Why are you talking like that?" she asked, noting his formal tone as she looked from one face to another. All the normal culprits were there, and they all wore forlorn expressions. There were two newcomers there, though. One was a short, slender man with a pair of shortswords strapped to his back, while the other was the stoic, matronly Verin who'd brought her to the council chambers.

For a moment, Carmen was confused until she saw something familiar leaning against the table. That's when it hit her. "W-what . . . What . . . What happened?"

She had crafted the Spear of the Dragon Lancer herself, and while she had created even more powerful weapons since, it held a special place in her heart. Because it had been a gift meant to keep her wife safe. If it was here, then . . .

"Oh, God . . ."

She sank to her knees, already having come to the only logical conclusion. Alyssa was gone. She was dead.

Suddenly, Roman was by her side, his hand on her back. "I'm sorry," he said. "I . . . I tried to save her."

"How?" she managed, looking up at him with tearful eyes.

Roman knelt beside her and said, "She died a hero."

"That's not what I asked. How did she die? I want the details."

Carmen hadn't forgotten the warning she'd passed on to Alyssa before she left for the tower. Back then, she'd told Alyssa to watch out for Roman, largely because they'd always had such differing views on how to run Easton.

He shook his head. "I know how you're feeling, Carmen. I've been where you are right now. It doesn't feel real, does it? Sometimes, I still look up and expect Trish to walk through the door. It's been more than a year, and . . . and I still haven't gotten over it."

Carmen clenched her fists, then repeated her question: "How did Alyssa die?"

It came out as more of a growl, and the tension in the room rose to unprecedented heights. Still, Roman didn't react negatively, even if there were more than a couple of hands subtly creeping toward weapons.

Then, he told her a pretty story about Alyssa sacrificing herself for the greater good. He described the circumstances, explaining how Alyssa had been speared through the back by a creature that canceled her self-buffs while draining her attributes. She was defenseless, and she died before Verin—apparently, the matronly woman was a Healer—could mend Alyssa's wounds.

All of it was perfectly believable. Alyssa had certainly been the type to sacrifice her own safety so her teammates could survive. Carmen had seen it play out on dozens of occasions, and she knew it was why Alyssa was so popular among most of the city's residents. They could recognize a hero when they saw one.

But in the back of her mind, Carmen felt suspicion take root. After all, Alyssa's death was nothing but a benefit for Roman. He'd wrung everything he could out of her, and now that the city seemed capable of defending itself, she was no longer necessary.

Or maybe that was just misplaced anger.

She knew herself well enough to recognize that she just wanted someone to blame. The reality was that the world was an incredibly dangerous place, and it was only a matter of time before Alyssa ran into something capable of killing her. Before, it had been easy to think of her as something akin to a chosen one. Everything had come so naturally to her.

But now she was gone.

Carmen knelt there for a long time, her eyes unseeing until, at last, she blinked. By that point, all the others—except for that slim man with the twin blades—were gone. Idly, Carmen recognized that he had a high-quality dagger at his waist. It was at least Simple grade. Maybe even Complex, which was unheard-of. Though with it in its sheath, she couldn't use Tradesman's Appraisal to get even basic information like the weapon's name.

That small distraction was enough to pull her out of her stupor, and she shook her head before saying, "Thank you for telling me."

She climbed to her feet, then grabbed the Spear of the Dragon Lancer. For a moment, Roman looked as if he was going to object. After all, such a weapon would normally have gone to the city's armory to be assigned to someone it might benefit. But her challenging glare must have told Roman that if he wanted to confiscate it, he would have to pry it free of her cold, dead fingers. He clearly didn't want to go down that road.

"Where are you going?" he asked when she turned to leave the room.

"First, I'm going to get Miggy and tell him that his mom's dead," she stated, the last word coming out ragged and barely audible. "Then, I'm going to Juan Carlos's bar so I can get well and truly drunk. You're welcome to join."

"I . . . The funeral arrangements are—"

"I'll take care of it," Carmen stated. "And I'll let you know where to show up. She always considered you a friend."

"She was my friend, too."

Then, without another word, Carmen turned and left the room, trying to figure out how she was going to tell her son the news.

3

GARDEN

A drizzle fell from the gray sky, accompanied by a fine mist that dampened the entire island. It was the sort of lazy rain that wasn't quite enough to drive one inside for the day, but too heavy to completely ignore. For Elijah, though, it was little different from any other day. He'd long since grown accustomed to much harsher elements, so as he tended his garden, he barely noticed the inclement weather.

A little more than a week had passed since his successful defense of the island, and he'd spent much of that time in well-earned relaxation. As much as he longed to explore the world and find civilization, the previous few months had certainly taken their toll. He needed to decompress, and there was no better way to do that than to lose himself in the task of nurturing his increasingly impressive garden.

There was something almost meditative about walking among the bushes, flaring Nature's Bounty as he went. From time to time, he was forced to pull weeds, though even those he preferred to leave alone. Because calling the Grove a garden was a bit of a misnomer. As beautiful as it had become, it was still a wild place, and taming that wilderness held little appeal for Elijah.

He preferred to leave it be, to let it grow as it would.

However, there were practical concerns, as well. He depended on the berries growing on the bushes he'd meticulously planted long ago. Certainly, he could survive from foraging and fishing, but there was a wide gap between simple persistence and flourishing. The berries—and the other wild edibles he'd managed to cultivate—represented the ability to veer away from the day-to-day struggle of wilderness survival.

After all, there was a reason humans had developed agriculture in the first place, and despite his preference for wild things, Elijah wasn't averse to carrying on that proud farming tradition. So, he tended his garden, pulling weeds as he went. From time to time, he would grab a ripe berry and pop it into his mouth, and it was on one such occasion that he got quite a surprise.

"Oh . . ."

The blackberry wasn't just sweeter than its fellows, though that was the first thing Elijah had noticed. He quickly moved past that observation when he felt a tiny surge of ethera race through his body. But there was something else there, as well. Something he couldn't quantify. One thing he did know was that it made him feel incredible, like that tiny spark of ethera had carried with it a little ball of pure adrenaline.

After gathering a couple, he carried them to the ancestral tree and called out, "Nerthus? You in there, man?"

For once, the little tree spirit actually responded. His appearances were still rare enough that Elijah usually didn't even try to contact him, but of late, they'd grown a bit more frequent. In addition, Nerthus looked a good deal larger, with more defined features, as well. Finally, the tree spirit's bark had taken on a much paler shade, mimicking the changes to the ancestral tree that had begun after it had absorbed the Shard of the World Tree that Elijah had received as a reward for defeating the tower.

"Yes?" the humanoid bundle of roots and branches asked.

Elijah held up one of the blackberries and explained what he'd felt. When he finished, he asked, "So, what's going on here?"

"It is as expected. I've told you that the Grove will change this island, yes?"

"You have."

"The ambient levels of ethera will rise and thicken, which comes with a host of benefits, both for you and the flora. One of those benefits is that many plants—especially within the Grove itself—will become pseudotreasures. That berry is one. It is a potent source of vitality that, given time, will help you heal more quickly and provide far more sustenance than any normal food. Be wary, though—as your Grove strengthens, so too will its value. Right now, it is fairly unremarkable in the grand scheme of the universe. But in a decade or two, it will be extremely valuable to many craftsmen. Alchemists, especially, would kill for such a ready source of ethera-rich pseudotreasures."

That was news to Elijah, but then again, basically everything he learned about his new world could qualify for that label. The reality was that, aside from the occasional explanations from Nerthus, he'd spent most of his time on the island flying blind. According to the tree spirit, he could change that by finding a Branch he could access in order to purchase some guides, but he didn't foresee that opportunity presenting itself anytime soon.

After all, it was a big world out there. Much bigger than Earth had been before feeling the touch of the World Tree, in fact. So, the chances that he would find a settlement with a Branch—other than the one across the strait, which came with its own problems—were fairly slim.

Still, he knew that was the only way he would get any significant amount of information. Nerthus was prohibited from saying too much, mostly because the System was structured to force people to gain knowledge either firsthand or through the guides it sold. It was something to do with that being the optimal way to ensure proper progression, and that restriction would remain in place for some time to come.

"So, eating these things isn't bad for me, right?" Elijah asked, looking down at the blackberry.

Nerthus answered, "No. The opposite, in fact. It will help prepare your body for the next step in your cultivation, and, in addition to providing sustenance, it will provide some degree of passive Regeneration. How much is dependent on your consumption as well as the power in the fruit."

"Wait—so you're saying that if I eat enough of these things, I can directly enhance my attributes?"

"Yes. If you were a Cook, you could create meals that would get even more out of those ingredients," Nerthus explained. "A truly skilled Chef can do even more, and with a wide variety of ingredients that augment attributes other than Regeneration. Of course, if you had either of those classes, you would not be a Druid, and as such, we wouldn't be having this conversation in the first place."

"But if I found someone who had a class like that?"

"Then your little Grove would be even more valuable," Nerthus said. "The same would be true for an Alchemist. However, I do warn you to be wary of any of those you might find. Many of them veer into devourer territory."

After that, Nerthus reached the limit of the information he could pass on, and soon retreated into his tree, leaving Elijah alone once again. He returned to his gardening, but he didn't get much done before he felt something interesting.

Ever since the ancestral tree had absorbed the Shard of the World Tree, the Grove had grown past the confines of the island. The boundaries had yet to reach more than a few dozen feet into the ocean, but Elijah hoped that it would soon encompass the tower, obviating the need for him to reconquer it sometime in the future. Nerthus claimed that would be the case, but Elijah was impatient for the tree spirit's prediction to come true.

In any case, the expansion of his Domain brought with it an awareness of the sea surrounding his island. Most of it was unremarkable—just rock, silt, and various forms of sea life. However, the Domain had just grown to encompass the mouth of an underwater cave that, according to his awareness, extended at least a few hundred feet below the seabed.

Elijah had been cave diving quite a few times in his life. Sometimes, it had been for work, but he'd done it for fun, as well. There was definitely something incredibly engaging about the act of exploration—especially when it was in a location that few, if any, others had ever experienced. So, the moment his Locus had touched the cave—more of a tunnel, really—he'd felt a deep sense of longing.

Partially, it was for a simpler time when he might've gone diving with friends. But it was also a call to adventure. For better or worse, his time in the tower, though deadly and exhausting, had awakened something inside of him. He wanted to explore new things. He needed to experience everything his new, magical world had to offer. And though he'd been putting off heading to the mainland—for good reasons, too—he didn't think there was any issue with seeing a new facet of his island.

He glanced at the gray sky. With the near-ubiquitous cloud cover obscuring the sun, it was sometimes difficult to accurately tell the time. Especially when Elijah often lost himself in whatever task he was performing. But he'd paid enough attention to recognize that it wouldn't be long before nightfall, so he resolved to spend the rest of his day tending to the garden. In the morning, though, he intended to explore the cave on the edge of his awareness.

So, with that, he continued his task until sunset, then headed back to his tree house where he enjoyed a meal of leftover fish stew and berries. After that, he took a shower—using his harsh homemade soap to thoroughly clean himself—then retired to his bedroom. For a while, he lay awake, just thinking about the world at large. As always, the persistent questions of how the rest of humanity had dealt with the world's transformation occupied his mind until, at last, he fell asleep.

That night, he dreamed of once again being trapped in the stomach of a giant killer whale. The next morning, he jerked awake, covered in cold sweat and with his heart pounding out of his chest.

Sighing, he massaged his temples. While he'd tried to move on from some of his experiences in the tower, some of those memories still crept up on him from time to time. It wasn't enough to counteract his enthusiasm for exploration or progression, but it was definitely a poignant reminder that nothing worthwhile ever came without a cost.

Certainly, he would continue to grow his power. And he wanted to see wonderful sights like he'd experienced in the Sea of Sorrows and the Primordial Jungle. The new world gave him that opportunity, and he fully intended to use it. However, he had to remember that that path wasn't without significant peril.

Elijah pushed himself out of his mossy bed and ran his hand through his blond curls. He'd need to cut his hair soon, he reasoned. While he didn't exactly have access to a barber, he had a knife and a couple of reasonably reflective surfaces. So, he could make do, even if he'd never grace any magazine covers.

If such things even existed anymore, which didn't seem likely.

Sighing, he rose to his feet, then slipped on a pair of homemade shorts. Autumn had already come, but his Constitution had grown enough that he could withstand fairly extreme climates without the benefit of heavy clothing. At a certain point, it would become extremely uncomfortable, but the temperatures hadn't quite dropped that low. Besides, he didn't want to swim around fully clothed.

Even as the sun peeked above the horizon, Elijah set about his morning routine. He went through his exercise regimen—he wasn't sure if it still helped very much, but almost two years of daily training had formed a habit. In any case, he spent most of the morning going through various calisthenics, then practicing his aim with Storm's Fury. After that, he enjoyed a breakfast of berries before, at last, he could finally get to the fun part of his day.

With that, he found himself racing across the island, staff in hand. He leaped over shallow gullies and bounded over fallen trees; he barely even had to look where he was going, he'd grown so used to sensing his environment with his Locus. Soon enough, he reached his destination, which was one of the beaches on the east side of the island. Without hesitation, he waded into the chilly water, then dove into the depths.

His Locus guiding him, Elijah cut through the salty water like a fish. With the Ring of Aquatic Travel, he didn't have to worry about holding his breath, so he quickly found the cave, which presented itself as a narrow crack—maybe three feet wide—that cut into the rocky seabed.

At the entrance to the cave, Elijah hesitated for a few moments. After all, he was well aware of how deadly cave diving could be. He was superhumanly durable now, though. And he couldn't drown. So, he expected it wouldn't be nearly as dangerous as it would've been before the world's transformation.

Without further ado, Elijah dove through the cave's entrance.

4

SPELUNKING

Cold darkness enveloped Elijah as he passed through the jagged mouth of the cave. He could still see, if only barely, and the current threatened to throw him into the sharp rocks. He kicked forward, grabbing hold of those rocks as he pulled himself through the tunnel.

Cave diving was not for the weak of heart, nor was it fit for the easily panicked. Not only did the diver have to be cognizant of his oxygen levels, but it was incredibly easy to lose oneself in the twisting turns of a submerged tunnel. Elijah didn't have to worry about the former, but the latter could probably get him killed. After all, though he could survive without food and water for a time, he was no immortal.

So, he kept his wits about him as he gradually pulled himself through the narrow tunnel. Soon, his Locus receded, and he had to rely on his more mundane senses. As he followed the cave's path, he noticed a slight decline that quickly grew far steeper until he was swimming down an almost vertical shaft. With every foot, his heart beat a little faster as he imagined all the monstrous things hidden in the darkness.

Elijah thought he could survive most threats—at least long enough to run away—but he hadn't experienced everything the world had to offer. Far from it, in fact. What if he ran into the underwater equivalent of that great raptor that had torn his plane apart so long ago? Or another creature like the panther that had once guarded his island? And that wasn't even considering the possibility that he might encounter one of the Voxx. After all, the most powerful of the interdimensional reptiles he'd encountered had come from the sea.

Still, Elijah continued on, confident in his own abilities. He'd conquered the tower, defeating creatures much more powerful than he was. So, he reasoned that, if push came to shove, he could repeat that feat in the real world. Still, he didn't savor the notion of being eaten by some sea creature, so he remained focused on his surroundings, concentrating as much on One with Nature as his more mundane senses. It worked, after a fashion, but it was far from ideal.

Slowly, the cave began to level out, and Elijah found himself with a pair of options. One branch of the tunnel continued down, while the other broke off to the right. He knew he was already pretty deep—maybe fifty feet below the seafloor—so he decided to check the latter branch. With that in mind, he turned to the right and continued on. However, the tunnel only continued for a few dozen more feet before it started to narrow.

Elijah persisted, steadily dragging himself along until he only had a few inches of clearance. When that happened, he was suddenly overwhelmed by a sense of claustrophobia. His heart raced, and if he hadn't been equipped with the Ring of Aquatic Travel, his breathing would have quickened into shallow and panicked pants, as well.

There was just something so powerfully primal about the fear of getting trapped in a tight space, and though Elijah had been cave diving a few times in the past, he certainly wasn't immune to his own human nature. So, it took him a few moments to master his fear and slowly back away.

More than anything, Elijah wished he could just take a few deep, calming breaths. An impossibility considering his situation, but the desire was there all the same.

Inch by inch, he pushed himself backward until he could flip over and retrace his proverbial steps. When he finally reached the fork, he considered returning to the surface but instead chose to resume his descent. So, he continued to pull himself down into the depths. At some point, the water grew still, and the darkness became even more oppressive; it was like he'd passed some ephemeral threshold into the mythological underworld. Any heat remaining in the water slowly dissipated with every passing inch until even Elijah's much enhanced Constitution began to falter.

Still, he went on.

In some ways, it felt almost like a dream. With no light, he couldn't see. With the numbing cold, he couldn't feel. Sound was muffled, and he certainly couldn't smell or taste anything but the salty water. But he could feel his surroundings. He was incapable of distinguishing between the microscopic creatures in the water and clinging to the walls of the cave, but he could feel their collective life force.

And it was comforting, knowing that even in such an inhospitable environment, life persisted.

It reminded Elijah of all the undiscovered creatures in the deepest parts of the ocean. They lived in a lightless world of crushing pressure, and yet, they thrived. If ever there was a testament to the enduring nature of life, then it would be found in the ocean's depths.

Such thoughts occupied Elijah's mind as his descent continued, and he reached something akin to a meditative state. Without much in the way of sensory input, he lost track of time. Indeed, he felt almost formless as he drifted ever downward. It was so hypnotic that he almost didn't notice when the slope leveled out. However, he couldn't help but see the subtle green glow hovering in the distance.

Elijah dragged himself forward, and the illumination loomed larger with every passing moment until it suffused everything. Then, he realized the source.

Tiny crystals, no bigger than thumbnails, lined the submerged tunnel. Elijah slowed to a stop, reached out, and ran a finger across the surface of one crystal. It felt like warm glass.

For a while, Elijah just floated there, drifting back and forth in the subtle current as he beheld the phenomenon. He was well acquainted with bioluminescence, but these crystals were unlike anything he'd ever seen. And the subtle aura of ethera they emitted told him that they were magical in nature.

As if there was ever any doubt. One glance, and he'd known.

Eventually, he resumed his path and continued through the tunnel. The crystals slowly grew larger until they were at least the size of his fist, and the illumination they cast followed suit, increasing in intensity until Elijah felt almost as if he was beneath the light of a green sun. Still, he kept going until, at last, he reached the end of the tunnel.

It didn't terminate in a dead end as he'd expected. Instead, it opened into a massive chamber, at least a hundred yards wide and only half filled with water. He swam to the surface, and when he broke through, he couldn't stop himself from taking a deep lungful of air. A mistake in normal times—who knew what gases might've been trapped in such an air pocket—but the danger proved unrealized because it was no different from the atmosphere of his island. Sure, it was a little stale, but that wasn't going to kill him.

In any case, Elijah was far more focused on his surroundings. The cave was roughly spherical, and the dome-shaped ceiling, which was about thirty or forty feet above him, was absolutely covered in more of the glowing green crystals. Verdant light danced across the surface of the water. To call it beautiful would have been completely underselling the awe in Elijah's heart.

He lay back, letting himself float on the surface as he stared up at the ceiling. The water was still cold enough to be uncomfortable, but he barely felt it. Instead, he was far too focused on the fact that he was looking at something he could confidently say that nobody had ever seen before.

And in that moment, Elijah was content.

Not just happy, because that was fleeting. Contentment was something else altogether, and though it didn't carry with it the intensity of most other emotions, it ran far deeper. Stress he didn't know he'd been carrying since his adventures within the tower melted away, and thus unburdened, he could truly appreciate the ethereal beauty before him.

More, he could see the wondrous nature of his new life for what it was.

Sure, he'd been forced to kill, and not just a little. But as he'd felt since the very beginning, that was just part of the circle of life. It felt a bit cliché to think of it in those terms, but there was a reason for the ubiquity of such sentiment. Some things had to die so others could live.

It had been true before the world's transformation, and it had become even more so afterward.

The funny thing was that he didn't really feel the weight of his actions—not in any way that was going to affect him. Only a week or so before, he'd killed almost fifty people. By all rights, it had been a massacre. And yet, he didn't feel the least bit guilty for it.

Elijah wasn't so naive as to believe that they'd all been terrible people, either. Most had probably just been following orders when they'd landed on the island. That didn't matter, though. They'd thrown their lot in with the sort of people who would kidnap and try to kill a sapient being, and for no other reason than to drain her power. That painted them all with the same brush, so when they'd come ashore intending to do the same to his Grove, he'd felt justified in his actions.

In fact, he was content in the knowledge that, given the same situation, he would make all the same choices. Admitting that he didn't really mind the killing—so long as he felt it was warranted—felt good, like he didn't have to lie to himself.

He also came to realize something he'd been dancing around for quite some time. When he'd first washed ashore, Elijah had been given a second chance at life. And throughout his time on the island, he'd used that opportunity to steadily claw his way forward. He had survived, and to his own surprise, he'd actually enjoyed most of it. Not the pain. Obviously. But the triumph. The discovery. The magic. The connection to nature he'd gained with his archetype. They all coalesced into one inescapable truth: He liked his new life.

And more than anything else, he wanted more.

He needed to experience new adventures. He craved that moment of triumph he'd felt after accomplishing what felt like the impossible. After overcoming long odds and defeating fearsome monsters. He wanted to gain more levels, to acquire new abilities. He wanted to find out what the higher stages of cultivation had to offer. And more than anything, he wanted to see more incredible things.

Elijah knew that path wasn't going to be a comfortable one, and he would probably experience plenty of pain along the way. But so long as he survived, he could take it.

"It'll be worth it," he said to himself, the sound of his voice carrying through the cave. The echo bounced off of the crystals, sending green power arcing from one to the other in a wave. It looked fearsome, but Elijah could feel that it wasn't dangerous. So, he couldn't help but grin at the sight.

And at his personal revelation. Or, rather, an admission.

For a long time, Elijah simply floated there, a contented smile playing across his face as he beheld the crystal cavern. Every now and then, he'd let out a subdued shout before he watched the green lightning dance across the ceiling.

But then, he felt something he'd been dreading since he'd let the little goblin mage leave his island alive. Someone had encroached upon his Domain.

Sighing, Elijah righted himself, then cast the teleport function of Ancestral Circle. Almost thirty seconds later, the spell's cast completed, and he appeared—still soaking wet—in the middle of his Grove. The invaders still hadn't moved from shore. Elijah could feel both of them standing beside their rowboat. Then, one of them planted something in the ground.

It took Elijah a moment to recognize the white flag. Did that mean the same thing for them as it did on Earth? Or was it something else? Elijah chose to believe the former but prepared himself for the latter.

In any case, he had no intention of meeting—or fighting—them in his homemade shorts. Instead, he'd sewn a garment for just such an occasion. It resembled a toga, but it represented the best of Elijah's tailoring capabilities. So, wanting to make a reasonably good impression, he retrieved the garment from his tree house, donned it, and then set off across the island, staff in hand.

Hopefully, it would turn out better than last time.

5

DIPLOMACY

Cold, clammy humidity hung thick in the air as autumn had begun to give way to winter's frigid grip. Still, as Elijah raced across his island, he was largely unaffected, save for the sweat on his brow. Even so, the robes he'd sewn were ill-fitting, and as he went, he had to take great care to keep them from snagging on the dense foliage. As a result, his progress was slower than if he'd been less clothed.

Oddly enough, he almost wished he could return to the nudity of his time in the tower. At least then he wouldn't have to worry about it. Instead, he could focus on the task at hand.

The two figures who'd arrived on his island still hadn't moved more than a few feet from their little boats, suggesting that they were waiting on him. The white flag supported that notion, though, as he approached, he remained wary of any traps. Sure, he could feel everything through his Locus, but he was also fairly ignorant of the world. For all he knew, there were ways around his extra-sensory perception. And he had no intention of walking into a trap.

Elijah took a few minutes to visually inspect the area, but to his relief, he found nothing out of the ordinary. So, without further delay, he headed toward the beach, stopping a few feet away from the tree line. From there, he studied the newcomers with his own two eyes. There were a pair of them—a goblin and a dwarf—but neither looked to be armed.

The goblin's skin was pale, with only the barest hint of a green tint. Both of his huge, bat-like ears bore multiple piercings that glittered gold and silver, but his features were a little less exaggerated than the other goblins Elijah had seen. He wore sturdy boots, slacks, and a black vest over a white shirt. In short, he looked strikingly normal, even despite his short stature and obvious goblinhood.

The dwarven woman next to him was the exact opposite. With heavy shoulders bulging with muscle, she wore a sleeveless tunic and a plaid kilt whose hem brushed against the rocky beach. More than that, her worn features and leathery skin told a story of a life filled with hard work.

But neither looked like a combatant, though Elijah had to admit that, due to his ignorance, he probably wasn't the best judge of such things. For all he knew, he was looking at the two most dangerous people in the world. He didn't think that was the case, but he really didn't have much basis for that judgment.

Elijah took a deep breath, then stepped out from the tree line. The pair flinched at his sudden appearance, but neither of them said anything as he approached. With each step, they grew more frightened until, at last, he was only ten feet away. He didn't intend to go any closer.

"Why are you here?" he demanded, planting the butt of his staff in the ground.

"Apologies," said the goblin, wringing his hands. His voice was fairly high-pitched but scratchy. Almost as if he was a preteen with a sore throat. "But we are emissaries from the Green Mountain Mining Guild."

"Is that supposed to mean anything to me?" Elijah asked.

"No. Not as such," stated the goblin. "But we have come to apologize."

"Oh?" Elijah asked.

"Yes. Eason Cabbot blatantly flouted our rules when he led his subordinates to this island," the goblin said. "He—"

"What about when he tried to kidnap and drain a dragon?" Elijah asked. "Was that against your rules, too?"

"W-what?"

"You heard me," he said.

"We . . . We knew nothing of this . . ."

"Oh, come off it, Ramik," huffed the dwarf. Her voice was gruff and her tone one of annoyance. "You knew the connivin' little bastard was up to somethin'. You might not've known what, but you knew somethin'."

"Carisa!"

"What? You ain't convincin' nobody with your little act. Just be straight with 'im like I said. He'll come around or he won't," she said. Then, she turned to face Elijah and said, "I'm Carisa. Head o' the miners. Meanin' I'm only second in command to Ramik there. 'Cept he knows if he steps out o' line, I'll straighten 'im out real quick like."

"You will do no such thing!" spat the goblin. "I am your superior, and I would appreciate it if you acted as such." Then, as if he'd just remembered Elijah was there, he went even paler than normal. He took a deep breath, then straightened his vest. "Right. As I was saying, the Green Mountain Mining Guild and Ironshore had no knowledge of Cabbot's misdeeds. If we had, we would have stopped him."

"Wouldn't've done much good," Carisa stated. "He had all the fighters on 'is side. Wasn't nothin' we could do to stop him. 'Cept Mr. Protector of the Grove over here did us a favor, yeah?"

"I didn't do anyone any favors," Elijah interjected, finally deigning to speak. "They invaded my island. I reacted."

"Some reaction," she muttered.

Elijah shrugged. "I don't like unannounced visitors. Which brings me to why you're here," he said. "I seem to recall telling that little goblin mage that I'd kill anybody who set foot on my island."

"And yet we still live," said Ramik.

"That could change."

The goblin swallowed hard in an exaggerated expression of fear.

"What do you want?" Elijah asked before either of his two visitors could speak again.

"An understandin'," said Carisa. "Maybe even an alliance."

At that, Elijah wanted to laugh out loud. His only real contact with the settlement had been the murder of nearly fifty people. To follow that up with diplomacy was more than a little surprising. Still, he kept his face expressionless.

"And what do you offer?" he asked.

"What do you want?" Ramik countered.

"Nothing," Elijah said. And he meant it. The island could provide everything he needed. Certainly, he intended to expand his horizons sometime in the near future, but they didn't need to know that. The less the people of Ironshore knew about his island, the better—at least as far as he was concerned.

But then again, if they'd come to him, they probably wanted to keep him happy.

"We needn't be enemies," Ramik said.

Elijah shrugged. "I'm content with being very distant neighbors. Like I said, I want people to stay away from my island," he responded. "That's it. I was fine with things the way they were. I stayed here, you all stayed over there. But then fifty people came to my island hoping to . . . I don't even know what they intended, but it wasn't good. I like this place the way it is, and I don't want anyone screwing with it."

"That seems reasonable," Ramik responded. "But let me ask you this—do you enjoy wearing rags? I suspect that you could use many things that we take for granted. That's what I'm offering. Clothing. Equipment. Soap—"

"I make my own soap."

"What? Really? I mean . . . Never mind that," Ramik went on. "I don't—"

Carisa interrupted, asking, "Yer a human, ain't you? A native, right?"

"I am."

"We can give you access to our Branch. Should be at least as advanced as any on the planet," she said.

Elijah didn't immediately respond. That was the one thing he really wanted more than anything else, largely so he could cure some of his ignorance. However, he could also admit that he wouldn't mind seeing what goods they had to offer. Perhaps some spices. Maybe something with caffeine. He definitely missed coffee. Or perhaps he could obtain some proper clothing. It was an attractive offer, but there was one thing that neither Ramik nor Carisa had mentioned.

"And what do you want from me?"

"Mutual defense," Ramik said. "You killed most of our fighters. We still have enough for basic defense, but if any truly powerful enemies attack, we will be vulnerable. I've sent for reinforcements, but those cost quite a bit of etherium, and I'll be honest—the coffers aren't precisely overflowing of late."

At that, he directed a pointed glare at Carisa.

"Don't look at me," she said before spitting on the ground. "Ain't my fault the ore's stubborn on this planet. We're gettin' there. Just takin' a bit longer'n we thought it would."

Ramik sighed. "This is neither the time nor the place to get into that," he said. "Mr. Protector, if—"

Elijah cringed at the moniker. If he'd had it to do over again, he certainly wouldn't have labeled himself in such a way. But there was nothing he could do about it now. So, he said, "My name is Elijah."

"Oh. Right. Elijah," the goblin repeated. "We would also like the opportunity to purchase any equipment you might have . . . ah . . . acquired during the previous raid."

That Elijah had no issues with. He'd already set aside a few pieces he thought might be valuable—an axe he intended to use for cutting down trees, a few extra daggers, and lots of leather and cloth—but the rest he had little use for. If he could simply sell them back to the people of Ironshore, it would solve some issues for him.

"I have no problem with the last part. The rest of it I'm going to have to give some thought. I don't think I'm revealing any secrets when I say that I don't trust you," Elijah said. "Your people came here to kill me and take what was mine. If they could have done it, they would have."

"Right, but—"

"I'm not finished," Elijah growled. "Even so, I'm not completely opposed to the idea of working together. I just need to give it some thought before I commit to anything. In the meantime, I would ask that you get back in your boat and return to Ironshore. I will bring the equipment across once I've made my decision."

For a moment, the goblin looked like he was going to say something else. However, Carisa beat him to it, saying, "Sounds fair 'nough."

Elijah just nodded, then turned around and retreated into the trees. He didn't stop, either. Instead, he just kept going, never turning back. However, he did keep tabs on his visitors, who resorted to arguing the moment he was out of earshot. That wasn't surprising; they seemed keen enough on bickering.

But then they boarded their little rowboat, and soon enough, they were on their way back to Ironshore. Elijah lost track of them when they passed out of his Locus.

When he got back to the Grove, he went straight to the ancestral tree and called for Nerthus. The little tree spirit had grown more active with every passing day, so he responded in only a few seconds.

"Yes?"

Elijah wasted no time before telling him what had happened. When he'd finished—which didn't take long—he asked, "So, any advice? I was thinking that it wouldn't hurt to sell the weapons back, at least."

"You need to access the Branch. Whatever concessions you must make, that should be the goal."

"Is it really that important?"

"It is. As I've said before, I am restricted in what information I can pass on. That is by design. On integrated worlds, the rules are much more flexible, but here, the origin of any knowledge must be the World Tree."

"Why?"

"Three reasons. The first is that the System is infallible. As such, any information it provides is guaranteed to be true. The same cannot be said for what might be passed on by settlers such as those goblins or gnomes. It is not difficult to manipulate people with bad information."

Elijah nodded. That much was true. Before the world had been transformed, humanity had been plagued by misinformation. Bad actors the world over had spent trillions of dollars in an effort to manipulate the populace via incomplete or outright false information. So, it stood to reason that the invaders—or settlers, as Nerthus categorized them—could do the same.

"And the second reason?"

"It is generally agreed that knowledge freely given does not promote the sort of growth necessary for the System's goals. As such, earning knowledge is preferable," Nerthus stated. "And finally, the System is an ethereal construct that needs fuel to function. The etherium spent on various functions accessible at any Branch goes toward that goal.

"Aside from that, what good is etherium? I mean, I know it's money, but does it have value other than what's assigned to it?"

"Of course. Etherium is a basic component of crafting," Nerthus explained. "Before you ask—no, I can't explain it to you."

Elijah sighed. It was just further evidence that he needed to access that Branch. Just like that, he made up his mind. He intended to approach any potential alliance with his eyes wide open, though. And if they stepped one toe out of line, he had no issues repeating his actions from the week before.

6

DROWNING

The hammer fell, sending sparks flying from the molten metal. Carmen knew it was too hot, that the result was going to be almost entirely unusable. But she didn't much care. Indeed, all she really wanted to do was hit something—anything—really, really hard. So, she had retreated to her forge, intending to lose herself in the process of shaping metal. Instead, she'd quickly made one mistake after another until she stopped even trying to do anything worthwhile.

With a growl, she reached down and grabbed the glowing bar of steel, then tossed it at the wall. It hit with another spray of sparks, then shattered entirely. That's when she let out a primal yell that sounded more like it came from a wild animal than a human woman. The moment the scream died in her throat, she sank to her knees and collapsed into a mess of sobbing tears.

Alyssa was never supposed to be the one to die. Even if everyone else was killed, Alyssa should have survived. Carmen had made sure that her wife had been equipped with all the best gear—armor the likes of which no one else in Easton could even think about making—and that wasn't even mentioning Alyssa's expertise. She was the best fighter in the city, and she'd proved her mettle in countless battles.

And yet, she had fallen.

She wasn't the only one, either. One of the Healers had died, and so had the lanky Wizard who'd been part of Alyssa's normal team.

Roman had spun a pretty tale. He'd talked about how brave Alyssa had been, about how she had sacrificed herself so the others could live. That certainly sounded like the woman Carmen had married, but still—she hadn't forgotten the growing animosity between Alyssa and Roman. That loomed over everything, casting frustrating doubt over the man's story.

Bending over, Carmen hung her head. Her sweat-soaked hair formed a curtain around her face as the tears continued to fall. She knew her suspicions were unfair. Roman had never done anything to suggest that he would betray Alyssa. In fact, despite their differences of opinion, the pair had been close friends. They had relied on one another at every turn.

Carmen knew she was just looking for someone to blame. The fact of the matter, though, was that there was no single guilty party. People died every day.

The world was dangerous and deadly, and Carmen needed to look no further than the situation itself. Going into the tower had always been a risk, and for once, Alyssa had paid the price for her gallant nature.

But just because Carmen knew there was no one to blame didn't mean she wasn't angry. That she didn't need to vent her frustrations on something. Anything. And given that the metal had proved to be a poor opponent, she decided to seek out a more satisfying foe. So, with tears still falling down her cheeks, she went to the corner where she found her armor.

It wasn't the same quality as the beautiful suit of plate she'd made for Alyssa. In fact, it looked just about as ordinary as any suit of armor could. Plain steel, with only a few embellishments to set it apart, the armor was workmanlike in both appearance and function. It suited Carmen perfectly, and she donned it with grim determination.

Once she'd strapped the various pieces into place, she retrieved a giant two-handed hammer from the storeroom. Like her armor, it didn't look like anything special. Indeed, it had a crude, almost unfinished look about it. But also like her armor, it was well crafted, and its quality exceeded any of her other creations, aside from the gear she'd made for Alyssa.

Thus armed and armored, Carmen grabbed a rucksack, then headed to the nearby home she'd shared with Alyssa and her son. Miguel was staying with friends for the night, so the house was deserted.

Confronted with that emptiness, Carmen once again felt on the verge of breaking down. The years after the world's transformation hadn't been easy, but as a family, they'd shared plenty of happy times—especially in that house. Now, it was empty, and it would never feel full again.

Forcing her emotions aside for the moment, Carmen gathered some provisions—just a few bottles of water and the dried meat Alyssa had always favored when she went on her patrols. Once she'd taken care of her supplies, she set off for the gate. When she got there, the pair of Guards tried to caution her against going out alone, but one glare was all it took for them to back down.

So, soon enough, Carmen was trekking down the well-trodden trails of the surrounding wilderness. At first, she had no real notion of where she was going. She just wanted to find something to kill. But in the back of her mind, in a place she didn't want to acknowledge, Carmen knew precisely where she was destined to end up.

And hours later, she stood in front of the derelict building she'd once called home. It had already been picked clean, and in the two years since it had been inhabited, the surrounding wilderness had reclaimed the single-story house. But it was still recognizable enough that Carmen couldn't look at it without tearing up again. She stood there for a while, just staring at it. Memories raced through her mind, each one encased in nearly impenetrable sadness.

She probably would have stayed longer if it wasn't for the massive creature charging down the street at her.

On the most basic of levels, it was a brown bear. However, like most of the local wildlife, the world's transformation had turned it into something else. Something bigger, faster, and far deadlier. Fortunately for Carmen, she'd changed, too.

Even as the monster charged at her, drool flying from its slavering jaws, Carmen pulled the massive hammer from her shoulder. For her first ten levels after Earth had been touched by the World Tree, Carmen had put every free point into Strength. And that attribute had been further enhanced after she'd gained her Blacksmith class. So, even though the hammer weighed north of a hundred pounds, she handled it like it was as light as a feather.

The bear monster closed with frightening speed, and if Carmen hadn't been so enveloped by her own grief and rage, she might've succumbed to fear. That wasn't what happened, though. Instead, she met the charging bear with a sweeping attack reminiscent of a softball swing, and the huge chunk of steel at the end of the hammer took the mutated animal directly in the face.

Carmen experienced a deep sense of satisfaction when she felt bones crunch under the blow. The bear stumbled, though its mass and momentum were so great that it still tackled her to the ground. Fortunately, her attack had shattered its jaw, so it couldn't bring its most potent weapons to the battle.

It still had claws, though.

So, Carmen dropped her weapon—it was useless when she was buried beneath a thousand pounds of furious ursine—and locked her own meaty hands around its wrists. Thus began a contest of strength. Woman against monstrous bear.

And for a moment, it looked like the bear might come out on top. Then, Carmen regained her leverage, and suddenly, the bear was losing. With a great heave, she flipped the creature onto its back and rolled atop it. Then, Carmen let out a mighty roar that dwarfed anything the bear could utter as she ripped her arms out to the side.

More bones cracked as the bear's joints couldn't handle the stress. It whimpered, suddenly aware of its own vulnerability. If Carmen had let it, the thing would have run. But she hadn't come out into the wilderness to wrestle bears. She'd come to kill something.

So, without further ado, she cocked her arm back, curled her fingers into a fist, and commenced with transforming her wishes into a reality. Over and over, her gauntleted fists descended, and slowly, she pummeled the monster's face into a bloody pulp. At first, it squirmed as it tried to escape, but soon enough, even that struggle fell away.

At some point, Carmen had stopped attacking a living monster, instead transitioning into beating a dead bear's corpse. But still, she persisted, screaming and growling and crying all the while.

It did no good, though.

Her frustration and grief remained as poignant and powerful as ever.

When she pulled away, her knuckles were sore and bloody beneath her armored gauntlets, and one of her hands was probably broken. Her one-sided attribute allocation meant that her Constitution couldn't really hold up to her Strength. But she'd get someone to heal her when she got back to Easton. For now, she grabbed the knife from her belt and started processing the creature.

That took quite some time; it was a large animal, after all, and she was no expert. However, over the next couple of hours, she finished the job, coming away with a decent-quality pelt and a few hundred pounds of good meat. Once she'd gotten everything she could out of the bear, she began the long trek back to town. Along the way, she had to fight two more times, though against nothing as menacing as the bear, and when she finally returned to Easton, she'd added a significant amount of meat to her haul.

She handed it over to the Guards and told them to distribute it accordingly. Then, she took her pelt to a man who'd taken the Leatherworker class and told him what she wanted made. It cost quite a few etherium, but he was amenable.

Finally, after washing the worst of the blood away, Carmen headed to one of the town's handful of taverns, where she quickly got down to the serious business of drinking herself into a stupor. While she was there, multiple acquaintances approached to give her their condolences, and for the most part, Carmen accepted them with as much grace as she could muster. However, at some point, she skated past mere drunkenness and into absolutely sloppy territory.

Which had always been the goal.

However, just before she let herself fall into unconsciousness, someone sat across from her at the table. She looked up with blurry eyes but didn't recognize the woman. "Don't think I'll be much company," she slurred.

Then, ethera gathered, and the woman cast a spell on Carmen. She never even had a chance to react before it enveloped her.

And gradually, her drunkenness faded away, replaced by horrible sobriety.

"What the fucking hell?" Carmen growled. "Hope you had a good goddamn reason for doing that because . . ."

That's when she recognized the woman. Verin. The Healer who'd been there with Alyssa when she'd died.

"I . . . I'm sorry," the older woman said, pushing her hair behind her ears. Her face was largely unlined, but she had a few gray streaks mixed in with the brown locks. "I didn't . . . I just wanted to talk."

"I don't. Or didn't me getting blackout drunk give you a goddamn hint?"

Verin's eyes found the table, and tears started to fall down her cheeks.

Carmen sighed. "Look—I didn't mean it like that, alright? Just don't start crying on me. Listen—just tell me what you want, alright? I'm all ears."

Verin looked up, her eyes glistening. "I was with her."

"I know. Roman told me."

"I should have . . . I should have saved her," Verin said. "I wish . . . I just wasn't strong enough. But I'm a Healer, right? That's my job. I should have saved her."

Carmen shook her head. With sobriety came terrible clarity, and she saw the day's actions for what they were—especially when she saw her own grief reflected in Verin's.

"Look—it's okay," she said. "You did everything you could have done."

The matronly Healer said nothing.

"You're new around here, right? You just got here a couple of weeks before the tower."

Carmen didn't know what else to say. She didn't want to be the one to comfort someone else. She wasn't capable of it, and even if she was, that was a road she had no interest in traveling. So, she'd changed the subject.

"Yes. I came with a group of refugees. Some of us were allowed in, but . . . others were not," she said. "Because of what I did in the tower, Roman is letting the rest in."

"Well, at least something good came of it," Carmen said. And indeed, she meant it. Not only had they kept the tower from overflowing and burying them beneath a horde of Voxx, but it had saved a few refugees, too. Alyssa would have been proud of that. She took a deep breath, then said, "Look—I'm sure you mean well and everything, but I really can't do this right now. So, I'm going to go. I hope . . . I hope you get what you want out of all this. We can always use good Healers."

"T-thank you," Verin said, her gaze back on the wooden table.

Carmen just shook her head and pushed herself to her feet. After paying her tab—with a single copper etherium—she headed back home. She was done feeling sorry for herself. Now, she needed to focus on what really mattered—making the world a safer place for Miguel.

7

CHANGE IS IN THE AIR

A distinct chill laced the morning air as Elijah hefted a large boulder above his head. Judging by its size, the mass of rock was at least a few hundred pounds, and Elijah let out a loud grunt as he locked his elbows out before dropping it to the loamy ground. The moment he was free of his burden, his shoulders sagged in exhaustion. He'd been working out with that boulder for almost an hour, and it had certainly taken its toll. So, he channeled ethera through his soul and into Touch of Nature, sending a pulse of healing magic through his body.

It was only mildly effective in combating his fatigue, but as he'd learned since the very beginning of his time on the island, that strategy certainly helped to mitigate his recovery times. He spent the next few minutes stretching his tight muscles before taking off at a light jog that took him to the beach, where he didn't hesitate to dive into the ocean.

Over the next couple of hours, he swam a circuit around the island. Once, he wouldn't have dared any such feat—the fear of mutated marine life had been enough to keep him from even considering it—but ever since his time in the tower, he'd moved past those concerns. He was still wary, but with his Locus extending almost fifty yards from shore, he would know about any threat well before it posed any real danger.

Once he'd completed his circuit, Elijah climbed out of the ocean. His arms and legs were burning with exhaustion, but another pulse of Touch of Nature served to alleviate that, at least to some small degree. Still, he needed to rest a bit before he concluded his training regimen. With that in mind, he returned to his Grove, where he spent the next hour or so tending to his garden with Nature's Bounty.

The process was meditative as well as restorative—not to mention necessary—so by the time he'd finished, he was ready for the more enjoyable, if frustrating portion of his training.

Once he'd finished up with the garden, he left the Grove behind and headed for his old cabin. When he reached it, he saw that the derelict building was in just as poor of shape as it had always been, though the simple repairs he'd made—like closing off the collapsed wall by leaning a mixture of branches and moss against the roof—had fallen by the wayside. Likely, one of the frequent storms that plagued the area had torn the makeshift wall down.

The sight brought with it a degree of nostalgia. At times, it felt as if only a few days had passed since he'd washed ashore and taken refuge in the ruined structure. At others, it felt even more distant than the two-plus years that had passed since then. Still, without that cabin, Elijah probably wouldn't have survived, and if he had, it would have been significantly more difficult and a good deal less comfortable. So, if he ever met the original builder, he would shower that person with all the gratitude he could muster.

In any case, he wasn't there to reminisce about days past. Instead, just like when he'd gotten his first attack spell, Elijah had taken to using the area for training. So, without further hesitation, he embraced Shape of the Guardian and shifted into the curious ape-bear-lizard hybrid to which he'd gained access at level thirty.

A couple of days after he'd dealt with the invaders, Elijah had finally taken the opportunity to truly inspect his new form. And he hadn't been disappointed. With thick red-and-black scales, the new shape was monstrous in size. If he decided to push himself fully upright, Elijah estimated that the form was at least nine feet tall and heavily muscled. There was a significant layer of fat, too—not unlike a grizzly bear, in that respect.

The face was a little harder to describe in earthly terms, but if he forced himself to compare it to something familiar, he would have said that, with its spiny protrusions, it resembled a bearded dragon—which felt somewhat appropriate, given the nature of his Dragon Core.

By comparison, the scaled body was easier to categorize as distinctly simian in shape. With long arms, stumpy legs, and a powerful torso, the shape looked like it belonged to the world's largest, scaliest ape.

It also came with a significant issue, as specified by the description:

Shape of the Guardian **Archetype: Druid** **Class: Animist** **Level: 30** **Take on the form of a stalwart guardian, vastly increasing your Strength and Constitution attributes. Spellcasting is suspended while Shape of the Guardian is active.**	
Guardian's Renewal	**Instantly and completely regenerate. Cooldown affected by Regeneration attribute. Current cooldown: Once per week.**

On the surface, it all looked great. And it was, which was reflected in his status:

Name	Elijah Hart		
Level	30		
Archetype	Druid		
Class	Animist		
Specialization	N/A		
Alignment	N/A		
Strength	62 (31)		
Dexterity	40 (30)		
Constitution	72 (31)		
Ethera	39		
Regeneration	53 (33)		
Attunement	Nature		
Cultivation Stage: Cultivator			
Body	Core	Mind	Soul
Wood	Hatchling	Opal	Neophyte

After reaching level thirty, Elijah had been happy to find that his limit for augmentations had increased to three, not including One with Nature or Essence of the Wolf. So, he could keep Essence of the Monkey, Essence of the Boar, and Aura of Renewal active at all times—which he did. However, even with Essence of the Monkey increasing his Dexterity by ten points, there was a huge disparity between his power and coordination. So, while he was capable of incredibly rapid movement, he had difficulty controlling himself. The disparity was especially difficult to endure after spending so much time with his balance of attributes skewing more toward immense coordination.

The problem had presented itself during the fight with the gnomish leader of the invaders, and in hindsight, the only reason Elijah had managed to win that battle was because of a gross power disparity. He expected that he and Cabbot had been similarly leveled, but Elijah had the benefit of his comparatively advanced cultivation, so he got far more out of his attributes than the gnome had. Couple that with the overpowered nature of Shape of the Guardian—especially with Guardian's Renewal effectively bringing him back from the brink of death—and it wasn't difficult to understand how he'd won.

But it definitely hadn't been skill that saw him through to victory because, as Elijah had discovered every time he tried to use Shape of the Guardian, he was incredibly clumsy in the new form.

It was an issue he was determined to remedy.

Thus, he'd quickly incorporated it into his training regimen. He'd made some progress, but he knew he had a long way to go. So, he quickly got to it.

In his experience, nothing built hand-eye coordination quite like juggling, so Elijah had gathered a multitude of rocks for just that purpose. They weren't identical or anything—not like juggling balls usually were—but that worked in his favor. Or, rather, it made things much more difficult, which in turn made the exercise that much more effective. Still, it was a frustrating experience, and more than once, he'd used his incredible strength to chuck rocks off into the distance.

But he persisted, as much out of a stubborn refusal to give in to the limitations of the form as it was due to a desire to improve. Either way worked, but it definitely made for a very different mindset.

For almost two hours, Elijah kept at it until he'd finally had enough. Then, he moved on to engaging in various agility drills he'd learned over the years playing sports. These were slightly easier because he could ride a wave of momentum until completion. However, he tried to vary things just enough to throw off his own rhythm so that he forced himself to learn to control his body better.

Once he was finished with that, Elijah shadowboxed. He'd engaged in the drill often enough in the past that it should have come easily to him, but due to the disparity between his Strength and Dexterity, as well as the odd anatomy of the form, it was much more difficult than it should have been. However, just like with the juggling, he persisted through those frustrations, hoping that so long as he kept at it, he would learn to deal with the imbalanced attributes.

By its very nature, the form would never be particularly coordinated. That was an inescapable fact. And yet, Elijah hoped that repetitive practice would help him to work around the lack of coordination at least enough that he could control his bulky body. Because, as it stood, he had trouble even running in anything but a straight line, which meant that he would be a sitting duck for any agile foe.

After a little more than an hour of shadowboxing, Elijah finally arrived at the most hated part of his workout. At one point, he'd enjoyed yoga. There was something meditative about it that had always given him a sense of peace. But in his guardian form, the practice was far too frustrating to allow for anything even approaching that lofty state.

If anyone else would have been there, they would have probably gotten a good giggle out of watching a nine-foot-tall ape lizard trying to contort itself into various yoga poses. Elijah could acknowledge that it probably looked incredibly silly. However, as he tried to wrangle his body into each position, his frustration continued to mount until, at last, he'd had enough. With a bestial roar, he launched himself from the warrior pose and into a nearby tree. His foreclaw swept out, destroying the trunk of the tree in an explosion of splinters.

He watched as the tree tipped over, then fell. Slowly, his anger faded until, at last, his mind stilled to the point that he could make sense of what he'd just done. Ever since he'd gained Shape of the Predator, Elijah had known that his forms came with appropriate instincts. As a mist panther, it had manifested almost immediately when he'd lost himself in hunting a hare. Later, he'd nearly lost his humanity altogether in the Primordial Jungle. And presumably, the scaled-panther form that the shape had become when he'd attained his Dragon Core would show similar tendencies.

It was the form of a hunter, and once he assumed that shape, his instincts followed suit.

Now, the guardian form had shown its own colors. It was a stalwart, powerful beast, but he could easily envision a scenario where he lost himself to its ferocity. He'd have to keep that in mind, lest he do something he'd regret.

Like knocking down a perfectly innocent tree.

Or killing an annoying person.

With a bestial sigh, Elijah let the form drop. He'd had enough training with the scaled-ape form. Instead, he needed to work on something he'd put off for far too long.

In the Sea of Sorrows, he had been deprived of his predator form. As a result, he'd been forced to fight as a human, which had put him at a distinct disadvantage—not least because his attributes were distinctly inferior in his natural shape. However, it was also because, until that point, he'd relied on his mist-panther form in almost every physical confrontation. So, he just wasn't used to fighting as a human.

And certainly, he'd gotten by, but during those long days, he'd made a vow to himself to remedy his situation through training. Thus, he'd decided to practice with his staff. He knew that, if he ever had to fight someone like Cabbot in his human form, he'd never come out on top. He just didn't have the attributes or abilities to do that. But he hoped to develop his technique to the point where he could at least hold his own long enough to bring his various spells to bear.

The problem with that was that he had almost no experience fighting with a staff, and as a result, when he decided to train, he felt like a little kid swinging a stick around. Which wasn't so far from the truth, really. The only difference was that, with at least some fighting experience, he had some notion of what might work. So, over the past week, he'd developed a few drills so he could practice strikes and blocks while incorporating some boxing footwork.

Was it perfect?

Far from it.

But it was the best he could do with the resources he had. So, as the sun dipped toward the horizon, Elijah occupied himself with flailing his staff around. He tried to maintain some semblance of discipline and technique, but the results were, at best, mixed. Still, he kept at it until night finally fell.

As darkness enveloped the forest, Elijah returned to the Grove, where he made another circuit of his garden—and the trees that constituted his Ancestral Circle—while flaring Nature's Bounty. Finally, he ended his day with a meal of berries and fish-and-mushroom stew. All in all, it was a good day, but he suspected that it would take many more before he saw any real results.

In the meantime, though, he intended to take Ramik and Carisa up on their offer. He'd already bound the weapons together with some of his homemade cordage—he wasn't going to waste the looted rope on something like that—and he planned to head to Ironshore at first light.

With that in mind, he took a long, cold shower—he certainly missed hot water something fierce—then went to bed.

8

A WARM WELCOME

The next morning dawned crisp and cool, but Elijah was hesitant to extract himself from his warm, rabbit-fur blankets. Still, he was a creature of habit, and he had many tasks to accomplish before heading to Ironshore. So, he groaned as he threw the comfortable bedding aside and pushed himself to his feet.

Soon enough, he began his morning routine. Starting with a leftover-fish-stew breakfast and ending with an abbreviated version of his training regimen, it wasn't long before Elijah was donning his best outfit. It was a toga, just like the one he'd worn for the first meeting, but the stitching was a little tighter and the fit a little better. Still, he knew he was never going to be much of a tailor, which highlighted one of his goals for the day.

If he did nothing else, he intended to purchase some proper clothing. To that end, Elijah found the little basket where he kept his pilfered etherium and dumped it all in one of his homemade satchels. Then, he gathered the looted weapons in an awkward bundle before heading to the beach where the invaders' incursion had begun.

The rowboats were all exactly where he'd left them, so he selected the sturdiest one and shoved it into the surf. The water was frigid, but Elijah had grown used to it during his daily swims, so it was only mildly uncomfortable. Likely, that had as much to do with his Constitution as it did his routine. In any case, he pushed the small vessel out to sea, then hopped inside and started rowing across the strait.

As he went, Elijah was reminded of the last time he'd crossed over to the mainland. Back then, he'd been on a mission to rescue a dragon from people intent on draining her for their own cultivation. That had ended with Elijah killing quite a few gnomish Ritualists, saving the dragon, and obtaining a Dragon Core. That Core cultivation had, in turn, given him the strength to kill the invaders.

He sighed as he continued to row.

So much had happened, and in so little time. Once, he'd struggled to even place on the power ladder, but now? He'd progressed into the top twenty-five, and given the advanced state of his cultivation—which Nerthus claimed should have been impossible on such a young world—Elijah felt comfortable in saying that he was one of the most powerful people on Earth.

Which was insane.

Almost as if to reassure himself, he opened the ladder and found himself in the thirty-second position:

Planetary Power Rankings (Earth)

Oscar Ramirez—Level 38
Sadie Song—Level 37
Hu Shui—Level 35
Ram Khandu—Level 35
Anupriya Pandey—Level 34
Kimberly Jackson—Level 33
Abigail Lowrey—Level 33
Michael King—Level 33
Gunnar Lindstrom—Level 33
Thor Gunderson—Level 32
Niko Song—Level 32

. . .

. . .

. . .

Elijah Hart—Level 30

. . .

. . .

. . .

Carmen Rodriguez—Level 21

Oscar Ramirez, whoever he was, still maintained the top spot, and most of the other names were unchanged. However, Elijah noticed that one of the Songs had dropped off the list entirely. It didn't take a genius to intuit that they were now dead. Given what he'd been through so far, Elijah expected that to happen more often, too.

He kept reading the names until he got to his, and initially, intended to close the window. But then a new name jumped out at him. Carmen Rodriguez. His sister-in-law. The oars came to a stop, and as he stared at that line, the boat just drifted back and forth in the gentle current.

Carmen was alive. But what did that mean? Surely, she wouldn't have let anything happen to his sister. Definitely not to Miguel. In fact, if something had gone wrong with Elijah's nephew, he felt confident that Carmen would have descended into apathy or, in a worst-case scenario, suicidal thoughts. No—if Carmen was alive, then the rest of her family and by extension, Elijah's—had to have made it, as well.

A broad grin spread across his face as he realized just how much he'd dreaded finding out his family's fate. Now, he knew. He just knew that Alyssa and Miguel were okay, and that made everything so much easier. So, with that buoying his mood, he resumed his rowing, propelling the little rowboat across the strait.

Still, it took quite some time to cover the distance, so he had plenty of opportunity to think. Mostly, his thoughts centered on Alyssa, Carmen, and Miguel, and he found himself wondering how they had survived. Had they formed a community with other survivors outside of Seattle? Or had they gone into the city itself? More, what classes had they gotten? Miguel was only ten or eleven years old—by Elijah's calculation, at least—but had he gotten an arche-type when the world had transformed?

Elijah had no answers to any of his questions, but he couldn't help but ask them in his own mind. And like that, he eventually found himself completing his journey and approaching the Ironshore docks.

They weren't terribly impressive, at least compared to what Elijah had seen in the old world. However, they were functional enough, and the long docks seemed capable of berthing at least a half dozen of the whaling ships he'd seen sailing from the small city.

Elijah navigated to one of the shorter docks, keenly aware of all the peo-ple—mostly gnomes, dwarves, and goblins—watching his every move. Some-one called out to him, but he ignored the shout. Instead, he pulled up to the dock, then used a rope attached to the rowboat to tie off. Then, he reached down and heaved the bundle of weapons onto the wooden planks. They landed with a clanking thud, but Elijah paid the sound little attention. Instead, he was prepared to shift to his guardian form at a moment's notice.

His caution proved unnecessary because, only a few moments after he'd landed, a small figure—even for a gnome, he was minuscule—scurried in his direction. When he got close, he nervously smoothed his long mustache and said, "Welcome, Protector of the Grove, to our humble town!" He bowed deeply. "I have sent for Overseer Ramik. I am Uban, the dockmaster."

"Good to meet you, Uban," Elijah said, climbing out of the boat. His bare feet slapped against the dock, reminding him that he wasn't wearing any shoes. The lack certainly hadn't been a problem back on his island, but now, with every passing second, he grew distinctly more aware of his state of dress. By compari-son, Uban wore what Elijah would have classified as Victorian garb. The cut was a bit wrong, and his wide-brimmed hat reminded him of a bolero, but it somehow fit the aesthetic. In any case, Elijah's homemade toga was, in a word, shabby to the point of being classified as rags.

Which it kind of was, considering that he'd made the garment from repur-posed Ritualist's robes.

Whatever the case, that was an issue that had contributed to his decision to visit Ironshore in the first place. Hopefully, he could find replacement clothing—and much more—while he was in town.

"You don't have to use that whole Protector of the Grove stuff," he said. "Just call me Elijah."

"Oh . . . Okay," said the anxious gnome. "Elijah."

After that, the little gnome tried to make nervous small talk, but he was obviously too anxious to succeed. So, Elijah tried his best to seem welcoming and kind, but with his lack of social interaction over the past couple of years, he was more than a little out of practice. He was nearly certain that the smile he meant to be reassuring came across as a little demented.

As a result, he felt no small degree of relief when Ramik approached. Elijah nodded to him and said, "I brought your weapons. What'll you give me for them?"

"Ah . . . There are some . . . Um . . . These are all Unranked grade," Ramik stated. "The best we can do is five silver etherium per weapon."

Elijah had no idea if that was an appropriate price, so he took a moment to think it over. He must've looked a bit hostile because Ramik quickly cleared his throat and amended his previous offer to seven silver. Elijah accepted that, then watched as someone else—a dwarf—sorted through the weapons and gave the goblin overseer a count. Ramik accepted that, then counted out seventy-seven silver coins, which he handed to Elijah. Once those had been deposited in his homemade satchel, he told the goblin what he wanted.

"First things first, I need to go to the Branch," Elijah said. "Then, I want to get some new clothes. Something durable. Maybe a good pack, too. Seeds, if you have them. And some spices. After that, if I have money left over, I want to buy a woodworking kit. Knives and files and such. Can you provide all of that?"

Ramik tapped his lip. "The clothes, certainly. And we're lucky enough to have a high-level Leatherworker in town, so the pack won't be a problem, either. As for the seeds . . . maybe. We have some Farmers, but I don't know if they'll be willing to part with any of their seeds. Spices, I'm afraid, won't be possible. Not unless you want to go through the Branch Market."

"I might just do that," Elijah stated. He'd been living without proper spices for so long that the idea of even basic seasoning seemed positively decadent. But he wasn't going to go broke just for a little paprika. "And the tools?"

Ramik said that he could accommodate that, too. So, without further delay, the little goblin—and his couple of dwarven guards—led Elijah through Ironshore and to the large building that seemed like the small town's hub.

He didn't know what to expect, but as they progressed through the building, Elijah was a little surprised to find that it was largely normal. Sure, some of the architectural choices seemed a little odd, and it certainly wasn't sized for someone of his height, but it definitely wasn't so abnormal that it seemed alien.

The same, however, could not be said for the crystalline tree that was the Branch.

"It's beautiful," he muttered to himself, wide-eyed as he took it in.

Ramik asked, "Is this the first time you've seen one?"

"It is."

"This one is a little more advanced than what you would see in a native settlement," the goblin stated with pride. "It is an import from my home world."

"I see," Elijah lied. He didn't want to show the depth of his ignorance, so he kept his questions to himself. But he did ask one that couldn't be avoided: "How do I access it?"

"Just touch it."

Elijah approached, trying to ignore the stern-looking dwarf that stood watch. He expected that the robed individual was one of the Envoys of the Cult of the World Tree Nerthus had mentioned. As such, he wanted to avoid offending her. So, he nodded and asked, "May I?"

"You may," she replied in a gruff voice. "Don't be expectin' special treatment from now on, though. You come back 'ere, and you wait just like everybody else, ya hear?"

Elijah nodded. He'd had no idea that he was skipping to the front of a line, but he wasn't going to refuse now that it had been arranged. So, he stepped forward and laid one gentle hand on the crystal tree's trunk.

Immediately, he became aware of a series of notifications waiting to be opened. He cycled through them, and as he did, he recognized them as menus meant to help him navigate the Branch's various functions. There were almost a dozen headings, but most were inaccessible to him. Instead, only five were available: the Market, the Bank, the Knowledge Base, the Regional Map, and the Communications Apparatus.

The first destination was the Bank. From Nerthus, he knew that each time he'd killed something, the system had marked him for reward. And the Bank was where he could access those rewards.

Copper	Silver	Gold	Platinum
321	92	11	0

"Can I deposit the coins I already have into the Bank?" Elijah asked, glancing in the Envoy's direction.

"You may. Simply think it and the Branch will transfer any coins you have on your person to the Bank."

Elijah followed the dwarven woman's directions, and with a stir of ethera, the coins he had in his pack disappeared. When he looked at the readout for his balance, he was unsurprised to see that it had changed slightly:

Copper	Silver	Gold	Platinum
362	179	11	0

Satisfied, Elijah moved to the next order of business: accessing the Knowledge Base. To his surprise, there were hundreds of topics ranging from crafting methods to faction information, with some of the guides carrying hefty price tags. So, he satisfied himself with subjects pertaining to the system itself. Still, he spent three gold on almost two dozen guides before he finally settled on one called "A Practical Guide to Progression." It was touted as a sort of progression-for-idiots instruction manual, and Elijah eagerly paid the fifteen silver to gain access.

When he'd finished, twenty-two crystalline leaves grew from the tree's branches, but Elijah wasn't finished. He still wanted to check out the Market, the Regional Map, and the Communications Apparatus. He hoped they might give him some insight into where his sister might have ended up.

As it turned out, all three topics were largely useless for him. The Regional Map only showed one other settlement, and it was almost two hundred miles away. It was also the only accessible target for communications, though at an exorbitant cost of fifty silver etherium per message. The Market was a little better, but Elijah held off on buying any of the few items available to him. He still had more practical concerns, and he didn't want to spend all his money on frivolity.

So, with that done, he collected the leaves, tossed them into his satchel, and let Ramik lead him away from the Branch and to what he dubbed the Crafting District.

9

SHOPPING SPREE

In preparation for what he hoped would be a shopping spree, Elijah had kept a decent number of etherium coins out. At Ramik's suggestion, though, he restricted himself to a few dozen copper coins and ten silver.

"You shouldn't need more than that," the little goblin said, checking what looked like a pocket watch he'd pulled from his vest pocket. "But if you do, you can always return to the Branch and withdraw more."

"What's that?" Elijah asked, curiously nodding at the device.

"Oh. I apologize for the rudeness," Ramik answered. "But all this talk of money prompted me to check my own available etherium. This is an enchanted coin-storage device called a folio. It doesn't actually hold etherium, but instead allows you to exchange promissory notes with other people. If you had one of these, it would obviate the need to carry coins on your person."

"How does it work? And where can I get one?"

"It only stores information," Ramik said with a small smile. "It maintains a thin connection to the Branch, allowing one to transfer wealth without physically exchanging coins."

"Like a credit card," Elijah reasoned. It sounded remarkably similar, and just as convenient as his old debit card.

"I have no idea what that is."

"Sorry. My world—before all of this—had a similar system. Though we used a different currency."

"Ah. I see. As to where you might acquire a folio, I can show you to an appropriate tinkering shop. You will still have to get it paired to your personal Bank, and it likely won't be inexpensive."

"Oh. Okay," Elijah said, already preparing himself to do without. He had no real notion of how much his money was really worth, but he couldn't imagine that it was a lot. So, he moved on to the next subject, asking, "So, what about clothes? I don't know if you noticed, but I'm kind of wearing rags here."

He tried to soften the statement with a slight grin, but Ramik still went a little greener than normal as his eyes found the persistent bloodstains on Elijah's toga. He'd scrubbed the cloth as well as he could manage, but blood tended to be quite difficult to wash away. He'd also hoped that the cloth's dark material would hide it.

Clearly, he'd been wrong.

Suddenly, he realized what he must look like to the residents of Ironshore. In the beginning, he'd hoped that most of them would be ignorant of his exploits, but judging by the fearful looks that had followed him since his arrival in the small town, that just wasn't the case. So, that, combined with his curious manner of dress, massive-in-comparison size, and apparent disdain for grooming, had probably given people the wrong impression about him.

"I wouldn't say no to a barber, either," he remarked.

"I think we could arrange that," Ramik said, tucking his folio away.

Elijah ran his hand through his curly hair, adding, "You don't have to escort me around. I can find my own way."

"Ah, well, I think it's best if I show you where to find everything. The Black Sky mercenaries weren't popular. Not exactly. But they still had friends."

That was the first time Elijah had heard the name of the group who'd assaulted his island, and for some reason, he wasn't surprised to find that they had been classified as mercenaries. That fit with what he'd seen.

After that, Ramik led him down the street and toward a nearby building. Elijah had spent some time exploring the small city in his predator form, but in the light of day, everything looked so much nicer. But then again, he'd been a little distracted by his mission to rescue the dragon the last time he'd been in Ironshore.

In any case, he was pleasantly surprised by how clean and orderly the little town was—it really did look like a mix of a settlement out of an old Western and something he'd see in a modern fantasy movie. That impression was only supported by the presence of tiny gnomes and green goblins. Dwarves, by comparison, could almost pass for short, particularly hirsute, and broad humans.

Elijah couldn't help but gawk a little as he followed Ramik into what turned out to be a barbershop manned by a trio of swarthy gnomes. They were all absolutely tiny, had blisteringly white hair, and eyebrows that looked like not-so-small caterpillars of the same hue. Elijah would have put a few of his coins on the idea that they were related in some way. Perhaps even brothers, given their similar features.

"Oi! This the one, then?" asked one of them.

"Course it is, you dolt! How many o' them you thinks is runnin' round 'ere?" asked another.

"Don't kill us, Mr. Protector," said the third. "We ain't got nothin' to do with no Black Sky bastards. I was just sayin' the other day as how we ought to kick 'em out, I was. Send 'em back where they come from, I said."

"You ain't said no such thing, Brok."

"Did so!"

"I ain't never heard so much as a peep of that kind o' talk."

"Wasn't talkin' to you when I said it, was I? Nope. I was talkin' to ol' Derkins. You can ask 'im, too. He'll tell you the same, he will."

"Gentlemen," interjected Ramik. All three went silent in the space of a heartbeat, telling Elijah that the goblin was held in no small esteem. "Mr. Elijah requires your services."

"Oh," said Brok, narrowing his eyes. Then, they widened. "Oh. You need a little trim, you do. Step right up, big fella. We'll get you sorted in a hurry, we will."

As he spoke, he gestured to a chair that looked like it'd been sized to fit a dwarf. Elijah had never been a giant—in fact, he was considered a little below average in the height department, at least for a human being—but he was skeptical that he'd fit. Still, he followed the gnome's instructions and miraculously wedged himself into place.

What followed was the oddest twenty minutes of Elijah's relatively young life. He'd had plenty of haircuts through the years, but the way Brok did it was certainly a novel experience. On the surface, some of it was familiar. The gnome used scissors just like any other barber Elijah had ever seen. However, those shears weren't wielded in the gnome's hands. Instead, they floated around seemingly of their own accord as Brok gestured here and there.

At first, Elijah was a little leery of the sharp scissors—and how close they came to his ears—but it quickly became apparent that Brok was in complete control. So, he let himself relax a little as he listened to the three brothers drone on and on about one thing or another.

If Elijah was honest, it felt good, just hearing other people talk. He'd had a few conversations with Nerthus over the months since being stranded on the island, but they were few and far between. Most of the time, he'd been all alone, with no one for company but himself. And though he wasn't about to go insane from the lack of human contact, he definitely recognized that it was no way for a human being to live. In short, it was nice just being around other people—even if those other people were bickering among themselves about things he didn't really understand.

Elijah ended up paying a few copper etherium for the service, and judging by Ramik's narrowed eyes, he'd gotten ripped off. However, a few measly coins were a small price to pay for something he'd very much needed.

Next, Ramik led a freshly shorn Elijah a few streets over and into a storefront that was obviously a tailor's premises. Soon enough, a pudgy, matronly female dwarf stomped out, put her hands on her hips, then demanded, "What is this, then?"

"Um . . ."

Seeing that Elijah was out of his element, Ramik stepped up, saying, "Mari, this is Elijah. Our friend and potential ally from the island."

"The island? What island are you . . ."

Her face went white, and she took a step back.

"He needs some clothing. Simple grade, if you have the materials."

For a few seconds, she didn't respond. Clearly, she was frightened of Elijah, but he had no idea how to combat that impression. So, he remained silent as she worked her way through her feelings. In the end, it was probably Ramik's presence that got her to come around, but even then, she still didn't look happy to have Elijah in her shop.

That was fine, though. He'd never really expected to be accepted in Ironshore, but so long as he got what he needed out of them, he'd be happy. In fact, he'd already accomplished his primary goal by buying the various guides from the Branch. Those would hopefully go a long way to cure his ignorance and give him some much-needed direction going forward. Everything else was just icing on the cake, as far as Elijah was concerned.

Still, the idea of getting some proper clothes was definitely attractive, especially if he intended to encounter more people anytime soon. The notion of meeting other humans while wearing nothing but a bloodstained toga stitched together from rags wasn't precisely appealing.

Finally, she said, "Seven silver. Each. I can modify some trousers for him. A few shirts. No boots, though. His feet are too big for goblin- or gnome-sized shoes and far too narrow for anything meant for a dwarf. And I don't have the materials for anything special order."

After that, she disappeared into the back, leaving Elijah to examine the wares on display in her shop. The clothes were a fairly simple design, and they seemed high-quality, if mundane. When Mari returned, she had a clear pane of glass in one hand and a pad with a stylus in the other.

She held the glass up, reminding Elijah of people taking photos with their smartphones, then said, "Hmm. The pants are going to be a bit short. Mid-calf, at best. Can't stretch the materials any more than that, so it'll just have to do."

Elijah wasn't exactly keen on wearing what sounded a lot like capri pants, but he wasn't going to argue with the dwarven woman. She already didn't like him—that much was clear—so he didn't want to push his luck. So, he agreed before asking, "That piece of glass—that's for measurements, right?"

"It is. Also lets me apply one of my abilities to inspect items other than clothing," she said. "Nice staff, by the way. Shame it's bound to you. You could sell it for quite a few etherium. Who made it?"

"I did."

She narrowed her eyes, then said, "Interesting. Clothes will be ready in a couple of hours. Now, shoo."

Elijah didn't need any other prompting, and he left the shop with Ramik only a moment later. Their next stop was a Leatherworker who sold Elijah a miraculous pack that could accommodate almost twice the volume its exterior would suggest it could hold. In addition, it was a Simple-grade item, so it was much more durable than more mundane packs. The only downside was that it cost Elijah most of his remaining silver, which meant that for any more shopping, he'd have to return to the Branch.

Before that, Ramik took him to purchase his own folio. His first impression of Ramik's device seemed accurate, and the item he ended up buying for himself looked like a pewter pocket watch. When he opened it, though, he didn't see a clock face; instead, there were a series of dials meant to indicate how much etherium he had in his Bank. At present, all the dials were on zero, but that was because he had yet to pair it with the Branch.

Which was, by necessity, the next stop. This time, Elijah was forced to awkwardly wait in line, just as the Envoy had promised. He didn't mind, though. It gave him some time to fiddle with his pack, which was an endless source of wonder for him. He'd been using magic for quite some time, but a bag that seemed to house a much bigger space than it should just seemed more miraculous.

Apparently, such containers weren't uncommon in the wider universe, but on Earth, with its low level of ethera density, they would be quite limited in their function as well as potency. That Ironshore had one as versatile as it was turned out to be a stroke of luck, which explained why it had been so expensive.

After Elijah had paired his folio with the Branch, he and Ramik finished up his shopping. He probably spent more money than he should have, but in the end, he acquired almost everything on his list. The lone exception was, predictably, spices. He got a few, but Ironshore simply didn't have enough to spare.

Finally, Ramik asked, "I don't mean to be presumptuous, but would you like to join me for a meal? There are a few people who wish to speak with you."

Elijah almost refused outright, but then he thought better of it. The people of Ironshore—aside from the ones who'd attacked his island—had been decent enough to him. So, he felt that he should return the favor. He wasn't about to commit to any alliances, but the idea of cultivating a decent relationship with his neighbors seemed more attractive than ever before.

So, he said, "That sounds nice. I'm starving."

10

A MEAL

The smell of smoked meats greeted Elijah before the restaurant even came into sight. His mouth watered as he remembered all the barbecue joints he'd sampled over the course of his life. His infrequent forays into vegetarianism—usually taken at the insistence of a girlfriend or his more environmentally conscious coworkers—had consistently been squandered by his love of well-cooked meat. He was a born carnivore, and no amount of social pressure could ever really change that, even if he'd made a decent effort at it from time to time.

But now, after having to subsist for more than two years with nothing but his own terrible cooking for comfort, he couldn't stop his mouth from watering the moment those savory smells graced his nostrils.

Thankfully, he didn't have to wait long before they reached the restaurant. It was a squat structure that took up an entire corner of an intersection of two major thoroughfares, and judging by the number of people entering and exiting the building, it was one of Ironshore's more popular destinations.

The interior was packed with dwarves, gnomes, goblins, and the odd elf, all of whom sat at a pair of long tables that reminded Elijah of cafeterias he'd seen during his high school years. The only difference, aside from the clientele, was that instead of being made of plastic and stainless steel, those tables were constructed of scrubbed wood.

Of course, the moment the diners saw Elijah, their conversations came to a poignant halt as each and every eye turned to behold the interloper in their midst. Ramik seemed to have anticipated this, and he quickly led Elijah across the main room and to a private dining area. There, Elijah found at least one familiar face among the five other people already seated at a more formal-looking table.

Carisa nodded to him, and said, "Welcome to the Stuck Pig. Best Cook in town runs the joint."

"I could smell it from a block away," Elijah admitted. He gave her a reassuring smile before adding, "Believe me when I say it almost brought tears to my eyes."

Soon enough, Ramik had guided Elijah to a chair, and the moment he sat, he realized what his next project should be. Sure, Nerthus had grown a few chairs in his tree house, but if he wanted to sit in his garden, he had to do so on the ground. Already, his mind whirled with plans for building the perfect chair.

It wasn't until a few seconds later that he realized that he'd been staring off into space, and that everyone was looking at him.

Elijah cleared his throat, then said, "Sorry. I've been alone for a long, long time, and I sometimes get a bit lost in my own head."

"How long?" asked Carisa.

Elijah shrugged. "Honestly, I'm not exactly sure," he said. "Time got a bit funny there for a while. I think it's been around two years. Except Nerthus, of course, but he doesn't really count."

"Why?" asked one of the other goblins. Elijah noted that she had conniving eyes, so he marked her as untrustworthy. But that wasn't so different from all the rest of them. Not really, at least. Even Ramik and Carisa, both of whom had actually helped him, had yet to earn his trust.

"Who is Nerthus?" asked the fourth diner. He was another dwarf, and judging by the way he kept glancing toward Carisa, the pair were either related or a couple. Elijah didn't know enough about dwarven physiology or mannerisms to make a judgment about which one was more likely.

"Just a friend. He's not important," Elijah said. "These are some nice chairs, by the way. You wouldn't know who made them, would you? I'd love to get the plans."

"Chairs?"

"Yeah. I don't have any chairs on my island. Well, I do, but they're not exactly where I want them, you know? I was thinking of building a couple. Everyone needs a hobby, I guess, and I suppose I could make chair building mine. Though after I finish one chair, I don't know if I'll want to build more. That's the ticket, I think. Figuring out what you want to keep doing, I mean. I keep trying to fill my time with different things, but after doing it once, I'm done with it. Like when I made my soap. It was a fun and diverting project, but I don't think I ever really want to do it again. At least until I need more soap, I guess."

Everyone just stared at him like he'd grown a third ear. But unlike with Sara the dragon, Elijah hadn't just started running off at the mouth on accident. Instead, he'd done it for a reason—to throw them off and keep them from focusing on his slip of the tongue. He hadn't intended to mention Nerthus. Nor had he meant to awkwardly stare off into space.

As it turned out, the group was willing to forgive his seeming eccentricity, and they soon turned their attention to the reason they'd invited him to the meal in the first place. They wanted an alliance—desperately, it seemed. When Elijah had killed the Black Sky mercenaries who'd tried to invade his island, he'd robbed Ironshore of much of their defense force. As such, they were vulnerable—and they knew it.

To them, Elijah represented a solution to that problem. After all, he was powerful enough to kill almost fifty people, all by himself. Surely, he could protect them from anything that might come after them until they managed to contract more mercenaries.

Either way, they spent the next fifteen minutes trying to forge an alliance with Elijah. For his part, he was content with a pact of nonaggression, so he didn't commit to anything one way or another. Fortunately, it wasn't long until the food arrived.

Elijah's eyes lit up as one tray of steaming meat after another was brought in by the restaurant's waitstaff. They were all goblins, identifiable by their simple, if identical red outfits, but Elijah was admittedly unconcerned with anything but the food they served. Not only was there plenty of meat—it looked like pork, but it might've been something else—slathered in some sort of red sauce, but there were also tureens filled with various vegetables. When he saw the rest of the diners serving their own plates, Elijah didn't hesitate to join them, piling his own plate high with everything he saw.

Over the course of his life, Elijah had eaten plenty of great meals. From the simple—like the home-cooked meals he'd once enjoyed with his family—to the borderline ostentatious, like eating at five-star restaurants in celebration of special occasions, he'd enjoyed some of the best Earth had to offer.

None of it came close to what he tasted in Ironshore's best restaurant. With the grace of hindsight, Elijah could admit that his enjoyment was based at least partially on the fact that he'd been eating charred crab and poorly prepared fish stew for most of the past two years. But unbeknownst to him, it was also the effect someone with the Cook class could have on food preparation.

Either way, he would remember it as the best meal he'd ever eaten, and it was almost enough to push him over the edge and into an alliance, if only it meant that he could enjoy their food a little more often.

"I think I might have to kidnap your Cook and put them to work on my island," he joked. The levity didn't quite make it through, though, and he got a couple of frightened looks before he pointed out that he was, in fact, joking. That got a couple of nervous laughs, telling him in no uncertain terms how they saw him.

To them, he was a dangerous and unpredictable force that was responsible for mass murder. Did it matter that he had no intention of attacking anyone who didn't try to attack him first? No. Nuance was easily outpaced by fear, and never was that more obvious than during that wonderful meal.

As a result, Elijah was at least a little relieved when it came to an end. With a promise that he would give the alliance all due consideration, he and Ramik left the others behind. Without any other errands to run—and with daylight already starting to fade—Elijah and the goblin stopped by the clothier so he could pick up his clothes.

Mari, the Tailor, handed him a few large parcels, telling him that she had put together three full outfits for him. He thanked her, paid the fee—plus a bit extra for her trouble—and then told Ramik that he was ready to return to his island.

The goblin took that in stride and escorted him through town and back to the dock. Once there, Ramik broached the subject of the alliance. "We really could use your assistance," he said. "I know you are hesitant to—"

"Look," Elijah said. "I'm not saying I don't want an alliance. I'm not sure. But if you need me, just send someone to the island. Don't stray from the beach, and I'll be there as soon as possible. As far as mutual defense—I'll do what I can. I'm not saying I'll come to your rescue, but I'm not saying I won't, either."

Ramik sighed. "That will have to do, then."

Elijah climbed into the rowboat, then added, "But I want to reiterate. Just because we're playing nice doesn't mean I've forgotten that your people were the aggressors. I know you claim not to have had anything to do with Cabbot and his mercenaries, and I'm inclined to believe you. But if anyone comes to my island looking for trouble, trust me when I say that they'll get more than they want."

With that, he pushed off and started rowing across the strait.

As he went, Elijah considered the proposed alliance. It seemed to him that Ironshore didn't really have much to offer that he couldn't get for himself. Sure, he liked having access to a Branch, but he'd exhausted the possibilities of the easily attainable guides. To go any deeper, he'd need quite a lot of time to sort through the seemingly endless possibilities. Still with the crystalline leaves in his pack, he had more information to study now than he could get through in a year.

And he'd gotten everything else he needed for the time being.

So, why would he ally himself with them, except as an expression of social responsibility? Could he sit idly by and watch them be overrun by some unnamed enemy? What if the Voxx attacked them? Or some pack of dangerously mutated animals? Or worse, another settlement?

No. Elijah knew himself well enough to recognize that he couldn't do that. Did that make him some doomed white knight? Maybe. It certainly wasn't conducive to self-preservation. However, he simply didn't want to be the sort of person who could stand by and watch people being killed just because he couldn't find any reason to intervene. If he could help, he would. Basic decency dictated at least that much commitment.

But he had no intention of committing to some sort of official alliance. More than anything, he wanted to be left alone—at least until he didn't—and the best way to do that was to keep to himself and maintain a sense of danger that would hopefully keep the people of Ironshore away.

With that in mind, Elijah crossed the strait, arriving back on his island just before the sun settled below the horizon.

11

EXPLORATION

The crystalline leaf glittered in the faint light of Elijah's tree house, but he was no longer fascinated by the thing's structure. It was just an information-delivery device, little different from a book, and as such, he was far more interested in the knowledge it contained. Figuring out how to use the leaves had taken Elijah a few hours, and it was only when Nerthus stepped in to explain it that he'd managed to unlock the information stored within.

Looking back, Elijah should have figured it out on his own. The idea—to simply inject a bit of ethera into the item, much as he would with one of his spells—wasn't complicated. However, after returning from Ironshore, he was emotionally exhausted, and he'd let that affect his thought processes. Once Nerthus had stepped in, though, his mood improved, and he set about learning everything he could.

Like everything else in the new world, the leaves were tied to the System, and as such, they sent information directly into his mind, opening windows not unlike his notifications, that he could read at his own pace.

"I might have overdone it with the guides," he muttered to himself, tossing the glittering leaf onto his bed and lying back. So far, he'd only made it through a single one, and even then, he hadn't absorbed half the information he probably should have. Despite his experience with academia, Elijah had never enjoyed studying. He could do it, as evidenced by the degrees he'd earned, but it was always an exercise in frustration.

The first leaf he'd chosen to read was, predictably, the one dedicated to giving an overview of progression, and at the most basic level, he understood it well enough. Still, he looked at the page still hovering in his mind:

Whether they are Warriors or crafters, Scholars or mages, each person is subject to the Divine System, which eases the burden of progression and provides an easily quantifiable means of tracking and guiding an individual's strength.

The generally accepted tiers of power are as follows:

Level 1–125	Mortal
Level 126–250	Ascendent
Level 251–500	Demigod
Level 501–1000	Deity
Level 1000+	Transcendent

As he'd read the information on each individual tier, Elijah had learned that Mortals made up the vast majority of the population. However, there was a huge difference between a level one and someone who'd reached the peak of said tier.

Before a person progressed to Ascendent, they would be given the opportunity to choose a specialization. The progression through the associated levels would also come with an even sharper increase in attributes and the power of skills, spells, and abilities. And upon reaching the one-hundred and twenty-fifth level, a person would have the opportunity to evolve their class into a more powerful—and often better-focused—variant.

The same could be said for reaching Demigod status, when a person's class would go through its second evolution. Then, it would once again evolve upon progressing to the Deity tier. The information about becoming a Transcendent was a little spotty, largely because few people ever reached those heights. And the ones who did weren't contributing to guides. If they were, Elijah didn't have access to that information, and even if he did, a fraction of the associated cost would be enough to bankrupt him many times over.

In any case, he didn't think he'd have to worry about that kind of thing anytime soon. Progressing through the Mortal Realm was supposed to take years, but a single line had given Elijah hope that his ascent would be a little quicker:

> **On newly integrated worlds, progress may be accelerated due to higher ethera density and increased opportunity.**

Basically, he interpreted that as meaning that he would have more foes to fight, and thus, more experience—or kill energy—to absorb. So far, that had proved to be the case, and he expected that when he set off to explore, it would be even more dramatic.

The Ascendent Realm was known to take much longer to cross than the Mortal Realm, and even the talented often stumbled along the way. That wasn't surprising to Elijah. In a journey that would take multiple decades, people would inevitably lose motivation or exhaust their own talent. More would be distracted by mundane concerns. Even the increase in longevity that came with reaching the Ascendent Realm wasn't enough to combat the many obstacles in the way of reaching Demigod status.

The same could be said for the path to becoming a Deity, though it was even more arduous and, outside of a few rare exceptions, always took centuries.

As he'd already noted, information on reaching the Transcendent Realm was thin on the ground, though the guide did note that, with everything after Ascendent, it wasn't enough to simply reach the appropriate level of power. There was some kind of trial required, as well, and with each realm of power, those trials grew more difficult.

Basically, everything he'd learned told Elijah that if he wanted to reach the peak, it was going to be the product of centuries. So, while it was interesting to contemplate, he knew he'd be better off focusing on the immediate future.

To that end, he'd continued his study, discovering the item grades, enchantment tiers, and more importantly, information regarding cultivation. According to the guide, there were nine levels of each facet of cultivation. For Mind, Soul, and Body, the levels were standardized, but with the Core, it was individualized. There were many types of Core cultivation—some common and others far rarer—but nothing he'd read indicated that anyone else had anything like his Dragon Core.

Nerthus had indicated as much, but he'd still half expected to see it listed among the examples in the guide. When it wasn't, it started to dawn on Elijah just how much of an advantage Sara's mother had bestowed upon him.

In the end, he spent almost three days perusing the various guides, and he'd come away much less ignorant than he'd been before going to Ironshore. And yet, he knew there was a nearly infinite amount of knowledge still out there. Some subjects the guides had barely brushed on—like the Voxx or the various races that comprised the universe's population—but Elijah felt certain that there was a lot more that wasn't even mentioned.

In short, he couldn't learn everything in a day or two of intense study. Not surprising, really. Even on Earth, which was just a single planet, it was impossible to learn everything about everything. So, a universe made of hundreds—if not thousands—of inhabited planets was that much more complex.

Still, it was nice to have some of the most basic information at his disposal.

However, he'd reached the end of his patience. Before his visit to Ironshore, Elijah had made plans to explore the surrounding area and, hopefully, eventually reunite with his family. Those intentions hadn't changed. So, it was with some anticipation that he levered himself out of bed, gathered the scattered leaves, and replaced them in a basket he'd woven. Then, he shoved that into his pack.

After that, he set about preparing provisions for a journey. First, he went to the kitchen where he gathered some fish fillets he'd smoked, a bunch of berries from his garden, and an earthen jug full of water. The last was a new addition and the result of his latest project; it probably would have been easier to simply go back to Ironshore and buy the equivalent, but he'd chosen not to, as much so that he wouldn't grow dependent on the small city as because he took pleasure in his own self-sufficiency.

In the end, it was a satisfying project, even if the results weren't as successful as some of his previous efforts. The jug, which was made from clay he'd harvested from near his stream, could hold liquid just fine, but due to a mishap with the baking process, it was a little misshapen. That didn't affect the usefulness, but the aesthetics left a lot to be desired.

As he loaded the jug into the pack, Elijah was once again impressed by the pack's vast carrying capacity. It was at least twice the size its exterior suggested, which meant that he could carry plenty of supplies. And he did, packing it full of everything he thought he might need. Then, Elijah donned one of the outfits he'd bought in Ironshore. The style of the clothing was uncomplicated and workmanlike, featuring a shirt that laced down to mid-chest and a pair of pants that didn't quite reach his ankles. Unsurprisingly, considering the complexity of the common zipper, the fastenings were limited to laces and buttons. The fabric was soft enough to be comfortable, but tough enough that Elijah suspected the clothing would resist normal wear and tear. On top of that, the Tailor had specified that each piece was Simple grade, which he'd since learned was the lowest level of magical equipment. Typically, the limited level of magic in those items only meant that it was more resistant to damage than it otherwise would be, but that was fine by Elijah. It wasn't as if he was going to run around in armor, after all.

Once he was dressed and everything had been packed away, Elijah took one last look around the tree house as he tried to remember anything he might've forgotten. That effort didn't result in any epiphanies, so after calling out to Nerthus—and getting no response—he decided to stop delaying his departure. With that in mind, he climbed down the steps and took a look at the ancestral tree. Its color had continued to change over the previous weeks, and its bark had turned almost completely white. In addition, the leaves had taken on a blue color, giving Elijah the impression that the Shard of the World Tree was still being absorbed. He spared a moment to wonder what would happen when it finished, but he had no real context to make predictions. He just knew that Nerthus had implied that it would be a fundamental transformation, which was exciting enough that Elijah was impatient to see results.

In any case, he didn't remain there long before he set off across the island, with the eventual destination of the beach where he'd stashed his collection of rowboats. The trip only took a few minutes, and before he knew it, he was standing on the beach next to his rowboat. The sun had already risen high in the sky, which meant that he'd reach the other shore by midafternoon at the latest. So, not wanting to put it off, he pushed the little boat out into the surf, hopped in, and started to row.

The crossing went quickly, aided by Elijah's inflated attributes, and he soon found himself pulling the rowboat onto shore. He'd considered taking it into Ironshore and leaving it there for safekeeping. However, he'd decided not to because he didn't really want them to know he wasn't on the island. Sure, leaving it untended on the shore meant that it probably wouldn't be there when he returned—unless he did so within a couple of days—but that wasn't a huge deal. He had a multitude of other boats on the island, and he could always use Ancestral Circle to return. And if push came to shove, he had no issue with swimming the distance, even if he didn't relish the notion.

In any case, it was better to be safe than sorry. He wanted to trust Ramik and the others, but he would have been a fool to extend that trust so early in their relationship.

Once Elijah had pulled the rowboat ashore and stashed it past the tree line, he took a deep breath, then used Shape of the Predator. In a lot of ways, he was just as comfortable in his scaled-panther form as he was as a human—and that was the problem. It was so easy to lose himself in the shape's wild instincts. After nearly doing so in the Primordial Jungle, he'd made a concerted effort to assert his humanity, but the animalistic mindset always hovered just out of sight, ready to pounce like the predator to which it belonged.

However, as wary as he was of using the form too much, Elijah couldn't deny that it was unmatched for wilderness traversal. Even without Guise of the Unseen, he was difficult to track, and with that ability enhancing his stealth, he was all but impossible to perceive.

Fortunately, his new clothing as well as his pack and staff transformed with him, which meant he could move light and fast as he embarked upon the initial stages of exploration. Hopefully, he would find something interesting and, perhaps, a few hints as to where to find his family. With that in mind, he set off, keeping his senses trained on the environment as he began his journey of exploration.

12

SPIDERS

The rainstorm started only an hour after Elijah had begun his trek inland, though with the dense canopy of a temperate rainforest above, only scattered drops of precipitation made it to the ground. However, as was common to the region, humidity clouded the atmosphere, and dewy wetness clung to every leaf. Elijah was only barely affected, though; his scales weren't as warm as his old form's coat of fur had been, but they were still largely impervious to the elements.

He slipped through the forest, keeping the awareness granted by One with Nature at the forefront of his mind. Back on the island, where he knew every last blade of grass on an intimate level, such concentration wasn't necessary. But now that he was on the mainland, he slipped back into the same frame of mind that had let him survive the most dangerous parts of the tower.

At first, he circled Ironshore, as much to get back into the proper frame of mind as to check up on his would-be allies. Their efforts at deforestation had slowed to a crawl, probably because they'd progressed past the need for wooden structures. Instead, they'd begun to replace those with sturdier stone and what seemed like a magical form of concrete. There were still hunting parties out and about, but that wasn't surprising. Not only was most of the wildlife dangerous and territorial, but the animals were also ready sources of meat. Ironshore had no herd animals Elijah had seen, so they were still dependent on wild game for their protein. Likely, that would continue for some time, though fishing would probably overtake hunting as the primary source of meat going forward.

Or at least that's how it usually worked with human coastal settlements. Perhaps other worlds had developed differently.

After making certain that there were no real threats in the immediate area, Elijah started moving toward the only town he'd seen on the Branch's map function. Without context, he knew it would still be difficult to find the settlement, but he figured it was the best place to start his search for Seattle, which he hoped would lead him to Easton, where he could find his sister.

There was a problem, though. Ironshore abutted a sizable mountain range, so Elijah couldn't simply travel in a straight line. Instead, he had to find a pass, and that search took up the next three days. Most of the time, he remained in his predator form and hunted whichever small animals he could find. However, he did make a point to resume his human form for at least an hour each day, lest he fall into the same trap that had threatened to rob him of his humanity back in the Keledge Tower.

For the most part, he went unmolested. He could've fought a few dangerous-looking animals—like a sizable boar that he found eating a giant stag it had killed—but he chose to silence his more murderous impulses.

That wasn't to say he didn't fight.

He certainly did, though he confined his efforts to when he sensed a Voxxian trail. On three separate occasions, he followed that acrid stench to its owner, and when he got close enough, he used Predator Strike to kill each reptilian monster.

It wasn't so different from how he'd hunted them on his island, though it was more difficult in a couple of ways. First, each of them was stronger than any of the other spontaneous manifestations he'd seen on the island. As a result, in all but one case, he was forced to follow up his initial attack with a second killing blow. In addition, they were slightly more difficult to track because he didn't have the benefit of his Locus to guide him. Still, he made do and accomplished his goal.

Eventually, Elijah found a pass that cut through the mountain range. It had clearly been used by a herd of some sort of animals, and it was only by following their trail that he was able to find the pass. However, they had used it long enough in the past that their scent had all but dissipated, and Elijah was incapable of identifying the animals by what was left.

Still, he had no issues using their trail as a guide, and so, he continued along until he saw something that brought him up short.

From a distance, it looked almost like the entire area had been covered by thick frost. Elijah pulled to a stop so he could study the phenomenon, and soon enough, he recognized it for what it was. Gossamer webs, thin and delicate, covered everything in front of him.

More importantly, he saw a few dark shapes, each one the size of a golden retriever and with eight horribly spindly legs, poised to pounce on anything stupid enough to wander into their domain. He looked past them and saw a few dozen large cocoons that he suspected contained the herd animals that had preceded him.

Setting up behind a boulder, Elijah crouched low, his thick, alligator-like tail sweeping back and forth in anticipation as he watched. For a long time, nothing changed, but then, a bird—it looked like a sparrow, but it was quite a bit larger than any version of that bird Elijah had ever seen—landed. It grabbed at something on the ground, then tried to lift off, but its feet were caught in the web. It screeched and flapped its wings, but no matter how much it struggled, it couldn't free itself.

A moment later, a half dozen spiders descended on it. The ill-fated avian creature stopped moving a few seconds later, and the arachnids—which resembled tarantulas, but with dark-green instead of brown coloring—quickly dragged it away, wrapped it in spider silk, then left it with the rest of their prey.

Elijah continued to watch, and though he felt confident that he could pick his way through the webs, he wasn't absolutely certain he could do so while avoiding the spiders. Which meant that he had no intention of trying.

He'd long since come to the conclusion that versatility was the hallmark of his archetype. He could heal passably well—though with restrictions—cast decently damaging spells, and through his two animal forms, either become a stealthy skirmisher or a stalwart defender. He didn't think he could do any of those things as well as a specialist might, but with his Dragon Core boosting his abilities by a significant degree, he could do well enough that it didn't matter.

And that versatility gave him the ability to attack each situation with a wide variety of tactics. So, sure—attacking the spider's nest in his predator form was too reckless to contemplate. However, there was nothing that said he couldn't do so in his natural form. So, still crouched behind the boulder, he allowed himself to shift back into a human. Then, hefting his staff, he peeked out from behind the huge rock.

The pass still looked the same, but without the enhanced senses of his predator form, he had difficulty picking out the motionless spiders. It didn't matter. For what he had planned, he wouldn't even need to aim.

So, without further hesitation, Elijah dragged ethera from his Core, filtered it through his Soul, and flooded Calamity with power.

Spell: Calamity	**Bury your enemies beneath the power of nature. Conjure a natural disaster appropriate to your environment. Only usable in caster form.**

He released it, letting the spell envelop the nest. The spiders reacted to the swirl of ethera, but they were incapable of escaping the coming cataclysm. The ground shook, and dark clouds swirled overhead, heralding the impending disaster. The earth opened, swallowing the nest even as lightning split the sky. The spiders went wild, screaming in pain and fury as they were caught in the storm of lightning, cutting wind, and roiling earth, but they couldn't combat the power of Elijah's spell, and one by one, they fell before its might.

It only lasted a few seconds before the air cleared and the earth quieted, leaving only the smell of ozone and cooked spider behind. However, there were a few that managed to survive, though none were in good shape. So, Elijah stepped out from behind the boulder, took aim with his staff, and repeatedly cast Storm's Fury, killing the survivors.

And just like that, the spider's nest went quiet. As he surveyed the scene of the one-sided battle, deep relief flooded his mind. He hadn't realized it before, but the sight of the spiders had left him feeling a sense of wrongness he couldn't explain.

He should have known that the relief wouldn't remain, but he was too busy patting himself on the back for gaining a level to even see the shadow moving in the distance. Not at first, at least. But then, Elijah saw what was rapidly approaching, and he nearly collapsed in fear.

"Spiders really aren't supposed to be that big," he mumbled to himself, as that same sense of foreboding returned.

Indeed, the creature skittering toward him was far too large and fearsome to be allowed, and from its bulbous and furry abdomen to the writhing chelicerae, it was at least ten feet long. With its sprawling legs, it seemed even more massive.

Was it the mother, and all the smaller creatures were simply its offspring? Or was there something else going on? Elijah had no idea, and he didn't have the time to think it through because the creature was quickly closing the gap.

His Mind spun as he sucked Ethera down into his Soul where it was redirected into his Core in an attempt to regenerate as much energy as possible. Meanwhile, he embraced Snaring Roots, loosing the spell as quickly as he could. At the spider's feet sprouted a multitude of roots that quickly wrapped themselves around the monster's feet. However, either the spell was too weak, or the spider was just too strong because it quickly ripped free; those roots were soon replaced by more, but Elijah recognized that the spell would do nothing more than slow it down for a few seconds.

Hopefully, that would be enough.

He didn't have enough ethera to fuel Shape of the Predator, which still took more than half of his Core's contents. But Shape of the Guardian took far less, and he had just enough to power the transformation.

But he hesitated.

The smart move probably would have been to run away, regenerate, and come back when he was more prepared. He was already thinking of how he could whittle the thing down with repeated uses of Storm's Fury or attack it with a stealth-boosted Predator Strike.

And yet, Elijah held his ground. Partially, it was due to a need to test Shape of the Guardian's potential. He'd spent some time working on maneuvering in that transformed state, and he hadn't had a chance to put all that training to work. But mostly, he chose to continue the engagement because he simply didn't want to back down. He felt confident that he could survive, given his ability to heal via Guardian's Renewal and the increased movement speed granted by Essence of the Wolf.

Still, Elijah hoped it wouldn't come to that.

In the space of a second, he had fueled Shape of the Guardian and begun the transformation. Meanwhile, the spider ripped through Snaring Roots in its desperation to reach Elijah.

Even as it continued to tear itself free of the constantly regrowing roots, Elijah's body transformed. By the time the arachnid reached him, Elijah had fully taken on the Shape of the Guardian, which presented as a strange amalgam of reptile and ape, though one with far more mass than should have been possible.

Elijah loped forward, using his hands for balance as he raced to meet the spider before it could completely recover from its entrapment. He hit it with the full weight of his massive body, knocking it backward with a shoulder tackle that sent it tumbling across the rocky terrain.

But a single blow—even with his enhanced weight and strength—wasn't enough to take out a monster so huge, and it quickly righted itself, screeched in fury, then skittered back into the fray. Elijah met it with a vicious uppercut with all his weight behind it. It flipped backward, but the creature wasn't without its own tricks. A thick strand of webbing shot out from the spinnerets attached to the back of its abdomen, hitting Elijah square in the chest.

And then he was yanked from his feet by the spider's momentum. Before he could rise, the creature had righted course, bounding off the sloping boundary of the pass and directly at the recovering Elijah.

He had only a moment's warning before he felt its fangs cut through his scaly armor and into his flesh, injecting him with its venom.

13

SLUGFEST

Fire raced through Elijah's body, melting his muscles from the inside out. And on instinct, he very nearly used Guardian's Renewal.

Guardian's Renewal	Instantly and completely regenerate. Cooldown affected by Regeneration attribute. Current cooldown: Once per week.

But he caught himself before he activated the ability. It had a lengthy cooldown, and so, it was best saved for emergencies. And while he was in agony as the venom coursed through him, liquifying and necrotizing his flesh, he knew he could endure much more than that. So, he shoved the pain to the back of his mind and focused on the fight at hand.

The decision was made in an instant, which meant that by the time he retook control, the spider's fangs were still buried in his meaty shoulder. Which was fortuitous because that put it within reach of Elijah's claws.

In his guardian form, his claws weren't nearly as sharp as they were as a predator. Nor could he activate Venom Strike, which meant he only had the strength of his limbs on which to rely. Fortunately, the form came with a significant boost to his Strength, and with the spider already in his grasp, he could leverage that attribute to its fullest capacity without having to worry about his lacking coordination.

So, he reached out and grabbed the first thing he could, which happened to be the monster's chelicerae. Elijah's fingers wrapped around the meaty mouthparts, and with the other hand, he grasped the thing's foremost leg. It writhed in his hand, but his grip was like iron.

Then, with all the power he could bring to bear, he pulled.

The mouthparts came loose in a shower of thick light-blue blood, and Elijah got a brief look at the pale flesh beneath the harder exoskeleton. The glance didn't last long because, only an instant later, the spider lashed out with panicked fury that sent Elijah tumbling backward until he hit the nearby boulder that had most recently acted as his hiding place.

The impact knocked the breath from his lungs, and he felt multiple ribs crack before he fell on his face. For a second, stars flashed before his eyes, and he struggled to make sense of his situation, but his Regeneration, augmented by Aura of Renewal, quickly showed its worth, and it only took a few moments for the worst of the concussion to clear.

When it did, he pushed himself to his feet—wincing with the pain of his broken ribs—and coughed up foamy blood. But as much as he wanted to use Guardian's Renewal, he held off. He could still function with what was obviously a punctured lung, and the spider's venom, while painful, wouldn't incapacitate him anytime soon. Even now, his augmented Regeneration attribute was hard at work counteracting it.

He shook his head, clearing the cobwebs as he stared across the pass at the still-panicking spider. For a moment, Elijah took pity on the creature. It hadn't really asked for the battle. In fact, the argument could be made that he was the aggressor. But whatever pity he felt was quickly quashed by the pain coursing through his muscles. On top of that, he couldn't ignore that pervasive sense of wrongness that enveloped his mind every time he looked at the oversize arachnid.

Besides, he had long since come to the realization that killing was just part of the natural world. And yet, just because he was resigned to the necessity of killing, it didn't mean that he wanted to watch the creature suffer. So, it was with renewed determination that he raced forward in an apelike gait. Though after the spider's venom had robbed him of most of the mobility in his right arm, it was a bit off-balance.

As he turned his approach into a charge, the spider mastered its panic and skittered forward to meet him. The resulting clash was titanic, and Elijah felt it rattle his teeth. Beneath its fur, the spider had the benefit of a chitinous exoskeleton protecting its most vital parts. Elijah still had his scales and high Constitution, but it wasn't nearly as durable as the spider's natural armor.

But armor or no, the force each combatant could bring to bear was monumental, and soon enough, the sound of cracking carapace filled the air as Elijah hammered his fist into the monster's head and thorax. Meanwhile, it used its own legs like spears, jabbing them into Elijah with ruthless precision.

The first time Elijah had used Shape of the Guardian against Cabbot, the gnomish berserker had been largely incapable of penetrating his scales. That wasn't the case with the spider, which was far and away more powerful. Elijah had no capability of determining another entity's level, but he knew that, on the most basic of levels, the spider was more powerful than him.

In fact, it reminded him of the guardian orca he'd fought back in the Sea of Sorrows, though that context didn't really do it justice, given that Elijah himself had grown more powerful since then. In any case, he didn't have time to think about relative strength. Instead, it was all he could handle to simply endure the spider's attacks while trying to punish it with his own.

But gradually, he found himself losing ground.

Bit by bit, the venom, combined with the spider's persistent attacks, wore him down. However, Elijah did plenty of damage of his own, and though the spider was clearly winning the battle, doing so required that a steep price be paid. To Elijah, it felt like some of the old heavyweight boxing bouts he'd seen growing up. Two powerful fighters trading blows until one simply outlasted the other.

As a spectator, those sorts of bouts turned into gruesome, awe-inspiring displays of perseverance, and as a participant, it wasn't so different, save that he traded awe for exhaustion.

Long minutes passed as the pair hammered one another with blows that would crack boulders, and yet, neither backed away. With the understanding that to lose was to die, neither even considered concession. Instead, they both threw everything they had into the fight, and soon enough, the minutes passed into more than an hour.

On both sides, endurance began to lag, and the blows lost some of their impact. And yet, they both persisted, harnessing every ounce of their waning strength in the effort to dispatch the other.

Blood—red from Elijah, and light blue from the spider—flew as flesh was rent, and slowly, the gap between the two widened. With fatigue mounting, Elijah found that he could avoid fewer and fewer blows. The spider slowed, as well, but at a much more gradual pace.

The writing was on the wall.

Elijah had picked a fight he couldn't win.

For a moment, he considered fleeing. If he used everything he had in an all-out assault, he could get enough room to dash away. The spider might follow, but Elijah was banking on it retaining some of its instincts. Spiders favored ambush as a hunting method, and as such, they were poor pursuers. Elijah could only hope that the mutated version before him was hampered by those same limitations.

Yet, Elijah hesitated, and for one simple reason: He wanted to win.

But was winning a battle worth the increasingly real risk of death? Sure, he could probably use Guardian's Renewal and win the fight. But was it worth using an ability with such a long cooldown?

No.

Despite his current form, Elijah wasn't some heavyweight brute meant to trade blows with enormous and powerful monsters. His strengths were rooted in his versatility. And he chastised himself for forgetting that.

So, without further hesitation, he altered his strategy. Instead of returning the spider's assault with attacks of his own, he started looking for openings. And soon enough, one presented itself, and he pounced, grabbing hold of its legs and, harnessing every point of his Strength attribute, heaved it off the ground. Then, he spun like he was an Olympic hammer thrower and tossed the spider into the distance.

In the past, he might've followed that attack up with a charge and a heavy blow. But with his new strategy in mind, Elijah did the opposite. He pivoted, then sprinted away. The off-balance spider gathered itself for pursuit, but by that point, Elijah had already begun his descent down the pass. There was no way the monster could catch him, especially when, around thirty seconds later, Essence of the Wolf kicked in, increasing his movement speed by twenty percent.

Soon enough, the spider recognized the futility of its pursuit and gave up on the chase. Still, Elijah kept going for a little while longer until, at last, he switched back to his human form and cast Healing Rain. It soothed his injuries and served to counteract the venom coursing through his body, but the spell wasn't nearly strong enough to heal him in any reasonable amount of time. So, he used Touch of Nature, harnessing his Ethera to send life-giving vitality throughout his injured body.

The first cast only served to stop the bleeding from the multitude of wounds Elijah had sustained. However, he had plenty of ethera to keep going, and after the sixth cast, the spider's venom had been nullified. It took a few more to reverse the damage it had wreaked, but Elijah kept at it until, with only a third of his ethera remaining, he had brought himself back to perfect health.

And this time, he hadn't even added any new scars to his collection, which was progress, as far as he was concerned.

He sat near a scraggly tree and focused on his Mind, funneling ethera into his Soul. As he always did, he pushed against the boundaries of his cultivation, forcing the aperture ever wider. According to the basic guides he'd read, that was the accepted method to prepare the Mind for the next stage of cultivation. But while Elijah would take any improvement he could, he was more focused on regenerating the energy in his Core a little more quickly.

So, he cleared his thoughts and pulled as much ethera into his system as he could, and over the next half hour, he regained enough energy to fuel Shape of the Predator. So, after only a few more minutes—he wanted a little buffer in case he needed to shift back into his human form and cast a quick heal—he embraced the spell and transformed himself into a scaled panther.

Once he'd assumed that form, Elijah used Guise of the Unseen, then stalked across the pass and returned to the battleground he'd left behind a few hours before. After his use of Calamity, the earth had settled, but the smaller spiders' corpses—as well as the remnants of their prey—remained. Elijah spent the next few minutes watching for movement, but he saw no sign of the larger spider.

So, he padded forward on silent feet and sniffed at some of the drying blood it had left behind. That familiarized him with the scent, so he had no issues following the wounded spider's trail up the pass and into a large cave. There, he found the monster curled into a ball. Gossamer webs coated almost the entirety of the cave's interior, and Elijah knew enough about spiders to recognize the danger that represented. Even if it wouldn't catch him like it would smaller prey, if he stepped on that collection of webs, he would almost assuredly alert the spider.

And that would ruin his plans.

So, with slow and delicate steps, Elijah silently stalked through the cave. With his heightened Dexterity, he had almost perfect control of his body—especially when it came to something that, from an instinctive perspective, came so easily to the scaled-panther form—so while it took time, Elijah's progress was never in question.

Once he drew to within a few feet of the injured spider, Elijah took a few moments to simply admire the creature for what it was. He'd never been much of an arachnologist, but he'd have been a fool not to acknowledge how impressive spiders were. The one in front of him was even more so, and not just because of its size. It wasn't difficult to imagine that it had ruled the pass ever since the world had been transformed, and it probably would have continued to do so if Elijah hadn't come along.

In a way, it was sad, the loss of such a magnificent creature.

But such was the law of nature.

Maybe he could have simply let it live. Certainly, now that Calamity had cleared the way of smaller spiders and their webs, he could keep going without much issue. But what about the next time? If the spider was allowed to recover, Elijah might not get another chance to kill it. And if he tried to use the pass again, who was to say that it wouldn't be the one to come out on top? After all, animals could progress, just like the sentient races. They didn't have the benefit of the system, but they could still grow stronger—at least according to Elijah's experiences as well as the basic information provided by his guides.

No—he needed to kill it while he had the opportunity.

So, after using Predator Strike and Venom Strike, he pounced. With his Strength and the enhancement provided by the first ability, his claws went through the creature's head with comparative ease. Still, though, it didn't immediately die.

Instead, it flailed, nearly catching Elijah with one of its spear-like legs. He bounded out of the way, using the cave's wall to reverse course before hitting it again. This time, his claws weren't nearly as effective, but the attack still carried with it another dose of the neurotoxin associated with Venom Strike.

Elijah kept moving, leaping off the spider's back and racing across the cave. Then, he reversed course and crouched low, watching the spider's continued flailing. It found him a moment later, then surged forward. But Elijah was too quick, and he easily dodged, returning the spider's attempted attack with one of his own.

Like that, the fight continued. Each time Elijah's claws made contact with the monster's furry carapace, he delivered another dose of neurotoxin. However, even as injured as it was—the result of the previous fight as well as Elijah's continued attacks—the battle didn't end quickly. Instead, Elijah balanced on a knife's edge as he narrowly avoided one assault after another. Eventually, the spider's movements began to flag, but Elijah continued his own efforts unchecked.

It was then that Elijah realized that, back when he'd been in his guardian form, he hadn't been nearly as close to defeating the spider as he'd thought. Even if he'd used Guardian's Renewal, the rejuvenating effect likely wouldn't have been enough to fuel his survival.

But now?

He only had to keep going, and his scaled-panther form would see him through to the end.

Over the next half hour, Elijah persisted, and the spider slowly lost the battle to the neurotoxin. And, as fatigue started to work against Elijah, the spider finally succumbed to its wounds, collapsing in a mass of legs and furry carapace.

Elijah skidded to a stop, but he didn't immediately approach. He didn't think the monster was intelligent enough to play dead, but he didn't intend to take any chances. So, he waited until a wave of kill energy washed over him, confirming the monster's death, before he let himself relax.

Congratulations! You have reached level thirty-two. Attribute points allocated according to your class.

If Elijah hadn't been convinced of the monster's power, then the fact that it gave him most of a level on its own served to confirm that it was no run-of-the-mill beast. But for now, he was more interested in the next notification he expected. However, when it didn't come, he realized that his assumption that he'd get a new spell at level thirty-two clearly wasn't accurate. So, it was with a little disappointment that he left the cave and continued on his way.

14

A DEAD CIVILIZATION

The spiders weren't the last threat Elijah faced as he traversed the pass, but they were the deadliest. Along the way, he ran into a couple more Voxx, which he dealt with accordingly, but he avoided any other dangers, aside from those posed by the terrain itself. On more than one occasion, he was forced to climb up or down steep cliffs or leap across gaping chasms, but in every instance, he found a way to traverse the obstacles.

And then, days later, he finally began his descent. It took a further couple of days to reach the other side of the mountain range, and when he did, he found himself back in the woods. However, instead of the temperate rainforest with which he'd grown accustomed, he'd come to a boreal forest, with tall pine trees and rocky terrain peppered with a multitude of placid lakes.

The temperature also experienced a significant decline, though Elijah wasn't certain if that was due to the regional climate or if it was winter tightening its grip. Whatever the case, he keenly felt the cold, even with the advantage of his animalistic endurance and inflated attributes.

That prompted some experimentation with Ward of the Seasons:

Spell: Ward of the Seasons	Harness the power of the seasons, increasing resistance to elemental damage (Water, Earth, Fire, Air).

However, to his disappointment, the augmentation did nothing to cut the cold. According to his guides, that sort of thing wasn't unexpected, and the spell had never been meant to abate environmental effects. Instead, it was intended to protect him from hostile spells. Still, he'd hoped that it would prove special, and he was sorely disappointed when it did nothing to protect him from the cold. Hopefully, it would prove useful in the future.

The forest itself, which had distinctly less undergrowth than the tangled mess he'd left behind, was much easier to traverse, so he made good time as he slowly left the mountains behind. The whole time, he kept a keen sense of his island in the back of his mind; he was ready to teleport back via Ancestral

Circle at a moment's notice. Fortunately, no such necessity presented itself, allowing him to continue his efforts at exploration.

After another week, Elijah started to see signs of civilization. At first, it was only a few roads here and there, but soon enough, he came upon the first cluster of buildings alongside what had once been a stretch of interstate highway. The on- and off-ramp had survived, as had a gas station and a Burger King. Both were in a state of advanced disrepair, suggesting that it had been quite some time—years, perhaps—since they'd been inhabited.

Still, Elijah spent a few hours inspecting both, and he found precisely what he'd feared when he stumbled upon a pile of old human bones. They bore deep grooves that were probably teeth marks, but beyond that, Elijah had no evidence to support any theories concerning how they had died.

It was further confirmation that the world had not weathered the transformation very well. Of course, Elijah had expected as much. He'd had to fight tooth and nail to survive, and though he acknowledged that his path was probably more difficult than most, it wasn't difficult to imagine that the rest of humanity hadn't escaped the end of the world as everyone knew it unscathed.

Partially, it was a function of civilization. In the United States—and most other developed countries, as well—the fact was that people had moved on from many of the skills they would need once everything stopped working. Survival skills had become a hobby rather than a necessity, and as such, few people could call themselves experts.

Sure, there were plenty of people out there who could adjust. But there were probably just as many who would've starved to death once their local supermarkets ran out of viable food. Many more would have died from avoidable diseases and, as sad as it was to say, the chaotic opportunism that came on the heels of any disaster.

And that wasn't even considering the mutated wildlife, the other races who'd chosen to descend upon Earth in hopes of building a better life, and the spontaneously manifesting Voxx. All of it coincided to create a world where survival was probably the exception to the rule rather than the default expectation.

Those thoughts accompanied Elijah as he continued to encounter the remnants of a dead civilization. Sometimes, it was just a stray house or two—clearly, the area had been rural—but every now and then, he'd find an entire deserted neighborhood. Where the people had gone was no mystery; he found their remains, as well. Often, they were clustered together as if they'd tried to take solace in numbers. Those were usually accompanied by rudimentary attempts at defenses. Cars that had been pushed together, boxes, wooden pallets—they'd used everything they could to create walls.

But it obviously hadn't worked because each instance Elijah stumbled upon featured the remains of the would-be holdouts.

At first, Elijah let it all send him spiraling into melancholy, but as the days wore on, he grew progressively more numb to it until he just accepted that most of humanity had already died. There were clearly survivors. The ladder was proof enough of that, but Elijah kept going back to his previous supposition that the endurance of human life was, at best, rare.

In any case, as he continued his increasingly depressing exploration, he found himself wondering if he'd actually lucked out by being stranded on a deserted island. The panther had protected him—mostly—from anything truly dangerous, which had allowed him to get a handle on the situation. Without that, he'd have probably died fairly early on.

Almost three weeks after he'd left the pass behind, Elijah stumbled on something he never expected. He crouched behind a disused gas station pump as he looked across an overgrown street at the low-slung building that had, once upon a time, been a Walmart. The sign had been ripped down, and trees—still barely more than saplings—sprouted from cracks in the parking lot's concrete. But that wasn't what drew his attention.

He'd seen a few such buildings, and he'd even raided a couple, finding nothing that he could use. But what made this one unique was that it was clearly occupied. Not by people, though. Instead, the residents were gray-skinned, tusked creatures that Elijah could only call orcs.

They carried primitive weapons and wore very little in the way of clothing. Most were only clad in loincloths, in fact. But there were hundreds of them engaged in what looked like a primitive sort of tribal life that reminded Elijah of the various races of protohumans. He wasn't certain if that was an accurate impression, but it was the first thing that came to mind when he saw their heavy brows, sloped foreheads, and jutting jaws.

Cloaked in Guise of the Unseen, Elijah watched them for a few hours before he decided to move on. The orcs weren't hurting anyone, and though he knew from the guides he'd read that they tended to be quite warlike, they were isolated enough that he didn't think they would be a problem for anyone.

Besides, what was he going to do? Fight an entire settlement on his own?

The idea wasn't just laughable—it was suicidal.

So, once he'd confirmed that the orcs were just living their lives, Elijah moved on. And over the next couple of weeks, he continued to explore. Along the way, he saw more evidence of humanity's rapid fall. In one instance, he came across an abandoned settlement that had been built around an old prison. It was reasonably well-developed, suggesting that the occupants had made it for a while, at least. But like everywhere else Elijah had found, it was entirely abandoned.

Still, he spent a few days exploring the disused settlement, finding few clues as to why its people had left.

Over time, he did find a few useful items, though. Like the collection of glass jugs that could hold a gallon of water each. His clay version had already begun to fall apart, so he was extremely thankful for the new additions. Elijah had also raided an old hardware store, taking a wide variety of tools he thought would be valuable for his continued survival. The only limit was the room in his pack, and even though it was a little more than twice as large as the exterior suggested, it still wouldn't hold everything he wanted to take.

But mostly, he just continued to explore, killing Voxx whenever he came across one of their trails. As a scaled panther, he found dispatching most of them easy enough, though he did encounter a few that managed to survive his initial ambush long enough to pose a serious problem. Elijah still won those fights, but he didn't do so without incurring injuries himself.

Fortunately, he had the tools to deal with that, and his healing spells got quite a workout.

In a lot of ways, it reminded him of his first year on the island. Technically, the wilderness was a good deal more dangerous. Everywhere he went, there were creatures that wanted to kill him. However, he had the ability to mitigate that danger—either before or after it manifested—and he soon found himself adapting to it. Just like he had adapted to the necessities of survival on the island.

Before Elijah knew it, winter had truly come, and with it came frequently inclement weather. Snowstorms, freezing rain, and miserably cold sleet were almost as common as clear days, and often, the temperatures dipped well below freezing. He was somewhat protected from the elements by his high Constitution, but even with that, it got to the point where he considered going home and waiting the winter out.

In fact, he was on the verge of making just such a decision when, at last, he reached the settlement that had been listed on the Branch's Regional Map.

Called Norcastle, it had clearly gotten its name from the ancient castle at its center. However, even from a distance, Elijah could recognize the multitude of newer structures surrounding the large stone fort. In addition, there was a sizable wall that looked like it had been constructed of cinder blocks encircling the entire town, which was even larger than Ironshore, both in terms of area as well as apparent population. As Elijah settled down to observe the city, he estimated that it was home to at least ten thousand people, but probably somewhere closer to twice that many.

From an ethnic perspective, it was a bit of a melting pot, and Elijah saw people of all different skin tones. However, there were no nonhumans in evidence, which suggested that everyone there was a native of Earth.

In the distance, Elijah saw some cultivated fields and farmsteads, but they were too far away for him to see any details, even with Eyes of the Eagle. And there were people constantly coming and going through the large main gate, many of whom carried game or gathered resources. For the most part, it looked like a thriving town.

Except for all the bodies.

Just outside of town, there were workers digging a huge hole in the ground. Elijah might've discounted it as a well or something of the sort, but next to it was a huge pile of white-wrapped corpses. Maybe a hundred of them, all in various states of decomposition.

Clearly, there was something wrong with Norcastle.

The question was whether or not Elijah wanted to get involved. He needed to get into the city; that much was certain. They had a Branch, and hopefully, it would lead him to more settlements. He certainly didn't think he'd find Seattle so quickly, but if he kept going, he'd eventually stumble across some information that might lead him in the right direction. Considering that the world had been transformed, with the terrain having been randomized and expanded, the search for Seattle would probably take years, but he had to believe it was possible.

However, as a healer, didn't he have some sort of responsibility to help people who needed it? He'd done it in the tower, and without question, so why did he hesitate when it was in the real world?

The answer, he realized, was simple. In the tower, he'd known the rules. Or at least he'd thought so. But in the real world, there were no rules. The people down in Norcastle might meet his attempts at helping them with hostility.

In the end, though, Elijah didn't want to live in fear. Even if those fears were valid, he couldn't let them dictate his actions. If, for whatever reason, the people of Norcastle chose to turn on him, he would react accordingly. But until then, he would do what he could to help.

With that decided, he let his scaled-panther form fall away, then strode toward the town.

15

A NEW PURPOSE

Carmen knelt next to her forge, staring at the smoldering coals. The apparatus was mostly enclosed, which meant that it was insanely hot, but due to her technique Resist Fire, she barely felt it. She'd yet to truly test the resistance to its fullest extent, but she suspected that she could shove her hand into a normal fire without any detriment.

But inside her forge was no normal fire.

Instead, the forge had been carefully assembled from blocks enchanted by a true Bricklayer, and the fire itself burned ethera-soaked coal. It wasn't quite a graded item, in and of itself, but it wasn't truly mundane, either. As a result, the fire was more than just fire, and hopefully, that would help with the forging process.

Once Carmen was satisfied with the state of the flame, she pushed herself upright and grabbed a specially prepared bar of steel. It had been merged, via Meld Metals, with titanium she'd harvested from a wrecked and abandoned sports car one of the scavenging teams had found, and then, she'd mixed it with a bit of aluminum. The result was an alloy that shouldn't have been possible.

She had further refined the resulting alloy by using Decontaminate and Refine Material multiple times. Finally, she had used Ethereal Infusion for two hours a day for two weeks, bathing it in ethera until it practically glowed with magic.

Hopefully, it would be enough to take her crafting to the next level.

The bar of metal had a silvery sheen and was almost ten feet long, two inches deep, and at least four inches wide, and if she hadn't invested so heavily in her Strength attribute, there was little chance she would have been able to lift it, much less work with the metal. For what she intended to create, that excess weight was more than appropriate.

With a grunt, she shoved one end into the enchanted flame. Then, she waited for it to heat up before removing it. After slamming it onto her anvil, Carmen used her summoned hammer to fold a ten-inch piece over, then back again. Over and over, she repeated the process until, finally, it broke free. She set the smaller piece aside, then shoved the end of the bar back into the forge.

Normally, Carmen would have just cut it with a saw, but the alloy was far too hard for any of her tools, so she'd had to resort to more of a brute-force method. And over the next few hours, she repeated the process until she had twelve identical pieces. She stacked the ingots on top of one another, then used Bind to bind them all together.

"Better than forge welding," she muttered.

But she wasn't done. So, grabbing the brick of dense alloy with a pair of heavy-duty tongs, she thrust it back into the forge. Once it had reached the proper temperature—which took far longer than it should have, likely due to the innately magical material—she pulled it out and started to hammer.

Gradually, using various other summoned tools in conjunction with her hammer, she shaped the hunk of metal into a rough approximation of a war hammer. However, because of its size, Carmen knew that only someone with immense strength would ever be able to wield the massive weapon.

Which was perfectly within her expectations.

Once she'd achieved the rough shape, she started in with smaller tools, giving the item a more refined appearance. One side was big, brutish, and aggressive, while the opposite bore a long, tapered spike. Meanwhile, the top looked almost like the tip of a spear. When she'd finished with the hammer's head, she started in on the haft, which was also made of the same alloy.

Finally, she attached the two via Bind, finishing the base weapon.

But that was only the beginning, and after she heat-treated the entire thing—quenching it in oil she'd also treated with Ethereal Infusion—Carmen started in on the engraving. At first, she'd intended to do that before hardening the weapon, but according to the guides she'd bought from the Branch, that was a suboptimal path. So, even though it was much more difficult to carve embellishments into the hardened metal, Carmen was more than willing to endure the hardship if it meant a better result was possible.

Gradually, the carving, which was nothing more than Celtic-style whorls, took shape, and it complemented the pattern of the folded metal. Once that was finished, Carmen took the teeth of a Voxxian beast and used Bind to merge them in a ring around the base of the hammerhead.

With the two embellishments finished—her current limit—Carmen started in on the enchantment. At present, she only had two available. One for durability, and the other for power. She chose the latter, reasoning that the alloy and sturdy construction would make it functionally indestructible with her current Strength.

Finally, she wrapped the grip in supple leather she'd gotten from a local Leatherworker, finishing the weapon.

> **Congratulations! You have created a unique item, Destroyer.**
> **Overall Grade: Simple (Low)**
> **Enchantment Grade: F**

"Finally!" Carmen sighed. She'd made hundreds of weapons since she'd created the Spear of the Dragon Lancer, and she'd yet to exceed its grade of Crude. "Until now," she amended.

The weapon itself was impressive, but that was largely due to the ethera wafting off of it. From a visual perspective, it was primitive and brutish. But that suited Carmen just fine. It was a weapon meant to kill, and in that endeavor, it would be very effective.

"I suppose congratulations are in order?" came a voice from the forge's door.

Carmen whipped around, hefting the hammer in a fighter's stance. She was far from the most effective combatant in Easton, but due to her high level, she could definitely hold her own. On top of that, she'd spent quite a bit of time working on her ability to wield the hammer, so she thought she was a match for all but the city's elites.

Not so with the man standing in her doorway.

"What do you want, Roman?" she asked.

He sighed. "Most people call me chancellor now."

"I'm not most people, chief."

He ran his hand through his dark hair and said, "You're definitely not. How have you been?"

"I'm getting by."

Indeed, ever since her brief outburst of self-destruction following Alyssa's death, Carmen had thrown herself into her work. And that effort had paid off, sending her level skyrocketing past everyone else in town. She had even managed to reach the ladder, which was something no one else in Easton had accomplished.

As a result, she had a waiting list for her services a mile long. Everyone in the city—and even some of the nearby smaller towns with whom they'd established trade relations—wanted a weapon made by her. So, she had money, power, and the ability to advance her craft by experimenting with expensive materials.

The only thing she didn't have was Alyssa.

No. Aside from Miguel, who was increasingly busy with training for when he acquired an archetype of his own, she had no one. Whatever friendships she'd managed to cultivate had fallen by the wayside, leaving her with nothing but her forge for company.

"That's a nice weapon," Roman said. "Personal use?"

She nodded. "I still like to do my part on patrol."

The statement was a bit misleading. While she did participate in her fair share of patrols, her reasoning had nothing to do with communal safety. Instead, she reveled in giving herself over to the violence. Without that release, she would have long since done something incredibly self-destructive.

"You don't have to, you know."

"I'm aware."

He sighed again. "Carmen, I know I've said this before, but—"

"What do you want, chief?"

"I can't just want to check on my friend?"

"Is that what we are?" she asked. "I don't dislike you, Roman. I really don't. But we were never close. At best, we were acquaintances, and we've grown further apart since Alyssa died. I haven't seen you since her memorial. So, I'll ask again—what do you want? And please, for both our sakes, stop bullshitting me."

"I want to offer you a job."

"I do consulting on potential commissions every Thursday. You can come by the shop and—"

"This isn't about you making weapons or armor," he stated. "This is about a unique opportunity. Last week, some of our Scouts discovered an abandoned iron mine. It's about two hundred miles south of here."

"Okay?"

"The ethera density there is like nothing we've seen before. And they found this," he said, tossing something underhanded to Carmen. She caught it easily, her Dexterity more than up to the task. But the moment it touched her skin, she let out a little gasp of surprise.

"What is this?"

"I was hoping you could tell me," he said.

Carmen opened her hand and gazed at the item resting on her palm. The bulk of the small ball of earth was just normal rock, but there was a vein of some sort of metal passing through the center. It pulsed with ethera strong enough to make her carefully prepared steel-titanium-aluminum alloy seem mundane by comparison.

She used Tradesman's Appraisal, but because the bit of ore wasn't her creation, the technique gave her almost no useful information. "Give me a minute," she said before crossing the forge to the bloomery she'd built.

"What is that?" asked Roman, following her.

"It's a special furnace meant for smelting," she said. "You're in luck. I had to build this a few months ago so I could smelt copper more easily. Now shut up."

"I'll remind you that I'm the chancellor of this—"

"It's my forge. Shut up or get out. I don't care who you are."

Thankfully, he went silent, which let Carmen get to work. The process of smelting wasn't nearly as complicated as most people thought. It started with heating the ore up to an appropriate temperature, reducing it with something like charcoal along the way. Once it was hot enough, the blacksmith simply needed to beat it with a hammer until there was only pure metal left over.

Of course, that was only if the ore behaved similarly to iron, which wasn't a guarantee. If it was more like gold or silver, she would have to add another couple of steps to the process. However, given that Roman had described it as coming from an abandoned iron mine, Carmen was hopeful that it would react the same.

Thankfully, that hope proved well-founded when she saw the bits of metal collecting at the bottom of the furnace. Soon enough, the process was complete, and Carmen extracted the bloom—which was a combination of slag, metal, and other impurities—and put on the finishing touches via further refinement.

That meant lots of heating and hammering, which she took to with gusto. Eventually, she had a little less than a pound of gleaming green metal. She used Tradesman's Appraisal:

Cold Iron
Overall Grade: Simple
Enchantment Grade: N/A

"It's called cold iron," Carmen said, holding the piece of green metal with her tongs. "And this little lump might just be worth more than this entire forge. If I had enough of it, I might even be able to make Complex items."

Roman nodded. "Then it's settled," he said. "We must protect that mine at all costs."

"Okay? What does that have to do with me? I mean, don't get me wrong—I want to work with this stuff, but that mine isn't—"

"I want you to run it," he said. "I intend to spare no expense in getting that mine up and running. We have a few Scholar archetypes we think might make good miners."

"And they want that?"

"They want to eat. They want shelter. They want advancement. This is how they get it," Roman stated. "They're useless right now, and you know as well as anyone just how thin our margins are. We start letting people freeload, and—"

"I don't want to talk about this, Roman. I resigned from the council because I'm not cut out for leadership. I just want to work my forge in peace."

"This is important. We secure this mine and use it to make weapons, and we'll have a leg up on everyone else in the region. Maybe the world," he said. "Or do you think people are just going to let us be? There are roving war bands out there. And we've gotten word of budding kingdoms. If we don't do the same, they'll wash over us like a tidal wave."

Carmen didn't doubt him. She wasn't nearly as idealistic as Alyssa had been. She was a historian, and so, she knew just how ruthless people could be when it came to power. It wasn't a question of if someone would try to conquer everything but, rather, when. Still, she had little interest in running anything, let alone a mine.

"I get ten percent," she said.

"Of what?"

"The cold iron. I need materials."

"Five."

"Seven."

"Deal," Roman said.

"And I want a full contingent of warriors. Real Carpenters, too."

"Don't worry. I don't intend to half-ass this, Carmen," Roman stated with a wide smile that didn't really touch his eyes. But then again, most of his emotions failed to do so. Not since Trish had died. "You'll get everything you need to make this a success. I guarantee it."

16

PLAGUE

Standing before the Norcastle main gate, Sam Harvin shifted uncomfortably as he tried to adjust his armor. It was a new addition, and he still hadn't grown accustomed to wearing it. But according to his captain, it was strong enough to stand up to Voxxian claws and teeth, so Sam was more than willing to endure a little discomfort.

"Quit fidgeting," said his partner, Lorelai. She was a middle-aged woman with gray-streaked black hair, and she reminded him of nothing so much as a middle school teacher. Not surprising, considering that it really hadn't been that long ago since he'd been in one of those classrooms. "Nobody's going to take you seriously if you keep messing with your armor. And look alive. We have a job to do, in case you forgot."

He rolled his eyes, saying, "I know."

"You say that, but the fact that I have to keep reminding you to pay attention tells me that you don't really take this seriously. We're the first line of defense if we see another attack."

"I know," he groaned. Indeed, that had been hammered into him during the six weeks of training he'd endured after awakening his archetype. Not for the first time, he wished he'd chosen one of the noncombat options, but he'd been too enamored with the idea of becoming a powerful fighter—maybe even getting the Champion class—that he'd never even considered anything but becoming a Warrior, and then, upon reaching level ten, the Guard class.

He'd regretted it ever since. Sure, he was stronger, faster, and more durable than he'd ever been, but his levels had lagged behind his peers' who'd chosen noncombat archetypes. For instance, his older sister's friend Jess had been offered a Healer archetype, which she'd parlayed into a powerful variant class called Lightkeeper. Since then, her levels had shot up—but then again, that was true of all the town's Healers.

"You're doing it again," cautioned Lorelai, jerking him back to attention. "Pay attention or I'm going to recommend you for punishment duty."

"I was paying attention," he lied. The problem was that, while he knew the wilderness was dangerous, he didn't have the firsthand experience with it that most of the town's citizens did. After the world had been transformed, he, his sister, and his mother had taken shelter in the local church. So, while others were fighting for their lives against suddenly mutated animals or monstrous creatures from some other reality, he'd been safe and sound in the ancient castle turned cathedral.

Then, over the following couple of years, that church had become the centerpiece of what would become Norcastle. So, unlike most of the others, he'd never had to deal with the dangers the new world represented. Sure, like everyone else, he knew what was out there. But knowing and experiencing were two different things, and Sam's first real brush with true danger had only occurred after he'd chosen his archetype and set himself down the path to becoming a Guard.

That hadn't ended well—he'd struggled to even hold his ground during the curated hunting expeditions the city's defense force used to train combatants— and he'd been regretting his choices ever since.

A slap on the back of his head once again brought him back to reality. He was about to say something to Lorelai that he would no doubt regret when he caught sight of something moving near the tree line. He squinted, using Enhanced Sight to zoom in on the anomaly, and asked, "Is that a person?"

Lorelai, who'd been glaring at him, followed his line of sight and focused in on the person striding out of the forest. "I think it is," she said. "Is it one of the gatherers? Or a hunter?"

"I don't think so," Sam said, tightening his grip on his spear. Outsiders weren't completely unheard-of. There were a few small settlements in the region, and Norcastle had even played host to an emissary from another city a few hundred miles away. However, almost no one was stupid enough to traipse around the wilderness alone. "You don't recognize him, do you?"

Lorelai said that she didn't, which worried Sam. She was annoying and a bit of a hard-ass, but Lorelai was very good at her job. And she had a great memory, especially when it came to people. Sam would have been surprised if she hadn't memorized the faces of every single hunter or gatherer who'd left the city during her shift.

Soon, the figure came close enough that Sam recognized him as a short, sandy-haired man wearing curiously anachronistic clothing and carrying a staff. But there was something about the way he carried himself that put Sam on edge. He couldn't pinpoint exactly what was bothering him until Lorelai pointed out, "He's completely relaxed."

People didn't exactly avoid the wilderness. Plenty of locals still ventured outside the city's walls, and with some degree of regularity. However, when they did so, it was with significant caution. Sam had learned to recognize it. Shifting eyes. Tense shoulders. Careful steps. Everyone who left Norcastle knew that they were walking into danger.

But this man? He was completely at ease.

As he drew closer, Sam took in more details. The newcomer had a beard, though it looked like it had been inexpertly hacked short. His blond hair was curly and had grown over his ears. And his complexion was fair, but with just enough tint to suggest that he spent most of his life outdoors. He wore a large pack on his back, and his wooden staff looked more like a series of twisted roots than a straight shaft.

"He's not wearing shoes," said Lorelai.

Sam glanced at the man's feet, and sure enough, his pants ended above his ankles. Below that was nothing but bare skin.

"Weird."

"Very."

The man finally got close enough that Sam could use Inspect, which was one of his Guard skills:

Name: Elijah Hart **Archetype: Healer** **Level: 18**

"A Healer?" Sam muttered. "By himself?"

"That name sounds vaguely familiar," Lorelai remarked.

"You think he's from around here?"

"No," she said. "Maybe he passed through, though. Look alive. He's almost here."

Almost as soon as she finished the sentence, the man raised a scarred hand in a friendly wave and said, "Hello!"

He stopped in front of them and gave Lorelai a welcoming smile. Then, he glanced at Sam, dismissed him with a nod, then turned his attention back on Lorelai before saying, "Sorry. Not from around here. This is Norcastle, right?"

"It is," said Lorelai.

"Where did you come from?" asked Sam.

"Oh, here and there. Most recently from a town called Ironshore."

"State your business," said Lorelai.

"Well, two things. First, it looks like you've got some issues here I can maybe help with," he said, gesturing with his staff toward a passing corpse wagon. Sam had gotten so used to them that he barely even noticed their comings and goings. "What's going on? Is it some kind of sickness? Were you attacked?"

"Plague," Sam said. "We don't—"

"You said two things. What was the other?" asked Lorelai.

"Oh. Well, I'm looking for Seattle. I have family there," he said. "Outside of it, if I'm honest. And I'm just trying to figure which way to go."

That was a common enough issue, and one with which Sam could readily relate. His own father had been away on business when the world changed, and he'd often considered setting out to search for him. However, his good sense had always won out; after all, the world was an incredibly dangerous place, and anyone who decided to trek across the wilderness was either stupid, suicidal, or incredibly competent. Maybe all three.

Lorelai said, "Haven't heard anything about Seattle. A part of San Francisco ended up about a thousand miles from here, but we haven't really heard anything but rumors out of there."

Elijah's shoulders sagged as he shook his head and said, "Kind of expected that. So, can I come in? I'm a Healer, and like I said, I might be able to help with your plague problem. Plus, I definitely wouldn't say no to a nice meal and maybe a shower. If not, I'll just be on my way."

There were no restrictions on who could enter the city, so they really didn't have the authority to deny him entry. However, Sam couldn't help but be a bit suspicious of the man. Not just because of his odd attire—his clothing definitely wasn't modern, and the lack of footwear was even weirder—but also because he'd been wandering around the wilderness alone. Even the Rangers and Explorers were required to adhere to a buddy system.

So, even though Sam knew he didn't have much to fear from a Healer—especially one that was only level eighteen—he couldn't help but feel a sense of unease when he looked at the newcomer. Maybe it was the extensive scarring on his hand. How badly must he have been injured that, even as a Healer, it had left its mark?

Even as Sam was considering stopping Elijah, Lorelai spoke up: "Normally, there's a one-copper fee for entering the city, but since you're a Healer, we'll waive it."

"No need," said Elijah, slinging his pack off his shoulder and rummaging inside. He reached in all the way up to his shoulder, which, given the size of the bag, didn't seem possible. There must've been some sort of optical illusion at play. In any case, the Healer quickly withdrew a handful of copper coins and handed one each to Lorelai and Sam. "So, can you point me to the nearest hospital or whatever? I really do think I can help out."

Lorelai gave him directions, even offering to have someone guide him there. However, Hart insisted that he could find his own way. So, after only a couple more minutes, they sent him on his way.

When he was gone, Sam asked, "You sure that was a good idea? He seemed . . . I don't know . . ."

"Dangerous," Lorelai said. "You felt it, same as me."

"Then why'd you let him in?"

"He's a Healer, and he wants to help," the other Guard stated. "That's enough. If we don't stop this . . . plague, there won't be a Norcastle left in a year."

"It's that bad?"

"You really should pay more attention, Sam," she said, her expression far softer than usual. "If you keep sticking your head in the sand, something is going to kill you. I won't always be here to protect you."

"I know, Lorelai."

"I think you believe that. Anyway, eyes forward. That big group of hunters that left this morning should start filing in soon."

And with that, Sam fixed his gaze on the surrounding wilderness, still wondering if they'd made a mistake letting the scarred Healer into the city.

Elijah strolled through the gate, and the moment he turned a corner, he let out a massive sigh of relief. Until that moment, he'd yet to trust the Ring of Anonymity to conceal his identity, so he had no idea if it would even work. Of course, he had no reason to doubt the ring's efficacy, but it was still a nerve-racking experience.

According to the guides he'd bought from the Branch, anyone with the Guard class had the ability to discern someone's identity, including level and archetype. So, if anyone was going to see through his Ring of Anonymity, then the pair at the gate would have. That they hadn't was just further confirmation that the item was the real deal.

Though he did belatedly remember that, while toying with the ring, he'd changed his surname back to the genuine version. Hopefully, that hadn't raised any red flags, but in the interest of not taking any further chances, Elijah changed it back to Smith.

Once that was done, he took another deep breath, then straightened back to his full height and looked around. The city was much larger than he'd initially suspected, and it sprawled for quite some distance in every direction. In addition, it seemed to have a population to match its size, and even so close to the gate, Elijah saw more than a few pedestrians.

He also saw carts carrying dozens of corpses, each wrapped in white cloth. The passersby gave the wagons—each one pulled by a few burly men or women—a wide berth, but Elijah couldn't fail to notice the furtive glances they cast toward each passing cart.

Otherwise, the city looked much as he'd seen from afar. Which was to say that most of the buildings were clearly newly constructed. For a moment, Elijah considered trying to find a hotel in which to stay the night. Or maybe a restaurant. However, the sight of the bodies had reminded him that Norcastle had a deadly crisis on their hands, and there was a good chance that he could help.

So, with that in mind, he strode down the street. Fortunately, it hadn't rained in some time, so the dirt streets were dry. He didn't usually mind walking around barefoot—after two years, he was used to it—but if the streets had been muddy, he might've changed his tune. In any case, he got quite a few curious glances as he followed the Guard's directions to a large three-story building near the center of the city.

The moment he caught sight of it, he knew he'd reached the hospital. Part of that certainty was due to the big red cross decorating the sign out front, but the steadily moving line of sick people gave it away, as well.

He advanced, stepping across the street and nimbly avoiding the passing hand-pulled carts—most of these bearing mundane goods instead of bodies—and pedestrians along the way. Soon enough, he found himself approaching the building's main entrance, where another pair of Guards stood. Both wore makeshift masks over their haggard faces.

"Stop right there, buddy," one of them said. She was actually taller than Elijah, which wasn't terribly uncommon. He'd never been a big man, after all. "Back of the line."

Elijah continued forward, saying, "The Guard at the gate told me to come here. I'm a—"

The other Guard, who was a square-jawed man wearing a spiteful expression, hefted his cudgel and swung it at Elijah. He didn't hesitate and parried the attack with his staff. Before the Guard could react, Elijah had turned the parry into a low swing that ended with the Guard's legs being swept out from under him. It happened in the space of an instant; Elijah hadn't even meant to react, but his instincts, earned after spending years in the wild, had won out.

Seeing the other Guard preparing to attack, Elijah shoved his staff under her chin and said, "I'm not in the habit of letting people attack me. So, please— let's just leave this here, okay? I don't want to hurt anyone."

By that point, the fallen Guard had scrambled to his feet. His face was red from clear embarrassment, and he spat, "Do you have any idea what you've done?"

"Yeah. I took it easy on you. Now, before you two do something stupid, let me explain what's going on. I'm a Healer. I was told to come here and help out. If you don't want it, that's fine. I'll go on my way. But judging by everything I've seen so far, you could definitely use my help."

"Wait—you're a Healer?" the female Guard said. Then, her eyes briefly unfocused—a sign that Elijah took as her using an ability, probably the one meant to identify him. The other one didn't have the presence of mind to even do that much. Instead, he looked like he was half a step away from attacking Elijah again. "You are. And only eighteen? How did you put Garret down like that?"

"I know kung fu."

"Wait, what?"

"Kung fu. Martial arts. I'm a black belt."

"You are?"

"Sure. My hands are deadly weapons," Elijah said. "My feet, too, but nobody ever asks about those."

She glanced down at his bare feet and muttered, "Huh?"

"Screw this guy, Holly. We don't have to—"

Holly rolled her eyes and said, "Shut up, Garret."

"You're not my boss!" he growled.

"He's a Healer, idiot. We need as many of those as we can get. Now, shut up. Or I'm going to shut you up. Got it?" Holly said. Garret clamped his mouth shut. He clearly didn't like it, but Holly just as clearly didn't care. To Elijah, she asked, "Are you really a black belt?"

"God, no. But I can handle myself okay," he replied with a grin that he hoped was disarming. From experience, he recognized that it probably came off as a bit cocky. Or maybe deranged, given his lack of social contact over the past couple of years. "Anyway, is it alright if I go on in? And who do I talk to about what the situation is? I think we can maybe knock this plague thing out in an afternoon."

She cocked her head to the side and said, "At level eighteen? Color me skeptical. But you're more than welcome to give it a try. God knows we could use the help."

Then, she gave him directions on how to find Jess, one of the Healers on duty. Elijah thanked her for her help, gave Garret a grin, then headed inside. The building was large, but it didn't have many twists or turns, so he quickly found his way to the appropriate room—which was a huge gymnasium-size space containing at least a hundred occupied beds. Elijah only got one step inside before a familiar smell wafted into his nose.

"Voxx," he muttered to himself as he realized that he might've just stepped into a situation he couldn't handle.

17

MIRACLES

The acrid stench Elijah associated with the Voxx filled his nostrils, reminding him of past battles. The smell of human misery reminded him that something else was at play, though. So, after only a few moments of hesitation, he pushed forward, his bare feet sounding loud against the cold tiles.

"Sir? Can I help you?" came a high-pitched voice. Elijah turned to see a pretty woman with dark skin. If he'd had to guess, he would have said that she was in her mid-twenties, but long, stressful hours had robbed her of some of her youthful vitality. "You really shouldn't be in here, especially dressed like that."

Elijah looked down at his attire. "What's wrong with what I'm wearing?" he asked.

The woman wore purple scrubs that had been mended in a few spots and a pair of comfortable-looking sneakers. "You're barefoot. In a hospital. Surely you can't think that's appropriate."

"Oh. Right. I keep forgetting about that," Elijah said, self-consciously wiggling his toes. Unfortunately, his bare feet were a necessity. One with Nature required him to be in contact with the ground, and while being indoors didn't seem to deactivate it, for some reason, wearing shoes—or any kind of foot coverings—did. It was a quirk of the System, and one he'd yet to find a way around. So, for now, he needed to remain barefoot, though he hoped to one day find a means of subverting the spell's requirements.

Though he supposed he should count himself lucky that it didn't deactivate when he leaped into the air or stepped foot on man-made surfaces. Otherwise, the seesawing of his effective attributes would've driven him insane.

"Occupational hazard, I'm afraid," he said. "Anyway, I'm Elijah."

She frowned at him, then said, "Jess. What are you doing here?"

He ran his hand through his hair. "I'm a Healer."

"Seriously?" she asked dubiously. "You don't look like any Healer I've ever seen."

"And you've seen all sorts of Healers, have you?"

"Well, no. But none of them I know walk around barefoot. Or looking like they stepped out of a Renaissance faire."

"Ouch. My outfit's not that bad. The dwarven lady who made it was very skilled."

"Dwarven?"

"Never mind that." Letting his staff fall against his chest, he slapped his hands together and said, "Alright. I'm full of ethera and ready to heal. Where can I set up? Now, I feel obligated to inform you that my spells—well, one of them at least—can get a bit messy, so it's probably best if I set up somewhere with a drain in the floor. Like a locker room. Or maybe outside. I don't know. This is your turf, so I'll let you decide."

"What are you talking about? How can a healing spell be messy?" She narrowed her big brown eyes and crossed her arms. "Wait. Are you messing with me? Did Sam send you here? This is a serious place with seriously ill people. If you—"

Elijah gripped his staff and said, "Whoa. I really am a Healer. You people really are the suspicious sort. Makes a guy feel a little unwelcome, if I'm honest."

"Prove it."

Elijah rolled his eyes. "So little trust," he muttered. "You could just get one of those Guards outside to identify me."

"Or you could heal someone." She looked back at the room full of patients, then pointed at one. "That one. He's already been healed, but there's still a little bit of the plague left in him."

"Why didn't you heal it all?" Elijah asked.

"Ethera. I'm running on fumes here," she said. "Same as the other four Healers. If it wasn't for us, the plague would've already killed everyone in town. But even with everything we've done, there's a limit to our Ethera, and . . . well . . . we can't get to everyone in time. Not even close."

Elijah could hear the frustration in her voice, and what's more, he understood it. He'd felt something similar when the panther had died. Despite all the power they'd been given—and it was miraculous what healing could do—there were still limits.

"Do you care if I get the room wet?" Elijah asked.

"Why would the room get wet?"

"It's part of my spell. Well, one of my spells."

"Is it real water?"

"As opposed to fake water?"

She shrugged. "Some of our Sorcerers can conjure ice," she said. "But it disappears after a few minutes. Same with rocks. We learned that the hard way when someone tried to build a wall out of conjured earth."

Elijah cocked his head to the side, then rubbed the back of his neck in embarrassment. "You know what? I've never even bothered to pay attention to whether or not the water sticks around," he said, a little ashamed that he hadn't tested that facet of Healing Rain. But in his defense, the climate of the island was that of a temperate rainforest, so it was almost always wet, raining, or both. And when he'd used the spell in the tower, he'd either been underwater or he'd had other things on his mind. "Best assume it's real, I guess."

She let out a tired sigh, then said, "Fine. Follow me."

Without another word, she turned around and strode away. Elijah followed, hurrying to catch up. With Essence of the Wolf active, he had no issues keeping pace as they crossed the room. Soon enough, she led him into another hallway, and he asked, "Where're we headed? Someplace special? I've been—"

Elijah's words died in his mouth the moment they passed into another room. The stench of the corruption was so strong that he very nearly gagged the moment he stepped over the threshold. But even then, the smell was nothing compared to the sight of three figures, each one looking as if they were rotting alive as they lay on soiled hospital beds.

"What the . . ."

"These are the worst," she said. "We've been trying our best to keep them alive, but . . . no matter what we do, the plague just keeps coming back. If you want to prove you're a Healer, then here's where you should start because if you can't do anything for them, they're probably going to die within the next hour. When they get this bad, we just make them comfortable because . . . because it would take too much ethera to heal them. If we even can."

"Jesus," Elijah muttered, studying the unfortunate trio. Two of them were men, and the last was a woman. However, there was nothing to suggest that they were in any way connected. Indeed, if it wasn't for the thick black tendrils spreading across their mostly naked skin, they would've looked mostly normal. The only saving grace was that they were at least unconscious.

But Elijah's every sense told him that they were anything but ordinary.

Not only did the smell of the Voxxian corruption—and Elijah was certain that's what it was—hang thick in the air, but he could also feel it sliding across his skin like he'd been dunked into a box of squirming maggots. The sour, acidic taste tickling his tongue was even worse, though. In short, being in that room—which was only about fifteen feet across—was one of the most unpleasant things Elijah had ever endured.

And he'd been digested in the stomach of a monstrous orca, so that was saying something.

"Go nuts," Jess said, gesturing to the nest of corruption.

Elijah shook his head, swallowed hard, then stepped forward. Without further hesitation, he ensured that Aura of Renewal was active so that he could be at peak Regeneration, then cast Healing Rain.

Storm clouds gathered, wreathing the ceiling in dark fog. Then, the first drop of rain fell. Then another. Soon after, a deluge of water poured forth from the clouds, and each drop that hit one of the patients did so with a sizzle.

Elijah stepped through the rain, then laid his hand on the first patient. She was older—maybe forty or so—and her body had clearly been ravaged by her illness. In a lot of ways, it reminded him of his time being treated for cancer. Back then, he'd had to sit in his oncologist's office as they pumped him full of dangerous chemicals. But he hadn't done so alone. There were always one or two other people in there undergoing the same dubious treatment, and Elijah had watched as those familiar faces succumbed to the horrors of chemotherapy. The woman laid out beneath him was little different, with sunken cheeks, pallid skin, and loose flesh that suggested rapid weight loss.

And then there were the black tendrils of corruption.

It all made Elijah sick. But instead of vomiting like he wanted to, he swallowed his discomfort and laid his hand on the woman's forearm. It was cold and clammy to the touch.

She almost felt like she'd already surrendered to death, but the shallow rise and fall of her chest told him differently.

For a second, he just let himself feel her moist skin. Then, he drew ethera from his Core and funneled it into Touch of Nature. The healing power of the spell raced out of him and into the woman. The effect was immediate.

She gasped, her eyes shooting open as her hand snapped out. Elijah could have dodged—the woman couldn't move very quickly, after all—but he let her wrap her fingers around his forearm. Her eyes locked onto his, and she croaked, "Kill . . . me . . ."

Elijah ignored her. He could practically feel her pain it was so palpable.

Since the very beginning, Elijah had been using Touch of Nature to cure himself of various diseases. At first, the spell had been used to eradicate various parasites he'd picked up from drinking tainted water, but he'd used it to similar effect dozens of times throughout his years on the island. So, if he knew nothing else about how the spell interacted with a patient, he knew precisely how it went about counteracting disease.

For specific injuries, he had to guide the spell, but with disease—especially one that suffused the entire patient's body—it was more akin to flooding the recipient with ephemeral vitality and forcing the body's natural recovery into overdrive.

Which was precisely what happened.

The first cast didn't really do much. But under the effects of Healing Rain, combined with a second cast of Touch of Nature, he sent the black tendrils into a retreat. The next cast pushed them back further. And the fourth banished them altogether. Elijah was fairly sure that the woman was cured—though she was still disoriented—but he cast Touch of Nature a final time before he pulled away.

He glanced back at Jess, who stood on the other side of the doorway, her mouth agape, and he said, "I think that takes care of her. You might want to get her somewhere else so it doesn't reoccur."

"What did you do?" she asked.

"Healed her," he stated. "Why? Can't you do the same thing?"

"Not like that."

"Oh. Well, call me special, then. I'll take care of these others, then we can move to the big room. Unless you don't want me making it rain in there, in which case we probably need to set up some sort of—"

"Wait—you still have ethera?"

"Sure," Elijah said, checking the state of his Core. He could still cast Touch of Nature a dozen more times before he ran dry, but his Regeneration was high enough—especially with Aura of Renewal augmenting it—that it wouldn't take that long to recover.

Not for the first time, he wished that Touch of Nature was a little more potent. But then, he supposed that it would probably cost more ethera, so it would almost assuredly even out.

"I can keep going for a while," he said. "And the rain is persistent, so it'll keep coming down for . . . I don't know . . . another hour, maybe? After that, I'll have to cast it again, but by then, I should have plenty of ethera recovered."

"But . . . But how do you have . . . If I did what you just did, I'd be out for the rest of the day . . ."

Elijah shrugged again, then gave her a grin before saying, "Like I said—I'm special, I guess. Now, if you don't mind, I'm going to save a couple of lives." He winked at her. "Because that's what heroes do."

She snorted in laughter. "That . . . was terrible."

"Really? It sounded cool in my head."

"Did it?"

"No. Not really. But in my defense, I've only really had goblins and a tree to talk to for a while, so my conversational skills are a little out of practice. Oh, and a gnome or two. A few dwarves, too, but they're not great conversationalists."

"You might be the oddest man I've ever met," Jess said as she positioned herself behind the healed woman's gurney. It was the sort that one would find in hospitals, so it was equipped with wheels. "And I know actual Wizards."

Elijah shrugged, then knelt beside the second patient. "If you're going to be anything, be the best version of that you can be. That's what my dad used to tell me. So, I'll take that as the compliment it was obviously meant to be."

"I'm going to go out on a limb and guess that he probably wasn't talking about being weird," she said, pushing the woman toward the door.

Elijah cast Touch of Nature on his latest patient, then glanced at Jess and said, "Maybe not, but I've decided to embrace it anyway. Besides, who wants to be normal, right? Odd is so much better. Sexier, too, I'm told."

She stopped. "Did you just hit on me? Here?"

He shrugged. "Maybe. That all depends on your reaction. If it's disgust, then of course I wasn't coming on to you. I'm offended that you would even suggest such a thing. But if you're even mildly interested, then I'm one hundred percent flirting. Or trying to. Like I said, I'm a bit out of practice."

She just shook her head and continued to wheel the woman away.

Elijah glanced at the comatose man he intended to heal and said, "That went well, right? I think it went well."

Then, he laid his hand on the man's arm and cast Touch of Nature.

18

NORCASTLE

Gentle drops of Healing Rain fell upon Elijah's head as he forced the aperture of his Mind ever wider. Ethera flooded through his Mind, cascading through his Soul and into his Core. But he needed more, so he continued to pull against the ambient ethera in an attempt to force the aperture wider; it was no use, though. There was something missing. A vitally important piece of the puzzle that he simply didn't possess.

Still, he kept at it, steadily stretching the aperture as much as he could. It was only a minuscule improvement over his passive Regeneration, but over time, it made a significant difference. Besides, he felt like he was on the right track regarding the improvement of that facet of his cultivation. As for the others, he was still unsure how to progress. Hopefully, he would gain some insight in the near future because he found himself itching for improvement.

A touch on his shoulder jerked him from his meditative state, and his eyes fluttered open. It took a moment for them to refocus, but when they did, he saw the familiar confines of the hospital's main room. The beds had been arranged around him in an effort to maximize the number he could reach with Healing Rain, but even so, he and the other Healers had been forced to steadily cycle the patients.

"Is that all of them?" he asked.

He'd been at it for a few days, and in that time, he'd lost count of the number of people he'd healed. Hundreds, at the least. Maybe thousands. Most he healed via Healing Rain, but some of the worst cases had required the application of Touch of Nature. The other Healers had done their parts as well, but if Elijah had learned anything since coming to Norcastle, it was that his spells were far and away more efficient than most. On top of that, his relatively high level—hidden though it was by his Ring of Anonymity—gave him far more Ethera with which to operate. So, as a result, he'd done the work of at least ten other Healers.

But even that was insufficient to adequately explain his contribution. Because of his Dragon Core, his spells were twice as potent as they otherwise would be. On top of that, he gained a significant boost from his overall level of cultivation. So, a spell like Healing Rain, which had once struggled to mend even minor wounds, had become a powerful tool for healing.

There was something else at play, too, though Elijah hesitated to commit to the idea. Still, he suspected that lower-level people were easier to heal than those who'd progressed further. His efforts in healing his own wounds suggested as much, and that notion seemed to have been confirmed by the ease with which he'd healed some of the less powerful people in the Norcastle hospital.

It was a subject he would need to address next time he visited a Branch. Perhaps he could find a guide that would give him more definitive answers. And failing that, there was always Nerthus to ask.

Jess, who was flanked by another exhausted Healer, said, "That's it. For now. They'll all be back, though."

"That sounds like firsthand experience talking."

"It is," she sighed.

The other Healer—an elderly man with nothing but a ring of gray fringe on his head—said, "At first, the number of patients ebbed and flowed. We would make progress and think we eradicated the disease altogether. Then, a few days later, it would return worse than before."

"Do you know what's causing it?"

Jess shook her head. "We've looked, too. Combed the whole city. We've exterminated all the pests, tested the water, even the food. But we haven't found anything that could be the cause."

Elijah nodded along. "But we're done for a little while, right?" he asked.

"We are."

He felt his shoulders sag. Just because his Constitution and Regeneration gave him the ability to keep going for quite some time without rest didn't mean that it was pleasant. He felt just as exhausted as the others looked.

"Is there someplace I can rest? Maybe get a good meal?"

"What kind of meal?"

Elijah pushed himself to his feet, then ran his hand through his hair. "I don't know. Not sure what choices there are. Like I said before, I've been a little cut off from society for a while. The last properly cooked meal I had was made by gnomes. Or was it goblins? I can't remember. Anyway . . . Yeah . . ."

"I can't tell if you're serious, joking, or a little crazy," she said.

"Probably all three," the older Healer groused. "Lot of that going around since the world ended."

Elijah raised a finger and said, "Pizza. That's what I want. Any suggestions? You have pizza here, right?"

"With goat cheese. All our cows got eaten," Jess said. The older man just shook his head and left.

"What's his deal?" Elijah asked. Then, before Jess could answer, he said, "You know what? Never mind. It's not hard to figure out. So, you want to have some pizza with me? Or are you going to leave me all alone to find my way in the big city?"

He gave her his best fake pout, which drew a laugh. "You are terrible at this," Jess remarked with a shake of her head.

"But is it working? It might just be a pickup tactic. Kind of like negging. But, you know, reverse."

"Self-negging."

"Or I might just be terrible at flirting. You never know."

"Plus, the setting really isn't doing you any favors," she acknowledged. "But you know what? Sure. I'll have some pizza with you. It's expensive, though."

He shrugged. "I've got money."

Indeed, he'd withdrawn enough etherium back in Ironshore that he shouldn't have to worry about whether or not he could afford a meal. Thankfully, Norcastle had adopted it as its basic currency, largely because the city itself used it to buy various items through the Branch Market. The coins had other uses—primarily in crafting—but none of the city's tradespeople had progressed to the point where they could use them.

Or so Elijah assumed.

Either way, he had money, and he wasn't opposed to using it to pay for a shared meal between him and Jess. He certainly wasn't interested in her in anything but a superficial way, but he had spent the majority of the past two years alone. So, her company certainly looked enticing from where he was standing.

In any case, after the pair took a few minutes to clean up in the hospital's bathrooms, Jess led him through the city and to Norcastle's only pizza joint. It wasn't much different from the surrounding buildings—just a cube-like structure made of sturdy cinder blocks—but the owner had made some attempts to differentiate it from all the rest. Beneath a red awning that stretched across the facade were a series of wooden tables and crudely constructed chairs.

It was also incredibly crowded, with every table occupied. Fortunately, Jess knew the owner, who quickly made room for them in the back.

At first, the conversation was confined to lighthearted banter, but eventually, Jess asked, "So, what's your story, anyway? Where did you really come from? And how did you survive the wilderness? I've seen what's out there, and I can't imagine going more than a mile or two from the city, especially not alone."

For a moment, Elijah considered lying. Or simply refusing to answer. But despite Nerthus's warnings to keep his circumstances hidden, he decided that he didn't really want to live like that. Sure, he'd keep some things under his belt. He had no intention of revealing his ability to shape-shift into powerful animal forms. However, he didn't see any issues with giving her the broad strokes.

So, he said, "When the World Tree touched Earth, I was flying home to die."

Then, he explained the basics of how he'd spent the past couple of years. He omitted quite a few details—like the specifics of his class, the panther guardian, and the tower. He did mention Ironshore, though only in the vaguest of terms, and he explained that it was almost entirely populated by gnomes, dwarves, and goblins.

"Wait, are you serious?" she asked. "There are actual gnomes?"

"All of that, and you latch on to the gnomes?"

"I think they're cool," she said unapologetically. "And cute. Back when we actually had video games, I used to always play as a gnome."

"Well, I'm sure they'll appreciate fetishization of their entire race," he said lightheartedly, which earned him a playful roll of Jess's eyes. "But yeah—there are gnomes, though I admit I'm not a huge fan. I had a bad experience with one."

Indeed, Elijah's opinion of the little people would forever be tainted by Cabbot. His views on mohawks were similarly affected, though he didn't say that to Jess.

After she asked a few more questions, it was his turn to throw some in her direction, so he asked, "So, what did you do before this?"

"Medical school. I was almost finished, too. Then the world ended, and . . . Well, you know the rest. Death, destruction, and eventually, survival. I lost . . . a lot of people."

Elijah reached across the table and gripped her hand. "I'm sorry."

She shook her head, sniffed loudly, then wiped her eyes before saying, "It's fine. I've come to terms with it. Everybody lost somebody, and we lose more every day. You know, it's funny. If you'd have asked me before all this happened, I would've probably thought it sounded kind of cool. Me and my friends used to joke about the zombie apocalypse and how we'd survive, you know? But now? I would give just about anything to just go back to the way everything used to be. Back to my boring little life."

Elijah wanted to agree with her. He truly did. But he knew it would be a lie. For better or worse, now that he had tasted what the new world—or universe, really—had to offer, he wanted more. He didn't enjoy the pain he'd had to endure. Nor was he looking forward to the inevitability of more. And yet, he was excited for the future in a way he'd never been back in Hawaii.

Then there was the fact that when Earth felt the World Tree's touch, it had given him a new life. Before, he'd been dying of cancer. He'd only had a few weeks to live. But now, he had a full life ahead of him.

Maybe it was a selfish way to look at it, but he was strangely okay with how everything had turned out. Even if it meant that millions—or billions—had died. Tragic, sure. But what was done was done. There was no going back. And Elijah intended to make the most out of the chance he'd been given.

But he didn't say that. Instead, he just nodded and muttered vaguely comforting things until their pizza arrived. That proved to be the highlight of the night. It was easy to forget just how perfect of a food pizza really was, but the moment he took that first bite, Elijah was reminded of that indisputable fact.

"That good, huh?" asked Jess after watching him devour the first piece.

"You have no idea. I spent most of the last two years surviving on mushrooms and badly cooked crab," he said, stuffing another piece into his mouth. "I don't even mind the goat cheese. And what is this meat?"

"Venison sausage," she said. "There's a huge herd of deer that roam across the plains about forty miles south of here. We send hunters down there pretty consistently, though they have to be really careful because the deer are supposedly extremely dangerous now."

"Mmm," he mumbled around a mouthful of glorious pizza.

After that, the evening wore on. For his part, Elijah ate far more than his fair share of pizza, even insisting on meeting the owner, whom he showered with effusive praise—and a handful of etherium. Meanwhile, Jess lightened up, especially when Elijah started talking about his Grove. He didn't reveal its magical nature, but he still spoke of it with enough enthusiasm that Jess couldn't help but mirror it.

Then, after a couple of hours of pizza and conversation, Elijah asked, "So, your place? Or am I staying in a hotel tonight?"

She rolled her eyes. "I think you know the answer to that."

"Alright. But I have to warn you—I have a tendency to snore. If you can—"

With a chuckle, she tossed a napkin at him. He caught it deftly. "You know I'm kidding, right? Unless you're interested. In which case . . ."

Another amused roll of her eyes told him all he needed to know. Perhaps he was on the right track, but she wasn't interested in making a night out of it. Which was fine. But Elijah did have one other question. "So, when did all this plague stuff start, anyway? Nobody could ever give me a good answer."

"About a month ago," Jess answered.

"Was there anything about the days before that that stick out? Anything at all?"

She shook her head. "Not that I know about. But I'm probably not the best person to answer that. You'd probably need to ask Captain Essex. He's in charge of the city's defense and keeps order in town. If anyone knows about . . . strange occurrences, it would be him. Why? Do you think you have an idea about what's causing the plague?"

Elijah shrugged. "Nothing concrete. It's just that I smelled something familiar when I saw those first patients. But if anyone in this city had seen anything like what I'm thinking of . . . Well, everyone would know about it. In any case, I think I'm going to find that hotel you mentioned and get some sleep. I might get you to introduce me to this Captain Essex in the morning, though. If you don't mind, I mean."

"Sure. If you think you can help figure out the source, I'll do whatever you want."

"Whatever I want? Well, in that case—"

"Get your mind out of the gutter."

She said it with a note of annoyance, but Elijah saw the interest in her eyes. That was enough to buoy his mood for the entire walk to the hotel. In fact, he was distracted enough that he briefly forgot about the horrible suffering he'd witnessed over the past few days.

19

DEFINING THE SOURCE

That night, Elijah went to bed a little disappointed, and for a couple of reasons. Obviously, he would've preferred it if Jess had joined him; her company had only hammered home just how lonely he'd been since washing ashore on his island. And while he could ignore it most of the time, the connection he'd forged with the former medical student was just electric enough to send his imagination running wild with possibilities.

The other reason for his ill attitude was the inn room itself. Despite the fact that he'd been camping in the wilderness for the past couple of months, he still remembered his mossy bed back on the island, and the inn's mattress just couldn't measure up to Nerthus's work. Still, he was exhausted enough that it was only mildly disappointing, and what's more, he'd slept in worse.

So, even though he wasn't as comfortable—or satisfied—as he might've hoped, Elijah spent a restful enough night, and the next morning, he felt reenergized. When he awoke, he pushed himself upright and looked around. The room was spartan, with only a bed, a utilitarian nightstand, and a bathroom. However, Norcastle had running water—apparently, Plumber was an actual class, and the city had a couple who'd managed to supply it with water via their creations—so he quickly jumped in the shower, then changed into one of his spare outfits.

As always, he had no shoes. Most of the time, Elijah barely noticed, but in the city, his unshod feet were noteworthy enough that other people definitely did. It didn't matter, though. If everything went according to plan, he wouldn't be staying much longer.

So, after dressing, Elijah gathered his things and left the room behind. His bare feet slapped against the wooden floor as he traversed the short hallway and entered the stairwell before descending a couple of flights of stairs and exiting into the hotel's common room. There, he found the proprietor standing behind a bar, where she was manning a griddle.

The heavyset woman glanced over her shoulder and asked, "What can I get for you?"

"Whatever's easiest," Elijah said. "Just so long as it's hot."

"Got sausage and pancakes. Even some real maple syrup."

"That sounds great."

He watched as the woman got to work, and he sensed a barely noticeable swirl of ethera accompanying her actions. Clearly, she had some sort of technique associated with cooking; perhaps she even had the Chef class. If that was the case, Elijah was truly looking forward to breakfast.

After all, he hadn't forgotten the meal he'd enjoyed back in Ironshore. While the woman cooked, Elijah took a look at his status:

Name	Elijah Hart		
Level	34		
Archetype	Druid		
Class	Animist		
Specialization	N/A		
Alignment	N/A		
Strength	35		
Dexterity	34		
Constitution	35		
Ethera	43		
Regeneration	37		
Attunement	Nature		
Cultivation Stage: Cultivator			
Body	Core	Mind	Soul
Wood	Hatchling	Opal	Neophyte

During his time healing the plague-stricken patients back in the hospital, Elijah had gained two more levels. Distressingly, though, he still hadn't been awarded another spell. The last one he'd gotten was at level thirty, and that was Shape of the Guardian. If he hadn't read guides that said that he would, indeed, get more spells going forward, he might've been even more worried. However, he knew it was only a matter of time before he acquired some new tools for his tool kit.

Still, he had high hopes for level thirty-five. In the beginning, he'd gained spells every level, but after reaching the tenth, the frequency had been reduced by half. After he hadn't gotten a spell at thirty-two, he'd hoped the pattern would continue, and he'd get one at thirty-four. But now that that hadn't happened, he could only hope that it would happen at level thirty-five.

For now, though, his attributes had continued to rise by one point each level. As the innkeeper continued to cook, a few other guests descended from their rooms above and took seats around the common room. Whoever had built the hotel had clearly taken inspiration from old school inns rather than modern hotels, because the business was clearly as much a tavern and restaurant as it was a lodging.

As he waited, Elijah cast Essence of the Boar, increasing his Constitution attribute by ten points. The same for Essence of the Monkey, though it increased Dexterity instead. Finally, he topped it all off with Aura of Renewal, then Essence of the Wolf. He already had One with Nature active, as well. Once he was fully enhanced, he looked at his status again, and he was pleased to see the state of his attributes.

Elijah couldn't quantify the effect of each point, but after having reached such lofty heights, he knew he was approaching superhuman levels of strength, coordination, and durability. Still, he had no real context for how he might stack up against more focused individuals. Given that, according to the guides he'd read, each class gave attribute bonuses according to its nature, there was every chance that others might be quite a bit more powerful than him.

As he saw it, that was the source of his greatest strength as well as his biggest weakness. On the one hand, he had the versatility to respond well to a wide variety of situations. However, on the other, he lacked specialization, so he would be at a disadvantage against more focused classes. Still, he hoped that his cultivation and Dragon Core might prove the difference if it ever came down to that.

Soon enough, the innkeeper served him, and Elijah proceeded to eat what felt like a mountain of pancakes and sausage before paying her a couple of copper etherium and excusing himself. After that, he left the hotel—or inn, really—and headed toward the hospital where he was supposed to meet Jess.

He arrived a little earlier than anticipated, so he spent the next half hour focusing on his Mind cultivation. It was still stubbornly resistant to his attempts at advancement, which served to solidify his certainty that he was missing something important. However, none of the guides he'd bought from the Branch back in Ironshore had specified any viable cultivation techniques.

"What are you doing?" came Jess's voice.

Elijah opened his eyes to see that she was, once again, wearing her purple scrubs and sneakers, and she looked just as good as she had the night before.

"Cultivating."

"What? How?"

Elijah explained what he knew, which was precious little, really. His own advancement had been contingent on a series of strange events, the unmatched ethera density on his island, and Nerthus's help. However, he told Jess what he could, ending with, "I'm still trying to figure it all out. There might be some guides available at your Branch's Knowledge Base. I don't know how that works, though, because the only one I've used was transplanted here from somewhere else. So, it was probably more advanced than yours."

"I wouldn't know anything about that. Branch access is very tightly regulated. Only the mayor's inner circle really use it, except to access the Bank," she said. "Not even Captain Essex and his people get to, so I'm pretty sure someone like me has no chance."

"Huh."

That definitely threw a monkey wrench in Elijah's plans. He'd intended to at least access the Regional Map in the hopes of finding the next closest settlement, but now, he realized that that might not be possible.

After that, Jess insisted on taking him to the barracks where Captain Essex and his people were housed. She wanted to get back to the hospital as soon as possible—even if the plague had been taken care of for the time being, people got injured all the time, and she took her job very seriously. So, neither of them really spoke on the way.

Which was fine with Elijah because he quickly lost himself in thought. He didn't like the idea of Branch access being restricted. The Knowledge Base alone held the keys to survival, and that wasn't even considering the things that could be bought in the Branch Market. That regular people couldn't use those functions was more than a little troubling.

But Elijah couldn't really do anything to change that. For now, he had more than enough on his plate, what with finding the source of the plague and searching out any hints as to the whereabouts of his sister. So, he had little interest in getting distracted trying to interfere in something he didn't really understand. For all he knew, the mayor had good reasons to restrict access to the Branch.

Still, he didn't like it, and that wasn't going to change just because he didn't want to dive into the deep end of Norcastle's problems.

After about fifteen minutes of walking through the city—during which time, Elijah confirmed his first impressions of the city and its population—they reached a large building attached to the wall. The gate was only a few hundred yards away, so the barracks were close enough that they could respond to any developing situations.

"Follow me. And don't say anything weird, okay? Captain Essex doesn't really put up with disrespect."

"I never say anything weird. And stop looking at me like that. There, that raised-eyebrow thing. Super disrespectful."

She sighed and rolled her eyes, muttering something that, to Elijah, sounded curiously like, "This is a huge mistake."

But Elijah was certain he'd heard her wrong.

He followed her inside, and she spoke to a receptionist who, in turn, told them to wait while she presumably went to speak to the captain. A couple of minutes later, the plump woman returned and told Jess to go ahead. Elijah followed in her wake, looking around as they passed through a bare hall. He also paid attention to One with Nature, though he felt nothing out of the ordinary.

Not until the captain's office came within his range. At that moment, he felt the swirl of ethera that suggested a powerful person was on the other side of that door. The feeling wasn't as strong as he'd felt from Ramik back in Ironshore, but it was potent enough to give Elijah pause.

In any case, he stood to the side as Jess knocked on the door. A moment later, a rough voice bade her enter, which she did. Elijah followed into the office and was unsurprised to see a pale, broad-shouldered man sitting behind an old metal desk reminiscent of the one his fourth-grade teacher, Mrs. Bliss, had used.

Elijah stood to the side as Jess introduced him, making certain to mention his efforts at healing the plague victims.

"Which is why I agreed to this meeting. Thank you, Mr. Hart. You saved a lot of lives over the past few days."

Elijah shrugged, leaning on his staff as he said, "Least I could do. But I don't want it to all be for nothing. So, I've decided to see if I can figure out the source."

"You think you can?" Essex asked, narrowing his eyes in suspicion.

"I believe so, yes. But I need you to answer a couple of questions for me, if you can. It'll help me narrow things down."

Essex gestured for him to go on.

Elijah asked, "Have you or your people been in contact with the Voxx?"

Even without One with Nature, Elijah couldn't have missed the sudden tension in the man's face. Or the fact that he glanced at Jess, then said, "Miss Roy, if you would please give us some privacy . . ."

Jess said, "What is the Voxx?"

"Please, Miss Roy. This is need-to-know information. I promise you will receive an explanation when appropriate."

"I'm just going to tell her the moment I leave," Elijah stated. "So, you may as well let her stay."

Essex ground his teeth so hard that Elijah could hear it. Or maybe he'd simply sensed it via One with Nature. Sometimes, it was difficult to tell the difference. In any case, the man didn't look happy to be pushed against a wall. He almost growled, "And if I tell you that the consequences for doing so could be very detrimental to your health?"

Elijah looked the man in the eye and said, "I'm unconcerned with what you deem dangerous."

For a long moment, the pair of men stared at one another, neither willing to back down. Finally, Essex deflated and said, "Fine. On your head be it, then. Just know that you're putting her in danger, as well. Some knowledge is—"

"Dangerous, sure," Elijah stated. Then, he turned to Jess and said, "The Voxx are interdimensional lizards who invade our world in one of three ways. Sometimes, they simply manifest as singular entities. Those are the least deadly. Basically pests. Most of the time. But they have the chance, albeit a small one, to manifest something much, much stronger. The most powerful creature I've ever seen came from one of those. I think."

Essex seemed to take issue with that assessment, and he said, "I beg to differ on that account. They are dangerous creatures who can—"

"Sure, they're dangerous. But nothing compared to the next ones. Those come from dimensional rifts. Those are temporary rips in the fabric of our reality. If you can go in and defeat the monster inside, you'll close them. And get a reward. But the Voxxian creature inside can be pretty strong," Elijah explained. "If you don't close them, they corrupt the environment and drive the local wildlife crazy. I've also read that they can burst, creating a minisurge."

"And where did you read this?"

"A guide I bought from the Branch Knowledge Base," Elijah lied. In reality, it had been explained to him by Nerthus. "Anyway, the third type is worse. If you've got a tower around here, which is what I suspect, then it'll go a long way to explaining things. So, please, tell me the truth, Captain Essex—are we dealing with a tower? Or is it just a dimensional rift?"

"What is a tower? I mean, I know what a tower is. But I feel like I'm missing some context," Jess admitted.

"A tower is like a dimensional rift on steroids," Elijah said. "The system erects towers around them, which drains the ethera by creating a complex environment that can be challenged by—"

"Is it like a video game dungeon?" she asked, interrupting him.

"Uh . . . I guess? I was never much of a video game guy," Elijah said. "But the problem is that if those towers are left unattended, they will eventually burst into surges. And they'll keep spilling more Voxxian monsters out until someone goes in, challenges the tower, and conquers it. That drains the ethera—at least for a while—and keeps the Voxx from passing over." He turned to the captain and asked, "That about the shape of things?"

Essex nodded. "It is," he said tersely.

"Tower or rift?"

"Tower," he said. "We've sent three teams inside. None have come back out."

Elijah groaned. "And you've been dealing with the surges, right? I'm guessing some of your people got injured, and that's how they got infected with the plague, huh?" he guessed. Given what he knew, it was the only thing that made sense. Or, rather, it was the only problem with a potential solution. If the Voxx weren't responsible, then the plague could've almost literally been caused by anything. In that case, he'd have to chalk it up as a loss and move on; at the same time, he'd advise anyone healthy to do the same.

But then Essex said, "It only happened one time. Just a single injured Warrior. Since then, we've been careful. We don't get close to the monsters. But the plague keeps coming back."

Elijah shook his head. There were a host of potential explanations, but it probably came down to magic. The Voxx spread corruption wherever they went, and this particular tower seemed to house a virulent version.

"Alright, then. I guess I know what I need to do."

"What?" asked Essex as Elijah turned to leave.

Elijah glanced back at the man and said, "Well, I'm going to conquer the tower. Obviously."

He didn't wait for a response before he left the office and turned down the hall, his mind already whirling with potential plans for defeating the tower. It was only after he'd gone a few steps when he realized that the downside of what he hoped was a cool exit meant that he'd never actually gotten directions to the tower. He was just about to turn around and sheepishly return to the captain's office when Jess caught up to him.

Then, the captain followed soon after. "Wait!" the man said, reaching out to grab Elijah's arm.

Elijah didn't react well to that, and he quickly jerked away. In only a second, he had his staff in the man's face. "Please don't grab me. I get jumpy," he said.

Essex backed away, raising his hands in surrender. "I'm not a threat to you."

"Sure you're not," Elijah said. "But you know what? I don't care. Just tell me where to find this tower. I'll run on over, conquer it, then be on my way. The good thing is that it won't surge while I'm inside, and after I beat it, you'll need to use that break to get stronger."

"Why?"

"Because even if I conquer it, it's not going to stop. It'll be a while before it comes back, but you'll be right in this same situation in a few months. Maybe a year. But it's not a bad thing. Towers are great for levels. I've read that, in other parts of the universe, they're seen as strategic resources."

Indeed, ever since Elijah had recovered from his previous tower run, he'd thought about revisiting the challenge. He had expected that foray into another tower to be the one near his island, but the thought process remained the same. In the last tower, he'd gained ten levels. If he could repeat that feat in this current challenge, he'd put himself at the top of the power ladder. That was enough of a reason on its own, but couple that with a good cause, and Elijah's decision was easy enough.

"We can send someone with you. There are a few talented—"

"No, thanks. They'll just slow me down. All I need from you is some supplies and a map. Oh, and when I get back, I want access to your Branch."

"I can't—"

"Nonnegotiable, cap'n."

"Please don't call me that. It's Captain Essex."

"That's what I said. Cap'n Essex."

The man groaned, massaging his forehead. "Fine. I'm skeptical you'll even survive, but if you happen to surprise me, I'll make sure you get access. In the meantime, if you'll wait here, I'll get you everything else you'll need."

"Sounds like we have a deal, cap'n."

Essex didn't respond. Aside from another groan, at least. But that surely had nothing to do with Elijah. Once Essex left, Elijah and Jess went back to the man's office, where they waited for him to make good on his promises.

Once they were there, Jess remarked, "Is that what you call respectful?"

"Sure. Why? Did it not come off as respectful?"

20

DIFFERENT PATHS

As the sun rose high into a cloudless winter sky, Elijah looked down on the corpse of small-town Americana. A strip of a street, overgrown with weeds and other vegetation, sliced between two rows of abandoned businesses. From a distance, Elijah couldn't identify them all, but he recognized the striped pole of a barbershop, a few signs declaring the names of the businesses, and a handful of rusting automobiles. The structures themselves were no more than two stories tall, many with glass fronts shaded by rotting cloth awnings, the remnants of which fluttered in the breeze.

Once, it might have been a quaint little town, but now, it was nothing more than the crumbling ruins of a lost world. Elijah knelt by the tree line, hundreds of yards away, and used Eyes of the Eagle to study the ruins, but he saw nothing out of the ordinary. In fact, he'd passed through a handful of similarly abandoned towns on his journey from Ironshore to Norcastle, and he knew he'd seen only a fraction of what was out there.

Likely, whole cities had been laid to waste.

If the transformed wildlife hadn't done the trick, then people certainly would have. Elijah had seen how people reacted in even mundane times of crisis. Looting. Murder. Tribalism. It was all so commonplace as to have become cliché. And with something like what had happened after Earth had been touched by the World Tree, it would inevitably be worse. It didn't take much of an imagination to envision a situation where a particularly strong despot came to power.

And there wouldn't be anything to keep them from doing whatever they wanted to do. No government. No law enforcement. Just chaos and anarchy, which always favored the amoral.

But there had to be some hope. As often as Elijah had seen evil rise, he'd also seen plenty of instances where people had come together to support one another. It had happened in Norcastle. Hopefully, that would prove to be the rule, rather than the exception. Still, Elijah couldn't look down at that snippet of a once-thriving town and feel anything but a sense of poignant loss.

It wasn't just for the people who'd died, though that was a significant part of it. Added to that was the cultural loss, as well. Would it survive? What Elijah had seen in Norcastle suggested that it wouldn't—at least not intact. Bits and pieces would persevere, but the world as Elijah and everyone else had known it was gone. Never was there a more apt representation of that fact than the ruins of the abandoned town in the distance.

With a sigh, Elijah rose to his feet and ran his hand through his hair. It had been almost an entire day since he'd left Norcastle behind, and according to the map Essex had given him, he was incredibly close to the tower. Soon enough, he intended to enter it, and then, he'd spend the next days or weeks fighting for his life.

When he thought of it in those terms, he almost turned around and left it all behind. By all rights, he shouldn't have committed himself to the quest. However, the fact remained that, over the course of the two-plus years since he'd been stranded on that island, he had changed. Not only had he gained magical powers and the ability to shape-shift into powerful animal forms, but he'd also attained nearly superhuman strength, endurance, and coordination. But it was more than that. Those were important, but even more impactful was his shifting mindset.

Things that should have terrified him he simply took as a matter of course. He wanted to enter that tower in order to save Norcastle from the plagued Voxx. That was a given. But his decision to challenge it was also seeded by a need to advance. He wanted to get stronger, and a tower was the best place to do that.

But more than that, even, was Elijah's need to seek a challenge. To balance on the edge of life and death and come out on top. That was the real benefit of conquering the Keledge Tower near his island. It had changed him, body, mind, and soul. And he wanted to experience that feeling, that sensation of overcoming adversity and conquering what should have been unbeatable, again.

Since then, he'd learned that most towers were only challenged by groups of people. As many as six individuals could enter the same tower, which meant that most people wouldn't dare try with less. The notion of going alone was unthinkable except at the highest echelons of power when finding peers became exceedingly difficult.

That he'd managed to conquer the tower by himself was a feat worthy of praise. That he wanted to try to repeat that accomplishment was a little insane, though he felt that there were two factors in his favor. First was the versatility of his class. By virtue of his varied spell book as well as his animal forms, he was suited to combat a wide variety of situations. So, going alone wasn't the detriment that it would be for, say, a Warrior whose ability to heal would be very limited. With his Dragon Core, he felt even more strongly about his chances.

But the second factor was arguably more important. Nerthus had informed him that a tower's relative strength was based on ethera density. They were graded according to the density, much like items. The lowest-ranked tower was Simple grade, but they could reach as high as Miraculous grade. And while

Elijah didn't think that the tower he'd conquered was the highest grade possible, he knew it couldn't have been the lowest, either. That certainty was based primarily on the fact that the ethera on and around his island was far denser than what he felt in the Norcastle region. By extension, any tower that would have manifested would have to be much weaker than one near his island. Of course, complicating matters was the fact that enemies within a tower adjusted according to the level of the person—or people—challenging it, so Elijah wasn't certain how things would work out.

Whatever the case, there hadn't been much information available concerning towers, so he'd need to experience quite a few before he could come to any viable conclusions.

In pursuit of that endeavor, he needed to find the Norcastle region's tower.

So, to that end, Elijah strode forward with a confident gait. He crossed a wide meadow before reaching the outskirts of the ruined town. The moment he passed the first building, though, he felt a steep rise in the ambient ethera. It didn't feel like a dimensional rift, though. There was no mistaking that much. Rifts—and towers, to an extent—felt wrong in a way nothing else really could. This, by comparison, felt natural.

But even though his senses told him to relax, Elijah kept his guard up as he progressed through the town. Originally, he'd intended to scavenge anything useful, but he quickly saw that the stores on either side of the street had long since been picked clean. Likely, the people of Norcastle were responsible.

Still, Elijah continued to check each building. He wasn't certain what he hoped to find—in fact, he had almost everything he needed—but he wasn't going to pass up a golden opportunity just because he lacked imagination or foresight. So, he went through each abandoned store with a proverbial fine-tooth comb.

And he found nothing of note.

But as he searched the small town, Elijah felt the density of the ambient ethera continuously increase. Eventually, he was following that more than he was looking for anything useful, and after almost two hours, he finally found the source.

He caught a quick glimpse of it through the broken windows of an old appliance store before he hastily ducked back out of sight, his heart beating out of his chest. In only a second, he'd already channeled ethera into Shape of the Predator, and it only took a few more moments before he once again assumed the form of a scaled panther. When he did, he embraced the Guise of the Unseen, hiding himself from view.

Only then did he allow himself to relax.

He waited for almost a minute before his heartbeat slowed down. Then, crouching low and trusting his ability to keep him hidden, he slithered out from cover and searched for the creature that, before, he'd only glimpsed.

And there it was, in the back of the store, looming over a broken washing machine. Most of the store itself was empty, obviously having been plundered by Norcastle's scavengers. They had electricity, even if it was obviously in short supply, so the appliances were still useful for them.

In any case, Elijah wasn't even remotely concerned with those sorts of mundane thoughts. Because a bear had mistaken the appliance store for a cave.

It wasn't just any bear, though. The thing was enormous—at least the size of a polar bear—with mottled black-and-red fur. But Elijah's gaze quickly flicked past the creature, and he saw the reason the enormous ursine had settled in the store. At first glance, it was obviously a mushroom. Red and white, with a stereotypically thick stalk and a bulbous cap, it was easily identifiable as a fly amanita. However, with a diameter of at least six feet, it was many times larger than any mushroom Elijah had ever seen.

And it was clearly the source of the thickened ethera. Elijah could feel it with every cell in his body.

Nerthus had often spoken of natural treasures. The ancestral tree with which the spirit was linked was one such treasure, but he'd also intimated that the transformed world would be full of them. Once, Elijah had wondered how he might identify such a treasure. Now, though? Looking at that enormous mushroom—and, more importantly, feeling the waves of dense ethera pulsing off of it—Elijah no longer wondered.

But what was he supposed to do with it?

More importantly, whatever he decided, how was he going to deal with the bear? Was it an intelligent guardian like the panther had been? Or was it just a mutated animal? More importantly, did it matter? Because, judging by the bear's size—and, more urgently, the feeling Elijah got when he looked at the thing—it was just as powerful as the panther had been. So, the source of that power, or rather, its origin, was somewhat a moot point.

Elijah settled back on his haunches and watched, though the bear seemed lethargic. Probably due to winter's onset. It wouldn't be long before winter storms and blizzards swept through the region, and it didn't take a biologist to suppose that the bear was settling down for hibernation. Perhaps that would give Elijah an opportunity.

At first, he considered attacking the creature with every weapon he had at his disposal. Perhaps he could even take it out before it had a chance to respond. However, even if that was possible—which he doubted—Elijah's thoughts traced a different path. The bear had done nothing to him, and he couldn't stomach the idea of killing it for the simple crime of existing.

With the spiders, his hand had been forced by that sense of wrongness he'd felt when looking at them. In addition, they were in the way, and he couldn't have gotten through the pass without dealing with them. But the situation with the bear was different. It had done nothing to him. It didn't really pose a threat to him, either. In fact, he could easily bypass the overgrown ursine and continue on his way.

And he would have, if it wasn't for the call of that amanita.

So, if he didn't want to kill the bear—or couldn't—Elijah needed to find a different path to getting what he wanted. And it didn't take him long to remember how he'd originally befriended the panther. A little fish could go a long way toward building a friendship.

With that in mind, Elijah retreated and quickly set off toward a stream he'd passed a few hours before stumbling upon the ruins of the nameless town. By the time he reached the stream, though, night had begun to fall, so he chose to set up camp rather than approach the bear at night.

He built a fire, then settled in to eat a supper of smoked fish, a few berries and mushrooms he'd gathered along the way, and a piece of flatbread he'd gotten back in Norcastle. It was not a pleasant dinner, and he was once again reminded of the meals he'd eaten back in the city. Or of the berries he grew on his island.

It was at that moment that he realized just how much he missed his Grove. He wanted to sleep in his bed. He wanted to tend to his garden. To catch his fish. He even wanted to eat his crabs. At some point, it had gone from a place where he'd washed ashore to an actual home.

Thoughts of his Grove settled onto his mind until, at last, he fell asleep. Somewhere around midnight, he was awoken by something tickling against One with Nature, but when he looked around, he saw that the culprit was just a raccoon. Elijah didn't shoo it away, and the small creature approached cautiously.

It sniffed his extended hand, then skittered backward a foot or so. But it didn't flee. Instead, it came back, a little more confidently than it had before. Over and over, it repeated the same motions until, at last, it seemed to accept that Elijah wasn't going to hurt it. Then, it settled down next to him, curled up at his hip, then promptly fell asleep.

Elijah knew that was unnatural behavior for just about any wild animal, much less a raccoon. They were nocturnal, so the fact that it was sleeping at night was a bit of a red flag. So, with as gentle a touch as he could manage, Elijah reached out and used Touch of Nature on the little ball of fur.

Immediately, he felt a host of parasites in the thing's stomach. They might've been worms. Or something else native to the new world. However, they were sucking the life right out of the little creature. So, Elijah used his healing ability to banish the parasites.

Idly, he wondered how that worked. How did the spell know not to heal the parasites instead of the raccoon? Was it based on his perception? He'd done something similar with himself on enough occasions that that explanation made as much sense as any other, but he resolved to ask Nerthus when he returned to the Grove.

In the meantime, he healed his new friend, and when he'd finished, the little raccoon fell into an even deeper slumber. Elijah did, as well, though he was careful to once again ensure that One with Nature was active so that the passive awareness it granted would alert him of any threats. That took him all the way until morning, when the raccoon stirred, waking him.

Elijah opened his eyes and glanced at the little critter and, with a yawn, asked, "Feeling better?"

It predictably didn't answer. Instead, it just scurried away, disappearing into a nearby bush.

"No—don't thank me. It was the least I could do," he muttered to himself. Then, he shook his head and let a wry smile play across his face as he said, "What did I even expect? A talking raccoon? C'mon, Elijah. You know better than that."

With that, he reached into his pack and retrieved his homemade fishing line. He'd always intended to get some back in Ironshore, but in all the hustle and bustle of buying the rest of his supplies, he'd forgotten. Still, his handmade line and hooks were more than capable of doing the job. So, he got to his feet, then headed toward the stream.

That's when he realized that his equipment was poorly suited for the job at hand. He saw the fish, but they simply weren't inclined to be caught. So, after spending almost an hour in a fruitless attempt at fishing, Elijah shifted into his guardian form and channeled his inner bear.

And with his incredible Strength pushing his body to ridiculous heights, he had no issues with slapping the water so hard that it stunned the nimble fish. After that, it was simple to grab them and toss them onto shore. Before another hour had passed, he had almost two dozen silvery trout.

Hopefully, that would be enough.

However, before he headed back to the town with his intended offering, he gutted one of the fish, filleted it, then roasted the results over his fire. He still wasn't a good cook, but brook trout were difficult to screw up too badly. Once that was done, he broke his fast, then wove some cordage through the trouts' mouths before slinging the lot over his shoulder and heading back to town.

His plan was simple enough.

Bears were already intelligent creatures, and they had a long history of peaceful coexistence with humans. Sure, they were wild animals, and they should always be treated as such, but so long as he played his cards right, Elijah felt certain that his offering of food, coupled with the subtle pacifying effect of One with Nature, would see him through to an alliance with the hulking creature.

Even so, he was more than a little nervous when the appliance store came into view. He could still see the bear—or more, the shadow of the creature— inside. But even when he approached, slowly and deliberately, the monstrous animal didn't respond. Then, suddenly, it lifted its massive head and sniffed the air.

"I'm a friend," Elijah said in an even tone. The bear sniffed again, then shifted its bulk. Elijah knew just how quickly bears could move, so he was on guard. As it turned out, it wasn't necessary. The bear eyed him for a long moment, then huffed and settled back down.

Elijah relaxed.

A little.

But he knew he was still on thin ice, so he pulled the bundle of fish off his back, then tossed it at the bear's front paws.

"All yours," he said.

The bear wasted no time before digging in and devouring one fish after another. Elijah sat down, his back to the wall, and crossed his legs. He could spring to his feet in less than an instant, and he had a full Core of ethera, so he felt confident that he could escape at a moment's notice. But he didn't want to.

Instead, he was compelled to coexist with the creature. Whether it was by virtue of his archetype or something else, he wasn't sure. But it was there, all the same.

More importantly, with the bear seemingly having accepted his presence, Elijah could bask in the dense ethera wafting off the giant mushroom. And the moment he let himself feel it—really feel it—he realized that it was the piece of the puzzle he'd been missing in his attempts at advancing his Mind cultivation.

21

QUARTZ

Waves of dense ethera crashed against Elijah's mind, threatening to envelop and overwhelm him, and yet, he endured, bracing himself for each impact. It was the only thing that kept him from being completely engulfed by the magical energy. Just before the latest wave slammed into him, he opened the aperture of his Mind as wide as he could. The results were predictable, and yet, still surprising. The flow of dense ethera threatened to rip him apart as it rushed through his Mind and into his Soul. There most of it dissipated, evaporating into nothing before a trickle entered his core.

He held the aperture open for only a second, but in that time, he very nearly tore his Mind to pieces. When he closed his Mind, he collapsed into panting exhaustion as his hands slammed into the mud-covered floor of the appliance store. For a few seconds, he knelt there, his mind and body twisting into knots. Gradually, though, he mastered himself, and after a couple of minutes, he managed to force his eyes open.

Elijah flinched back when he saw a wet snout and a pair of glistening brown eyes only a handful of inches from his face. The bear wasn't having it. Instead, it advanced, then snorted, sending a mist of mucus and other wet gooeyness to coat his face.

"Oh, come on, man . . ."

It snorted again, then sat on its backside like a trained circus bear.

"Seriously? Again? I just fed you," Elijah complained. That got a low growl in response. "Don't give me that. You're perfectly capable of hunting your own food. I can't spend all my time fishing. I'm on the clock here."

Indeed, he'd been trying to cultivate his Mind and reach the next stage for the past three days, and he knew that if he didn't make a breakthrough soon, he'd need to move on without reaching his goal. The tower was still a threat, and if he didn't challenge it soon, another surge would come. And then, more people would die.

His cultivation wasn't worth that.

Elijah told himself that he would've already gotten to the next stage if it wasn't for the bear's greed. His plan of offering it a meal had backfired, and now, it expected him to run off and catch some fish each time its stomach rumbled.

And given its size, that was quite a frequent occurrence. So far, he'd acquiesced to the animal's demands, mostly because it was a bear the size of a Honda Civic. But he was nearing the end of his rope.

Still, once he managed to get his body and mind under control, Elijah pushed himself to his feet, gathered his staff and pack, then shifted into his scaled-panther form. He didn't do so for its stealth or combat capabilities; rather, he knew that, of his three forms—human, scaled panther, and guardian—the predator form was by far the fastest.

That was because it increased both his Strength and Dexterity attributes by a significant amount. So, that form, coupled with his personal enhancements and Essence of the Wolf, gave him the ability to traverse the terrain with incredible alacrity.

So, he reached the stream in only a few minutes. When he did, he quickly started swatting the fish out of the water. Fishing in his scaled-panther form required a different strategy than doing so as a guardian, but it was at least as efficient.

Soon enough, Elijah had caught almost thirty fish.

Once he'd gotten enough, he switched back to his human form, threw the fish into his pack—he didn't like it, but that was the best and most efficient way to get a lot of fish to the bear—then shifted back into his predator form for the trip back.

Predictably, he found the bear right where he'd left him.

"This is it," he said, resuming his human form and tossing the fish at the ursine. "No more until I finish."

The bear snorted, then started to noisily devour the offered pile of fish. Not for the first time, Elijah considered shifting back into one of his animal forms and attacking the greedy, slothful beast. But he suspected that that wouldn't end well for either of them. So, he restrained himself, then crossed the abandoned appliance store and set himself atop a mostly destroyed dishwasher.

That was as close as he could get to the amanita without actually touching it—which would be a mistake, as he'd found out on his first day in the appliance store. Even a tiny brush against the thing's cap had made Elijah so ill that it had taken so many casts of Touch of Nature to heal him that his Core had gone dry.

And in the interim, he'd been miserable, spewing from both ends. It had taken every ounce of his self-control to keep himself casting. No—he had no interest in repeating that, so he got as close as he dared, then settled back down to meditate.

As it had every time in the vicinity of the enormous mushroom, the moment he opened the aperture of his Mind, the ethera came pouring in. Elijah's first instinct was to flinch away from the torrent—he had the first few times—but he shoved that instinct aside and forced the aperture of his Mind to remain open.

The ethera flooded his Soul, then slowly began to seep through his pores before dissipating back into the air. Over and over, Elijah flexed the aperture, forcing it wider and wider until it became physically painful. Still, he kept going, and soon enough, he started to pull against the current. He needed more ethera. So, with one half of his mind, he grabbed ahold of the torrent of ethera, pulling it with all his might. And with the other half, he forced the aperture wider.

The ethera filled him, Body, Mind, and Soul.

And yet, he still didn't progress. He felt confident that the effect of his cultivation on his Regeneration had been increased, but it wasn't enough to push him over the edge to the next stage.

Something was missing.

With most of his conscious thought occupied with the Mind exercises, Elijah had trouble focusing on the problem at hand. However, soon enough, an errant thought skittered across his mind. To achieve the Opal Mind, he'd had to channel ethera into the partition he'd created so he could deal with the effects of his Locus. So, what if that was what was missing? What if he needed to bolster that partition?

Desperate to make progress, Elijah did just that, breaking the flow of ethera into two. One went into his Soul, then misted into the air. But the other went into the partition he'd created.

Most of the time, Elijah didn't even think about it. It was just there, and it kept him from being overwhelmed by the sheer volume of information that came with his Domain. However, as he focused on it, he couldn't deny that it was a beautiful, almost tangible thing. Elijah wasn't certain if he was simply imagining it, or if it truly was the webwork of ethera that it seemed to be, but he latched on to the idea that it was the latter.

And he used the onslaught of ethera to enhance it.

Soon enough, one strand of ethera became two. And two became three. The web slowly transitioned into a three-dimensional thing that encompassed his entire Mind. Before, it had simply separated it into two halves, but by the time Elijah was finished, it had become something far more complex.

Still, it wasn't until he received a notification that he recognized it for what it was:

Congratulations! You have cultivated a Quartz Mind!

Quartz.

The ethereal structure in his mind looked like a faceted gem. A rough one, barely more than a natural stone, but it was unmistakable. On top of that, instead of two separate pieces, it had been divided into nine. And in the center of each one was a miniature aperture. None were as large or as wide as their predecessor, but collectively, they could handle far more ethera.

Elijah couldn't be certain, but after a little testing, he guessed that the effect of his Regeneration on his ability to regain ethera had been improved by at least twenty-five percent. It wasn't quite as dramatic as it had been when he'd first cultivated the Opal Mind, but it was a sizable increase, nonetheless.

He was tempted to stay and see if he could work on the rest of his cultivation, but there were two problems with that. The first was that he didn't really have any hints as to how he might go about it. He'd tried to simply repeat the actions that had put him on the path of cultivation in the first place, but he'd had very limited success. So, he would have to spend precious time figuring it out before he could even make any progress. It had taken months of practice—every chance he'd gotten, he had cultivated his Mind—to prepare for the final push into Quartz. And he suspected it would be a similar path with the other facets of cultivation.

However, more pressing was the simple fact that he needed to enter the tower sooner rather than later or the people of Norcastle would suffer the consequences of his inaction. He couldn't stomach having that on his conscience, so after he'd gotten a handle on the new structure of his Quartz Mind, Elijah pushed himself to his feet.

"Well, that's it," he said to the bear, who hadn't bothered to move. It had only opened a single eye. "I guess . . . Well, goodbye. No more free fish for you."

If the great beast cared at all, it gave no indication. So, with a sigh and a shake of his head, Elijah slipped off the old dishwasher, gathered his things, then reapplied his various enhancements. Once Essence of the Monkey, Aura of Renewal, and Essence of the Boar had been activated, he embraced Essence of the Wolf, then slipped into Shape of the Predator before leaving the little town behind.

Over the next day and a half, Elijah traversed the wilderness. As always, he killed any Voxx he found—which was only two, but he exterminated both of them with extreme prejudice. And slowly, he homed in on the location of the tower. As it turned out, the map was a little off, but with Elijah's incredible traversal speed, he had little trouble finding the structure.

Unlike the first tower Elijah had challenged, which presented as a giant headless statue just offshore of his island, the latest tower took the shape of a featureless green obelisk. Its sides were entirely smooth, to the point where Elijah couldn't even see the seams of whatever stone that had been used in its construction. At its base were four smaller pillars, each about twenty feet tall and ending in a tapered point.

The tower itself was at least twenty times that height, and it reminded Elijah of nothing so much as the Washington Monument back in the District of Columbia. He'd only been to Washington, DC, once, and that was back when he was in high school, but he distinctly remembered how awe-inspiring the giant monument to America's first president was. The green obelisk definitely had that same aura about it, and Elijah couldn't help but feel a bit intimidated by the simple majesty on display.

And that feeling was further enhanced by the thick ethera hanging in the air. It was nothing compared to the island, but it was much denser than anywhere else in the region, save for the immediate area around the amanita. Even if he hadn't known what the obelisk represented, the density of the ambient ethera would have screamed its importance.

For the next hour, Elijah slowly circled the structure. He quickly found the door—a simple square opening that led into impenetrable darkness—but he ignored it at first. Instead, he wanted to get the lay of the land so that when he managed to conquer the tower, he would know what he was exiting into.

As it turned out, there wasn't anything notable about the area. A few scattered trees decorated the meadow in which it was located, but Elijah couldn't find any wildlife. Likely, they'd all been scared away by the surges.

So, after he'd satisfied his curiosity, Elijah took a deep breath, checked his supplies for what felt like the hundredth time, then strode forward and into the tower.

22

THE BACK DOOR

One moment, Elijah was striding across a meadow and through a big, blocky doorway, and the next, his bare foot touched down in something warm, wet, and squishy. That alone would have been bad enough—especially when it got between his toes—but what made it even worse was the horrid stench that suddenly enveloped him.

"Oh, God," he muttered to himself as he tried not to gag.

He was markedly unsuccessful, especially when he had the chance to truly take in his surroundings. Before him stretched a wide body of water, from the center of which rose a steep edifice topped by a menacing wall. The water itself wasn't an inviting or placid lake. Instead, it was a seething moat, below the surface of which writhed something Elijah's instincts told him was absolutely deadly.

That water was also the source of the horrible stench tickling his nostrils. For a moment, Elijah had difficulty placing it; it was like rotten eggs mixed with vomit and hot garbage. But after only a few seconds, he recognized the smell for what it was.

"Sulfur." He sighed, though he knew there was more to the smell than that.

It was an odor usually associated with swamps, but after a brief look around, he discounted that possibility. The lake—or moat, really—notwithstanding, the area was incredibly arid, with very little in the way of vegetation to be found. Instead, large rocky pillars jutted up from the ground, twisting high into the sky, which was discolored by a setting sun.

Beneath Elijah's feet was mud, or at least he hoped that was all there was, considering that, across the expanse of roiling water, Elijah saw a wide grate from which flowed some sort of disgusting sludge.

The moment he realized that the area was inhabited, he shifted into his scaled-panther form, then embraced Guise of the Unseen. And it was just in time, too, because only a few seconds later, a loud screech filled his ears before a wide shadow fell over him. He looked up to see an enormous winged creature soaring a hundred or so feet above his position.

At a glance, it looked like a bat, but there were two issues with that assessment. First, even if his perspective was a little skewed by the distance, he judged its wingspan to reach at least thirty feet. Maybe as much as fifty. And that would make it ten times the size of even the largest bat back on Earth.

But that was within Elijah's experience. He'd seen plenty of oversize animals, so he knew that his concept of proper size wasn't really relevant in terms of identifying creatures. After all, he only had to remember the size of the crabs on his island to confirm just how much larger things could get in his new world.

In any case, he was far more concerned with the second problem with his initial identification. He was no chiropterologist, but he felt confident that bats weren't supposed to have horns. Of course, that could have been a mutation, too. He'd seen hares with horns back on his island, so who was to say that giant bats couldn't have them, as well?

Elijah watched as the enormous horned bat glided toward one of the jutting towers along the wall, where it landed. Just before it passed out of view, he caught a glimpse of something big and bulky upon the creature's back, but he had neither the time nor the visual acuity to identify the rider.

Only once he'd gotten his bearings did Elijah bother to read the notification he'd received upon entering the tower:

> **Welcome to Reaver's Citadel, Level One. To advance to Level Two, complete the task before you.**

Reaver's Citadel was obviously the keep positioned at the top of the plateau in the center of the lake. Elijah read the next notification:

> **Task: Reach the dungeon and defeat the Warden.**
> **Optional: Free the prisoner.**

The moment Elijah read that there was an optional goal, he knew he was going to try to accomplish it. Largely, that was because he knew that the towers graded performance, and the System created rewards based on that. For instance, he'd gotten an S grade for completing the Keledge Tower, and his reward had been the Shard of the World Tree, which Nerthus had claimed was a treasure the likes of which shouldn't have existed on such a newly integrated world.

And Elijah certainly wasn't immune to the call of cool new equipment. His rings had already proved useful—though he'd belatedly realized that leaving his name the same on his false identity as the listing on the ladder had probably been enough to out him as more than he appeared to be—so he figured that any new rewards would probably be just as beneficial. And if he was going to get a reward, he preferred that it was as high-quality as he could get, which meant that he needed to not only conquer the tower, but he needed to do so in a way that the system recognized as extraordinary.

So, he needed to complete the optional task. Of course, he'd have probably done so anyway, just based on the way it was phrased. And the environment. He wasn't sure what sort of people might live in such a place, but he suspected that they wouldn't be a welcoming bunch—especially with a name like Reaver's Citadel, which was quite evocative in all the wrong ways.

So, it stood to reason that any prisoner of theirs might just turn out to be Elijah's ally.

Or maybe he was completely off base, in which case he'd need to reevaluate as he progressed through the tower.

In any case, he couldn't afford to stand around doing nothing. So, after getting his bearings, Elijah decided to circle the moat in order to further investigate the situation. A few feet from the waterline, there was a sharp rise of about five feet, so Elijah crested that and looked around a little more.

Most of the terrain was much the same as his first impressions had indicated. However, in the distance, he saw a few squat structures standing next to a long bridge that stretched across the water and to a yawning gate built into the base of the plateau. Deciding that that was probably the easiest way in, Elijah stalked forward.

Even with Guise of the Unseen masking his presence, he took great care to use the natural landscape to his advantage. He flitted from one rocky outcropping to the next, and as he did so, he was reminded of the American Southwest. Specifically, he thought of the time he and his family had visited the Colorado Plateau when he was only a teenager. There, he'd gotten his first taste of the desert, with its huge rock formations and arid climate. The area surrounding Reaver's Citadel was reminiscent of that, though the terrain bore a deep-red color he'd never seen from an earthly landscape.

As he slowly approached what he soon recognized as guardhouses, the light began to fail. Dusk took hold, and Elijah got his first glimpse of the creatures who called Reaver's Citadel home.

The pair of humanoids guarding the bridge were both at least ten feet tall, and their body types were reminiscent of powerlifters—all solid, heavy muscle beneath a layer of fat. More importantly, they were clearly not human. With jutting tusks, bald heads, and huge pointed ears, the creatures were most appropriately labeled as ogres. Perhaps they were actually members of some other species, but Elijah could think of no name more suitable for the hulking humanoids.

Both ogres wore pitch-black metallic armor that looked more like cast iron than anything else. However, Elijah had enough sense to suppose that it was likely far more powerful than mundane iron. At the very least, it would be as strong as high-carbon steel, and that was if it wasn't magical in nature. If it was, Elijah really had no gauge for what to expect, except that he didn't want to find the limits of their equipment.

Instead, he skirted around the guardhouses, avoiding notice as he continued along the edge of the moat. The smell continued to be an issue, but he ignored it as he circled the moat. By the time he'd reached his original position—or a close approximation of it—night had fallen, but he'd found nothing else of note.

So, as far as he could tell, he had two options.

The first was to try to sneak past those two guards, cross the bridge, and enter the citadel that way. He had no idea what was on the other side of the bridge, but he suspected that he'd find more ogres, at the very least. There was a good chance that there were other defenses, as well, though he couldn't speak to what form they might take.

Which led him to the other option, which centered on him crossing the moat and slipping through one of the grates and into what he hoped were drainage tunnels. They looked like they were large enough to accommodate even his guardian form, so Elijah didn't think he'd have any issues fitting.

But still, that wasn't his first objection to that option. No—that distinction belonged to the smell. That, coupled with the sight of that sludge slowly oozing out of the tunnels, gave him a good idea what was going on, and he could confidently say that it was absolutely disgusting.

Perhaps it wasn't meant for sewage. Maybe his nose had fooled him on that front. But he didn't think so, and for that reason, he shied away from what was obviously the optimal path. With that in mind, he found himself crouched approximately twenty feet from the two ogre guards.

That close, they looked even larger and far more menacing than they had from a distance, and Elijah's eyes kept flicking toward the huge battle-axes they wore strapped to their backs. It wasn't difficult to imagine that, with their obvious strength, the creatures were more than capable of bisecting him with a single blow.

He crept close, taking one careful step at a time. With Guise of the Unseen, Elijah felt confident that he wouldn't remain undetectable—especially at night—but he knew it was far from perfect. If he put one foot out of line, it would all fall apart. Fortunately, he had ample experience sneaking around.

As it turned out, his confidence was entirely misplaced.

The moment he came within ten feet of one of the guardhouses—and the pair of ogres stationed on either side of the bridge's entrance—a blindingly white light erupted into being. Suddenly, Elijah felt his stealth being stripped away and exposing him to the hulking ogres. For the longest of instants, he stared at them, and they stared right back at him. Then, confusion turned to rage, and without any more warning, the closest ogre ripped the axe off its back and leaped forward with a bestial roar.

Elijah's instincts had been honed by much worse circumstances. In the Sea of Sorrows and the Primordial Jungle, he'd often had to deal with ambush predators, so his reaction to the charging ogre was completely intuitive. He crouched low, then dodged to the side just in time to avoid the descending blade of the ogre's axe. The miss threw the creature off-balance, opening it up for a counterattack, but Elijah had no intention of getting into a straight fight.

Instead, he used the opening to gather his wits and dash away. Both of the ogres roared angry challenges, but Elijah paid them no attention. Instead, he raced along the terrain, dodging behind rocky protrusions at every opportunity until, at last, the white light faded. But even then, he didn't slow.

He kept running well after the reactivation of Essence of the Wolf told him that he'd exited combat. In fact, he circled the moat, racing across the terrain for miles along the circumference of the roiling body of water until, at last, he felt his safety was assured. Only then did he let himself slow to a stop.

Elijah knew how fortunate he was to have escaped. Perhaps he could have defeated the ogres, but he knew it would have been a Pyrrhic victory. Doubtless, that blindingly white light had been an alarm, of sorts, and like all alarms, it would have brought with it some sort of response. It wasn't difficult to imagine that, if he'd stayed and fought, he would have quickly been buried under a mountain of bulky ogres.

No—retreat had been the right choice.

But now, if he was going to accomplish his task, he only had one available option.

Once he'd caught his breath, Elijah shifted back to his human form and, after using Eyes of the Eagle to look at the nearest grate, muttered, "I really don't want to do this."

He didn't have much choice, though. So, he took a deep breath, getting a nose full of the foul odor in the process, then settled in to regenerate his ethera. Once his core was completely full, he renewed his enhancements, then switched to his guardian shape.

What it lacked in stealth, the form made up for in sheer durability. The scaled-ape form had one other thing going for it, and that was the fact that it was much better suited to swimming than the predator form.

Shaking his head, Elijah loped forward and waded into the water.

23

OOZES OF INDETERMINATE ORIGIN

The water was warm.

And not the sort of warm one usually experienced in a bath but, rather, the kind that usually came when someone urinated in a pool. That was to say that it was absolutely disgusting, and it was made even more so by the stench invading Elijah's nostrils. It was so horrid that, for a brief moment, he considered going back. However, it only took the memory of those monstrous ogres—or, more importantly, the enormous weapons they wielded—to keep Elijah paddling forward.

Then, only twenty feet from shore, something brushed against his leg. It was only a tentative touch, but it was more than enough to hasten Elijah's stroke. Even as he put his immense Strength to work, the water bubbled all around him. Suddenly, a hundred tentacles, each tipped with a hand of tinier and even more horrifying tendrils, burst from the water.

Elijah lashed out, slashing the closest with his foreclaws. They fell like wheat before a scythe, though with far more white, pus-like gore than would come from any harvested plant, clearing his way. He didn't squander that brief opening, and with a mighty heave of his long arms, he cut through the water. Behind him, something roiled and splashed, but Elijah knew better than to look back. He had no interest in identifying whatever monster he'd disturbed.

One with Nature had already given him more information about the nigh-unidentifiable monstrosity than he ever wanted. He couldn't get a good picture, but he could sense a tangle of slimy tentacles and way too many eyes, which was more than enough to speed him along.

The sound of splashing chased him through the water, but Elijah barely stayed ahead as he clambered toward the grate. His heart beat out of his chest as the tentacled creature tickled his heels, but he narrowly managed to reach the grate before it closed in on him. After grabbing hold of one of the bars, he levered himself out of the water and onto the thin ledge of the grate. Without hesitation, he yanked against the bar.

And yet, it didn't move.

With the tentacle monster bearing down on him, Elijah gripped the bar with both hands, then pulled with every point of his inflated Strength attribute.

It creaked under the stress, but still, it held fast. A tentacle whipped out of the water and lashed his leg, then wrapped around his foot.

It yanked.

Elijah held on to the bar, and before the tentacle monster could pull him back into the water, he let out a grunt and summoned an enormous level of Strength, likely due to the adrenaline pumping through his veins. The bar screamed in protest, but Elijah kept pulling until, a moment later, it budged. It only moved half an inch, but it was like the breaking of a dam. With its integrity having been sundered, the bar quickly surrendered to his massive Strength.

However, it didn't break free.

Instead, for all his efforts, it only bent just enough to widen the gap by a few extra inches. Elijah hoped it would be enough. So, he ripped his leg free of the tentacle—which dislodged quite a few of his scales—and, before more could descend upon him, shifted back into his human form and narrowly squeezed between the bars.

He barely made it before a dozen slimy tentacles fell upon the spot he'd just vacated.

Elijah rolled, then scrambled backward as he beheld the monster he'd only just escaped. And it was a true horror, with hundreds of bulbous eyes, a body that looked like a cross between a bullfrog and an octopus, and dozens of slimy, grasping tentacles.

Suddenly, his decision to cross the moat seemed ill-advised. But in his defense, he'd had no idea what horrors the water held, and he'd been riding high on the seeming invincibility of his guardian form. But looking at that thing, Elijah knew that if he hadn't escaped its grasp, it was more than capable of killing him.

That, more than anything else he'd seen so far, hammered home just how much he had underestimated the tower. Certainly, he had every reason to think he could defeat it. However, he wouldn't do so easily, and if he didn't take just as much care as he had back in the Keledge Tower, he would end up just like the teams Captain Essex had sent into Reaver's Citadel.

Elijah continued to back away, though the tentacle monster seemed incapable—or at least unwilling—to send its tendrils through the grate. For that, Elijah was grateful, but he wasn't going to trust it too far. So, he made certain to keep an eye on the creature until it retreated into the water. He still didn't relax, though. Instead, after seeing the shallow wound on his leg, Elijah cast Healing Rain and settled in to regenerate his ethera.

He wasn't missing much, but he didn't want to progress until he was at his best.

A few minutes later, the wound had healed, and he was in as good a condition as he could be. So, pushing himself to his feet, he took stock of his surroundings. The tunnel was made of well-worn stone, and it was absolutely covered in thick green algae. Otherwise, it looked unremarkable, save for the stream of sludge flowing down its center.

Elijah could see bits and pieces of bone in the bubbling goo, but otherwise, it was mostly unidentifiable. Or, rather, he didn't want to think about what it probably was. Instead, he positioned himself on the edge of the tunnel where he could at least avoid stepping in it, then embraced Shape of the Predator.

He shifted into a scaled panther, which, due to its horizontal posture, made the pipe seem far less confining. After he'd assumed the proper form, he used Guise of the Unseen before setting off down the tunnel.

For the first hundred feet, it was unremarkable and flat, but soon enough, the passage took on a sharp incline. That was within Elijah's expectations, but what he hadn't counted on was the slick algae that made climbing that slope a pain. In the end, he had to deploy his claws and treat it like he was climbing a tree. Fortunately, his talons were sharp enough that they could gouge their way through stone, but that method meant his pace was much slower than it otherwise would've been.

In any case, Elijah chalked it up to the price he had to pay and continued on. For a while, nothing changed, and his path was entirely unobstructed, but then he reached a large circular chamber positioned at the intersection of tunnels. Inside, the ground leveled off, but the interior of the circle was a wide cesspool.

More importantly, there was a collection of gelatinous creatures half submerged in that slurry of waste and water. Elijah hesitated at the tunnel's exit, remaining mostly hidden by the declining slope. He peeked over the lip and observed the amorphous blobs.

The largest was the size of a beach ball, but the smallest Elijah could see was only about a foot across. The rest—he counted ten of them, but he suspected there were many more beneath the surface of the cesspool—were somewhere in between, with the majority skewing closer to the largest than the smallest. On the surface, they looked mostly harmless, but Elijah knew better than to trust that notion. Nothing in the tower was harmless. Even the mostly benign Ulthrak on the first level of the Keledge Tower had been capable of killing him, and none of his experiences in either the Sea of Sorrows or the Primordial Jungle had suggested anything but more of the same.

No—those harmless-looking balls of sludge were dangerous, even if Elijah had no idea how that danger might be presented. Still, he had no intention of finding out, so he continued to observe their behavior until he'd established that the things didn't really do anything. Perhaps they fed on the miasma of water and waste. Or maybe they didn't eat at all.

After all, there was nothing to suggest that the environments within towers had to be working ecosystems. For all Elijah knew, they were just there to hinder anyone who tried to enter the citadel by sewer. Fortunately, Guise of the

Unseen seemed capable of hiding him from their senses, so he hoped that he would be able to bypass them altogether.

With that in mind, he gradually padded forward until he'd crested the lip dividing the chamber from the descending tunnel. There, he paused, ready to flee at a moment's notice. But the oozes didn't react to his presence at all. The closest was twenty feet away, so perhaps he was outside their sensory range.

Once he'd fully progressed into the chamber, he looked around, and it only took a few moments for him to work out how everything fit together. If he thought of the circular chamber as a clock, then at the twelve, three, six, and nine o'clock positions, there were tunnels leading down, presumably to empty into the moat. Between each pair was another tunnel that sloped upward. Elijah felt certain that those would lead him into the citadel.

That seemed to establish the route he needed to take, so while keeping a close eye on the oozes, he carefully crept toward the closest tunnel that led upward. Thankfully, the room wasn't that large, and with the way everything was positioned, he didn't have far to go. Still, he had no interest in drawing the attention of the oozes, so he took his time as he covered that short distance.

He was well used to moving stealthily, but the relatively close proximity of the oozes—as well as their indeterminate nature—certainly ratcheted up the anxiety. So, Elijah was more than a little relieved when he finally reached his destination. Still, he didn't relax. Instead, he stopped at the mouth of the tunnel and settled in to observe.

It was a good thing, too, because only a few moments later, a bulbous ooze came trundling down the tunnel, leaving a disgusting trail of slimy sludge in its wake. It moved deceptively fast, and its arrival was so surprising that Elijah almost found himself in a head-on collision. However, he sinuously dipped out of the way just in time for the thing to pass.

Still, the thing splattered a bit of sludge on him with its passage, and Elijah had to suppress a pained yelp when it started eating through his scales. He suppressed it, then quickly scurried up the tunnel until he was out of range. Once he'd reached relative safety, he shifted out of his predator form.

Unsurprisingly, that only made things worse, largely because he was no longer protected by his durable scales. Still, he pushed the pain aside just long enough to unsling his pack and retrieve one of his jugs of water. Then, biting his lip, he washed the ooze away before, at last, using Touch of Nature.

Distressingly, it took three casts of the healing spell before the pain faded, and another couple before the damage was reversed. That, as much as anything, told Elijah that his choice to avoid those oozes was the correct one.

But he knew he wasn't out of the woods yet. That last ooze had come from somewhere, and he had a feeling that it wasn't a one-time thing. So, as soon as he'd healed, he only paused long enough to allow himself to regenerate enough ethera to fuel Shape of the Predator. Once he had enough in his core, he cast the spell, resumed his scaled-panther form, then embraced Guise of the Unseen.

Thus hidden, he mounted the upward slope and continued on his way.

It only took a couple of minutes of gradual progress before he saw another ooze sliding toward him. With no other way to avoid it, Elijah leaped, then used the side of the tunnel to vault over the thing. Still, he came close enough that he was sprayed by a few more drops of that caustic ooze.

But this time, Elijah didn't intend to take the time to heal. Instead, as soon as his feet hit the ground, he raced up the incline. Moving as quickly as he could without discarding his stealth altogether, he soon reached a switchback. There, he saw a couple more oozes, though these two were moving back and forth in the tiny square space.

Elijah paused only long enough to discern the pattern, then put that knowledge to good use as he timed his passage to narrowly miss them both. He did pick up a few more drops of caustic mucus, though; that just added to his mounting pain as he continued on his way.

Over and over, he repeated the same steps until, at last, he passed beneath another iron grate. Looking up, it took him a few moments to discern that it was a drain that ran the length of the floor above. He followed it for a few seconds until he finally found the source of all those oozes.

Just above was a huge humanoid creature with toxic-green skin and bulbous features. More distressingly, it was absolutely covered in what looked like pus-filled boils. Elijah watched as one burst, but instead of spewing liquid, it erupted with one of the familiar oozes. The thing quickly slipped through the grate and began its long trek toward the cesspool far below.

For his part, Elijah easily avoided it as it went on its way, but his mind churned with questions. The most prevalent one, though, had to do with the fact that the huge monster—which he'd decided to think of as a troll—was bound by thick iron chains.

Was this the prisoner he was meant to free?

24

A POTENTIAL ALLY

A steady flow of gelatinous sludge dripped down into the drainage tunnel. The smell alone was enough to turn Elijah's stomach, but he was even more concerned with the persistent drops clinging to his scales. Most of them were confined to his upturned face, which made it all the worse.

Further complicating his situation was the enduring pain of the caustic ooze still burning its way through his scales. It wasn't enough to derail his thoughts—especially after he'd spent so much time in the belly of an orca— but it was just distracting enough to be a constant irritation. Elijah ignored it, though not without a significant expenditure of willpower.

Thankfully, that was where his Mind cultivation came in handy. In addition to increasing the effect of his Regeneration attribute—and by no small degree— it had also further partitioned his mind into nine distinct sections. It wasn't quite like having nine brains working for him, but it did give him the ability to quarantine distractions in such a way as to let him focus on the task at hand.

One of those sections was dedicated to the awareness of his Domain back on the island, another focused on One with Nature, and a third housed the pain waging a steady war through his body. The other six were entirely focused on climbing the tunnel wall toward a shaft that would lead him to the floor above.

Inch by inch, he climbed, moving so deliberately that it took him a full min- ute to move each foot. His caution wasn't unfounded, either. The troll, despite its clear captivity, was the size of a fully grown bull elephant, and Elijah wanted nothing more than to avoid its notice. One slipup, and the thing could flatten him without even trying to. And if he actually drew the thing's ire? He didn't want to consider that.

So, he climbed, and he hid, cloaked by Guise of the Unseen, and eventually, he reached the six-foot shaft that led topside. It was only about two feet wide, which meant that in his scaled-panther form, it would be a tight fit. However, he didn't dare shift back into his smaller human form. Doing so would rob him of his stealth, and that would almost assuredly spell disaster. With that in mind, he resigned him- self to a brief bout of claustrophobia as he wedged himself into place.

The going was tough, mostly because he couldn't extend his claws more than an inch or two. However, Elijah was nothing if not persistent, and he slowly covered the distance to the top of the shaft. Fortunately, the grate meant to cover the top had rusted away, meaning that he could barely fit through.

Still, it was an even tighter fit than the shaft itself, and as he dragged himself through, the shards of rusted iron that had once been the grate scraped painfully against his scales. The remnants of the grate were incapable of piercing his natural armor, but it was still incredibly uncomfortable. He shifted that discomfort into another partition in his mind.

Meanwhile, the troll's pustules continued to burst, sending a steady stream of oozes to collect in the cistern far below. And even though the massive creature was only ten feet away, Elijah forced himself to ignore it, save for a basic awareness of its position.

In the end, that sliver of attention saved his life.

Elijah had no idea what had alerted the troll, but one second, the thing was sitting and staring into nothing, and the next, an enormous fist was falling in Elijah's direction. He ripped himself free of the shaft, the sudden movement tearing one of his scales free, then launched himself to the side, narrowly avoiding the descending fist.

It hit with thunderous impact, shaking the floor and sending Elijah off-balance. He quickly righted himself—partially due to his inflated Dexterity attribute, but also because of the instincts of the scaled panther whose form he'd taken—then bounded away. The troll roared in fury, erupting into violent motion as it dove for the intruder.

Elijah used every point of Strength he possessed to propel himself forward, but the troll's might clearly outstripped his own. The result was inevitable. Elijah knew it even as he felt the monster gaining on him with every passing millisecond.

But just before it caught up, the sound of rattling chains heralded Elijah's saving grace. The bindings pulled taut, stopping the troll in its tracks. It roared in frustration, anger, and obvious agony as it reached out with dirty, meaty fingers, but by that point, Elijah was far out of range and sheltering on the other side of the room, where he turned to face the bound monster.

It was entirely contained by the thick chains attached to the shackles on its wrists and ankles, but still, Elijah wasn't as worried about the metal as he was about the brickwork to which the bindings were attached. However, it quickly became clear that he was worried about nothing.

Well—not nothing.

The troll was certainly worth every ounce of trepidation Elijah could muster. And yet, it was obviously incapable of attaining its freedom. Otherwise, it would have already done so.

In any case, it certainly presented a problem in that it had clearly detected him. Until he lost its attention, he wouldn't be slipping back into the sheltering embrace of Guise of the Unseen. With that in mind, he reluctantly turned his back on the slavering monster and took stock of his location.

The good thing was that the room was plenty big enough for the both of them. Bound as it was, the troll couldn't reach past the room's halfway mark. But the good news came with a significant degree of ill tidings, largely due to the fact that the room looked like nothing so much as a jail cell. Aside from the tentative confirmation that the troll was the prisoner his optional task had charged him with freeing, that meant that Elijah was trapped.

The room's lone exit—which was big enough to permit passage from something even as large as the troll—stood on the other side of the cell, and it was barred by a door made of ancient timbers bound by thick iron bands. Elijah finally let Shape of the Predator fall away and resumed his human form. His bare feet were silent against the cold and clammy stone floor as he crossed the intervening distance and grabbed hold of the door's ringlike handle. To Elijah's dismay, when he tried to push or pull it open, it remained steadfastly stuck in place, assuredly due to a lock on the other side.

"Stuck," he muttered to himself, confident that his voice wouldn't carry over the sound of the still-raging troll. He fell to his haunches, then began the arduous task of healing himself from his previous contact with the oozes. As before, the caustic burns stubbornly resisted his efforts, but he pushed through it, using far more ethera than healing such small wounds should have required.

Meanwhile, the troll continued to growl and spit, but Elijah mostly ignored it. Bound as it was, the monster posed little danger. However, he wasn't so arrogant that he didn't devote one of the nine facets of his Mind to keeping tabs on the creature.

It was due to this small bit of attention that he came to realize that the monster wasn't simply angry. Nor was it feral. It was in pain, a factor made obvious by its bloodshot eyes and the increased volume of its screams that accompanied each popped pustule.

Elijah crouched, his staff across his knees as he gave the situation some thought. The nature of towers was a little confusing. On the one hand, the environments were clearly manufactured, and that meant that there were intended paths to victory. However, on the other, there were less obvious ways to overcome each obstacle. So, he wasn't limited by the System's intentions.

But the fact that his task had mentioned the prisoner meant that it might be the key to victory—at least for the first task.

Elijah was busy giving that some thought when the sound of a turning lock assaulted his ears. Or maybe he'd felt the ogre on the other side via One with Nature. Sometimes, his senses mingled together, obscuring the actual source. Either way, he leaped to his feet and, at the same time, shifted into a scaled panther.

It was just in time, too, because at that moment, the door swung open, admitting an ogre. However, this ogre wasn't like the others. It was just as tall, but instead of being built like a powerlifter, its body type could best be described as morbidly obese. Roles of fat cascaded down its body, squishing together until Elijah couldn't tell where one ended and another began.

He just had time to note its attire—a fur-covered loincloth held in place by a thick leather belt—before he sprang into motion. His claws flashed, ripping into the ogre's stomach. The flesh parted easily, spilling blood and fat onto the floor, but it wasn't the disemboweling blow Elijah had hoped it would be.

More, the ogre responded far more quickly than its body type might've suggested, and its fist smashed against a bounding Elijah midair, the impact hitting him in the ribs and sending him skidding across the jail cell's stone floor. He came to a sudden stop when he slammed into the wall. He felt his bones crack under the impact, but he shunted the agonizing pain into its own facet of his Mind, and it was a good thing, too, because he needed all of his available concentration to avoid the ogre's follow-up blow.

He leaped to the side as its pudgy foot came crashing down, narrowly missing his darting form. But Elijah knew better than to fight an entirely defensive battle, so he dashed in, raking his claws across the back of the ogre's leg. Muscle split under the influence of Elijah's claws, and the ogre stumbled.

That allowed him to leap upon its back, where he dug his claws into its bulbous flesh. Then, snapping out like a striking snake, he latched his jaws on to the base of its skull. Harnessing every point of Strength he could muster, he flexed the muscles of his jaws, and after a brief moment of resistance, he was rewarded with the sound—and feel—of crushing bone.

The ogre flailed as it desperately tried to dislodge him. However, the creature's pudgy arms were just inflexible enough to keep it from reaching him. So, even as Elijah clamped down on its skull, it slammed its back against the wall. With the full weight of its massive body behind the blow, the force it brought to bear was enough to crush multiple of Elijah's bones.

Still, he held on, knowing that if he let go, the creature would be free to finish him off. He was already too injured to continue the fight in any other way, so he continued to flex his jaw even while the ogre crushed him against the wall. Gradually, those cracking bones began to shatter, and then, suddenly, the integrity of the skull collapsed entirely, giving Elijah free access to the brains they were meant to protect.

The taste of iron and salt played across his tongue as his teeth ripped apart the ogre's brain. Still, it remained upright for a few moments until, at last, it could go on no longer. It fell forward, hitting the ground with a thunderous crash that threw Elijah free.

A second after he rolled to a stop, he tried to rise, but too many of his bones were broken. The partition in his Mind was incapable of holding back the tide of pain, and for a brief second, it enveloped him. Ruthlessly, Elijah thrust it back where it belonged, and with the weight of his willpower holding it in place, he let his body shift back to human form.

The moment he did, he realized just how dire his situation was. He hadn't been so injured since being digested by the orca guardian back in the Sea of Sorrows. He forced himself to look down at his body; one of his legs had been turned the wrong way and one of the bone shards had broken through the skin—a sure sign of a compound fracture and probably a dislocated knee, as well. He knew that it was even more serious than it appeared because, left like that, the blood flow would likely be interrupted, and the leg would die out.

In addition to that, he had multiple broken ribs as well as what felt like someone stabbing him in his lower back. Finally, there were multiple other contusions, each signaling another problem. The only solace was that, even with all his broken ribs, it didn't feel like any had punctured his lungs.

"Silver linings," he muttered to himself as he looked up at the still-growling troll. At least he wasn't covered in a bunch of caustic blisters like his cellmate.

With a pained breath, Elijah channeled ethera from his Core and through his Soul, fueling a cast of Healing Rain. A wave of relief washed over him as the soothing precipitation fell on his injuries, but he knew it wouldn't be enough to heal him. Indeed, even Touch of Nature wouldn't do anything until he embarked on the arduous task of setting his broken bones.

So, that was what he did.

Reaching down, he grabbed his lower leg, then gently twisted it. Pain lanced through his shin and up the entirety of his leg. Nausea followed soon after, making him feel like vomiting. However, he persisted, knowing that if he wanted to keep his leg, it had to be done. At first, it wouldn't move, though. A gentle tug wasn't enough. He needed something altogether more violent.

So, taking a deep breath, and with tears in his eyes, Elijah wrenched it back into place. He let out a loud, agonized cry, and for a moment, he blacked out from sheer shock. But he recovered his wits soon after, then continued the agonizing task of setting his broken bones.

Being melted by stomach acid was painful, but there was something altogether different—and arguably worse—about the pain he was forced to endure while setting those bones. Some of that was due to the fact that he was in complete control of it, which made things so much worse. But it was also the differing nature of the pain. Either way, he wouldn't have wished either situation on even his worst enemies.

Even so, Elijah kept going until, at last, he'd accomplished the feat.

After that, it was a simple task of continuously casting Touch of Nature until he ran low on ethera. Then, he rested until he'd regained enough to repeat the cycle. Over and over, he kept going until, at last, he managed to banish the pain altogether. Not long after that, he'd healed himself entirely.

Once that was done, he sagged against the wall and glanced over at the troll. Over the hours—or it might've been as much as a day—since Elijah had begun his healing, the creature had grown accustomed to his presence. It still wasn't in a good mood, but it had at least stopped growling.

Elijah was staring vacantly at the creature when something occurred to him.

Healing Rain had a diameter of around thirty feet, which meant that its edge extended just enough to affect the troll's lower legs. And to Elijah's surprise, where the rejuvenating precipitation had fallen—continuously over the past day—the cysts had all but disappeared.

Was that why the troll had calmed down? The rest of its body was still just as disgustingly infected as the rest, but those legs—they almost looked healthy.

Elijah glanced at the door, then back at the troll.

He still hadn't accomplished the first task, which was to defeat the Warden. That meant that the ogre he'd killed wasn't the guardian of the level—which was troubling, given how close it had come to killing him. Certainly, it hadn't been an optimal fight; the monster had come upon him when he was incapable of using Guise of the Unseen—or Predator Strike—but it was still a healthy reminder that towers were meant to be challenged by entire groups, and the difficulty reflected that.

So, it was entirely possible that the Warden—wherever it was—might be far too strong for Elijah to defeat alone. Still—he didn't have to be alone, did he? There was a potential ally only a dozen or so feet away.

Elijah glanced back at the troll, and as he did, an idea began to take shape.

25

ON THE ROAD

Snow fell, gently drifting down from the slate gray sky as Carmen steadily trudged along beside the pickup truck. As heavily laden as it was, the vehicle could barely move more than a few miles per hour, and even that was only possible because of the incredible accomplishments of a few Engineers. Electric motors still worked after the apocalypse, but far less efficiently than they had in the past. As a result, even electric cars—or trucks, in this case—were vastly underpowered. Still, considering that they'd yet to find any proper beasts of burden—and if they did discover a herd of horses or oxen, they would probably be mutated and wild—it was the best way to move large quantities of gear, supplies, and goods.

The truck itself was one of seven they'd commandeered for the trip out to the mine, though even that number seemed inadequate, considering how much they needed to do to get the settlement up and running. Fortunately, Easton's Scouts as well as the men and women who worked as laborers had already cut a path through the wilderness. It wasn't a road—not precisely—but it would make resupply much easier.

Of course, that wasn't why Roman and his cronies had been so adamant about its construction. They didn't care about what went to the mining settlement; instead, they were only concerned about what came out. Roman had big plans for how he intended to use the cold iron to catapult his budding kingdom to the top of the region's pecking order.

That was fine by Carmen because, after Alyssa's death, she'd begun to pull back from the settlement she'd helped found. And in that time, things had changed so much that she barely recognized it anymore. By all accounts, it was a successful city. They were well set up for security, and nobody really went hungry anymore. However, it was so far removed from the culture they'd lost in the apocalypse that it felt like an entirely different world.

Many of the freedoms modern society had taken for granted had been discarded. Any criticism of the city's leadership—or of Roman himself—was met with swift reprisal in the form of banishment. The logic was that if someone disagreed with the way things were run, they could try to make their own way.

Some had left voluntarily, but even more had been cast out into the wilderness, kicking and screaming all the way. Carmen could understand it, too, and from both sides. In Roman's favor was the undeniable fact that his methods had turned Easton into a safe haven, and one of the few that existed amid the chaos of a changed and much more dangerous world. He provided protection and stability when both were in short supply. From his perspective, they had only survived because of his efforts, so having the methods by which he provided that survival questioned was tantamount to a slap in the face.

Even so, the idea that someone could be sentenced to death—because that's what banishment usually meant—over spoken criticism was absolutely abhorrent. And making it even worse was that Carmen knew that if Alyssa had been there, she wouldn't have allowed it to happen.

But at least Roman had come around on the subject of Scholars and the subset of classes that came from the archetype. In the beginning, the benefits those people offered were far outweighed by the cost of keeping them safe and fed while supporting their progression. Now, though, Easton had the resources to spare, and what's more, they'd developed a need for the sort of people who could ease the burden of bureaucracy.

They still weren't treated particularly well—at least not in comparison to crafters or combatants—but at least they weren't refused entry altogether, which was a step up from the previous policy.

Whatever the case, Carmen had no interest in politics. She just wanted to get to the mine, get it working properly, and then progress along her own path while raising her son. However, she couldn't escape the reality that Roman's policies could very well affect Miguel, so she knew she didn't have the luxury of just ignoring them.

For now, though, she could focus on the things she could control.

To that end, she continued to walk aside the slow-moving truck. She was far from the first line of defense—there were dozens of Scouts and other combatants traveling along with the convoy—but she remained alert regardless. She had also been wearing her armor almost constantly since leaving Easton a week before, and even if it was well fitted, she was eager to get to their destination so she could go back to normal attire.

It wasn't that it was too heavy. Her Strength attribute was more than capable of bearing the weight. But wearing a full suit of plate armor for twelve hours out of each day was incredibly uncomfortable. The only upside was that the experience had already prompted her to incorporate some changes into her designs.

Just as she was solidifying some of her plans in her mind, one of the Scouts burst through the dense foliage, skidding to a stop just in front of Carmen. "What is it now?" she demanded.

The Scout—a stout young man who'd only just gained his class—said, "Incoming. Apes of some kind." He pointed back the way he'd come, saying, "The others are slowing them down."

"How many?" asked Carmen, her grip tightening on Destroyer's haft. Over the weeks since she'd finished forging it, the hammer had proved its worth a hundred times over. Crossing the threshold from Crude to Simple grade had been a quantitative leap forward, and one she was more than capable of exploiting in battle.

"Ten at least. Maybe as many as twenty."

"Incoming!" Carmen bellowed in warning. The response was well practiced as the trucks ground to a halt and the members of the caravan readied themselves for battle. Because the threat was omnidirectional, the bulk of the responding force joined Carmen and the Scout, but they knew better than to leave the other directions undefended. The result was a lopsided deployment with Carmen at the head.

There were a few decently strong combatants at her flanks, but none were the cream of Easton's crop. Indeed, almost everyone she'd been given were, at best, green. At worst, they were the sort of below-average specimens Roman would have been glad to send away.

Whatever the case, Carmen was by far the highest-level person in the entire caravan, and even as a crafter, that meant she could bring quite a bit of force to bear. With her high-quality armor and powerful weapon, she was the linchpin of any defense effort.

As such, she positioned herself to take the brunt of any attack.

Behind her, the Scholars and children took up their bows, slings, and other ranged weapons. They wouldn't do much damage, but when everyone's lives were at stake, everything counted.

Over the week since they'd been on the road, the convoy had been forced to respond to a multitude of attacks, and from a wide variety of sources including carnivorous deer, curiously aggressive beavers, and a few Voxx. So, their response was well practiced. Still, they hadn't escaped unscathed, and even with the pair of Healers included within their number, they'd lost a few people.

Such was life in their new world.

The incoming threat was heralded by the sound of a fighting retreat. Men and women shouted, as much as a response to the battle as to announce their positions to the waiting caravanners. Then, the first few burst from the dense foliage on the side of the path and took up positions among the defenders. Another dozen joined them before, at last, the enemy arrived.

They looked like chimps, though as was the case with most wildlife, they'd been mutated by the onset of ethera that had transformed the world. Their already impressive musculature was denser and more prominent, and they had grown sharp tusks, as well.

But at least they were no larger than normal.

The idea of a gorilla-sized chimp was a truly terrifying concept.

In any case, Carmen didn't have much time to consider such things before the first screeching chimp threw itself at her. She met its charge with a herculean swing of her hammer. With her lopsided attributes, it would've been easy to think that she couldn't move with alacrity. However, that simply wasn't true. Because of her high Strength, she was capable of momentous bursts of speed; the only downside was that, without comparable Dexterity, those sorts of maneuvers were incredibly difficult to control. That was why she had chosen a broad-headed hammer as her personal weapon.

Swinging Destroyer didn't really require fine motor control, after all.

The head of the hammer took the overly muscular chimp directly in its tusked face, and the momentum of the blow sent it tumbling back the way it came. It didn't stop until it hit the trunk of a tall pine tree, the impact shaking loose a cascade of pine cones and needles. But the creature wasn't killed.

In fact, it was only stunned.

That was the problem with the mutated wildlife. They were dangerous, sure, but they were also incredibly durable. Even with everyone's increased attributes, combating those animals often took an application of force that, in the old world, would have easily killed any organic being unlucky enough to find itself on the wrong end of those attacks.

After that first attack, the other chimps fell upon the defenders. All around, people activated various skills. Some were subtle—like a gentle flow of ethera around a weapon—but others were a little more bombastic. However, Carmen hadn't been allowed any dedicated mages. Those, according to Roman, were necessary for Easton's defense, and they were too vulnerable to send out into the wilderness.

So, the fight took a lot longer than it otherwise would have if they'd had access to the sort of devastating spells a Wizard or Elementalist could bring to a fight.

Still, Carmen fought on, wading into the battle secure in the knowledge that her armor would protect her. Others couldn't say as much, and the sounds of wounded combatants joined in with the chimps' screeches. She ignored that, though.

At one point, she might've tried to be everywhere at once, but that was a path to ruin. She wasn't a dedicated combatant, and as such, she could only rely on her equipment and high attributes to see her through.

Others weren't so limited, though no one was high enough level to truly affect the battle alone. As a result, teamwork and organized tactics proved to be the deciding factor. The chimps were powerful—far more so than any individual in the convoy—but they were also animals. As such, they didn't fight with anything approaching a cohesive strategy, and that difference saw the defenders through to victory.

Still, it took hours until, at last, there were only a few left. Those were quickly dispatched until only a single wounded chimp faced off against Carmen. It was the biggest and strongest of the entire pack, and so, it would be the last to fall.

Carmen stepped forward, slamming her hammer into its side. It tried to dodge, but it could do nothing to avoid the follow-up attack.

With a sledgehammer strike that absolutely destroyed the skull of the last chimp, Carmen finished the battle. Looking around, she saw a few injured warriors, but miraculously, none had died. That was probably due to the Healers' intervention, but it may well have been because of the group's experience. They'd fought quite a few battles along the way, so it would've been odd if they didn't get better at it.

She glanced back toward the truck to see Miguel standing in the bed, bow in hand and mostly empty quiver at his hip. He didn't have an archetype yet, but he'd already proved himself a talented archer—which was just fine by Carmen. Anything that kept him out of the thick of battle was great, especially if it gave him the tools to survive when things inevitably went wrong.

To that end, he'd been training with the Scouts and even taking lessons from some of the other combatants. The problem was that most of them had, only a few years before, led absolutely ordinary lives doing mundane jobs. There was only so much Miguel could learn from construction workers or accountants.

Even so, in the two and a half years since the apocalypse had begun, Miguel had learned to handle himself with a handful of weapons. And he'd continue to train with those until he was given the opportunity to choose an archetype when he turned fifteen. That was still a few years away, but Carmen hoped that he would learn enough to set himself apart and gain a host of solid options.

She quickly found the man in charge of the combatants. Technically, he had equal standing with her, but Colt had made it clear from the very beginning that he saw her as the expedition's true leader. Largely, this was based on the immense respect with which he'd held Alyssa, but it was also the result of his single-minded pursuit of personal strength. Either way, she appreciated it, if for no other reason than that she knew just how disastrous having two leaders could be.

The man himself was a little over average height, with relatively narrow shoulders, a thick black beard, and only stubble on his head. In his hand was a katana that Carmen had forged herself; it was still Crude grade, but it was still one of her better pieces, and she knew from experience that Colt was well suited to using it.

In terms of levels, he was in the top five combatants in Easton, but in terms of actual skill, he was probably the most dangerous person in the settlement. Which was probably why Roman had sent him away. Like Alyssa before him, he'd made a habit of throwing himself into the thick of things, and his reputation had seen quite a boost because of his penchant for saving people.

Perhaps that was what would've happened to Alyssa, if she had lived. Maybe Roman would have sent her away, too.

Colt took off the wide-brimmed cowboy hat that was his personal affectation and wiped his forearm across his forehead before saying, "Could've been a lot worse."

"Yeah. How far do we have until we get there?" she asked. "Because we can't keep going like this indefinitely."

"A day. Maybe two before the Scouts get into range. Another couple of days for the rest of us."

Carmen shook her head. "To think, there was a time when we would've been able to make the whole trip in a day. Wish these hunks of junk could go a little faster."

Colt spat on the ground and said, "Not really my department. You want someone or something cut in half, I'm your guy. You want to figure out how to make cars run right? That's more like your thing."

"I'm no Engineer. I just smack hot metal with a hammer," Carmen pointed out as she watched Colt use a spare bit of cloth to clean the blood and bits of chimp flesh from his blade. "If it was just a normal engine, I could maybe do something. But these electric motors?" She shook her head, then said, "I've heard that there are some Engineers back home who are trying to implement ethera into the process. I'm not sure how that works, but I think I speak for everyone when I say I hope they figure it out soon."

"Won't get any argument from me."

With that, they began the process of tending to the wounded and getting moving again. Soon enough, the sun started to dip below the horizon, and Carmen called for a halt. After spending the next hour making camp, she settled in with Miguel next to a fire.

After Alyssa's death, he barely spoke anymore. Hopefully, getting the mine set up would give them both a fresh start.

26

TROLL ON THE LOOSE

The odious smell that permeated the dungeon had grown no less pervasive, but as Elijah stalked forward, he endeavored to ignore it. On either side of the hall were more cages, each of them similar to the one in which he'd left the troll. However, they were mostly empty, and the ones that were occupied contained only corpses of fearsome beasts. The only creatures Elijah recognized were smaller trolls, but even those were so plague stricken that he could barely make the connection between them and the sole living monster within the dungeon.

Certainly, he hadn't intended to empathize with that creature, but after seeing what had happened to the other prisoners within the dungeon, he couldn't help but feel sorry for the troll. Whatever it had done to earn its captivity certainly wasn't enough to force it to endure the torturous existence with which it had been afflicted. Making it worse was that, according to the Ulthraks back in the Keledge Tower, there was a good chance that a real consciousness was buried somewhere inside that monstrous form.

The thought sent a shiver up Elijah's spine.

Gradually, he progressed through the dungeon, memorizing the twists and turns of its disgusting hallways along the way. He saw a few more ogre jailers, but there was nothing to indicate that any of them were the Warden he sought to complete his task. Still, after exiting the troll's cell and leaving its curiously attentive gaze behind, Elijah had no issues hiding from the ogre jailers.

But it only took the memory of his previous fight to tell him that attacking those bulky creatures was a mistake. Even with the benefit of Predator Strike on his side, getting through those thick layers of fat and muscle was a tall task. Perhaps he could kill them on his own, but there was enough doubt that he couldn't commit to that path. After all, if he failed to quickly kill one, his would-be victim would almost assuredly raise the alarm. In that event, Elijah's chances of survival would fall to almost nothing.

So, he chose caution instead.

As he continued to stalk through the dungeon, he flared One with Nature as much as possible. And he discovered something he'd already suspected: It was far less effective indoors than it was in the more natural world. Back in Ironshore—and then in Norcastle—he'd noticed as much, but being in

Reaver's Citadel confirmed that the spell worked much better in the untamed wilderness.

Still, it wasn't completely ineffective, and it still gave his attributes an invisible boost. Fortunately, his other enhancements worked the same as always, bolstering his Dexterity, Regeneration, and Constitution by a significant degree. That made his task much easier, and he managed to avoid detection until, at last, he'd mapped the entire dungeon.

And what he'd discovered wasn't ideal.

First, there was only one exit, and that was guarded by four ogres wearing black iron armor like the ones he'd seen standing sentry at the gatehouses outside. Otherwise, there were four jailers scattered throughout the dungeon, as well. But their presence wasn't what truly worried him.

No—that distinction belonged to his discovery of the Warden. He'd expected another ogre, but what he'd found was something altogether different. Elijah hid in the corner of what could only be called a torture room, where he stared at a black-skinned elf. The man was short and slender, with prominently tapered ears and a mane of thick white hair.

Like many of the ogres Elijah had seen, he wore a suit of bulky black armor, though his had been embellished with a series of silver whorls that sparkled with blue ethera. Elijah didn't have to study it for long before he became convinced that it was magical in nature. So was the slender sword at his hip, which glimmered with the same silvery metal.

However, Elijah was less concerned with the elf's attire—or race, for that matter—than the fact that he was gleefully torturing what looked like a taller, bulkier goblin. Even more disturbingly, the Warden wasn't asking any questions. He didn't seek information. Instead, he was clearly tormenting the creature for no more reason than because he wanted to hear it scream.

Even if Elijah hadn't been tasked with killing the elf, he would have committed himself to that endeavor right then and there. Killing was often necessary. That was the cost of survival. Even torture, for some misguided individuals, might hold some value as an interrogation method. He'd heard that it didn't really work, but Elijah could at least follow the logic that would lead someone down that road. But torture for torture's sake was absolutely abhorrent, and Elijah had no intention of letting it continue.

Still, he knew he couldn't attack without a plan, so he retreated through those same halls and back to the jail cell where he'd killed the ogre jailer. After he'd slain the creature, Elijah had shifted into his scaled-ape form and tossed the heavy corpse to the troll as a distraction. As one monster fed on the remains of another, Elijah had resumed his human form, rushed forward, and cast Healing Rain.

The troll had ignored him, and over the course of the spell's duration, those painfully popping pustules of pestilent pus had slowly shrunk. They weren't entirely gone, but the troll looked as if it was in far less pain. Moreover, the formation of the cysts—and the oozes that came from them—had become less frequent, suggesting that Elijah's efforts hadn't been for naught.

It also looked a good deal less infuriated, which was key for Elijah's plan.

After resuming his human form, he raised his hand in what he hoped was a placating gesture, then stepped forward. The troll shifted, obviously noticing Elijah's progress. But it didn't rush him, so he took another step. Then another when it showed no further reaction. Finally, Elijah was close enough that another cast of his spell would envelop the creature, so he used Healing Rain, then retreated.

Even as heavy drops of rejuvenating precipitation fell, Elijah crouched on the other side of the cell. He knew better than to expect to have tamed the troll. A single meal and a little healing could only do so much, after all. So, he never allowed his awareness to waver. At the same time, he studied the cell itself—a task only possible because of his faceted Quartz Mind. If he'd tried to pay attention to so many things—his Domain, One with Nature, the cell, and the troll—before he'd advanced his cultivation, he would've no doubt been lost in the weeds. But now, it was a simple task to compartmentalize the disparate thoughts.

Still, he was pushing the limits of his Mind by fostering even those simple strains of thought. Perhaps once he advanced to the next stage, the facets would expand and allow for more complex thinking. For now, though, anything more than cataloguing sensory input required the full weight of his Mind.

The cell itself was a simple rectangular room made of the same stone common across the rest of the dungeon. Most of the floor was covered in a thick layer of algae that even crept a few feet up the walls. However, it was densest near the drainage grate—and the shaft probably meant for waste disposal—that split the cell in two.

The troll was confined by shackles on its thick wrists and ankles, which were in turn attached to the wall via bulky, black iron chains. Elijah only had eyes for the thick locks holding those bonds together, largely because, after killing the jailer and looting the corpse, he had the means to free the creature.

Or so he expected.

He glanced down at the key in his hand and contemplated how he might accomplish that feat. At first, he'd hoped that healing and feeding the troll might engender some sense of cooperation, but that clearly wasn't going to happen. It would tolerate his presence only so long as it couldn't kill him. The moment it was freed, he would become its target.

Was the optional part of the task a fool's errand?

Was there no way to complete it?

Elijah knew that towers could accommodate up to six people, and that they were usually meant to be challenged by those groups. Entering into such a situation alone was regarded as only a step above suicidal, largely because the challenges necessary for completion not only required incredible power, but they usually necessitated a wide variety of skills, as well. So, he had no doubts that there were probably classes that could easily combat and conquer his current dilemma.

But he just didn't have the necessary skills to pacify the monster. If it had been an animal, perhaps it would have been possible. He could have treated it like the bear guarding the amanita he'd encountered. But the troll was clearly something else. It wasn't sapient, but it wasn't an animal, either. Or if it was, it was intelligent enough not to fall prey to the placating manipulation of One with Nature.

Elijah continued to ponder the problem as Healing Rain did its work. When the spell faded, he darted close and recast it. The troll tolerated him, and yet, Elijah knew that if he tarried for even a second too long, it would destroy him.

After the third cast, he started to wonder why he was even bothering with healing the creature. It wasn't real. And as far as he knew, the moment he conquered the dungeon, the troll would reset just like everything else. Yet, he couldn't just ignore its suffering. So, he continued along, reapplying Healing Rain four more times over the next few hours. And in that way, the troll was healed.

It was only when he saw the way the now-healthy troll strained the plates attaching the chains to the wall that a plan began to take shape. It wasn't ideal. He knew that there were a host of ways it could go wrong. But he also suspected that, without the assistance the troll could provide, he stood little chance of bypassing the guards, much less killing the Warden.

Was it possible?

Certainly. But just as surely, his victory in those circumstances was far from probable.

So he latched on to another, arguably just as dangerous, plan. But given that it didn't involve him attacking an entity of entirely unknown strength, he preferred it over squaring off against the Warden in a straight fight.

As soon as Elijah saw that the troll had been completely healed, he settled down to renew his stores of ethera. Flexing every facet of his Quartz Mind, he dragged nine streams of energy through his Soul and into his Core, enhancing his Regeneration by a good amount. It took no small degree of concentration, but it was effective, so long as he wasn't too distracted.

Gradually, his Core refilled, and after he renewed his augmentations—Essence of the Monkey, Essence of the Boar, Aura of Renewal, One with Nature, and finally, Essence of the Wolf—he embraced Shape of the Guardian and shifted into the scaled-ape form. Without hesitation, he launched himself forward, harnessing every point of his enhanced Strength attribute.

And considering the augmentation provided by the guardian form, he could bring quite a bit of power to bear. He launched himself forward, accelerating like a sports car before slamming into the wall with incredible force. The troll, for all its wariness, never even had a chance to react before Elijah kicked off the wall and threw himself to the other side of the cell, where he skidded for a few feet before his momentum ended in a collision with the other wall.

Shifting back into his human form, he immediately cast Touch of Nature as he shook his mangled hand. His Constitution attribute was incredible in his guardian form, but the anatomy of whatever creature upon which it had been based was not suited for punching like a human. Instead, it was meant to pummel its opponents like a gorilla. Or rip and tear with its claws. As a result of misusing his body, he'd broken a couple of bones in his hand.

But that was what his healing spells were for, and after two casts, he managed to mend his bones. At that point, he took a look at his handiwork, and when he laid his eyes on the brickwork surrounding the anchor, he felt a mixture of disappointment and encouragement. The first was due to the fact that, for all the power he'd managed to harness, the results were decidedly minor. A few tiny cracks, and that was it.

However, he was also encouraged by that small effect, if only because it proved that his plan was a viable one.

Now, though, the troll was awake and aware, which made his job that much more difficult. He'd surprised it once, but that seemed like . . . Wait . . . What was it doing?

The troll had shifted to the side. It could only move a few feet, but the meaning seemed clear. It was giving Elijah a free shot. Did it understand what he was doing? That seemed to be the case, but . . .

Well, Elijah wasn't going to look a gift horse in the mouth. So, after healing himself and regenerating the ethera he'd spent in the process, he shifted back to his guardian form and once again launched himself at the anchor. This time, he used his palm to strike the wall, which seemed to bear the impact much better than his delicate knuckles. It was also a little less effective, but that initial punch had served to weaken the brickwork enough that it didn't matter overmuch.

Over and over, Elijah threw himself at the wall until he jarred the first anchor loose. And with that proof of concept buoying his efforts, he wasted no time before assaulting the other three.

It took quite some time, and periodically, Elijah was forced to shift back into his human form in order to heal the damage he was doing to his own body. He also tried to use the key on the troll's shackles, but predictably, it slapped him across the room the moment he started groping around its wrist. Still, he eventually managed to accomplish his goal.

It was just in time, too, because only a few moments after he'd regenerated his ethera, the door to the cell let out a screech as someone opened it. Elijah didn't hesitate to enact the next part of his plan, which began and ended with him diving down the descending shaft just in time to avoid being seen. He dug his fingers into the algae-covered walls, arresting his momentum as the sound of footsteps thundered in his ears.

"Look not sick no more," came a deep baritone.

"Look same to me."

"You no see good."

"Yeah? You ugly!"

"You ugly!"

A second later, Elijah heard something that sounded like someone had slapped a side of beef, which was followed by a noise not unlike a deflating bellows. Then, the second ogre said, "No call me ugly or you get more fist!"

The other ogre began to offer a wheezing response when it was cut off by the sound of crumbling mortar, clinking chains, and cantankerous troll. It was music to Elijah's ears.

27

DISTRACTION

The floor of the cell shook with titanic battle as the two ogres clashed with the freed troll. Warbling screams filled the air, suggesting that things were not going well for the jailers. That was as expected; the troll wasn't just larger, but it had looked far sturdier, as well. Still, even if the winner had been assured—which was no certain thing—Elijah had no intentions of letting it play out.

Not without having his say.

So, wedged in the shaft, he shifted his way up until only his head poked above the floor. When he did, he saw precisely what he had expected. The massive troll had everything it could handle as it fended off the other two creatures, but it was clearly in control of the fight. The ogres were powerful enough to hold their own, though, and it looked like it was going to be a long, drawn-out fight.

Elijah aimed to change that.

So, without further hesitation, he gripped the Staff of Natural Harmony and channeled ethera into Swarm.

Spell: Swarm	Conjure a swarm of pests that infect your enemies with appropriate afflictions.

The spell wasn't as immediately devastating as Calamity. However, it had the benefit of being far more subtle, which was precisely what he needed at the moment. He released the spell, and a few seconds later, a few biting flies manifested before landing on the broad, naked back of one of the ogre jailers. A second or two later, it was joined by a veritable horde—or, appropriately, a swarm—of flies.

The bulk of the group of little insects attacked the same ogre, but the nature of a swarm meant that there were plenty of others for the other jailer as well as the troll. Now that the troll had been freed, and he'd gotten the appropriate credit, he thought nothing of using it for his ends. Certainly, he didn't want to watch it suffer, but that didn't mean he would spare the aggressive creature out of some misguided sense of friendship.

If it lived, that was fine. But if it ended up dying, Elijah wanted his afflictions to ensure that he got at least some kill energy from its passing. Besides, he needed it angry and raging, or it wouldn't be much of a distraction.

The flies didn't last long, and by the time they dissipated into motes of ethera, Elijah had already retreated into the shaft where he hoped to avoid notice long enough that he could exit combat.

Meanwhile, the battle continued, and through the use of One with Nature, he kept track of the three combatants' conditions. The ogres had clearly gotten the worst of it, and the one who'd shouldered the brunt of the impact of Swarm looked like it was only a hair's breadth from passing out. Wet, clammy skin, splotchy cheeks, and unsteady legs were only the most apparent of its symptoms, and Elijah knew that it certainly wasn't fighting at full strength.

The same could be said for the other ogre jailer as well as the troll, but there was enough of a difference that it was clear which ogre would fall first. It ended up coming sooner rather than later, when the troll hammered the ogre with a giant, meaty fist that sent it splattering against the wall. Even as the masonry crumbled, the troll pounced, hammering the unfortunate ogre with all its might.

Elijah only caught glimpses here and there—all via One with Nature—but he got the impression that the pummeling was similar to what one might see from an enraged grizzly bear. In any case, the ogre was done for, and though it continued to fend the troll off with all the effort it could muster, its fellow could read the writing on the wall.

And when it did, the remaining ogre jailer didn't swoop in to save its comrade. Instead, he turned tail and ran, dashing through the door as quickly as its generously meaty proportions would allow. At first, the troll paid it no mind, but the moment it finally finished with its gruesome and single-minded task, it whirled around to look for another victim. When it didn't find one, the formerly imprisoned troll let out a frustrated roar, then squeezed through the cell door—no small feat, given its larger size—and took off down the hall.

Elijah waited a few moments before he climbed out of the shaft, and the moment he saw the devastation that had been wreaked on the cell, his reticence to engage the ogres or the troll in battle was reaffirmed. The walls were cracked, with one of them covered in blood, and large chunks of brick had been torn away. But that was nothing compared to the state of the ogre the troll had killed.

From the shoulders down, it was much the same as Elijah had expected. Just a large, corpulent body composed of equal parts fat and muscle. However, from the neck up was just a mass of unidentifiable meat and exposed bone. The troll hadn't just beaten the thing to death. Indeed, he'd rendered it entirely unrecognizable. Seeing that, it was easy for Elijah to imagine the troll venting its rage and frustration on the unlucky ogre.

Elijah wasted no more time inspecting the site of the battle. Instead, he quickly shifted into the Shape of the Predator and slipped into the Guise of the Unseen. Only then did the tension in his mind dissipate, and he slipped from the cell, secure in his own invisibility. As soon as he did, he saw more evidence of the troll's passage. Unlike the cell's door, the corridor was easily large enough to accommodate even the enormous troll, and yet, it looked like the creature had gone out of its way to smash into everything it saw.

More cracked walls were the most obvious sign of its ire, but it had also torn torches from their sconces and dented other cell doors. Elijah followed the trail of destruction as he made his way through the dungeon, his passage accompanied by the echoing sounds of the ongoing battle up ahead. Along the way, he saw the bodies of the remaining ogre jailers; the troll had clearly used the weight of surprise to tip the battle in its favor, and it had dispatched the unarmored creatures without even slowing down.

Elijah padded forward, his feet silent as he crept from one flickering shadow to the next. He knew it wasn't strictly necessary—Guise of the Unseen as well as his form's ability to change color was enough to render him nearly invisible—but he didn't want to take any chances. As such, his progress was much slower than it likely should have been. Even so, he reached the source of the noise only a handful of minutes later.

By the time he caught sight of the troll, Elijah couldn't help but let out a silent gasp of horror. It bore hundreds of wounds. Some were small—pinpricks for a creature of its size—but some gaped open, with huge flaps of skin flopping around with every movement. Its opponents hadn't fared any better, though.

Four armored ogre guards encircled the troll, harrying it with their massive weapons. However, despite their brutish appearance, the ogres displayed no small degree of cooperation and finesse, hemming the creature in and slowly whittling it down with the superior reach of their axes and the weight of numbers.

That simply would not do.

So, Elijah retreated to the chamber's door, then ducked out of sight before resuming his human form. Then, he once again used Swarm, sending a cascade of biting flies to inflict their afflictions on the ogre guards. Fortunately, their armor proved no obstacle to the tiny insects, and before the swarm dissipated, the four remaining guards—one had been completely incapacitated, but it was still alive, while another slumped against the wall, its body misshapen and unmoving—had been infected.

And even in that short span, the effect had already made itself known. A woozy guard didn't move quite quickly enough to avoid the troll's sudden attack, and as a result, it ended up being slammed against the wall with the force of a runaway train. Predictably, it didn't survive intact, and even from so far away, Elijah could hear cracking bones over the sound of twisting metal.

That was when Elijah shifted back into his scaled-panther form, automatically embracing Guise of the Unseen the moment it was available. Then, he settled in to wait. However, even with the numbers tilting slightly more in favor of the troll, it quickly became clear that it was destined to lose.

The afflicted ogres couldn't move quite as quickly as before, but the troll hadn't escaped the swarm unscathed, either. So, while it wasn't as affected as the guards—probably due to a better Constitution attribute or some other inherent regenerative trait of being a troll—the gap hadn't widened enough to give it an appreciable advantage. The fight continued on, settling into a standstill, which meant that Elijah had little choice but to act.

After all, it was only a matter of time before the Warden responded. And if that dark elf added its weight to the battle, the troll's fate would be sealed. Elijah knew he needed to act before then because, if he didn't have the troll as a distraction, he knew precisely how the fight would go. Perhaps he could use hit-and-run tactics to thin the ogres' numbers, but in a relatively small and enclosed space, he wasn't so sure that was a viable strategy. And that was saying nothing of whether or not they could implement an alarm similar to the one that had outed him at the guardhouse outside.

If that happened, he would surely die.

So, with those issues pressing down on him, Elijah did the only thing he could.

He attacked.

Targeting the first ogre proved to be quite difficult, largely because it never quit moving. Moreover, he wanted to time his attack such that he wouldn't be seen; to that end, he needed to use the troll as a shield from the other two ogres. So, he waited for the perfect moment, and when it presented itself, he pounced.

Striking out like an ambushing cat, he used Predator Strike before slashing his claws across the back of the ogre's ankle. Then, even as it wailed in anger and pain, he dashed away, slipping through the door before the thing could wheel around. There, he waited until, thirty seconds later, he heard the sound of crunching metal before Essence of the Wolf kicked back in.

Now that he was out of combat, Elijah once again embraced Guise of the Unseen before creeping back into the chamber. True to his expectations, the troll had overcome the wounded guard, and the ogre now lay in a crumpled and motionless heap only a few feet from the other dead guard.

There were only two remaining, and the troll seemed more than capable of overcoming those odds.

Still, Elijah wasn't going to leave that up to chance. So, he once again set himself up for another strategic attack, and when it presented itself, he launched himself forward and sliced through the ogre's hamstrings. However, it was only when he whipped around to dart back into the safety of the hallway that he realized that he'd pushed his luck a little too far.

The elf, its dull, black iron armor glowing with ethera, leveled its silver sword in his direction. It started to say something, but Elijah had no interest in hearing some villain's monologue.

So, mid-stride, he shifted back into his human form and preemptively cast Healing Rain. The spell was wide enough to encompass half the room, and even as the storm clouds gathered, Elijah embraced Shape of the Guardian.

The call for stealth had faded.

Now was the time for unmitigated strength.

As he felt his body shifting, Elijah slammed into the wide-eyed elf, but by the time he'd completed his transformation, the creature had recovered his wits enough to once again attempt to speak. And Elijah responded appropriately by harnessing every point of his inflated Strength and ramming his open palm into the elf's chest.

A sound like a gong announced contact, and a moment later, the slight creature rocketed backward, hitting the wall with bone-crunching force. Elijah wasted no time before bounding forward, grabbing the stunned elf around the waist, then spinning in place like an Olympic hammer thrower before launching him down the hall.

Elijah didn't wait for his opponent to land before he raced back into the room and threw himself at the injured ogre. His shoulder hit the monster in the hip, eliciting a howl of anger and pain. It hammered a fist against Elijah's back, knocking the breath from his lungs, but he was too close for the ogre to bring its massive weapon to bear. So, he bunched his legs and drove himself, as well as the ogre, into the wall.

More bones broke, but more importantly, the guard was stunned by the sudden impact. That gave Elijah the chance he'd been looking for, so he reared back and brought his clasped hands down on the monster with every ounce of power he could summon. Other than extending the ogre's dazed state, the blow did little good. However, Elijah persisted, repeating the attack.

When that didn't finish the guard off, he did it again.

And again after that.

Over and over, he smashed his scaly fists into the ogre's exposed head. And after the sixth such attack, he was finally rewarded with the feel of a shattering skull beneath his claws. Still, he gave it one more blow for good measure. That one cracked the ogre's skull open like an overripe melon, splattering brain, blood, and bone across the wall.

Still, he seethed with a need to keep going. To rip that corpse to pieces with every ounce of his power. Yet, he pushed that aside and forced himself to disengage.

He was just in time to see the elf's snarling face as it drove its silver sword into his chest.

28

SHOWDOWN

Pain lanced through Elijah's chest as the blade parted his scales and sliced deep into the meat of his torso only to erupt from his back an instant later. The sheer force of the attack drove him backward until he thudded against the wall, sending a spiderweb of cracks arcing out from the point of impact. Dust and debris rained down on his head as the sword pinned him in place.

Panicked, he lashed out, his claws raking against the elf's face. But they never reached his dark skin. The creature smirked and leaned on the hilt of his blade, twisting it cruelly.

"Beast," he growled, his voice melodious yet menacing. "You dare strike me?!"

Elijah hissed and spat as he tried to escape, but his peril was absolute. He couldn't wrench himself free of the sword, no matter how hard he pulled. But more distressingly, he felt something being dragged out of him. It wasn't just ethera. It was something far more vital. His life force, perhaps. He felt weaker with every passing second.

Desperate to stop that pull, Elijah reached out, his long arms moving with incredible speed until he wrapped his claws around the elf's wrist. Then, he yanked.

The elf clearly hadn't expected that, and the result was a slight stumble in Elijah's direction. It wasn't much, but it was just enough to put him in range of Elijah's sharp fangs. His jaws snapped shut with undeniable power, and the elf's invisible shield shattered.

The Warden threw himself backward, mitigating some of the damage, but when he recovered only a moment later, long, jagged strips of flesh still hung from his ruined face. Elijah used that small opening to grab hold of the sword and pull. It took every ounce of strength he could bring to bear, but he still managed to yank it free.

Then, he roared.

At that very moment, the injured troll, having dispatched the final ogre with a thunderous punch, joined the battle. It rushed the still-reeling elf, aiming a massive blow in his direction. However, just before it closed the distance, the Warden regained his wits and thrust his hand at the monster.

Bands of red energy exploded from his fingertips, wrapping around the charging troll's limbs. Then, the elf yanked his arm back, sending the enormous creature flying across the room only to collide with the wall. It didn't stop there, though. Instead, it crashed through the wall, sending bricks flying in an explosion of momentum.

Elijah raced forward, raising the sword in an attack. However, he was no swordsman, and his scaled-ape form was ill-suited for using weapons. As a result, his intended blow was clumsy and fated for failure. Still, he had surprise on his side, and due to that, he very nearly made contact. The elf moved like a striking snake, though, and despite his heavy-looking armor, he managed to dodge Elijah's attack with inches to spare.

But he could do nothing to allay Elijah's charging momentum, which took the form of a shoulder tackle that sent the slender elf flying backward. He hit the ground a half dozen feet away, but he didn't skid to a stop until he hit the wall on the other side of the room. Elijah threw the sword aside, then pounced.

He never reached his target.

With a snarl, the Warden swept his hand out, and once again, red bands erupted from his fingers. This time, though, they were aimed at Elijah. For his part, he tried to dodge, but the ribbons of energy seemed to have a mind of their own, following his every move until they slithered around his limbs.

And then he was flying through the air, just like the troll before him. He caromed off the remnants of the shattered wall, then cartwheeled across the neighboring cell until he came to rest two dozen feet into the room.

The guardian shape was incredibly durable. Elijah knew from experience that he could endure all sorts of damage in the scaled-ape form. With his hard scales, dense bones, and enhanced Constitution, he was like a living tank. However, the limits of his endurance had clearly met their match because he could already feel multiple broken bones as well as a multitude of shattered scales.

And that wasn't even considering the internal damage.

He struggled to rise, but he let out a growl of pure agony as his leg collapsed the moment he tried to put weight on it. It was broken in multiple places, he was sure.

Elijah looked up to see that the elf had recovered his sword and was hacking at the grievously wounded troll. The monster's battle with the ogres as well as the aftereffects of Swarm's afflictions had clearly put the creature at a vast disadvantage, and the elf was more than strong enough to exploit the effects of its many injuries.

More troublingly, each fall of the Warden's sword came with a swirl of ethera that snaked around his body before being absorbed. With every strike, the elf's wounds healed a little.

Elijah knew that if he let that continue, he'd never have a chance of winning the fight. Certainly, he could use Guardian's Renewal and heal himself before either resuming the battle or retreating long enough to reenter stealth. However, by that point, the Warden would have completely healed.

And even with an ambush, Elijah doubted his chances of defeating the elf if he had the chance to recover. Moreover, he wasn't sure if the elf would allow his retreat. Those red ribbons of energy—a spell, obviously—had been inescapable. Who was to say what other abilities the elf possessed?

No—Elijah needed to put everything on the line, and all at once, or he would never defeat the Warden, much less conquer the tower.

With that in mind, he activated Guardian's Renewal. Instantly, his bones mended, and his flesh was restored. In seconds, he was whole, hale, and ready to continue the fight. However, he had no intention of doing so in his scaled-ape form. Its endurance and strength had already proved a poor match. So, he had other plans.

Having regained his health, Elijah shifted back into his human form. The moment he did, he yanked ethera from his Core and cast Swarm. The spell took a decent portion of his available ethera, but due to his cultivation and ever-increasing Core size—which came with each point of the associated attribute—it wasn't nearly as much as it once had been. So, even as the biting flies manifested, he embraced another spell.

Spell: **Calamity**	**Bury your enemies beneath the power of nature. Conjure a natural disaster appropriate to your environment. Only usable in caster form.**

Ethera drained out of his Core at a rapid pace, flooding the spell with power. Then, Elijah released it, and all hell broke loose. The ground was sundered, the stale air suddenly broke into sharp gusts that would rend flesh, and lightning filled the air. Meanwhile, Elijah was already casting another spell.

This time, he preemptively cast Healing Rain before using the last of his ethera to shift into the Shape of the Predator. As his scaled-panther shape replaced his human form, Elijah raced toward the door. The elf—and the troll, who still clung to life despite having its head mostly severed—was too distracted to notice his departure.

Fortunately, the System took that into account because, the second he was out of view, he felt Essence of the Wolf increase his movement speed, which told him that he'd left combat. So, he wasted no time before slipping into the Guise of the Unseen and returning whence he had come.

Neither Calamity nor Swarm were long-lasting spells, but only a few seconds had passed. So, the elf and the troll were still very much occupied. The elf had redoubled his efforts at hacking through the troll, clearly hoping that the draining ability could outpace the damage of Elijah's spells.

And it was mostly working.

However, everything went wrong for the Warden when, at last, the troll succumbed to the cascade of damage and passed away. Suddenly, the elf's efforts were for naught—obviously, his victim needed to be alive to facilitate his draining spell—and it was at that moment that Elijah embraced Predator Strike and pounced.

Instead of focusing on harrying attacks as he had against the ogres, Elijah leaped onto the elf's back, latched his powerful jaws on to the nape of his neck, then squeezed.

Since the transformation—or evolution, perhaps—of the predator form, Elijah had spent quite a lot of time examining his physiology. In a lot of ways, it resembled the big cat it had once been, which was why he referred to it as a scaled panther. However, that characterization was a bit of a misnomer, especially when it came the structure of his head.

Most big cats could only muster around a thousand pounds per square inch of bite force. Even before the form's evolution, Elijah knew he far exceeded that, especially under the effect of Predator Strike. However, he still felt like that was just a multiplier on the limitations of basic physiology.

The new scaled-panther form had a jaw more like a crocodile, and as such, in that shape, he could bring an absolutely incredible amount of force to bear. With the modifier of Predator Strike working in his favor, that degree of pressure went from incredible to astounding.

Elijah knew that. He had come to rely on it. And yet, he was still surprised when the elf's head popped like a grape. The Warden fell, collapsing into a boneless heap atop the troll it had worked so hard to kill.

Elijah leaped free, shocked at how easily the elf had died. He'd been gearing up for a long, epic battle where he would be forced to dart back and forth and wear the Warden down. And what he'd gotten was a sudden and somewhat anticlimactic end.

Not that he was complaining.

And after a few moments, he saw evidence of why the elf had succumbed so quickly when he noticed the dark tendrils tracing a spiderweb of discoloration up what was left of its neck. Clearly, the affliction of Swarm had weakened him. Cataclysm had contributed, as well. Though Elijah had only intended the two spells as distractions, they were obviously more powerful than he'd expected them to be.

After letting out a hiss of relief, Elijah embraced Guise of the Unseen once again and turned to see if there were any other threats. He'd already accounted for everyone in the dungeon, but there was nothing to say that they couldn't get reinforcements from the citadel above. When nothing came for another five minutes, he finally let himself relax.

He'd sustained no damage since using Guardian's Renewal, so he was still in perfect health. Still, he switched back to his caster form and spent some time in meditation so he could regain his spent ethera. When that was done, he set about looting the ogres as well as the Warden.

The ogre guards had very little Elijah could take with him. Their armor and weapons were far too bulky, and they'd carried nothing but a couple of copper etherium in their belt pouches. He collected what loot he could, then turned his attention to the elf.

Fortunately, the sword fit in his pack, though try as he might, he couldn't remove the Warden's armor. It was almost as if it was part of the elf's body. So, after spending far longer than he probably should have trying to pry it loose, he marked it up as a lost cost. However, he did retrieve another set of keys that he hoped would come in handy going forward. He also looted a pair of silver etherium, which he added to his collection.

With that, he felt that he was finished with the floor—especially considering that he'd finally accomplished the task. However, before he advanced and retrieved what he hoped would be a useful reward, he had to take care of something important.

The experience had pushed him over the edge and into level thirty-five. And with that level, he had finally gotten his first spell in quite some time.

As he looked at the resulting notification, he couldn't help but smile at the achievement.

29

BRAMBLES

The smell of death and decay hung heavy in the air as Elijah crouched in the cell where he'd defeated the Warden. The corpses of the troll, dark elf, and ogres were a long way from decomposition, but to Elijah, they still smelled of rot.

Perhaps that was just his imagination.

Or given the things he'd seen in the other cells, maybe not. Either way, he was eager to leave it all behind for more pleasant environs. However, before he could do that, he had a few tasks before him. The first concerned the fact that, by virtue of killing the Warden and the troll he'd temporarily saved, he'd finally reached level thirty-five. And that advancement had come with a host of advantages.

As always, he'd gained another point in each of his attributes, enhancing his already-impressive status further past the human standard:

Name	Elijah Hart
Level	35
Archetype	Druid
Class	Animist
Specialization	N/A
Alignment	N/A
Strength	36
Dexterity	45 (35)
Constitution	46 (36)
Ethera	44
Regeneration	58 (38)
Attunement	Nature

Cultivation Stage: Cultivator			
Body	**Core**	**Mind**	**Soul**
Wood	**Hatchling**	**Quartz**	**Neophyte**

Of course, his attributes didn't tell the full story of his advancement. Due to both One with Nature and his cultivation, his attributes all meant much more than the numbers might suggest. He still wasn't certain exactly how much those factors affected him, but he knew that it was significant.

And if he managed to advance the rest of his cultivation, the gap between his apparent and effective attributes would only grow wider. To his annoyance, though, he still wasn't entirely sure how to go about furthering his cultivation. He'd tried variations on the methods he'd used to take the first step in each category, but those had so far yielded no results. He supposed he just needed to keep at it, and maybe he would unlock the secret.

But in the back of his mind, he hoped that, eventually, Nerthus would be able to tell him more. Or perhaps he could purchase a guide from the Branch, though that came with other issues—largely, that there was so much information contained within the Knowledge Base that it made finding all but the shallowest information almost impossible. Either way, he suspected that continuing to progress his cultivation would be a difficult road. If it was easy, then everyone would have done it. And though he couldn't be certain, Elijah didn't think anyone in Ironshore had made strides in that department, supporting the notion that it would take more than a few lucky guesses to break through to the next cultivation stages.

Still, there was hope.

After all, he'd already reached the second stage in the cultivation of his Mind. That was proof that he could do the same with the other components of cultivation.

Even so, his attributes were still progressing nicely, especially when he was under the influence of his various enhancements. He shuddered to think of where he would be without them.

"Dead," he muttered to himself. "I would be dead."

Ironically, the enhancement that had probably served him best during battle didn't even show up in his status. Essence of the Wolf had proved itself a vital component of his tool kit on so many occasions that he knew that, without a shadow of a doubt, he would have died dozens of times over without it. Not only did it increase his movement speed—which was incredibly valuable, as he'd proved in the Primordial Maze as well as many other times since then—but it also gave him an easily understood indicator of when he entered and dropped out of combat. That was precisely the information he needed in order to properly time the use of Guise of the Unseen.

For what felt like the thousandth time, he found himself grateful that he'd been granted the Druid archetype. Otherwise, there was no way he would have survived even a few weeks on the island, much less everything that had happened since then.

Two and a half years.

At times, it certainly didn't seem like it had been that long. But at others, it felt like an eternity had passed since he'd been on a plane and dying of cancer. He wasn't just a different person now. He felt like an entirely different species. However, it was at times like these that he found himself glancing at the power ladder and wondering about his family.

His sister-in-law's name was still on there, giving him comfort. Sure, he knew that Carmen Rodriguez wasn't a terribly uncommon name. There were probably thousands of women bearing that moniker. But Elijah knew in his gut that the one on the ladder was his sister's wife.

"Or maybe it's all just wishful thinking," he acknowledged aloud. After all, he needed to believe that Alyssa and Miguel were okay, and clinging to the notion of Carmen's survival as an indicator that they were still alive satisfied that need in a way no self-assurance could. It was something tangible that he could point to as evidence, and until he discovered otherwise, he would choose to believe that everyone he loved was still out there living their lives in the transformed world.

A pretty fantasy, perhaps, but it was one he needed to believe.

Idly, he wondered if they'd thought the same thing when seeing his name. Maybe they'd thrown a party when he'd popped onto the ladder. Or perhaps they hadn't noticed at all. Surely they had their own problems to deal with, and Elijah was well aware that everyone wouldn't be quite as obsessed with that ladder as he'd become.

Whatever the case, he couldn't afford to dwell on it. Instead, he had a tower to conquer, and before he did that, he needed to examine his latest spell:

Spell: Shield of Brambles	Shelter beneath nature's embrace, protecting yourself and damaging any who attack you.

The description was a little ambiguous for Elijah's taste, but he could sense a few things about the spell. First, it was an enhancement not unlike Essence of the Boar or Monkey, meaning that it would take up one of his three slots. That alone soured him on it a little. He liked his extra attributes, and now that he could use all the relevant spells to enhance them, he was loath to give them up.

Second, he could sense that there were two benefits to the spell. For one, it would shield him from some degree of damage. How much was yet to be seen, but any extra protection would be welcome. He hadn't forgotten how easily that magical sword had slid through his scales, after all. And that had been in his guardian form, which increased his Constitution by a fair amount.

He didn't want to think about the damage it would have done if he'd been in his human form. So, he couldn't dismiss the spell altogether, especially when it had a secondary function, which would somehow inflict damage on anyone who attacked him. He had no idea what form that would take or how severely it would injure his attackers, and the only way he was going to find out was to test it.

So, without further ado, Elijah canceled Essence of the Monkey, then cast Shield of Brambles. As he did so, he looked at his arm, and what he saw was simultaneously awe-inspiring as well as troubling. His skin turned slightly green, taking on the texture of bark. At the same time, tiny thorns—maybe a quarter of an inch long—sprouted all over his body. Strangely enough, they positioned themselves atop his clothes, which made for an odd sight.

Extending his index finger to one of the thorns, he was disappointed to find that it passed right through the protrusion. But then again, that shouldn't have been terribly surprising. The spell's description had specified that it only damaged those who attacked him, so it stood to reason that it would only become material in that event.

Which was more than a little frustrating. In a tower, he didn't have much chance to test a new ability. The margins for error were so thin that he just couldn't afford to use a suboptimal enhancement. Perhaps that would change. Maybe he would find a good opportunity to find its limitations. But for now, he would keep going with the same approach he'd used since the beginning of the tower.

So, he canceled Shield of Brambles, then reapplied Essence of the Monkey.

After ensuring that his other enhancements were active, he took the opportunity to explore the rest of the dungeon, paying close attention to the torture room. The giant goblin was exactly where Elijah had last seen it—which was to say that it was hanging from a torture rack—but it had already surrendered to death.

The room itself was a grotesquerie of torture equipment. Hooks, knives, and various other tools abounded; there was even something that looked suspiciously like an iron maiden in the corner. Despite the fact that some of the implements had the potential of being somewhat useful, Elijah declined to take them with him. He told himself that they were all too bulky and that they would take up too much room in his pack. But in the back of his mind, he knew the real reason lay in their intended purpose.

However, he did find a small chest containing a few gems, a handful of etherium—both copper and silver—and a shiny dagger with a ruby embedded in the pommel. Like the sword he'd taken from the Warden, it felt magical, though Elijah had no idea what form that magic might take.

Perhaps he could get one of those tablets that Mari, the Tailor back in Iron-shore, had used to inspect his staff. She'd said something about it utilizing her techniques, so he suspected he wouldn't be able to use it.

Either way, he hoped to find someone who could help him out by identifying the weapons he'd looted. Maybe he could even sell them for a decent number of coins. He wasn't hurting for money or anything, but he'd seen the price of some of those guides. More, he wanted to be in position to buy things he might need in the future, and from his experience, one could never have enough money. That was true in the old world, and he suspected it would be the same moving forward.

In any case, he finished his perusal of whatever the torture room had to offer, then left it behind as quickly as possible. Soon enough, he found himself standing before the gate leading up to the citadel above. He had no idea what to expect up there, but he knew it would tax his abilities.

So, he took a deep breath, then used one of the keys from the Warden's key chain to unlock the gate. It swung open with an ominous creak, but as horror-movie-esque as the sound was, nothing jumped out at him.

Now that the need for thumbs had been obviated, he replaced the key chain in his pack, took his staff in hand, and shifted into the Shape of the Predator. Then, after embracing Guise of the Unseen, he padded forward. The moment he passed through the gate, he felt himself shift slightly. It only lasted an instant, and when the feeling passed, the stairwell beyond the gate looked no different than it had from the other side. Yet, he knew that he'd stepped into the next level of the tower.

Hammering that home was a simple silver box that had suddenly appeared before him. Almost as soon as he noticed his reward for defeating the previous floor, a notification flashed before his eyes:

> **Congratulations! You have completed Level One of Reaver's Citadel.**
> **Grade: B.**
> **To progress further, complete the task before you and reach Level Three.**

His grade was a little disappointing, especially after he'd gone to such lengths to complete the optional task. However, when he thought about it, Elijah could guess why he hadn't gotten full marks. After all, he'd only killed a few of the monsters himself. That had to have counted against him. In any case, he moved on to the next notification that appeared before his inner eye:

> **Task: Defeat the Five Lieutenants.**

That certainly didn't sound promising. If the Five Lieutenants were anything like the Warden, he had his work cut out for him. And this time, he didn't think he'd have the benefit of a semifriendly troll to act as a distraction. Still, he'd gotten this far, and he had to believe he had what it took to conquer the tower.

Hopefully, his reward would help with that. So, he quickly shifted back to human form, then bent down and unlatched the small chest. Inside was a simple red strip of cloth.

Reward for completing Level One of Reaver's Citadel:
Sash of the Whirlwind

Elijah reached in and retrieved the strip of cloth. It was a little more than three feet long, so he could easily wrap it around his slim waist. But when he put it on, tying it in place, he immediately felt the item's effect.

A wide smile spread across his face. He couldn't deny the utility of his previous rewards. The Ring of Anonymity and the Ring of Aquatic Travel had both served him well enough. Though, by his own admission, the latter had proved far more useful than the former so far. The jury was still out on the Shard of the World Tree he'd given to Nerthus, but given the tree spirit's reaction, it was probably the most valuable of his rewards.

However, based on his initial impressions, the Sash of the Whirlwind would be even more immediately impactful.

30

THE WRONG END OF A SWARM

After Elijah tied the Sash of the Whirlwind around his waist, he looked at his status. What he saw was incredible—a boost of three points to both Strength and Dexterity—but what he felt was even more impressive. It was difficult to explain, but he felt faster and more energetic than even that small boost would have suggested. Indeed, the effect was so prominent that he felt almost as if the world was moving just a little bit slower than normal.

His predator and guardian forms both came with significant attribute boosts, so he knew very well what those felt like. This was something entirely different, and unless he missed his guess, it would prove to be life altering, at least in terms of his combat ability.

Once again, he cursed his inability to inspect his items. Sure, he knew the name, but contrary to what had been the case with the Ring of Anonymity and the Ring of Aquatic Travel, the label did nothing to hint at its purpose. Even so, if that influx of speed that he felt was any indication, the name still felt appropriate enough.

For a few minutes, Elijah practiced moving with the new sash, but he quickly tired of the game. He wouldn't be able to properly test it until he found some enemies. So, with that in mind, he once again shifted into his scaled-panther form and climbed the moldy stairs and into the darkness beyond.

With One with Nature, he could feel most of his surroundings, but even so, he kept his every sense trained on his immediate vicinity. Like that, he crested the first flight of stairs and reached a small rectangular platform. There was nothing there, so Elijah quickly mounted the set of stairs leading up and in the direction he'd just come. Soon enough, he found another switchback. Then another until, finally, he reached a thick wooden door banded with black iron.

Stepping close, he tried to extend his senses to the room beyond, but he felt nothing past the door. So, he adopted his human form, then retrieved the Warden's key ring from where he'd stashed it in his pack. After that, it only took a few tries to find the proper key, which he used to unlock the door. Then, he pushed it open to reveal a dark room filled with crates and barrels.

He stepped inside, and the door slammed shut behind him.

The moment it did, Elijah felt a thousand presences flare to life around him. One with Nature didn't tell him much about what they were, but he could feel their long, fat, and furry bodies. More importantly, he sensed that they were aggressive, and that they'd targeted him as their potential prey.

Without hesitation, Elijah preemptively cast Healing Rain, then canceled Essence of the Monkey before using Shield of Brambles. Finally, he cast Shape of the Guardian. Shape of the Predator was great for dealing damage, but with the size of the horde bearing down on him, Elijah knew he couldn't avoid taking damage himself. For that, the scaled-ape form was far superior.

Discarding Essence of the Monkey in favor of Shield of Brambles followed a similar logic. A few extra points of Dexterity weren't going to help him very much in his current situation, but a little extra mitigation and whatever reflective damage came with the spell would be far more useful. In fact, it was just such an occasion—an onslaught of smaller, numerous enemies—for which he'd preemptively decided to use Shield of Brambles. It was just a twist of fate that it had come so quickly after he'd gotten the spell.

Or maybe not. The towers were curated, after all, so there was a good chance that it had somehow noticed the acquisition of the spell and given him a perfect chance to use it. Elijah had no idea, and he was in no position to ponder a question to which he didn't think he'd ever get an answer.

Even as those thoughts crossed his mind, his transformation into a scaled ape completed, and just in time for him to meet his opponents. The first one launched itself high into the air, clearly with the intention of clawing out his eyes. However, with the seeming time dilation afforded by his new Sash of the Whirlwind, Elijah saw it coming from a mile away. Still, his foresight was only enough to allow him to turn his head before the furry bullet hit him in the side of the face.

Elijah's scales protected him from the thing's sharp teeth, but the sheer force of its impact sent him stumbling.

The rodent—and it was definitely a foot-long rat, bulging with muscle—wasn't so lucky. The second it hit him, a giant thorn ejected from Elijah's scales, piercing it through the chest. It only went about an inch deep before breaking off, but that was more than enough to send the little monster screeching in pain as it fell to the stone floor.

A quick but vicious stomp ended that, and he felt the monster's bones crunching underfoot. He also felt its innards oozing between his talons, but thankfully, he didn't have any time to think about that before another little rodent hit him. Then another. Dozens came, all at once, but they met the same end as the first. Pierced through by thorns, they all fell to the floor, where Elijah stomped them to death.

None of them were particularly dangerous. Not individually. However, that was mostly because they only got one bite in. However, Elijah knew that, without the extra armor provided by Shield of Brambles or his enhanced Constitution, he never could have withstood the onslaught. Even with all his advantages—and in his scaled-ape form, he was almost perfectly suited for that kind of battle—it was still an incredibly painful fight. The rodents were equipped with sharp teeth as well as enhanced Strength, so while they had trouble getting all the way through his scales, their bites were still anything but comfortable.

But as always, Elijah endured. The small wounds they did manage to inflict were healed quickly enough by Healing Rain, so he was never in much danger. That would have changed had he been in his human or scaled-panther forms, though. It wasn't difficult to imagine being ripped to shreds under that barrage of sharp teeth and claws.

Even in his guardian form, the fight would have gone very differently if Shield of Brambles hadn't proved its worth by incapacitating the little beasts.

By the time he squished the last one underfoot, Elijah had long since lost track of how many he'd killed. Hundreds, surely, though he didn't think the number exceeded a thousand. Regardless, he slew so many that he actually gained another level, putting him at thirty-six. When the last of the swarm of rodents had died, Elijah let his shoulders sag in relief and fatigue.

He hadn't really had to put forth much effort. He wasn't that tired, either. However, there was just something about being constantly nibbled to death that brought with it an exhaustion all its own. Yet, he couldn't allow himself to rest for more than a couple of minutes before he moved on, exploring the room in which he'd found himself.

Remaining in his scaled-ape form, Elijah loped from one end of the room to the other, surmising that it was a cellar of sorts. He did discover that the crates were filled with foodstuffs—mostly moldy bread and bits of dried meat—and the barrels contained some foul-smelling liquid he took to be beer of a sort. He didn't taste it, though, so he couldn't be certain.

Instead, after shifting back to his human form, he retrieved one of his jugs from his pack and drank deeply before satisfying his own hunger by dipping into his own travel rations. They were mostly tasteless, but he did savor one of the berries he'd brought from his Grove. After almost two months of travel, he didn't have many left, so he'd resolved to eat them sparingly.

The tart flavor reminded him of home, though, and more than ever, Elijah found himself missing his Grove. Certainly, his thirst for adventure hadn't faded, but he couldn't deny that he also craved the comforts and safety of home.

Once he'd satisfied his hunger and slaked his thirst, Elijah rose from his haunches and headed toward a stairway he'd found during his previous examination of the room. It was short, ending in a pair of doors embedded in the roof, confirming his deduction that he was in a cellar. However, that presented a problem in that he was quite sure that on the other side of those doors were enemies. And not the sort he could kill as easily as the rat swarm.

Mentally preparing himself to respond to any threats, Elijah took a deep breath, then reached out to unlatch the doors before pushing one open.

He poked his head out just enough to see the confines of a broad, empty hallway before scrambling through. After slowly letting the door close behind him, Elijah shifted into the Shape of the Predator, then adopted Guise of the Unseen before stepping into a deep shadow near the wall. It was just in time, too, because only a few seconds later, he heard the heavy tromp of boots and the clinking sound of metal clashing against metal coming down the hallway.

A moment later, an armored ogre appeared. He already had his weapon out, but he'd nonchalantly let the massive broadsword rest on his shoulder as he marched down the spacious hall. Elijah didn't dare move a muscle as he hid in the shadow of what he now recognized as a tall, narrow statue depicting another dark elf. This one had the same elven features that the Warden had possessed, but he wore an imperious scowl. Elijah wondered if the elf depicted in the statue was likely the final foe he'd have to defeat if he wanted to conquer the tower.

Before he could worry about that, though, he needed to defeat five lieutenants.

To that end, he waited—holding his breath the whole time—as the enormous ogre stomped down the hall. Guise of the Unseen had proved itself hundreds of times, and he trusted the ability implicitly. However, the close proximity of the gargantuan—and deadly—ogre was enough to send his heart beating out of his chest. Yet the ability remained just as effective as ever because the ogre never even glanced in his direction. Still, Elijah didn't relax until it turned a corner and was out of sight for more than thirty seconds.

For a few more seconds after that, he remained still as he let his heart rate normalize. When it did, he took another deep, hissing breath, then padded forward on silent feet. Staying low to the ground, he practically slithered to the end of the hall, then peeked around the corner. The coast was clear, so he continued on.

As Elijah progressed, he studied his surroundings with a keen eye. The structure itself was much the same as he'd encountered below. Just unadorned stone walls, without much in the way of decoration. However, it was free of the algae that pervaded the sewer and dungeon, which told him that the denizens at least understood the value of cleanliness. Every so often, he'd pass by a tapestry depicting ogres in battle. The style was extremely primitive, but it was easy enough to make out the subjects.

Then there were the statues, each one representing the same dark elf. Some had him standing stoic guard, a giant sword with its tip planted into the ground. Others showed him in the middle of battle, sword raised high and with a snarl on his sharp-featured face. It was a not-so-subtle hint of what was to come.

Finally, after spending quite some time wandering the halls—and seeing more than a dozen ogre guards along the way—Elijah found an unlocked door. It wasn't the first he'd encountered, but it was the only one that was occupied. He crept through the door, seeing a tall, gangly man sitting behind a desk with his head in his hands.

Elijah slipped around the edge of the room, preparing himself to attack. He used Predator Strike, then Venom Strike for good measure. However, just before he pounced, he noticed the heavy shackles on the man's ankles. From those iron cuffs stretched a pair of thick chains leashing him to a couple of rings beneath the desk.

That's when Elijah stopped to really study the man. He was bald, and his skin held a waxy sheen. Upon his body were a collection of rags—dirty, dusty, and frayed. But more than anything, Elijah noticed that the man was weeping.

He was a prisoner, just like the troll had been.

For a moment, Elijah considered attacking anyway, but he discarded that notion as disgusting. The man was clearly human, and the idea of killing an unarmed and helpless captive crossed almost all of Elijah's lines. On top of that, he didn't sense that the prisoner was very powerful, so he wouldn't even get much experience for it. So, there was little to gain from killing the man, which gave Elijah two choices.

One, he could simply leave the prisoner behind.

Or two, he could free the man and use him as a source of information.

The former was, on the surface, the smarter option. There were a ton of ways freeing the prisoner could backfire, and Elijah wasn't so certain of his own strength that he wanted to make the task before him more difficult. However, the second was appealing, as well. The possibility of gaining the upper hand through information was enticing, all on its own.

Ultimately, though, the decision came down to one thing. Elijah knew that towers were structured very deliberately. The presence of the prisoner was important, and he suspected that freeing the man would prove, if not necessary, then important going forward. That was enough to push Elijah into the second option.

So, without further hesitation, Elijah backed away—just out of reach of the man's chains—then let his predator form fall away. With it went Guise of the Unseen, completely exposing him. However, the prisoner was too engrossed in his own misery to even notice the sudden appearance of another human being.

Elijah cast Healing Rain, which encompassed the entire room. Then, even as the first drops fell and the man looked up, he said, "Hello. I'm Elijah. You look like you could use some help."

31

THE OLD MAN AND THE OGRES

The prisoner looked up with heavy-lidded eyes, his face creased from advanced age, and locked his gaze onto Elijah. He opened his mouth as if to speak, revealing a mouth devoid of teeth, then let out a rasping cackle that quickly turned into a coughing fit. Elijah's instincts told him to step in, to offer comfort to the elderly man, but he pushed that urge aside. Looks, he knew, could be deceptive, and he had no idea what capabilities the old prisoner possessed.

"Help?" the man croaked, disbelief evident in his rough voice. "There is no help. Only the sweet release of death. Will you deliver me, stranger? I am willing. I will not resist."

His chains clinked as he held his hands out in submission, but still, Elijah was wary. So, he asked, "Do you know that you're in a tower?"

"Tower? No. That is impossible. I remember . . . Oh . . . Goddess and her Empire, I remember the Reavers descending upon my village. They took us all. I resisted. I tried to save them. But I was powerless. I lived, even when I should have died. There . . . Th-there is no one else left. Just me . . ."

Elijah considered the cost of the man's endurance. His ordeal had clearly robbed him of the necessary faculties to see the truth of his circumstances. Briefly, Elijah wondered what that meant for when this fragment of his soul returned to the host—if it ever would—but he couldn't afford to ponder such things. Every moment he spent without the shelter of Guise of the Unseen was another opportunity for his enemies to find him. So, as much as he wanted to help the old man see the truth, he simply didn't have the time nor the opportunity.

So, he moved on, asking, "Why did they spare you? What do you do in here?"

The man had already begun to babble about empires, curses, and goddesses, so Elijah had to snap his fingers in front of his face before he looked up. When he did, no recognition was apparent on his face. Clearly, the elderly man's mind was gone.

Deciding to use a familiar tactic, Elijah unslung his pack and retrieved a jug of water. He took a drink, then handed it over. "Drink. It's safe," he prompted.

The old man didn't need any more prodding, and an instant later, he was sputtering under the onslaught of water as he tried to drink too much at once.

Yet, the fact that he spilled more than actually went down his throat didn't seem to deter him one bit. Finally, after emptying the entire jug, the man seemed to remember that Elijah was there, and he narrowed his eyes, asking, "Who are you?"

"My name is Elijah."

"Why are you here?"

"I think you know," Elijah guessed. When the old man didn't offer a response, Elijah went on, "I'm here to kill the lieutenants, and then the Reaver."

Once again, the elderly man's eyes narrowed to slits. Suddenly, he burst into laughter that soon became another coughing fit. This time, Elijah had no trouble ignoring his own helpful nature as the old man muttered, "Kill the All-Devouring Reaver . . . As if . . . Ha!"

"Are you finished? Because if you keep going on like this, the ogres are probably going to come investigate. I'm pretty sure I can take at least a couple of them," Elijah lied. "But you? They'll smash you to bits. Maybe that's what you want. I don't know. But I need your help. A lot of people depend on my success."

"I did that once," the man mused. "Tried to take it all on my shoulders. I could not bear the weight. And . . . I . . . I don't remember much more than that. Is that not odd?"

"That's because you're in a tower."

"Not possible. If this were a tower, and you were a challenger, you would not be alone," he said.

Elijah shrugged. "Maybe I do things a little differently. It doesn't matter, though. Look—these ogres imprisoned you, right? They killed people you cared about, didn't they? Don't you want revenge?"

"Of course."

"Then help me," Elijah urgently insisted. "Give me information and maybe I can make them pay for what they did to you. I could even save you."

"I am beyond saving, and there is no possibility of your success. No—better to just give in and beg for a quick death. No suffering."

"I'll risk it. Tell me about the lieutenants."

"Monsters all. Tuk and Tok are mages, masters of fire and ice, and their domains reflect their chosen elements," the old man stated.

"Domains? They have domains?"

That got the prisoner's attention. "No. The wings of the citadel in which they live and work. Not true Domains. If they were, then you would die even more quickly. I am surprised you know of such things," he said. "Where did you hear of them?"

"Here or there," Elijah answered, already filing away the information. "What about the others?"

It didn't get any better from there. Now that the old man was talking, he was more than willing to give Elijah all the information he could desire. Each lieutenant commanded a separate wing of the citadel. To the north was Tuk, with his fire. Tok—who was apparently Tuk's twin brother or something—commanded frost to the south. Meanwhile, to the east was a dark elf named Tulariel who held dominion over shadow. A high elf named Avasil, who was a master of light, was to the west. Finally, on the next floor up was a domineering ogre who was supposedly the strongest warrior the citadel had to offer. He was known only as the Champion.

The ogre warrior guarded the way to the Reaver who was almost assuredly the final obstacle to conquering the tower. So, even if Elijah found a way to bypass his task to slay the other lieutenants, he would still have to defeat the Champion.

Once the old man had finished his explanation—which Elijah was convinced was the whole reason he existed within the tower—he said, "Now that I've answered your questions, I have a request for you."

"I don't think the keys I stole will work on those—"

"Kill me."

"W-what?"

"Please. Kill me. If it is a tower, then I will be that much closer to having fulfilled my purpose. One day, I will be freed to rejoin myself in the outside world, and I will be all the richer for it. But if it is not a tower, I do not wish to live another day. It is . . . too painful, physically and emotionally. Please . . . I would do it myself, but . . ."

He pulled the chains taut, showing that he only had a few extra inches of movement.

"Why do they keep you here?" Elijah asked.

"I translate texts," the man said. "The . . . Reaver is something of a student of the occult. From time to time, he descends from his perch and requests a translation of some obscure text. Yet another reason I must die. Those . . . books, nothing good can come of them. Fell rituals, soul magic, and daemonic pacts. You mustn't—"

"Real demons? As in the elder race?"

He gave a rasping chuckle. "No. Someone like him, as powerful as he is compared to the likes of us, could never command one of the elders," the man said. "He makes pacts with beings from Alta Terra. The Underrealm. They use that pact as a tether to allow them to traverse the World Tree and enter this realm."

Elijah told the old man that he didn't understand. To that, the prisoner simply shook his head and said, "The universe you know, the one in which we live, is called Mortalum. Above is Pruina, the Ice Fortress, Silvara, the Wilderness, and Aesira, also called the Realm of Sky. Below us is Ignis, Nilfara, The Umbra, and the Etherium. And below even that is the Underrealm, located in the roots of the World Tree. It is there from which the Reaver's demons hail. They are alien creatures with fell powers of corruption, and they can only pass into this realm by virtue of an invitation."

"The pacts you mentioned," Elijah reasoned. It didn't take a genius to make that connection.

The old man nodded. "You will likely never see the other planes," he said. "Few natives of Mortalum do. To even survive, you must become an Ascendent at the very least, though even then, it is dangerous to the extreme. Not that going to the other planes is ever safe. Even for Demigods."

"What about Deities and Transcendents?"

The man snorted. "What do I know about those lofty existences, hmm?" he asked, a little more personality showing through. Was he getting comfortable? Or was it a ruse to get Elijah to do what he wanted?

"Probably more than me," Elijah admitted deprecatingly.

The old man snorted again, but he didn't extend the conversation. A few seconds passed before he asked, "So, will you do it?"

"I . . ."

Suddenly, Elijah was reminded that it wouldn't be his first experience with mercy killing. Not only had he done so while hunting with his father throughout his childhood, but more memorably, he'd killed the panther guardian he'd been incapable of saving. More than once, he'd replayed those events in his mind, and he knew precisely how many mistakes he'd made that day.

But this was different.

He could save the old man. With a few casts of Touch of Nature, Elijah could heal him. Then, he could find some way to free the prisoner from those shackles. He was smart. Resourceful. He could figure it out.

"Don't."

"What?" asked Elijah.

"You cannot free me."

"Why? I've done—"

"If you do, I will kill you," the old man said in a low voice. When he looked up and saw Elijah's puzzled expression, he went on: "Oh—this is not the real me. It is, but these chains, they weaken me. Drain my ethera until there's nothing left. Freed, I would recover, and the beast would take over."

"What beast?"

"One of those demons we were talking about," he said. "I was one of the Reaver's first experiments. His first sacrifice. He offered me up, and with these chains, I was incapable of resisting. The stupid creature never expected to take over a bound body, though. It was restricted and drained, just as I was. He lets it out from time to time, using it to translate demonic rituals. If it was at full strength, I would not be aware during those periods. But now? I know everything it does. I know how it thinks. I know its cravings as my own. The moment these chains are removed, it will take over, and it will wreak havoc on this entire citadel. I am already dead. Finishing the job will be a mercy. It cannot survive without me to anchor it to this plane."

While listening, Elijah had felt his heart sink. He knew what he had to do. Certainly, the old man could be lying. But it didn't seem likely. Besides, Elijah kept reminding himself that killing the man wouldn't be permanent. He was just a sliver of a soul borrowed by the System and thrust into the tower so as to give it authenticity. Or variety. Regardless of the reason, it didn't really matter. The fact was that there was no good reason for Elijah to refuse the man's request.

And there were plenty of reasons to do it.

Except it felt wrong in ways logic and reasoning couldn't touch. For all his life, Elijah had been told killing another person was wrong. So, even with the mitigating factors of the situation, he couldn't help but hesitate.

Sure, he had killed, and often. All those gnomes, goblins, and dwarves had fallen by his hand, and that wasn't even considering the things he'd done in the tower. Yet, there was something entirely different about those, and Elijah was at least honest enough with himself to admit that it was based on the fact that they weren't human.

He closed his eyes and took in a deep breath. When he opened them, he was resolved to do what was necessary. So, he said, "I need you to close your eyes."

The old man looked a little surprised at the request, but then nodded, saying, "I understand."

When the prisoner's eyelids fell, Elijah used Shape of the Predator to adopt the scaled-panther form. Then, because the old man's eyes were closed, it only took a few seconds for him to slip out of combat. The moment he did, he let Guise of the Unseen envelop him. Thus cloaked in the stealth ability, he activated Predator Strike.

He padded into position, his feet silent. The old man clearly didn't hear him. He had no idea what was coming. Once Elijah was behind the man, he cocked his claw back, then swiped across the old prisoner's neck. The blow, which was augmented by Predator Strike, hit so swiftly and with such force that it decapitated the old man.

Even as the prisoner's head fell free, Elijah felt a tiny trickle of experience, telling him that the man was dead.

He let out a reptilian sigh, then noticed that the shackles had unlatched the moment the man died. Seeing that, Elijah wasted no time before gathering the chains, then shifting back to his human form so he could stow them away in his pack.

With that done, he waited a few moments to let his ethera regenerate, then shifted back into his scaled-panther form before once again adopting the Guise of the Unseen. Without another look back, he padded out into the hall and continued on his way. Still, even if he didn't look back, he would never forget the sight of that old man's headless body.

32

A MERCENARY MINDSET

Roman stood on the balcony, his hands clasped behind his back as he stared at the horizon. Below him, the city of Easton spread out for more than a mile. The old wall had been dismantled, and the area surrounding his palace—the former police station—had been meticulously redesigned. The Architects, Builders, and Sculptors had only had time to implement the new plans in an area of about two square blocks, but they covered more ground by the day.

"It truly is amazing how quickly people can work with these new classes," he remarked, careful to measure his words. With his position, he needed to maintain a certain aura of authority, and speaking like a small-town police chief was no longer appropriate. Instead, he struggled to channel a more imperious personality—even when he wasn't in public. He turned to Fiona, the Sorcerer who had become his closest adviser, and asked, "How long until they complete the Royal District?"

The mousy woman's expression didn't change as she answered, "Victor claims that it will be complete at the end of next month."

"And the new wall?" asked Roman, squinting into the distance. The wall in question was located a few miles away, but even from such a distance, it wasn't difficult to see. Roman had approved the plans himself, but it was still hard to believe such a thing was possible. Little more than the foundations had been completed, but when the wall was finished, it would stretch almost three hundred feet into the air and encircle the entire city. Even the outskirts.

"That will take longer," Fiona answered. "Six months. Perhaps a year."

"Unacceptable."

Fiona said, "We're pushing them, but the Arcane Researchers all agree that—"

Roman's glare was enough to send her sputtering to make excuses, and each one angered him even more. His knuckles whitened as his fists tightened, but he refused to shout. He was better than that. He needed to be steady. Strong. Immovable. Otherwise, he couldn't be a proper leader.

So, he listened as Fiona haltingly explained how the complexity of the wall's intended enchantments was slowing down its construction. The true issue was that he was dependent on a bunch of Scholars. Ever since Earth had felt the touch of the World Tree, their mere existence had been a thorn in his side.

In the beginning, his annoyance with their naive choice of archetype was born of simple practicality. When they lived in a world where every day was a struggle to survive, fighters and crafters were exponentially more useful than someone whose skills began and ended with the ability to remember things really well.

That was an intentional oversimplification, but the fact remained that Roman regarded anyone who chose the path of a Scholar as, at best, selfish. At worst, they were cowards. Most of them were idealistic idiots who refused to accept that the world had irrevocably changed and that their priorities should shift, as well.

Even if it was uncomfortable.

Even if it meant they'd have to do the sorts of things they often regarded as barbaric or beneath them.

Of course, Roman was no idiot. He understood the value such people could bring to a society. However, he also knew that, when food and security were in such short supply, Scholars and Researchers were a luxury they couldn't afford to overindulge. So, he'd made a lot of difficult choices. He'd indirectly killed thousands by refusing Scholars entry into Easton. Each one of those deaths weighed heavily on his shoulders, but that was what leadership often was— choosing between a collection of terrible options.

And now, the price of those choices had come due.

It had been months since he'd rescinded the moratorium on allowing new arrivals with Scholar archetypes into the city, and though the population of dedicated academics had grown significantly, few exceptional people had emerged. Some of his advisers had pointed out that some of that was due to the city's reputation. The world was disjointed and disconnected, but there was enough trade between Easton and a few other towns and cities that word of their discriminatory practices against Scholars had spread. Because of that, very few of those people even tried to enter the city anymore, opting for more accepting environments.

As a result, Easton's advancement had suffered, though Roman had some ideas on how to solve that problem. He only needed a little more time before he could implement those plans. In the meantime, they were forced to work with the tools they had on hand, which meant that development on a project like the wall was slow.

Still, Roman hoped it would be worth it, especially considering the resources they'd put into it. He'd lost count of how much etherium they'd spent—not to mention the physical cost of all the labor that had gone into it—to get even this far. And the price would only become more exorbitant before the project was completed.

"It will be worth it, sir," said Fiona. She was his right-hand woman, and as such, she knew him better than anyone else in Easton. Especially since Alyssa had met with her unavoidable fate. "When the wall is finished, we won't have to worry about spontaneous Voxx manifestations anymore. Not to mention that it will keep out the other monsters."

Indeed, even though the second was the traditional purpose of a wall—especially one as formidable as what they were building—the first benefit was the most important. Every week, Roman read reports about those spontaneous manifestations. Voxxian monsters suddenly appearing in people's homes, in businesses, and even in public squares. The city's guardsmen dealt with them as quickly as possible, but rare was the instance where one of the Voxx was killed without taking at least a couple of citizens with it.

"I know. That's why I green-lighted the project," he said, turning away. Then, he looked at his watch and asked, "Where is he? He should be here by now."

"I am," came a voice from nearby.

The moment the sound hit Roman's ear, he had his sword out of the sheath at his waist and three temporary enhancements singing through his body as the weapon sliced through the air. With supernatural control, he halted the blade's path as it touched Trace's throat. The Outlaw didn't flinch.

He knew Roman well enough to trust the Assassin's control. Roman rewarded that trust by only nicking the man's neck. It was a testament to Roman's passive ability Sharpened Blade that even that was possible, given Trace's level and Constitution. The man's Outlaw class was more well-rounded than most, which meant that he could fill a wide variety of roles, though with a trend toward stealth and utility.

That meant that, even though he wasn't as overpowering as people with more focused classes, he was dangerous in almost every situation. He'd proved that on many occasions, and if Roman had his way, he'd continue to do so in service of Easton's best interests.

"Not the welcome I expected," the man said, an air of nonchalance lacing his voice as he pushed the blade away with one finger. He ran that same finger across the tiny cut on his neck, wiping the blood away. Notably, the nick healed only a second later—some ability at work, Roman knew—and Trace grinned as he added, "I thought we were friends."

"I've told you not to sneak up on me," Roman responded. "If you continue to flout my instructions, I will have no choice but to act."

Trace chuckled. "So you keep saying. But then, you keep coming back to me. Some people might consider our relationship a little toxic," he said. "Far be it from me to make that kind of judgment, though."

Roman sheathed his sword a bit more forcefully than he otherwise might have. It was a high-quality weapon—one of the best available in Easton—but it was still only Crude. None of the other weaponsmiths in the city had managed to repeat Carmen's feat of creating a Simple-grade item. It wasn't for lack of trying, either. The highest level of the bunch didn't have Carmen's knack, and the ones who had the knack had yet to attain the necessary techniques. And the couple who had both were lazy, unmotivated, or lacked follow-through.

It was a good reminder that, by definition, most people were mediocre. Even in a world full of magic and wonder, that would remain true.

That, more than anything, made him regret sending Carmen away. However, he knew that she was a ticking time bomb that, if she remained in Easton, would eventually explode. It was only a matter of time before she discovered the truth of what had happened in that tower. He'd taken steps to mitigate the chances that someone would let the cat out of the bag, but Carmen was far too intelligent to fully believe the fabricated explanation for how Alyssa had died. All it would take would be a stray thought before her suspicions would begin to mount. From there, she'd put it all together.

Roman was certain of it.

So, he'd pushed her away from the city in the hopes that the distraction of running the mine would keep her from figuring things out, at least until he was ready to do what was necessary to deal with her.

It would have been easier to simply kill her and everyone who'd been in the tower. However, he hadn't quite reached the point where he'd resort to wanton murder to solve all his problems. Alyssa's death had been necessary. She was too popular. People had already begun to rally behind her. And it was inevitable that, sooner rather than later, they would decide that she'd make for a better leader than Roman.

Never mind that he was the only reason Easton had survived. He'd made all the unpopular choices. He had owned the sacrifices necessary for the city to make it through the events that had killed so many others. Without him, people would have starved. Without him making the hard choices, they would have been incapable of defending themselves. They'd have been weighed down by individual freedoms and freeloaders, and they'd have met a similar fate as dozens of other prospective settlements.

By comparison, Alyssa had set herself up as the hero. The person who leaped into battle, putting her own safety at risk to ensure the survival of others. She was the knight in shining armor who never had to make any of the unpopular choices.

It would've been so much easier if she'd done so out of a desire to undermine him. But Roman knew that wasn't the case. She'd simply acted according to her nature, and she'd never even realized that, whether she wanted it or not, she had set herself against him—at least in the eyes of the people.

The fact that she had often—and publicly—disagreed with him made the entire situation untenable.

But if Roman was honest with himself, he knew that at least part of his decision to remove her was based on her failure to protect Trish. Because of Alyssa's selective incompetence, his wife was gone, and even more than two years later, he still felt the loss so keenly that, when he was alone, his grief sometimes sent him spiraling into a level of depression he couldn't afford to let anyone else see.

Roman bore some responsibility, as well. He should have insisted that Trish stay behind. Up until that point, he'd sheltered her as closely as he was able. But she'd been adamant that she be allowed to do her part, and he had finally acquiesced to her demands. Largely, that decision was based on his trust in Alyssa. She would protect his wife. He'd been so certain of it.

And yet, Trish had died, setting Roman on a path that had ended with him ordering the death of his closest friend.

His only friend, really.

There were plenty of sycophants like Fiona, all scrambling for his approval in a selfish quest for more power and authority. He recognized them for what they were, but he also saw the benefits they could bring. So, he tolerated them. However, none could replace Alyssa, who'd always spoken her mind, even when it put her at odds with him. There was value in that, but it also set a dangerous precedent.

Opposition could not be allowed.

Not yet.

If they were divided, the city would fall. Roman knew that as surely as he'd ever known anything. Which brought him to why he'd summoned Trace to the palace. The man was uniquely qualified to do the job Roman had in mind.

"I have a proposal for you," he said.

"No offense, chief, but I'm not looking to get married," Trace said with the same crooked grin he almost always wore. "Nothing against you. You're great. Very handsome. I'm just not interested in that kind of—"

"Take this seriously," Roman interrupted.

"The world ended. Magic and monsters exist. If you're taking this seriously, you're doing it wrong."

Roman's grip tightened on the hilt of his sword, the threat of which Trace did not miss.

He held up his hands, saying, "Fine. Putting on my serious face. What's up? What do you have for me?"

"Like I said—a proposal. An opportunity. I want you to head up a new division of the government," Roman said. "Your focus will be information gathering and, if necessary, quiet removal of threats to the common good."

The decision had not been lightly made, but Roman felt confident that he'd made the right choice. Not only did Trace's class suit the role perfectly, but he also had a certain moral flexibility that would almost assuredly prove necessary.

Couple that with his connections throughout the city—the man seemed to know every lowlife in Easton—and he became the clear choice.

"That sounds an awful lot like secret police, chief," Trace said. "Not a great track record for those, historically speaking."

Roman didn't dispute that. "I will give you resources," he stated. "You will have top-tier equipment. Good people. Advancement opportunities. And, of course, you will be well compensated."

Trace grinned. "You had me at well compensated."

"That is literally the last thing he said," Fiona pointed out, her first contribution to the conversation.

"And the only thing that mattered," Trace stated. "Look—I'm a simple man. Pay me what I'm worth and I'll do whatever job you've got in mind."

"A true mercenary," Fiona said. "Don't you have any civic pride? Don't you care about the greater good?"

"If the money's right, sure. I can care about all sorts of things if you pay me enough."

"Disgusting."

"Practical."

"Enough," Roman said before the two could further their argument. Then, to Trace, he asked, "You'll take the job?"

"I will. And I promise I'll root out all the bad apples. Every last one," Trace said. "Now, let's talk more about my compensation. I assume there's a bonus for every traitor I find . . ."

33

PUTTING IN THE WORK

As Elijah slipped from one shadow to the next, every exhale brought with it a cloud of mist. The temperature had been falling for a while, and with every step, it had grown ever colder until frost decorated the rough columns on either side of the hall. He glanced up at the vaulted ceilings that had become common in this wing of the citadel, and he saw that small icicles had formed. In addition, when he saw one of the armor-clad ogre guards tromping down the hall, he noticed that the giant creature had donned a fur-lined cloak and heavy gloves.

Elijah felt none of the cold, though. The moment the temperature had begun to drop, he'd found an abandoned room where he'd shifted into his human form and replaced Essence of the Monkey with Ward of the Seasons.

Spell: Ward of the Seasons	Harness the power of the seasons, increasing resistance to elemental damage (Water, Earth, Fire, Air).

The effects were immediate, shielding him from the increasingly frigid temperatures and confirming what he'd already suspected. The frigid cold was magical in nature, so the enhancement had worked as an effective counter.

That boded well for what he knew he would have to do in order to conquer the tower. Still, Elijah needed to scout things out before he made any firm plans. So, he continued on, noting the patrol path of the guards along the way. They were pretty well spaced out, which was a great sign, but he didn't want to act upon the strategy slowly forming in his mind. For now, he was only gathering information.

Gradually, he passed through the halls. Every now and then, he would find branches, and he dedicated one facet of his Quartz Mind to keeping track of the layout as he explored the wing. And over time, Elijah noted the pattern, which roughly resembled a series of concentric hexagons with a circular chamber at the center. Each layer was connected by five larger halls that spread out from the center like spokes of a wheel.

Elijah couldn't enter the room itself, as it was blocked by a thin sheet of ice. He could break through, but doing so would assuredly draw the attention of the large shape—presumably, the ice ogre, Tok—he could just barely make out on the other side. He also noted that the ambient ethera had grown much thicker as he'd drawn closer to the creature's icy domain.

In any case, he couldn't see how to get to the lieutenant without garnering the attention of every ogre in the wing, so he quickly retreated.

Elijah remained in that wing long enough to completely map the layout and the pattern of the guards' patrols before he left it behind and headed to the northern section of the citadel. There, he found that the corridors followed a similar pattern, though instead of increasing cold, the temperatures quickly rose to sweltering levels.

And when Elijah finally reached the presumed lieutenant's chamber, the heat became visible, and the floor beneath his feet grew uncomfortably hot. And given the protection afforded by Ward of the Seasons, that was saying something. Without it, he felt positive that it would've been hot enough to blister, even with his enhanced Constitution. However, just like had been the case with the Tok's domain, visibility into Tuk's chamber was blocked. This time, though, instead of a sheet of ice, a wall of fire obscured his vision.

Fortunately, the layout of the wing was identical to the one dedicated to ice, so once Elijah confirmed that, he focused his attention on other things. The guards in the area had eschewed their armor completely, and they wore similar outfits—if loincloths qualified for that label—to the more rotund jailers back in the dungeon. However, even without the protection the black iron armor provided, they were still formidable foes.

Each one was slick with sweat and obviously miserable, though the fact that they weren't burned, even when they passed by the central chamber, was a testament to their inflated Constitution attribute as well as their fiery nature.

In any case, Elijah noted their patrol paths, then retreated to the milder environment surrounding the old prisoner's corpse. Once there, he commenced planning. The first obstacle was obviously the guards, and each one represented a potentially deadly battle. The troll had struggled with the ones down in the dungeon, but Elijah expected that that was largely due to the fact that it had been outnumbered. So, he reckoned that if he could get each of the guards alone, it would give him the best opportunity to defeat them.

And given that there were twelve such guards in each of the two wings— along with five patrolling his current location—that strategy was probably going to be a lot trickier than it might seem at first glance. Each wing was an expansive maze of corridors, but they weren't so spread out that he could fight a battle without getting the attention of that area's guards.

After giving the problem some thought, Elijah came up with a plan he thought would work. However, the viability depended on the relative intelligence of the ogres. If they were smart, there was no chance of it working. But if they were as dim as his experiences had led him to believe, then he had a chance. Without any other options—that he could think of, at least—Elijah retreated to the cellar, where he took a few minutes to renew the appropriate enhancements before preemptively casting Healing Rain, regenerating his ethera, and then shifting back into his scaled-panther form.

After applying Guise of the Unseen, he climbed the steps and positioned himself just outside the cellar. Once there, he crouched in one of the shadows and waited for his first victim.

Fortunately, there wasn't much of a delay before the steady clink of armor and the heavy clomp of ogre footsteps announced the imminent arrival of one of the patrolling guards. Soon enough, the hulking creature stepped into view, but Elijah remained completely stationary as he waited on his victim to arrive at the appropriate location.

One weighty stomp came after another until, at last, the monster drew even with Elijah's position.

That's when he activated Venom Strike and Predator Strike before he pounced, savaging the unsuspecting ogre's right knee. His claws bit deep between armor plates, ripping through meat and ligaments. The guard let out a shout of surprise and tried to wheel around so it could bring its massive cudgel to bear. By that point, though, Elijah had already darted into the cellar. He didn't descend the steps, but instead, he let out a low growl, just loud enough for the ogre to hear.

As he crouched there, he knew that he'd reached the moment of truth. If the ogre was smart, he would seek help. If he was as dumb as Elijah hoped, then the guard would follow the trail Elijah had left. He had plans for both scenarios, but he certainly preferred the latter. When it came to enemies, dumb was always better than smart.

For a moment, the ogre seemed confused, but then he realized where the growl had originated. Once he did, he wasted no more time before pursuing Elijah into the cellar. Unfortunately, the wound on its leg wasn't nearly as debilitating as Elijah had hoped, so he was caught by surprise by the ogre's rapid arrival.

Still, the time dilation effect of his Sash of the Whirlwind came in handy, allowing him to move just quickly enough to avoid the charging ogre. Even as Elijah bounded away, it became clear that the monster hadn't counted on the presence of steps. Overbalanced, the guard couldn't halt his momentum before clattering down the stairs and into the cellar. That's when Elijah pounced again, clawing and biting a handful of times in quick succession. He didn't care about doing immediate damage. Instead, he wanted to build up instances of Contagion.

For that, fast, shallow cuts were the best. And given his advantages—high Strength and Dexterity, coupled with the effects of his Sash of the Whirlwind— he was capable of moving extremely quickly. Even so, he very nearly pushed his luck too far, and he was forced to narrowly dodge the recovering ogre's backhanded blow.

Elijah raced away, shifting into his caster form before renewing Healing Rain. It drained only a tiny bit of ethera, but with the extra potency provided by his Dragon Core, it could potentially save his life. So, he preferred to keep it active during every fight he could. Once that was done, he turned his attention to the ogre and saw that it'd nearly recovered its feet. Elijah pushed ethera from his Core, through his Soul, and into Snaring Roots. Thick vines erupted from the ground, tangling the ogre's massive feet. It tried to rip free, and it succeeded in tearing through the first wave of roots. However, they were quickly replaced by more.

But even as one facet of his Quartz Mind kept an eye on his enemy, Elijah was pushing more ethera into another spell. Leveling his staff at the ogre, he let loose with Swarm, manifesting hundreds of biting flies that descended upon the ogre. The creature's armor offered little protection against the tiny insects, and soon enough, they slipped beneath the plates and delivered their afflictions.

The ogre bellowed, slapping its meaty hands against its own body in an attempt to smash the little bugs. It got quite a few of them, too. Yet, there were plenty that survived to get the job done.

As the ogre unsuccessfully attempted to deal with the insects, Elijah cast another spell. His ethera was getting low, so he didn't use Calamity or Storm's Fury. Instead, he used Shape of the Guardian to shift into the scaled-ape form, then launched himself at the distracted ogre.

He crashed into the monster in a vicious shoulder tackle before pummeling the prone creature with his fists. Between blows, he snapped out with his powerful jaws, and the sound of rending metal filled the air. It did little good, but Elijah was playing the long game. More evidence of that manifested when the ogre tried to fight back, clawing and punching, but each attack only resulted in painful thorns being embedded in its hands.

Elijah kept up the pressure, knowing good and well that if he let the ogre recover—even for a second—it would spell his doom. So, he continued to punch, bite, and kick—each attack buoyed by his immense Strength. Still, it wasn't until the combined effects of Contagion, Venom Strike, and Swarm had taken hold that Elijah truly started to win the battle.

The ogre's resistance weakened, and its bellowing cries turned into pained moans. And still, Elijah kept on. He didn't grow any stronger as the fight went on, but with the ogre's power being sapped by various afflictions, it certainly seemed like it.

Finally, after a few minutes that felt like hours, Elijah finished the creature off with a mighty bite that crushed the ogre's skull. That didn't kill it. The ogre was too durable for that. But its body went mostly limp, save for a series of uncontrolled spasms. Elijah lashed out again, and he felt more bones crunch beneath the might of his jaws. Still, he didn't feel an influx of kill energy, so he attacked again.

And again after that. In all, it took five more bites before the skull completely shattered like a melon.

A flood of experience washed over him, and as he backed away, he finally let himself relax. The fight had gone almost perfectly, and he had managed to keep the pressure up the entire time. The ogre had never had a chance to regain its balance. Still, it had taken far more damage to put it down than he'd ever expected.

But he'd done it.

That was all that mattered. Now, though, he needed to repeat the process. So, after taking a few minutes to drag the body out of the way—looting a pouch containing a couple of copper etherium as well—he settled down to recover his ethera and center his mind. A little less than an hour later, he headed out to repeat the process.

His next victim went down a little easier, though Elijah took a bit of damage because he stayed in predator form a little too long. Still, the few broken ribs he'd sustained when the ogre caught him with a wild kick were nothing that a little Healing Rain couldn't mend.

However, the third ogre very nearly killed him. Elijah didn't know if it was just a higher level than the others or some other overlooked factor was at play, but it endured his initial barrage without flinching. Then, it ripped through the entanglement of Snaring Roots before Elijah had even finished casting Swarm. So, he'd been forced to dodge while in caster form—a losing strategy if ever there was one. Predictably, he'd taken a hit, but fortunately, because he'd had an entire facet of his Quartz Mind focused on casting Swarm, he managed to complete the spell as he flew across the cellar and hit a cluster of barrels with bone-crushing force.

If Elijah hadn't had Shape of the Guardian ready with another facet of his Mind, he would have died then and there. However, as it happened, he managed to shift into a scaled ape just in time to meet the ogre's charge. It still wasn't ideal, but after that, the stacked afflictions combined with Shield of Brambles and the enhancements of his durable form was enough to tip the balance in his favor.

Even so, it was a long, hard-fought battle that pushed him to his limits. Afterward, he was forced to spend nearly ten hours healing himself before he was ready for the fourth battle. That went much better—in nearly perfect mimicry of the first fight—and Elijah finished it off without issue.

A couple of hours later, he managed to kill the final ogre guard in the area. Doing so pushed him to level thirty-seven, which, on the surface, wasn't nearly as beneficial as it might've once been. However, it put him one step closer to gaining a new ability, which was what he truly considered important at the moment.

Even more importantly, killing that sixth ogre meant that he could now focus on clearing the wings to the north and south. So, once he'd healed from the final battle, he took a few minutes to eat and drink before setting off toward the fire wing.

Hopefully, things would continue to go his way.

34

THAT BURNING SENSATION

The first time Elijah attacked one of the ogre guards in the fire wing, he got quite a surprise when it summoned a fireball and tossed it in his direction. Fortunately, he'd kept one facet of his Mind focused on the monster, so he narrowly managed to leap aside before the ball of flame swallowed him. Still, it represented a serious deviation from what he'd found clearing the first set of guards.

Regardless, the addition of spellcasting ability didn't change his general strategy, so even as his scales smoked from the near miss, he raced through the corridors to his carefully chosen battleground. He reached it after only half a minute, barreling through the door and slipping to the side just in time to avoid yet another arcing fireball. It splashed against the far wall as Elijah shifted into his human form and cocked back his staff.

The moment he caught a hint of the ogre passing through the doorway, Elijah swung his weapon with all the might he could muster. It cracked against the guard's kneecaps hard enough that it would have shattered a lesser staff. However, the Staff of Natural Harmony was a Simple-grade item, and so it was unnaturally durable. Still, to Elijah, it felt like he'd just hit a brick wall, and the impact sent incredibly painful vibrations through his hands and up his forearms.

But the tactic proved its viability when the ogre lost its balance and stumbled through the door. Already off-kilter, the guard couldn't mitigate the effect of Elijah's next attack, which came via a blow across the creature's broad back that sent it into an even more exaggerated stumble. That, in turn, ended with the guard falling flat on its face. Its momentum took it all the way to the far wall.

Elijah leveled his staff at the monster, then cast Snaring Roots. The resulting eruption of vegetation wrapped around the ogre's entire body, encasing it in a cocoon of thorny vines. That was far more effective than if the creature had remained upright because it robbed the ogre of any leverage. Even so, Elijah knew it would only last a few seconds, so he acted quickly, casting Swarm, then Healing Rain in quick succession.

He'd shunted the burning into its own facet of his Mind, so it didn't affect his cognitive abilities. However, he was still very much aware of it, and as a result, he was even more cognizant of the soothing precipitation that healed the damage.

Elijah got his next surprise when he saw that Swarm hadn't summoned the biting flies it had in the previous area. Instead, it had manifested hundreds of glowing orange spiders, each one emitting visible heat. They descended upon the prone ogre, their obviously painful bites sending its struggles to a new level of panic.

But Elijah barely noticed it. Instead, he was already shifting into the Shape of the Guardian. The transformation only took a second, but to his impatient mind, it was still too long. In the previous area, he'd come to enjoy the sense of power he felt in the scaled-ape form, so he was eager to resume that mighty shape.

The moment he felt his body complete its transformation, he loped forward, covering the ground in a couple of hopping steps before he descended upon the panicked and diseased ogre.

However, the moment he reached the creature, he got his second shock when the guard erupted into flames hot enough to burn the vines to ash. Fortunately, the swarm of spiders were clearly resistant to the fire because they were entirely unaffected. Unfortunately, Elijah was very much affected as the flames hit him like an exploding bomb.

Even with Ward of the Seasons active, his scales proved to be little protection against the eruption of fire. All along his front, they melted, but his exposure was blessedly brief as he was quickly tossed backward by a shock wave that sent him on a collision course with the wall on the other side of the room.

He hit with bone-crunching force, but his body held up surprisingly well to the blunt-force impact. Still, when the back of his head hit the stone wall, he saw stars. Whether it was due to his high Constitution or the ongoing effects of Healing Rain, Elijah wasn't sure, but he recovered quickly and picked himself up just in time to see the flaming ogre do the same.

It bellowed a challenge, slapping its chest with one fist. Then, it gave its bald head the same treatment, reminding Elijah of some of the more unhinged boxers he'd seen during his years participating in the sport.

Then it charged, once again taking Elijah by surprise, this time with how quickly it moved. But with the extra time afforded by the Sash of the Whirlwind, Elijah quickly got over his shock and reacted by dodging to the side. The ogre was afflicted with the same issues that affected Elijah when he was under the influence of Shape of the Guardian in that it had plenty of Strength to propel it forward at incredible speed but lacked the Dexterity to control that power, meaning that it had no chance of changing direction.

Or stopping.

The ogre hit the wall headfirst, knocking itself for a loop. It bounced back, then stumbled, shaking its head. That's when Elijah leaped forward, his claws lashing out with all the power he could muster. Fire licked at him as his short, sharp claws gouged into the guard's bare chest. Ward of the Seasons protected Elijah, though, allowing him to continue his attacks against the off-balance creature.

Once. Twice. Then three times. Each attack dug deeper into the ogre's flesh until Elijah felt bone. However, it was at that point that the guard regained its wits, and with extreme and explosive speed, it punched out. Its meaty fist took Elijah in the stomach with an uppercut that launched him toward the ceiling.

In the air, he lacked leverage to affect his own movement, so he could do nothing about his fall toward the ogre's follow-up attack that collided with his toothy snout. Once again, Elijah was sent flying across the room, stopping only when he collided with the wall with even more force than his first meeting with the barrier.

His breath left his lungs in a rush, and it felt like iron bands wrapped around his chest. Fortunately, Healing Rain persisted, soothing his injuries just enough to let him quickly regain his faculties. When he did, he saw something that gave him hope.

The ogre was clearly stronger than the guards he'd previously fought. Probably due to that fiery corona surrounding its body. However, Elijah could also see that the ability was a double-edged sword. Blisters had already begun to spread across the ogre's bare skin, and they were worsening by the second.

That meant that Elijah only had to endure.

That, in turn, meant that he was in for a painful run.

Yet, he didn't shy away. If he could deal with being digested inside an orca's stomach, then he could take whatever the fire ogres could dish out.

In theory.

In practice, the next few minutes were an exercise in torture. The two combatants went back and forth, trading one heavy blow for another. Elijah got in a few hits here and there, but most of the work was done by the still-ongoing afflictions as well as the fire that was the origin of the guard's explosive power.

Without any of his advantages—whether it was Ward of the Seasons, his enhancements, or his inflated Constitution—Elijah would have fallen prey to the ogre's attacks. However, they proved just enough to endure the worst of it until, gradually, the guard wore down. As the creature waned, Elijah's blows landed a little more often until he felt like he was fighting a one-sided battle.

Still, every time he drew close to the ogre, his body erupted into fiery agony.

So, by the time he finally downed the monster, he was drowning in so much pain that he could barely think straight. Still, every second that passed after the ogre's flames winked out, he was healed a little more by Healing Rain. That, along with his Quartz Mind, allowed him to drag himself out of that painful abyss. When he did, he shifted back to his human form and started casting Touch of Nature.

It took a few hours for him to return to normal, but he didn't immediately set off to pull another ogre to his chosen killing field. Instead, he took quite some time trying to center himself. In theory, enduring pain was just about willpower, but every person had limits. Eventually, enough agony would break anyone, and despite the fact that he'd progressed past human limitations, Elijah was no different.

But the more he thought about it, he realized that wasn't entirely true, either. By all rights, he should have been riddled with post-traumatic stress, and yet, once he'd recovered, his mind just skated away from all the worst parts of his ordeal. It had been the same with his time in the first tower, which had been incredibly taxing on his psyche. Now, though, he almost looked back on it with fondness.

Not the part where he'd been eaten alive by a mutant orca. Or when he'd almost lost himself to his feral side. Or when he'd had a chunk of his torso eaten by a giant snapping turtle. Or dozens of other life-and-death situations.

When he looked at it like that, he should have been a mess. And yet, he didn't feel wracked with anxiety. In fact, even now, only a couple of hours after enduring the fire ogre's attacks, he felt positively optimistic. Clearly, there was something else at play, but he had no idea what that might be.

Nor was Elijah terribly concerned with something that seemed helpful. He couldn't afford to deal with the psychological effects of his adventures, so it was probably better that something—likely the System or the cultivation of his Mind and Soul—had dulled it.

In any case, once Elijah had recovered—mentally and physically—he embarked on a painful and necessary quest to exterminate the fire ogres. The second was just as difficult as the first, but over time, he developed a viable strategy. It was a little more dangerous, but he found that using his caster form a little more generously made things much less painful. So long as he continuously cast Snaring Roots, weaving Storm's Fury in, he could remain mostly out of range of the ogres' flames.

Of course, he still made mistakes, and there were plenty of close calls. After those fights, he ended up looking a bit like Freddy Krueger. Fortunately, his healing spells kept him from scarring, but he did lose most of his hair.

More distressingly, he once again ended up naked when his outfit caught fire and burned to a crisp. After that, he stashed his pack in another room before resuming his quest in the nude. After all, he could easily repair his body. His expensive clothes were another story altogether.

By the halfway point, Elijah was more than ready to move on. At first, the pain he'd been forced to endure was counterbalanced by the struggle. However, as it had gotten easier, the process had become an unexciting slog. Or as unexciting as being burned alive ever could be, he reasoned.

Still, he had no choice but to finish it off, and for two reasons. First, he didn't dare fight the lieutenants while any of the guards still lived. He knew each one would strain his capabilities, so he didn't want to complicate matters by adding a few extra ogres to the mix. The second reason was just as practical, and it centered on the influx of kill energy he received with every slain guard. He'd already reached level thirty-seven, and he hoped that, by the time he finished off all the guards—in every wing—he would attain level forty and gain a new spell.

But first, he needed to finish the fire ogres. So, once he'd healed from the latest fight, he took a deep, steadying breath, and got back to work.

35

EVERY TOOL

Icicles hung from the ceiling, and thick frost coated every surface, but Elijah forced himself to ignore the biting cold as he raced through the corridor as quickly as he could manage. Behind him, two hulking ogres, both covered in icy spikes, followed with deceptive speed. Each stride of their long legs ate quite a bit of distance, and they had the Strength to propel their massive bodies forward with alarming alacrity. Still, Elijah narrowly outpaced them.

But he had no idea what to do next.

Two facets of his Mind whirled with one idea after another as he searched for some way to salvage the situation, but there were no clever tricks to be found. Especially when he turned a corner and ran headlong into two more icy ogres that should not have been there.

He ducked, sliding across the ice-slick floor as he avoided a similarly frost-coated axe as it descended on the spot he'd just vacated. It sent shards of ice flying, but by that point, Elijah was already leaping high into the air.

But not high enough.

Thinking quickly, he used Venom Strike before raking his claws across the face of yet another ice ogre. As it reeled back in pain, Elijah kicked off the creature's shoulder, bounded off the wall, then hit the ground running. The whole maneuver had only delayed him for a little more than a second, but even that was enough to give the pursuing ogres the chance to catch up. Fortunately, they hadn't expected to run into their fellows, either, and as a result, one pair collided with another, resulting in a tangled scrum of hulking monsters.

That was the opportunity Elijah had been waiting for.

He dug his claws into the floor, grinding to a stop. The instant his momentum had been arrested, he whipped around, shifting back to his human form. Even as his body morphed, he threw out his staff and shoved ethera into Calamity. He released it only a moment later, and the fury of nature descended upon the fallen ogres.

Lightning cracked. Thunder rolled. And the ground was rent asunder, ripping through the prone monsters without mercy. However, Elijah paid little attention to that. Instead, he was already casting a second spell. As he forced ethera into Swarm, hundreds of crystalline rats formed from the ice on the walls, then scurried forward to fall on the reeling ogres.

Even then, Elijah wasn't finished casting.

With the influx of levels as well as his advancement in cultivation, his Core had grown quite a bit larger than it had been in the beginning. That translated into the ability to cast more spells before he ran dry. So, he had plenty of fuel to use in the attempt to salvage the situation his carelessness had foisted upon him.

So, he channeled Storm's Fury through his staff, sending a thick bolt of lightning out to join the storm summoned by Calamity. It struck the closest ogre directly in the upturned face, sending a powerful electrical current arcing through the massive creature's body.

But it didn't stop there.

Because it was touching all the other ogres—who were conveniently clad in ice-covered iron, which made for a great conductor—the electrical current flowed from one to the other, effectively extending the single cast to four targets.

So, seeing how effective it was, Elijah cast it again. Then, he went for a third cast, but by that point, he knew he was pushing his luck as well as his Core's capacity. So, he stepped forward, cocked his staff back, and used Venom Strike before hitting the closest ogre in the face. The staff took the creature in the jaw, and Elijah was rewarded by the sound of breaking bones—or cracking ice, perhaps. More importantly, he delivered the neurotoxin of Venom Strike.

Ability: Venom Strike	Imbues an attack with a fast-acting neurotoxin. Usable in all forms. Damage doubled when in predator form.

He used it again before hitting the next closest ogre. However, the moment he connected, his good fortune truly did run out, and the first monster caught him with a wild backhand that sent him stumbling into the frosty wall. Elijah quickly recovered, but by that point, Calamity had ended, and despite the afflictions Swarm had delivered, the ogres had begun to pick themselves up from the floor.

That was when Elijah decided to once again run.

This time, though, he didn't switch into his predator form. Because he had an idea. Dashing to the end of the hall, he turned around to see that the first ogre had climbed to its feet. It stumbled forward in pursuit of Elijah, but its body lacked the Strength it had once possessed.

Elijah waited.

The next ogre found its feet, too. Then, the third. Finally, the fourth lurched upright. By that point, the first creature had reached the halfway point, but still, Elijah held his ground.

Just before the last monster resumed its own pursuit, Elijah cast Snaring Roots. The prickly vines exploded from the ground, eagerly wrapping around the already-weakened ogre's legs. For a moment, it looked confused that its legs wouldn't move, and then, it tipped back over. The vines continued to snake out, wrapping the ogre in a prone cocoon, but Elijah didn't stick around to watch.

Now that he'd slowed one down, he needed to run.

So, he took off down the corridor, turning down paths he'd memorized. The ogres followed. Although, because they were fighting the afflictions of Swarm as well as the neurotoxin of Venom Strike, their steps were slow and plodding. Due to that, Elijah easily managed to outpace them.

So, after a few more minutes dedicated to racing through the halls, he finally felt Essence of the Wolf take effect. When it did, he didn't hesitate to shift into his predator form, then adopt Guise of the Unseen. However, he didn't stop. Instead, he padded forward with as much speed as he could muster, then slipped into one of the empty side rooms.

It was just in time, too, because the first ogre thundered past the entrance only a second later, completely oblivious that it'd lost Elijah's trail. Even so, he didn't relax. That was what had nearly gotten him killed the first time.

But in his defense, how was he supposed to know that the ogres would be able to detect him? He still didn't even know what had prompted their discovery. One second, he'd been sneaking along as he searched for a way to separate them and kill them one by one, and the next, one of the huge creatures had wheeled around and aimed a herculean kick in his direction. It was only due to his faceted Mind that he had seen it coming and managed to leap aside.

What had followed was a desperate chase through the corridors that had mercifully just ended. But Elijah wasn't finished. Throughout his flight through the halls, one facet of his Mind had been working overtime trying to come up with a plan to make the best of the situation, and through some good fortune and quick thinking, he'd managed to engineer just such a chance.

Now, he needed to follow through.

So, after the second and third ogres rushed past, he crept out and sprinted down the hall to where he hoped to find the final ogre he'd bound with Snaring Roots. Only a few moments later, he got his wish when he nearly ran into the creature. Without hesitation, Elijah leaped, opened his mouth wide, and used Predator Strike before clamping down on the monster's head.

The ogre was wholly unprepared for the attack, and weakened as it was, the creature had little chance of stopping the forceful bite. Elijah flexed his jaw, and his teeth bit deep. When he yanked away, a chunk of flesh and bone came with him. The ogre lurched out of control, then crashed into the wall.

Elijah bounded free, then darted back in to slash his claws across the creature's hamstrings. Then, he repeated the motion on the ogre's ankles. The huge monster tumbled to the floor, cracking the ice along the way. In a panic, the ogre activated an ability that sent spikes of ice erupting from the ground, but they were unfocused and too slow to catch Elijah.

He dodged around them, then leaped on the ogre's back. Digging his claws between the plates of armor, he once again reared back, then struck forward with snapping jaws that tore another chunk from the base of the creature's skull. Knowing what was about to happen, he repeated the action, though this time, he didn't let go or try to tear free. Instead, he latched on with everything he could muster.

That's when the ogre managed to push itself to its knees, then launch itself backward, slamming Elijah against the wall. Still, he didn't let go. Even as he felt his bones creak under the impact, he raked his claws across the monster's back, digging deep even as he continued to apply pressure on the ogre's skull.

Letting out a hiss of mingled pain and fury, Elijah tapped into a well of well-earned willpower, and he was rewarded a moment later with the sound of a skull cracking. A second later, brains and plasma squirted into his mouth as the creature finally succumbed to its many injuries.

It collapsed, pinning Elijah against the wall so thoroughly that he was forced to switch into his guardian form to push it out of the way. After finally winning free, Elijah switched back to his caster form and ran back the way he'd come. As he did so, he channeled Touch of Nature in an attempt to heal his aching bones. He didn't think he'd broken anything, but it was close enough that he knew that ignoring the injuries would be a mistake.

His bare feet slapped against the icy floor, though he barely felt the cold. Ward of the Seasons, which had taken the place of Essence of the Monkey, had proved invaluable. Once, he'd considered the enhancement to be mostly useless because it did nothing to block the weather. However, in the ethera-induced cold of the citadel's ice and fire wings, it had become one of his most important spells.

He quickly found his way to another side room—they were all empty, and it felt almost like they'd been included more to make the citadel seem like a real place than to serve an actual purpose—where he settled into a corner and continued his healing. Fortunately, his injuries were minor compared to some of the damage he'd been forced to endure in the past, so it wasn't long before he was back to perfect condition.

As soon as he'd recovered his ethera, Elijah shifted back into his predator form, then set off through the corridors. After all, he still had quite a few ogres to hunt. Three of them were already wounded, and he hoped to take care of them first. However, he knew he couldn't afford to be picky. So, he stalked through the halls until, at last, he found his next victim.

As it turned out, the ogre was not one of the ones he'd already fought.

What followed was a systematic dismantling of the force of ogres manning the frost wing of the citadel. Elijah was ruthless as he slowly picked them apart using similar tactics to the plans he'd employed in the fire wing. However, unlike the fire ogres, the ice ogres' abilities tended more toward defense than doing extra damage, which played right into Elijah's hands.

So long as he only fought one at a time—which wasn't easy to arrange—the ogres couldn't do much to harm him while in guardian form. Of course, that also meant that each battle was a long, drawn-out affair where Elijah was forced to use every source of damage he could muster, including Shield of Brambles. Still, it was the safest way to proceed.

Ironically, the quickest way to deal with the ice ogres was in his human form, when he could chain cast his spells. However, it was simultaneously the most dangerous as well as the least efficient. Each battle he tried to fight in that manner left his Core completely drained, and the margin for error was slim enough that if he made even the slightest mistake, he'd end up splattered against the wall.

Somewhere in the middle was his scaled-panther form. Each fight began with him using Predator Strike and Venom Strike, but after that, he usually switched to one of his other forms for the rest of the battle. However, for a couple, he remained in his predator form, which proved to be effective but ultimately exhausting. It was also nearly as dangerous as fighting in his human form.

But he knew it was important to familiarize himself with all the tools at his disposal, so he focused on making each form work in his favor. In that way, he slowly whittled the ogres down, one by one, until he finally killed the last ice ogre in the wing.

That last kill came in his guardian form, when he repeatedly slammed a weakened ogre's head against a wall until it finally succumbed to all the damage he'd inflicted.

He sagged against the wall, his hissing breath coming in ragged gasps. He'd pushed himself incredibly hard, and as a result, he'd managed to not only clear the last of the ogres from the wing, but he'd also progressed to level thirty-nine. One more, and he'd get a new spell.

But now he had a decision to make. Would he challenge the two lieutenants? Or would he assault the next two wings? The remaining two wings were located up a set of stairs, so they were isolated from his current position. That also suggested that the two elves—one of light, and the other of shadow—were slightly above the ogres in the citadel's hierarchy.

In turn, that probably meant that their guards were a little more dangerous.

In the end, it came down to one simple fact—he wanted to be at his best when he fought the lieutenants, so that meant he needed to gain at least another level. And that, in turn, made his choice clear.

He needed to clear the other wings first, and then he could assault the lieutenants. Hopefully, whatever spell he gained at level forty would be enough to catapult him to victory.

36

LIGHT AND SHADOW

Stay on your side, fiend!" bellowed the blond elf. As he spoke, he brandished a long, slim sword that glinted in the flickering firelight. "If you cross, we will be forced to take action!"

The dark elf planted her hands on her hips and sneered, "You haven't the power to threaten me, cur."

"Call me cur once again and I shall—"

"Cur," she purred. "Filthy. Mangy. Obedient. Dog."

The blond elf's face screwed up in a rictus of anger, and he took a step forward. However, he stopped just before he stepped across the silver line cutting across the floor and dividing the chamber into two halves. Instead, he spat, "The Queen of Light shall hear of this, shadow!"

The dark-elf woman spread her arms out wide and bowed as she replied, "By all means, tell your decrepit mistress that you are a mangy cur. I shall back up the claim, should she seek a confirmation."

"You . . ."

Elijah backed away, having seen enough of the exchange. It wasn't the first time the two had traded insults, and he suspected it would not be the last, either. During his previous reconnaissance, he'd discovered a few key things. First, there was quite a lot of animosity between the two sets of elves. He had no idea if that was indicative of the rest of the universe, but high elves and dark elves very much hated one another.

Second, the two sides simply refused to pass from one wing to the other, instead rigidly remaining in their respective territories. The exchanges he'd overheard seemed to suggest that bad things would happen to whoever crossed that line, though he'd yet to discover what form those repercussions might take.

And finally, he had absolutely zero chance of using his previous strategy to take care of the two forces patrolling the light and shadow wings. For one, there were just too many elves, and each one was armed and armored and felt far more powerful than the ogres Elijah had killed. For another, he strongly suspected that any hostile actions would have both sides bearing down on him, and with unknown abilities.

No—he needed a different strategy, so he'd spent much of the past eight hours reconnoitering the area. During that time, the seeds of a proper plan had begun to take root, and Elijah felt that it would only take a bit of cultivation—the mundane sort—to create an opportunity to destroy all the elves in one go.

He'd probably lose out on some progress, but if things went right, he wouldn't be in nearly as much danger as he'd encountered while fighting the ogres.

But first, Elijah needed the right opportunity. So, as he waited, he continued to explore the wings. Cloaked in Guise of the Unseen, he could come and go as he pleased. Neither the light nor dark elves seemed capable of detecting him. If they could, he would've long since gotten their attention.

As he explored, he came to appreciate the mirrored decor. The shadow side was decorated all in black, with silver accents to give it shape. Meanwhile, the light wing was the opposite, with white stone and tiles featuring gold accents. It made for an interesting study in contrasts, and an aesthetic that Elijah could very much appreciate.

Still, the two wings were not without hidden dangers. In addition to the guards—which were ubiquitous—both wings featured themed traps. In the dark side, that meant shadows that often weren't shadows at all, but instead deep holes that ended in jagged spikes. The other wing had corridors criss-crossed with beams of light that Elijah suspected were capable of cutting a person in two.

Both obstacles made traversal of the wings in question an extraordinary pain, and keeping himself from falling afoul of those traps had definitely kept Elijah on his toes. Still, his impatience to progress and gain enough kill energy to get level forty had almost gotten him killed a couple of times. Only his copious experience had kept him from making deadly mistakes.

However, now that Elijah knew the dangers, he could avoid them easily enough. The biggest issue was that he was forced to go against his instincts and avoid the shadows. Fortunately, Guise of the Unseen as well as his chameleon-like natural camouflage was enough to help him avoid detection.

Otherwise, he found the chambers housing the two lieutenants, both of which were hidden by their native elements. For the shadow lieutenant Tulariel, that meant deep, impenetrable darkness. The light lieutenant was hidden by a sheet of white light. As usual, Elijah didn't dare cross the thresholds for fear of alerting the lieutenants as well as their underlings. With that suspicion in mind, Elijah knew he needed to take care of the guards before he engaged the lieutenants that were the subject of his task.

Eventually, he found himself following a lone dark elf as he approached the chamber at the center of the two wings. As normal, his patrol coincided with that of one of the light elves, and the pair commenced with their banter.

Elijah ignored it, instead waiting for the perfect time to implement his plan.

* * *

Par seethed at the mere sight of the uppity elven woman on the opposite side of the Sacred Line. She wore a contemptuous expression, and though that wasn't uncommon, it still set Par's blood to boiling. How dare she look at him like that? He had half a mind to leap across the line and show her the error of her ways.

And then, he would teach her the meaning of respect. By the time he was finished, she would be begging him for the mercy of death. He wouldn't give it, though. Instead, he would keep her as a pet. A broken warning for anyone who dared to berate the servants of the one true mistress.

Oh, yes. She would make quite the example.

That pretty little fantasy comforted him right up until he heard the elven woman speak. And then reality came crashing down on him when he realized that he was powerless to do anything about her impudence. The Sacred Line existed for a reason, and to cross it was to surrender to death. Par was angry. Furious, really. However, he was not stupid, and he knew better than to give in to his instincts.

He wasn't one of those fat ogres downstairs, after all.

He could think, and more importantly, he was more than capable of self-restraint. However, the little light elf was trying his patience with every moment she remained among the living.

"I thought I smelled something awful," she said, wrinkling her perfect nose. "Clearly, His Dark Reverence prefers unclean lackeys. Unsurprising, given his own proclivities."

Par clenched his fists in fury. "Your petty insults have no effect on me, wench."

"Insults? Nay! I merely worry for your hygiene, cousin," she said. "It is unsanitary to walk around in such a state. Unseemly, as well. Think of how your filth reflects upon your master's reputation. Though I suppose if he was worried for such things, he would not have set down his own path of decrepitude. Such a shame, for I hear he was once quite handsome. Now, though . . . Well, to say that it is a great loss is an understatement. Still, he has my pity, cousin. As do you."

"My master is—"

"You could convert," she said brightly. "Come to the light, cousin. We would welcome you with open arms. After a shower, of course. We wouldn't want your filth to spread."

"You are filthy!" he shouted.

"Such a pointed rejoinder. Surely, your wit knows no bounds."

Par stepped forward, coming right up to the Sacred Line. But he didn't dare cross. Not until his master completed his cultivation and decided to take the citadel for his own. When he did, not only would the blasphemous light elves fall, but so would that monstrous champion. The Reaver himself would find himself writhing beneath Tulariel's boot. The master of the citadel would beg for mercy, and yet, it would not be granted.

Because the Dark One was not merciful. Nor was he cruel. He was simply unstoppable. Irresistible. He would one day rule the world. And after that, the universe. Eventually, he would go to the Abyss and challenge the Ravener himself for dominance. Par was so certain of it that he couldn't keep a smile from spreading across his dark face.

"Do you crave insults, then? Enjoy them, do you?" sneered the blonde elf from only a few feet away. "If so, you will—"

"Prattle on, little elf. I know that my master will soon tear your entrails from your body and hold you up as an example of what happens when you follow the wrong path. You will be powerless to stop it. You will beg and plead, but it will do no good. When the master is finished with you, he will put a stop to your disgusting mistress's misdeeds. She will bow before him, or she will die like everyone else who has ever challenged my master. That, I promise, cousin."

She looked as if she was about to respond, but she clearly thought better of it. Instead, she stamped her foot, let out a huff, and turned on her heel before striding away. Par was just feeling a sense of triumph when he felt something grab him around the waist. He didn't even have time to react before he found himself sailing through the air.

Par windmilled his arms as he flew across the Sacred Line, only to collide with the retreating light-elf woman. The pair of slender armored figures clattered to the floor in a tangled heap. Before Par could extract himself, panic set in.

He had crossed the line.

His heart beat out of his chest as that terrifying realization took hold. He had done the unthinkable, putting himself at the mercy of the light elves. Panicked, he struggled to free himself and retreat, but he could not accomplish that feat before he felt a viselike grip around his throat. Fiery pain erupted from the light elf's touch, and an outraged shout tore free from her perfect lips.

"You dare?!"

"I didn't mean—"

He could choke out no further words because her grip tightened even farther. More, he felt the strength draining from his body. That was why no one crossed the line. To do so was to put oneself at the mercy of the enemy. For every second he remained on the wrong side, he would grow weaker until nothing but a husk remained.

The light elf was going to kill him far before that, though. He barely had an opportunity to wonder what had thrown him across the Sacred Line before the pain overtook all rational thought. However, he did catch sight of a pair of emerald eyes glinting from within the shadows of the connected hall.

* * *

Elijah watched as the dark elf died. He'd barely managed to retreat into the relative safety of the corridor before the two elves had collided, and it had been just in time to avoid the light elf's searching gaze. Now that the dark elf was dead, though, Elijah found himself once again nestled within the concealing embrace of Guise of the Unseen.

The attack—which had been undertaken in his guardian form—had gone off without a hitch, and though he'd hoped for a longer fight, the results were acceptable. The light elf pushed herself to her feet and, for a long moment, stared down at the withered elf in confusion. Clearly, she was having trouble figuring out why he'd seemingly thrown himself at her.

She was in the middle of trying to make sense of it all when the next part of Elijah's plan commenced, and a pair of dark elves rounded the corridor's corner and caught sight of the scene.

They erupted into motion a second later, charging into the chamber and demanding answers. The light elf tried to explain, but the pair were having none of it. Without any further delay, the pair launched themselves across the line, grabbed the light elf, and dragged her back to their side. They hadn't stayed long enough for the drain to take effect.

The light elf struggled. She screamed. But just as the dark elf had been weakened by being on the other side, so too was she diminished by the darkness. That, combined with the fact that she was outnumbered, sealed her doom.

Elijah watched as the elf's screams drew more attention, and from both sides. Soon enough, two dozen light elves faced off against just as many dark elves. They screamed insults at one another, each more disgusting than the last. And yet, they restrained themselves.

At first.

Soon enough, though, the insults reached a crescendo, and an enraged light elf screamed bloody murder before launching himself across the line. His fellows followed, and the silver line dividing the two halves of the chamber shattered into a thousand splinters. After that, the fight descended into a bloody melee that provided the perfect backdrop for Elijah to work his magic.

Still in the shadowy corridor, he shifted into his human form and cast two spells in quick succession. First came Swarm, summoning a flock of bats that descended upon the warring elves. Each bite delivered a powerful affliction that would hasten their demise. Meanwhile, Elijah cast Calamity, as well, adding to the chaos and delivering plenty of punishment all its own. The wind whipped into a frenzy, sending blades of air arcing through the mass of warriors, and lightning split the sky, electrocuting the unsuspecting elves.

Even as the two spells wreaked havoc upon the warriors, Elijah slipped back into his predator form, then retreated until he left combat. Then, he embraced Guise of the Unseen and returned to the impromptu battlefield. There, he saw the fruits of his labor. More than half the elves had already died, and the battle was still going strong.

Idly, he marveled at how little of a spark it had taken to set everything ablaze. The elves clearly hated one another, and it hadn't taken much to send them into a battle lust. Still, Elijah knew that it wouldn't be enough. Some would survive, and he'd have to finish the job himself.

Gradually, the battle wore on, but Elijah didn't act until only one survivor remained. For the normally slim dark elves, he was quite bulky, and his armor was stained with fresh blood. He jammed his sword into a prone light elf, using the blade to support his weight. Then, he let out a wheezing cackle of mingled incredulity and relief.

He was so occupied that he never even noticed Elijah's approach.

However, he couldn't ignore it when the Druid leaped upon his back, dug his claws in, and clamped his jaws down on the base of his skull. The dark elf tried to react, but he was so weakened that the force of Elijah's bite was enough to burst his skull. He fell dead without any further struggle, and Elijah leaped free, landing nimbly among the corpses.

He'd had a hand in killing each and every one of them, and yet, he'd struck only one killing blow. Still, he'd managed to accomplish his goals—to clear the wings while gaining enough experience to progress to level forty—and that was what was truly important.

Standing over the corpses of his enemies, he let himself return to his human form. Then, he inspected the results of his progression. He'd gained a new ability, and he was eager to inspect it.

Ability: **Iron Scales**	**Harden your scales, temporarily reducing all damage by 90%. Effectiveness dependent on relative Constitution versus the attacker's Strength for physical attacks and Ethera for magical attacks. Usable in guardian form. Duration dependent on Constitution. Current Duration: 4.2 seconds.**

Elijah read the ability's description with some degree of relief. He'd been a little afraid that he'd gain another enhancement. And while the increases to his attributes were helpful, they were not impactful enough to change a battle by themselves. However, if it worked the way he expected it to, Iron Scales was precisely what he thought he'd need in the coming battles.

37

OF TWO MINDS

Ice tickled the pads of Elijah's feet as he stalked through the frost wing. On the surface, it looked little different than when he'd left it behind the first time. However, the halls had grown even colder than before, and as a result, the ice coating the walls had thickened. The same escalation had been present in the fire wing, though he'd not investigated it very thoroughly because he intended to target the frost lieutenant first.

With that in mind, he'd set off through the worsening conditions, quickly finding the doorway that would lead to the lieutenant's chamber. He'd checked it before, so he knew that the door led to a long, twisting hall that terminated in a thin and obscuring sheet of ice. Before, he'd only given it a cursory inspection so he could verify the lieutenant's location before turning back, so he knew the way.

However, when he finally reached the lieutenant's quarters, he discovered that the ice sheet that had once guarded the entrance was gone. And the moment he saw inside the chamber, he got quite a shock.

Before, he'd only caught a glimpse of the lieutenant's blurry silhouette, and once he had confirmed that he was looking at another ogre, he'd turned back. However, now, in the blazing firelight, he could see that the creature was differentiated from the other ogres by one key characteristic.

It had two heads sitting atop its broad shoulders.

One was ice blue, while the other was a deep crimson.

It wasn't until he looked across the room and saw the telltale glow of overheated stone that he realized what was going on. The twin lieutenants, Tuk and Tok, shared a body. Elijah had no idea how that was supposed to work, but he was fairly sure that was what was going on. Still, he took the time to retrace his steps, return to the fire wing, and follow the mirrored path that eventually led back to the same chamber.

And the two-headed ogre that sat in what looked like a study.

The bulky creature was at least twelve feet tall, and its body type was somewhere between that of the guards and jailers. However, it was hidden beneath heavy purple robes that concealed more than they revealed.

Leaning against the wall near where the ogre sat was a metallic staff etched with swirling lines that glowed slightly. One half was blue, while the other was orange.

The study itself was exactly what Elijah would have suspected, with one wall dedicated to bookshelves that were packed full of huge, dusty tomes. The two-headed ogre sat in an oversize leather chair, with its—or their, perhaps—feet propped on an equally large ottoman. In one hand was a mug of something steaming, while in the other, it held one of the large tomes.

It looked almost peaceful, at least insofar as a twelve-foot monster with two heads could.

"Turn page. Done reading," barked one head.

"Not done yet. You not read whole thing."

"I skim. Read it before."

"You not read before."

"How you know?"

"I know."

"You stupid."

"You stupid!"

Suddenly, a massive hand slapped against the fire head. Tuk, unless Elijah was mistaken. Then, the other hand hit Tok in the face. After that, Elijah lost track of what was going on. It was an odd thing, watching a two-headed ogre punch and slap itself in the face. Odder still was when the faces started biting back.

Clearly, the pair of ogres didn't much care for one another.

More importantly, Elijah couldn't resist the opening he'd been afforded. So, he crept forward, activating both Venom Strike and Predator Strike along the way. He'd checked his enhancements before he'd entered the room, so he was entirely prepared for battle. Having no reason to delay—and every reason to attack while he had the advantage of a distraction—he pounced as soon as he was in range.

However, he didn't bother with the hobbling attacks he so often employed. Instead, he went in for the kill shot. Leaping high into the air, he opened his mouth as wide as it could go, then clamped down on Tuk's head. Then, harnessing every muscle in his powerful jaw, he squeezed.

With his cultivation, the natural biting power of the scaled-panther form, and the inflated attributes that came with Shape of the Predator, Elijah could bring quite a bit of force to bear. And it was downright terrifying when he used Predator Strike at the same time.

He used the full extent of that horrifying might to absolutely crush the first ogre's head between his jaws. Then, he was bounding away before the other head even had a chance to react.

Or so Elijah thought.

A giant shard of ice hit him midair, scraping across his scales and sending him spinning until he collided with the bookshelf. Even as a cascade of tomes fell upon him, Tok bellowed, "Brother! Argh!"

Elijah shot to his feet, feeling more than a twinge of pain in his side as the books rolled off of him. He rose just in time to see Tok stamp his foot on the ground, causing a series of icy stalagmites to erupt from the ground. Tiles shattered, sending an explosion of frost-rimmed stone flying across the room. Elijah turned, tucking his head as he was pelted with hundreds of shards. But his scales protected him from the incidental damage.

However, he had to bound out of the way in order to avoid the deadly spikes of ice. He narrowly dodged the spell, but he was sent crashing into the wall a second later by yet another flying icicle.

"You kill Tuk!"

Elijah had felt his shoulder pop out of socket upon impact, but he was otherwise in fighting shape. However, he knew he couldn't remain in his predator form. His speed was insufficient to completely dodge the flying ice spikes, and his defenses were incapable of standing up to the inevitable damage he would sustain.

So, he shifted.

But he didn't take on his guardian form. Instead, he resumed his caster shape, leveling his staff at the panicked ogre before he'd even completed the transformation. He let loose with Storm's Fury. The ogre was clearly surprised because it remained completely motionless as the lightning bolt tore across the room and hit it square in the chest.

The smell of burning flesh filled the air as the ogre was thrown from its feet. It didn't go far before hitting the ground on its back, but it was enough to give Elijah the opportunity to cast his next spell. Thorny vines burst from the ground, rapidly wrapping the ogre in writhing roots. The ogre wasn't nearly as strong as the guards had been—apparently, its casting abilities had come at the expense of some Strength—so it struggled to escape the thorny bonds.

After casting Healing Rain, Elijah ran forward, using Venom Strike along the way, and brought his staff down on the prone ogre's face. The creature's nose exploded into a bloody ruin, but more importantly, Elijah delivered yet another instance of neurotoxin. He used it again, and again after that—he wasn't worried about inflicting immediate damage. Rather, he only wanted to stack as much neurotoxin as he could.

Meanwhile, the soothing rain went to work on his injuries even as he whaled on the fallen monster. With one facet of his Mind, he kept track of how much time had passed, and just before Snaring Roots was scheduled to run its course, he leaped backward, casting Swarm along the way.

By that point, his stores of ethera had dipped past the halfway point, so he chose to use some of that to shift into his guardian form. The rest he would keep in reserve for an emergency.

As Elijah took on the shape of a scaled ape, the ogre was beset by frost spiders. Each bite delivered yet more venomous damage, and though the creature had escaped the bonds of Snaring Roots, it was completely incapable of stopping the swarm of spiders. Its panic gave Elijah plenty of time to finish his transformation, and by the time he loped forward, the creature was in sorry shape, indeed.

But the ogre was anything but defeated, as he proved a moment later when he raised his staff high into the air and shouted, "Blizz-ard!"

Immediately, the air temperature plummeted well past freezing. Despite Ward of the Seasons, Elijah felt the icy cold down to his very bones. In fact, he could feel it sapping his strength with every second. And that was before the swirl of snow and ice began. The whirlwind cut through Elijah with frigid fury, but the combination of his high Constitution and powerful enhancements was just enough to keep him on his feet.

He loped forward, hitting the ogre with a shoulder tackle that drove the creature to the floor. Elijah heard a sharp exhale of rushing air leave the ogre's chest, and he knew he had only a handful of moments to finish the fight. So, he raised his hands high and channeled his inner ape as he brought his fists down like hammers. He didn't pay much attention to precision. Instead, Elijah only cared about harnessing as much of his Strength as possible as he repeatedly pummeled the monster into submission.

The first few attacks were absorbed by the creature's copious flesh, but Elijah kept on until he felt bones crack beneath his balled fists. He kept going, knowing good and well that if he didn't keep the pressure up, the ogre would recover. Meanwhile, the frigid cold continued to assail him, threatening to undermine his vigor and vitality until the ogre could turn the tables. Elijah refused to let that happen.

So, he gave himself over to the fury, letting it consume one facet of his Quartz Mind. He focused on that, leaving the rest to other tasks. Like pulling him back before he let the animalistic rage completely overwhelm him. He'd come close before—in a different way back in the Primordial Jungle, but it was similar enough that he knew precisely how dangerous his feral instincts could be—and he refused to let it happen again.

Fortunately, with eight facets of his Mind on the job, he felt secure enough to give one over to the ferocious instincts that came with the guardian form.

Bones crunched, and organs burst beneath Elijah's fists. He knew it wasn't his sheer Strength at work. The creature had already been weakened by Swarm's afflictions, the neurotoxin of repeated instances of Venom Strike, and the gaping wound where its brother's head had once been. Still, Elijah was surprised at how easily the monster succumbed to his onslaught.

But he knew it was a little misleading.

Most people wouldn't have the protection of Ward of the Seasons, and he could feel that, without that enhancement, he would have already fallen to the intense cold. In addition, he had the advantage of versatility as well as his cultivation—including the powerful Dragon Core—on his side. With that providing context, his victory should not have been a surprise.

And yet, it was.

Elijah pummeled the monster until, at last, it perished. The icy storm persisted for a few moments after that, but it quickly dissipated. A second later, the ice it left behind started to melt.

Seeing that, Elijah picked himself up and watched as the storm continued to fade. The study was a mess, and most of the books had been completely destroyed. However, a few of them had managed to survive, so after resuming his human form, Elijah crossed the room and gathered them. In his hands, the tomes were absolutely enormous, and worse, they were in a language he could not understand. Evidently, the universal translation that had come with the System didn't include the written word.

"Or maybe just not this writing," he muttered to himself. It was the first time he'd spoken since killing the old prisoner. "God," he continued, running his hand along his scalp. "I really need some company for this kind of thing."

Indeed, the constant solitude had begun to wear on him, and he hadn't realized how much it had affected him until he'd met with the old man. In retrospect, it wasn't surprising. People were social animals, after all, and even the most solitary person needed some human contact.

Maybe he should have invited Jess along. If she'd seen him in action, perhaps she might've been a bit more amenable to his advances.

He swallowed hard, remembering all the killing he'd done.

"Yeah, probably not."

Besides, she likely wouldn't have survived the tower anyway. There was a reason none of Norcastle's teams had conquered it, after all.

Elijah shook his head and pushed past those thoughts. There was nothing to be gained from maudlin regrets or asking unanswerable questions. So, refocusing on his task, he crossed the room once again and found the ogre's staff. The thing was at least as big around as Elijah's biceps, and almost twice his height. A suitable size for an ogre, but for Elijah, it was unwieldy and ultimately useless.

However, he wasn't going to just leave it behind. The thing pulsed with power, suggesting that it would be valuable. Maybe not to a human, but surely there was someone who'd want it. After all, there were plenty of other races on Earth now. Maybe one of them was of a size to use a staff the size of a goalpost.

So, resolving to take it with him, Elijah hefted it onto one shoulder and took one last look around the room. There was nothing left that either hadn't been destroyed or simply wouldn't fit in his pack. Satisfied that he'd taken everything he could, he left the study behind and went in search of the next two lieutenants.

38

ILLUSIONS AND SHADOWS

Finishing the two-headed ogre that was Tuk and Tok had come with a couple of benefits. The first was the enormous staff Elijah had thrown over his shoulder, but even more importantly, he'd gained another level. Given that it had taken an entire wing of elves to progress to level forty, doing so from a single kill—or two, if he counted the twin heads as separate entities—was phenomenal efficiency. That gave Elijah a little more insight into how the System awarded kill energy, and he suspected that, even though the creatures were probably only a few levels higher than their guards, they awarded a lot more experience. Likely, it was something to do with ethera density, which translated into more power.

That made sense, though Elijah was still trying to wrap his head around how everything worked. For instance, he knew he gained experience from healing, but he'd also surmised that healing himself was useless for those purposes. In addition, the power of the entity he healed seemed to have some effect, as well.

Everything still didn't add up. Not completely. But he didn't have the time nor the inclination to investigate. Instead, he headed toward the stairs that would lead him to the next lieutenants. Before he ascended, though, he dropped his pack and the ogre's staff in the large central chamber. That way, he wouldn't have to worry about lugging everything around or damaging the sack.

Thus unburdened, Elijah checked his enhancements to ensure that everything he needed was active. At present, he was using Aura of Renewal, Essence of the Boar, and Shield of Brambles, as well as Essence of the Wolf and One with Nature. Once he was satisfied with everything, he shifted into the shape of the scaled panther, then proceeded up the steps before following a twisting hall that led to the light wing. Along the way, Elijah deftly avoided the slicing beams of light that crisscrossed the halls until he reached an intersection. Down one hall, he knew he would find the once-divided chamber that had become a graveyard for elves. He chose the other, which he'd already established would lead him to the light lieutenant.

That's when he embraced Guise of the Unseen, took a deep, steadying breath, then headed up. The path was fraught with even more beams of burning light, but Elijah's high Dexterity allowed him to maneuver his body well enough to avoid them. So, he reached the next lieutenant quickly and without incurring any additional damage.

The elf inside was precisely what he'd been led to expect. Avasil was beautiful, wearing a long, gossamer robe, and she seemed entirely at peace. Except for the huge basin of blood in front of which she stood. At first, Elijah tried to convince himself that it was some other red liquid, but the smell—which was augmented by his animalistic senses—was absolutely unmistakable.

After he allowed himself to accept the reality of the basin, which was at least four feet across and made of elaborately engraved stone, it didn't take long for him to look up and see the source of all that blood. Three bodies, all completely devoid of skin and entirely unrecognizable, hung from the ceiling. Every few seconds, a few drops of blood would drip down to land in the basin.

Avasil, meanwhile, paid them no heed. Instead, she occupied herself in much the same way the twin ogres had, which was to say that she was reading a book. However, neither the nearly incomprehensibly beautiful elf nor the bodies hanging from the ceiling were the most extraordinary details in Elijah's view. Instead, that label belonged to the fact that there were eight identical elves moving throughout the room. However, even their presence wasn't what alarmed Elijah. No—it was the fact that, despite their appearance, which was as solid-looking as anything else in the room, they were just as plainly fake.

It wasn't a single thing that told him they weren't real. Rather, it was a multitude of factors. The first that he'd noticed was the most important, though. None of them showed up in the sense granted by One with Nature. At first, he hadn't really understood what had triggered his instincts, but the discrepancy was jarring enough to send a tingle of unease up his spine.

But it was more than that.

There was no smell coming from any of them, save for the single elf standing near the basin, but other than that, they were perfectly realistic.

They were copies.

It only took Elijah a few seconds to make the connection. The lieutenant was a master of light, but instead of using the dangerous beams that existed throughout the rest of the wing, she had created illusions.

But they weren't real. Elijah could feel that through One with Nature. He couldn't quite put his finger on how he knew it, but he completely discounted the possibility that they were corporeal. Instead, he felt completely certain that they were like ghosts. For most people, they would make for a confusing mess, but Elijah could see through the deception. And as such, there was nothing keeping him from attacking the real lieutenant.

There was a part of him that was curious about what she was doing with the bodies and the blood. However, he wasn't so interested that he would pass up a golden opportunity to attack an unwary enemy. So, without further hesitation,

Elijah padded into the room, avoiding the illusions along the way, then positioned himself behind the elf.

It was telling about how far he'd come down the path of a killer that he didn't hesitate before leaping into action. After engaging Predator Strike as well as Venom Strike, Elijah pounced.

Even as his jaws closed around the elven woman's head, she let loose with a series of flashing lights that had him seeing stars. The illusions all screamed, and Elijah felt the light burning holes through his scales.

But it only lasted a second before he bit through Avasil's skull.

After that, the illusions let out one last scream before dissipating into motes of light. Then, a blaze of blinding light flashed before everything went dark.

Then, slowly, the flames flickered back to life, revealing a very different setting than the one he'd seen before he'd killed the elf. And she was definitely dead. He'd felt the influx of energy that heralded her death. Plus, he'd crushed her entire skull between his teeth, which was usually a good way to ensure something would cease living.

However, when Elijah looked down, instead of the beautiful elf—headless though she was—he saw a decrepit creature with pallid, flaky skin and a body that looked like it belonged to a desiccated corpse. The copies were predictably gone, but the illusion that had apparently extended to the entire room had disappeared, as well. Now, Elijah saw a bloodstained torture chamber that would have been at home in the dungeon where he'd killed the Warden.

Elijah pushed his disgust aside, focusing on what was really important—he'd managed to kill the light lieutenant without a real fight. Of course, it wouldn't have been possible without the unique advantage of One with Nature, proving the necessity of bringing the right tool for the job. For most people, that meant having a diverse group, but Elijah had to lean on his personal versatility instead.

It had worked so far, but he dreaded the day when he'd encounter a situation he simply wasn't equipped to handle. That day had yet to come, but he knew it would. Hopefully, he'd have even more skills and abilities when it did. For now, though, he needed to loot what he could, then head to the other wing where he would deal with Tulariel, the master of shadow.

Over the next few minutes, Elijah scoured the area. However, other than a few extra copper etherium, he found nothing of value. Even the books he'd seen had been illusory, so he quickly left the grisly chamber behind, retracing his steps as he headed toward the shadow wing.

That necessitated the traversal of the battlefield, where he was confronted with the results of his actions. Dead elves, each wearing elaborate armor that was impossible to remove, carpeted the floor, though Elijah pushed past them without a second glance. In a few facets of his Mind, though, he wondered if killing denizens of a tower counted as murder. On the surface, he was certain that it didn't. And yet, some vestiges of guilt remained, casting doubt on his certainty.

Fortunately, he quickly left that chamber behind and found his way through the shadow wing and to the room that housed Tulariel, the shadow lieutenant. In the Shape of the Predator, and with Guise of the Unseen cloaking his presence, Elijah observed the dark elf was in the middle of executing an elaborate sword kata. It was a truly impressive display of grace, balance, and skill, reminding Elijah of just how inadequate his efforts with the staff were.

It also lit a fire beneath him. Once he conquered the tower, he resolved to devote himself to better learning the weapon he'd adopted as his preference. At the moment, though, he had an elf to kill.

There was no justification for it. As far as Elijah could see, Tulariel was simply minding his own business. Unlike Elijah's previous encounter with Avasil in the light wing, there were no basins of blood or skinned corpses. Still, he knew precisely what he had to do, and the fact that the elf didn't overtly deserve it was irrelevant.

It was a fundamental aspect of nature's brutality that sometimes some creatures needed to die so others could live. Elijah understood that better than most, and he refused to let himself get tangled in doubts. Instead, he focused on the obstacle in his way, on the death that would allow him to live.

He lashed out like a striking snake, intending to end the fight the same way he'd overcome the last lieutenant. However, at the last second, Tulariel's battle instincts kicked in, obviously telling him that he was in mortal danger. Just before Elijah's jaws closed in, the dark elf dove forward, moving so quickly that Elijah couldn't even redirect his course.

After missing his target, he crashed into the floor, then dug his claws into the tiles, forcing himself to a stop just in time to see the dark elf dart in, slashing his sword across Elijah's unprotected flank. He shifted, avoiding the brunt of the blow—only possible because of the time dilation afforded by his Sash of the Whirlwind—and his scales deflected the sharp blade before it could penetrate too deeply.

However, the message was clear.

In the realm of speed, Elijah was woefully outmatched. The only solace was that, due to Shield of Brambles, Tulariel had been assaulted by a painful thorn for his trouble.

"A draconid? Here?" the elf breathed, yanking the thorn from his hand. He narrowed his eyes. "No. You are more than a mere beast, are you not?"

Elijah didn't answer. Instead, his mind whirled with potential strategies. The scaled-panther—or draconid, apparently—form was ill-suited to a straight fight. It was deadly so long as he had the advantage of surprise and kept his opponents on the back foot, but its defenses were too soft to stand up to even glancing blows.

No—as much as he wished he could remain in his favored form, he couldn't do so. But that presented a problem all its own, chiefly that both of his other forms, human and scaled ape, had weaknesses of their own. As a human, he was wholly dependent on ethera to do damage. However, that same pool of ethera was the only way he could endure damage. By comparison, the scaled-ape form was incapable of keeping up with the dark elf.

Still, it was his best shot.

So, without further ado, he initiated the shift from draconid to human. He only paused for a brief second before he cast Shape of the Guardian.

"What? A shape-shifter? What sort of monster are you?!"

Tulariel didn't ask any other questions before he launched himself forward with blistering speed. Elijah tried to avoid it, but mid-transformation, he was incapable of doing much more than protecting his head.

The sword sliced into his shoulder, stopping only when it hit the bone. However, by that point, Elijah's transformation into a scaled ape completed. He let out a roar, slapping the sword away and throwing himself at the elf. Tulariel's reflexes were up to the challenge, and he nimbly danced away, aiming a back-handed blow at Elijah for good measure. Fortunately, his scales were more than up to the task of deflecting the attack—largely because the elf was incapable of putting his full strength behind it—but he couldn't stop himself before colliding with the wall.

With a growl, Elijah tore himself away, then wheeled around to face the elf.

"A lamellar ape?"

Apparently, that was the true name of his guardian form, which would have been interesting if Elijah wasn't in a fight for his life against a superior and frustrating opponent.

Suddenly, he launched himself forward, hoping to take the elf by surprise. With all his Strength, he could move incredibly quickly. However, because his attributes were lopsided, that Strength was extremely difficult to control. And he didn't even have Essence of the Monkey to close some of the gap, either. So, the elf had little trouble spinning out of the way and landing yet another attack.

This one cut a few inches into Elijah's hip, telling him that, despite what that first attack might have suggested, the elf was more than capable of harming him. It would take a while, but it was possible.

Likely, even, considering that Elijah couldn't even catch the nimble swords-man, as became evident over the next few minutes of back-and-forth. Elijah's frustrations mounted as he missed the elf time and time again. Each charge was rewarded with yet another painful wound, as well, which only exacerbated Elijah's rage.

But he shunted that into one facet of his Mind, focusing the rest on coming up with a plan of attack. However, he kept coming back to one simple reality: Attacking was what was eventually going to get him killed. Instead, he needed to defend.

So, instead of once again charging after the elf, he slammed his fists into the ground and waited. The elf, realizing that something was the matter, hesitated.

However, he couldn't pass up an opportunity of attack, so he darted in, slashing his sword across Elijah's shoulder.

It clanged against his scales, doing nothing.

Ability: Iron Scales	Harden your scales, temporarily reducing all damage by 90%. Effectiveness dependent on relative Constitution versus the attacker's Strength for physical attacks and Ethera for magical attacks. Usable in guardian form. Duration dependent on Constitution. Current Duration: 4.2 seconds.

Using his latest ability made his scales incredibly durable, but only for a few brief seconds. However, because of his inflated Constitution, he felt that he could use it quite a few times before fatigue started to take hold. More importantly, he could counter the elf's attacks without even moving.

Tulariel retreated, pulling another thorn out of his forearm. Already, his body was peppered with lightly bleeding wounds, and if he wanted to kill Elijah, there would be many more where they'd come from. All Elijah had to do was take damage, and the thorns from Shield of Brambles would eventually wear the elf down.

And so the elf continued to attack. Elijah, for his part, practiced activating Iron Scales at the last second, and because of his Sash of the Whirlwind, he managed it well enough. Still, it was unsurprising when the elf had finally had enough.

He retreated, then refused to attack further.

"It seems we are at an impasse," Tulariel said.

"So we are," Elijah growled.

"You can speak?"

"I can."

"Are my subordinates dead?" was the elf's next question.

"They are," Elijah said. Speaking in the lamellar-ape form was unnatural, but he could manage it. "The light elves, too."

The elf cocked his head to the side, obviously surprised. Then, he grinned. "Small rewards, I suppose. Why have you attacked us?"

"Because I must," Elijah said. He knew better than to start going on about towers and tasks. It was unlikely that the elf would believe him, and even if he did, it would do little good. After all, it wasn't as if the creature intended to surrender. Nor could Elijah allow it. His task had been clear on that count.

Besides, Elijah had a plan to finish things in a hurry.

"Why? I can give you—"

Elijah canceled Shape of the Guardian, and before he'd even completed his transformation, he'd begun to cast a spell. Meanwhile, the elf recovered from his surprise and dashed in Elijah's direction. Still, the delay was just enough to allow the spell to complete.

Snaring Roots leaped from Elijah's staff, prompting a surge of lashing vines to erupt from the floor and wrap themselves around the elf. It wouldn't last long. Elijah knew that. But he hoped it would be just enough to give him one shot.

And he knew exactly how he was going to use that opening.

He ran forward, casting another spell along the way. He didn't have time for Storm's Fury or Swarm, and he didn't want to spend the ethera necessary to fuel Calamity. But that was fine. Long ago, he'd chosen his path, and though he would utilize those attack spells when necessary, he preferred his animal shapes.

So, he once again shifted into the lamellar-ape form, enhancing his Strength and Constitution to superhuman levels. The elf, trapped by the vines, tried to rip himself free and avoid the oncoming attack, but he was slowed just enough to allow Elijah one good attack.

And he used it well.

With his hands clasped together, Elijah raised his arms, then brought his fists down with thunderous fury. The elf lashed out with his sword, but it clanged off of Iron Scales just before Elijah's own attack fell. The impact of his fists crushed the elf's collarbone as well as a few ribs. It also sent him crashing to the ground where the remnants of Snaring Roots held him in place for Elijah's next blow.

It fell with inevitable force, crushing bones and rupturing flesh.

He hit the elf again.

And again after that.

Over and over, he repaid the elf for every attack he'd landed. And soon enough, the dark elf perished. Elijah stood over him, then let out a roar as he beat his chest with wild abandon.

The lieutenants were all dead. Now, he only needed to challenge the Champion before defeating the Reaver himself. Hopefully, he would be up for the task.

39

PLACE YOUR BETS

After examining the dark elf's corpse, Elijah came away with an extra sword and three silver etherium, which was the most he'd gotten from any individual kill. Fortunately, when he returned to where he'd left his equipment in the central chamber, he found that the blade was just small enough to fit inside his pack. So, he added it to his collection before settling down to rest and recuperate.

Because of his copious use of Iron Scales, he'd sustained very little actual damage. However, that same strategy had drained his stamina more thoroughly than anything he'd ever done. It felt like he'd just run two marathons back-to-back while carrying a sack of rocks over his shoulder, and he very much needed a few hours of downtime.

It also didn't help that he hadn't really slept since entering the tower, which, by his count, had been at least three days ago. Maybe as much as a week. Time felt a little squirrelly when he had nothing to mark the passage of each day. He was also hungry and thirsty, so he spent a little time taking care of his biological necessities—and eating his last Grove berry—before heading to one of the most isolated rooms he could find and settling down to take a nap.

It was a testament to how tired he was that he was able to fall asleep at all, and for the next few hours, Elijah slept like a contented baby. When he awoke, he felt ready to defeat the Champion and progress to the last level of the dungeon. So, he pushed himself upright, ate some mostly tasteless travel rations and drained one of his jugs of water. If he didn't conquer the tower soon, he would have to start rationing his water. He'd only brought a handful of glass jugs, and there were only a couple left.

Pushing that out of his mind, Elijah climbed to his feet and went through a brief calisthenics routine so he could work out the kinks in his stiff muscles. He'd healed all his injuries from the day before, but his body still paid the price. However, it only took a quick cast of Healing Rain and a little stretching to banish the resulting soreness. Once he'd done that, Elijah set off through the citadel and toward the stairs leading up to the Champion's wing.

The old prisoner had pointed it out, but Elijah hadn't needed it because the broad stairs were obviously important. At least forty feet wide at the base, they narrowed to only ten feet across after a hundred or so yards. From what Elijah had seen of the citadel's dimensions from the outside, the distances seemed impossible.

But magic was involved, so possible only seemed like a suggestion rather than a rule.

In any case, after getting himself into the right frame of mind, Elijah shouldered his two staves—one the enormous ogre's staff, and the other his Staff of Natural Harmony—then shifted his pack before embracing Shape of the Predator and slipping into the draconid form. Fortunately, the magic took care of the staves and his pack, leaving him free to progress up that long flight of intimidating stairs.

Once he reached the top, Elijah let Guise of the Predator settle across his shoulders before he approached the doors. To his surprise, the massive gilded doors opened inwardly of their own volition. However, Elijah could see nothing but a black field on the other side. So, he took a deep breath, then pushed through.

Unlike when he'd progressed from one level to the next, he felt no sense of displacement. Instead, it was like walking through any other doorway. However, as he passed the threshold, his vision cleared and he saw a large expanse of glittering gray sand.

More distressingly, Guise of the Unseen was forcibly canceled, leaving him entirely exposed. Elijah didn't even have a chance to look around before a bellowing voice bounced off the walls to assail his ears.

"Little draconid!" it roared. "I have watched you dismantle my would-be challengers, and I approve of your methods! However, if you wish to face me, you will need to prove yourself worthy against more varied opponents! Do you accept the challenge?"

Elijah had only dedicated one facet of his Mind to listening to the voice's declaration. The other eight were occupied with cataloging his surroundings. The floor was gray sand that glittered in the firelight of a hundred surrounding torches. The walls were tall and featureless, save for a sturdy gate on the other side of the circular room. However, the most surprising aspect was the fact that he could hear the din of hundreds—perhaps even thousands—of conversations.

"You must answer!"

Elijah finally found the source of the voice. He was an ogre, and yet, he was simultaneously larger and more muscular than any Elijah had seen below. Fifteen feet tall, with bulging muscles that made him look like a bodybuilder, the ogre wore nothing but a fur loincloth, hide boots that came up to mid-calf, and a leather harness crisscrossing his massive chest. Aside from a ragged scar that cut from his hairless scalp, diagonally across his face, and to the opposite jaw, his lumpy visage looked little different than the lesser ogres Elijah had so far encountered.

But even from so far away, he radiated power and authority as he stood on a platform atop the wall. Three elven women, all clad in gossamer robes, sat in elaborate chairs to either side of the massive ogre, and beyond the platform, Elijah saw the source of the din he'd heard before.

Hundreds of ogres and elves stood shoulder to shoulder in an enormous, bowl-shaped arena. That gave Elijah some insight into what sort of challenge the ogre offered. And given the point of the task he'd been given, it didn't take much for him to connect the dots. The path before him looked clear.

He just didn't like where it would lead him.

Elijah preferred to fight unfair battles. That was where he excelled. But with what was coming, he knew that wouldn't be possible. For the first time, he would be forced to fight on even terms. No tricks. No clever plans. Just him against whatever opponents the ogre sent his way. He didn't know if he could survive.

Still, it wasn't as if he had a choice.

The walls were too high to climb, and he couldn't go back the way he'd come. None of his spells could reach the ogre, either. So, he had no other option but to go along with the scenario.

Knowing what was coming, Elijah shifted into his human form. As he did, he was suddenly aware of his own nudity. He hadn't bothered dressing after defeating the ogres, largely because he hadn't seen the point. Now, though, with thousands of ogres and elves looking down on him, he regretted the oversight.

Pushing his embarrassment aside, he cast Healing Rain. Then, he ensured his enhancements were still active before raising his voice and shouting, "I accept your challenge!"

The crowd roared.

The ogre clapped.

And the gate opened.

A trio of tall goblinoid creatures strode forward.

"The challenger versus the Hobgoblin Trio!" announced the giant ogre. "Who will win? Place your bets now!"

The hobgoblins looked like their smaller counterparts, and yet, they were much larger. In addition, they had much more muscle and far more refined features. Still, each one wore a savage snarl on his face, and they all carried jagged and rusty swords.

Elijah had no intention of letting them get close. So, he used Snaring Roots, aiming just in front of them. Normally, he used the spell on a single opponent. However, it wasn't really that limited. Instead, the vines that it manifested would attack any enemy that came too close. So, when the hobgoblins did just that, the thorny vines lashed out, tangling their legs.

One tripped and fell on its face. Another was briefly immobilized. And the last attacked the vines with its jagged sword, hacking through the thick roots with savage ferocity.

But it was just enough to allow enough time for Elijah to cast Swarm. Hundreds of hornets, each the size of Elijah's thumb, swooped in, stinging the hobgoblins and delivering their afflictions. At the same time, he shifted into the Shape of the Guardian and raced forward. Using every point of Strength at his disposal, Elijah covered the ground in an instant. The immobilized hobgoblin that was his target stood no chance of dodging, and Elijah hit it like an out-of-control locomotive. The impact broke the comparatively slender hobgoblin's bones, and Elijah ended its life only a second later when he grabbed its head like he was palming a basketball and squeezed.

It popped like an overfilled water balloon, surprising even Elijah with its fragility.

However, he wasn't going to sit there and stare. Instead, he wheeled around and, with a roar, raced toward the hobgoblin who was still trying to cut itself loose. Elijah reached out, grabbed it by the waist, and spun around before tossing it into the crowd. He didn't see where the creature landed, but he felt the influx of kill energy that told him the hobgoblin was dead.

That left only one.

Elijah turned slowly before locking his eyes on his intended victim. These weren't enemies. They were prey. And Elijah intended to make that abundantly clear. Seeing the approach of a massive lamellar ape, the hobgoblin let out a terrified scream. For his savage side, the sound was music to Elijah's ears.

Before the hobgoblin could scramble away, Elijah leaped, and his arcing path ended when he landed upon the hobgoblin. Bones broke. Organs ruptured. And ultimately, the creature died an ignoble death.

Elijah bent down, scooped up the hobgoblin's corpse, and tossed it at the ogre. It didn't quite make it up to the platform, but it came close enough that the elven women flinched. The Champion—and that was who it had to be—pointedly did not, though.

"Impressive!" the ogre bellowed with a hearty laugh. "Very impressive. But how will you do against the next opponent?"

Elijah had no chance to answer before the gates opened once again, this time revealing a large reptilian creature. Its torso was humanoid, but the bottom half resembled an enormous snake.

Elijah didn't have much chance to study it, though, because the creature opened its mouth wide, then spat a glob of thick mucus in his direction. Elijah darted to the side, narrowly avoiding the projectile before rushing the snake man. It moved as quickly as its reptilian appearance would imply, and it managed to avoid Elijah's charge.

It lashed out, raking its claws across his shoulder as he barreled past. However, Elijah used Iron Scales at the last second, and the snake creature's claws clanged harmlessly.

"The naga are known for their speed and Dexterity as well as their potent venom. One nick can kill even the strongest warriors! Can our sturdy challenger compete with that? Place your bets!"

Elijah paid the ogre's commentary little heed as he dashed in, aiming to end the fight in only a second. However, the creature once again evaded him, though he did manage to activate Iron Scales before it raked its claws across his ribs.

Like that, the fight went on, with neither side capable of gaining an advantage. At least that was the case until Elijah finally had enough and switched to his draconid form in mid-stride. The increased Dexterity was all he needed to land a solid blow, and with his claws, he ripped a long gash in the naga's abdomen. Intestines spilled out, though Elijah was incapable of avoiding a retaliatory swipe that opened up a gash in his hind leg.

Fiery agony erupted from the wound, and his leg immediately spasmed. Yet, Elijah had endured pain before, and he managed to dash away before the naga warrior could follow it up. When he turned back to face the snakelike creature, he saw that it was struggling to gather its intestines. So, Elijah used that distraction to his advantage when he shifted into his human form, used Touch of Nature to counteract the monster's venom, then aimed Storm's Fury in the naga's direction.

The creature had no chance of dodging, and it took the resulting lightning bolt square in the chest. It flew backward, landing a few feet later in a coiled and twitching heap. Elijah didn't let up, though. Instead, he hit it with another Storm's Fury. And another after that. By the fourth, the creature's twitching had become a full-blown seizure, and it died only a few seconds later.

"Incredible!" yelled the ogre. "Absolutely astounding! But can the challenger stand up to the Forest King himself?"

Something huge, green, and monstrous crashed through the gate, knocking the metal doors aside and letting out an immense roar.

"Place your bets now!"

40

CHALLENGING A CHAMPION

In most cases, a frog alternates between disgusting and cute, depending on who's looking at it. Rarely are they considered horrifying, and yet, that was precisely the thought that crossed Elijah's mind as he barely managed to dodge a thick, rubbery tongue. It slapped against the body of one of his previous opponents—a mantis-like creature with organic scythes for hands—that he'd narrowly defeated only a few minutes before.

The frog's tongue stuck fast to the corpse's chitinous exoskeleton, but Elijah knew it would only be temporary. The tongues of amphibians—and the saliva they secreted—were a marvel of nature, and on Earth, frogs captured prey by covering them in said saliva, which was capable of transforming from liquid to solid and back, making for some of the stickiest substances in nature.

That meant that it wouldn't stay stuck to the mantis's body for long, so Elijah needed to act quickly and decisively. With that in mind, he aimed his staff at the frog—which was the size of a rhinoceros—and let loose with Storm's Fury. The lightning tore across the arena, disappearing into the frog's gaping mouth.

The creature let out a deep, croaking bellow of pain as its body was wracked with convulsions. As had been the case for the past ten fights, the giant ogre on the platform far above commented on Elijah's progress. However, he didn't hear it. Instead, he sprinted forward, hoping to take advantage of the frog's electricity-induced seizure. As he did so, one facet of his Mind completed the casting of Shape of the Predator, and over the space of three steps, he shifted into the draconid form.

He'd shifted a dozen or more times since the gauntlet had begun, and he suspected his latest transformation wouldn't be the last. Whatever the case, he crashed into the amphibian with snapping jaws and slicing talons that ripped into the creature's rubbery stomach with ease. Yet, he didn't get to anything important before the frog recovered and tried to hop away.

But Elijah had already seen that tactic, so he latched on with claws meant for climbing trees and went along for a ride. The panicked frog sailed high into the air, its arc taking it on an inevitable collision course with the wall. It smashed into the barrier with a wet squelch, and the impact very nearly jostled Elijah loose.

Nearly was not completely, though, and Elijah managed to hang on. More importantly, his tenacity was rewarded with an opportunity to truly dig into the stunned monster's belly. He dug deep, raking his claws across the wet and pliable flesh until, at last, he hit organs. Without skipping a beat, Elijah continued to tear into the frog's abdomen until he had completely submerged in its innards.

That was when the real work started.

Elijah didn't bother with trying to identify organs. Vaguely, he recognized some of them, but what they were was less important than inflicting as much damage as possible. So, he tore his way through the frog's guts one raking claw at a time. In the back of one facet of his Mind, he was aware of how disgusting it was. However, he'd long since moved past acknowledging that, adopting a philosophy of pragmatism.

Besides, he'd once been a biologist, so he could handle all sorts of grotesque sights, sounds, and as it turned out, tastes. More importantly than that, though, by that point, Elijah was exhausted enough to not care about anything except killing the monster as quickly as he could. So, that was what he did.

And eventually, he managed to finish it off, though it took far longer than Elijah would have expected. Like many of the other creatures he'd fought since Earth had been touched by the World Tree, the frog was clearly far more durable than any animal should have been. However, he'd long ago accepted that most of the biological knowledge he had accumulated over years of study was now useless.

After all, what use was any of that against dinosaurs made of roots? Or monstrous killer whales whose insides seemed to defy the laws of physics? Or, as was the case with his latest conquest, a giant frog who, according to everything Elijah knew about biomechanics, was so large that it should not have been able to bear its own weight.

In any case, Elijah felt a deep sense of relief when he finally climbed out of the monster's slimy gut. Once he did, he summoned Healing Rain, as much to wash the remnants of the frog's innards away as to treat any injuries.

Even as he basked in the rejuvenating precipitation, he heard the tenor of the crowd suddenly shift. For a moment, he didn't understand what was going on, but then Elijah picked up what they were saying.

"Champion! Champion!" they chanted, over and over, until the ogre finally bellowed for them to quiet down.

"This challenger has accomplished something impressive. For that, he has our praise!" shouted the ogre. The crowd went wild. "But! If he is to be called a champion, then he needs to do more than defeat a few hobgoblins. Indeed, he must become a challenger in truth. He must fight me!"

The enormous ogre then stepped forward and leaped from the platform. He landed in a spray of glittering gray sand only a moment later. By that point,

Elijah knew he was in trouble. The ogre was even larger than his first assessment had suggested—a trick of perspective, he was sure—and what's more, he was far more muscular than any of the other ogres Elijah had fought. He looked like a perfect warrior.

But the implications were clear. Elijah needed to kill the Champion if he wanted to complete the dungeon. There were no clever tricks to be played. No sneaking. No ambushes. Just him and the opponent.

If the fight had happened a few weeks before, he would have never had a chance. However, because he'd spent the past few days—or weeks, maybe—learning to use every facet of his tool kit, Elijah didn't even flinch at the challenge before him. Instead, he remained in place, letting the waters of Healing Rain wash away the remainder of his fatigue while he leveraged his Quartz Mind to increase his Regeneration as much as possible. The tiny vortexes at the center of each facet of his Mind eagerly drank the ambient ethera, funneling it through his Soul and into his Dragon Core.

Across the arena, the ogre beat its muscular chest and roared to the crowd. It was clear that the Champion was as much a showman as it was a fighter, especially considering that its bare chest had been oiled and its bald head shined to a dull gleam.

Not that that made it any less dangerous, of course. Elijah did find it amusing, though, and he was reminded of a professional wrestler. Perhaps that would change once the fight began.

Elijah rolled his shoulders, then checked his enhancements. The ogre looked so muscular that if he landed a single blow—even a glancing one—it would have dire consequences for Elijah, so he replaced Shield of Brambles with Essence of the Monkey. Beyond that, he had Essence of the Wolf, One with Nature, Aura of Renewal, and Essence of the Boar active.

With that, he was ready for the fight.

He stepped forward, leveled his staff, and summoned Calamity. Thunder rolled, and lightning struck as blades of wind swirled, kicking up sparkling gray dust and obscuring the ogre. Elijah couldn't see much, but he definitely noticed when the Champion came crashing through the maelstrom, its fists gleaming with purple energy.

Elijah hurriedly cast Snaring Roots, but they did nothing to stop the enormous ogre's vast momentum. It ripped through them, barely even slowing down. And yet, even that small delay allowed Elijah enough time to cast Swarm. Hundreds of fist-sized mosquitoes manifested, then flocked onto the Champion's oil-slick back, where they latched on and started doing the job for which they had been summoned.

Yet, few of those proboscises managed to penetrate the ogre's thick hide, and their inability mitigated the swarm's effect. Still, a few managed to break through, so the spell wasn't entirely useless.

Elijah cast Storm's Fury, sending a bolt of crackling lightning to hit the creature in the chest. That definitely did something, sending the ogre's muscles into involuntary contractions. However, that only slowed the monstrous humanoid down a little more than the roots, so Elijah had no choice but to rapidly shift into his lamellar-ape form.

He managed to complete the transformation just in time to meet the ogre's charge.

And get sent flying through the air to hit the wall hard enough to crack the bricks from which it had been constructed. Fortunately, he used Iron Scales just before the ogre made contact, but even ten percent of that punch was enough to make Elijah see stars.

He was still within the effective radius of Healing Rain, though, so it cleared up quickly. That was just in time for him to see the ogre once again bearing down on him. Elijah used Iron Scales once again, then leaped at the creature. The two collided with a titanic impact that shook the very ground, but Elijah definitely got the worst of it. Even with the protection afforded by Iron Scales, he had the breath driven from his chest by a momentous uppercut that took him in the gut.

That's when Elijah realized his mistake.

He'd gotten so used to fighting like a beast that he'd forgotten the years' worth of lessons he'd learned in the boxing gym. The lamellar-ape form wasn't perfectly suited for most of his techniques, but the general principles remained just as valid as they ever were before. So, when he regained his composure a second later, he stepped back into the fight with renewed confidence.

The ogre came in with a simple jab, but instead of simply taking the hit, Elijah shifted slightly to the side, letting it pass him by. Elijah returned the would-be blow with one of his own, whipping his own fist out to slap against the ogre's hip. With the size difference, that was the best spot he could reach, and though it wasn't ideal, it certainly threw the ogre off-balance.

Elijah followed it up by tapping into his bestial nature. His jaws snapped out, latching on to the ogre's exposed thigh, and ripping a chunk of its quadriceps muscle away. The Champion howled in pain and fury, but by the time it brought its own fists to bear, Elijah had danced away.

Awkwardly, by his standards. But it was effective enough to let him avoid the ogre's furious and ill-aimed punch. That further overbalanced the creature, which Elijah used to great advantage when he rushed in with a shoulder tackle that bent the Champion's knee the wrong way.

Its sudden collapse surprised Elijah, and that shock very nearly got him killed. Even as the ogre fell, it reached out, grabbed Elijah's shoulder, and yanked him off his feet. Before he knew what was happening, the creature had him pinned to the ground and was raining one herculean blow after another down on him.

Elijah used Iron Scales, but it could only do so much against such a powerful opponent. However, that damage reduction was just enough to keep Elijah from being pummeled into unconsciousness.

While one facet of his Quartz Mind focused on using Iron Scales at the appropriate time, another took care of keeping him moving just enough to avoid taking too solid of a blow. Still another housed his panic. The rest were wholly occupied with trying to think of a way out of the dire situation.

But as far as he could tell, there was only one shot.

He just didn't want to take it because, if he was wrong, a bad situation would turn to worse, which would probably mean the end of his struggle, and not in a way that would see him traipsing into the next level of the tower.

He didn't have much choice, though. The battle had turned in a hurry, and he had none of his usual tactics available. The creature had escaped his Calamity without issue, and Swarm had already dissipated without infecting the ogre with much in the way of afflictions.

So, he shifted.

Not because he wanted to take advantage of his draconid form. Rather, he transformed because that form was much, much smaller than the lamellar ape. As such, when the ogre's fist descended, it found only sand where Elijah's head had once been. Meanwhile, the smaller size also gave him just enough wiggle room to escape the ogre's grasp. He slithered out from beneath the creature, then leaped onto the wall.

Bounding off that surface, he launched himself at the slightly confused ogre. He landed lightly, then sank his claws into the monster's oiled back. The creature howled at the sudden pain, and it tried to dislodge the stubborn draconid, but to no effect.

Because Elijah had learned something about his opponent.

The ogre was strong. Far stronger than anything he'd ever encountered, and that was including the very first encounter with one of the Voxx. However, the Champion's attributes were lopsided, but not in the way Elijah's guardian form was. Instead of having a detriment of Dexterity, it instead lacked Constitution.

Normally, that wouldn't have been such a debilitating weakness. The monster was still plenty durable, and with its extremely high Strength and Dexterity, it could probably end most fights before they had a chance to really begin. Yet, Elijah was just capable of avoiding that fate, and he'd managed to find the ogre's weakness.

And now, on the Champion's back, he could finally exploit it to the fullest extent.

His claws bit deep, but his teeth went even deeper. He ripped into the monster's back, tearing it to ribbons even as he ripped huge chunks of muscle from its body. Bits of flesh flew through the air, and blood coated the gray sand, but Elijah refused to stop.

He couldn't afford to rest. Even the slightest pause would lift the pressure and allow the ogre to regain its equilibrium. Elijah couldn't let that happen, so he ripped and tore, bit and clawed until, at last, he found his way to the ogre's vulnerable organs.

He started with the intestines, but those were shredded in seconds. A foul and acrid stench filled Elijah's nostrils as he dug into the chest cavity, piercing lungs and finally latching on to the ogre's overlarge heart. He ripped it free, then, at last, bounded away. The ogre fell like a tree, hitting the ground with a massive impact that sent even more sand, blood, and guts into the air.

It was dead before it hit the ground.

Just like that, Elijah had won the battle and conquered the second floor of the tower.

41

THE REAVER

The crowd went silent, as if they were unsure how to react to the fall of the Champion. That silence stretched for what felt to Elijah like an eternity before, suddenly, they let out a collective roar that shook the very foundations of the arena. It wasn't simply deafening. Rather, it was a sound so loud—so visceral—that it was physically painful to endure. However, Elijah felt nothing but elation at his accomplishment. He basked in the crowd's approval, his chest heaving with excitement.

Then, he noticed a silver box glinting in the distance. It stood before the gate, his reward for another level conquered. The prideful satisfaction he felt was nothing new. He'd felt the same way, though to a lesser extent, upon winning bouts in his boxing days. Or when playing other sports as a kid. It was always addictive, and yet, it was usually fleeting, as well.

Not so this time.

Elijah knew how uncommon his accomplishments were. His first tower had been a series of misadventures he'd survived through cunning, good fortune, and simple endurance. However, the gauntlet he'd just run was no such thing. He'd fought, not via tricks or subterfuge, but in an even match against impossible odds.

And he had come out on top.

That he'd proved himself stronger than an entity like the Champion—much less the ten encounters through which he'd fought before facing off against the giant ogre—was a heady realization. Yet, Elijah knew he wasn't finished. There was still one more level left in the tower, and if he was going to conquer it and survive, he would need every aspect of his unique abilities.

So, with that sobering realization coursing through every facet of his Mind, he summoned Healing Rain and set about scrubbing himself clean. The water wouldn't persist longer than the spell's duration, but it still lasted long enough for an impromptu shower. He'd even packed a little of his homemade soap for just such an occasion.

He must've made for an odd sight, showering with his summoned rain cloud in the middle of an arena that, at present, housed quite a few dead bodies. But the crowd never stopped cheering, which told Elijah that they weren't even whatever passed for real people within a tower. Instead, they were just background noise. Meaningless, soulless, and inconsequential.

"I'll still take the cheers, though," he said to himself as he finished washing the soap—and all the viscera—from his body. The shower also served the purpose of reinvigorating and healing much of the damage he'd taken. However, he still had to use Touch of Nature to heal a few broken bones he'd sustained. All in all, though, he managed to make it out of the arena with far fewer injuries than he'd have suspected.

It was a rarity for him to get through a fight without being beaten, bloody, and on the brink of death, so he chose to enjoy it while he could. After all, he still had the Reaver to defeat, and he wasn't so naive as to think it would be any easier than the gauntlet he'd just endured. And given the fact that it would've only taken a mistake or two to send the previous battle careening in an entirely different direction, Elijah was wary of what he might have to suffer on the next level of the tower.

After he finished showering, he dressed in one of the outfits he'd bought back in Ironshore. He still had one that was undamaged, but he chose one that had already been subjected to quite a bit of wear and tear. As usual, he wore no shoes, as much because he didn't have any as because his spells seemed to work better so long as his feet remained unshod.

Clean and rejuvenated, he returned to the ogre's corpse and took the creature's money pouch, which he tossed into his pack. Then, he retrieved the giant staff he'd lugged up from the other wings, then shouldered it before heading toward his reward. The chest was a lot bigger than the ones he'd received in the past, and as he approached it, he noticed that it looked slightly more elaborate.

He leaned down, then unlatched the clasp that held it shut. The lid popped open of its own accord, revealing a leather bracer. The moment he opened the treasure chest, a notification popped up, too:

Congratulations! You have completed Level Two of Reaver's Citadel.
Grade: A.
To progress further, go through the gate and reach the third and final level.

Elijah pumped his fist in celebration at his grade. He'd only received a B for the previous level, but it seemed that he'd performed far better in his most recent challenge. The question remained as to how that would translate to his reward. The Sash of the Whirlwind had been invaluable so far, allowing him to move more quickly than ever before. Often, he likened it to time dilation, but it was really that his increased speed was accompanied by an adjusted perception of time. That gave him the opportunity to use his speed more efficiently.

Still, it wasn't a huge difference, and he suspected that was because of his decidedly average performance in the previous level. Now that he'd gotten a higher grade for the second, he hoped that the reward would be that much more powerful. So, it was with eager hands that he reached down and grabbed the leather bracer. When his fingers brushed against the item, an expected notification flashed before his inner eye:

**Reward for completing Level Two of Reaver's Citadel:
Silver Bracer of Rage**

As usual, it didn't give any indication as to what it would do. So, he picked the bracer up and turned it this way and that while inspecting it. As he'd already seen, the item was primarily made of black leather, but the back side, which was intended to protect his forearm, was plated silver. In addition, there were designs etched in silver thread across the whole thing. It reminded him of Celtic knots, but slightly off—as if it was a similar concept but developed by a different culture.

But it was an interesting look, he couldn't deny.

The inside of the bracer was lined with soft fur reminiscent of sheepskin, though with a silver sheen, and a leather lace on the bottom held the whole thing together.

Elijah unfastened it, then slipped the bracer onto his right arm. Once he tied the laces—awkwardly because he only had one hand to do it—he felt a surge of power. When he opened his status, he saw that his Strength had improved by seven points.

"Nice," he said to himself.

Given that Strength was the one of only two attributes that he couldn't directly boost via one of his enhancements, any help in that department was more than welcome. Still, he'd hoped for more. Even the Sash of the Whirlwind, which was supposed to be worse than the Silver Bracer of Rage—if the grades were meant to indicate anything—had an extra function in addition to the three points it gave him to both Strength and Dexterity. Sure, the attribute bonuses for the bracer were better by a point, but he'd hoped for an extra function.

Whatever the case, he intended to put the extra Strength to good use. After renewing his enhancements, he opened his status:

Name	Elijah Hart
Level	42
Archetype	Druid

Class	Animist		
Specialization	N/A		
Alignment	N/A		
Strength	53 (43)		
Dexterity	54 (42)		
Constitution	53 (43)		
Ethera	51		
Regeneration	65 (45)		
Attunement	Nature		
Cultivation Stage: Cultivator			
Body	Core	Mind	Soul
Wood	Hatchling	Quartz	Neophyte

His attributes were really getting up there, especially since he'd gained another level during the previous battle. One point per level in each category didn't seem like a lot, but it definitely added up. Getting extra attributes via his equipment was nice, as well, especially when it gave him an extra ten points in Strength and three in Dexterity. Added to all of that were the effects of his enhancements.

And when he shifted into his forms, the results were even more impressive. After all, Shape of the Guardian gave him thirty extra points in Strength and Constitution, which was an absolutely insane amount of power and durability. Similarly, Shape of the Predator gave bonuses to Strength and Dexterity, as well, so when he was in either of his animal forms, he was an absolute terror.

And even with all of that, he'd struggled with the ogre Champion.

That was a sobering thought, and it brought him back to the reality of his situation. He'd done well so far, but when he progressed to the next level, he'd be forced to fight the leader of the citadel. And Elijah knew it wouldn't be an easy battle. So, he pushed his self-congratulatory thoughts away and focused on the path ahead.

The gate was open, but he couldn't see much beyond the entrance. He stepped forward into the darkness, but he didn't immediately progress to the next level. Instead, he followed a long, low-ceilinged hall for a few hundred feet before it doubled back and sloped upward. He kept going, hitting multiple switchbacks until, at last, he reached another door.

He pushed it open, revealing a featureless black plain of impenetrable darkness. Knowing that it was the way to the next level, Elijah stepped through and felt the familiar displacement that had come with progressing between previous tower levels. It only lasted a moment before his bare foot hit something soft.

He looked down to see an elaborate rug. Another second, and he saw that he'd stepped into a richly decorated corridor. Lined with doors, the corridor was lit by flickering lamps, and it featured a host of small statues, oil paintings, and tapestries.

And that was just what Elijah saw at a glance.

Before he could study it further, though, he heard voices coming from nearby. So, he shifted into the Shape of the Predator, then adopted Guise of the Unseen only a second before two elves came into view. One was a dark elf, with onyx skin and white hair, but the other was a light elf, with blonde hair and a fair complexion. Clearly, the enmities of the previous level meant nothing here.

Fortunately, the elves were either too distracted to see him or completely incapable of piercing his Guise of the Unseen because they never even glanced in Elijah's direction. That allowed him to get a good look at the pair, and he was a bit surprised to see that they were devoid of the armor every other elf he'd seen within the tower wore. Instead, they were both dressed like they'd stepped out of a period drama.

The female elf with the blonde hair wore a gown of deep crimson, while the male dark elf was clad in pantaloons, a blue tunic, and actual hose. Both wore copious amounts of jewelry and quite a bit of dark makeup around their eyes.

Elijah waited for the pair to pass by, then followed at a discreet distance. He didn't know where he was going, so one direction was as good as any other. He trailed the two elves for a few minutes, listening to them chatter on about nothing as it became clear that they were a couple. Eventually, though, they led him to a pair of elaborately carved double doors, which they unhesitatingly stepped through.

From his position a half dozen yards behind them, Elijah only caught a brief glimpse of the room on the other side of the doors. But the moment he did, he realized that he'd found exactly what he was looking for.

Still, he waited for another elf to wander into the room, and he slipped inside before the door could close. After positioning himself in an out-of-the-way corner, Elijah took stock of the situation.

And it wasn't good.

Around a vast table laden with a feast were seated two dozen elves. And at the head was a man—not an elf—that was clearly the Reaver. If Elijah hadn't known from the man's commanding demeanor, he would have gotten the picture from the notification that popped up the moment he laid eyes on the black-clad man.

Task: Slay the Reaver without alerting his subjects.

42

GLUTTONY

If Elijah hadn't been keenly aware of how close he was to the elves—and more importantly, to the Reaver himself—he would've sworn that he was watching a high-budget fantasy movie. The table itself was polished wood, and it was piled high with so much food that Elijah questioned whether or not the elves could consume even a quarter of it. He saw whole roast pigs, tureens of buttery potatoes, and a host of other foods he couldn't identify but that looked amazingly appetizing.

Suddenly, he was reminded of how long it had been since he'd had a proper meal. During his trek to the tower, he'd eaten nothing but wild game and whatever edibles he could forage. He was used to that sort of diet, so he didn't mind, but it was woefully lacking compared to the feast laid out before him. It was especially pointed because of the sheer delight shown by the elves each time they took a bite.

More than once, he considered casting Calamity and clearing them out, just so he could take their meal. However, the task set by the tower had specified that he should kill the Reaver without alerting his subjects. He didn't think that failing the second part would result in anything dire, but he was certain that it would at least affect his eventual grade.

And he had no intention of taking a lesser reward if he could help it.

So, he settled into a corner and watched the progression of the feast, and over time, the elves grew increasingly drunker. The Reaver, though, abstained from alcohol. His cup—which was a jeweled thing that looked more like a chalice—only held water.

He also didn't eat nearly as much as the elves, who were positively gluttonous with their consumption. For his part, Elijah held his own hunger at bay through a sheer expression of willpower. It wasn't until it had been gnawing at one facet of his Mind for more than an hour that he realized just how unnatural it was.

Elijah had always enjoyed food. Simple or complex, the product of home cooking or a five-star restaurant—it didn't matter. He could always find something to appreciate. Even cooking wild game over an open fire was enough to get his salivary glands working overtime. And yet, he'd never felt an urge to eat, to consume, that was nearly as strong as what he experienced watching those elves gorge themselves. Perhaps it was because of his cultivation, or maybe it was something else entirely. But he knew that the hunger was wrong. That it was alien.

That it came from the Reaver.

The moment that thought crossed Elijah's Mind, he doubled down on his resistance. The challenge of the current level of the tower had already begun, and he'd almost fallen prey to it without even realizing that he was in danger.

Now that he knew what to look for, he could feel the tendrils of alien thoughts wrapping themselves around his Mind. And once he was aware, it was much easier to resist the hunger that had, only a few minutes before, seemed so potent.

He also saw the gluttonous elves for what they were. The slight crinkling around their eyes. The fearful glances toward the Reaver. The tears coating their cheeks. They weren't guests. They were prisoners, one and all.

But Elijah wasn't there to free them.

Instead, he watched as they continued to gorge themselves. The food gradually disappeared down their respective gullets until, at last, the first one passed out. Her stomach bulged obscenely, and using One with Nature, Elijah knew she was dead. She had literally eaten herself to death.

And she wasn't the last.

Over the next few hours, the elves dropped one by one until only the Reaver remained. Still, he sat at the head of the table like nothing had changed. He sipped at his water with a mild expression that bordered on boredom.

Then, finally, he stood. The legs of his chair scraped against the tile floor, loud in the silence the dead had left behind. He looked from one elf to the other, disappointment playing across his face. He ran his hand through his brown hair before letting out a tired sigh. Then, the air around him shimmered.

So did the ambient ethera.

And before Elijah's eyes, the Reaver transformed. His arms and legs extended, growing longer and skeletally thin. The same could be said for his hands, and soon enough, the fingers had doubled in length. More, they were tipped in jagged black claws.

The man's skin took on a gray hue, and his face remolded itself into a visage out of a horror movie. Like a mixture of man and bat, with long incisors extending to at least a few inches long, he looked like someone's twisted interpretation of a vampire.

However, when the man fell on the elves' corpses, Elijah found that the Reaver wasn't interested in blood.

Or not only blood, Elijah amended.

The ghoulish mockery of a man ate everything. It was a grotesque sight, watching that creature gorge itself, but Elijah didn't dare look away. Instead, he watched every last bite. And it was nearly enough to send his stomach into rebellion. He kept himself from vomiting, but it was a close thing.

Even so, Elijah's stomach twisted into knots as he watched the creature's macabre feast. The Reaver took special and obvious pleasure in consuming the elves' ruptured stomachs, but he seemed to quite enjoy every other bit of elf he consumed, as well. Even the bones, which crunched loudly beneath his powerful jaws. Or the intestines, which went down with a wet slurp. Eventually, Elijah stopped trying to identify the bits and pieces, but unfortunately, his biology background came back to haunt him.

Whatever the case, the only solace was that it couldn't last forever.

Eventually, the Reaver completed its feast, leaving only bloody chairs behind. It shifted back into a human form and returned to its chair. A moment later, a pair of ogres stomped into the room. Their body types resembled the jailers, which was to say that they were built like sumo wrestlers, though even more obese.

The pair waddled in and, without a word, started clearing the table. Very little food had survived the elves' forced gluttony, so they were mostly tasked with gathering used dishes. It took a few trips, but gradually, they accomplished their task. In the meantime, the Reaver sat at the head of the table, with a bored expression playing across his face as he sipped at his water.

Once everything had been cleared away, the Reaver pushed himself back to his feet and, without a word, left the dining room via a side door. A disgusted Elijah followed, intending to ambush the creature the moment he had a chance. However, even though he had already used Predator Strike as well as Venom Strike in preparation for the attack, he never got the chance.

Most of the time, the hall was deserted. Yet, each time Elijah verged on commencing his attack, an elf or ogre would be there. Usually, they shuffled past the Reaver quickly—obviously, they were engaged in their own tasks—but they were frustratingly spaced in such a way as to ensure that Elijah never had a clear opportunity to do what he very much wanted to do.

After a few minutes, during which the Reaver traversed the halls at an unhurried pace, he reached a pair of elaborate double doors. At first, Elijah thought he'd stumbled upon some sort of ritual room or something else of importance. However, when the Reaver threw the doors open, he saw another long, straight hall. It was at least fifty yards long, and from what Elijah could see, it was entirely empty.

Looking left, then right, Elijah ensured that no one else was around. Then, he crept forward, preparing to pounce. He knew precisely how he intended to attack; he only needed to do it.

Just before he was going to leap upon the creature's back, heavy footsteps announced a new arrival. Frustrated, Elijah whipped around to see the second-largest ogre he'd ever beheld. The creature was tall and broad, and he was clad in a full set of dark iron armor. Elijah could see nothing of the ogre's skin. Instead, he looked like a monstrous automaton.

"Remain in the hall," the Reaver said. "I feel something amiss, though I know not what it might be. Be wary."

The metal-clad monster grunted an affirmation, the sound confirming that it was, indeed, a living creature. Elijah had enough experience with that armor to recognize the futility in attacking such a creature. He could get through it, perhaps, but not in his draconid form. Even with Predator Strike, he would fail. He knew that as well as he could sense that the creature was much, much higher level than him.

Frustrated, Elijah slipped into the hall as he followed the Reaver. The corridor was nothing special, though Elijah felt curious abnormalities in the walls. Or, rather, he felt the tiny organisms that lived in the pits and grooves that shouldn't have been present in a solid wall.

He remained a few feet behind the Reaver as they traversed the hall until they reached another pair of double doors on the other end. There, the Reaver flung them open to reveal a large and richly furnished apartment. Thick velvet carpets and gold ornaments abounded, but the Reaver paid them no heed. Instead, the creature stepped inside, closing the door only an instant after Elijah had slipped in after his prey.

Just like that, Elijah had a golden opportunity. He had the Reaver alone. He only needed to finish him off before he reached the end of the hallway and that massive metal-clad guard.

Still, he didn't rush.

Elijah had always been a patient person. So, he waited and watched as the Reaver went farther into the apartment. After a few minutes of watching the monster go about its nightly routine, he finally got the opportunity he'd been waiting for. With the additional power of Predator Strike as well as Venom Strike singing through his claws, he pounced.

And missed entirely.

His claws swiped through the creature's human head, but he hit nothing but air. In the meantime, the Reaver screeched. It was a sound no human had ever uttered, and Elijah likened it to something that should've come from an insect. At the same time, the thing transformed—or perhaps it let the illusion of its human form lapse—showing Elijah his error. He'd been using his eyes when he should've relied on his other senses.

As a result, he'd been fooled by a formless illusion.

But now that the monster was in its natural form, that would no longer be a problem. So, even as the thing panicked, Elijah lashed out with his claws, using every point of Strength and Dexterity to get in as many attacks as possible before the monster reacted. When he finally bounded away, he left a ruin of bloody ribbons where the monster's emaciated thigh had once been.

But Elijah had pushed it a little too long, and he was forced to leap over the creature's retaliatory counterattack. It swung its long, thin arm with wild abandon, clipping Elijah's tail and throwing him off-balance. However, even though it sent him sliding across the bedroom, it wasn't enough to injure him.

That had never been the point, though.

When Elijah recovered, he saw that the Reaver had abandoned the fight altogether and was using its lengthy legs to sprint toward the apartment's exit. Elijah's heart jumped into his throat.

If the creature reached the guard, he wouldn't have just failed his task, which would end with him losing a potential reward. Instead, he'd run the risk of losing his life. The guard was dangerous enough on its own, but if the Reaver made it to the end of the hall, more help would be on its way. It wouldn't be long after that that Elijah would be buried under the weight of the entirety of the level's defenses.

He couldn't let that happen.

So, he launched himself after the Reaver, moving with every ounce of speed he could muster. His claws dug into the tiles and ripped the rich carpets apart as he tore across the room. But despite its awkward appearance, the Reaver was deceptively fast, and it remained just ahead of Elijah's pursuit.

When it reached the door, Elijah knew he had to change tactics.

Fortunately, he had just the tool for the job. So, he initiated a transformation back into his human form without breaking stride. The Reaver threw the doors open, then started down the hall.

But Elijah didn't let it get another step before he embraced Snaring Roots and cast the spell. Thick, thorny vines exploded from the floor, wrapping around the monster's thin legs. It ripped free, but for every vine it shredded, another took its place. For a brief second, it was immobile.

Elijah crashed into it, having initiated yet another transformation—this time, taking on the shape of a lamellar ape. The monster raked its claws across his chest, but Elijah had preemptively used Iron Scales, and the attack did nothing. The same couldn't be said for Elijah's own blows, which rained down on the monster's emaciated body with reckless and inevitable abandon. Bones cracked, and the monster screamed. Yet, despite the volume, no cavalry came running to the creature's rescue.

For a second, Elijah thought he'd won the battle.

But then, he heard a metallic click, and an instant later, a line of fiery agony erupted in his side.

43

NOT SO SIMPLE

Elijah twisted away from the lacerating pain, trying at the same time to keep a grip on the monster's bony shoulder. But he couldn't do both at the same time, so his hindbrain kicked in, forcing him to flee the agony cutting a long line into his scales. Against that, his Iron Scales were wholly insufficient, and he let out a roar of pain all his own. It joined the monster's anguished whimpers.

No matter how quickly Elijah moved, though, the pain persisted, and soon enough, he saw why. A small dart—no bigger than his human thumb—was embedded in his scales, and when he yanked it free, he found that a series of long, writhing white tendrils came with it. As they left his body, they left behind a stinging pain that felt like the world's most painful jellyfish sting.

From the inside.

The second the last of the tendrils had left his body to dangle from the dart, Elijah tossed the projectile aside. Or at least he tried to. However, the tendrils had left his entire side so numb that the best he could do was a slight shrug as he dropped the thing onto the carpeted floor. The tingling numbness spread quickly, encompassing the entire left side of his torso and all the way down his hip before, at last, slowing to a virtual stop.

But the effects didn't stop with simple numbness. Instead, with the sensation having spread to his chest, he soon found that his breathing had shallowed to the point where he knew he wasn't getting enough oxygen. That, in turn, caused him to panic.

In only a second, Elijah was panting with anxiety, with his mind whirling for a solution.

Meanwhile, the injured Reaver had begun to recover, its shattered bones shifting grotesquely as they reset. As it pushed itself to unsteady feet, it let out a hiss of pain. Then, it cocked its arm before following it up with a backhanded blow aimed at Elijah's face. He tried to dodge, but with half his body not working properly, he only managed to shift enough to avoid taking the attack head-on.

"Pitiful beast," the creature rasped as Elijah crashed to the floor. Then, it kicked him. "You attack me? In my home?! How dare you?!"

It kicked Elijah again. The blows didn't hurt. In fact, he couldn't even feel them, even if he knew they'd left some damage behind. Instead, the pervasive numbness had started spreading again, telling him that he needed to do something to stop it, lest he lose all bodily control.

So, between kicks, Elijah shifted back to his human form, then cast Touch of Nature, which pushed the numbness back just enough that he could roll out of the way of the next blow. He could do nothing about the follow-up kick that took him in his side and launched his much-lighter body into the wall.

Once again, via One with Nature, he felt the odd grooves in the wall. Suddenly, one facet of his mind arrived at the answer.

Traps.

There were traps in the walls. How could he have missed that? Why hadn't he paid more attention? If he had . . .

No. He couldn't go down that road. Instead, he used Touch of Nature once again, though a good portion of the spell's power went to healing his ribs. Meanwhile, the Reaver continued to rant about intruders and trespassers, spitting out insults that made him sound like an indignant aristocrat who'd stumbled upon a thief.

Which wasn't so far from the truth, really. Except that the aristocrat in question was a monstrous creature with skin like a cadaver and arms and legs that were about two sizes too long for its skeletally slender body.

As that useless thought skittered through one facet of Elijah's Quartz Mind, he used the others to search for a strategy to escape his dire situation. Because even with Touch of Nature, he was only barely able to push the numbness back. So, with the monstrous Reaver kicking him, he didn't have much opportunity to change his circumstances. Still, being launched a few feet away had given him just enough time to attempt a gambit.

So, he shifted his staff just enough to aim it at the Reaver's feet, then cast Storm's Fury. His aim left a lot to be desired, but he still managed to clip the monster's foot with his spell. That sent its leg into brief spasms, which gave Elijah an opening to cast Healing Rain. The nurturing precipitation fell from the sky, soothing Elijah's injuries and working toward pushing the numbness away.

It was incapable of doing the job alone, but with another application of Touch of Nature, he gained even more ground. More importantly, when the Reaver recovered a second later, the healing spells gave him the necessary control to avoid the worst part of the next kick. Though he did feel a rib shift a bit, even when he only took a glancing blow. It was healed a second later, and he continued with that strategy.

With another facet of his Mind, though, he started casting another spell.

Even as he shifted and rolled around on the floor, trying his best to dodge the Reaver's swinging kicks and stomping feet, a swarm of bloodsucking mosquitoes manifested and swooped down on the unsuspecting monster. It was a testament to how worked up the thing was that, at first, it didn't even notice the summoned insects.

Which made for a perfect scenario for the little creatures to do the maximum amount of damage.

Or at least that was how Elijah comforted himself as the Reaver's uncoordinated barrage of attacks continued. He wasn't just getting the snot kicked out of him. He was distracting and delaying the monster.

It was strategy, not incompetence.

Of course, he didn't quite believe that, even as one facet of his Mind tried to convince him of it.

After a handful of seconds, the Reaver finally noticed the mosquitoes sucking its blood. However, by that point, it was too late for it to stop the cascade of afflictions they brought with them. Soon after, it abandoned its quest to kick Elijah into submission, opting instead to try to dislodge the pesky insects. It was mostly unsuccessful in that endeavor, but more importantly, the thing's antics gave Elijah some much-needed breathing room to cast Touch of Nature a couple more times.

Soothing healing washed through him, banishing the numbness almost entirely. Tiny white tendrils were ejected from his body with every instance of the spell. If Elijah would have been a little less occupied with his own survival, he certainly would have been disgusted at the things that had been in his body. As it was, though, he was far too focused on the task at hand. Because now that the numbness had been overcome, he felt like he finally had an advantage.

So, after casting Touch of Nature one last time and healing the remaining damage, he swept his staff out, catching the Reaver mid-kick. With Elijah's still-impressive Strength working for him, he managed to knock the monster's leg out from under him.

The Reaver tipped over, but before it fell, it caught itself with one of its enormously long arms. Then, it skittered backward in a crab walk that took it farther down the hall. Elijah tried to cast Snaring Roots again, but he didn't have enough ethera to fuel the spell.

In fact, the constant healing had sapped almost the entire contents of his Core. He didn't remember spending so much ethera, but he supposed he must have gone into a daze or something.

Or maybe the numbing tendrils had had a secondary effect of draining his ethera.

In any case, the situation had changed, and he had no choice but to adapt. So, he used the one spell he could and once again shifted into the Shape of the Guardian. It had always been his least costly spell, and as such, it gave him the best chance to survive the encounter. As he threw himself to his feet, his body transformed, taking on the strange amalgamation of lizard and primate. Then, he raced after the Reaver.

The first trap he triggered almost took him by surprise, but he'd dedicated one facet of his Mind to keeping track of the changing conditions, and as a result, he became aware of it just in time to avoid the debilitating dart. It was a close enough call that he shifted another three facets of his Mind to that task. As he continued his pursuit of the monster, he was forced to react to more trap activations, twisting and turning his immense body as he sought to avoid a repeat of his first encounter with the darts.

He managed it.

Barely.

But it slowed him down to the point where he only barely managed to keep pace with the Reaver.

With the distance between his prey and the end of the long hall steadily shrinking, Elijah knew he needed to change tactics. So, he harnessed every point of Strength he possessed and flung himself down the hall. However, he didn't go directly at the monster. Instead, he bounded forward, bouncing from one wall to another and keeping just ahead of the traps. With his Strength, he could move incredibly quickly, but when he did that, he couldn't really control himself very well. So, he removed that part from the equation, just pointing himself in a direction and going. Like that, he stayed just ahead of the triggering traps, though he knew that if he slowed by even a millisecond, he would be peppered with darts.

So, he didn't slow, and as a result, he crashed into the Reaver in barely a couple of seconds. The creature was more than a little surprised at Elijah's rapid pursuit, so it didn't even react before it was bowled over. Elijah knew the danger hadn't ended, though, so he wrapped his hand around the monster's slim waist, then used the monster's body as an impromptu shield against the closest trap.

The darts thudded home in the Reaver's struggling body.

It did not possess Elijah's high Constitution. Almost immediately, one of its arms went limp, quickly followed by the rest of its body. In only a few seconds, it was a deadweight, flopping around like a corpse. But it lived. Elijah could sense that much.

Without knowing what else to do, Elijah returned the same way he'd come, traversing the hall on his way back to the Reaver's quarters. Along the way, he continued to use the monster as a shield, intercepting the darts as they came. With multiple facets of his Mind focused on the traps, he could anticipate their activation well enough to facilitate his passage.

By the time he reached the apartments, the Reaver had taken nine darts in various parts of its body, and as a result, it was only barely clinging to life. Elijah ended it by banging its head repeatedly against the ground. It took quite a few blows, but eventually, he managed to kill the thing.

The resultant experience gave him another level, but more importantly, the monster's death completed the final level of the tower.

He sighed, letting the creature fall from his claws. His shoulders slumped as he shifted back to his natural form and realized just how close he'd come to losing. He shuddered to think of what would have happened had he succumbed to those darts.

A few seconds later, a notification told him that he'd completed the last level:

> **Congratulations! You have completed Level Three of Reaver's Citadel.**
> **Grade: A.**
> **To complete the tower, progress to the exit.**

He was a little disappointed he hadn't gotten the highest possible grade, but he was a little too relieved for that to last more than a second or two. He'd conquered Reaver's Citadel, and though it hadn't been quite as harrowing as the Keledge Tower, it certainly hadn't been easy, either. His abilities had been stretched to their limits, and as a result, he'd been forced to learn how to use every tool in his kit.

That was the true reward.

Of course, there was a more tangible reward waiting for him, as well, and it only took a second for him to find the silver box. It was lying next to the huge ogre staff he'd dropped when he'd been forced to transform to his human form after his failed attempt at an ambush.

He bent down and opened the lid, resulting in another notification:

> **Reward for completing Level Three of Reaver Citadel:**
> **Claws of Gluttony**

The item inside was a strange one. At first glance, it looked like a disparate pile of black iron. However, when Elijah pulled it from the box, he realized that it was precisely what the name suggested. Composed of a single leather cuff that was connected to five distinct and hollow claws via a series of thin, black chains—it looked like an awkward thing to wear. That suspicion was confirmed when he tried it on, as well.

He checked his status, and once again, disappointment blossomed when the item didn't live up to his expectations. This time, he didn't even get any attribute bonuses. Indeed, the item seemed no more than ornamental in nature. So, he took it off and threw it into his pack.

Hopefully, he would soon find someone who could help him identify the items he'd acquired in the tower. And perhaps buy the ones he didn't need. If not, he would have to go back to Ironshore, where he knew he could get that kind of information.

Not that he wanted to do that just yet. He could travel between Ironshore and Norcastle much more quickly now that he knew where the second was located. However, it was still a long trip, and one he didn't want to reexperience just yet.

In any case, he scoured the Reaver's quarters, coming away a little disappointed with his haul. There was very little in the apartments that wasn't nailed down, and what he could take probably wasn't worth it. Still, he found some tiny golden statues that looked like they might be valuable, so he figured that it wasn't a total loss. He tossed those into his pack, as well, then set about searching for the exit.

The search only took him a few minutes, and he found the exit in the bathroom of all places. With a shrug, he stepped through the door and was transported back into the real world.

44

THE CONQUERING HERO RETURNS

It had been almost three weeks since the stranger had come out of nowhere, brought hundreds of people back from the brink of certain death, and then declared he would conquer the tower that had plagued Norcastle for months. In that time, Captain Orville Essex had begun to doubt his initial impression of the man. According to his Inspect ability, Elijah Smith was an unremarkable level-eighteen Healer. Yet, the way he'd moved, not to mention his feats in the hospital, had been at odds with that label.

Essex had chosen to trust his gut that something was amiss, and what's more, he had decided to put his faith in the man. He'd come to regret that in the intervening weeks, when the mayor and the goons he'd put on his council had taken issue with the fact that Essex hadn't let them know about the enigmatic Healer. More, they'd called his qualifications into question, casting doubt on his assessment of Elijah. They had even spread rumors about his ineptitude. After all, if he thought a level-eighteen Healer was special—aside from his ability to work in the hospital—then why would the citizens of Norcastle trust him with their security?

But the captain had held fast in his assessment. Elijah Smith was not normal. In fact, Essex suspected that the Healer had some ability or item meant to obfuscate his true class and level. That was the only explanation for his obviously high attributes. He'd subdued one of Essex's guards without skipping a beat, and what's more, he clearly had the ability to traverse the wilderness alone. That, combined with the reportedly ridiculous ethera pool that allowed him to heal far more than anyone else in the city, was enough to convince Essex that the man was special.

Was he special enough to conquer a tower that had, so far, killed more than two dozen of Norcastle's strongest fighters? That was the question that had kept Essex up at night.

"I should have insisted on sending some of my people with him," he muttered, staring at his desk.

Jess Roy, the other Healer who'd brought Elijah to Essex in the first place, sat across from him. As she had done every day since his departure, she'd come by to ask after the man's well-being. And as always, Essex had no answers. The tower had yet to erupt into another surge, so they knew the man was still alive. Beyond that, his fate was a complete mystery.

"You can't just send some people in to help him?" she asked.

Essex shook his head. "We've been over this. Even if you don't send the maximum number of people into a tower—which is six, apparently—it locks others out after a few hours. Last week, I sent some people up there to check, and they were blocked from getting in. He's still alive, but we can't help him. As long as it doesn't send another surge out, we know he's still alive, though."

"You still think he's that guy on the ladder," she said.

"I do," the captain responded, leaning back and running a hand through his hair. As he did, he pulled up the appropriate list:

Planetary Power Rankings (Earth)

Oscar Ramirez—Level 46
Sadie Song—Level 45
Hu Shui—Level 44
Ram Khandu—Level 44
Anupriya Pandey—Level 44
Elijah Hart—Level 44
Niko Song—Level 43
Thor Gunderson—Level 43
Kimberly Jackson—Level 42
Michael King—Level 41
Gunnar Lindstrom—Level 38

. . .

. . .

. . .

The power rankings kept going after that, but Essex wasn't concerned with any of those names. There were a few people within Norcastle who were knocking on the door of making it into the top one hundred, but they were still a few levels away. For his part, Essex didn't think any of them would ever reach those lofty heights. Even the best of them were only a little above average in terms of talent, and the gap between them and the best of the best kept growing wider. And the distance between the top ten and everyone else was a wide gulf that didn't look like it would ever be crossed.

Essex himself was only level twenty-four, and he'd had to make a concerted effort to get to that point. The same was true for his guards, and the only ones who'd made it to a higher level had done so by spending every waking moment hunting in the wilderness alongside like-minded people. That sort of attitude came with issues all its own, and most nights saw the captain lying awake wondering what would happen when those people figured out that the only thing keeping them in check was a sense of morality. One day—perhaps soon—someone powerful would decide that they were tired of following rules. And when that day came, Essex could only hope to minimize the casualties.

In any case, that was a problem for another day. Or hopefully, one that would never manifest. For now, he was focused on the eighth name on that list. Elijah Hart had gained a few levels over the past three weeks, and as a result, he'd jumped into the top ten—an impressive feat by any measure, given how set the general rankings usually were. Sure, the top ten jostled a place or two pretty frequently, but the names had remained mostly the same since the ladder had been introduced.

That supported the captain's theory that Elijah Hart and Elijah Smith were one and the same. After all, what better way to rapidly progress than to challenge a tower meant to be conquered by an entire group of people? Doing so alone was bound to result in some impressive gains, assuming the solitary challenger managed to live through the attempt.

"He didn't seem like one of the top ten most powerful people in the world," Jess stated. "He was just kind of weird."

Essex shook his head, then looked around at his office. The world had changed so much, and he knew he was on the verge of being left behind. He was too old to change the way he thought. Too set in his ways to adjust to the new realities of their transformed world. He didn't intend to give up, but he could see the writing on the wall.

But for now, he just wanted to protect the people who couldn't protect themselves. The innocents who'd taken refuge in Norcastle deserved a life where they didn't have to worry about plagues or monster attacks, and he'd long since decided to devote his life to that endeavor. However, if someone like Elijah Hart decided the world would be better off if Norcastle was wiped from the map, then Essex didn't think he could do much to stop him.

"The sort of person who gets onto a list like that is bound to be abnormal by definition," he stated. "I just hope he's peaceful."

"He was nice," Jess said. "Weird, but nice. Even when he was attacked, he didn't overreact. He just stopped him."

"Because he was never in danger," Essex stated. "But what if someone who can actually hurt him does something stupid? What if he decides to get serious with us? It would probably take the whole guard to stop him. He's probably left hundreds of bodies in his wake."

"He might've just healed his way to his level."

Once again, Essex shook his head. "I doubt that very much," he responded.

It was possible, certainly, but healing didn't work nearly as well for progression as killing. Largely, that was due to the fact that healing the same person over and over gave diminishing returns. There were ways around that, but the System was finicky enough that their experiments had yet to yield concrete results as to what worked and what didn't. It was entirely possible that it wasn't a set of hard-and-fast rules but, rather, a system of guidelines that were applied based on individual and unique situations.

But the biggest reason Essex doubted that Elijah had reached his level via healing alone was the fact that he hadn't even hesitated to say that he could conquer the tower. That kind of confidence only came from experience.

A terrifying prospect, given the difficulty even his best warriors had encountered with the surges of Voxx as well as the people who'd already failed to conquer the tower.

Just then, a knock on the open door announced the arrival of one of Essex's guards. When he looked up, the agitated woman said, "Captain. He's back. The Healer. And there's trouble."

"What?"

"Some of the mayor's men were at the gate when he arrived, and . . ."

"Oh, God," Essex said, leaping to his feet. He was running down the hall before the guardswoman had even turned around. And he had good reason for his haste, too. If the mayor's men acted the way they normally did, then there was a good chance that someone was going to end up dead.

Essex knew that he couldn't allow that to happen because, once blood was shed, there was little he could do to stop it. So, he ran, praying that he wasn't too late to stop the seemingly inevitable clash.

Elijah gripped his staff with white-knuckled fingers as he glared at the four men who'd chosen to bar his way. They were all burly, bearded, and armed, though Elijah didn't get the sense that they were terribly dangerous. It was only a vague feeling, but through his experiences, he'd learned to judge that sort of thing with some degree of accuracy.

"Look at 'im," said one. "Scared out of his mind, he is."

"'Bout to piss his pants, probably. You scared, little man?"

The other two just laughed.

The first—a balding man who looked like an NFL linebacker—stepped forward and pushed Elijah. Or he tried to, at least. Elijah saw it coming, but instead of lashing out with his staff—or worse, taking on one of his other forms and killing all four of the men—he just shifted slightly and avoided the man's hand. That overbalanced the fellow, and he stumbled a little before getting his feet back under him.

"You think you're clever, huh? Well, you ain't gettin' in here without payin' the toll. Two silver coins, or you can walk back wherever you came from."

"And give us that big stick. Looks expensive!" said one of the others.

Elijah already had a single copper etherium gripped in his other hand, so he held it up and said, "Last time I came here, this was the entry fee. Has that changed?"

The Guard, whom Elijah recognized as the same one he'd encountered the first time he had entered Norcastle, shook his head, though the burly bullies didn't see him.

"You pay us separate," the leader spat.

"Why?"

"What?"

"I asked why I should pay you."

"'Cause we'll beat you if you don't!" the man growled.

"Then I'm not paying for entry, right? I'd be paying to avoid having to teach you a lesson. Is that right?"

"What?"

"You don't hear very well, do you? Or maybe you're just incapable of understanding. I don't know. The point is that I'm not paying you just so I don't have to go through the trouble of beating you all within an inch of your lives. In fact, I don't think it's any trouble at all. You seem the types who need it, so I'll just consider it a public service."

"What?"

"You say that a lot."

"Huh?"

"Variation. Nice. Variety is the spice of life, I'm told. So, we doing this thing? I need to meet with Captain Essex, and you're kind of in my way," Elijah stated. "But I'll warn you right now—it's not going to be pleasant for you. I think I can hold back, but you're all kinds of weak, so I'm not making any promises."

"What?"

"Jesus, man. You're backsliding now," Elijah said to the clearly confused would-be bully. "Look—just let me past and it'll save you a beating. And a little advice? Just stop. You're going to pick a fight with someone who's perfectly willing to teach you the lessons I'm trying to avoid here."

That seemed to do it for the man. Clearly, his brain had short-circuited because he didn't even repeat his favorite word before launching himself at Elijah. However, because of his Sash of the Whirlwind, well-honed battle instincts, and his high attributes, to Elijah, the intended attack looked like it was moving in slow motion. So, he sidestepped the blow, then swung his Staff of Natural Harmony.

He didn't use all his Strength, but even so, the sound of a breaking bone echoed through the area as Elijah's staff hit the man's knee. The joint bent the wrong way, and the bully let out a scream of pure anguish as he lurched to the ground. The burly and bearded man collapsed, hitting the turf with a pitiful whimper.

His lackeys, who'd started forward at the same time, pulled to a stop a few feet away. Elijah raised his finger, saying, "Not another step or I won't heal him. If you still insist on fighting, things are going to get worse for all of you. A lot worse."

That—along with how easily he'd disabled their leader—brought them up short. So, keeping one facet of his Quartz Mind trained on the trio, Elijah knelt beside the fallen bully. Then, he tapped him on the head, saying, "Shut up. It's just a dislocated knee. And a broken kneecap. You'll be fine. Quit whining."

"You . . . Y-you asshole!" the man shouted, grabbing at Elijah. It was a weak attempt, and one that was easily slapped aside.

"Come on, man. Do you want me to heal you or not? If I leave you like this, I can guarantee you're going to walk with a limp the rest of your life. Maybe Jess and the other Healers can fix you up. I don't know. But with your attitude, I'm doubting it. So, this might be your best chance to avoid spending the rest of your days hobbling around."

That got through the man's thick skull, and he shut up after that.

Elijah wasn't going to heal him outright, though. For one, he didn't want to waste the ethera. For another, he didn't want to have to break more of the man's bones when he recovered. So, he used Healing Rain instead, then as the rain started to fall, he said, "Stay in the storm. It'll be a little cold, but it should be enough to heal you."

With that, he pushed himself to his feet, grabbed the giant ogre staff from where he'd let it fall, then stepped forward. When he reached the stunned guardsman, he apologized for the mess, then handed him the copper-etherium entry fee. After that, he strolled into the town. Just as he reached the first inter-section and turned toward the hospital, he saw Captain Essex speeding in his direction. Jess followed a few dozen feet behind.

When the older man reached him, Elijah grinned and said, "Oh, nice to see you, captain! I took care of your little tower issue. But you should probably keep sending people in there at regular intervals. It won't be quite as dangerous now that the ethera's been drained, but it'll still be a pain, so don't send your rookies in there."

Then, he stepped past the stunned captain and smiled broadly as Jess finally caught up. He said, "Hey! I've been thinking a lot about you, and I've decided to let you court me."

"Huh? Court?"

"I feel like I'm speaking a different language lately. Court. As in, attempt to date. I know, it's a stunning turn of events, but I think you've got a good shot," he said.

She burst out laughing. "You haven't changed a bit, have you?"

"You mean I'm still ruggedly handsome and incredibly charismatic?"

"Yeah. Sure. Let's go with that."

"I feel like you might be making fun of me."

"Oh, no—I would never do that."

"Good. I don't deal well with teasing. I have very thin skin."

45

CONSEQUENCES

A blanket of snow covered the roofs and collected in the shadowy alleys of Norcastle as Elijah was escorted through the town. From most of the eaves hung garlands and flickering lights, and evergreen wreaths festooned most of the doors. Red and green ribbons and streamers abounded, lending the city a festive spirit that felt infectious, even after the encounter with the thugs at the gate.

"I didn't realize it was Christmas," Elijah said softly as he took in the festive decorations. Indeed, his sense of time still hadn't recovered after his trips into towers and his long isolation. At one point, he'd tried to keep up with the passing months, but it had quickly grown impossible. Now, he usually only paid attention to the seasons, and only for practical reasons. The idea of celebrating holidays—especially ones with religious connotations—hadn't even crossed his mind since the world had been transformed.

Still, he wasn't immune to the Christmas spirit. Growing up, the holidays had always been a source of warm and comforting memories, and the world's transformation hadn't changed that fact.

"The mayor thinks it's important to celebrate the holidays. He thinks we'd lose sight of our past if we forget the things that used to be important," Essex said.

Jess added, "Plus, everyone likes Christmas."

"That, as well," Essex stated.

"Neat" was Elijah's response. He immediately regretted the word choice, but it was too late to change it, so he just let himself fall silent. Soon enough, they reached a large square, at the center of which was an enormous spruce tree that was at least forty feet tall and decorated with twinkling lights as well as red and green ornaments. "Went all out, huh?"

"I love it," Jess said, her bright smile showing off a pair of impressive dimples. "My favorite time of year."

After that, they left the square and headed in the direction of the guards' headquarters. Now that they'd left the main thoroughfare behind, the decorations became less prominent, but they were still there, just more subdued. Even the building that was their destination bore a festive wreath on the door.

They passed inside, then headed to the captain's office. Once the door was shut, Elijah leaned his massive ogre staff against the wall and let out a sigh. "That thing is just too big," he said. "So, what's up? Who were those guys out front? And am I going to have to kill them?"

"Please don't," Essex said.

"I mean, I don't want to, but . . ."

"They're the mayor's men," Jess said, flopping down in one of the chairs. "Do you really think you could? Kill them, I mean."

Elijah shrugged. "Probably. If they come at me all at once, I might have to reveal some of my secrets," he said, waggling his eyebrows. "But . . . Yeah. I think could do it. Why? You need some bullies killed?"

"What? No!" she said. "Of course not!"

"It probably wouldn't be much trouble. I could just nip on over and—"

Essex interrupted, "Please do not kill anyone in my city. Especially them. The mayor and his men aren't perfect, but without them, this city wouldn't exist. It's going to be difficult enough explaining what you just did as it is."

"I was just kidding."

"About murder," Essex pointed out.

"Yeah. Probably bad taste," Elijah admitted. "Won't happen again, cap'n."

"Please don't call me cap'n."

"Aye, aye," Elijah said, giving the man a poorly received salute. However, before Essex could say anything else, Elijah went on: "So, I guess you want to hear about the tower, huh? Turns out, it was a pain . . ."

He went on to describe—in detail—everything he'd seen inside. If Essex was going to send more people in, he needed to know everything. Perhaps that would give his subordinates—or possibly even him—the opportunity to survive. For their part, both Jess and Essex listened intently, with the latter even going so far as to take copious notes and asking plenty of questions. Due to his advanced Mind cultivation, Elijah had no problems remembering everything, so he gave Essex all the information he could want and more. By the end, more than three hours had passed, and Elijah was even more exhausted than after his bout in the tower's arena.

The problem was that he'd barely had any social interaction over the past couple of years, so when he did talk to other people, it was an exciting and sometimes frustrating experience where he often went overboard one way or the other. Sometimes, that manifested in poorly conceived jokes, but his issues with talking to Jess were another symptom of his psychological trauma. Elijah knew that, and yet, there wasn't much he could do about it except to try to work through those issues as best he could.

And that was exhausting, if ultimately necessary.

When he'd finally finished, he said, "And that's about it. Went in, killed some ogres and elves, fought a gladiator-style gauntlet, and killed this creepy

Slenderman-slash-vampire knockoff. But it wasn't about the enemies I killed. The real reward was the loot I got along the way."

"I don't think that's how the saying goes," Jess interjected.

Elijah shrugged. "Well, that's how it should go. Anyway, do you need to know anything else about the tower? Because I've been roughing it for a while now, and I'd love to get a nice meal and a real shower. Oh, and is there anyone around here who can identify items? Because I got some stuff in there that I'm not sure exactly what it does."

"I think that's all I need for now," Essex said. "But can I give you some advice?"

"Sure."

"However it is that you're concealing your identity, you should probably choose a different name. If I made the connection between your assumed identity and the power rankings, then someone else will, too."

"Oh," Elijah said. He'd accidentally left his real name on his assumed identity when he'd first arrived in Norcastle, but he'd changed it before he had gotten too far into the city. He hadn't even considered changing his first name, though. "I guess I'm just not really cut off for subterfuge."

"You should probably learn to be," Essex said.

Elijah sighed. "Probably right," he said, running a hand through his hair. It was greasy and more than a little unkempt, reminding him of just how little good his impromptu shower back in the tower had been. He pulled his hand away, looking at a bit of gore that had stuck to his finger. He shook it, sending the chunk of gray skin to plop against a wall. "Gross."

"Is there anything else we should know?"

"Nope," Elijah said brightly. "Oh, there's also a little abandoned town a few miles away. Your people should probably avoid it unless you want to die. There's a big, grumpy bear there. He's kind of a friend, actually. Or at least he tolerates me. I think that was probably the fish, though. But I like to think my winning personality had something to do with it. In any case, he's probably way more than any of you can handle, and I'd be very upset if someone took that as a challenge, if you know what I mean."

"I don't—"

"Don't mess with my bear buddy is what I'm saying. I can't stress this enough."

"We won't. But I can't control everyone," Essex stated.

Elijah nodded. "Alright. So, if there's nothing else?" There wasn't, so he grabbed both of his staves and said, "I'm going to get a shower and some rest. When can I visit the Branch of the World Tree?"

"I'll set it up. Just come back here when you're ready," Essex said.

With that, Elijah said goodbye to Jess, then headed back outside. By that point, the sun had begun to set, which made the holiday decorations that much more expressive. The sight brought with it a wave of nostalgia. In Hawaii, he hadn't been especially interested in Christmas. Certainly, he'd celebrated—everyone did—but it didn't carry the same cachet that it had back home.

But the holidays he'd shared with his family before his parents had died were some of his best memories. Those came with a certain sadness, though. Not only were they a grim reminder of his parents' untimely deaths, but it also brought his separation from his sister and her family into focus. Before the world had transformed, he'd always assumed he'd have plenty of time to reconnect, and there was always technology to fill the gap left by physical distance. After nearly having his wife stripped away by terminal cancer, he'd been forced to confront the realities of his choice to move so far away from home.

The isolation was especially difficult when his illness had forced him to abandon work. His coworkers had tried to keep in touch, but they were always just that—coworkers. Without the connective tissue of a shared career, they inevitably drifted away. He'd even lost his girlfriend's support, though that was more his fault than hers.

In any case, seeing the Christmas decorations of Norcastle brought with it a mixture of pain, nostalgia, and a little comfort. So, when he arrived at the hotel—or inn, really—Elijah wore a subdued smile. The innkeeper was just as brusque as before, but she remembered him, which made renting a room a little easier. Soon enough, he found his way upstairs where he took a long shower before going to bed.

He slept like a log, and when he awoke, he set about the task of emptying his pack and cataloging his loot. The two most important pieces were the staff and the Claws of Gluttony, though the sword he'd taken from the Warden was probably quite valuable, as well. Beyond that, he'd taken a few smaller weapons from the elves he'd set against one another. Finally, he had a large pile of loose copper coins as well as a few silver etherium.

He still wasn't certain what the sword or staff did, and he felt sure that he was missing something with the Claws of Gluttony, as well. However, as he'd told Essex, he had no way of figuring any of that out. So, that was at the top of his list regarding what to do for the rest of the day. After that, he needed to access the Branch and deposit his etherium as well as try to find out if there were any other towns nearby.

Because his resolution to find his sister hadn't faded. Sure, he'd been derailed a bit by his recent tower excursion, but now that Norcastle was safe, he was even more dedicated to hunting her down than ever. The only reason he wasn't more frantic was because of his assumption that his sister was safe and, perhaps more importantly, due to the fact that he had no idea how to find her. After being touched by the World Tree, Earth's terrain had been randomized and expanded, which meant that nothing was where it was supposed to be. Regardless, he would continue looking until he found his family.

So, after dressing in his cleanest clothes, he headed downstairs and settled in at the bar. The same cook greeted him, and he ordered a breakfast of sausage and oatmeal. While he waited for his food, Elijah glanced around the room and, to his frustration, found that quite a few of the patrons were watching him.

Sure, they tried to look like they weren't, but with his multifaceted Mind as well as One with Nature, Elijah could see through their thin subterfuge.

So, as he ate, he kept an eye on everyone. Most of the inn's diners were just normal people, but six of them stood out. Elijah couldn't quite put his finger on what made them different, but he suspected that each one had a few levels under their belt. And it didn't take a genius to figure out why they were there, especially after his actions the day before.

It seemed that, despite his efforts to help the city's people, his peaceful stay in Norcastle had come to an end. But Elijah had no interest in going on a rampage, so even though he could tell that none of the watchers had good intentions, he still took the time to enjoy his breakfast before heading back upstairs.

The moment he was in his room, he threw open the window, checked to make certain that he hadn't left anything behind, then shifted into his draconid form. After that, he embraced Guise of the Unseen before leaping through the window and landing in the alley beside the building. There, he settled into the shadows to wait.

Only ten minutes later, he heard a ruckus before the heavy tromp of boots announced that someone had entered his room up above. A few seconds after that, he saw one of the men from the inn's common room poke his head out the window and let out a curse.

Elijah only had to wait a little longer before the hostile men and women stormed out of the inn and spread out, presumably to look for him. But he knew they wouldn't find him. So, he waited until their search took them down the street before he set off across the city.

He didn't intend to stick around Norcastle for much longer, but he still needed some information before he set off back into the wilderness. More, he intended to check on Jess and Essex to make sure they were okay.

Because if they weren't, bad things were going to happen to whoever had hurt them.

46

THE RIGHT DIRECTION

The frigid air reminded Elijah of the recently departed tower, though there were enough differences that he didn't start experiencing flashbacks. For one, he increasingly thought that he was immune to post-traumatic stress. Certainly, in the immediate aftermath of some horrible experience, he felt the full weight of his trauma. More than once, those instances had very nearly broken him—at least temporarily. However, the more distance between him and what should have been life-altering trauma, the more he could look at it from the perspective of an observer. He knew he should feel differently. Everything he'd ever learned about human psychology told him as much. And yet, he didn't, lending weight to his budding theory that the influx of ethera had come with some sort of inoculation to the psychological impact of life-and-death struggle.

Or maybe it was his cultivation. It might've even been his archetype. As a steward of nature, he had a unique perspective on the struggle inherent in nature, so perhaps that insight was enough to alter the way he processed the things he'd been forced to do. Either way, he was grateful for it. Without that ability to keep going despite everything he'd been through, he would have long since succumbed. And if that had been the case, there's no chance he would have survived.

In addition to that seeming inoculation to the psychological consequences of his decisions, the other reason he didn't descend into flashbacks was because of the clear blue sky. It was the sort of morning that only seemed to come in winter, and freezing though it was, there was a certain crisp beauty to it that certainly had never been present in the tower.

But the irritation and murderous thoughts were similar. In the tower, he'd aimed those feelings at ogres and elves, but in Norcastle, the target landed squarely on the backs of the mayor's men who'd been sent to harass him.

Or kill him.

Maybe they even thought to kidnap him. Elijah had no idea what their goals were, but he had seen enough to recognize that the realization of those goals would be bad news for him.

Not that they had any chance at all. They were weak, blundering idiots, and they posed no threat to him. Even in his human form, which was markedly weaker than either of his other shapes, he could tear them apart with ease. And he was sorely tempted to exercise his superiority, as well. There were only two things holding him back, one of which was simple morality. Defending his grove was one thing. So was fighting his way through a tower. But when he had the option of simply leaving? No—he couldn't make himself take lethal steps if he had that option in front of him.

The other issue was that Essex had made it clear that the mayor and his thugs had done good things in service of the city's residents. Elijah didn't know what form that took, but the captain had been adamant that Norcastle couldn't survive without them. That was enough to bring Elijah up short and push the worst of his natural inclinations to the side.

Of course, that wouldn't remain the case if they'd hurt Essex or Jess. Or any of the other Healers at the hospital. Elijah was hesitant to kill other human beings, but he wouldn't hold back if they were the first to cross those lines.

So, he stalked through the town, and despite the city streets being bathed in bright sunlight, none of the other pedestrians could see him. They were completely unaware of the predator in their midst, and that fact excited his draconid instincts like nothing else could.

But he pushed those wild impulses aside and focused on the task at hand. At first, he'd followed a few of the thugs who'd meant to ambush him, but he'd quickly lost interest when they gave up on the chase and returned to the castle at Norcastle's center. Elijah could have followed, but he thought another tactic was appropriate, which was why he found himself traversing the city on his way to the hospital.

Once he reached the building in question, he waited a few minutes for an opportunity to slip inside. When one didn't present itself, he circled the structure until he found an open window on the second floor. Using his sharp claws like he was climbing a tree, he vaulted to the window and slipped inside. From there, it was easy enough to find Jess.

She was perfectly fine, which was quite a relief. However, he didn't immediately confront her. Instead, he waited until she was alone before he shifted back to his human form and said, "Don't scream."

Of course, she screamed.

Or tried to. But before more than a peep could escape from between her lips, he had himself pressed against her, with his hand over her mouth. "I said not to scream," he repeated. "I'm going to let you go. Please, for the love of God, don't scream. Okay?"

She nodded.

Elijah let her go and backed away. That moment of closeness had felt nice, though. Way nicer than he would have expected. But he had been alone for quite some time, so maybe he should have known how much a little human contact would mean to him. In any case, he pushed that aside and said, "I saw that you have some visitors in the hospital. Want to tell me what's going on?"

Jess didn't answer. Instead, she punched him—inexpertly—in the chest. Then, she hit him again. "Don't ever do that again!" she hissed. "I thought I was about to die! And where did you even come from? How did you get in here? I swear, if you—"

Elijah took the first couple of hits, but then he caught her wrists as gently as he could. "I came in through one of the windows, okay? And I couldn't very well use the front door, could I? I saw the goons out there," he said. "And the ones inside, too. What the hell is going on?"

"Let me go," she said with a calm iciness that brooked no hesitation.

Elijah pulled away and held his hands up in surrender. "I'm sorry. I just can't afford to let you take all your frustrations out on me. I'm sure those idiots out there are going to notice if you're gone for too long," he said, looking around the storage room. It was large enough to accommodate the two of them, but only just.

"It's your fault."

"What is?"

"That they're here," she said. "They're the mayor's men."

"I saw two women."

She rolled her big brown eyes. "It's a figure of speech," Jess said. "It doesn't literally mean that they're all male."

"People. You should call them people so you can avoid these kinds of—"

"Fine! People!" she interrupted, and with some vehemence. "You are so frustrating to talk to sometimes!"

"Just take a deep breath," Elijah said, his hands still in the air. He had his staff in one of them, and the butt hovered dangerously close to what looked like a shelf full of cleaning chemicals. "Woosah."

"What does that mean?"

Thinking it was probably safe, he lowered his hands. Fortunately, Jess didn't react to that. "I saw it in a movie once."

"What does that have to do . . . You know what? Never mind. You need to get out of the city," she said. "The mayor is after you. I don't know exactly what he wants to do, but I can guarantee it won't be good."

"I could just kill him."

"What? No! You can't kill him. He's . . . It's complicated, okay? I mean, he's an asshole, but he's also the reason a lot of people are still alive."

"Counterpoint, he sent people to probably kill me. And it wouldn't even be that hard. Probably. I haven't really killed any humans though, so . . . Yeah," he said, trailing off when he saw the expression of horror on Jess's face. "Not that I want to kill people. I just . . . I mean . . . Okay. I won't kill anybody unless they deserve it."

"That's . . . a good policy."

"And just so we're clear, the mayor and his goons don't deserve it, right?"

"They do not."

"Alright. Noted. Just maiming and crippling. I can do that."

"No."

"I was . . . I was mostly joking," Elijah lied.

"I think you'd better leave," Jess said.

"Ouch."

"It's not like that. It's just that . . . I mean . . . With everything going on, it's probably best. Not that we don't appreciate what you did."

"Sure seems like nobody appreciates it," Elijah said, more than a little annoyed. He'd done nothing but try to help the people of Norcastle, and now he was getting chased off? That wasn't right.

"We do. I swear, we do," she said, stepping forward and gripping his arm. "This is for your good as much as it is for anyone else's."

"I promise you, it's not," he said, gently pushing her hand away. All the playful quirkiness was gone from his voice as he continued: "But I get it. I'm dangerous and weird, and I scare people, right? Or maybe the mayor heard about what I did—either in the tower or the hospital—and he wants to use me. Either way, if I stay here, I'm going to have to make it clear why that's a bad idea. So, you're right. I should probably leave. I just wish it would have ended differently."

She looked down. "Me, too."

Elijah shook his head, then said, "Don't freak out."

Without any more warning, he used Shape of the Predator, assuming his draconid form. To her credit, Jess didn't scream, but she definitely reacted with some alarm, pushing herself against the wall in an effort to get as far away from him as she possibly could. Of course, that just highlighted an issue Elijah hadn't anticipated.

So, he canceled the transformation, shifting back to his human form. Then, he said, "Okay, so I had this cool thing planned where I was just going to transform into a draconid, then disappear. But that's not possible because, apparently, you being all freaked out by it counted as me being in combat. Which . . . you know . . . ouch. That hurts. But whatever. I get it. Giant lizard-dragon monster, right? Of course you'd be scared. But it does raise an issue, chiefly that I need you to leave the room first so I can use my stealth ability."

"What kind of a Healer are you?"

"I'm technically not one. I'm a Druid. Totally different thing. Better, in my opinion, but your archetype is totally cool, too. So . . . unless you want to, you know, give me a proper goodbye . . ."

"Not going to happen," she said, snorting a chuckle.

He shrugged and grinned. "Didn't really expect it, but you can't blame a guy for trying. But I do need you to tear yourself away from me. I won't get past those thugs without going on a killing spree if I'm unable to use stealth."

"Just take care of yourself, okay? And come back. Maybe we can . . . you know . . . see what happens," she said. Then, before he could respond, she left the room.

The moment she did, he whispered to himself, "That went really well."

Even as he said it, he shifted back into his draconid form and adopted Guise of the Unseen. A moment later, he was padding through the hospital toward the window he'd used as an entrance. He took a few seconds to watch Jess, who was cut off by one of the goons, but her responses to his questions were acceptable enough that he let her go a moment later. So, seeing that she was fine, Elijah left her and the hospital behind.

One facet of his Mind paid attention to his surroundings as he traversed the city, but the majority of his thoughts were on the Healer. He'd never really expected anything to happen. Maybe if he'd stuck around a little longer, but he knew that, even in the best of times, he was an acquired taste. He'd been a lot smoother before the world changed, but two solitary years had a way of affecting a man's personality. He still hadn't returned to what he'd once considered his normal demeanor, and he wasn't certain that he ever would.

But that was fine.

It might make things a little lonely going forward, but hopefully, the more time he spent around people, the easier it would become.

In any case, Elijah soon crossed the town, barely noticing the festive decorations along the way, and soon arrived at the guards' quarters. It only took a little patience to wait for an opportunity to enter and make his way to Essex's office. It was empty, but that didn't stop Elijah from heading inside and waiting on the captain.

An hour later, the man himself showed up. Upon entering, he shut the door, then plopped down in the chair behind his desk. A second later, he'd opened the drawer to retrieve a bottle of whiskey.

Elijah let Guise of the Unseen and Shape of the Predator drop at the same time. The captain reacted quickly, yanking a long dagger from his belt. But Elijah slapped it away with one of his staves. The other, he balanced on his shoulder as he said, "Calm down, captain. I'm just here for a little information."

"How did you get in here?"

"Just waltzed right in. Nobody even tried to stop me," Elijah said. "But never mind that. There are some things I need to know, and I think I'm correct in assuming that I'm not going to get the Branch access you promised."

He sighed. "I'm sorry. If it makes you feel any better, I did try to—"

"It doesn't," Elijah said. In a perfect world, he could have just walked into the castle and accessed the Branch, permission or not. But that just wasn't possible. The Envoy who was inevitably there could deny him access. Or worse. Ramik had implied that Envoys had complete dominion around their Branches, which meant that Elijah couldn't just force his way in and take what he wanted.

He continued, "In fact, it makes me feel like you took advantage of me. Here I was thinking we had a deal. Shame on me, I suppose. But here's the thing—you still have information I need. Even if I can't access the Branch, you can help me out."

"What do you need to know?"

"Are there any other settlements nearby?" Elijah asked. "Ones with Branches, I mean."

"No. Not that we're close enough to connect with, but there were some refugees that came from the east. They said that the population is denser in that direction, but it's also more dangerous."

"I can deal with danger," Elijah said. "Did they say anything about what towns or cities are there? I'm looking for Seattle."

"Oh."

"Oh, what?"

"I have heard some things about Seattle," Essex stated. "It's in that direction. Vaguely. But I don't know if you really want to go there."

"Why not?"

"It's a war zone," Essex stated. "A bunch of different factions. I don't know much beyond that."

"Who does?"

"Nobody here. The group who came from there died about four months ago," the captain explained. "They never integrated with the rest of the population. They didn't trust us, and they ended up being some of the first to die from the plague."

"Crap," Elijah said. Then, he sighed. He'd come in search of a direction, and he'd gotten that much. Still, he'd hoped for a little more. "Any luck with item identification?"

"Sorry, no. All the crafters are loyal to the mayor, so . . ."

"So, if I go to them, they'll run to tell his people. Great. Well," he sighed. "I guess that's it, then. I wish I could say I've enjoyed my stay in your town, but the last bit where people were trying to hunt me down and kill or capture me kind of soured me on Norcastle. I'm sure you understand."

"I'm sorry it happened like this. If I was in charge, I would have done things very differently," the captain responded. Then, he looked Elijah in the eyes. "Take care of yourself, Mr. Hart. I have a feeling that things are going to get a lot worse for you before they get better."

Elijah shrugged. "Story of my life. I'll survive."

47

BAD OMENS

"Don't like this one bit," growled Kurik as he knelt next to the tracks. He cast his gaze over the pass, seeing a story that had played out months before. There were hundreds of tiny arachnid corpses, all in various states of decay. He recognized the invasive species, which, on his home world, had been referred to as sovereign spiders. Typically, the monsters were incredibly territorial, and left unchecked, they were capable of approaching sapience. They had no natural predators, largely due to the fact that their flesh was infused with poison that would painfully kill anyone or anything that ingested it. As a result, there was little reason for natural predators to have evolved.

But something had killed the budding community, as evidenced by the piles of corpses and half-rotted webs.

"We found somethin', boss!" came a shout from up the pass.

The dwarf pushed himself to his feet, then knocked the dust from his pants before following the shout to its origin. The pass was narrow, but it was more than large enough to accommodate Kurik and his team of Scouts. They had been tasked with finding a way through the mountains, and it appeared that they had discovered just that. However, the spider corpses had brought them all up short.

After a few moments, he found his way to a yawning cave. From experience, he knew it would have been a perfect location for a sovereign-spider queen to nest. But judging by the smell, something large was rotting inside. Kurik didn't need to lay eyes on the corpse to know what he would find.

But he'd always been thorough, which was why he'd been given leadership over the Scouts of Ironshore. It was also why he'd survived as long as he had. So, he squared his shoulders and headed through the mouth of the cave. Only a moment later, his dwarven eyes adjusted to the lack of light, and he saw the rotting corpse of a full-grown sovereign-spider queen.

He also saw his subordinate, Rasana, kneeling next to the thing. She was short, even for a gnome, and her blue hair stood in stark contrast to the hulking monster's corpse in front of her. She looked back, her eyes shining, and grinned. "It's a real queen, Kurik! Do you know what this means?"

"That somethin' even nastier is out here," he muttered.

"No. I mean, yes. Of course that's a possibility. But I'm talking about the venom!" she went on. "Do you know what we could do with something that strong?"

"Poison somethin'?"

"No! Well, yes. But I talked to old Biggle—you know, the Alchemist—and he said that a potent poison is the only thing he's missing for a Body-cultivation potion!" she said, her words spilling out in a rush. "With the amount I could get from this big of a specimen, I bet he could make ten or maybe even fifteen doses! That's huge, Kurik! Like, super huge!"

Kurik didn't need her to tell him the value of cultivation. Back home, his people would make pilgrimages to the lava pits far below the city and use the dense ambient ethera as well as the lava itself to spark the evolution into the first stage. Of course, even that had required alchemical assistance for all but the most naturally gifted, so he was well aware of how valuable something like that could be.

"Seems less than optimal," he muttered. He and the rest of his clan had been exiled before he'd ever had a chance to start his own cultivation, and he'd all but given up on taking the first steps down that road. However, a newly integrated world offered many opportunities, which was why it was like a magnet for outcasts like him.

Like everyone in Ironshore, really.

"I think it would be brilliant!" she squeaked. Even after more than two years living side by side with gnomes, Kurik still wasn't quite used to them. None of them had proper beards, and they were far too excitable. Still, he didn't want to be prejudiced, so he'd tried his best to be as accepting of the other races as possible. Because of that, he had one of the most evenly integrated squads in the entire city. "Imagine actually achieving Body of Wood stage. It would change everything."

Kurik wasn't so sure if he'd accept a poison-based Body-cultivation potion even if it was available. A proper dwarf used fire, after all. Any dwarf who used anything else, regardless of how advanced their cultivation, was worthy of mistrust. Or at least that had been the case back home.

But he wasn't back home anymore. He was on Earth, and he needed to adjust his expectations accordingly.

"What killed her?" he asked, wanting to change the subject.

"Looks like an animal of some sort," the little gnome answered, pushing herself to her feet. "But I don't think I'd want to meet the sort of creature that could do this to a queen sovereign spider. You see the evidence of poison, right? Sovereign spiders are naturally resistant, so it would've had to have been an extremely powerful toxin."

"Or just a lot of it," Kurik interjected.

"Right," Rasana agreed. "Either way, it's very interesting."

Kurik had some ideas about who was responsible, but he didn't give those thoughts voice. The entity who called the mist-wreathed and recently named Isle of Slaughter home was not to be mentioned, lest he visit some calamity upon their heads. Still, he'd heard some stories from the goblin Calix who was the lone survivor of the expedition sent to that island. Unless she'd been drinking, she never spoke of the massacre she had witnessed, but that changed when she was in her cups. So, Kurik had made it his business to facilitate that by spending a few nights buying her one drink after another. After all, if there was some murderous monster living only a couple of miles away, he needed to know. He'd rather take his chances in the wilderness than ignore that sort of threat.

What he'd learned had very nearly sent him running. But then the human had visited their city, and during that time, he'd acted perfectly reasonable. So, Kurik had resolved to stay. But he had also decided to take no chances at risking that man's ire.

Whatever the case, he'd learned enough to match the human's fighting style with the old wounds he saw on the spider's corpse. Certainly, it could have been his fears manifesting to make connections that weren't there, but Kurik had always prided himself on his ability to look at things objectively. More than that, he trusted the instincts that told him that he was looking at the aftermath of that man's passage.

He was just about to order Rasana to organize the processing of the monster's corpse when another member of his team raced into the cave. Pavi was a goblin, but unlike his more urbane brethren, he'd taken a liking to the outdoors. That had translated into his joining Kurik's scouting team.

Pavi bent down, catching his breath as he said, "Boss. There's tracks up ahead. You need to come see."

"What kind?"

"I'm not sure, but there's a lot of them," the goblin panted. "I think . . . I know I'm not the most experienced, but . . ."

"Spit it out."

"Hundreds. Maybe thousands, boss. I don't know what made the tracks, but there were a lot of them."

"Show me."

After that, Pavi led him outside and up the trail through the pass. After a few minutes, they came upon the tracks Pavi had mentioned, and Kurik saw precisely why the young goblin was so alarmed. There weren't just hundreds of tracks. There were thousands leading to a rough path that ran perpendicular to the main trail. A few felled trees lay nearby, telling Kurik yet another story.

But most troubling of all was that he recognized the tracks. Not wanting to believe his own first impressions, he knelt at the edge of the trail and examined an isolated footprint. That confirmed his fears.

"Orcs," he said.

"Orcs?" Pavi echoed. "Here? Where'd they come from?"

"I don't know," Kurik admitted, pushing himself back to his feet. He ran his hand through his auburn hair, then let out a sigh. "Gather the other scouts."

"But—"

"Now, Pavi. We might already be too late."

"For what?"

"Do you know anything about orcs?" Kurik asked. The goblin admitted that he didn't, so Kurik went on: "They have a very distinct cycle of social development. When they first appear, they're little more than intelligent beasts. Like the crag apes back home. But if a pack grows past a certain point, they start working together. Their society starts to evolve, becoming a primitive tribe. For a while, that's how they stay. But if they're left alone for too long, they go to the next phase."

"What's that?"

"Conquest. Throughout the universe, on every planet connected to the World Tree, orcs are considered a menace that must be eradicated the moment they're found. Otherwise, they will rapidly grow into a force that will sweep across a planet, conquering everything in their path. Eventually, they will develop sapience. Do they not teach the story of the Dred Empire on your world?"

"Nobody taught us anything where I'm from," Pavi stated.

"Well, they should. This many orc tracks means only one thing," Kurik said before pausing for a moment. When he continued, his voice was grim, "Ironshore is in grave danger."

After that, the young goblin sped off to gather the others. Meanwhile, Kurik waited, his mind churning with a host of possibilities. Each one was worse than the last, so by the time his ten underlings joined him, he was on the verge of panic. Still, he kept his wits about him as he gave out his instructions.

Two of his Scouts he sent back to Ironshore. Six were tasked with following the tracks to their origin. Meanwhile, he and Pavi—who happened to be the stealthiest of all the Scouts, save for Kurik himself—would follow the tracks until they found the orcs who'd used the pass. With any luck, they would have missed Ironshore altogether, but even as that thought crossed his mind, Kurik knew that it was a long shot.

Once everyone had their orders, they set off into the wilderness. For his part, Kurik led Pavi along the alternate path for almost a mile until they reached another trail that led down the mountain. It showed plenty of signs of having been used, but not recently. That was somewhat comforting, but Kurik knew enough about orcs to know that it wouldn't last. If they'd sent a war party out, there was assuredly a village in the other direction.

Still, he didn't want to make any assumptions, so he continued to follow the tracks, using Camouflage to mask his passage. Pavi did the same, though his ability wasn't as advanced as Kurik's.

For the rest of the day, they descended the mountain on the crooked and winding path used by the orcs, and just before nightfall, they found their quarry. The orcs were big, with prominent brows, sloped foreheads, gray skin, and jutting tusks. More distressingly, they were all wearing primitive clothing and carrying stone-bladed weapons. That suggested that they'd reached a reasonably advanced stage of development.

As he knelt in the bushes a few dozen yards away, Kurik could only take solace in the group's size. There were just twenty orcs there, which was far more than he could fight alone. But even with the bulk of Ironshore's defenders having been slain by the man on the island, they had enough capable warriors to fend off such a group.

Still, after Kurik had seen everything there was to see, he and Pavi circled around the group of orcs and continued down the narrow pass. Unfortunately, it quickly became clear that the group they'd encountered was only one among many. Over the next day, they found a dozen more like it until, at last, they reached the base of the mountain.

There, they encountered the bulk of the orcs' forces.

A hundred or more fires burned among a forest of primitive tents. But more distressing was the sheer number of orcs present. If there were less than five thousand, Kurik would have been incredibly surprised, and he suspected that the true number was probably twice that.

After he'd observed enough, Kurik grabbed the terrified young goblin Scout's arm and guided him away. He didn't relax until they were miles into the wilderness and, even then, only slightly.

He said, "Pavi, I want you to promise me something."

"What is it, boss?"

"What's about to happen to Ironshore is going to be horrific. I intend to fight until the very end, but if it comes down to it, I want you to promise me that you'll gather as many people as you can and flee."

"But, boss . . ."

"Those orcs there are more than we could've handled before we lost the mercenaries," he said. "We have almost no chance of winning now. You owe it to yourself to escape what's coming."

"What about you?"

He fingered the axe at his waist. "Orcs are good for leveling, I'm told. I intend to see for myself."

48

UNFORGIVABLE SIN

The smell of pine needles hung in the air, and regret danced in Elijah's mind as he padded through the forest. He'd left Norcastle without making the mayor's guards pay for their transgressions, and he sorely wished he'd taken a different tactic. However, as vicious as his need for justice was, they had done nothing more than inconvenience him. And by all accounts, the mayor was a big part of the reason the city's residents had survived.

Elijah didn't have much of a problem with killing. He'd done it enough to get past any compunctions he might have had in that arena. However, he drew the line at senseless violence, which was how he would have categorized killing or maiming the mayor and the people sent to harass him.

So, as much as it galled his pride to let them off without punishment, he pushed those thoughts away and focused on his surroundings.

Fortunately, his draconid form wasn't cold-blooded like other reptiles, so he could easily endure the frigid temperatures. Yet, just because the weather wasn't harmful, it didn't mean it was particularly pleasant. At least he was used to it after spending most of the past two years outdoors.

Still, as he traversed the forest, he was more than a little cranky, which was why he decided to go a little out of his way to revisit the guardian bear and the amanita that had facilitated his Mind cultivation. Perhaps he could spend a few days to see if it could do the same for the other parts of his cultivation. As powerful as his Quartz Mind was, Elijah couldn't help but believe that progressing to the next stage of Body would be even more impactful. And if he could do the same for his Dragon Core? That would be a game changer for him.

With those thoughts occupying a few facets of his Mind, Elijah quickly covered the familiar ground between Norcastle and the small town he'd visited on the way to the tower. After a little while, he reached the stream where he'd caught so many fish, but in the middle of winter, it had mostly frozen over—a testament to the region's frigid climate.

Leaving the frozen stream behind, Elijah kept going until he caught sight of the small town. It had snowed the night before, so the slice of long-lost Americana was covered in a white blanket. Yet, it only took Elijah a few seconds to recognize that something was out of place. He couldn't quite put his finger on precisely what was wrong, but still, he couldn't escape the notion that something terrible had happened. So, after embracing Guise of the Unseen, he slipped down the slope and entered the city at a light trot.

Along the way, he noticed a host of unfamiliar smells—animals who'd come through the area, he was certain—but there were two other easily identifiable scents present. The first was the acrid stench of decay that seemed to pervade everything in the area, but the second was the all-too-familiar smell of humans.

Elijah's stomach tied itself into knots as he came to the most likely conclusion, and yet, he refused to acknowledge it. Instead, he explored the whole town, taking extra time as he inspected every building. All the while, he knew it was a subconscious effort to avoid the inevitable discovery awaiting him at the end of his search. However, he could only delay so long before he found himself staring at the old appliance store.

Or what was left of it.

The collection of washing machines, dishwashers, ovens, and microwaves had spilled into the street as if they'd been carried out on a tidal wave. Most bore some degree of damage, and a few had been completely ripped apart. Their innards had been scattered across the road and partially buried beneath the snow.

Elijah knew what he would find, but he needed confirmation. His heart pounded in his chest as he crept forward, nimbly leaping from one fallen hunk of machinery to another. Meanwhile, the stomach-churning odor of oily decay clung to everything, growing more powerful with every step he took into the appliance store.

And then, he saw what remained of the bear. Of his onetime friend.

It was just a pile of offal and bone. The once-mighty creature had been skinned, and half its body had been butchered. Whoever had killed it clearly hadn't had the ability to take everything, though, so quite a bit of the corpse remained intact. Though without the bear's glorious pelt, it made for a pitiful sight.

Elijah stared at it for a long while, and with every passing moment, his pulse quickened. Rationally, he knew that the bear's death was no great tragedy. It was entirely possible that it had attacked someone who'd stumbled upon its lair. Maybe the killers had been acting in self-defense.

And yet, Elijah's anger continued to mount. Perhaps it was because, somewhere in the back of one facet of his Mind, he recognized the signs that someone had deliberately hunted the bear. Or maybe, after his period of peaceful coexistence with the beast, he simply couldn't look at its death objectively. Whatever the case, his anger reached a crescendo when he saw what had happened to the amanita.

It had been hacked to pieces. What remained had rotted, so the pile of decaying fungus was barely recognizable. In addition, the aura that had surrounded it was almost completely gone, leaving behind only a tiny swell in the density of the ambient ethera.

As he stared at the aftermath, Elijah seethed, especially when he saw the remnants of broken spears and arrows lying around. He turned away from the scene, letting his anger envelope him.

Elijah told himself that his anger wasn't rooted in the fact that they'd killed the bear. He had killed plenty of animals himself, so he didn't begrudge someone for hunting. However, what truly set him off was the waste. They'd barely harvested a quarter of the animal, suggesting that the purpose of the kill hadn't been for food or resources. Rather, it had been an attempt to gain levels.

Or maybe even for the challenge itself.

Worse yet, there was a possibility that they had killed the bear just because they could. Because they enjoyed the act of slaughter. Perhaps they liked watching the bear suffer, then took joy in hacking the amanita to pieces. Elijah had no idea which camp the killers fell into, but in his frustrated anger, he had difficulty imagining that they were justified.

In any case, he didn't waste much more time before setting off. But he didn't head in the direction of the next town. Instead, he looked for the killers' trail. Soon enough, he found precisely what he was looking for and proceeded to follow it out of town.

Fortunately, the trail was still fresh enough that, through his heightened senses and the increased concentration afforded by his Quartz Mind, he had no difficulty following the tracks. Still, he didn't catch up to them until well past sunset. When he did, he approached under the concealment of Guise of the Unseen and watched the murderers who had killed the creature whom, in Elijah's anger, he'd begun to remember far more fondly than was probably warranted.

Rooker sat on the overturned log, staring at the flickering flames as a bit of bear roasted on a spit. The fat and grease trickled down the juicy hunk of meat, and when they hit the fire, they sizzled. It looked delicious, and it smelled even better. However, even if it was more nourishing than most meat, a couple of meals had never been the goal. Instead, he and his boys had been contracted by an elven Alchemist named Breeze to harvest the giant mushroom that had very nearly killed all four of them. If they hadn't had the benefit of the poison-resistance potion, they'd have dropped dead before they even got close to the horrible thing.

But they'd persisted, and they'd filled the specially prepared sacks with bits of mushroom flesh. They'd even had to leave a little behind because they didn't have enough room. So, their job was done, and in only a few weeks, they'd get the Body-cultivation potions they had been promised.

Killing the bear had just been a well-deserved bonus.

The dumb beast had put up quite a fight, too, and their Healer, Richard, still hadn't recovered enough ethera to completely mend their wounds. Rooker was the only one who'd managed to make it through entirely intact, but that was only because of his high Constitution as well as the Jerkin of Resilience that he'd gotten as the reward for conquering the tower back home.

He'd been the only survivor of that one, and yet, he'd come out on top. Like always. That was the key benefit of his Stalwart Defender class, after all.

A clatter yanked his attention away from the roasting meat to see the pair of damage dealers—Tommy and Vic—fooling around with the bear's pelt. Tommy, the spellcaster of the group, had the thing draped over his shoulders with its head functioning as a gruesome hood.

"Knock it off, you two," he growled. He was the highest level among them, so he had taken his position as their leader. And given that he was only a couple of levels from making it onto the ladder, the others respected him in a way they wouldn't have with anyone else. Still, all three were young and immature, so he often felt like he was babysitting his sister's kids.

Of course, Michelle hadn't made it through the apocalypse. Neither had his nieces or nephews. But he didn't like to think about that. No—the world had changed, and if he wanted to survive more than a few more years, he needed to keep his eyes facing forward. That was why he'd taken the job offered by the Alchemist.

Normally, he wouldn't have even spoken to one of the elves. They mostly kept to themselves, but they'd also refused to help when so many humans were reeling from the world's transformation. That was hard to forget.

Not for Rooker, though. He was a pragmatist, through and through, and he'd have done the same thing in the elves' places. In fact, he had done exactly that when he'd chosen to withhold his own assistance when it might've saved some of his neighbors. If they couldn't survive on their own, then they didn't deserve his help. More, he couldn't afford to offer it. Not if he wanted to ensure his own survival, at least. The moment the apocalypse had hit—or the World Tree had touched Earth, as he'd learned—it had become an every-man-for-himself sort of situation. That was especially true after he'd lost his family.

But Rooker didn't like to think about that, so he pushed the thought out of his mind. It was at that moment that he heard a rustle in the nearby bushes. Knowing precisely how dangerous the wilderness could be, he whipped around, yanking his axe from the loop on his belt. "Who's there?!" he demanded.

At the same time, the two knuckleheads left their fooling around behind and leveled their own weapons in the direction Rooker was facing. For his part, Richard quickly retreated behind Rooker. As a Healer, the once-pudgy man was barely capable of defending himself, much less fighting anything more dangerous than a bunny, so he was almost entirely reliant on the others.

For Rooker's part, he didn't care about the man at all. But he liked the idea of having a Healer in his pocket in case things got dicey.

"I come in peace," came a man's voice. It was a little rough, but clear as a bell. Then, the owner of that voice stepped out of the wilderness. He held a staff that looked like twined roots, and his clothes were oddly cut but unremarkable, save that the pants ended just above the man's ankles. He was handsome, though a little rough around the edges, with curly blond hair and a beard that looked like it hadn't been trimmed in some time. However, there were two true oddities about him that made Rooker look twice.

First, his feet were bare. What would drive someone to walk around the forest in the dead of night without any shoes Rooker had no idea, but the characteristic was strange enough to make him do a double take. Second, the hand gripping the staff was scarred, and to Rooker, it looked as if he'd been seriously burned. The scarring went past his wrist and disappeared beneath his sleeve.

"Stop right there," Rooker growled, gesturing with his axe.

The man did. "Didn't mean to sneak up on you. I just saw your fire and figured I'd drop in and say hello," he stated. Then, he gave a half-hearted wave and said, "So, hello, I guess."

"What do you want?" Rooker asked.

"I . . . I just told you?"

Rooker blinked. "What're you doing out here? It's not safe."

The scarred man gave a shrug. "Kind of my thing. I'm looking for my sister. You wouldn't know where Seattle ended up, would you? I think there's a city called Tom's Town a hundred miles or so south of here. I was thinking of heading there first, then seeing if I can find any more information on Seattle."

"East," Richard said from his position behind Rooker. He'd relaxed a little, and for good reason. It was just one man, after all. Of course, there could be others nearby, but Rooker didn't think so. If that was the case, they'd have just attacked without bothering with a ruse. "I heard Seattle ended up east of here. Not even next to the ocean anymore."

"Really? Wasn't expecting that," the newcomer said. "Thanks. I'll probably still head south first since I'm so close, but . . . Yeah. That's helpful information."

"You're a Healer?" asked Vic. He was the only one in the group with the ability to identify people, though it only told him a person's archetype. How that related to his Stalker class Rooker had no idea, but it was a useful enough ability to have.

"Oh. Yeah. Why? You need healing?" the man asked.

"You have spare ethera?" asked Richard.

The stranger shrugged. "Depends on a few things. Like what's that on the spit right there?" he asked.

"Bear," grunted Rooker. "Killed this high-level fucker a little while ago. This is the last of the meat we could take. Shame, too. He was big. Only reason we were able to kill him at all is because of this sleep poison we got from an Alchemist. It was a pain getting in close enough to get it in him, but once we did, it knocked him right out."

"Oh. So, were you just hunting, then?"

"No," blurted Richard. "We were hired to harvest this—"

Rooker cut the Healer off with a glare. "We were on a job," he said slowly. "That's it. Details aren't important."

The man shrugged again. "Mind if I lower my arms? My Strength is a bit lacking, so my shoulders are screaming at me right now."

Rooker nodded, and the man dropped his arms, then rolled his shoulders. "You want some?" he asked the man, gesturing to the hunk of bear meat roasting over the fire. "Plenty to go around. And Richard could use a little help with the healing. The boys over there are—"

Just then, the man pointed his staff at Richard—who'd moved out from behind Rooker. The ethera in the area shuddered before a thick bolt of lightning erupted from the stranger's staff, then hit Richard directly in the chest. He was flung backward with enough violence that, when he struck a nearby tree, the sound of cracking bones echoed through the campsite.

For a brief moment, everyone was stunned by what had happened. And then, suddenly, everyone erupted into motion. Vic yanked his dagger from the sheath at his waist—the idiot's bow wasn't even strung—then launched himself at the man. Meanwhile, Tommy raised his hands high into the air as he began casting a spell.

He never got the chance.

The Stalwart Defender was already moving to intercept him, but he was far too slow. Rooker watched as the man transformed, taking on the form of some sort of scaled nightmare that looked as if someone had crossed a panther with a crocodile, but far sleeker than either of those descriptors would normally indicate.

The man—or monster—hit Tommy like he was shot out of a cannon. With claws and teeth, the monster ripped through the spellcaster like he was made of paper. Blood and viscera misted into the air, but the nightmare didn't stop. Instead, it disappeared into the darkness on the other side.

"What the fuck . . . W-what the fuck was that?!" Vic pleaded, sliding to a stop. He jerked around, looking this way and that, but he clearly didn't see anything. The creature's scales were dark, so it was perfectly suited to hide in the shadows.

"I don't know," Rooker said, already using spells and abilities to accentuate his already-stout defenses. Some of them were intended to protect comparatively more vulnerable teammates, and they had diminishing returns when he used them on himself. However, he almost never blessed anyone else with his defensive abilities.

It was every man for himself, after all. He didn't care if his teammates survived, so long as he walked away intact. In fact, he preferred it that way because, if he was the only one left, he wouldn't have to split any rewards.

"Is Richard still alive?"

"Fuck if I know, man!" Vic shouted. "I don't know. I don't know . . ."

"Pull yourself together."

"You pull yourself together, asshole! It just went through Tommy like it was—"

He slapped his hand against his neck, then tapered off. He was trying to look everywhere at once, but Rooker had already written the man off. So, he backed himself against a tree and set his feet. By that point, he'd layered four defensive abilities, one atop the other to create a veritable cocoon of protection. So, he was ready for whatever that monster could throw at him.

Meanwhile, Vic continued to panic, muttering to himself the whole while. Every now and again, he'd slap his hand against any bit of exposed skin, but Rooker wasn't certain if that was a nervous tic or if a swarm of mosquitoes had descended upon them. Whatever the case, he wasn't concerned with a few insects.

Or at least, that was the case until Vic fell to his knees and vomited. In the firelight, it was difficult to tell, but Rooker thought he saw blood in the resultant puddle. He shouted for Vic, but the man pitched forward onto his face, collapsing into convulsions. He went still a second later.

Suddenly, Rooker felt very alone.

So very alone. And tired. He wanted nothing more than to go back in time and hold his daughter again. Or his wife. They'd had their problems. He'd been a terrible husband back then. But if he could just go back, he would change. No more drinking. No more cheating. He would never lay a hand on either of them again. He just wanted a second chance.

"Why?" came a deep, rumbling voice. Rooker looked up to see another monstrosity looming in the shadows. It was enormous, with hints of scales and a face like a spiny lizard. But it was shaped more like an ape, with long arms and squat legs.

"Show yourself, monster!" Rooker bellowed with all the false bravado he could muster.

"I'm not hiding," the creature growled, stepping into the firelight. It was just as awful and intimidating as Rooker's first impression had suggested. "Tell me why you killed the bear. The mushroom, I understand. But the bear was innocent. Once it was unconscious, you could have left it."

"Leave it? Why?" Rooker asked, confused. "It was a monster. Monsters give experience. That's the world we live in."

"And you? Will you give experience when I kill you?"

"W-what?" the Stalwart Defender asked, his confident facade breaking.

"I was going to let you live," the monster stated, its gravelly voice rattling Rooker's bones. "You just wanted the mushroom, and the bear was in the way. But you killed it when you didn't have to. I won't let that pass."

With that, the monster erupted into motion. Rooker used his final ability, manifesting an ethereal shield a foot in front of him. The monster didn't even slow down as it shattered the plane of magical force, then crashed into its owner. Rooker's defenses were useless against the powerful monster, and it ripped through him with ease. Still, he managed to get a couple of blows in of his own, though they clanged off the creature's skin with the sound of metal on metal.

And then, the creature grabbed his head with one of its massive claws.

That's when it started squeezing. At first Rooker's Constitution was up to the task, but the power the monster could bring to bear was absolutely overbearing. And soon enough, the integrity of his skull collapsed, and he knew no more.

49

PESTS

With mixed emotions dancing in her heart, Carmen watched her son as he trained with the practice spear she had made for him. A few years before, she'd have never condoned such a thing. Back then, even combat sports like boxing or mixed martial arts had been off the table, and she had actively forbidden him from playing football. There was too much chance of permanent injury, especially to Miguel's all-important brain, for her to sign off on those sorts of things.

But now, the world had irrevocably changed, and she knew better than most that if they didn't change with it, they would become fodder for those who had adapted more fully. Or for some sort of monster, of which there were plenty. The reality was that, if she wanted to prepare Miguel to thrive, she needed to ensure that he had the tools to do so. That meant training him with weapons as well as ensuring that his normal education continued apace. In addition, she'd begun to teach him the rudiments of crafting—at least as much as she had learned—and bought plenty of guides so he would know as much about the System as possible.

Still, it felt so odd, worrying about his combat ability. That was a remnant of the old world, though, and Carmen had to remind herself to push it away so that it didn't infect her perception of reality. The moment the World Tree had touched Earth, the entire paradigm had shifted, and the world had become a place where nothing was assured.

A pang of regret sliced through her heart.

She'd learned that lesson the hard way. Alyssa had been the best person she'd ever known, and yet, she'd died anyway. Not for the first time, she wondered what had really happened in that tower. Roman's story made sense. It was a dangerous place, and if anyone would have sacrificed herself so others would live, it was Alyssa. However, there was a degree of doubt she couldn't quite push aside. Roman had had every reason to get rid of Alyssa. His grip on Easton was stronger now than it had ever been while Alyssa was alive.

Yet, there was one problem with that line of thinking. Roman and Alyssa had been friends for a long time even before the world had ended. And Alyssa had been convinced that Roman was a good man. She had thrown her support behind him at every turn. That kind of bond wasn't easily discarded.

Besides, Carmen had seen Roman's face during Alyssa's memorial service. That kind of grief was difficult to fake, especially for a man like Roman.

Even so, she'd once warned Alyssa to remain wary of the man, and for good reason. So, she was of two minds on the subject of whether or not to trust Roman's version of events.

Not that it mattered.

She needed to move on, both for her sake and for her son's good. He hadn't taken Alyssa's death well, and if Carmen started wallowing in her own depression—which was the inevitable path that would take—it would only push Miguel to do the same. So, as much as she wanted to dwell on the death of her wife, being a responsible mother came first. With that in mind, Carmen watched Miguel sparring with one of the warriors who'd been sent to protect the mine.

The small town they'd built around the mine had grown to include three main buildings as well as a handful of houses for the workers. And with what they'd found so far, there was every reason to expect that growth to continue. Carmen suspected that, one day, it might become a full-blown city to rival Easton itself.

But that hinged on the continued exploration of the mine.

Almost as soon as that thought crossed Carmen's mind, she heard someone approach. "What is it now?" she asked, glancing back to see Colt drawing closer. "I'm busy."

"I know," he said, removing his hat and wiping his forearm across his sweaty forehead. His other hand rested on the hilt of the katana at his hip. She knew from experience that he could have that blade out in the blink of an eye, and he was quite adept at using it. The man characterized himself as a samurai, even claiming to follow the Bushido code—which was a bit odd, considering that he looked every inch the cowboy, with his wide-brimmed hat and leather duster. But oddities had become the norm, and all Carmen really cared about was his competence. In that arena, she couldn't have asked for a better second-in-command.

"Just one day," she said, sighing as she pushed herself to her feet. She'd been sitting on an old tree stump near the training grounds she'd established. There, the warriors as well as any children who'd come along could practice their martial skills. She stretched her back with a groan. "Just one day was all I wanted. Can't even give me that, can you?"

"Sorry, ma'am. But the miners ran into some problems," he said with his characteristic drawl.

"Big problems or little problems?"

"I don't come to you with the little ones, ma'am."

She sighed in annoyance. "Stop calling me ma'am. You're making me feel like I'm some old crone. You're older than I am, for God's sake," she said.

"Yes, ma'am."

Carmen just shook her head. That was the thing about Colt. He wouldn't change for anyone, which was probably why she appreciated him so much. It was also why he'd been sent to the Silverswift Mine. Why it had been named that, Carmen had no idea, but she'd discovered some documentation in an abandoned office near the entrance that labeled it such. Odd, considering that it had been an iron mine, but Carmen had no interest in thinking of a name herself. So, she'd kept the old name, as ill-fitting as it was.

The budding settlement had taken a similarly silly—but much more under-standable—name when someone had started referring to it as Silverado.

"I hate that our village is named after a stupid pickup truck," she muttered to herself.

"I don't think that's where the name came from, ma'am."

"I know that, Colt," she said. "Alright. Show me this problem."

"Yes, ma'am," he drawled. Then, after Carmen waved at Miguel—he was fine in the training ground, given that there were a few Warriors with decent levels around—the pair set off for the mine's entrance. It was less than a quarter of a mile away, so they covered the distance quickly enough, passing through the burgeoning settlement along the way. Carmen was pleased to see that everyone was busy either processing the little ore they'd managed to mine or working on the town's infrastructure. If they'd been slacking off, she might've had a few choice words for her people.

Soon enough, they reached the mine's entrance. When they'd first arrived, it was only a few feet wide, and it had experienced a cave-in sometime in the recent past. However, through arduous labor—most of which had required Carmen's personal participation—they had managed to clear the debris and widen the entrance by a considerable amount.

But that wasn't what Carmen was focused on. Instead, her attention lay solely on the group of fighters and miners who were congregated at the entrance. A few of them showed clear signs of having recently engaged in combat, and one of the expedition's two Healers sat nearby, clearly exhausted.

"What happened?" she asked as they approached.

"Some critters attacked us, ma'am," Colt answered. "Don't rightly know what they were, but they were small and vicious. Big, sharp teeth, too."

"Like gremlins or goblins?"

"No. Critters," he reiterated. "Like the movie from the eighties."

"Never saw it," she stated. "Well before my time."

"Freaked me out as a kid," Colt said. "Maybe that's why I thought of 'em when the miners described what they saw."

"Probably. Unless eighties movie monsters are real now," she joked half-heartedly. "If we encounter Freddy Krueger in there, I'm done. We don't need the ore that badly."

"I think everyone would agree with that one, ma'am."

They reached the group a few moments later, and Carmen asked what had happened. The first to answer was a rawboned woman with high cheekbones that, if she wasn't covered in dirt and blood, would've made her look like a runway model. Or that would have been the case if she wasn't so clearly used to hard labor, which was made evident by her well-defined muscles and calloused hands.

She said, "We were expanding one of the new tunnels, following a thick strain of that cold iron. That's when they hit us, hard and fast. We killed a couple, but there were way too many. We had to retreat."

"Laney, right?" asked Carmen. If she remembered correctly, the woman was in charge of the third shift of miners, but she'd not learned much else about her. Or anyone else, really. She could put a few names to faces, but she had spent much of the trip from Easton to Silverado in the grip of depression. It wasn't until they'd started work on the budding town that she had begun to come out of it.

"That's right," she said. "Miner extraordinaire. Actually, I'm a Scholar. Haven't gotten my class yet, though, so I ended up having to volunteer for labor to stay useful. You know how it goes."

A few others among the miners nodded along. Carmen knew just how common that story was. It didn't make sense. Scholars were ill-suited to manual work, and yet, they formed the bulk of Easton's labor force. Like Laney, most of them hadn't had much of a choice. If they wanted to remain in Easton, let alone earn their keep, they had to do whatever it was the city needed them to do. And given Roman's prejudice against Scholars, that usually meant that those with that archetype were relegated to all the worst jobs.

It was a damned waste, but Carmen was in no position to do anything about that sort of ridiculous thinking. Moreover, she didn't think she'd be very successful in changing anyone's mind, given that the city owed its continued prosperity—and more importantly, its security—to Roman and his policies.

The existence of the critters wasn't a surprise. Ever since they'd first begun exploration of the mine, they'd known that something had expanded the system of tunnels that had existed since before the touch of the World Tree had changed the world. So, having to clear the creatures out had always been an inevitability, though one she'd hoped would wait until her people were a little better prepared.

"Alright. Here's what we're going to do," she said. "I want a group of three Warriors to come with me into the tunnels. We'll hunt down as many of these critters as we can, but our real objective is to find wherever they're nested and put them down. Sound good?"

There was a murmur of agreement from the miners, but Carmen was only really interested in Colt's response. He said, "It needs to be done, so we'll do it."

"Gather two more. Best we've got for close quarters," Carmen said. "I'm going to get my armor."

She wasn't like the people with combat classes. Certainly, she could hang with them well enough, but only if she had proper equipment. Without her armor, she really only had her Strength to set her apart. The rest of her attributes were, at best, mediocre, and none of her skills translated to combat. Still, she could hold her own, but she knew that the gap would continue to widen as humanity progressed. Eventually, she wouldn't even be in the same realm as people with actual combat skills.

For now, though, she could handle herself well enough, so she headed back to her office-slash-home and donned her armor. Despite having been through quite a bit of fighting on the way to the mine, it didn't show any wear and tear. Once Carmen was wearing her armor, she glanced at her massive hammer. However, she chose to leave it behind because, in the tunnels, she wouldn't have any room to swing it. Instead, she would rely on Summon Tool and use the much smaller blacksmith's hammer she could manifest.

It wouldn't pack quite the punch of her Simple-grade weapon, but it would still do the trick.

Thus armed and armored, Carmen headed back to the entrance of the mine to await Colt and the two other combatants that would accompany them on their critter hunt. As it turned out, he chose a pair of Warrior archetypes. One had a Brawler class and specialized in hand-to-hand fighting, while the other was a Vigilante who favored a longsword. He also had an ability that allowed him to identify creatures, which Colt reasoned would come in handy.

"Tiffany," Colt said, nodding toward the Brawler. Then, he indicated the Vigilante as he continued: "And Brett have been with us for more than a year. I trust them."

"Well, then I do, too," Carmen said. "Let's do this thing."

50

ARGOS

The morning air held a distinct chill as Elijah leaped over a burbling stream. When he reached the other side, he slowed to a stop before shifting into his human form. With a sigh, he unshouldered his pack, setting his two staves aside as he squatted next to the stream. After dipping his hands into the water, he splashed his face.

How long had it been since he'd killed the group of hunters? Two days? Three? It might've even been a week. After he'd slaughtered the leader, who'd been a little more durable than Elijah had expected, he'd taken the time to loot the corpses, coming away with nothing worthwhile besides a few extra etherium that he added to the pile at the bottom of his pack. Other than that, he'd also taken the sacks of mushroom flesh as well as the bear's pelt. Everything else he'd left behind, as much because he didn't want to strip the bodies due to his limited carrying capacity.

However, one thing he did carry with him was the guilt.

Despite the justifications that kept playing through his mind, the fact was that he'd unhesitatingly murdered four people filled his mind with questions. Certainly, he'd killed before, and far more than he ever could have imagined possible in the years preceding the world's transformation. But they'd all been gnomes and goblins and elves. Or they had been the pseudo-real people populating the towers. But these last four were humans, just like him. And he wasn't so far removed from the civilized existence that had once characterized his life that he didn't find it at least somewhat repulsive.

At the end of the day, he was a murderer. Sure, he had his reasons, and for the most part, he accepted them as just. But most was not all, and Elijah was still trying to deal with the psychological ramifications of his actions.

The worst part was that, given the same set of factors, he would make the same choice every single time. Those men had flippantly killed the bear for no more reason than that they could, and that was something he refused to accept. What that said about him and his place in the new world Elijah wasn't certain, but he knew his heart well enough to recognize that he would continue along that path, even if it one day made him a monster.

Perhaps that was why he'd become a Druid in the first place, because he had the capacity to look at the world from that perspective. And because he had the wherewithal to act, even if it meant going places most people would not.

In any case, Elijah bore the stain of guilt—faint though it was—that would require some time to wash away. In the meantime, though, he felt a more immediate need to wash himself of the inevitable filth that came from spending more than a week living and hunting in the wilderness. So, without further ado, he quickly undressed, then retrieved the much-diminished bar of homemade soap from his pack before stepping into the frigid stream and taking an impromptu bath.

He even cast Healing Rain to assist in the process. Even as dirt, mud, and congealed blood were washed from his body, so too was his fatigue as well as the worst of the guilt clinging to his psyche. It didn't magically disappear, but the symbolic nature of his wilderness shower gave him both the context as well as the time to come to terms with his actions.

And unsurprisingly, he was fine with what he'd done.

In a vacuum, murder was wrong. He knew that. But he couldn't bring himself to regret killing the hunters. From what he'd seen, the world was a better place without them.

So, by the time he had finished, he was clean in body, mind, and spirit. In the aftermath, he propped himself against a boulder and let himself relax for the first time since the night he'd rid the world of the hunters' stain. With the sun warming him, it was only a matter of time before he dozed off.

He didn't dream, but when he awoke, a sense of contentment enveloped his mind. He also couldn't help but notice that he'd attracted a small audience. A squirrel the size of a beaver sat on the limb of a nearby oak tree, chittering down at him with mingled annoyance, curiosity, and fear.

Elijah sighed, then pushed himself to his feet. As he dusted himself off, the squirrel's chittering grew more urgent. Finally, Elijah said, "Fine, fine. I'm getting out of your territory, you little tyrant."

That didn't placate the creature, and it didn't cease its tirade until Elijah retrieved his staves and pack, then took on his draconid form. The moment he did, the squirrel went silent before fleeing through the forest's canopy. Elijah just shook his scaly head before taking off in the opposite direction.

As the days wore on, the forest thinned, and more evidence of a fallen civilization presented itself. The remnants of old roads bore dozens of abandoned automobiles. Some seemed mostly intact, but others had clearly been ripped apart by powerful beasts. Still others showed signs of salvage, having been dismantled for parts. That was an encouraging sign even if Elijah didn't see any evidence of current occupation in the area.

As he kept an easterly heading, he started seeing more and more proof of human habitation. However, he couldn't ignore one simple fact—the actual signs he saw were not in English. By virtue of the System's translation feature, he could read them, but he still recognized that they were written in a language he shouldn't have been capable of understanding. He did know enough to recognize that it was Greek, though.

Which made no sense, considering that his island was in the American Pacific Northwest. But then again, the world had been transformed, and its geography had been rearranged. So, with that framing his expectations, it should not have been surprising to suddenly stumble upon a region that had once been located on the other side of the world. In any case, Elijah couldn't complain, especially with the steadily rising temperatures he'd experienced since descending from the more mountainous region around Norcastle.

It wasn't warm, per se. But it was much more temperate.

Along the way, he ran into Voxx from time to time, but none of them were particularly strong. So, even though he killed each one that he found, they only provided a trickle of experience.

He shook his head at that. Hanging out with actual human beings had resulted in him changing some of his terminology. Instead of referring to the influx of ethera he received upon killing an enemy as kill energy, he had begun to think of it using a gaming term that was popular in Norcastle. Experience. It seemed fitting enough.

Regardless of terminology, the result was that he hadn't gained a single level since leaving the tower, and as a result, he found that he was a little irritable at the lack of progress. That was odd, too. He'd gone weeks between levels back on his island, and that hadn't bothered him. Perhaps he was growing addicted to progression. Or more probably, it was an issue of mindset. Back home, he didn't feel the need to constantly progress because, well, it was home. But in the wilderness? Things were different.

In any case, he didn't intend to go out of his way to hunt powerful beasts just to gain a few levels here and there. If he did, he would be no better than the hunters he'd found so disgusting. But killing Voxx—even the weak versions he kept stumbling upon—was always a nice distraction.

He hoped it would prove profitable, too. He knew that each kill was recorded by the System, so he likely had quite a sizable reward waiting for him to visit a Branch. Not that he had much to spend it on, of course. There were a few things he wouldn't mind buying back in Ironshore, and he'd forgone purchasing quite a few guides that looked useful because they were incredibly expensive, so there was always something he'd need to buy.

More than anything, though, he wanted to find someone—anyone—to identify the loot he'd taken from the tower. He was still carrying the giant ogre staff, and he had a small arsenal of swords and daggers in his pack. Finally, there was the curious reward he'd gotten upon defeating the Reaver and conquering the tower. The Claws of Gluttony didn't have an overt purpose, but he was certain that they would be somehow useful. He just needed someone to help him discover what form that usefulness might take.

Those thoughts occupied one facet of Elijah's mind, while the others were free to focus on his environment. His diligence bore fruit as he hunted his way across the region, and eventually, he came upon a road that led into a moderately sized Greek town. From a distance, Elijah could see people going to and fro, but none of them strayed outside the city's stone wall without a couple of armed Warriors to protect them.

As Elijah drew closer—under the Guise of the Unseen—he couldn't ignore the fact that the surrounding fields had been left untended. Moreover, there were a handful of empty paddocks that had clearly been used for livestock. And finally, he saw the locals' furtive glances and hurried gaits. Clearly, they were afraid of something, though Elijah couldn't figure out what it was.

Because, other than the humans in and around the city, the immediate region was almost entirely deserted. There were birds and a few squirrels chittering and chattering in the trees, but on the ground, there was nothing. No hares. No deer. Elijah picked up the scent of a few Voxx, but after following those trails, he found that the monsters had long since been killed.

As he explored, Elijah saw a couple of signs that declared the town to be Argos, which sounded vaguely familiar. In any case, he quickly exhausted the possibilities of the surrounding wilderness and fields, so he prepared himself to enter the city proper. Though, once he made that decision, he came upon a difficult choice.

Did he want to enter the town as a human and risk something like what had happened back in Norcastle? Or would he prefer to slip in under the Guise of the Unseen, access the Branch—if there was one—then slip back out without any of the residents, aside from whoever manned the Branch itself, being the wiser.

In the end, though, Elijah's decision came down to two factors. First, he had no intention of slinking around like a thief for the rest of his life. His draconid form was powerful, and he would use it accordingly. However, letting himself fall into the habit of always being unseen was not healthy, and it held little appeal for him. He wanted to talk to actual people. He wanted to socialize. He wanted to drink and eat and do all the things he'd missed during his solitary confinement on his island.

Second, Elijah didn't think he could accomplish his goals while flying entirely under the radar. The Branch's attendant—or Envoy of the Cult of the World Tree, he'd learned back in Ironshore—would doubtless know of his presence the moment he came into range of the Branch. But more, he wanted to identify his items—and maybe even sell some of them—resupply, get some information, and perhaps most importantly of all, sleep in a real bed.

He couldn't do any of those things while in his draconid form.

So, without any further hesitation, Elijah retreated out of sight of the Guards manning the gate, then let his draconid form slide away. After that, he took a deep breath, tried to smooth down his unkempt hair, then set off on a path that would take him to the city's entrance.

Soon enough, the Guards caught sight of him, but they didn't react with the hostility he might have expected. Instead, they simply watched his approach with grim resignation.

51

ATTICUS'S ARSENAL

What are you doing out so late?!" the grizzled Guard barked. He had a tanned complexion and a great, bushy, black beard. It was almost as if he'd grown such magnificent facial hair in order to make up for the lack of hair on his head. Otherwise, he was short and stocky, wearing a leather breastplate and carrying a shield and spear. "Do you have a death wish, boy? At your level, you're lucky you didn't meet the beast!"

"The beast?" Elijah asked, adjusting the giant ogre staff he had propped over one shoulder. His other staff he used as a walking stick. "What kind of beast?"

Indeed, he hadn't sensed any other creatures in the area, so the notion that there was some sort of beast around was something of a surprise. However, on second thought, it was entirely possible that some great predator had killed or scared off any other animals.

"The man-eater," the other Guard said in a quiet voice. She was taller than her partner, with similarly dark hair and a nearly identical complexion. However, she was wearing a helmet, so Elijah couldn't get a good look at her face. "Now, in with you. You don't want to be out after dark. That's when it's most active."

Elijah asked, "Do I need to pay or . . ."

"What? No. Of course not," said the bearded Guard. "In with you now. We're about to lock up."

Elijah knew better than to argue, so he thanked the pair, then stepped through the gate. As soon as he did, a horn sounded, loud enough to echo for miles, and behind him, the gate creaked closed. He did notice that there was a smaller door set into the gate, but it was barred shut, as well. Soon, the entire city would be locked down, likely as a defense against the man-eater the Guards had mentioned.

Pushing those thoughts to their own facet of his Mind, Elijah looked around as he strode into Argos. The architecture was what he would have expected from a Mediterranean city, with red-tiled roofs and stucco walls. Yet, there were only a few remaining bits of evidence that it had once been a modern town. The streets were populated by pedestrians and handcarts, without a car in sight. However, there were still electrical lights, and Elijah even heard a few stereos playing music.

The people themselves wore an odd collection of old and new. There were plenty of old sports jerseys, blue jeans, and tee-shirts, but there were also oddly cut trousers, shirts, skirts, and dresses, as well. Elijah even saw a few robes that looked like they would've been at home in a movie about fantastical wizards. Fortunately, he wasn't the only one carrying a staff. In fact, the vast majority of the pedestrians were armed with at least daggers. Quite a few had swords, axes, and spears.

There were also plenty of Guards present, and though they eyed everyone with stoic purpose, Elijah saw no evidence of overt corruption. It was a nice reminder that, sometimes, people could be good and effective at keeping order. He hoped that would turn out to be the rule, rather than the exception he'd seen in Norcastle. Yet, for all of that, Elijah saw anxiety etched on every face. Each furtive glance told him that the population was uneasy.

Elijah strolled through the city, the butt of his Staff of Natural Harmony thudding against the flagged streets along the way. The architecture of the city was impressive in its diversity. From what he had seen from afar, he had expected a picturesque Mediterranean town, and there was certainly some of that present. However, there were plenty of modern, soulless buildings that would have been at home in any Midwestern strip mall, as well.

The bland curse of modernity, he reasoned.

In any case, Elijah spent the next few hours just wandering around. It was nice, just being around people for once. He'd gotten a taste of it back in Norcastle, but he'd jumped from one crisis to another without stepping back and letting himself enjoy the benefits of civilization. There was just something comforting about being surrounded by other human beings. Most people took that for granted. Even those who preferred to stay away from crowds took solace in the knowledge that they weren't really alone. As isolated as they were, they knew that, if they so chose, they could have a conversation with their neighbors. They could meet up with friends. They could go see family. Many chose to eschew those benefits of living in a connected society, but the fact that the option was there was more important than exercising it.

The highlight of the city was a large statue that, according to an engraving on the plinth, was meant to depict Heracles. Further, it was supposed to be an exact copy of the famous *Farnese Hercules* statue. That it had survived the transformation of the world filled Elijah with a sense of gratitude. Even though it was a copy, its endurance felt like an assurance that Earth's culture and mythology wouldn't be completely lost.

Of course, billions of people had likely perished in the transition—and thousands more probably died each day—so there would be an undeniable effect going forward. Hopefully, humans would maintain some connection with the world they'd lost.

Eventually, Elijah's wandering took him to what looked like an armory. The sign out front declared it to be Atticus's Arsenal, which was perfect for ticking off one item on his to-do list. He still needed help identifying the items he'd looted, and he expected that a weapons shop would be perfectly suited to such an endeavor. So, it was with some anticipation that he stepped through the front door of the shop.

Inside, he found a dozen racks filled with weapons of every sort. Some were clearly low quality, which meant that they were bad examples of even Unranked items, but others were just as obviously higher grade. And there was one sword on display that drew Elijah's eye like no other. It was situated in a glass cabinet, but even with that barrier blocking his senses, Elijah could feel the ethera dancing around it.

"You've got a good eye, friend," came a male voice. Elijah glanced over to see a man leaning against a doorframe. He was tall and well muscled, with the build of an athlete. On his head was a mop of curly black hair, and he had the same olive complexion that seemed so common amongst the town's residents. One thing that set him apart was a large, hawkish nose that gave his face an aggressive cast that it would've otherwise lacked. Other than that, Elijah noted that he was clean-shaven, with a strong jaw and a slightly pointed chin. The man wiped his hands with a rag he then stuffed into his pocket, and continued, "That's my baby. Came from an actual tower. It's the blade of a true hero like Heracles himself."

"You conquered a tower?" Elijah asked, surprised and awed. He'd beaten two himself, but he'd half expected that he was unique. It only took a moment's thought to realize how silly it was. The world didn't revolve around him, and while he was strong, there were probably plenty of people out there who could accomplish similar feats. In fact, the last time he'd looked at the ladder, he'd seen that there were at least eight other people who were higher level than him, so the idea that his experiences were unique was ridiculous.

The man laughed jovially, then said, "Me? No. I'm just a humble merchant. The man who looted it died a few weeks after conquering the tower." He sobered, then shook his head. "Great man. A great loss."

"How did he die?"

"You're not from around here, are you?"

Elijah shook his head. "What gave it away?" he asked.

"What didn't? Don't have many blonds in Argos. A few, but it's a not that large of a town, so I know most of them. Plus, I'd have noticed a man walking around in the middle of winter without shoes."

"Oh. That."

"So, where'd you come from?"

"Most recently, Norcastle," Elijah said. He saw no reason to lie. Or maybe he just didn't like the idea of dishonesty. Either way, he wouldn't shy away from hiding his identity when necessary, but the notion of lying about every facet of his existence was so unappealing that he'd rather deal with the consequences of having his every secret known than try to keep up with a web of lies that would inevitably unravel at all the wrong times. "But before that, I was living just outside a town called Ironshore."

"Norcastle. Heard that name once or twice. Never been, but . . . Well, travel isn't as easy as it used to be, is it?" the man remarked. "Wish it was different, though. Staying cooped up in a little town like this is not the life I'd have envisioned. But enough about that. What can I do for you? No offense, but you don't look much like a sword swinger, if you know what I mean. The Healer tag doesn't help, I'll grant, but I suppose it takes all kinds. For all I know, you're going for a Paladin class or something."

"Oh. Right." Elijah had completely forgotten about his Ring of Anonymity. However, at least he hadn't made the same mistake he'd made when he'd first entered Norcastle. Back then, he'd forgotten to change his surname, which had gotten back to Essex, leading the captain to guess his identity. Now, he was comfortably ensconced in the false identity of Elijah Smith, the level-eighteen Healer. "Yeah. Blades really aren't my thing. I just thought it felt powerful."

"Getting a similar vibe from those two staves you're carrying. The big one's a bit weaker than the twisty one, but both are strong. High Crude, at least. Maybe even low Simple," the man said. "I'd have to examine them properly to tell for sure, though." He stepped forward, offering his hand. "Sorry. Name's Atticus, just like on the sign out front. Atticus Ariti."

Elijah took the man's hand and gave it a firm squeeze. "Elijah Smith."

"Sure you are."

"Huh?"

"Don't know how you're doing it, but I'll eat my socks if you're only level eighteen. And if that's false, I'm willing to bet that the rest is, too. But it's fine, Elijah. I'll respect your privacy. Any merchant worth his salt would do the same," Atticus said.

Elijah's first instinct was to dispute the man's claim. However, he'd just finished acknowledging how much he hated dishonesty, so he said, "How did you know? About my level, I mean?"

"Two things. Most people don't go waltzing through the wilderness without a few friends to watch their backs. Most don't go far from the city at all. So, that was the first clue. Second was that you're glowing with powerful items. Even your pants are decent quality, and that's not considering the hot spots. Like those staves. The two rings on your fingers. That pack. The bracer there. Can't hide that kind of thing from somebody like me."

"Like you?"

"Oh. That's my class."

"Which is?"

The man gave him a crooked grin. "We just met, friend. Not going to show you all my secrets, am I? So, let's get to why you wandered into my shop. You don't need weapons, so . . ."

"Fair enough," Elijah said. "I need some items identified. I'm also looking to sell a few pieces. You in a position to help me with that?"

"Friend, you came to the right place. Let me show you to my office," Atticus said.

If Elijah wasn't completely certain that he could take the man out if necessary, he would've been a bit more cautious. So, he followed the arms merchant through the doorway at the back of the building and into a large storage area. There were crates lining every wall, and in the center was a long wooden table, upon which were a few curios and a giant ledger. Atticus planted himself on the other side of the table, then slammed the enormous book shut. Despite the surprising sound, Elijah didn't even flinch.

"Nerves of steel on you, huh?"

"Something like that," Elijah admitted.

"Well, let's see what you've got," Atticus said with a sweeping motion that indicated Elijah should place whatever wares he possessed onto the table. So, he started with the giant ogre staff. It wouldn't completely fit, so a foot or so of its length hung off the ends of the table in both directions. Atticus leaned forward and squinted before announcing, "Staff of Twin Forms. Low Simple grade. Enhances fire and ice spells by eighteen percent. Nice find. No bond necessary."

"Bond?"

"Yes. You get the benefit without the necessity of bonding it. That makes it more valuable because the owner can just resell it once he outgrows it. Or she, I suppose. Equal opportunity and all that," Atticus explained.

"Uh . . . How do you bond items?"

For a moment, Atticus stared at him like he'd asked the dumbest question imaginable. Then, he laughed. "Oh, don't tell me you've just been walking around with unbound items!" he exclaimed, having figured Elijah out. "No—that other staff is definitely bound. So are the rings. I can see that much. But the other items you're wearing . . . Oh, this isn't great, friend. Not great at all. Didn't you wonder why you weren't getting the full effects?"

"Just tell me how to bond them. Please."

"I'll be happy to," the arms dealer said. "I'm always ready to help my customers. You are a customer, aren't you? I'd hate to give you all this vital information and have you leave without doing any business."

Elijah sighed. "I'm definitely selling the staff. No question about that," he stated. "All I ask is that you give me a fair deal."

"Hmm," Atticus responded, leaning closer to the staff once again. "I can give you two silver. It would be more, but the thing is too big for most people. I'm sure if you bonded it, it would size to fit, but then you'd lose the main selling point. In fact, I'm not sure I even want it. Probably only useful to some of the crafters, and even then, only as scrap. Or as an example. Yes, I'm certain. It's going to be taken apart for sure. Still, I offered already, so . . . Yes. I can do two silver. Friend prices, of course."

Elijah knew he was being taken advantage of, but he wasn't really attached to the staff in the first place. It was a nice curio, but ultimately, it wasn't something he could use. So, he said, "Fine. Two silver etherium. You have a folio?"

"Not sure what that is, friend, but we can settle up at the town Branch once we're done here," Atticus said, already putting the staff away. "Now, as promised, because we're such good friends and you're now a loyal customer, I'll let you in on the closely guarded secret of bonding an item. Just drip a bit of blood on the item in question, then run some ethera through it."

"Really? That's it?"

"That's it, friend. Now, I'm going to assume that none of the items you're actively wearing are for sale. That belt looks very interesting, though. Very interesting indeed."

"No. But I do have these," Elijah said, unshouldering his pack. He reached inside—noting that the merchant was very interested in the pack itself—then retrieved the weapons he'd looted from the elves. He set them on the table, then ended with the sword he'd taken from the Warden. "All for sale."

Atticus's eyes widened at the treasure trove of weaponry. Each one of them was higher quality than most of his wares, so he stood to increase the value of his stock by quite a bit.

"Where did you get these?" the merchant asked, leaning close to one of the daggers.

"Here and there. You have your secrets, and I have mine. Anything notable about them?"

"They're all high Crude," he said. "On the edge of being Simple grade. Just called Crude steel daggers and swords. But they're all extremely durable. Better than most of what we have here in town. I'll give you one silver etherium each."

"Hmm."

"Plus two copper for each."

"Alright. But that doesn't include the sword here," Elijah said, pointing to the weapon he'd taken from the Warden. "It's better than the rest."

"Yes. Right. It's Simple grade. Called the Punisher," Atticus explained. "When bonded, it provides an extra two points to Dexterity. It also has a secondary effect called Pain Spike. I'm not certain what it does, but it sounds pretty self-explanatory to me. I can give you ten silver, but that's my hard cap on a single item. It's not quite as good as Challenger's Call out there, but that's probably a good thing."

Elijah nodded. "Alright. We'll add that to the tally. That's all I'm selling, though," he said. "But I do need you to identify a couple of things."

Atticus agreed, though he said he would charge a nominal fee for each service. It only turned out to be a few coppers, so Elijah wasn't worried about that. The first item he had the merchant identify was the Claws of Gluttony, which garnered quite a reaction.

"Simple grade again. Medium, though. This is the best weapon I've ever seen," Atticus said, his voice filled with awe. "It's . . . It has a passive ability attached to it. Only activates when bonded. Oh . . ."

"What?"

"I'm sorry, friend, but unless you're a bare-knuckle brawler, you're out of luck. And I can't afford to buy something like this unless you're willing to sell it for a fraction of its worth," Atticus stated.

"What's the effect?"

"It increases all unarmed damage by nine percent," he said. "But it also has an effect called Anticoagulant. I'm thinking it causes extra bleeding as a damage-over-time or weakening effect."

Elijah nodded. "Seems powerful," he said.

"For the right person, most certainly," Atticus said. "Not many people fighting with their hands, though. Almost everyone picks up a blade or at least a club. Our Guards favor the spear on account of our heritage. But the hero doesn't need a weapon, I'm told."

"Hero?"

"Goes by Atlas. Mightiest warrior in the village. He's hunting the man-eater right now. Sad because he's surely going to die."

"What? Why?"

"Because everyone else has," Atticus said. "But enough of that. Do you have anything else you need identified before we head to the Branch and settle up?"

Elijah did. First came the Silver Bracer of Rage, which turned out to have an additional effect that was unsurprisingly called Rage. Elijah didn't know what it did, but Atticus had some insight into that sort of thing. "It's probably a berserking ability," he said. "Increased attributes or damage at the cost of control. There are a few abilities like that."

The final item Elijah had Atticus identify was the Sash of the Whirlwind. It had no extra effects, but Elijah did learn that the time dilation was called Haste. However, it was limited to only two percent when unbonded. Once Elijah bonded the item, it would increase to five percent. The attribute bonuses would remain the same.

"Interesting," Elijah said, retying the sash around his waist.

"I believe you might be the best-equipped person I've ever seen, and you're not even wearing any proper armor," Atticus said with a shake of his head. "I'm sure there's a story behind all of that."

Elijah shrugged. "I got stranded in the middle of nowhere when the world changed, so I had to fend for myself. I guess there are benefits to that," he said. "If you manage to survive."

Atticus laughed, then clapped Elijah on the shoulder. "You're not wrong, friend. The survival is the tricky part, I'm sure. Now, come on. Let's get you paid."

52

GOOD COMPANY

Atticus slapped Elijah on the back and proclaimed, "You aren't so bad of a guy, friend. And best of all, you're rich! So you can buy dinner!"

"Uh . . . alright?" Elijah said, depositing a few crystalline leaves into his sack. They were guides that he'd bought that would hopefully shed some light on a few topics that were still a mystery to him. Those same guides had been available back in Ironshore, but they had been much more expensive. Vaguely, he remembered Ramik mentioning that Ironshore's Branch had been imported, so perhaps that had something to do with the increased cost.

Whatever the case, with the prices of those guides, he felt like he was stealing. Unfortunately, there was almost nothing available on the Market, and there was only one town listed on the map, and it was at the very edge of the range. Still, it would give Elijah a good starting point for his continued search for his sister.

He had also added quite a few coins to his tally, especially after Atticus had paid him. He checked his folio:

Copper	Silver	Gold	Platinum
114	422	17	0

Even after buying the guides, Elijah was a lot richer than when he'd left Ironshore. He supposed that conquering a tower alone was a good way to earn money, though he was still unsure of how he was intended to spend his wealth. He had everything he needed—so far—and he had a feeling that acquiring new equipment and supplies would only grow easier as he progressed in levels.

"What do you suggest?" he asked. "I don't know anything about Greek food."

"Oh, you're in for a treat, my friend!" said the jovial Atticus. Despite shelling out quite a few coins, he was in a great mood. That probably meant that he'd gotten the better of Elijah in their dealings, but that wasn't so concerning. He had plenty of money, after all, and he was more concerned with getting the items off his hands—especially the giant ogre staff—than he was about getting the absolute most money he could out of selling them. Still, he intended to make an attempt at contextualizing prices going forward; that way, he could avoid getting ripped off by less reputable merchants. "I know the best restaurant in Argos. The finest moussaka you'll ever taste. You'll see, friend. You will see."

Elijah just nodded, saying, "Sounds good. I've never had moussaka."

"Then you're in for a treat!"

After that, Atticus dragged him from the building containing the Branch. It was located in a central location, but the structure itself was little different from the rest of the city. By the time they stepped out into the street, night had begun to fall, and as they strode along, Elijah noticed the prevalence of elderly women sitting on the residential buildings' balconies. As they passed, the old women would lean in close to one another, clearly gossiping about him. A few even pointed, making him feel incredibly self-conscious.

Atticus assured him that it was nothing to worry about. Instead, it was just a characteristic common among older Greek women. Even if he'd been absolutely normal—which he decidedly was not, considering his blond hair and odd attire—he would have become a source of gossip.

Eventually, Atticus led him to a restaurant. In front of the building, there were a half dozen tables, at which various diners dug into their meals. Elijah didn't recognize many of the dishes served, but he was no expert on Greek cuisine, so that was unsurprising. Atticus obviously knew the owner because he greeted the portly, heavily bearded man with a jovial hug. He introduced Elijah as a good friend.

The owner—who was named Nikolas—escorted them to a private table in the back. There, Atticus and Elijah took seats on opposite sides.

"It's nice, yeah?" Atticus asked.

"Better than any place I've eaten lately," Elijah answered honestly. The last time he'd eaten a meal at a proper restaurant had been back in Norcastle, and even that had been the inn where he'd stayed. Before that, he'd had pizza with Jess the night before he'd left for the tower.

"That's the spirit. So, what's your story?" asked Atticus, leaning in eagerly.

"Who says I have a story?"

"Everyone has a story, friend. You're more powerful than you have any right to be, you have special treasure I've never seen before, and you're walking around out in the wilderness alone. If anyone has a story, it's you," he stated.

Elijah sighed. "The long and short of it is that I was stranded alone when the World Tree incorporated Earth. So, I ended up having to spend the next two years—I think; time got a bit funny—trying to survive. A couple of towers later, and I'm here."

"A couple of towers? Where's your team?"

"No team," Elijah said. "Just me."

"Seems like there's a story there, too."

"Not an interesting one," Elijah lied. "So, what about you? How'd you end up here?"

"Born and raised in Argos. I moved to Athens a few years back, but I was back home visiting my mother when everything changed," he said. Then, his face fell. "She didn't make it. Giant rat creature. They were bad there for a while, but then they just . . . stopped. Most people think they went elsewhere, but I don't know. I think something killed them. Same with the cats."

"The cats?"

"Argos used to be lousy with them. It was an issue in the first six months or so, but then, they started disappearing until there weren't any left. Dogs went next. Now, anything smaller than a mule disappears after a few days. Nobody knows what's happening."

"Interesting," Elijah said.

"Eh. Just life in the apocalypse, right? I'm sure you've seen stranger things," Atticus said.

Just then, Nikolas arrived bearing two plates of what looked like lasagna. However, the smells were all wrong, It was obviously the moussaka Atticus had mentioned, so once the owner left them alone, he wasted no time in digging in.

And it was glorious.

"What is this, and why have I never had it? It's amazing!"

"It's moussaka, friend. Eggplant lasagna with lamb. The national dish of Greece."

"Is it really?" asked Elijah around a mouthful of the delicious dish.

Atticus laughed. "I don't know, but it should be. Now eat, friend. Eat and be merry!"

After that invitation, Elijah had no compunctions about doing precisely that. Before he knew it, his plate was clean. However, it didn't take long before Nikolas returned with another serving. In all, Elijah ate three helpings as well as a dessert of baklava. Through it all, Atticus proved an amiable companion, though he did continuously ask for details about Elijah's exploits.

For his part, Elijah revealed a few more bits about what he'd been through, including his misadventures in Norcastle.

"That's your problem, friend," announced Atticus with a laugh. He gestured with a fork as he continued: "You should have bowed to them. People like that, they expect subservience. When they don't get it, they react with violence."

"Can't really argue with that assessment," Elijah acknowledged.

"So, where are you going after this? Do you seek another tower? Or are you here to hunt the man-eater?"

Elijah shook his head. "No more towers."

"The man-eater, then."

"Everyone keeps mentioning that. What is it?"

Atticus leaned in and, in a stage whisper, said, "There are two schools of thought on that, friend. Some people believe it's just some evolved beast. No different from any other. We had issues with wolves a few months back, for instance. But me? I think different."

Elijah raised an eyebrow. "Oh? What do you think it is?"

"Have you ever heard of the Nemean lion?"

"One of the twelve labors of Heracles, right?" guessed Elijah, intrigued.

"Indeed, friend. Impenetrable hide. Claws sharper than any mortal sword. Sprung from the moon goddess, Selene."

"And you think this creature is here?" asked Elijah.

"We have history with the Nemean lion around here. Just north of here was the town of Cleonae, where the hero received his quest," Atticus explained. "This System made monsters real. The hero Atlas slew a minotaur not three months past. Who says the System is not a tool of Olympus, eh? The gods are angry that we've moved on without them, and they sent their monsters to punish us."

"You believe that?" asked Elijah, his dubiousness apparent.

Atticus shrugged, then grinned. "I've no idea, friend, but it's as good an explanation as any, eh? Besides, something is killing people out there. That's indisputable. So, the question remains—are you here to hunt our monster? I fear Atlas is already gone, and with him out of the picture . . ."

Elijah didn't know how to respond. On the one hand, he had no issues hunting a monster. In fact, that seemed right up his alley. However, from his perspective, it was far more likely that the monster in question was just a guardian beast who was protecting its territory. In that case, there was no way Elijah would hunt it, even if it was killing people.

But there was another possibility for handling the situation, wasn't there? What if he befriended the creature, then used Ancestral Circle to take it back to the Grove? It would be difficult, but he'd done it before with Sara the dragon. Besides, the creature would probably be much happier in his Grove, right?

It was certainly something to think about, and before Elijah even knew it, he had already decided to check it out. He was self-aware enough to know that part of that was due to what had happened to the bear. If he'd done the same for that guardian beast, it would still be alive.

"I can look into it," he said. "But I can't really guarantee anything. Chances are I won't even find anything out there."

"You will. I'm sure of it."

"What makes you so certain?"

"A good feeling. Now, let us drink!" he said, raising his mug of beer.

Elijah tried to beg off, but in the end, the boisterous merchant insisted. Fortunately, Elijah's Constitution and Regeneration were high enough that beer really couldn't inebriate him—not unless he went seriously overboard, at least.

Just to be sure, though, he continuously healed himself via Touch of Nature. He wanted to trust Atticus, but getting drunk with a stranger seemed far too reckless, even for Elijah.

So, he drank with the merchant, and as he did, he felt much of the tension he'd carried melt away. It wasn't the alcohol, per se. Rather, it was just being around people who weren't looking to exploit or kill him. In fact, there were moments when he felt like he was back home with his friends and coworkers, just hanging out and having a good time.

But before long, the night came to an end, and he helped a very unsteady Atticus back to his shop. Apparently, he lived on the floor above, so Elijah had no qualms about leaving the merchant to find his own way to bed. Meanwhile, he quickly found an inn where he rented a room from an annoyed innkeeper.

"Sorry about how late it is," he said, sliding an extra couple of copper coins to the frowning woman. "I got caught up with a friend."

She snorted. "Lose your shoes, too?"

"Uh . . . I don't have any shoes."

"That's quite an oversight."

Elijah looked down at his bare feet. "Yeah. You're probably right."

Then, he took the key from the crotchety old woman and headed up the nearby stairs to the room he'd rented. To his surprise, there were no villains there to ambush him. No sudden issues. Nothing but a bed, a nightstand, and a pitcher of cold water. Over the next few minutes, he undressed, then used the pitcher of water to wash himself as best he could. He knew it was inadequate, but the small inn was the only place that was open so late. So, he figured that beggars couldn't be choosers, and he made do with what he had.

Once he was done, he collapsed onto the bed and fell asleep before more than a minute had passed.

53

LADENIA

Elijah missed his own bed.

And the tree house. The Grove, too. Even Nerthus. When he'd first washed ashore on that island, he'd have never expected to think of it as home, and yet, from the moment he'd departed, he had begun to miss all the things that had grown so familiar. Certainly, he didn't miss the monster attacks or the starvation that had plagued his first few weeks, but his Grove had come a long way since then. It was easily as comfortable as his apartment back in Hawaii.

As he lay in the hotel's thin-mattressed bed, he cast the whole of his Mind back to his Domain. Thanks to his Locus, he always knew what was going on back on the island, but he usually kept that information sequestered in its own facet of his Mind. But every now and again, he liked to turn his full attention to the goings-on back home.

When he did, he was gratified to sense that it was much the same as always. His Domain had continued to grow, and it had even encompassed the tower. However, the rate of growth had begun to slow, and he suspected that it would peter out within a hundred yards of the island's shores. Even that was an incredible amount of territory, though, and what's more, he could sense the tower's excess ethera draining into the Grove itself. That was just as Nerthus had predicted, and he expected that it would keep the tower from overflowing in a surge of Voxx.

"That's a relief and a half," he said to himself as he stared up at the ceiling, his hands behind his head. For a long time, he just enjoyed the safety and security of civilization while keeping his Mind focused on his Locus. It was oddly comforting, knowing everything that was happening back home.

If Elijah was honest, he'd half expected to have already been called home for one reason or another. But the people of Ironshore had remained on their side of the strait, seemingly content to live separately. A good thing, too, because as much as he craved the comforts of home, he still had a goal ahead of him. Finding his sister remained at the top of his list. Fortunately, Carmen's name was still on the power rankings, and he took great solace in the implication that his sister, as well as Miguel, was still out there and safe.

After all, there was no way that Carmen would let anything happen to Alyssa. Not so long as she was alive, which she clearly was because she'd actually gained a couple of levels in the past few weeks. That was enough to put at least some of his anxiety to rest.

With that thought, Elijah pushed himself out of bed and looked around the room. The night before, he'd barely noticed his surroundings, but he was pleasantly surprised to find that the room was extremely clean, if a little sparsely decorated. As he'd noted before going to sleep, there was no bathroom attached to the room, so he quickly went down the hall to take advantage of the communal toilet. Fortunately, he was an early riser, and so, he didn't have to wait his turn.

Once he was finished, he went back to his room and took another bird bath with the provided pitcher of water, then headed downstairs. As was the case with the last hotel where he'd stayed, the bottom floor functioned as a restaurant, but to his disdain, the surly innkeeper wasn't cooking to order. Instead, a few minutes after he sat down, she stopped in to serve him some flatbread that had been topped with tomatoes and drizzled in olive oil.

"What is this?" he asked, trying his best not to sound disappointed. He wanted bacon and eggs, or at least something a little heartier than a bit of bread.

"Ladenia," the woman answered. "Good. Eat."

Without further explanation, she left him to his meal.

"At least there's coffee," he said, reaching out to grab the cup she'd left behind. When he took a sip of the hot beverage, he was taken back to the world before everything had changed. It had been so long since he'd enjoyed a real cup of coffee that he'd almost forgotten how much he loved the bitter brew. Even without sugar, it was amazing, and he almost forgot about the ladenia. But then his stomach started rumbling, and he gave it a shot.

"Oh my God," he muttered around his first bite. First of all, there was a lot more going on than simple bread and tomatoes. There were onions and herbs on the fluffy flatbread, too. And of course, the olive oil set it all off. Elijah quickly forgot about his previous objections as he tore through the entire meal in what felt like seconds. As he swallowed the last bite, he signaled the innkeeper and asked for seconds.

Strangely, his obvious enjoyment of the food cut through her surly demeanor, and she actually favored him with a smile. "I have something else for you. Wait."

Before she left, she refilled his coffee cup and patted him on the head like he was a child. But given her advanced age, she was probably old enough to have been his grandmother, so he didn't take offense. Especially if she kept bringing him delicious food and coffee—if she did that, he would take whatever she wanted to dish out.

Soon after, she returned and set a plate in front of him. He looked at the round, pancake-like dish in front of him and asked, "What is this?"

It certainly didn't smell like a pancake, and it had nuts sprinkled on top. There was also honey drizzled across the whole thing.

"It's called sfakianopita," she said, beaming. She waved her hand, adding, "Eat. It's good."

By that point, Elijah trusted the older woman's judgment, so he dug in. And predictably, it was amazing. It was soft and crispy and flaky, all at once. And the cheese and honey and nuts all played perfectly together.

"I think you're my new favorite person in the world," he said, grinning at the woman as he continued to chew. Meanwhile, he was trying to think of a way to coax the woman back to his island. He was top ten on the power ladder, wasn't he? That meant he was famous and powerful. Surely, he deserved a personal cook.

For her part, the woman just smiled knowingly. There was no trace of the curmudgeonly innkeeper he'd met the night before. Instead, she'd been replaced by a kindly old grandmother. Elijah knew which one he preferred.

Regrettably, by the time he finished the small pancake-like pie, he was absolutely stuffed. Still, before he left on the day's mission—he still hadn't forgotten about the supposed man-eater stalking the countryside—the innkeeper thrust a basket into his hands, telling him, "Egg muffins. For later."

Elijah wasn't going to turn her down, so he took the basket with gratitude and handed her a couple more cooper etherium. Of course, she tried to refuse, but he insisted, closing her fist around the coins and saying, "That was the best breakfast I've had in years. Thank you."

And he meant it, too. Of course, he could count on one hand the number of times he'd eaten anything but leftover fish stew, crab, or a few berries, so that probably wasn't the compliment it seemed. Still, he was as satisfied with the meal as he'd ever been.

After that, Elijah grabbed his staff from where he'd leaned it against the table and set off. As he started through the city, he once again noticed the prevalence of older women sitting on balconies and presumably gossiping about everything they saw. He gave one group a wave and a smile, which set them off into excited whispers. His contented grin widened at that, and he kept on going until he reached the gate.

When he passed the guards, they reminded him to be back inside before nightfall. Otherwise, he would risk the ire of the man-eater. Elijah assured them that he would do just that, then strode off toward the tree line in the distance. As he did, he saw an olive grove on the other side of town. That explained where all the olive oil had come from, at least.

Once Elijah reached the concealment of the trees, he took a few minutes to find a secluded glen where he settled down on a fallen log. There, he started emptying his pack. After all, he now knew that, because he hadn't bonded his items, he wasn't getting their full use. So, he quickly got down to the business he hadn't even known he had neglected, pricking his fingers and thrusting his ethera into his magical equipment.

It was a bit embarrassing that he hadn't figured it out on his own, but it only took a moment for him to realize that it was nothing to be ashamed of. After all, it would've taken quite an intuitive leap—or some odd coincidence—for him to figure the process out.

"I mean, who goes and smears blood on their fancy new sash, right?" he asked the forest. Predictably, it did not answer. "Nobody. That's who."

In any case, he quickly did as Atticus had described, dripping blood onto the item and shoving some ethera into the sash. A moment later, when he tied it around his waist, he felt something new. It wasn't a huge difference, but the Haste effect was still more potent than it had been before. Next, he bonded the Claws of Gluttony before slipping the awkward thing onto his hand. While he wasn't going to run around punching things in his human form, he fought unarmed in his other shapes. So, he expected that the effect would work just fine. And Elijah certainly wouldn't refuse a straight nine percent increase to his damage, let alone the Anticoagulant effect.

Finally, he bound his bracer. When he did, he became immediately aware of the Rage effect. With a thought, he could activate it. However, he intuitively knew that once he did, the ability would go on cooldown for six hours. So, he needed to be careful about using it.

With all that done, he embraced Shape of the Predator, and once he'd assumed his draconid form, he looked down at his claws. The set on the right—the ones that corresponded with the Claws of Gluttony—had taken on a distinctly metallic sheen. That seemed to confirm that, if he wanted to take advantage of the weapon, he'd need to attack with that paw. It was not ideal, but still better than nothing.

He suspected it would be more effective in his lamellar-ape form, largely because he was more dependent on his claws in that shape. Still, he wasn't going to refuse any extra source of damage.

Now that his items had been bound, and he was fighting at peak strength, Elijah decided to finally get started on the task at hand. So, he took on the Guise of the Unseen and set off through the woods. During his conversation with Atticus, he'd discovered that the last recorded man-eater attacks had been in the olive groves, so that was the direction Elijah headed. As he did, he kept an entire facet of his Quartz Mind dedicated to parsing the data he received from One with Nature. The effective radius still wasn't more than a dozen feet or so, but he'd found the extrasensory perception to be invaluable, nonetheless.

Yet, even with that on his side, he found nothing until he reached the groves. There, he encountered plenty of twitchy and anxious workers. However, there was no sign of the man-eater. So, Elijah kept going, slowly making his way through the olive groves until he reached the edge. That was where the hero Atlas had gone hunting the monster, so Elijah had always figured that was where he would end up.

Soon enough, he'd left the olive groves behind, though even miles from the city, he still hadn't found any evidence of the monster. In fact, other than birds and a few tree-dwelling creatures, there were no animals at all. The day wore on and as his search continued, he encountered more of the same.

Until, at last, he smelled blood. One whiff, and he knew that it had originated with a human, as well. He expected that he'd finally found Atlas's trail, and judging by the spatter of blood, it seemed that the hero was injured.

So, Elijah followed the smell, pausing every now and again to make certain that he wasn't walking into a trap. Even so, he didn't sense anything amiss, so he continued to track the injured hero until, finally, he caught sight of him.

And he was nothing like what Elijah had expected.

When he'd heard the name Atlas, he'd envisioned a huge, strapping man with bulging muscles capable of bearing the weight of the world on his shoulders. However, the person huddled against a boulder and sitting in a pool of his own blood looked little bigger than a child. Even to Elijah, who was below-average size, the boy looked slim to the point of malnutrition. He wore round spectacles and had a mop of curly black hair that made him look like a member of a boy band.

He was clutching a long, thin stick, and his eyes flicked around as if he was expecting to be attacked at any moment. That was probably smart because his bloody clothing and multitude of wounds suggested that he'd already gotten the worst of some enemy's attention. And judging by how twitchy he was, whatever had mauled him was still out there.

For a moment, Elijah considered waiting to see if the enemy—probably the man-eater—would show itself, but the idea of using a dying teenager as bait just didn't sit right with him. So, he let Shape of the Predator fall away, and he said, "Aren't you a little young to be out here all by yourself?"

"No! You idiot! Run away! It's going to—"

Before Elijah could even cast Healing Rain or approach the young man, something slammed into his back, sending him pitching forward into the loamy forest turf.

54

THE NEMEAN LION

Pain erupted in Elijah's back as his attacker brought incredibly sharp claws to bear. Due to his high Constitution, he wasn't killed outright, but the claws still scraped against his ribs. As the creature—whatever it was—tore his flesh to ribbons, one facet of Elijah's Mind focused on casting Shape of the Guardian. The second he finished the spell, his body started to morph.

First, he grew scales. Then, his arms extended, his hands becoming vicious claws. His legs didn't grow any shorter, but the effect was the same due to the lengthening of his torso and the sheer amount of muscle that came with the form of the lamellar ape. The moment the transformation was complete, Elijah used Iron Scales. It didn't do anything for the ruin that had already been wreaked on his back, but it would hopefully prevent more damage in the immediate future.

But only for a few seconds. Then, he would have to cast it again, which was not a viable strategy. Using the ability in quick succession would drain his stamina very rapidly, and if he employed that approach, he would quickly wear himself out. As a result, he was on the clock.

With that timer occupying one facet of his Mind, Elijah used the second of solace granted by his ability to shove himself to his feet. With his long arms, he tried to dislodge the creature on his back, but it was both too small and too awkwardly positioned. Even with his extended reach, he couldn't get ahold of the thing. After spying the nearest tree, he launched himself backward. Just before he crashed into the massive trunk, the little monster on his back leaped free.

That was when Elijah got his first look at the thing.

"Is that a house cat?" he murmured, his transformed voice coming out as more of a growl.

Indeed, the supposed monster was clearly a house cat, though Elijah wasn't certain of the breed. With an extraordinarily fluffy coat of tawny fur, it would've looked like a stuffed animal if it wasn't for the blood splattered across its chest. The animal was also more than twice the size of any house cat Elijah had ever seen, which meant that its stature was similar to a mountain lion.

"Don't hurt her!" screamed the boy, his voice cracking. Then, he added, "No, Artemis! Bad girl! Leave the man . . . er . . . monster alone!"

The cat, which Elijah belatedly recognized as a Maine coon, briefly shifted its focus to the boy. That gave Elijah an opening he wasn't going to squander. So, he launched himself forward, intending to end the fight with a single blow. With the increased Haste effect from Sash of the Whirlwind, Elijah moved with incredible alacrity, and he managed to take the distracted cat by surprise.

His claws glinted metallically as they swept out, but when he made contact with the little monster's tawny fur, he got the surprise of a lifetime. The sound of metal scratching against metal filled the air, and though the momentum of the blow sent the cat sailing through the air, the attack did not bear the results Elijah had anticipated.

The little creature twisted, hitting a tree feetfirst, then launched itself back at Elijah. He barely had time to once again use Iron Scales before it hit him like a launched missile. Despite its comparatively small size—after all, even a house cat as big as a bobcat was tiny compared to his lamellar-ape form—the impact of its attack sent him staggering backward. Then, it savaged his chest with its sharp claws, though most of the damage was mitigated by the still-ongoing Iron Scales.

But it was set to end soon.

To avoid having his chest shredded as thoroughly as his back, Elijah clambered for a grip on the little creature, and to his surprise, he managed to grab ahold of its great, bushy tail. However, when he did, he felt something that, once again, filled him with surprise. Instead of fluffy fur, the cat was covered in something more akin to the bristles of a steel brush. When his claws closed around the tail, he felt those bristles painfully digging into his palm. Yet, he wasn't going to let such a perfect opportunity go to waste. So, despite the annoying pain, his grip tightened. And when he had a good hold of the tail, he ripped the creature away from his chest and slammed it against the ground.

Once.

Twice.

Three times, channeling his inner Hulk. The little monster yowled in agony, but Elijah wasn't rewarded with the sound of breaking bones. Instead of being crippled by being slammed into the ground multiple times, the cat had gone wild, clawing anything that came into range. That meant that, as soon as Iron Scales wore off, the creature tore into his wrist and forearm.

Elijah's Constitution was high, so those claws didn't sever tendons, but even if it wasn't permanently damaging, it was more than enough to frustrate him. However, just before he took his anger out on the cat via another slamming attack, something hit Elijah in his already-wounded back. The smell of sizzling meat assailed his nose before the blistering agony reached his Mind. And when it did, he reacted reflexively, loosening his grip just enough that the cat was able to wriggle free.

"Leave her alone!" screamed the boy.

Elijah stumbled to his knees as the flesh of his back smoldered. Then, another attack landed, and the molten pain shot through the roof. He collapsed onto his chest as another fireball sailed overhead, hitting a nearby tree and setting it alight. Elijah tried to rise, but with the muscles in his back having been destroyed, he couldn't move more than a few inches.

His options were limited. Touch of Nature was powerful, but the healing it offered was far from instantaneous. Given that he could scarcely move, and he had two enemies bearing down on him, that just wouldn't work. So, without any other choices he could see, Elijah used Guardian's Renewal.

Guardian's Renewal	**Instantly and completely regenerate. Cooldown affected by Regeneration attribute. Current cooldown: Once per 6.7 days.**

The ability was instant, and his body immediately recovered. Muscles mended, flesh reformed, and his scales were quickly restored. Yet a lingering pain persisted, almost as if he had a pulled muscle. As far as Elijah knew, that shouldn't have been possible. Fortunately, it wasn't enough to hinder him, but in one facet of his Mind, he was definitely concerned.

More distressing was what he finally allowed himself to notice. The pervasive, sickly sweet scent of rot filled the air, and beneath the cat's fur was a series of familiar black tendrils. Now that he saw it—albeit only barely—Elijah knew the source. He'd seen such a thing before, and the encounter had been significant and terrifying enough that he would never forget it. Clearly, the cat had run afoul of a dimensional rift, which had infected it with the madness Elijah had seen from the bear back on his island. Back then, he'd managed to close the rift before it had spread too much, but from the looks of it, wherever the cat had been infected had probably been there for quite some time.

"W-what? How?" breathed the boy.

Elijah rose to his feet, completely restored. That prompted another attack from the young man, who summoned a ball of blue-white fire and tossed it in Elijah's direction. Now that he could see it coming, he had no issues dodging it, and when he did, Elijah darted forward to wrap his massive claw around the young man's waist. At the same time, the cat managed to push itself to its feet and flee into the surrounding forest. It used some sort of ability because it even disappeared from One with Nature far before it had time to leave the area of effect.

So, with only one enemy left, Elijah turned his full attention to the young man. He squeezed, then growled, "Why did you attack me?"

"Please . . . She's just sick . . . She's not . . . She's not bad! Don't hurt her!"

The fury of the lamellar ape threatened to overwhelm Elijah, but he shoved it aside in favor of human calm. Still, he was prepared to rip the young man in two if the situation called for it. In fact, he craved that outcome in ways he didn't want to think about.

"Explain," he growled.

"She's . . . She's my only friend! Please don't hurt her anymore!"

"I won't," Elijah snarled. He fully realized that the statement was entirely contrary to his tone, but he didn't dare switch back to his much more vulnerable human form. That fire would have eaten a hole through him in a second if he hadn't been in his guardian shape. He unsuccessfully tried to soften his voice as he once again prompted, "Explain. Now."

"O-okay. Okay. Just . . . Just don't hurt her . . ."

Then, the young man launched into what sounded to Elijah like an unlikely tale. According to Atlas—which Elijah surmised was the boy's name—the animal was his cat, Artemis. Just after Earth had experienced the touch of the World Tree, the cat had started to level via hunting various pests in Argos. It had also become the young man's protector, keeping him safe until he was old enough to take an archetype. He'd chosen the Sorcerer archetype, though he didn't specify his class. Elijah got the feeling that most people kept that information to themselves, at least in Argos.

"Then, Artemis started hunting other cats. Even dogs," Atlas explained. "She kept getting stronger, too. So did I. And when we found out about the tower, I was one of the people asked to go. I . . . I was the only one who made it back. When I did, Artemis was gone. And all the animals in the city had been killed. I don't know if that was before or after she got . . . infected."

Elijah sighed, which came out more like a growl. Then, he finally let the young man fall from his grip and made a choice that, in a vacuum, was probably stupid. However, the alternative was something he didn't want to consider. He shifted back to his human form, which caused Atlas to scramble backward in fear.

Holding up a hand, Elijah said, "Calm down. I'm going to heal you, okay? And then you're going to show me where the rift is. Once I close it, we'll find your cat, and I'll try to remove the infection."

"What? How? You're not a Healer."

"You're not wrong. But I'm close enough," Elijah responded, already casting Healing Rain. As the soothing precipitation started to fall, he added, "See? Healing Rain. Feels good, right? I'm here to help."

Elijah was well aware that his bedside manner left a little to be desired, but he hoped that his calm tone, human visage, and healing would bridge the gap and allow the young man to trust him—at least enough that he wouldn't start tossing more of those blue-white fireballs at him.

"I . . . I . . ."

He didn't get anything else out before Elijah took a step forward and laid his hand on the young man's shoulder. He wasn't going to push his luck by insisting on a proper examination, so he settled for the untargeted form of Touch of Nature. That was usually fine for self-healing, but when he was trying to mend someone else's injuries, it was decidedly less effective. Still, he made do, suffusing the young man's body with rejuvenating energy.

Atlas gasped and flinched before he was beset by a series of tremors as his body mended. In the end, it took six casts of Touch of Nature to heal the boy, which was a testament to Atlas's level of power.

"That . . . Most people have trouble healing me," he muttered, looking down at his bloodstained clothes. "Because of my class . . ."

Elijah could tell that the young man didn't want to talk about that, so he asked, "What's your real name? And don't tell me it's really Atlas. I know that's bullshit."

"Oh. It's Isaak. The Atlas thing wasn't my idea."

"Well, Isaak," Elijah said, holding out his hand. "I'm Elijah." When the young man grasped his hand, he pulled Isaak to his feet and added, "Nice to meet you. Now, let's go find that rift. With any luck, we'll have your cat healed by the end of the day."

55

A DIFFERENT KIND OF CHALLENGE

The forest was silent, but Elijah felt the corruption of the nearby dimensional rift. It was clearly a higher grade than the one he'd entered back on his island, which didn't bode well for the difficulties ahead. Even as he focused on that with one facet of his Mind, the other partitions in his Quartz Mind monitored his surroundings. One facet was trained on Isaak, who walked beside him, but the rest were entirely focused on the environment. He didn't want to get ambushed again, and One with Nature seemed incapable of detecting the corrupted cat.

"So, why did Artemis attack you?" he asked, following the strengthening trail of corruption. Now that he was looking for it, it was easier to track, and he knew it was closer than expected.

"She was a good girl, at first," he said. "She even protected me. But . . . once she disappeared, and I figured out what was happening, I knew I needed to help her. Or stop her . . ."

Elijah stopped, then turned to put his hand on the boy's shoulder. He was taller than Elijah, but he held himself with a stoop. "Listen. You need to accept that this might not turn out like you want it to," he said, trying to be as compassionate as possible. The cat wasn't just the boy's pet. That was his friend. His guardian. Better than most, Elijah could understand how important that could be, which was probably why he was so sympathetic to the young man's situation. It had probably saved Isaak's life, if Elijah was honest. "I'm going to try to heal her, and I think I have a good shot. But I've never done this, and there's every chance that I won't be able to. If that's the case . . ."

"I know," the boy said, his eyes adopting a steely glint that flashed behind his round spectacles. In that moment, Elijah could see the determination that had allowed Isaak to survive the tower. "I'm prepared to do what's necessary."

"Good."

After that, Isaak explained how the cat had spent the past week toying with him. It wasn't simple cruelty, either, though that was part of Artemis's motivation. In addition, it had been using Isaak as bait, wounding him and waiting on other monsters or animals to investigate the smell of what they thought was a wounded animal. When they came around, Artemis pounced.

It was a viable hunting method, though one that Elijah found disturbing for a number of reasons he didn't want to contemplate. However, he did find himself wondering if it was an expression of the cat's natural cruelty or if the corruption had twisted it into something it never should have been.

Whatever the case, he listened to Isaak's explanation with equanimity as they approached the rip in the dimensional membrane that connected their world with the Void. One of the guides he'd bought back in Argos had elaborated on the nature of the universe, which he'd added to the explanation he'd gotten from Nerthus. He already knew that the World Tree connected multiple universes—nine, in fact—but the space between those universes was referred to as the Abyss. It was uncharted territory ruled by an entity called the Ravener. There wasn't much information on that creature—or god, as it seemed—but the guide wasn't shy about calling it the enemy.

The space on the other side of the dimensional rift was, like the towers, a result of the System's intervention. So, instead of directly connecting the normal universes with the Void, it acted as both a barrier and a bridge between dimensions. In many ways, it was exactly the same as the towers, but on a much smaller scale.

Even so, Elijah had also learned that they could be much more dangerous than towers, and for a variety of reasons. Mostly, though, it was due to the fact that people often underestimated those dangers, but also because the levels of the creatures inside were completely independent of the challenger. That was a departure from the nature of the towers, the levels of which scaled according to the levels of the people trying to conquer it.

Of course, that didn't mean that a level twenty could jump into a tower and defeat nothing but creatures of that level. Instead, the guide described the tower denizens as "appropriately leveled to provide a difficult challenge to an entire group of would-be conquerors." That was further muddled by the grades of towers, but that seemed to be less based on levels than on real power.

It was all a little confusing to Elijah, but the gist of it was that most towers were theoretically surmountable by a well-tuned group. However, challenging and defeating the higher-grade towers was much more difficult and only appropriate for the best of the best.

Every time he dug deeper into the universe—or multiverse, he amended— the more he saw how little he understood. There were so many layers that it would take a lifetime to explore them all. But that shouldn't have been surprising. Even before the touch of the World Tree, Earth had been complex enough to take a lifetime to understand, and that was with the knowledge of all of human civilization to build upon. It only stood to reason that a multiverse that was composed of not just multiple planets, but multiple universes, would be infinitely more complex.

So, he'd resolved to take things one step at a time and work with whatever snippets of information he could acquire. Anything else would be too overwhelming to contemplate.

With that in mind, he and Isaak continued to follow the trail until, at last, they discovered the tear in the dimensional fabric. It manifested as a large, ragged rip hanging in the air. Through it, Elijah could see nothing but darkness, though he knew what to expect on the other side. Spreading out from that rip were black tendrils of corruption that looked like glistening vines. They reached about thirty feet in every direction, and the moment Elijah stepped within that circle, he felt the corruption skyrocket.

Isaak let out a gasp. "I don't like this," he mumbled. "I don't like it one bit."

"You get used to it," Elijah lied. "Just try to ignore it." He turned to the young man and continued, "You don't have to do this. I can go in alone."

"No. I need to help."

Elijah admired the boy's courage. "Fine. You remember what I told you, right? We're going into a space between worlds where we'll have to fight something, just like in the tower, but on a smaller scale."

"I understand."

"Okay—you're a mage, right? Like, you sling fireballs."

"Soulfire."

"What?"

"It's soulfire. It eats away at a person's ethera while doing . . . a lot of damage. I've never seen anything survive after I hit it."

"I survived."

"I know," the boy said with a visible tremor. "I can also increase Regeneration. And I have an ability called Soulfire Explosion. If I use it, everything dies, and I'm out of commission for the rest of the fight. Last time, I had to spend a week in recovery."

"Do you have anything else noteworthy?"

"I have a couple of self-buffs," he said. "One called Arcane Shield that can block a few attacks. One called Shackle that kind of roots a bad guy in place. There are a couple more, like Fireball and Ice Explosion that I don't use that much. I normally just use Soulfire Dart, like the one I hit you with."

"Alright. So, I'm going to try something, then," Elijah said. Then, he cast Essence of the Boar, Essence of the Wolf, and Aura of Regeneration on the young man. The enhancements stuck, but when he tried to use Essence of the Monkey on Isaak, it wouldn't take hold.

Still, that was enough to elicit a gasp of surprise from Isaak. "What was that? I feel . . . better. Like, a lot better."

"One increases your Constitution, another your movement speed, and the last is called Aura of Regeneration. It increases your Regeneration quite a bit,"

Elijah explained. Then, he cast the enhancements on himself, though he added Essence of the Monkey to his own list. He still couldn't use everything all at once, but he hoped that when he got a few more levels, that would change.

Of course, he also kept One with Nature active, as well, but that was always the case.

Isaak responded by casting an enhancement of his own, and when Elijah looked at his status, he saw that his Regeneration had increased by another fifteen points. That was incredible, considering that Isaak probably hadn't advanced his cultivation like Elijah had. And if he had, he certainly didn't have the benefit of the powerful Dragon Core. So, the base spell was definitely powerful.

With that, the pair were ready for the challenge of the dimensional rift. So, without further hesitation, they stepped inside.

For a brief instant, Elijah felt like he was being ripped into a million pieces. He'd experienced much the same in his first trip into a dimensional rift, so he had expected it. However, Isaak clearly hadn't, and his response was predictable. He let out a long, piercing scream before falling to one knee and sobbing. Elijah left him there for a few seconds before kneeling beside the boy. He put his hand on Isaak's back and said, "It's okay. It's over. Now, eyes up. This isn't like the last time I was in one of these."

The setting was similar. Populated by jagged rocks that looked distressingly like obsidian, the ground was otherwise barren. In the distance, he could see huge peaks of gray stone, and just as before, there were a multitude of purple rivers of energy. A few dozen feet away, Elijah saw what looked like purple anemones waving in the motionless air.

More importantly, he saw his opponent.

The Voxxian monster was small. Maybe three feet tall but built of solid muscle and coated in dark-green scales. It cocked its head to the side, gazing at Elijah with obvious curiosity.

"On your feet, Isaak."

The moment he uttered those words, the little creature let out a screech, then charged Elijah. For his part, he immediately shifted into his lamellar-ape form and leaped forward into battle. He met the monster's charge with a herculean punch that sent it skidding across the rocky ground. It shattered the jagged shards of obsidian with its passage, only coming to a stop thirty feet away when its momentum was met by a larger black edifice.

But it wasn't dead.

Not yet, at least.

Isaak had recovered from the pain of passing through the dimensional rift, and he'd already tossed a Soulfire Dart at the prone creature. The little ball of blue-and-white fire moved extremely slowly, but the fallen Voxx was too stunned to take advantage of that weakness. The Soulfire Dart hit it in the shoulder, then quickly enveloped the creature. It screeched again, but the sound quickly died away, replaced by the sizzle of broiling flesh. Only a few moments later, it was dead, leaving behind only a charred and unrecognizable husk.

"Is that it?" the young man asked, panting with excitement and fear. Elijah looked back to see Isaak pushing his spectacles back into place. "I expected it to be harder."

"No. We didn't get a notification."

Just then, the ground rumbled, and via One with Nature, Elijah felt two distinct presences flare into existence. A moment later, two creatures erupted from the rocky ground.

Both of them screeched, then launched themselves into a charge that mirrored the previous monster's attack. However, these two Voxx were slightly different than the one that had come before. Not only were they noticeably larger and more muscular, but they featured sharper-looking claws.

"Upgrades," Elijah muttered before leaping forward. However, the creatures were smart enough not to meet his charge head-on. Instead, the second he moved in their direction, they split. One went for Isaak, while the other intended to confront Elijah. Knowing that the young man wasn't built to take hits, Elijah pivoted, springing sideways and tackling the other monster. However, the first quickly adjusted and darted toward Isaak.

Even as Elijah grabbed hold of the monster and started pummeling it into submission, the other reached Isaak. But to his surprise, the young man's shield held through the monster's first blow, and he responded by hitting it with another Soulfire Dart. Just like that, the monster ended up like the first—charred and crispy. Elijah's opponent died a few moments later.

But almost as soon as it went down, he felt the next wave of monsters. Three more burst from the ground a second later, confirming the nature of the rift's challenge.

"It's a gauntlet," he shouted. "Conserve your Ethera as best you can. I think we're going to be here for a while!"

56

A BATTLE OF ENDURANCE

Three Voxxian monsters clambered across Elijah's broad back, biting and clawing for purchase. He'd just used Iron Scales, so they stood no chance of actually harming him. However, the same couldn't be said for Isaak, who was running in circles as he tried to avoid yet another creature. He was not doing a good job of it, either, because the thing kept catching up and biting him. The only reason he hadn't already fallen was the ethereal shield that protected his body.

Eljiah couldn't worry about the boy, though. He had to trust that Isaak could take care of himself because he was already starting to feel the strain of using Iron Scales too many times in quick succession. If something didn't change—and soon—he would fall from sheer exhaustion. So, with that in mind, he reached back with one long arm and snatched at the much-smaller Voxx. It dodged nimbly and continued its gnashing attack.

So, he tipped over and slammed himself into the ground, back first. Two of the monsters scattered, leaping from his back just in time to avoid being flattened. However, the third wasn't so lucky. Bones crunched as the full weight of Elijah's guardian shape squashed the creature. It didn't die, but it certainly wasn't recovering from that anytime soon.

More importantly, Elijah had a brief moment to enact the next part of his hastily conceived plan. Without hesitation, he shifted back into his human form and cast two spells. The first was Healing Rain, which he hoped would be enough to keep both himself and Isaak healed for the time being. The next was Snaring Roots, which he aimed at the boy's pursuer. Thick, thorny, and purple vines erupted from the ground, wrapping around the small creature and locking it into place.

Meanwhile, the remaining two Voxx reversed course and made a beeline toward the suddenly vulnerable Elijah. He met the first one with a baseball swing of his staff that sent it skidding to the side, but that opened him for the other's attack. Elijah raised his arm just in time to keep it from tearing into his torso, but when it crunched down on his forearm, he let out a cry of anger and agony. Without aiming, he used Storm's Fury, and a bolt of lightning descended from the sky. It hit the creature clinging to his arm, sending it into convulsions, and he used that brief opening to fling it away.

The second it flew free, Elijah canceled Essence of the Monkey and used Shield of Brambles. After that, he shifted back into his lamellar-ape form; the transformation completed just before the two creatures returned to the fight, but this time, Elijah was ready for them. He didn't even bother keeping them off him. Instead, he was perfectly willing to endure their attacks. With Iron Scales active, they did almost no damage, and every time they bit or clawed—which was quite a lot, considering their favored form of frenzied attacks—they got sharp thorns for their troubles.

In seconds, they were coated in a dozen rivulets of blood.

At the same time, Elijah stomped on the injured Voxx that was still struggling to rise despite its plethora of broken bones. He ended its life with a generous application of force directed at its vulnerable skull. It couldn't avoid the blow, so it died after only a few more seconds.

That left three, two of which were covered in their own blood from a hundred reflective thorn attacks. The third was still struggling with the roots as Isaak finally realized that he was no longer being chased. To his credit, the second he had an opening, he took aim at the struggling monster and let loose with one of his balls of soulfire. Even with its limbs wrapped in writhing vines, the creature managed to dodge the oncoming spell.

Mostly.

It still took a glancing blow, which, for any other spell, might have been an issue. With soulfire, though, it was more than enough. The monster howled in agony as, in the space of a second, its arm melted entirely. However, the remainder of the ball of soulfire hit the roots, burning them to a crisp and freeing the creature. It stumbled as it tore loose from the remaining tendrils of vegetation.

For his part, Elijah couldn't afford to watch the unfolding battle between the young man and Voxx. He was far too busy with his own opponents. Thankfully, the multitude of wounds—small though they were—had begun to take their toll, and the two Voxxian creatures had slowed considerably. That allowed Elijah to reach back and grab one of them by the loose skin on the back of its neck. His claws dug into its hide as it attempted to wriggle free, but he wasn't having that. Despite its efforts at escape, Elijah's grip held, and he proceeded to slam the creature into the rocky ground.

The first instance broke bones, but the second shattered them. The third ruptured organs, and the fourth took its life. He let out a roar as he tossed it away, turning his attention to his remaining attacker. It wasn't long before it went the way of its partner, broken and dead.

At that moment, Isaak finally finished his target off, as well, using a whip of pure soulfire to slice through the creature. It fell into two disgusting halves that squelched when they hit the ground.

"What was that?"

"It's called Soul Whip," he said. "I . . . I'm not good with aiming it, so I can't use it unless they're close."

"You didn't mention that before," Elijah accused, his lamellar-ape voice low and growly.

The young man shrugged. "I wasn't sure if I might need it against you," he admitted self-consciously.

"That . . . makes a lot of sense."

"You're not mad at me?" Isaak asked.

Elijah shrugged his massive shoulders, saying, "Can't blame you. You don't know me. I don't know you. But I'll tell you this right now—you use that thing on me, and we're going to have a big problem."

Isaak swallowed hard. "I'm not . . . I wouldn't . . ."

"Look alive. Next wave is coming soon."

Just then, a massive rumble shook the ground, and Elijah felt dozens of presences swimming through the earth toward the surface. He knew exactly how to deal with that, so before they could complete their ascent, he shifted back to his human form and cast Calamity. Even as the wind began to blow, he shifted back to his guardian shape and readied himself for the coming struggle.

As it turned out, he needn't have worried.

The second the creatures—and there were more than ten—surfaced, Calamity descended upon them in all its disastrous fury. The wind howled as it cut them to pieces, and the earth buckled beneath them. And all the while, Elijah stood back, using his massive form to shield the young man.

In the end, all but three of the Voxxian monsters perished in the Calamity, and the trio of survivors were in no shape to fight back when Elijah went in to finish them off. They were much smaller than the previous wave—maybe three feet tall, at most—but they still looked extremely dangerous, with their sharp claws and biting teeth. Elijah pummeled them to death without hesitation.

When he returned to his position in front of Isaak, the curly-haired young man was in awe. "You just . . . How did you . . . What level are you?"

"Don't worry about that," Elijah responded. "Besides, levels aren't everything."

Before he could elaborate, a deep, resounding roar cut across the landscape, bouncing off the jagged obsidian rocks to make it seem like it was coming from everywhere all at once. But Elijah didn't need to rely on his aural senses to recognize the source. He could see it coming right for him.

It was big.

Bigger even than the monster that had nearly killed the panther back on his island. It also only had one set of arms, which somehow made it look even more fearsome. Elijah had just enough time to notice a huge sail-like set of spines on its back before it crashed into him. He met its charge with one of his own, though the impact with the twelve-foot-tall monster sent him flying backward like he'd been hit by an eighteen-wheeler.

Isaak lashed out with his Soul Whip, though to much lesser effect than against the other monsters. The tendril of blue-white fire wrapped around the Voxxian monster's leg, setting it to sizzling, yet that was where the damage ended. Still, it must have been quite painful because the monster let out a shuddering scream of pure agony before it backhanded Isaak. Blood arced, and the young man went flying away.

Elijah's mind went white with fury, and he sprang to his feet and launched himself at the monster. He hit with the force of a charging bull, knocking the Voxxian monster into a stumble. However, it recovered quickly, raking its claws across Elijah's back. Even with a hastily activated Iron Scales, Elijah felt his hide part beneath its sharp talons.

But he wasn't without claws of his own.

He snapped out his fists, ripping and tearing with all the fury he could muster. With the additional potency from his Claws of Gluttony, he managed to do quite a bit of damage before the monster lashed out with its foot, kicking him across the landscape. He tumbled, flipping over three times before hitting an escarpment of jagged black rock. It shattered, and a few bits lodged between his scales as his momentum took him a few feet farther.

Fortunately, he was durable enough that the damage was minor, and he recovered his feet only a second later. As he did, he saw the huge monster's unhurried approach. It almost looked like it was enjoying it. Or perhaps Elijah was simply anthropomorphizing the macabre smile playing across its semi-reptilian face.

Whatever the case, he wasn't going to waste the opportunity represented by the distance between them. So, without even pushing himself to his feet, Elijah once again shifted to his natural form and cast Swarm. Then, knowing that he needed all the damage he could get, he cast Essence of the Monkey, willing it to replace Shield of Brambles before he cast Shape of the Predator.

Assuming his draconid form took a lot more mana than taking on the shape of the lamellar ape, but he knew he couldn't win if he fought on the huge monster's terms. He needed to change the paradigm, and the Shape of the Predator offered the best chance to do that.

The giant Voxxian monster reached him just as the transformation completed, and he narrowly bounded out of the way of what would have been a devastating slash. Yet, because of Haste and his increased control, he easily dodged it before springing off a nearby shard of jagged stone and leaping onto the monster's back. There, he dug his foreclaws into its shoulders and raked with his back claws.

Elijah only managed a few good gouges before he saw another attack coming his way. So, he leaped free and sprinted away.

Meanwhile, as the monster followed with its lumbering steps, a swarm of tiny glowing bugs descended on it, delivering a payload of afflictions as it loped after Elijah. He had no trouble keeping ahead of the creature, but when he got too far away, the scaly monster lost interest and started toward the still-prone Isaak. So, he darted back in, raking his claws across the Voxxian monster's legs—as much to get the thing's attention as it was to do damage.

It worked, and he slowly led the creature away from the hopefully recovering Isaak. Healing Rain was still going, so if he hadn't already succumbed to his injuries, there was a good chance that he would live. So long as Elijah dealt with the monster. So, he continued like that for a few minutes, darting in every so often to keep the creature's attention as well as to do whatever damage he could muster.

Meanwhile, every time he attacked the monster, he stacked instances of Contagion as well as Anticoagulant from the Claws of Gluttony. In addition, the afflictions from the Swarm were busy working on the monster, as well.

Gradually, Elijah whittled the monster down. It was slow, though. Very, very slow. And he got into trouble more than a few times when he underestimated the monster's speed. It was so easy to forget that massive Strength—which the monster clearly possessed—translated into explosive, if often short-lived and barely controlled, bursts of speed. So, on more than one occasion, Elijah found himself on the wrong end of that equation. Still, each time, he managed to escape with only a few scrapes.

Until, almost twenty minutes later, it caught him with a backhand that crushed his ribs and sent him tumbling across the landscape. As it happened, he ended up near where the battle had begun, but to his shock, Isaak was nowhere to be seen. He couldn't give that much thought, though, because the moment the monster had sensed even a hint of weakness, it had become rejuvenated. The sluggishness of its many injuries briefly forgotten, it charged Elijah with renewed fury.

Elijah forced himself to his feet, but one of his legs was broken, and Healing Rain had long since run its course. With his mobility cut to almost nothing, he had no choice but to initiate a shift into his lamellar-ape form and hope he could endure whatever punishment the creature dished out.

So, he did, noting that his Ethera had gotten extremely low due to his constant shifting back and forth as well as the copious use of his spells. He would need to be more cognizant of that going forward.

But for now, he had other things on his mind.

Like the monster bearing down on him.

His transformation completed just in time for him to once again meet the charge. However, in this instance, he was at an even more distinct disadvantage due to his broken leg. Even so, Elijah took the hit as well as possible, rolling with the blow to dissipate the impact. The injured Voxx was still stronger than him, though, and he definitely got the worst of the clash.

He landed flat on his back, his head hitting with enough impact to make everything fuzzy. When he recovered his wits, he saw the massive monster looming over him. It once again wore the disgusting grin upon its face.

It laughed, a sound like clinking glass.

Elijah tried to pick himself up, but the creature stomped down on his chest with its entire weight. Elijah felt his ribs creak as he struggled to breathe. It cocked its arm back, clearly intending to level a fatal blow. Elijah struggled, his claws raking against the monster's ankle as he tried to free himself.

It was useless.

Every facet of Elijah's mind whirled with potential solutions. He considered shifting again. He could probably wiggle out from under the monster's foot if he took on his human form. Yet, with it so close, there was almost no chance he'd win free. And without the increased Constitution that came with his guardian form, there was no way he could endure the monster's attacks.

For similar reasons, he couldn't shift into his predator form, either.

Those thoughts—and a hundred others like them—writhed in Elijah's mind, but he could think of nothing. No clever plans. No new powers. He was going to die.

Then, a flash of white-and-blue light announced his salvation before a ball of soulfire hit the monster in the back. It sizzled, filling the air with the smell of charred meat. And for the briefest of moments it let up the pressure on Elijah's chest.

He used that opening—slim though it was—to roll free. Then, with only one leg, he pushed off and threw himself at the off-balance monster. He hit it with a shoulder tackle that drove it backward. It tripped over the nearby escarpment, then tumbled to its back. Elijah latched on to its chest, riding it to the ground, and when it hit, he pummeled it with every point of Strength he could muster.

Between blows, Isaak—ragged and looking as if he was barely hanging on to life—tossed another ball of soulfire at the monster's head. It hit the struggling creature and melted its scales. Elijah kept going, and Isaak refused to let up, either, though one facet of his Mind recognized that Isaak had fallen. Elijah feared the worst, though he couldn't spare the attention to worry about the young man's fate.

When Elijah saw that his blows weren't doing enough damage, he activated the Rage ability of his Silver Bracer of Rage. His mind was flooded with fury as his attributes skyrocketed. He didn't have the presence of mind to check his Strength, but blows that had once felt completely ineffective were suddenly dislodging scales and breaking bones. The Voxxian monster struggled, yet just as had been the case with Elijah only a few moments before, it couldn't escape.

He roared in berserk fury as he continued to smash his fists into the monster, not stopping even after it had finally succumbed. In fact, Elijah didn't let up until, finally, the effect of Rage dissipated, leaving him feeling even more drained than if he'd used Iron Scales a dozen times.

His shoulders sagged as he looked up to see that Isaak's form had gone unnaturally still. That cut through the last vestiges of his enraged state, and with that clarity, he forced himself back into his human form. Dragging his broken leg, he stumbled toward the fallen young man, hoping that he wasn't too late to save him.

57

FUTILITY

He was dead.

"Help him!" Carmen shouted, whipping her head around. But the Healer she had brought into the mines was busy performing triage on another Warrior. Meanwhile, Colt and Tiffany stood at the head of the tunnel, defending them against a tide of critters. There were hundreds of them, each the size of a basketball and with teeth like razors. Alone, they weren't that dangerous to anyone with a few levels under their belt. But in the numbers they'd found within the mine's tunnels, they were like terrestrial piranhas that could strip the meat from their prey's bones in a matter of minutes.

At first, the expedition to exterminate the pests had been safe enough. For the first few days, the group, which consisted of Carmen, Colt, Tiffany, and Brett, had been more than enough to deal with the scattered creatures. However, after a week of constant exploration of the tunnels, which included quite a lot of backtracking and frequent trips back to the surface in order to rest, they had finally discovered the nest.

And it was both awful and awe-inspiring. The cavern had contained thousands of the little monsters, each of which were capable of downing a level-fifteen warrior. None of her group were that low of a level, but to Carmen, the second she'd laid eyes on the colony of little terrors, she'd known they weren't up to the task. So, like any good commander, she'd called for a retreat.

That had gone well enough, and in the following days, she'd begun to assemble an assault team. More, she'd sent a runner back to Easton begging for more Healers.

She had yet to hear back from Roman, which wasn't that surprising. It was an arduous journey made even worse by the onset of winter. So, it made perfect sense that no one had returned.

Yet, Carmen's hand had been forced when groups of the critters—they were actually called terrestrial molaks, according to Brett, whose Vigilante class gave him an ability to identify enemies—started to surface. The first time they had, the critters had killed one of the Guards and maimed a couple who'd been on a walk through the town. That had necessitated a response. So, Carmen had commandeered the services of one of the town's two Healers, gathered a handful of Warriors, and set off to exterminate the pests.

It had not gone well.

The mistake was forging ahead and having their Elementalist set fire to the nest. Before they'd done that, Carmen and the others had rigged the surrounding tunnels to collapse, so they thought they could trap the creatures inside and burn them to death. And at first, it had worked well enough, with hundreds of the little monsters perishing in Logan's summoned flames.

That was one thing that had changed with the apocalypse. Conventional combustion was far less effective than it once had been, which was why gas cars and guns didn't really work as they once had. However, magical flames picked up the slack, and once set, they could use the ambient ethera as fuel. So, Logan's fires burned hot and fast, enveloping the entire cavern in seconds.

The group was busy patting themselves on the back when a trio of much larger molaks came crashing through the debris blocking the tunnels and giving the rest of the critters an escape route.

More distressingly, it gave them a free shot at the people who'd attempted to engineer their deaths. Her people had fought valiantly, and yet, there had been far too many molaks. So, Carmen had organized a fighting retreat, eventually taking shelter in a small cavern with a single narrow and easily defensible entrance. Since then, they'd fought a steady stream of the critters, taking a plethora of wounds along the way.

The Healer—Keith—had done everything he could, but it was obvious that it would only be a matter of time before he ran low on ethera. In the meantime, the wounded continued to pile up, overwhelming even his magic.

Carmen checked the young man's pulse and found nothing. Still, she hoped that Keith could do something. So, she reached down and grabbed the body around the waist before throwing it—no, him—over her armored shoulder. He didn't react at all. As she ran across the small cavern, Carmen tried to convince herself that her burden was simply unconscious. Keith would save him. She just knew it.

So, when she reached the Healer, who already had three patients, she gently laid the body down and begged, "Please . . . Please tell me you can help him . . ."

Keith took one look at the young man, his eyes flicking down to the gaping wound in his chest, then shook his head. "I'm sorry," he croaked. "He's already gone. Even if he wasn't, I don't have the Ethera to . . . I can't do anything about that kind of injury."

He hung his head. Whether it was exhaustion or shame, Carmen had no idea, but for her part, she felt both. Everyone had put their faith in her, and she'd rewarded that trust by getting people killed. Three were already dead, and she had no idea if the critters had made it outside. If they had . . .

No.

She refused to go down that road. She'd done everything she could, and at every turn, she'd made the choices she thought appropriate. She couldn't let herself drown in self-pity or guilt. That didn't help anyone.

So, she reached out and gripped Keith's bony shoulder, giving it a reassuring squeeze. He really was a thin man, largely because he'd been a member of one of the groups of refugees that had initially been denied entry into Easton; it was only recently that his people had been allowed in, and his condition reflected that. He wasn't precisely unhealthy, but he clearly hadn't been flourishing, either.

Carmen had hoped to provide him a fresh start.

Now, he was watching the people who depended on his miraculous healing ability die. That was going to take a toll.

"You're doing everything you can," she said. "Keep it up."

Then, she ran a hand through her hair—she had no idea where her helmet had gone—and when she pulled her hand away, she saw that it was bloody. It didn't matter. She was still on her feet, and she wouldn't trouble the Healer for a mere scratch. Before Keith could notice, she stepped away and returned to the entrance. There, she saw Colt hard at work. Most of the time, he simply sliced the little monsters to ribbons with precise, perfectly controlled attacks. However, from time to time, he would use one of his techniques, and one of the larger critters would simply fall to chunks.

He called it Blade Storm, and the way he described it, it manifested thirteen razor-sharp blades of ethera that cut his target to pieces. It was expensive to use, but it was as sure of a kill as any ability could guarantee.

By comparison, the rawboned Tiffany's hands were bloody and from her knuckles grew a series of ethereal claws. When she punched, they ripped jagged wounds in the creatures' coarse-furred hides.

She had a few other abilities that she rarely used, which was common for the combatants. Most of them didn't have enough experience to use anything but their go-to skills, spells, and abilities, which were often enough to deal with the typical threats they saw during routine patrols. This was different, though, and it highlighted a huge issue with how they were training the potential fighters.

But that was a concern for another day. For now, Carmen stepped up and shouldered the exhausted Tiffany aside. As she did, she growled, "My turn."

Then, she manifested her blacksmithing hammer with Summon Tool and planted herself beside Colt. It wasn't long before she was forced to use the crafting tool for its adapted purpose when she crushed a critter's spine. The little round creatures had odd anatomy, but she'd fought them enough by that point that she knew precisely where to hit them to do the most damage possible. She employed that knowledge to great effect as she stoically stood vigil, shoulder to shoulder with Colt.

At some point, one of the other Warriors replaced Colt, but Carmen barely noticed. Instead, she focused entirely on the task at hand, which meant using her immense Strength to pummel the monsters to death. Because she was used to long hours at the forge, she barely grew fatigued, and she didn't have any combat skills or abilities, so she never ran low on ethera. As a result, Carmen felt like she could keep going indefinitely.

Of course, that wasn't true.

Eventually, she would grow tired. But that point was a long way off.

In addition, she took almost no damage due to the high quality of her armor. If the rest of her people had been wearing something similar, perhaps they could have avoided casualties altogether. But she'd been too caught up in wanting to be properly compensated for her work. All the best crafters were, largely because they all thought the danger had passed. Clearly, they were wrong, and they needed to get back to the basics of collective survival. When Easton had first been founded, everyone had contributed without thought for how it would personally benefit each of them individually. And that was fine, in a vacuum. People deserved to earn a living. Yet, the world was still changing, and everyone's lives were still balanced on the edge of a knife. Carmen—and the other crafters—needed to do what they could to keep people from falling over that edge.

Those thoughts flitted through Carmen's mind as she monotonously slaughtered one critter after another. It wasn't until she realized that she stood alone against the tide that she began to realize how dire their situation was. She'd been fighting for hours, and so had everyone else. They'd picked up one wound after another until, one by one, they'd fallen. She couldn't look back to check if they were dead or simply wounded, but she feared the worst.

That thought crashed into her mind, and in that moment, something broke. She didn't grow any stronger. Her fatigue, thin though it was, didn't wash away. Instead, it was like she experienced a rush of adrenaline that, later, she would liken to what a parent might feel when she saw her child being threatened. In those sorts of situations, people had been known to lift cars, and Carmen's physical abilities skyrocketed along those same lines.

Suddenly, every fall of her hammer sent a critter splattering against the ground. At the same time, her fury—or frustration, perhaps—climbed to unprecedented levels. She took that out on the monsters before her.

And for a while, it was enough to convince her that she was going to win.

But reality came crashing down on her when that surge of adrenaline faded, and her arms started to feel like they were encased in lead. She slowed, and her blows lost their lethality. Still, she pushed on, trying to force the strength back into her muscles. It didn't work.

A critter latched on to her arm. Then, as she was trying to dislodge it, another crunched down on her leg. She kicked it away, but another soon replaced it. Then another after that. She kept swinging, screaming all the while. From somewhere behind her, she heard a scream, and she felt the weak activation of skills. Yet, she couldn't even turn to see what was going on, much less help the people who'd chosen to put their faith in her.

Just as she felt a monster latch on to her neck, sending a gout of blood gushing into its greedy mouth, she spared a thought for Alyssa. She wasn't sure if she believed in an afterlife, but in a world of magic and monsters, the idea didn't seem as silly as it once might have. And while she didn't want to leave Miguel, she couldn't deny that there was a part of her that welcomed death and the possibility of being reunited with the woman she loved.

The moment that thought crossed her mind, she felt a surge of rotten guilt envelop her. She was better than that. She needed to be. Miguel needed her to be stronger.

With a roar, she grabbed the critter and tossed it aside before ramming into the nearby wall and squashing the trio of monsters clinging to that side of her body. Then, she did the same to the other side. Over and over, she let the critters latch on to her, then she used her own body as a hammer and the wall as an anvil. Like that, dozens died, but she certainly didn't escape unscathed.

Her armor had limits, after all. And it couldn't cover everything. Her growing fatigue hadn't disappeared, either.

No—that brief surge had given her a few moments more, but it wasn't enough. It wasn't nearly enough.

Still, Carmen fought on until she felt the effects of blood loss and exhaustion drive her to her knees. The first time it happened, she forced herself back to her feet with a swell of forced energy, but it didn't last long.

It couldn't.

Soon enough, she fell and couldn't regain her feet. Even so, she never stopped swinging her hammer. Even when her blows lost all strength, she refused to give in.

Finally, she fell and couldn't force herself to rise.

Briefly, Carmen felt sharp teeth on the back of her head, but then, there was something different.

Blistering heat washed over her. Because of Resist Fire, which was no doubt intended to help her endure the heat associated with magical forges, she was unharmed. The same couldn't be said for the critters, and the smell of burning fur filled Carmen's nostrils. Once the confusion passed, she looked up to see a hellish scene.

Monsters burned, some of them so hotly that they actually melted. Amid that stood a man, tall and thin and wearing a red-and-white robe. Carmen recognized him from somewhere, but in her exhausted state, she couldn't quite place him. However, she certainly remembered the person beside him. Or rather, the morning star at the woman's waist.

"Verin," she muttered.

It was the Healer who'd been with Alyssa when she'd died. That probably meant something, but now that the threat was ended, even that mystery couldn't keep Carmen from slipping into unconsciousness.

58

A NEGLECTED PURPOSE

Purple lightning flashed in the sky as the smell of death filled Elijah's nostrils. He stumbled toward the fallen Isaak, dread and despair mingling in his heart as he let his guardian form fall away. With each staggering step, pain lanced up his broken leg, but he forced himself to ignore it, and as soon as his transformation completed, he summoned Healing Rain. A storm of soothing precipitation gathered, dumping its rejuvenating payload on Elijah and Isaak alike.

But the young man wasn't moving, and when Elijah finally reached him, he found that Isaak's breathing had stalled.

"No . . ."

He reached out, and as soon as he laid his hand on the boy's chest, he used Touch of Nature. It pulsed, and Isaak's body seized at the injection of healing ethera. Yet, Elijah could tell that it hadn't worked. Forcing life into a corpse wouldn't do anything. Dead was, after all, dead.

Yet Elijah refused to accept it.

So, he channeled it again. And again after that. Each time, the boy's body jerked like he'd just been subjected to the electrical current of a defibrillator. However, the moment the flow of ethera ceased, he went limp. Elijah gritted his teeth and continued his efforts. Over and over, he kept going until there were only wisps of ethera left in his Core. He pulled on more, flexing his Mind and Soul for all they were worth.

But it wasn't enough.

Tears traced lines through the dirt and dried blood on Elijah's cheeks as he tilted his head back and screamed.

That didn't do any good, either.

It just wasn't fair. Nothing was. The world had become a cruel place where a young man like Isaak had been tasked with becoming a hero. He was just a boy, and yet, he'd marched into danger and answered the call of heroism. And then, he'd died unceremoniously, and for no other reason than that Elijah was incapable of saving him.

Of protecting him.

Ever since he'd killed those hunters, Elijah had felt that something was wrong. That everything was skewed. He'd avenged the bear, killing people that, in his head, he'd pegged as villains.

But were they?

Elijah really had no idea. The reality was that he'd reacted based on frustration and, he could admit to himself, a false sense of companionship. For so long, he'd been alone, and in retrospect, it was easy for him to anthropomorphize the creature. Yet, the bear would probably have tried to kill him if he hadn't continuously brought it food. The same was true of the panther he remembered far more fondly than reality suggested.

More than once, Elijah had thought himself immune to the stress that came from his traumatic existence. But he wasn't. Not anymore than anyone else, at least. He'd just processed it differently. And that flawed method had led him down a road that eventually pushed him into killing a group of hunters that may or may not have deserved what he'd done to them.

Did he feel guilty about it?

No. He did not. Not truly. Yet, he knew that, in the future, he needed to think things through, rather than react based on his ultimately flawed feelings. He also needed to be cognizant of his tendency to lose context. Animals were animals, and people were people. And in the changed world, he couldn't blame humanity—or the various other sapient races—for killing. That was probably the only way anyone was going to survive.

What the hunters had done still didn't sit well with him, though. He didn't like it, and he suspected he never would. However, that didn't mean they had deserved to die.

Thoughts like that flitted through Elijah's mind as he struggled to absorb enough ethera to fuel more attempts at healing the fallen Isaak. He knew it was useless. But just like with the bear, he had latched on to the young man in a way that probably wasn't warranted by the situation. They barely knew one another, after all. But in Elijah's mind, the boy had taken on the role of a little brother.

Or a nephew.

Hopefully, if Miguel was in a similar situation, someone would try just as hard to help him.

So, Elijah kept going well past the point when he should have stopped. Then, after some interminable time, Isaak's eyes shot open. His hand shot out, and Elijah only recognized the danger at the last second. He dove to the side just in time to avoid taking a ball of soulfire to the face.

He didn't care, though.

"You're alive!"

"What?" panted Isaak. "How? Of course I'm alive."

"What?"

"It's . . . Um . . . It's an ability. A spell. It kind of keeps me alive. It's called Stored Soul. Think of it like a second life. So long as I cast it before a fight, I can survive fatal damage. I go into a coma for a while, but . . . Yeah. It's saved my life three times so far. It goes on cooldown after activation, though. It'll be a month before I can use it again," Isaak said, the words spilling out all at once.

"You probably shouldn't tell strangers that," Elijah pointed out.

"You're not a stranger, though. You saved me."

Elijah shrugged. "We're even, then. You saved me, too."

"I did, didn't I?" the young man said, grinning. He tried to get up but winced. "Oh. I guess I'm not completely healed, huh? How long have been here? It usually takes a week for me to wake up from the coma."

"It's been about an hour. Maybe two since the monster died," Elijah said. It made sense. Likely, the influx of healing had shortened the duration of the coma. He picked himself up, saying, "Don't move. I want to finish healing you."

"Uh . . . I think we should probably get out of here."

"Why? There aren't any more monsters."

Isaak pointed at the sky. Elijah followed the gesture to see that it had broken into a million jagged pieces, revealing an abyssal blackness that did not look good. It was as if they were inside a broken snow globe, except that it was intended to keep something out rather than in.

"Yeah. You're probably right . . ."

With that, Elijah reached down and helped Isaak to his feet. Then, they hobbled back to the entrance, where a pair of white crystals floated in the air. Elijah touched one, and Isaak touched the other. That prompted a notification to appear before Elijah's mind's eye:

Congratulations! By closing a Minor Dimensional Rift, you have done a great service to your world. Thus, you have earned a reward. Lesser Rejuvenation Potion awarded.

"Whoa," exclaimed Isaak, looking at the vial in his hand. "This is . . . This is amazing."

Elijah was less enthused.

"Yippee," he muttered to himself. He could already heal himself, so he didn't see a whole lot of use for a potion that would do the same thing. Others clearly didn't have that option, so it must have been very valuable. However, he would've much preferred an attribute potion like he'd gotten the last time he'd closed a minor dimensional rift. He sighed, pocketing the potion as he said, "Beggars can't be choosers, I guess."

After that, the pair left the rift behind, and when they stepped back into the world, the rip in reality dissipated, and the black tendrils of corruption dissolved. Elijah was less concerned about that than the giant cat barreling toward him.

He pushed Isaak aside and took the furious feline's leaping charge right in the chest. It only managed to rake its claws across his unprotected skin a few times before Elijah managed to reposition his hands and shove the thing away. The cat was big, but Elijah's Strength attribute was well past the peak of humanity. As such, dislodging an eighty-pound cat wasn't nearly as difficult as it would have been before the world had changed.

The creature went flying away, bounced off the trunk of a tree, then came rocketing back at Elijah. He met it with an overhand swing of his staff that ended with the cat hitting the ground with enough force to leave it stunned. That's when Elijah dropped his staff and pounced on the cat, wrapping his arms around its torso.

He could feel the corruption pulsing through it.

"Don't kill her!"

"I'm not!" Elijah growled, straining to hold the struggling cat still. He hadn't escaped its initial pounce unscathed, and he was bleeding pretty profusely. Even so, he had the animal at his mercy. "I'm going to heal it. Her. I'm going to try to heal her. Just . . . Just be prepared for if it doesn't work . . ."

With that, Elijah cast Healing Rain. It barely cost any ethera, especially considering the sheer volume of healing it could offer. It was especially efficient, considering that the spell was healing him, the cat, and Isaak, all at the same time. But for now, he was mostly concerned with banishing the corruption from Artemis the cat.

He focused as hard as he could, channeling Touch of Nature into the overgrown feline. It went wild, bucking and hissing and raking its claws across his arms. With Elijah holding it off the ground, it couldn't get any leverage, though.

He cast the spell again, trying his best to guide it toward the corruption. But the moment the two clashed, he knew it wouldn't do any good. The thick corruption wasn't a disease or a virus. Indeed, it didn't feel like anything else Elijah had ever experienced. Even calling it corruption felt wrong. It was so fundamentally different from anything else he'd ever experienced, as a result, Elijah struggled to even contextualize it.

Alien was the best he came up with, but even that implied that it was of their universe. It wasn't. It was from somewhere else—whatever was on the other side of that rift. Not the place where they'd fought the Voxxian monsters. No—that was just a bridge. Instead, the corruption was from wherever that bridge led.

Still, he kept trying to heal, but to no effect. The cat wasn't diseased. It wasn't unhealthy. It was just different.

Desperate to find something that worked, Elijah shouted, "Isaak! Take the potion from my right pocket. I need you to pour that down Artemis's throat. Can you do that without getting cut to ribbons?"

He nodded, saying something about his Arcane Shield. Then, he followed Elijah's directions, finding the vial and uncorking it. The moment he did so, Elijah felt the power emitting from it. Then, Isaak reached in and awkwardly dragged the cat's mouth open. It hissed and spit and tried to claw him, but each time it did, it was met with a shimmering blue shield. Eventually, Isaak managed to pour the concoction down Artemis's throat.

Instantly, he felt the difference. The potion was more than simple healing. It exceeded what Elijah could do by a fair amount, adding some other characteristic that he simply couldn't identify. However, what he could tell was that the moment the potion went down Artemis's throat, the corruption had started to retreat.

But it wasn't enough.

Elijah felt the darkness rally as the effect of the potion started to dissipate. So, he spat, "The other one!"

To his credit, Isaak didn't hesitate, which told Elijah just how much the young man loved his cat. Isaak yanked his own potion from his pocket and added that to the mix, as well. As he did so, Elijah forced as much ethera as he could muster into repeated castings of Touch of Nature.

And finally, it worked.

Slowly.

The cat continued to struggle, but soon, its yowls weakened and its wriggling lost vigor. Elijah continued to pour ethera into his healing spells, and miraculously, the corruption retreated, then began to dissipate. Just as he was about to run out of energy, the last of the otherworldly taint dissolved, leaving only a healthy cat behind.

But it was absolutely exhausted, and the creature immediately went limp, passing out.

Elijah felt like doing the same, but instead, he gave Isaak a tired smile as he said, "She's going to be okay. I think."

"I hope so. Do you have any idea what those potions were?" Isaak asked, grinning like a giddy idiot.

"Uh . . . Rejuvenation potions is what the notification said. Why? What's so special about them?"

"They're kind of like a cure-all. I think I remember someone who had an identification skill saying that the description claimed that 'no affliction can endure a rejuvenation potion.' Those things are priceless," Isaak stated.

Elijah shrugged and scratched behind the cat's ear. Even out cold, it let out a contented purr. "Worth it," he said, and he could tell that Isaak completely agreed.

59

LEVELS AND REWARDS

Are you sure?" asked Isaak, looking around the darkening forest.

"It's fine. I sleep outside all the time," Elijah said, sitting beside the small fire he'd built. Artemis was draped over his lap, sound asleep. Because she was so much larger than any house cat had a right to be, she didn't quite fit in his lap, but that clearly didn't bother her very much. And if Elijah was honest, he didn't mind, either. "I spent an entire winter sleeping outside once. Don't recommend it one little bit. Of course, I've got a pretty awesome tree house now."

"You live in a tree house?"

"I think I'm selling it short here. Not a house in a tree. A house made out of a tree. That's a very important distinction, I'm pretty sure," Elijah pointed out. As he spoke, he idly scratched behind the cat's ear.

"What are you?" asked Isaak.

"Uh . . . A human being. Well, as much of a human as any of us are anymore," Elijah answered. He tilted his head to the side and scratched his chin. "Though with cultivation in the mix, I'm not really sure how true that is. I mean, I feel human. But a Body of Wood doesn't really sound like a very human thing to have. More tree territory, if I'm honest. Or Pinocchio. Pre-real-boy shenanigans, of course."

"I was . . . I was talking about your class," Isaak clarified.

"Oh. I'm a Druid. Well, technically, that's my archetype, but that's good enough."

"Does that mean you're a protector of nature?" asked the young man. "Or is it more like the Celtic druids?"

"The first," Elijah answered, reaching into his bag. He still had some travel rations in there, down near the bottom. So, he reached in almost up to his shoulder and grabbed the jerky wrapped in wax paper. When he pulled it out, he offered some to Isaak. "Jerky? I'm not sure what kind of animal it's from, but it's not bad. A bit peppery for my taste, but it's better than eating crab every day."

"Crab?"

"Yeah. Used to love it. But fun fact about crab—when you eat it every single day for more than a year, it kind of loses its luster, if you know what I mean. Maybe if I'd had proper spices, but those are hard to come by out in the wilderness. Best I could do was some salt from boiling seawater, wild garlic, and a few odds and ends I gathered," Elijah babbled. "It was edible, but only just. Didn't really help that I've never been much of a cook. My dad used to tell me I could burn water, and he wasn't that far off."

As Elijah spoke, Isaak tore a chunk of the jerky away and scooted a bit closer to the fire. It was still on the tail end of winter, and though the temperatures had begun to rise, nights remained quite chilly.

"I don't know anybody else who can do what you do. Are you on the power-ranking list?" asked Isaak.

Elijah considered lying, and his good sense told him to do just that. However, he'd never been much for dishonesty, especially with someone who had saved his life earlier that day. Besides, the notion of constantly lying about who he was just left a bad taste in his mouth. So, he said, "Yeah. Top ten, actually. What about you?"

He hadn't even checked, but given the boy's obvious power, it seemed likely.

"I was in the nineties for a little while after the tower," he stated. "But I haven't hunted that much lately. I just . . ."

The young man trailed off, and Elijah understood precisely why. It didn't take a psychiatrist to recognize the inevitable consequences of the trauma the boy had been through.

"It's okay. You don't have to talk about it," Elijah said.

For a long moment, Isaak just stared into the crackling fire. Then, in a low voice, he said, "I was the only survivor. I shouldn't have made it, either. I was the first to go down. Too slow. My shield didn't hold. The monster . . . I think it was a werewolf or something . . . It was too fast, and it targeted me first. Stored Soul saved me, and when I woke up, everyone was already dead. But the monster, it was wounded. Barely alive. I killed it, and I got the rewards." He laughed harshly. "A stupid sword I couldn't even use."

"I saw it."

"Ridiculous thing, right?" Isaak said, shaking his head. "After that, everyone started calling me a hero. Someone said I was like Atlas, standing with the world on his shoulders, and it stuck. Me. A Titan. Even stupider than the sword. Before the world changed, I was a nobody. Worse than nobody. I spent all my time playing online games and avoiding . . . everything. But now I'm supposed to be a hero or something. I don't know how to do that."

"Me, neither," Elijah admitted.

"What? You saved me. You saved Artemis. You are a hero," Isaak insisted, leaning forward, his eyes glistening.

Elijah just shook his head. "I'm definitely not what you think I am, kid," he said. Then, he stood, careful not to wake the cat cradled in his arms. He stepped toward Isaak and deposited Artemis beside him. The cat woke up and yowled in his direction, but he ignored it. "I'm going for a walk. I'll make sure nothing messes with you."

"What? Did I say . . ."

Elijah ignored the rest of the boy's question, instead slipping into the trees and shifting into his predator form. He had Guise of the Unseen wrapped around him within a couple of steps. But he didn't go anywhere. Instead, he just turned around and watched over Isaak, who looked incredibly small and young, sitting there beside the fire.

The boy was also naive.

The fact that he thought of Elijah as a hero was laughable, especially considering that not that long ago, he'd killed four people for no more of a crime than hunting a bear and picking a mushroom.

There was more to it than that, he knew. Far more. On top of his trauma and his tendency to anthropomorphize animals, he suspected that his attitude was being affected by something far greater than himself. Was that the effect of his archetype? Or was it something more ephemeral? Had he truly gone wild? Or was he simply making excuses for indulging in his most violent tendencies?

The truth was that he didn't know, and that scared him. Because for better or worse, Elijah knew he had the power to become something incredibly scary. Without rules or restraint, he would be a monster not unlike the Voxx. Just pure destruction in human form. After leaving Norcastle, he'd been patting himself on the back for taking Jess's advice and refusing to rise to the mayor's unspoken challenge. But in retrospect, it was easy to leave the town behind because he just didn't care enough to react.

Pride wasn't Elijah's sin, after all.

But his frustration had left him primed to react poorly when he'd come upon the bear's corpse, and he'd given in to the anger.

The rest was history, and not the sort any sane person would look upon favorably.

As Elijah considered his actions—and how to avoid falling into that trap again—he watched the young man fall asleep. Artemis pretended like she was asleep, as well, but in his draconid form, Elijah could tell that she was awake and alert, likely to guard Isaak from any potential predators.

It made him think of the panther who'd died what felt like a lifetime ago, which brought his thoughts back to the bear. Neither had deserved to die, but in retrospect, he could understand the motivation to hunt them. The world was a dangerous place, and unless humanity grabbed at whatever power it could, people would die. If not to the dangerous wildlife, then to the nonhuman settlements like Ironshore. Some of those people were assuredly aggressive.

Even so, Elijah couldn't stomach the idea of hunting something for no more reason than to gain experience. Doing so for food was acceptable. For defense, too. Even for dominance. But just for experience? It just left him feeling queasy, and for reasons he couldn't quite articulate. He only knew he didn't like it.

To distract himself from that, Elijah focused on something he'd not let himself acknowledge while with Isaak. Since leaving Norcastle, he'd gained four more levels. The first was when he'd killed the four hunters, and the other three had come in the dimensional rift. Normally, four levels wouldn't have excited him—after all, it wasn't as if he needed to allocate his attribute points anymore—but in this case, he'd finally hit the level-forty-five threshold. And that meant that he'd gotten a new spell.

Spell: Essence of the Lion	**Channel the might of the lion, increasing Strength attribute by ten (10) points. Usable on allies.**

It was a familiar format, largely because he had similar enhancements meant to augment his other attributes. The lone holdout was Ethera, and he wasn't certain if he'd ever get something like that. However, he could already think of tons of situations where having the extra Strength that came with Essence of the Lion would come in handy. The only drawback was that he couldn't use all his enhancements at once.

Yet, if he ever found himself fighting as a member of a group, he could pick and choose the enhancements he bestowed upon other people, tailoring the augmentations to the person's archetype, class, or role.

And who knew? Perhaps at level fifty he would gain another slot.

Once he finished examining the new spell—which didn't take long, considering how similar it was to the others in the Essence line—Elijah decided to take a look at his full status for the first time in quite a while.

Name	**Elijah Hart**
Level	45
Archetype	Druid
Class	Animist
Specialization	N/A
Alignment	N/A
Strength	56 (46)
Dexterity	78 (45)
Constitution	56 (46)
Ethera	54

Regeneration	68 (48)		
Attunement	Nature		
Cultivation Stage: Cultivator			
Body	Core	Mind	Soul
Wood	Hatchling	Quartz	Neophyte

His attributes had continued to grow by one point for every level, and combined with his equipment and enhancement spells, he felt like he was in a good place. And in his draconid form, it was even more dramatic.

But he had to wonder about the other people on the ladder. Were their attributes just as impressive? He knew his archetype was rare, and he believed his class was, as well. On top of that, with his Dragon Core, his enhancement spells were that much more effective. So, he felt confident that he could stand toe-to-toe with any of them, even the ones ahead of him on the list.

Yet, it stood to reason that they'd all experienced their own lucky encounters, as well. Perhaps their cultivation was just as advanced as his. Or maybe more so. The reality was that he had no idea, and so far, he'd yet to find an opportunity to answer the questions strangling his thoughts.

And perhaps he never would.

The world was a big place, after all. What were the odds that he'd actually run into another high ranker?

Slim, Elijah knew.

But still, he expected that it would eventually happen. Power drew power, and strength challenged strength. It was naive in the extreme to suspect that there wouldn't be friction between those high-ranking people. Competitive natures dictated as much, and that was discounting the possibility that someone might see their fellow people as a means of progression.

No—he knew he would run into them at some point. He just needed to be ready for when the inevitable came to pass.

Until then, though, he had other things on his mind. He still needed to find Alyssa, and despite having spent the past months exploring and fighting his way across hundreds of miles, he still didn't feel any closer to accomplishing that goal.

But he would.

He believed that because he didn't want to contemplate any other possibility. With that at the forefront of his mind, Elijah switched back to his human form and returned to the campsite. There, he settled down to watch over the now-sleeping young man and his cat.

60

A HEARTY WELCOME AND
AN AWKWARD SITUATION

Morning sunlight filtered through the forest's canopy as a dewy chill carpeted the forest floor. Somewhere up above, a bird chirped, and in the distance, a squirrel chittered, painting the morning with a cold yet idyllic brush. Elijah sat with his back to the trunk of a tree, his head tilted upward as he enjoyed the peaceful atmosphere for what it represented. He looked across the campsite to see Artemis staring back at him from her position cuddled next to Isaak.

She was a dangerous creature.

He knew that down to his very core. Even without the corruption of the dimensional rift infecting her, Artemis was a peerless predator. Due to that undeniable fact, Elijah was hesitant to leave her behind. The chances that she would end up killing someone were high enough that taking her back to his island was probably the most responsible path he could take. And yet, he couldn't bring himself to make that decision.

For one, he didn't have the heart to separate Artemis from her owner. Or perhaps she was the owner in this situation. Regardless, it seemed that neither would accept being parted from the other's company. So, if Elijah took one, he'd need to take the other.

And he had no interest in doing that.

Not only would having another person underfoot, trampling his Grove, be far more trouble than it was worth, but the prudence of that course of action was extremely questionable. Elijah knew he wasn't great company, and sentencing someone else to the sort of solitude he'd endured was a cruelty he refused to contemplate.

No—that wasn't a path he intended to explore.

Perhaps Artemis would hurt someone, but maybe not. Elijah couldn't be responsible for the whole world, after all. It wasn't his problem to solve. He'd already done enough by saving her and Isaak, and if he was honest, he was eager to get back on the proverbial road and hunt down his sister, Carmen, and Miguel.

Because, if nothing else, the bond between Isaak and Artemis had proved the value of having trustworthy people around. Even if those people happened to be overgrown and deadly house cats.

More than anything, he wanted to just unload his problems onto someone, but he didn't think many therapists had survived the touch of the World Tree. Not many of anything had, as far as he could tell. But as a substitute, his sister would do just fine. Certainly, she'd played that role before, and he'd done the same for her.

But that was back before he'd run away to Hawaii.

Of course, he'd never characterized it like that. On the surface, taking that job had made perfect sense. It was in his field, and it was paradise, after all. But in reality, Elijah could admit that he'd just wanted to get far away from all the trappings of familiarity that reminded him of the parents he'd lost far too soon.

It was a mistake, and one he'd acknowledged on more than one occasion. Being diagnosed with terminal cancer tended to prompt introspection, and as he was dying, he'd most regretted losing touch with his sister.

Now, he had a chance to rectify that mistake, and with all the things going through his mind, he needed the support of family more than ever.

Finally, about an hour after dawn, Isaak's eyes fluttered open, and he pushed himself upright. "I can't believe I slept all night," he muttered, stretching. He ran his hand through his curly black hair, smacking his lips as he yawned. "Didn't you need to rest? I could have stood watch."

"It's fine," Elijah answered. "Not the first all-nighter I've ever pulled. At least I have the attributes to soften the blow now."

He reached into his pack and retrieved one of his glass jugs, which he handed to Isaak. The boy took it gratefully and, after taking a long swig, wiped his arm across his mouth. "We should head back to the city. My sister is probably worried sick."

"Sister?" asked Elijah. "You never mentioned a sister."

He shrugged. "Must have slipped my mind," the young man said. "She didn't want me to come out here looking for Artemis. She's kind of protective like that."

"This is an older sister, right?"

"Please don't."

"Don't what?"

"Look, I'm grateful for what you did for me. But please don't go after my sister," he said. "She's . . . Just don't, okay?"

"What makes you think—"

"That look. I've seen it enough to know exactly what it means. Delilah was always popular."

"Was that because of her looks or . . ."

Isaak just shook his head. Elijah tried to babble an excuse—his social graces might have been a bit rusty, but he was still aware that he'd crossed a line—but he ended up going off on a tangent about how big his Grove was. It was not an effective conversational path, and by the time they started back to the city, Isaak was visibly annoyed.

Artemis just followed along, but Elijah got the feeling she was judging him, too. But that might have just been the fact that she was still a cat, if an overgrown one.

Still, Elijah wouldn't let that dampen his spirits. After all, he'd successfully completed the mission he'd set for himself, gained a couple of levels and a new spell, and to top it all off, a beautiful woman was waiting back in Argos to show him how grateful she was that he'd saved her little brother.

And he'd saved a couple of lives, which, now that it was done, didn't seem quite as important as all the rest.

"I hate how much you're smiling," Isaak muttered as they drew within sight of the gate. Elijah pointedly ignored him.

The same two Guards were working the gate, and to Elijah's surprise, they recognized him straight away. They were far more excited about Isaak's return, which meant quite a lot of backslapping and jovial declarations as to the hero's valor. Artemis hadn't even stopped. Instead, she'd disappeared through the gate to wander the city. Hopefully, she wouldn't kill anyone. Or at least nobody that didn't deserve it.

Once they made it past the two enthusiastic Guards, Elijah and Isaak made their way through the city. As they went, the same old ladies sat on their balconies exchanging gossip. Meanwhile, Isaak received the celebrity treatment, which he endured with as much grace as could be expected. Still, Elijah could recognize the tightness of frustration in the young man's shoulders.

One good thing was that, apparently, Greek people liked to show their appreciation with food, which meant that by the time they reached Isaak's home, they'd been loaded down with various fruits and a couple of hearty meat pies. The smell alone was enough to set Elijah's mouth to watering, so when Isaak invited him inside, he was more than happy to take advantage of the young man's hospitality.

It had nothing at all to do with the possibility of meeting the boy's goddess of a sister.

Unfortunately, by the time he finished his meat pie, no such sister had presented herself. So, without any reason to hang around, he said his goodbyes and headed back into town. For a couple of hours, he just wandered around enjoying the atmosphere. He enjoyed the wilderness, and he was a bit solitary by nature, but Elijah could appreciate civilization as much as the next guy— especially when everyone was so friendly.

It was such a departure from what he'd experienced back in Norcastle that he couldn't help but make the comparison. Where one town had responded to the world's transformation with petty cronyism and corruption, another had pulled together in solidarity. The existence of somewhere like Argos was enough to color Elijah's expectations with a fair amount of optimism.

Eventually, he made his way to Atticus's shop, where he found the eponymous owner closing a deal with a man in a heavy purple robe. Elijah recognized the ogre staff the man was in the process of buying, so he gave Atticus a quick thumbs-up.

He didn't mean to eavesdrop, but he definitely overheard the final price the two agreed upon, and it was quite a bit higher than what Atticus had paid. So, once the purple-robed would-be wizard departed the shop, he asked, "Was everything you told me about that staff a lie?"

"Welcome back, my friend!"

"Oh, don't 'my friend' me. You paid me two silvers for that stick, and you just charged him fourteen."

"He overpaid, friend."

"Or you underpaid."

"I would never!" he said, clutching his chest as if stabbed.

Elijah rolled his eyes and said, "Whatever. What's a few silvers between friends, right? But maybe you can help me with identifying a couple of other items."

"More treasure already? Did you go to the tower, then?"

"No," Elijah answered. "Just some things I didn't know what to do with before. Still don't, honestly. But figuring out what they are is probably the first step."

With that, the two men headed into the back room. There, Elijah rummaged in his pack until he found the two items that were his goal. The first was the bear's pelt, which he set onto the table.

"Dire-bear pelt," Atticus stated, with a note of surprise. "Simple grade. Where did you get this?"

"Oh, out and about. What about this?" he asked, setting the pack containing the amanita flesh onto the table. "It's an enchanted sack, but inside is what's left of a natural treasure. I wouldn't open it if I were you, though. It'll almost certainly make you sick."

"Can't identify it, then. The pack is Crude grade, though. Called a preservation sack. You might have more luck with an Alchemist, but we don't have any living in the city limits."

"Does that imply there's one outside the city?"

Atticus nodded. "There's one that lives in a commune about forty miles to the south, on the edge of the swamp. I've never met him, but I've heard weird stories," he said.

"What kind?"

"The cult-y kind. I don't know anything else, but people certainly don't hold him in high esteem, friend. Name is Konstantinos. Don't know any more, and I'll be honest—I don't want to know."

"Fair enough," Elijah said. "Oh, took care of the man-eater, by the way. Turns out, you had a dimensional rift. It's closed now."

After that statement, Atticus begged Elijah to tell him more. And for his part, Elijah parlayed that into a meal, which the two took at a local tavern. By the time he was done telling the story—in as self-deprecating way as possible—the pair had already finished their meals and were deep into a night of drinking.

Which was why Elijah didn't even notice the newcomer until she tapped him on the shoulder. He turned around a little too quickly and almost stumbled directly into a woman's chest. He caught himself just in time, then pulsed Touch of Nature to rid himself of the effects of the alcohol.

Then, he realized where he was staring, so he looked up and into the eyes of the goddess he'd envisioned earlier. She looked a little like Isaak, though far more mature and infinitely more feminine. However, she was far from some dainty maid. Instead, she was a striking Amazon, with thick shoulders and a Warrior's physique.

"You're smaller than I expected," she said with a smirk. "Cute, too. Isaak didn't mention that."

"Uh . . . Delilah?"

"Oh, so he mentioned me. Good."

Then, without further explanation, she wrapped her arms around him, hugging him tight. His bones creaked under her high Strength, but with the orientation of his face—which was positioned in the center of her chest—he couldn't really complain.

When she finally released him, Atticus cleared his throat and slurred, "I think I deserve a hug, too. Whatever he did, I did it twice as much."

Delilah ignored him, which didn't seem to bother the weapons dealer at all. Or that was the impression Elijah got when Atticus turned his attention back to the mug of beer in front of him. Meanwhile, he got a good look at Delilah.

She wore a boiled-leather cuirass and a skirt composed of leather strips. From the knees down, she wore brass greaves, which left her thighs on display.

And from Elijah's still slightly drunken perspective, they were great thighs.

In fact, everything about her was great, even if she was almost a foot taller than him. She probably weighed more, too. But that didn't dissuade him at all. Instead, he found it quite interesting.

But in his defense, outside of Jess, who'd never really considered giving him the time of day, he'd not had much of an opportunity to mingle with the opposite sex in more than two years.

So, of course, he put his foot in his mouth.

"Yeah, I can see why you're popular."

"What?" she asked, narrowing her eyes in confusion. "What do you mean by popular?"

"Oh. It's something your brother said."

"You were talking about me with my brother?"

"Of course. I think he meant to fix us up. I tried to talk him out of it, but he insisted. Said we'd make a great couple."

"Did he now?"

"More or less."

"I'm thinking it was less more than more," she stated.

"I'm far too drunk to make sense of what you just said. So, I don't have a room yet, but there's an inn around here where the owner loves me," he went on. "I'm sure—"

"You think you can handle me?" she asked, her eyes twinkling.

"Definitely," Elijah said with a grin of his own.

Then, without hesitation, she dipped down, wrapped her arms around his waist, and threw him over her shoulder. With his Sash of the Whirlwind, Elijah probably could have avoided it, but in his human form, his Strength and Dexterity weren't quite high enough to make use of the item's Haste.

Besides, he wasn't all that displeased with the sudden shift because it at least gave him a nice view of her backside.

Still, he made a show of resistance, claiming, "I was just joking!"

"I wasn't."

Then, she was marching outside and to the house where he'd left Isaak earlier that day. Nobody in the streets batted an eyelash at the clear abduction, which Elijah would later learn was due to Delilah's well-known proclivities. She was a straightforward woman and, apparently, not averse to taking what she wanted.

And at that moment, she wanted Elijah.

Yet, despite the lack of dignity in its beginning, Elijah couldn't think of any reason to object to what he hoped would prove to be a very eventful night and a much-needed release.

<h1 style="text-align:center">61</h1>

THE MORNING AFTER

Sunlight filtered through the curtains, illuminating the dancing dust motes in the air. For a moment, Carmen had no idea where she was, and she reached for a partner that wasn't there. Then, everything came crashing down on her like a tidal wave, and she suddenly felt very alone.

That lasted right up until she saw Miguel curled up in a chair, his mother's old spear leaning against the wall next to him. That brought all sorts of mixed feelings, but the most prevalent was that she couldn't afford to lose herself in the still-poignant grief that came every time she thought of Alyssa. She had a responsibility to the living, including Miguel and all the people of Silverado who'd entrusted her with their safety as well as their potential prosperity.

She shifted, and her muscles screamed at her for the mistake. Groaning, she persisted, propping herself up on the pillow. That noise woke Miguel, whose eyes fluttered open sleepily. Just like his mother, he took a moment to remember where he was, but when his eyes found Carmen, they widened in surprise.

"Mom! You're awake!" he shouted, launching himself from the chair. In less than a second, he crashed into her, burying his face in her shoulder as he hugged her as tightly as his little arms could allow. He'd put on a bit of muscle since he'd started training, but he still wasn't strong enough to really affect Carmen.

Physically, at least. Emotionally, he had all the power in the world.

Even though it caused some degree of pain, Carmen wrapped her arms around her son and returned his hug with one of her own. She didn't even realize she was crying until her tears started to drip onto his mop of black hair. She sniffed loudly, then said, "I'm sorry, sweetie. I'm so sorry."

"For what?" he asked, pulling away. Carmen didn't want to release him, but she also didn't want to smother him. When they locked eyes, she saw the evident confusion implied by his question.

"I made a dumb decision. I shouldn't have gone into that mine," she said. "But I know my limits now. I won't leave you ever again."

Then, she hugged him again.

"But, Mom, you saved all those people," he said, his voice muffled by its close proximity to her chest. "Everybody says you're a hero."

Hero.

People had called Alyssa that, too. But that had gotten her killed. Carmen didn't care what people thought of her. In fact, a sudden epiphany told her that, in the grand scheme of things, she didn't care about anything nearly as much as providing Miguel with an opportunity to grow up in a safe environment. That meant that she couldn't just throw herself into dangerous situations, regardless of what she saw as her responsibility.

Not only did that put her in unnecessary danger, which in turn increased the odds of turning Miguel into an orphan, but it was also a waste of her talents. She was strong, and she could hold her own in battle. Yet, if she had been focusing on the things she did best, then the people who'd followed her into that mine would have been far better equipped to meet the dangers therein.

As a result, as Carmen had fought what she thought was a fruitless battle, she'd made the choice that, if she managed to survive, she would devote herself to giving her people the tools they needed to do the jobs for which they were suited. They were the Warriors. She was the crafter. And as much as she wanted to do her part as a fighter, she needed to remember that she'd chosen her path long ago, and now she needed to walk it.

All of that flitted through her mind as she held Miguel, and in that moment, she had to admit that her own selfish desire to protect her son played a part in that resolution, as well.

Before she could respond to her son's remarks, the door to the room—which Carmen belatedly recognized as the town's infirmary—opened to admit a familiar face.

Verin looked much the same as she had when she'd fetched Carmen so Roman could deliver the news of Alyssa's death, which meant that she was an older matronly woman with a thick brown-and-gray braid and a stout figure. She was unarmored, and the morning star she normally wore at her waist was nowhere to be seen.

The woman gave Carmen a tight smile that didn't touch her eyes as she asked, "How are you feeling?"

"Like I was in an eighteen-car pileup," Carmen admitted. "I'm sore all over."

"That's normal."

"Is everyone else okay?" Carmen asked, rather than talk about her own condition. She was still among the living, which meant that she would recover. In any case, she was far more worried about whether or not everyone else had made it out alive.

Verin shook her head. "We saved as many as we could, but . . ."

"Who?"

"Brett Thomas," she said. "He fought until the very end, but by the time we arrived, he was already dead."

Carmen's heart jumped into her throat. Over the course of the battle, the Vigilante had proved himself a dozen times over. He was a talented fighter, and

Carmen had thought he would be the last to succumb. Perhaps he wouldn't have died if he'd had proper armor.

"Anyone else?" she asked.

"Nora Lassiter and Misha Addison."

"I remember Nora, but the other . . ."

"She came with me," Verin said. "We were in such a hurry that some of my people were caught off guard by the number of monsters. Misha was our Knight, and she's the only reason we arrived in time to save everyone else."

"Oh. I'm sorry," Carmen said, shaking her head. To Miguel, she said, "Sweetie, why don't you go get me something to drink?"

"But, Mom . . ."

Carmen knew he wanted to stay and listen in, but she didn't think it was appropriate for a boy his age to hear a casualty report. So, she gave him her best mom look, cutting off any further objections. He did move extra slowly on his way out, though, just to make sure everyone knew he wasn't happy about being excluded.

Once Miguel was out of the room, Carmen got the full report of the injured. A few people had lost limbs, but aside from Brett, Nora, and Misha, everyone else had survived. Verin credited Keith, the other Healer, for that. And Carmen herself, of course. The story of how she'd single-handedly held the entrance had already begun to make the rounds. It was made even more plausible by the tales of how, despite only being a crafter, she'd fought side by side with the combatants on the trip from Easton to Silverado. That had done wonders for her reputation, and her status as a hero had been cemented by her exploits in the mine.

And Carmen hated it.

To move on, she asked Verin for the whole story of how she had come to arrive in the mines. And to her surprise, it was only partially as she expected. Apparently, the messenger she'd sent back to Easton had never actually made it to the city. Instead, he had been intercepted by Verin's patrol, and the older woman had taken it upon herself to respond. After that, they'd come as quickly as possible, and when they had arrived, they had found a town in disarray and a few Warriors holding off a tide of critters who were trying to spill out into Silverado.

"Then we fought our way through until we found you. We would have gotten there sooner, but Devin had to stop a few times to recover his ethera," Verin explained.

"So, Roman doesn't know what happened here?"

Verin shook her head. "I think it's best he doesn't know you and I met again," she said, looking away.

"Why?"

"I can't talk about it here. But if I asked, would you meet me and some other people back in Easton? In a month or two, I mean. There are some things you need to know," Verin said.

"What kinds of things?" Carmen asked.

"The kinds of things that will explain why Alyssa had to die."

At first, Carmen didn't react. But then, she threw herself from the bed with all the Strength she could muster. It was considerable, and as a result, she moved so quickly that Verin couldn't react before Carmen rammed into her, clamping her hand around the older woman's throat.

Carmen didn't stop until she'd slammed Verin against the wall hard enough to shake the building. Leaning in, she growled, "What did you just say?"

The sound of a glass hitting the floor jerked Carmen's attention toward the door, where she saw Miguel staring at her, wide-eyed and in shock. "Mom?" he breathed.

"Miguel, go get Colt. Now."

"But, Mom, why—"

"Don't ask questions. Just go. Now."

Miguel clearly wanted to disobey, but when he saw his mother's face, he thought better of it. The moment he raced from the room, Carmen turned her attention back to Verin, who'd started to turn blue from lack of oxygen.

"I'm not letting you go until Colt's here to back me up," she hissed. "But if you know what's good for you, you'd better think long and hard about telling me absolutely everything. You don't know me, so I'll explain it to you in the clearest way possible. I am usually an easygoing person. I don't get angry very quickly. But one thing sure to set me off is my family. So, if you know anything about how my wife died that you haven't told me, then I suggest you tell me the moment I let you go. Got it?"

Verin tried to nod, but Carmen's viselike grip prevented her head from moving more than an inch or two.

Just then, Colt arrived, wearing a hospital gown and his hat and with his sheathed sword in one hand. Miguel followed after him, out of breath. Colt took less than a moment to take stock of the situation before saying, "Miggy, I'm going to need you to do me a huge favor. You good with that, boss?"

Miguel nodded, saying, "Yes, sir!"

"Close that door and guard it with your life," he said. "Anybody tries to come in here, I want you to scream bloody murder. Got that?"

Miguel said that he understood, then hastened to obey the Samurai's orders. When the door slammed shut, Carmen said, "Colt. If she tries anything, I want you to use Blade Storm and cut her into a hundred pieces."

He unsheathed his sword, saying, "Yes, ma'am."

Carmen released Verin, and the older woman fell to the ground, gasping for air. Clearly, she hadn't worked on her Constitution very much. A mistake, but an understandable one for someone who could heal herself from any injury. In any case, Carmen wasn't concerned with the woman's deficiencies. Instead, she'd latched on to her words.

Ever since the world had been transformed, Carmen had mistrusted Roman. She'd tried to give him the benefit of the doubt, but the combination of his questionable policies as well as the way he'd treated his wife had always left a bad taste in Carmen's mouth. Then, he'd taken a hard-line stance against Scholars, which, while better in the short run, was a surefire way to create a regressive society that would never meet its potential.

But with monsters knocking on the door and issues like starvation becoming a real threat, standing up for people who couldn't really pull their weight wasn't a priority for most people. It wasn't until Easton had moved past the immediate survival stage that she'd begun to advocate for the Scholars. It had been met with little success, and that only because of Alyssa.

It wasn't the only thing the two had disagreed on. But Alyssa had always trusted Roman. After all, they'd been friends and coworkers for years before the apocalypse had reared its ugly head. So, while they were prone to animated disagreements, the two still trusted one another.

Carmen had seen Roman in a different light, though, and she had even warned Alyssa of the dangers of going into the tower. Yet, when Roman had brought news of Alyssa's death, she'd simply accepted the story due to shock and a desperate need to believe that her wife had died for a purpose.

In the back of her mind, though, she'd never quite abandoned the notion that Roman had engineered it somehow. That he had betrayed Alyssa. So, when Verin had uttered those words, "why Alyssa had to die," something inside of Carmen had snapped into place. Suddenly, Roman's story didn't seem so believable.

"Tell me everything," she spat, glaring down at the woman whom she'd already found guilty by association.

And Verin did as she'd been ordered, spilling the story with a mix of eagerness and shame that Carmen found repulsive. Or maybe that was due to what she had to say.

Verin explained how Roman had approached her just before the trip into the tower, promising that her people would be given a place in Easton if she went along with what he had planned. At the time, Verin didn't have any choice but to do it. She had more than a hundred people—some of whom were friends and family—depending on her. So, she went in knowing that something bad would happen.

"I didn't think he was going to kill her," she mumbled. "I swear . . . I just thought . . . I don't know . . ."

It was either a lie or naivete. "Go on. Tell me how he did it."

Verin continued, explaining in brutal detail how Trace had stabbed Alyssa in the back. "He had this dagger that we'd gotten from the other level," she said. "But that just made it easier. He already had another plan to make it happen. That dagger made her vulnerable, and then . . . Then Roman . . . did it."

"How?"

"You . . . Y-you don't want to know . . ."

"Tell me!" Carmen roared, kicking Verin in the side. She didn't hold back, either. In her state, she couldn't have, even if she'd wanted to. And she did not want to.

Verin coughed, spitting up blood, but she didn't dare embrace any skills. Not with Colt standing there ready to cut her to pieces. He would, too. Everyone knew how much he'd idolized Alyssa, and he had transferred much of that devotion to Carmen in her stead.

"H-he . . . He beheaded her," Verin stammered. Then, she looked up with tears in her eyes. "I'm sorry. I'm so . . . s-so sorry. I didn't know he was going to . . . I thought . . . I thought I could maybe let him do it, then heal her, but . . . she . . . she was gone, and . . ."

"Kill her."

"Ma'am?"

"Kill her, Colt. Do it or I'm going to beat her to death with my bare hands. I don't want Miguel to see me like that."

"With all due respect, ma'am, I don't think that's a good idea."

"Fine," Carmen said. "If you can't stomach it, I can."

And then she embarked on a quest to do just that. She only got one good kick in before Colt wrapped his arms around her and pulled her away. Carmen was incredibly strong, but he had all the leverage. Still, she could have broken free, and she would have if she hadn't been interrupted by a garbled cry coming from the broken woman at her feet.

"I know how to get revenge on him!"

Carmen tore free, but that sentence had torn a hole in her resolve. So, she growled, "How?"

She knew good and well that Roman's position was nearly unassailable. Not only was he one of the highest levels in Easton—he wasn't quite on the power ladder, but he was close—but he also had the weight of the entire government on his side. That meant that to get to him, one needed to either be prepared for a suicide run, or . . .

"There's a resistance," Verin said. "Mostly people who were loyal to your wife, but there are people who lost friends and loved ones to his policies. I can . . . I can put you in touch with them. I can help you! I'm sorry! I just wanted to save—"

Carmen had heard enough. Or perhaps she'd finally lost whatever thread of civility she had left. Whatever the case, she suddenly had her summoned blacksmithing hammer in her hand. Even as it descended, Colt tried to stop her.

He wasn't quick enough, though.

Just before the blow landed, Carmen caught sight of Verin's surprised face. Had she really expected to be forgiven? Had she truly thought Carmen could ignore that confession? If so, then she didn't know whom she was dealing with.

The hammer crushed the Healer's skull with a sickening crunch that sent splatters of brain and fragments of bone against the wall. Then, Carmen hit her again. Roaring in inarticulate rage, she continued to pummel the woman's skull until it was little more than a slurry of blood, bone, and brain matter.

By the time she'd finished, she was hoarse. Pushing a bloody lock of hair out of her face, she turned to a stunned Colt and said, "I need you to find out who these rebels are. I'd very much like to meet them."

Colt swallowed hard, then said, "Yes, ma'am."

"And Colt."

"Ma'am?"

"Don't let Miggy in here, okay? He doesn't need to see this."

"Y-yes, ma'am."

62

A ONE-TIME THING

It was a good morning.

That was the most prevalent thought in every facet of Elijah's Mind as he lay on his side, his head propped on one hand as he beheld the goddess he'd met the night before. As she dressed, this time in normal clothes as opposed to the Wonder Woman getup she'd worn when she had accosted him, she gave him a small smirk. "What?" she asked.

"Do you think there's a Prostitute class?" he asked.

Her eyes narrowed dangerously. "Come again."

"What?" he said. Then, it hit him what he'd just suggested. "No! I didn't mean you! It's just that I was thinking about it last night, and—"

"And you think I'm a whore? I'll have you know that I'm a well-respected member of this community, and I do not have a Prostitute class!" she shouted. Her eyes went to the spear propped against the wall.

Before she could take a step toward it, Elijah leaped to his feet, just in case he needed to defend himself. He didn't think getting stabbed would kill him, but he didn't want to experience it regardless. He held his hands out in surrender. "Wait. That's not what I meant!"

She stopped, put her hands on her hips, and demanded, "Then explain it. If I don't like your explanation, there's always the spear. And believe me, I've got a good measure of your attributes, so I'm fairly sure you're not getting away if I don't want you to."

"Do men run away from you often?" he couldn't stop himself from asking.

"Not successfully."

Elijah could believe it, too. While he had no idea what level Delilah was, she'd certainly proved that her physical attributes were up to just about any task. He'd only spent one night with her—and it was definitely a pleasurable one— but he was sore in places he didn't even know existed. To call her strong would have been an understatement.

If he was in a bit less desperate of a situation, he might've wondered why she wasn't on the power ladder, but as it was, he was far too concerned with explaining himself.

"It was just an idle thought, okay? I'm weird. We've established that. I sometimes lose track of things," he said.

"Do better," she said, taking a step toward the spear.

"Okay! Okay," he said. "I spent a long time alone. Like, a long time. Longer than you can imagine. So, I sort of lost some of my . . . uh . . . social graces. I'm trying to get them back, but it's a work in progress. What I meant when I asked about that . . . other class was that there seem to be classes for all sorts of other professions. And that's supposed to be the oldest one, right? I'm sure that wherever the System came from had lonely people who would pay for companionship, right? It seems like there'd be just as much call for someone with that kind of class as there is for, say, a Carpenter. Or an Archivist. Or whatever other noncombat classes are out there."

"Just idle curiosity, then. That's your final answer, huh?"

"I should warn you that I am a powerful warrior, and I will defend myself if necessary," he said. That's when he realized that he was probably twenty pounds lighter than her, a couple of inches shorter, and as they'd established the night before, lacking more than a few points in Strength.

He was also still naked, which he only realized when Delilah's eyes flicked down to his most private bits. But he stubbornly refused to cover up. She'd seen all there was to see, anyway. It wasn't as if he had anything to hide after the night they'd spent together.

"You really believe that, huh?" she asked, cocking her head to the side. "Scrawny thing like you."

"Uh . . . I spent two years with barely enough food to survive," he said. "I think I'm in pretty good shape, all things considered. And let's not even talk about when I got digested by a whale. Or whale monster, I guess. I was down to skin and bones after that."

"A whale monster? Where in the world did you encounter a whale monster?"

"In the Sea of Sorrows. Or something like that. I forget the name, if I'm honest," he said, hopping off the bed. "My point is that you shouldn't make light of someone who's been through what I've been through. Bad form and all that." She narrowed her eyes again, and he added, "My other point is that in no way, shape, or form did I mean to impugn your reputation. If I did, I apologize wholeheartedly and throw myself upon your generous mercy."

He ended with as dramatic a bow as he could muster.

"You're not getting laid again."

"What?"

"You heard me. It was fun. I had a great time," she said. "But this was always going to be a one-time thing."

"Ugh. I feel used."

"Because you were," she pointed out. "Look—do you have any idea how few men my age are still around in Argos? Not many. Do you know why?"

Elijah shook his head, though he did take a moment to find his underpants, which were hanging from a standing lamp. Classy.

"Who do you think the first ones called to defend the city were? The young, healthy men. And who do you think were the first ones to die when the Voxx started surging? Yeah. You guessed it," she said, her expression suddenly hard. "It was almost overnight that the average age in Argos rose by fifteen years. So, when somebody new comes in and saves my little brother, well . . . A girl has needs."

Elijah guessed, "But a girl doesn't want commitment."

"Just so. I've got plans," she said. "Me and Isaak are going to travel once we both get a few more levels under our belts. We want to see the world."

Elijah understood wanderlust better than most. He had no intention of sitting still, even after he found his family. Yet, he also didn't want to be responsible for two strangers, even if they were reasonably capable. Isaak had proved himself, and he suspected that Delilah was nearly as strong in her own way. But Elijah was on a different level, and he didn't want to saddle himself with that kind of responsibility.

"It's not you," Delilah said. "It's me. I don't want to have to carry anyone."

Elijah almost laughed at that, but he remembered his manners well enough to keep that to himself. Instead, he just gave her a feigned sad smile and said, "I understand. I hope you both find exactly what you're looking for."

After that, Delilah finished dressing. When Elijah hesitated to do the same—aside from his hastily donned underwear—Delilah cleared her throat pointedly. That's when he remembered that they were in her room. Clearly, she had no intention of leaving him behind, so he quickly apologized and dressed, gathering his things without much fanfare. Once that was done, they shared an awkward goodbye, then Delilah led him downstairs and past Isaak, who was pointedly ignoring everything as he sat at the table eating a piece of fruit. Elijah had no intention of extending that awkwardness, so he just gave a half-hearted wave before Delilah practically pushed him from the house.

A couple of old women sitting on the neighboring front porch sniggered at his treatment, so he just gave them a shrug before heading on his way. It wasn't long before his path took him to the Branch, where he deposited his coins and spent a few minutes perusing the Knowledge Base as well as the Regional Map. He bought a couple of extra guides—one on crafting and the other called "Guidelines for Entering a Newly Touched World," which he surmised was intended for people traveling from other worlds to ones that had been recently touched by the World Tree. He hoped that would give him some insight in case he encountered more off-worlders.

On the map, he found his next target, which was called Kalajma. That didn't sound Greek, so he suspected that it had come from a completely different part of the world. Which was both exciting and daunting. Elijah hadn't experienced a lot of different cultures in his short life, but he knew just how easy it was to say or do the wrong thing when you didn't know the societal rules. Still, if it was half as friendly as Argos had been, then he expected he would enjoy the new town.

Once he'd copied a rough facsimile of the map into a notebook he'd bought back in Ironshore, Elijah thanked the Envoy and went on his way. Before he decided what to do, Elijah stopped by a café, where he enjoyed a cup of coffee. As he sat there, he became keenly aware that someone was watching him. So, he focused on One with Nature, and he found a familiar presence in the nearby alley.

He didn't immediately go check it out, though. Instead, he continued to enjoy his coffee, chuckling softly when his visitor started pacing impatiently. However, Elijah didn't want to push things too far—especially because he knew what his friend was capable of—so instead of ordering another cup, he paid his bill, leaving an extra copper etherium as a tip, then headed into the alley.

"What?"

Predictably, his stalker didn't answer, but that was more due to the fact that cats typically couldn't speak rather than any intention of rudeness. Artemis just stared at him flatly, then approached.

"I'm not taking you with me," he said, kneeling down to pet the cat. When he did, he was reminded that the fur on her back felt like metal bristles, which sort of took the fun out of the whole thing. Still, he was careful to show her the positive attention she obviously craved as he said, "You need to stay with Isaak. Protect him. He's strong, but he's vulnerable. If you—"

"Are you giving my cat an explanation like she can actually understand you?" came Isaak's voice.

"Huh?" Elijah asked, forcing himself to calmly look back. "No. You must have been hearing things. I wouldn't . . . You know what? Sure. I was explaining to Artemis that she can't come with me."

"Pretty sure she doesn't want to go with you," Isaak said, stepping forward. He seemed a lot more confident than he had in the woods. But that was probably because he was more comfortable in the city where everyone saw him as a hero. Or maybe it was because Argos was only home to one monster, and now that Artemis had been cured of the corruption, she wasn't going to start attacking people.

Probably.

Cats being cats, one could never be sure, but Elijah felt reasonably confident that Artemis wouldn't just haul off and start hunting people. Especially so long as Isaak was around.

In any case, Artemis raised her head primly and sashayed past Elijah to leap into Isaak's arms. Considering her size, that was quite a feat, but Isaak didn't seem to have much difficulty holding the cat. What was obvious was that Artemis didn't have any intention of leaving her friend, which just highlighted how silly Elijah felt.

"Just one of those days." He sighed. "What's up, then? Need me to save you from something else?"

Isaak held his cat close as he said, "No. I just . . . I just wanted to thank you again. I know you didn't have to help me. Most people wouldn't have, especially after I hit you with that soulfire ball. But you did. And . . . Well . . . Thanks. If you ever need me for anything, I'll be here."

Elijah nodded, but he really didn't know how to respond to that.

"Also, please stay away from my sister."

"What? Why? I mean, she came for me!"

"Ugh. Please just . . . No. Just no."

"I didn't do anything wrong!"

Isaak just shook his head. Then, he cleared his throat before asking, "Where are you going to go?"

Elijah was more than happy to move the conversational topic to something else, and he said, "There's a town a few hundred miles from here. It's called Kalajma. That's the next stop."

"I thought you wanted to go to Seattle."

"I do," he said. "And how do you know that?"

Indeed, he'd never revealed his plans to Isaak. Suddenly, he was suspicious.

"Delilah told me. She said you told her about it last night."

"We didn't do much talking last night."

"Gross."

"Where did you really hear it?" Elijah asked.

"Fine. It was from Atticus. When we got back into town, someone told me that you two had gotten kind of friendly. So, I went over there today and asked about you," Isaak said. "He told me about Seattle."

"What else did he tell you?"

"Nothing!" Isaak said, taking a step back.

"Easy, kid. I'm not going to attack you. Jesus. People are so paranoid. Like I'd just murder a kid in the middle of town," he muttered. "Just don't tell anybody else, okay? I'm not exactly hiding here, but I don't need my business all over town."

"You might've made friends with the wrong person, then. Everybody knows Atticus is the town gossip," Isaak revealed.

"Of course he is," Elijah said, running his hand down his face in exasperation. In reality, it wasn't really that surprising. In retrospect, it wasn't even that frustrating. Atticus was just a friendly guy who was probably on good terms with everyone in town. Of course he'd talk. Elijah could just hope that he hadn't revealed all his secrets. "It's fine. I'm leaving anyway, and I don't know if I'll ever come this way again."

"Don't you want to know where Seattle is? It's to the southeast. Close to five hundred miles, though. At least according to the last peddler that came through here," Isaak explained. "He seemed pretty sure about it, though, and from what I understand, it's not a good situation down there. But that was more than a year ago, so I'm sure things have changed."

"Do you know anything else about it?"

Isaak shook his head. "And that's secondhand information. For all I know, the peddler was lying. But he seemed sure that Seattle was in that direction, and I don't see why he would lie about that part."

"Me, neither."

After that, the conversation went on for a few more minutes, but it was clear that Isaak didn't have any more information. So, Elijah said goodbye, patted the cat on its bristly head, then set off to the southeast. Hopefully, before too long, he would reach Seattle and find his sister.

So, it was with some degree of optimism that he left Argos behind and set off into the wilderness.

63

THE LOOMING THREAT

Kurik dove aside, rolling away just in time to avoid the orc's descending axe. The stone blade thudded into the loamy turf, sending an explosion of black soil and dead leaves into the air. The monster roared in frustration as it yanked the massive blade out of the ground, but it had dug into the roots of a nearby oak tree, so the motion wasn't quite as smooth as it should have been.

That was the only opening Kurik needed.

The dwarf dashed in, drawing his one-handed axe from the loop at his belt. He swung, and with a sickening thunk, the blade bit deep into the off-balance orc's knee. It was like hacking at an ancient tree, but Kurik ripped it away, keeping his momentum going as the orc finally retrieved his massive weapon from where it had become embedded in the ground.

Kurik skidded to a stop, twisting back to face his opponent.

The orc was almost twice as tall as him, and broader across the shoulders, as well. The heavily muscled creature wore nothing but a loincloth and the hide of some animal across its shoulders, and its weapon was about as primitive as any Kurik had ever seen. Stone bladed and with a haft made from the femur of a monstrous animal, it looked too large even for the huge orc.

And it was, often overbalancing the monster.

Though that didn't mean it wasn't deadly. If he found himself on the wrong end of that blade, he knew he'd end up bisected. No—he had to fight smart.

Fortunately, he was well prepared for such a battle. Through his long years, he'd fought so many oversize opponents that he'd lost count. That was the life of a dwarf, after all. Or any of the shorter-statured races. He made up for it with sheer durability and, some would say, stubbornness.

The real advantage was upstairs, though.

So, with that in mind, Kurik slowly retreated, holding his axe in an easy grip he'd learned from his long-dead father. Then, he crooked his finger at the hulking monster and said, "C'mon, you big idjit. I'm right here waitin' fer ya."

The orc didn't need any further invitation, and with an echoing roar that Kurik hoped none of the other orcs in the area had heard, it threw itself forward. So, Kurik did the only sensible thing: He turned on his heel and ran, leaping over a fallen and rotted tree, then sliding down the dew-slick slope on the other side. The monster barreled through the tree, sending decomposing splinters flying before realizing its mistake and tumbling down the slope after Kurik.

That gave the dwarf a few extra seconds to stretch his lead, though he didn't dare glance back. That would only slow him down, and he knew that the huge creature was possessed of enough Strength to throw itself forward with incredibly quickness. Certainly, it couldn't control that speed, but that wouldn't do much to help Kurik on a straightaway.

So, he continued to sprint, nimbly avoiding the worst of the area's thick underbrush. It was like a tropical jungle it was so dense. But Kurik was an experienced Scout, and he knew how to move in all sorts of terrain. He was at home in the forest, so he didn't have any trouble keeping ahead of the orc.

The chase continued for about thirty more seconds before he saw a small mark on one of the trees as he darted past. Grinned, leaped over a barely noticeable depression, then skidded to a stop.

The orc came only a few seconds later, roaring in bestial fury as it caromed off of trees and ripped its way through the dense foliage. Then, it hit the depression and disappeared. Less than an instant later, a pained yowl filled the air. But Kurik didn't immediately approach. Instead, he waited for a few more seconds to see if the creature was going to climb out of the trap.

It didn't, but not for lack of trying. Agonized screams, frustrated growls, and the sound of digging greeted Kurik's ears, but the monster seemed to have been confined to the pit. In most cases, Kurik would have waited a little longer. Many animals were more than capable of pretending they'd been caught so that they could turn the situation around on a careless hunter. He'd seen it happen, and more than once.

But orcs were too stupid—or perhaps single-minded—for that kind of thing. At their current stage of development, they could barely even use tools, much less think strategically. Yet, they were dangerous monsters, and what's worse, Kurik knew that Ironshore wasn't prepared to meet such a threat.

Not with most of their security forces having been killed in an ill-fated attempt to snatch some natural treasure out from under a powerful guardian. Kurik had seen the man for himself, and though he didn't think much of what he'd seen, he knew well enough to respect his deeds. A full fifty people had gone to that island, and only one had returned. Kurik knew better than to tempt those odds.

Of course, he wouldn't have gone hunting on that island anyway. Just wasn't worth it, as far as he was concerned. There were other ways to advance that didn't involve fighting a guardian on his own turf. Less deadly ways.

Kurik wasn't a coward. He'd fight when necessary, and if he thought the odds were in his favor. But trying to take more than a dwarf's share was what had gotten his clan banished in the first place. It was why he'd spent his formative years without a father, and ultimately, it was why he'd ended up in Ironshore looking for a fresh start.

He crept forward, keeping on his toes as he approached the pit. And when he looked down, he saw precisely what he'd expected. The pit itself was almost ten feet deep and lined with sharpened sticks. But it was more than just a hole in the ground. It was augmented by two of his abilities.

The first was Conceal Trap, which was why the orc had never detected it.

Ability: Conceal Trap	Create an illusion to hide a trap. Lasts thirty (30) minutes. Potency of the illusion is based on Dexterity.

Kurik's Dexterity was fairly high for his level, which meant that, when he used the technique, his traps were almost entirely undetectable for someone near his level. The orc had him by three levels, but it clearly hadn't the wits to see through Conceal Trap.

The second ability was the one that really gave the trap some punch, though:

Ability: Venom Trap	Augment an existing trap with potent venom. Choose type: Paralysis Neurotoxin Necrotic (Current)

The ability was an incredible boon for any hunter. Normally, he used the paralysis type of venom—after all, he didn't want to ruin the meat of his prey. However, now that he was hunting orcs, he knew he needed to use the most powerful venom available to him. When he'd originally received the ability, it had been nearly useless. But over time, he'd discovered that he could add potential types to the ability; the only caveat was that he had to experience it himself.

The necrotic venom had come from a scorpion native to his home world called a lava dredger. Normally, they were fairly peaceful creatures, but when agitated, they would strike. But it only took one hit and their victims were goners. To endure it, Kurik had been forced to commission an expensive healing potion, but in the years since, it had proved invaluable.

"Hurts, don't it? I still remember that sting," he said, looking down at the orc. Already, the venom had infected it, and because it'd been stabbed by the stakes in multiple places, the venomous skill had worked extremely quickly. The thing would be dead in less than a minute, unless it possessed some sort of healing ability.

Which it almost certainly didn't.

Kurik had killed enough orcs over the past few weeks to be as sure about that as he was about anything else in his new world.

Ever since he'd reported the orc invasion to the mayor as well as Ironshore's ruling council, he'd been tasked with keeping an eye on the horde while killing as many as he could. The rest of his scouting team was doing the same, and to date, they'd slaughtered almost a hundred of the monsters. Yet, there were still plenty left.

Their primary purpose wasn't fighting a war, though. Instead, they were meant to watch for signs that the orcs had detected Ironshore. The boundary field they'd set up upon arrival kept the worst of the monster population away, but it could only do so much against semisentient creatures like orcs. The moment the orcs got a whiff of such a juicy target—even if it was rendered faint by the boundary field—they'd come running, and in full force.

And that eventuality, which they'd hoped they could avoid, had clearly come. The orcish horde had shifted and begun their march toward Ironshore. By Kurik's estimation, they were no more than two or three weeks away, which meant that he needed to hightail it back to the city and warn them.

But what that would accomplish he didn't know. They couldn't stand up to the oncoming horde. Not even if the security forces were still intact. He knew that the city's leaders had pooled all their etherium in order to hire more, but they could scarcely afford the teleportation fee for any force that would make a difference, much less enough to actually get them to come.

No. Ironshore was doomed.

Kurik knew it, and if he was a smart dwarf, he would have already fled into the wilderness. Yet, he hadn't because, if he was honest, he was tired of running away. That was what he'd done when his people were exiled. And he'd done it again when the opportunity to come to a new world had crossed his path. That wasn't how he wanted to spend the rest of his life.

So, Kurik waited until the orc had succumbed to the venom of his trap, then headed back toward Ironshore. Along the way, he met up with his squad. Most of them had greatly benefited from the ongoing hunt—so had Kurik—which, in normal circumstances, would have been cause for celebration. But now? None of them were thinking of anything but the coming fight.

As a result, it was a somber group that headed back to Ironshore.

Ramik glanced up at the gray sky and watched the roiling clouds that heralded a coming storm. He let out a sigh, then glanced at his closest friend and said, "Storm's coming."

Carisa let out a snort. "Storms're always comin'," she said in her characteristic brogue. "Be a lot more interestin' if you said it wasn't 'bout to rain."

The goblin shook his head, then removed his glasses. With a handkerchief he took from his pocket, he wiped the priceless lenses. They weren't intended to correct his vision—he'd had that fixed long ago—but, rather, to give him some insight into the flow of ambient ethera. For instance, when he looked across the strait at the guardian's island, he could see just how special of a place it really was. Through the lenses, the island practically glowed with potential. It was nearly enough to awaken the avarice in his heart, but he only had to remember Eason Cabbot's fate to recognize just how bad of an idea it was to pursue that line of thought.

"It was meant to be a metaphor," he explained. "But I suppose it was a terrible one."

"What do ye want to do?" she asked.

"Do we have any choice?" was his responding question. "The guardian said—"

"He said he might help. Not that he would."

"But might is better than we've gotten from anyone else," Ramik stated. "There are ten thousand bloodthirsty orcs coming this way, Carisa. Do you know what an orc horde can do?"

"I've read the same stories as you."

"Then no. I've seen it. On my home world. I was only a child, but I remember it so keenly. They swept across the countryside, conquering and devouring everything they could find. Some people say they are descended from the great Ravener himself." He shook his head, continuing, "But they're just monsters, Carisa. Deadly, dreadful monsters that only know aggression," he explained. "We stopped them. Barely. But a lot of good goblins lost their lives in that fight."

Indeed, his own family, once prominent members of a successful merchant guild, had been devastated. From there, they'd experienced a precipitous fall from grace, ending with Ramik leading what was left of his family into the new world. They weren't even part of the guild anymore.

But Ramik had vowed to return the Lendar'i family back to prominence if it was the last thing he did. The Green Mountain Mining Guild had given them the opportunity to do just that, and though they weren't members, that could change soon enough. He just had to defend the town from an orcish invasion.

A tall task, especially given that his entire security force had been killed. Certainly, everyone in town had at least some ability in combat. Nobody came to a new world without that. However, those meager abilities wouldn't count for much against a ravening horde of orcs.

Because of that, he'd used the Branch's limited communication capability to ask for support, but the guild's hub had only told him that they would take it into consideration. That was code for "Fend for yourself."

The reality was that Ironshore was operating on a razor-thin budget as it was, and because they'd yet to find anything truly valuable, it was probably easier for the Green Mountain Mining Guild to cut ties and leave them to their own devices. If they managed to survive, then that was great. But if not, then they wouldn't have sunk any more etherium into the venture.

It was just good business.

Terrible from a compassion standpoint, of course, but that was normal. Guilds weren't charities, after all.

"You think he can stop 'em?"

Ramik shrugged his shoulders, then replaced his glasses. "I don't know. He's strong. I felt it."

"He also killed Cabbot and his folks."

"Cabbot was an idiot who was convinced he was far more powerful than he actually was," Ramik spat. "When I saw who he was, I thought that we had lucked out. An Eason. Here. Yet, I quickly discovered why he'd ended up on a frontier world with all the rest of us desperate people."

"I ain't desperate. I just felt the call of adventure," Carisa insisted.

That was blatantly untrue. Ramik had seen her file. She was a competent enough miner and engineer, but the dwarven woman was anything but reliable. She'd left a string of misdeeds in her past, the same as almost everyone in Ironshore. The same as anyone who chose to come to a newly touched world.

They were wild, lawless places that catered to the desperate and depraved, and more often than not the dangers outweighed the potential rewards. But still, like Ramik, they came because they had no other options. For him, it was either take his chances on Earth or spend the rest of his life wallowing in mediocrity.

And that latter was the best-case scenario if he'd stayed on his home world.

"I think we have to try," he said, still gazing across the strait at the island. "He may not help us, but our backs are against the wall, Carisa. We need him."

"Aight," she said. "I'll fetch us a boat, and we'll go for a little visit. Let's just hope he don't kill us on sight."

"He wouldn't."

"You sure 'bout that?" she asked, raising one bushy eyebrow.

"I'm . . . not," he admitted. But then, he straightened his coat, pushed his shoulders back, and said, "But we can't let that dissuade us."

"Aight," she said again. "Sounds good to me. He didn't kill us last time, so here's hopin' he'll keep to that."

64

A MAN NEEDS A CODE

Elijah knelt atop the hill, looking out across the valley. It was an idyllic scene, with lush vegetation and a gentle stream cutting through the center of the dell. Despite the drizzling rain that had pervaded the region since he'd left Argos a couple of days before, sunlight still bathed the hollow, giving it a surreal, yet comfortable atmosphere. The only thing marring the landscape was the crumbling skyscraper standing in an asphalt clearing on the eastern side of the valley.

Ignoring the obvious damage, it would have been at home as part of any major city's skyline, though Elijah didn't recognize it. Still, it was so incongruous that it sparked his curiosity to the point that he felt obligated to check it out.

Running his hand through his hair, he let out a low sigh. Every time he decided to investigate one oddity or another, he ended up getting sidetracked from his primary quest. It had happened in Norcastle with healing the plague-stricken townspeople and the tower, then again in Argos. He knew that if he kept giving in to his wanderlust, he'd never find his sister.

And now that he knew where to find Seattle, he was more eager for a reunion than ever. After all, Easton had been just outside of the city, so hopefully finding Seattle would mean finding that small town, as well. Even if the two locations had been separated by Earth's sudden transformation, it would at least give him some degree of verifiable progress. Because so far, he'd felt like he was just wandering randomly and hoping for a clue to point him in the right direction.

Which was precisely what he'd gotten. Now, he just needed to not ignore it.

Still, the mystery of the skyscraper called to him, and in the end, he decided that a quick look wouldn't hurt. So, Elijah shifted into his draconid form, then set off down the hill and into the valley. With Essence of the Wolf working in conjunction with his high attributes, he covered the ground incredibly quickly. He didn't have much context for his actual speed, but if he traveled any slower than a thirty-mile-an-hour jog, he would have been surprised. He could go much faster if he fully exerted himself, though that was always a little disconcerting. It would also quickly exhaust him.

In any case, he slowed down as he descended into the valley, if for no other reason than because it was a pleasant setting. So often, it was easy to forget just how miraculous nature could be. Once, it had been common for people to lock themselves in their homes and stare at one screen or another without ever enjoying what the Earth had to offer. Likely, people in cities were still unwilling to venture out into the wilderness, albeit for a different reason. Now, it was due to the dangers inherent in the wilds rather than laziness, depression, or the habits of a screen-addicted society.

Those thoughts flitted through one facet of Elijah's Mind as he beheld the wonders of the idyllic valley. Birds chirped, and small animals chittered. Meanwhile, he could feel everything all around him. Even the trees felt more alive and aware than normal, which was both welcome and a little disconcerting.

Eventually, he reached the stream, where he stopped to drink and wash. As he did so, he cast his mind back to the events of the past few weeks. It had begun with his flight from Norcastle, and it had ended with his night with Delilah. Somewhere in the middle of it all, his awareness of his place in the world had begun to coalesce.

In hindsight, he wished he hadn't killed those hunters. Not because he didn't think they deserved it. He fully believed that they had. Yet, he also knew that his perspective was skewed by his compromised mental state. He'd let that drive him to do something that he now regretted.

From a philosophical perspective, Elijah knew he needed to accept that people would hunt the wildlife in order to advance. Progression was as necessary a part of survival as food or water, and without it, people would stagnate and eventually die when they encountered some hostile situation they couldn't handle.

That was the world now. And as much as it pained him to see something like the bear killed, it was a fact of life he would have to accept going forward. That didn't mean he had to do those sorts of things himself, but he could at least look the other way while others did. The same was true of natural treasures, though given what he'd experienced so far, the idea of consuming something for a one-time benefit when you could instead bathe in the ethera it emitted indefinitely was the height of stupidity.

Yet, Elijah knew he couldn't do anything about that. He could govern his own actions, but he would not run around like some ecopolice hell-bent on punishing people for their crimes against nature. Down that road lay disaster, both for his own mental health as well as the likelihood he would be tolerated by the rest of the population.

But one thing Elijah did know was that he enjoyed helping people. That had begun with the Ulthraks in the first level of his island's tower, and it had only grown more prevalent when he'd helped heal the people in Easton. The same could be said when he'd fought his way through Reaver's Citadel, and then saved Isaak and Artemis.

In a world where so much had been destroyed and so many lives had been lost, he liked the idea that he could affect positive change. He could save people.

He could rescue and heal them. With the power he'd earned, he could do miraculous things, and he refused to let that go to waste.

Did that make him naive? Perhaps. And maybe it would one day come back to bite him. But he wouldn't want to live with himself if he ever became the sort of person who could see a chance to save someone and simply turn away. It would take a truly damaged person to end up like that.

He liked to think that his parents had raised him better than to let that sort of attitude take hold.

Those thoughts and more occupied Elijah's mind as he idled near the stream. Eventually, he caught a couple of fish, made camp, and had a peaceful meal, all thoughts of the nearby skyscraper briefly forgotten.

As night began to take hold, he decided to tackle the skyscraper in the morning. For now, though, he was content.

Which was why it took him a few moments to recognize the warning in his Mind. The source wasn't his immediate surroundings. Rather, someone had landed on his island. Through his Locus, he could feel the familiar figures of Ramik and Carisa planting a white flag on his beach.

Elijah's initial reaction was one of annoyance. He'd told them to stay away from his island, and yet, there they were. However, that only lasted for a moment before he came to terms with the fact that his irritation was more about the fact that his foray into the wider world had been interrupted. Clearly, the people of Ironshore needed help, and they were willing to ask him to intervene in whatever problem they'd found.

Through his Domain, he watched the pair standing on the shore and waiting. They didn't stray from the beach where they'd landed, which further reinforced Elijah's surety that they'd come in peace.

So, he had an option to either ignore them and hope they simply went away, or he could use Ancestral Circle and teleport back to his Grove so he could see what they wanted. But even before he'd posed the question to himself, Elijah knew what he was going to do. So, it was with some residual irritation that he gathered his things, making sure that he smothered the fire before embracing Ancestral Circle and teleporting back to his Grove.

When he reappeared, he stumbled to his knees at the influx of dense ethera. It took him a few seconds of deep breathing to reacclimate. Had it grown thicker? Or had he simply grown accustomed to the thinner ambient ethera in other parts of the world? He resolved to ask Nerthus after seeing what Ramik and Carisa wanted.

However, he did take a second to snatch a berry from one of the Grove's bushes and pop it into his mouth. It was sweeter than ever, and he experienced a slight jolt of energy and vitality the moment he swallowed.

"Oh, it's good to be home," he said. Despite his annoyance at having been called back, he couldn't deny that much. Even though his bed—and the shower—called to him, Elijah knew he needed to take care of business first. So, he shifted into his draconid form and took off across the island at close to full speed. Anywhere else, he couldn't have traveled through such dense forest at top speed, but with the knowledge of the terrain he received from his Locus, he could have gone even faster.

The result was that he arrived at the beach—or, rather, the tree line nearby—only a few minutes later. Predictably, Ramik and Carisa remained near their boat, nervously looking around.

"You think he's comin'?" asked the dwarven woman.

The goblin shook his head, then straightened his coat. "My answer is the same as the last ten times you have asked, Carisa," he said in his prim voice. "I have no idea. If he hasn't responded in the next hour, we will have to return to Ironshore and prepare to either flee or fight back."

"If we fight, we die," Carisa stated. "We have no fighters, other than that squad of Scouts. And they ain't much for a straight fight."

"Again, I am aware."

"Hope he shows up soon. I'm hungry," Carisa said, leaning against the rowboat they'd used to reach the island.

That statement prompted Elijah to wonder if he should return to his Grove and gather some more berries, but ultimately, he decided against it. The moment either of them tasted his berries, they'd know just how special the island was. As far as he was concerned, they didn't need any more incentive to visit, so he chose to simply shift into his human form and step out from the tree line, his Staff of Natural Harmony in hand. As he did, he asked, "What do you want?"

The pair flinched away from him, but both quickly mastered themselves. Ramik was the first to speak. "Thank you for coming," he said with a bow of his head.

"Skip the pleasantries. I was busy. What do you want?"

"Very well," Ramik said, adjusting his glasses. "As you are . . . ah . . . aware, our security force was . . . Well, we no longer have a security force. We have attempted to hire more, but the teleportation fees to a newly touched world are exorbitant. The only reason any of us are here was because of the settlement incentive, which covered the fees for anyone who met the requirements. Otherwise, we—"

"We can't hire nobody else," Carisa interrupted. "We got a few people who can fight, but not enough to do what needs doin'."

Ramik cut his eyes at the muscular dwarf. "Right. That is what I was saying," he went on. Then, he looked back at Elijah and continued, "We have been training people, but it's not enough."

"Enough for what?"

"Orcs," Ramik answered. "A horde has invaded and are coming for Ironshore."

Immediately, Elijah thought back to the tribe of orc-like creatures he'd seen on the other side of the mountain range. They had settled in an abandoned Walmart, but it didn't take an intuitive leap to come to the conclusion that those monsters and the ones described by Ramik were one and the same.

The goblin went on to explain the nature of an orc horde and how it posed a unique threat to not just Ironshore, but to all surrounding areas. That included Elijah's island, which meant that he really didn't have much of a choice but to help.

Not that he would have refused, anyway. Certainly, the mohawked gnome and his warriors had come from Ironshore, but the rest of the population had made it clear that he'd been a rogue element. On top of that, they'd been kind to him—likely because they were terrified, but still, that mattered. And, of course, his previous resolution to help where he could loomed large in his mind.

So, he asked, "How long until they reach Ironshore?"

"A couple of weeks. Perhaps three," Ramik said. "But it could be as few as five days before we see their scouts."

Elijah nodded. "Alright. I'll help," he said.

"Just like that?" asked a surprised Ramik.

"I told you he'd help," Carisa said.

Elijah shrugged. "Feels like we're in this together, for now," he said, wanting to maintain an air of mystery and danger. "But I expect cooperation and some degree of compensation. We'll discuss that later."

Ramik nodded, and after a few more awkward exchanges, the pair boarded their boat and rowed out into the strait. When Elijah lost sight of them, he let himself relax.

A whole horde of orcs.

He had his work cut out for him. But for now, he just wanted to go back to his Grove, talk to Nerthus, and then sleep in his own bed. Tomorrow, he would worry about fighting what sounded like a war.

65

REBELLION

Are you sure?" asked Carmen, looking around Easton. It had been months since the last time she had visited, and in that time, the city had once again transformed. It was difficult to believe that only a few years before, it had been nothing more than a sleepy suburb. Now, it was a walled city that had to house at least a hundred thousand people. Probably a lot more. "Because if you're wrong . . ."

Colt nodded. "Sure as I can be," he responded, his hand on the hilt of his katana. The duster he always wore had been pushed back to allow for easy access to the sword. Underneath, he wore a set of chain mail Carmen had made herself. It wasn't her best work—she still wasn't great with the delicate process of making that type of armor—but, as a low-Simple-grade item, it was head and shoulders above average. "Didn't have a ton of information to go on."

It would have been easy to take that statement as a reprimand for her actions regarding Verin, and in fact, she'd admonished herself enough as it was. Colt knew that better than most, and Carmen was well aware that he didn't mean the statement as anything but informative.

Not that Carmen regretted her actions, per se. Verin had deserved to die. So did Roman. However, the timing could have been better. As it happened, her rash reaction to learning what had really happened in that tower had robbed her of the opportunity to learn more about the so-called rebels. So, after interrogating Verin's squad—and to no avail—she'd been forced to send Colt to search things out. Fortunately, he had a background as a bounty hunter, which he was quick to point out was not as exciting as it sounded, so he was a natural choice as an investigator.

Still, she'd spent the following weeks on pins and needles as he'd gone back to Easton to investigate. When he'd returned with the identities of the rebels, Carmen had been relieved. However, when he'd revealed that he'd already set up a meeting, she couldn't help but be a little suspicious.

That had followed her all the way back to Easton and to the tavern door in front of her. It was located in what had once been the least developed part of the city, and in a lot of ways, it still was. But as much as she had grown to hate Roman, she couldn't deny that his policies were effective. Exclusionary and oppressive, but effective, nonetheless. Because as far as she had seen, the city was incredibly clean, the people looked well-fed, and most of all, they were safe.

Of course, there were Guards on every street corner, each one wearing a blue-and-white uniform and sporting a decent level, and someone had decided to get the propaganda machine going. Even in the small portion of the city Carmen had seen, she'd passed four statues in various stages of construction. Each one depicted Roman in some sort of heroic pose. More than that, she'd seen a host of banners and flags that reminded her of Soviet-era propaganda.

And finally, she'd noticed more than one poorly disguised member of a secret police. If she'd seen that many, then she could extrapolate that there were far more scattered throughout the population. Easton had become a fascist police state in every way that mattered, but with that had come safety, which was likely the only reason anyone tolerated it.

At least at first. But after years, the pervasive propaganda had assuredly done its work. Carmen hesitated to call the population brainwashed, but they had certainly been manipulated. Even without that, though, the world was such a dangerous place that giving up freedom in favor of security was a valid option.

So long as you weren't one of the undesirables.

There were plenty of those, too. People who'd only done the bare minimum. The ones who'd chosen less-than-optimal classes or archetypes. The untalented. The lazy. The apathetic. The disabled. The list went on and on. For anyone who didn't fit Roman's narrow definition of usefulness, Easton was hell.

But at least they were protected from the monsters on the other side of the walls.

That was the first problem. The second was that anyone who was strong enough to be useful was well-treated and, as a result, had few reasons to buck Roman's authority. Sure, there were likely a few people here and there who would object based on empathy, but from everything she'd ever seen of human nature, Carmen knew those would be the exception rather than the rule.

That meant that any potential rebellion would already start from well behind, making its viability that much less likely. Carmen knew these things, and yet, she didn't care. Roman needed to die. She was committed to that endeavor to such a degree that she was willing to ignore everything else if it gave her a chance to see it through.

"I wish I was wearing my armor," she muttered. Indeed, it wasn't uncommon for people to walk around Easton wearing armor or carrying weapons, but it did tend to get the attention of the Guards. As she was trying to avoid such notice, Carmen had left her armor and hammer back in Silverado. She sighed. "You first. I'll follow."

Colt nodded, then opened the door. A cacophony of noise swept out of the building and overwhelmed Carmen. The tall Samurai stepped inside, and

Carmen followed. Fortunately, the tavern, which was called the Flailing Fortune, was busy enough that two new entrants weren't enough to garner any undue attention. The pair went straight to the bar, where they ordered a pair of drinks. Then, once the bartender served them, Colt said, "I'm lookin' for somethin' special."

"Brothel's down the street."

"Not what I was talkin' about. I hear there's a special meeting downstairs. Real special, you hear? Be mighty obliged if you'd let 'em know that Carmen Rodriguez is here, and she wants in."

The bartender, who Carmen noted was young enough that his poor excuse for a mustache hadn't really filled in yet, swallowed hard, then took a step back. A second later, he glanced at Carmen, and recognition dawned in his expression. His face went pale. "I don't know what you're talking about."

Carmen rolled her eyes and leaned forward. "Listen. What's your name?"

"Pete."

"Look, Pete. I'm pretty sure I already know where this little get-together is," she stated. Her eyes flicked toward a door in the back that looked like it led downstairs. The bartender's eyes followed that small gesture, and he went even paler. "So, here's the thing. I've come to help. So, run along down there and let them know I'm here. That way, we can avoid them scattering across the city. I don't want to have to chase anyone down." She gave him a smile that she was sure didn't touch her eyes and said, "Short legs, you know. Not built for running people down."

A moment of indecision passed, followed by a pregnant silence. Then, finally, he let out a deep breath before saying, "Fine. Alright. I'll go let them know."

"'S all we ask," drawled Colt.

Then, Pete took yet another steadying breath before heading toward the door. Colt said, "You see the bouncer?"

"Yep," Carmen said, taking a drink of her beer. It was not the highest-quality stuff, but it was more than they had back in Silverado. "Is he coming this way?"

"Not yet. Think they'll rabbit?"

Carmen shrugged. "Dunno. Maybe. I was on the council."

As far as the public was concerned, she and Roman were thick as thieves. Of course, they had no idea that he was responsible for the murder of her wife, which was an important bit of context.

"Means you're valuable. If you wanted 'em gone, you wouldn't've come yourself. You'd send those secret police."

"You saw them, too?"

"Couldn't miss 'em. Lost 'em before we came, though. Sure of that much," he said. As he did, his eyes flicked toward the door, and he said, "Here we go."

Carmen tensed. She didn't have a bunch of combat abilities or spells like real fighters, but she made up for it with her high level. That gap would close soon, she was sure, but for now, she could hold her own. As such, she was ready to use Summon Tool the moment she felt threatened.

Pete came back to the bar, looking slightly more relaxed. When he reached them, he said, "You can go down. They said that you'd . . . uh . . . better not be trying anything. 'Cause they got some powerful fighters down there. Real heavy hitters."

"Noted," Carmen said. "Colt."

"Yes, ma'am," he said, sweeping his coat back and swaggering toward the door. To Carmen, he looked like a gunfighter from an old Western, which should have been a little silly. Yet, he made it work, radiating an aura of pure danger that told anyone looking for trouble that he was ready for just that. By comparison, Carmen felt clunky and clumsy.

Or like a little girl playacting as a dangerous fighter.

Perhaps he felt like a little boy playing cowboys, but she doubted it. Colt was a lot of things, but unconfident was definitely not one of them.

Either way, she followed him to the door, where they both descended a set of stairs that terminated in another door. Carmen could hear muffled conversation on the other side, but she couldn't make out any actual words.

Colt led the way, pushing through the door. But the second he stepped through, he whipped his katana out and to the side. "Easy there, fella," he said, circling so that Carmen could get through. Just then, someone moved across the doorway, but Carmen had expected it. So, she barreled into him—or her, she supposed—slamming them against the wall. Her hand found their throat.

"Like my friend said, easy. We're not here to fight," she said, finally taking in the attacker. He was average height, but with heavy shoulders. Out of the corner of her eye, Carmen saw that Colt had his blade against another, much taller would-be attacker's throat. Behind her were three other people. Presumably, they were who she'd come to see. So, she said, "Now, I'm going to let this guy go. If he tries to attack again, we're not holding back. Got it? We're just here to talk."

"Very well," came a strong voice.

Carmen stepped back, releasing the attacker. He fell to the ground, gasping for air. Already, his neck had begun to purple. Meanwhile, Colt stepped away from his target, as well, sheathing his sword so quickly that Carmen had trouble tracking the movement.

Trusting that he would watch her back, she turned to face the three people. There was one man and two women, though she didn't recognize any of them.

"Are you here to kill us as you did Verin?" asked one of the women. She had close-cut gray hair and wore decidedly shabby clothing.

"Do I have a reason to want you dead?" she asked. Apparently word of Carmen's clash with the Healer had somehow gotten back to the city. Hopefully, it had yet to reach Roman's ears.

"Perhaps," the older woman stated, leaning forward. There was a table separating them from Carmen, but with her Strength, that wouldn't be much of a barrier. The room was lit by a series of candles on the table, casting the entire area in deep, flickering shadows. "You are one of his lackeys, are you not? One of the founders of this city, in fact."

"I am. A founder, I mean. Makes it all the more difficult to see what it's become," Carmen stated evenly. "I'll just come out and say what I'm here to say. I'm not one to dance around the facts. So, here it is. I know you're planning some sort of rebellion or resistance. I want in. If you know who I am, then you know what I can offer."

"Why?" asked the lone male across the table. He was tall, with a severe appearance. More, he was missing an arm, suggesting some tragic story that Carmen didn't care about.

"Do I need a reason other than the obvious?"

"Yes," said the woman. "The city isn't much different than when you were assigned to the mining colony. Worse, perhaps, but not much. What changed to set you on this path? And why did you kill Verin, if not to punish her for fomenting rebellion?"

"Because she helped kill the woman I loved," Carmen answered simply. "Roman, too. And a guy named Trace. I don't care all that much about your rebellion, if I'm honest. Sure, it's sad, and it all sucks. But I can't deny that Roman has given people safety when there wasn't much of that available. I disagreed with some of his policies, and I argued against them when I was on the council. I was overruled, so I left it behind."

She leaned forward, her hands on the table. The two fighters tensed behind her. "All I care about is killing Roman. And that little weasel Trace, too. You give me that, and I'll make sure you have the best-equipped rebellion in the world. So long as I get a chance to stand over him as he's bleeding out on the ground, I'll give you the means to accomplish your goals. That's what I offer, and that's what I want in return. So, are we on the same page?"

The woman glanced at her companions, then back at Carmen. As she did, she said, "I think we can work with that."

66

CALM BEFORE THE STORM

For a few minutes, Elijah stood on the beach watching the crashing waves as the storm rolled in, bathing him in a deluge of precipitation. Spring had already taken hold, but the rain still felt like frigid needles against his skin. However, some of that discomfort was mitigated by the blanket of dense ethera that covered the island. The difference between what he'd felt in the valley he'd recently left behind and the power emanating from his Grove was so stark that he wondered how he could've felt comfortable in the former.

But it didn't take him long to figure it out. The drop had been so gradual that he'd barely noticed it in real time. It was like the old wives' tale of the boiling frog, and it really put his unique situation into perspective. Certainly, he could have simply left the Grove behind and made his way through the world. But it was his home, and what's more, it was special in a way that he had yet to truly appreciate. So, even if he was willing to let the people of Ironshore fend for themselves—and likely fail—he couldn't stomach the thought of ceding his Grove to the impending tide of vicious orcs.

He remained in place for a while, letting the cold rain soak him through. Then, he sighed and turned back to the tree line. Before he'd taken two steps, Elijah had shifted back into his draconid form, after which he raced across the island and to his Grove. When he reached the circle of trees, he noticed that the ancestral tree at its center had continued its transformation.

With stark-blue leaves and bark of purest white, it looked both alien and familiar. However, it also felt like home in a way he couldn't quite explain. So, he stepped into the Grove with gratitude in his heart. As he did, he couldn't help but notice the state of his garden, which had grown far more than he ever would have expected—especially because it had done so in winter. He could suspect that it was feeding more off of the ambient ethera wafting from the ancestral tree than via normal biological processes. What that meant for the plants themselves he had no idea.

He plucked another berry, popping it into his mouth and savoring the tartly sweet taste as he pulsed Nature's Bounty. It didn't even come close to covering the entire garden of bushes and other plants, but it still felt like a return to normality. So, he took solace in that as he strode toward the tree. When he reached it, he called out, "Nerthus? You in there, bud?"

"I told you before that I can leave the tree more frequently now," came the tree spirit's familiar voice from behind. As Elijah turned, he couldn't help but notice that it had grown slightly deeper. The reason for that became apparent a moment later when he saw that the tiny tree spirit had nearly doubled in size, topping out at a little taller than Elijah's waist. "I cannot come and go as I please, but I have far more freedom now that the ancestral tree has reached early maturity."

"Early maturity?" asked Elijah. Then, he said, "Good to see you, by the way. I hope you're doing well?"

"I am, thank you for asking," Nerthus answered with a bow of his head. Then, he explained, "For an ancestral tree, maturity is a difficult thing to quantify. For some, that stage is reached very quickly. For others, it takes years. However, for all of them, stepping past that point to become an elder is a long and arduous process that most will never achieve. Most that do have the benefit of an ideal environment as well as the protection of a Druid. Or someone equivalent."

"So, this tree will grow more powerful?" Elijah asked.

"Indeed. Its progress will be much slower now, but it has finally borne a seed," Nerthus said excitedly.

"There were seeds before, remember?"

"Those were mundane," Nerthus stated. "Unranked. This seed is much different. More powerful. It is difficult to tell, but it is at least Complex grade. Perhaps even Sophisticated. With a natural treasure such as the seed of an ancestral tree that has absorbed a Shard of the World Tree, the grading system lacks nuance."

"I see," Elijah lied. As far as he knew, the grading system for items, towers, and natural treasures was well established.

"You do not. The seed is connected to its progenitor. They are separate, but they are also a single entity," Nerthus explained. "And that entity is connected to the World Tree in ways the Divine System is not meant to fully understand."

"What does that mean from a practical perspective, though?"

"If you plant the seed, it will eventually connect to its progenitor through the World Tree, extending the boundaries of your Domain."

"Oh. I like that" was Elijah's lacking response. "I suppose it'll raise the ethereal density in that area, too, huh?"

"It will, though not to the degree of the original grove," Nerthus said.

Elijah sat down and leaned his back against the tree. "So," he said. "Theoretically, I could take that seed, plant it elsewhere and, eventually, get similar benefits to what I have here?"

"Yes."

"And what would happen if some disaster struck here?"

Nerthus gasped. "Why do you ask that?"

Elijah sighed, then explained the situation with the orcs—or at least what he knew of it. When he'd finished, he said, "I was just thinking that if things start looking really bad, I could grab the seed and run."

"You cannot do that."

"Why?" he asked. "I mean, I don't want to. Just to be clear, I intend to fight. But there's a good chance we're going to lose, and I want a backup plan just in case."

"That is understandable, but it is neither possible nor advisable," Nerthus stated. "If this tree dies, then its progeny will lose the majority of its power. You will be incapable of creating another grove after that."

"But—"

For the first time ever, Nerthus interrupted Elijah, saying, "The reason it is inadvisable has nothing to do with that, however. Instead, it concerns the nature of orcs. They are spawned from the System, usually using some local beast as a template. They evolve quickly, becoming intelligent enough to create a rudimentary society. From the very beginning, though, they have one goal— to conquer. Some say they are a test created by the System. Others claim that they are tainted by the Void. Regardless of their true origin, they are a plague that must be eradicated before it is too late."

"Too late for what?"

"The survival of your planet," Nerthus answered. "They will conquer and consume until there is nothing left. Then, once they've grown strong enough, they will set off into the wider universe to do the same. By that point, only the truly powerful will be capable of dealing with them, and even then, it is no sure thing. You mustn't ignore this threat, or you could very well lose this planet before it is even fully developed."

Elijah sighed. "And I assume that nobody can help us, huh? Like the dragon lady who gave me my Core, maybe."

"The System's restrictions cannot be overcome. Sending even one person here after the initial rush would cost many fortunes. Perhaps some powerful faction will respond to the threat when Earth is fully integrated, but by that point, the orcs will have already won," Nerthus answered.

Back in Argos, Elijah had bought a guide explaining—in broad terms— what happened when the World Tree touched a new planet. For a short time, low-level people were permitted to travel to what the System called the frontier, and for a negligible cost. However, after that, the cost of doing so became exorbitant to the point that very few could afford it. On top of that, only people under level twenty-five could come at all, and those over a certain level were too powerful to exist on a planet like Earth without destroying it with their mere presence.

That wouldn't last, though. After the planet's ethereal density stabilized, a countdown would begin until it was opened up to the rest of the universes. Sometimes, that took a hundred years, but it wasn't uncommon to take much longer. Elijah had no idea how long it would be for Earth—no one did—but he knew it wouldn't be anytime soon.

That was both comforting and distressing. The former because it meant that some powerful despot couldn't descend on Earth and enslave everyone. The latter because benevolent factions couldn't help with problems like the orcs. It was a double-edged system, and Elijah couldn't decide whether he liked it or not.

But the facts were clear—he had no real choice but to fight.

"I have two other things you might be able to help me with," he said. Then, he explained what had happened with the hunters. He did so as neutrally as he could, ending with his acquisition of the bear's pelt and the mushroom flesh.

"The mushroom is useless for us," Nerthus said, shaking his head sadly. "An Alchemist may be able to make use of it, though. The pelt is a different case. May I see it?"

Elijah nodded, then reached into his pack. The pelt was all the way at the bottom, so it took him a couple of minutes to remove everything. When he finally retrieved the item in question, he laid it out before Nerthus.

"It was a powerful creature," the tree spirit said. "What do you intend to do with it?"

"I was going to ask you about that. I almost just buried it," Elijah admitted. "Kind of a memorial—"

"You mustn't do that."

"What? I thought you'd support that sort of thing."

Nerthus shook his head. "The death of such a creature is a sad thing. However, nothing we can do will change that. There is no dishonor or shame in using its body or eating its flesh. Though if a weakling were to consume the meat from such a powerful beast, they would almost assuredly be negatively affected. Perhaps they would even perish due to the influx of potent ethera."

"That can happen?"

"It can."

Elijah shook his head. "So, if I'm not going to bury it, maybe I should . . . make a cloak out of it," he said.

"I see. If you choose that route, may I suggest that you leave it here for a few weeks?" Nerthus asked. "Then, once it is saturated in potent ethera, treat the hide as you did your staff. In that way, any item created from it will be much more powerful and tailored to your needs."

"Interesting," Elijah said. "Would that work with other items?"

Nerthus shook his head. "Only resources," he answered. "And then, only if those resources were once living."

Despite the restrictions, it still seemed like it could be a significant boon. However, like the creation of his Staff of Natural Harmony, preparing the hide would take time. It would also require materials that he didn't have. Fortunately, the hunters had done one thing right by already fleshing the hide, which meant that Elijah could get by with storing it in his tree house for now.

So, after only a little more conversation with Nerthus, Elijah made his way to his home, climbed the stairs, and unpacked. After that, he gratefully took a shower before, at last, heading to bed.

Yet, as tired as he was, he couldn't sleep. Instead, he just lay in bed and stared at the lightly glowing flowers as he contemplated the coming fight. A hundred ideas on how to deal with the orcs flitted through each facet of his Quartz Mind, but the fact was that he had too little information to create a proper strategy.

Hopefully, he would address that lack tomorrow when he headed back to Ironshore.

Eventually, the comfortable bed did its job, and he finally let himself relax. Once he did, he drifted off to sleep.

67

ERRANDS

The next morning, Elijah's eyes fluttered open, and for a moment, he forgot the weight of responsibility resting on his shoulders. In those brief few seconds, he raised one hand, letting the warm blanket of dense ethera envelop him as he let the first rays of the morning sun dance across his fingers.

But it couldn't last.

He knew he was on the clock in terms of preparation for the coming orc invasion, and as such, he didn't have time to lie abed. So, with some degree of frustration, he pushed himself out of bed and dressed for the day. He chose his least dirty outfit, which still wasn't precisely clean, and vowed to find some easy way to do laundry in Ironshore. Once that was done, he gathered his things before heading downstairs and to his Grove, where he enjoyed a breakfast of berries while walking through the garden and flaring Nature's Bounty.

It wasn't necessary. The bushes had already reached the point where they were self-sufficient, which meant that his efforts only had a limited effect on their growth. Yet it calmed him, bringing back memories of days he'd spent trying to coax the bushes and other plants to fruition. He took a few minutes to converse with Nerthus, as well, though he didn't broach any important subjects. Instead, he simply wanted to make the tree spirit feel better about their partnership because, during his travels, he'd come to the conclusion that he'd treated Nerthus more as a means to an end than an actual friend. He aimed to change that going forward.

Soon enough, when the sun had pushed fully above the horizon, Elijah gathered a bunch of berries in his pack, then bade Nerthus goodbye before heading to the beach where he'd stored his collection of rowboats. Despite his neglect, the small vessels still looked in good repair, so he pushed one into the surf and began the journey across the strait. As he did so, he sensed a couple of large fish—one that was much larger than the boat—swim by beneath him. Yet, none of them paid Elijah's passage any heed. They were too focused on their own lives, which presumably included hunting for prey large enough to sustain them.

Like that, Elijah covered the distance to Ironshore's dock, where he was greeted by more than a few hostile stares. The city itself hadn't changed all that much, save that it had developed a little more, with some of the buildings having grown, both in terms of size as well as architectural complexity. Indeed, it looked like a proper city now instead of something that would have been at home in the Wild West.

But while there were plenty of fearful glances still directed his way, there was plenty of anger there, as well. Fortunately, one of the dock Guards recognized him—after all, how could they mistake him for anyone else?—and asked him to remain at the dock while she fetched Ramik.

What followed was an awkward few minutes where Elijah tried not to notice all the aggressive glares. To him, it looked like the dockworkers as well as the few sailors present were only a few inches from tossing rotten produce at him and running him out of town.

Soon, Ramik arrived, though, and when the distinguished-looking goblin did, the people reluctantly went back to their business. "What's going on with them?" Elijah asked.

"They blame you," the goblin answered with a shake of his head. "If you hadn't killed the mercenaries . . ."

"What was I supposed to do? Just let them kill me?" he asked.

The question was a little misleading. For all he knew, Cabbot hadn't come to the island with murder on his mind. The presence of his private army seemed to counter that presumption, but Elijah had every reason to suspect that if he'd simply run away, Cabbot would have let him. Still, there was no way he would have let the greedy gnome destroy his Grove and use it for his own progression. So, the point was moot.

"No. Of course not. But the public, they don't know all the facts," Ramik stated. "Even though we've spread the story, some disbelieve. Others give credence to rumors. The point is that the people are woefully misinformed, as well as frightened. They want to blame someone, and you are the easiest target."

That made sense to Elijah, at least. Everything he'd been through, both before and after Earth experienced the touch of the World Tree, suggested that people were rarely great judges of where to place blame. Especially when there was someone as different as Elijah around.

"Is it going to be a problem?"

"No," Ramik said firmly. "We have enough Guards to keep order."

"Alright. I have a few errands I want to run," he said. "Then, I want to check out the horde myself. Once we do that, maybe we can develop a strategy."

"Oh. I thought . . ."

"That I'd just snap my fingers and make the problem disappear?" asked Elijah.

"No. Of course not. I . . . No. You are right. Expecting you to deal with them alone was wrong," he said. "I apologize. We will do our part."

The conversation went on for a few more moments, but nothing of import was said. So, it wasn't long before Elijah found himself heading into the city. Notably, there were a couple of Guards trailing him. He didn't mind, though, because as he headed to his first destination, he became convinced that, without the Guards, he would have been attacked. Or at least confronted. He had no desire to deal with that, so he was grateful for the Guards' dissuading presence.

In any case, he quickly found his way to Mari's tailoring shop. When he entered, the matronly dwarf looked up from where she was arranging some of her wares, gave him a short look, and said, "Still haven't gotten any shoes, have you? Barbaric."

Elijah shrugged. "I thought about buying some in another town, but it just felt weird," he admitted. "I don't think I'm meant for footwear."

"If you say so. What do you want? Perhaps some cleaning powder for your clothing? All the gods know you need it," she stated.

"Uh . . . Is that just soap? Because I have plenty of that, and—"

"No. It's an alchemical solution. Sprinkle some on your clothes and it'll clean them," she stated. "Not as good as a proper self-cleaning enchantment, but better than doing it the old-fashioned way. I suggest you go visit that crazy old coot of an Alchemist if you're really interested in buying some. I have a few pouches in the back, but my prices won't be kind."

"Oh. Okay. But no. I was coming here to ask if you know anything about tanning hides," he said. "I've done it without ethera before, but I'm wondering if there's something else I should be doing."

She shrugged. "Tanning solution is something Biggle can provide," she said.

"I was more thinking of using natural methods."

"Ah. Then you're going to want some brains," she said. "Preferably of a sentient creature. More ethera, you see."

Elijah was well aware of the brain-tanning method, and on top of that, he knew he was about to have to kill a lot of orcs, all of which satisfied the sentience requirement. It was a gruesome thought, especially considering that orcs so closely resembled people. Yet, Elijah couldn't allow himself to fall into the trap of looking at them like that. Instead, he intended to treat them much the same way he'd treated the ogres and dark elves in his most recent tower run.

Which was to say that he was going to try to see them as enemies rather than people. It had worked for armies going back throughout all of human history, so Elijah hoped it would work for him, as well. Otherwise, there was every chance he was going to add quite a lot of trauma to his already-significant psychological burden during the coming conflict.

"Is there anything else I should know?" he asked.

"What do you plan to do with this hide you're curing? I assume it's special, or you wouldn't bother."

He shrugged. "A cloak, maybe. I don't know," he admitted. "Maybe some bearskin pants or something."

"No—a cloak is good," Mari said, tapping her finger against her chin. "Yes, lots of possibilities there. I could even tailor it to your specific needs, provided we have the proper materials. Those wouldn't be difficult for someone like you to acquire, I'm certain."

"You want to make a cloak for me?" he asked.

"Of course. I could even tan it, if you like."

"No. I need to do that myself," Elijah stated. "But no offense, why would you do that? I got the feeling that you didn't much care for me."

"Don't be silly. You're to be our great protector, are you not? What sort of citizen would I be if I didn't offer my services. Not for free, of course. Obviously. But I will make you a great deal," she said. "Is there anything else you need? Some new clothes, perhaps?"

Elijah shrugged. "Unless you have something better than what I'm wearing, probably not," he responded. "But thank you. I'll probably take you up on your offer. Probably not until after . . . you know . . . what's coming."

"Of course, of course. I'm sure you'll be victorious."

Elijah definitely didn't like the dwarven woman's sudden change of tone. When he'd visited before, her attitude was best described as terse. Still, she had a Tailor class, which meant that she could probably do things with that bear hide that he could only dream of. He could stitch things together, but that was the extent of his talent in sewing. So, he already knew he would take advantage of Mari's offer.

After only a little more conversation, he exited Mari's shop, promising to return with the hide when he'd finished preparing it. His next stop was on the other side of town, so he, along with his Guards, quickly set off. Along the way, Elijah couldn't ignore how unpopular he was. It also didn't help that he stuck out like a sore thumb, considering he was the only human in town.

Fortunately, he reached his destination only fifteen minutes later, though it was not what he'd expected.

Set at least a hundred yards away from the next closest building, the Alchemist's shop—or was it a home, perhaps?—sat atop a low hill. A winding path led to a small fence, on the other side of which was an overgrown garden teeming with ethera. Elijah marched up the winding path, and when he reached the low gate that he could have stepped over if he so desired, he called out, "Biggle? Can I come in?"

There was a small, muffled explosion, followed by a shouted expletive, after which a squeaky voice spat, "Drat! I almost had it!"

Then, Elijah heard the sound of clinking glassware and the thud of something extremely heavy before the door to the little cottage banged open, revealing a tiny gnome. He was maybe two feet tall and built like a toddler, yet he had a great, white beard, thick eyebrows that looked like pale caterpillars, and a bulbous nose. There wasn't a bit of hair on his head, and the tips of his mustache smoldered as if they'd just been on fire.

He stomped out, demanding, "What do you want? I swear by all the gods that—"

That's when he caught sight of Elijah. Recognition dawned, and the gnome went pale. "W-what . . . What are you . . . Please don't kill me! I got nothing against nature! All my ingredients are sourced from cruelty-free—"

"I need your help," Elijah said. "I don't care about any of that. I just need some cleaning powder. I also have something that might interest you."

"What? You're a Druid, aren't you?"

"How did you know that?"

"It's obvious to anybody who's paying attention," Biggle answered. "Are you really not here to avenge the death of your floral friends?"

Elijah rolled his eyes. "I'm not. I just told you why I'm here."

Biggle narrowed his twinkling blue eyes. "Hmm. A reasonable Druid. Never thought I'd see the day. But it's a new world and a new attitude, I say," he said. "Well, come on in. Don't mind the tentacula. It's just playful."

Elijah looked back at his Guards, both of which took a step back and shook their heads. "We'll stay out here," the female dwarf said. "Right, Marv?"

"Policy," he grunted.

Elijah nodded, saying, "Sure. Policy. I understand."

Then, he opened the gate and marched through. As he did, he focused on One with Nature and discovered that most of the plants were mobile. He suspected that they were carnivorous, as well, judging by the unique smell of predation. Still, none of them attacked him, which he counted as a lucky break. It unnerved Biggle, too, who said, "Wish they'd stop biting me like that . . ."

In any case, Elijah quickly followed the gnome inside the cottage, which was absolutely strewn with what looked like chemistry equipment and cooking supplies. There were pots and pans, cauldrons, beakers, vials, and what looked like Bunsen burners. In addition, bundles of herbs hung from the beams on the ceiling, and there were huge barrels lining the walls. On the shelves were all sorts of jars bearing labels like "newt eyes" and "giant's toes."

And it smelled like a wet foot.

"Sorry about the mess. And the smell. I've been doing some experiments, hoping to make a breakthrough, and they have not been going well," the little gnome said. "You know how it is. One drop of basilisk saliva too many, and the whole thing goes up in smoke."

As he spoke, he climbed atop a stool so he could more or less look Elijah in the eye, and he asked, "So—what can I do for you? You wanted cleaning powder, yeah? Can't blame you on that one. No offense, but you smell worse than a three-day-old bobtik."

"Uh . . ."

"Right. You wouldn't know what that is, would you? A bobtik is a swamp monster with a curious life cycle where it starts to decay almost as soon as it hatches," Biggle explained. "By the third day, they have the most pungent aroma. But that's when you have to harvest them, or you'll miss peak efficiency. So—you also said you had something for me? I'm not interested in any more kelp. I have plenty."

It took Elijah a moment to catch up, but when he did, he unshouldered his pack and said, "I have this mushroom. Well, most of it, at least. It's contained in a specially made satchel right now."

"Hmm . . . I'm always interested in mushrooms. Was quite a mycologist back in the day, you know? World-renowned, some might say. Not this world, though. Another world. You wouldn't know it."

Ignoring the gnome's babbling, Elijah reached into his pack and retrieved the sack containing the mushroom flesh. He set it before the Alchemist, saying, "That satchel is keeping its aura contained. Otherwise, it would've probably killed a few people on the way here."

Biggle's eyebrows twitched. "And where did you get this sack?" he asked innocently.

"I killed the four hunters who had harvested the mushroom," Elijah answered honestly. "I don't know where they got it."

"Oh."

"Yeah."

"Right. So, let's see what you've got here," the Alchemist said. Then, he unbuckled the strap and flipped the top open. Immediately, the entire room was bathed in dense ethera. It wasn't quite as strong as it had been when the mushroom was still whole, but it was still enough to elicit a slight feeling of nausea. After using that same ethera to fuel his cultivation, Elijah was used to it, though. However, he did notice that with every passing instant, it felt noticeably weaker.

Biggle slammed the bag shut.

"Is that something you can use?" Elijah asked, already knowing the answer to that question.

"Of course it is. That's a high-Simple-grade natural treasure," Biggle stated. "There's nothing else like that in the surrounding area. And if there is, it won't last through the orcs' invasion."

"So, it's valuable."

"Extremely. With this, I could create a powerful Body-cultivation potion. It might even be enough to push someone to the halfway mark."

"Of the first stage?"

"Yes. Of course."

"Alright. This is the deal. If you want to take it, great. If not, I'll go elsewhere. You give me half of what you make from it, and the mushroom's yours," Elijah said.

"Half? I wouldn't make any profit! Best I could do is a quarter."

After that, the haggling commenced, and it didn't end until they'd settled on a third of what Biggle created from the mushroom, plus a ten-pound sack of cleaning powder. Elijah thought he got the better of the deal, but then again, it seemed that Biggle thought the same thing. So, who was to say who won the negotiation?

In the end, though, Elijah was satisfied, and that was all that really mattered. After Biggle told him that the potion would be ready in a few weeks, Elijah departed and, along with his Guards, headed to the center of the city. There, they led him to an administrative building, inside of which he met a surly looking dwarf with spiky auburn hair and a short beard.

"Name's Kurik," the dwarf said, holding out a hand. "Can't say as I blame ya for killin' Cabbot. He was a right cunt."

"Oh," Elijah said, taking Kurik's rough hand in his own. "Yeah. I guess he was."

After that, Ramik explained that Kurik was the highest-level combatant in the entire town. He was apparently some sort of Ranger variant, which meant he was more of a scout than a fighter. However, now that Elijah had killed their entire security force, Kurik had been forced into the latter role.

"I got thirty good Scouts under me," Kurik stated. "Another ten that ain't worth spit, but they're still better than nothin'."

"And of the fifteen hundred residents of Ironshore, two-thirds are combat capable," Ramik explained. "Some to a lesser degree than others."

Elijah remembered the barbers he'd met during his second visit to Ironshore and nodded. He didn't think they'd contribute much to a fight. "Will they still fight?"

"All but the little ones," Ramik answered. "The more mature among the children will be used as runners, both for messages as well as supplies. However, there are a few who are not old enough to do even that. We intend to house them here until the fighting is done."

Or until everyone was overrun by orcs.

"Alright," Elijah said. He didn't know much about war, so he was prepared to bow to their judgment. "I guess I need to see these orcs with my own two eyes."

"Right. I'll lead you," Kurik said.

And not long after that, the pair were traveling through the wilderness. As they went, Elijah refrained from using his draconid form. He was certain that Kurik and his squad of Scouts knew about his ability to shape-shift, but he didn't want to give away any of his secrets, just in case they were leading him into an ambush.

As it turned out, two days later, he discovered that the residents of Ironshore had been entirely truthful as to the nature of the threat. He stood on a hill, crouching low at the tree line, and looking out at a camp containing thousands of orcs.

"God. This is going to get really ugly, isn't it?" he muttered, using Eyes of the Eagle to get a good look at the creatures.

Beside him, Kurik said, "Damn right it is. Damn right."

68

ESCALATION

Horns blew, and flags rippled in the wind of some officiant's spell. The richest and most influential people in Easton stood nearby, drinking and dancing, completely unaware that the world—indeed, the universe—was passing them by. They all thought that the danger had passed, that they were safe. They believed that, after having survived the past few years, they could simply go back to old customs, as if the world would soon return to normal.

But as Roman stared down at the Seal of Authority, he knew it was all a misguided fantasy.

There was no such thing as normal. One could never stop striving. The days of humanity standing on the shoulders of past generations were long gone, and now, people needed to forge their own path through an unfamiliar and expansive universe. That was what drove him. That was the reason he couldn't relax. Theirs was a dangerous and deadly world filled with all the worst sorts of monsters. And he was the only one standing between his people and total annihilation.

More than anything, he wished that Alyssa could have seen that. But she'd insisted on questioning his authority, on pushing against his every decision. She had championed the weak and protected the insubordinate, and all the while, monsters were knocking at the door. It was madness that she couldn't see the danger she represented. She would have turned on him, Roman was certain of it, and when she did, she would have had enough support to get everyone in Easton killed.

Her death had been necessary.

Regrettable, certainly. It had been the hardest thing he'd ever had to do. Even after the betrayal that was her inability to prevent Trish's death, he still cared deeply about Alyssa. She had been his only true friend. But that was a sacrifice he was willing to make. As a selfless leader, that was the burden he was forced to bear.

All of that and more washed through Roman's mind as he watched his people celebrate an accomplishment that was not theirs.

The wall had finally been completed, and as such, the city within was safe from the formation of minor rifts or spontaneous manifestations of Voxx. It was a tremendous feat of engineering, enchanting, and architecture. Yet, it could do nothing about the virus that had already begun to take root within his city.

"Congratulations, boss," came a grating voice Roman did not want to hear. "The sheep are safe, but what now?"

Roman didn't turn. "What do you want, Trace?" he asked, slipping the Seal of Authority into his vest pocket.

"Maybe I just wanted to make small talk with the big man in charge," the Outlaw said, stepping forward until he stood shoulder to shoulder with his superior. Out of the corner of his eye, Roman saw Trace's garish attire. The man flouted the notion of a uniform, making alterations that made him stand out. It was still the same blue-and-white outfit, with black boots and a badge of authority on the chest. However, the cut was anything but normal, with a long blue coat with a dragon stitched on the back. If it was anyone else, Roman would have had him whipped.

Or killed.

Yet Trace was valuable, and they both knew it. So, he got away with things no other person could. For now. Soon, there would come a point when the man went too far.

"In that case, leave," Roman stated. "I'm not in the mood for your foolishness."

"You really take all this seriously, don't you? If you say that's how you've always talked, I'll call you a liar."

"Normally, people who say such things end up dead," Roman said, refusing to rise to the Outlaw's bait. He had changed his speech patterns, but that was a necessity. His people deserved more than the small-town sheriff he'd been. They needed dignity. Respectability. They needed a king.

"Ain't that the truth."

"What do you want, Trace?"

A surge of ethera announced the activation of some sort of ability, but Roman wasn't afraid. The Seal of Authority gave him plenty of leeway so he didn't have to react to every ripple in the ambient ethera. Still, he cut his eyes at Trace.

"Don't get all antsy," the man said. "I know better than to mess with you here. It's just an ability meant to prevent eavesdropping."

"That's new."

"Is it? Maybe I've just kept it in reserve all this time."

That was the problem with Trace. He was an incredibly useful man to have around, ruthless and efficient in what he chose to do. However, he was untrustworthy as well as secretive, meaning that he was unpredictable.

Roman hid his irritation by adopting an at-rest stance, with his hands behind his back. His eyes never wavered from the affluent people who'd attended the party he'd never wanted to host. But Fiona had insisted, saying that it was a display of power as well as a way to keep the idiots happy. He acknowledged that she had a much better head for such things, so he'd chosen to trust her judgment. Still, he could barely hide his irritation.

"Speak your mind."

"You are absolutely no fun. You know that, right? Fine. I've traced the traitors to a tavern in the southern district," Trace stated. "Mostly the usual suspects. You know the ones."

Indeed, even with Alyssa dead, he'd had to deal with no shortage of naysayers and dissidents. Even as they sheltered beneath his wing, they complained about the manner in which he provided for their safety. It was maddening. He'd given them everything. By all rights, their lives were his to do with as he pleased. Yet, treason had bloomed, vivid and poisonous.

The only solace was that they were easy to keep track of. Roman already knew who the leaders were, even if he was unaware of the methods they intended to use. That was where Trace came in.

"That is not news," he said.

"No," Trace said, running his hand through his hair. "No, it's not. But the people they're meeting with—that might interest you quite a bit."

"Who?"

"Who do you think? Who has more reason to hate you than anyone else?" Trace asked.

"Carmen."

"Bingo," Trace said.

"Does she know?"

"Does it matter?" the Outlaw asked. "She was always a loose end. We should've clipped that thread a long time ago."

Roman finally turned away. He knew he should have killed Carmen the moment he came back from that tower. Yet, his soft heart had stayed his hand. It wasn't that he cared so much about the woman herself. He'd never particularly liked her in the first place. But he refused to orphan her child.

Not unless he was forced to do so.

"What happened afterward?" Roman asked.

"She left," Trace answered. "Headed out of the city, presumably back to Silverado."

"Interesting. Did you have her followed?" Roman asked.

"Of course. Two of my best girls," he said.

Roman ground his teeth. Trace's depravities regarding his female underlings were well-known, and they were a visible stain on the reputation of the government. And as the ultimate authority within Easton, the man's reputation was a blight on Roman's, as well. Yet, he was too useful to hold accountable.

For now.

Eventually, Trace would outlive his usefulness. At that point, Roman would make him pay for every crime he'd committed. And he would enjoy it.

"I want you to go to Silverado and keep an eye on what she's up to," Roman ordered.

"Want me to just kill her? Because I'm assuming you don't want me to just waltz into that little mining camp and announce I'm there on a mission of espionage."

"You will remain unseen."

"So, is that a no on the killing? Because if we're just going to put her down, I wouldn't mind trying my hand with her. She's a bit thick for my tastes. Too many muscles. But like I always say, I'll try anything once."

Roman's hand shot out, faster than most people could even track, and his fingers clamped around Trace's throat. The Outlaw tried to activate an ability, but Roman used one of the functions of the Seal of Authority, ending it immediately. He hated using the cooldown for something so mundane, but making a point was important. Besides, it would cycle in a week.

He lifted Trace from the ground, and as the other man's feet dangled a few inches from the polished tile floor, Roman growled, "You will not touch her. If you harm her without my say-so, I will make you wish for death. You know what I can do."

With that, he released the Outlaw, who fell to the floor in a gasping heap.

For his part, Roman returned to his previous stance, looking for all the world as if he'd never even moved.

"Jesus fucking Christ, man," Trace croaked, massaging his throat. "I was just joking. You didn't have to go all evil emperor on me."

"I am not evil. I am necessary."

"Sure," Trace muttered. "I believe you. But do they?"

Roman had already seen precisely what Trace was referring to. A few of the guests had noticed his outburst, but the moment they realized that he was staring back at them, they hastily returned to their little bubble of affluent ignorance.

"They do not care," he stated.

Trace picked himself up off the floor, then dusted himself off as he said, "Because they're terrified."

"So long as they are obedient, it doesn't matter to me."

Indeed, Roman had long since moved past the need to be loved by his people. Most of them would never see the things he did to ensure their lives continued. They were blissfully unaware of the sacrifices he'd endured, the difficult decisions he'd been forced to make. For someone like him, love had never been on the table.

Fear, though—that was attainable. Natural, even. And most importantly, fear kept people in line. He'd learned that in his previous career, and it was a lesson that was still applicable in his current endeavor.

"Damn, man. They're well trained," remarked Trace with a shake of his head.

"Do you understand my instructions?"

"Yeah. I got it. But for the record, you could've just told me to leave her be. You didn't have to do what you did."

"Yes, I did. You may go. Now."

For a moment, Trace looked as if he was going to argue, but then thought better of it. Assuredly, the previous lesson was on his mind. In any case, the man turned on his heel and marched out of the ballroom.

When he did, Roman went back to his stoic attendance of the celebratory party. Soon enough, he found the Seal of Authority back in his hand. On the surface, the pendant was nothing special. Just a few extra attribute points. However, when he'd bound it, he'd discovered two separate abilities. One he'd used on Trace, locking down the Outlaw's abilities. It only lasted for a few seconds, but with that much time, Roman could do all sorts of damage.

But the other ability it granted was far more important, as anyone who tried to attack him in his city would quickly discover.

The thought had just crossed his mind when he saw Fiona approaching. She was dressed in an emerald dress that clung to her waifish body, accentuating what few curves she possessed. More than once, she'd made it clear that she was interested in more than a professional relationship with Roman, but he'd never even considered taking advantage of her in such a way.

He was better than that.

She asked, "What did the weasel want?"

"He wished to congratulate me on the completion of the wall," Roman lied easily.

"Huh. Unexpected, but I suppose it shouldn't be. It's a great accomplishment," she said. "And just in time, too. That roaming war band is getting closer. Did you give any thought to their demands?"

"I won't pay a ransom for my city's protection. If they attack, we will defeat them," Roman stated unequivocally. Indeed, the war band's leader, a man who called himself Laramie, had recently sent an emissary demanding that Easton pay a tithe. He referred to it as a protection fee, but the implication was clear. Pay willingly or it would be taken. Roman hadn't even needed to consider it in order to refuse, which he did by virtue of beheading the emissary and launching his body over the wall.

"The wall will protect us," Fiona said, taking a sip.

"It will," he said. And if it didn't, they had plenty of fighters. If they failed, then Roman would have to use the seal's second ability. Either way, anyone who attacked Easton would quickly discover the error of their ways.

69

HARASSMENT

The night hung heavy in the air as Kurik crouched atop a thick branch, looking down at the game trail. For the past day, he and his squad had steadily engaged in a campaign of guerrilla warfare against the orcs. They had killed dozens, and yet, their efforts paled in comparison to their ally's.

At one point, Kurik had doubted that a single person could make enough difference to turn the tides of the coming conflict. No longer did he harbor such doubt because he'd gotten a small peek at what the man was capable of, and he'd come away both impressed and horrified. Kurik pushed those thoughts aside. He couldn't afford to be distracted because he heard his prey finally coming into range.

He'd been stalking the orc for the last hour, and he'd finally managed to bait the hulking creature into following him. Now, he only had to wait as the monster crept down the trail. It made an attempt at concealment, and it was clearly capable of moving through the thick terrain with some degree of stealth. However, to Kurik's keen eyes, it was entirely exposed.

Just when it passed beneath him, Kurik leaped from his position on the branch. His axe flashed with his Eagle's Talon ability, which augmented his melee damage by forty percent for a single strike. The caveat was that he could only use it while striking from above. It was a very limited ability, but under the right circumstances, it was devastating, as well.

Never was that clearer than when his axe cleaved through the orc's shoulder, cutting diagonally across its torso and digging deep into its chest. It would have gone farther if it wasn't for the thing's dense bones and high Constitution. In any case, Kurik's momentum bore the monster to the ground, and he ended up on top of the bulky and bleeding monster.

Orcs were notoriously hard to kill, and even the devastating attack he'd just delivered wasn't enough to finish it off. So, he reared back, intending to deliver a killing blow.

But before he could, he heard a twig snap behind him. Knowing what that signified, he dove forward in a roll that narrowly let him avoid a descending club. He came up running, recognizing that he'd already lost the fight. A pair of orcs crashed through the underbrush behind him, both bellowing in rage as they left their fellow behind.

Hopefully, it would bleed to death, but Kurik had fought enough orcs by that point to know how unlikely that was. If they weren't killed outright, they would recover. Not to full strength—they weren't trolls, after all—but enough that they could keep on fighting. Still, as much as he regretted the necessity of leaving the kill unfinished, Kurik knew his own abilities well enough to recognize that he couldn't stand up to a single orc in straight combat, much less two.

So, he ran.

As he did so, he went over his options. He had a couple of traps nearby, and both had been enhanced with his ability. Yet, he didn't want to use them unless absolutely necessary. The fact was that each time he used the ability, it took a significant amount of ethera, so he'd begun to ration his abilities. As a result, he was forced to rely on other tactics, which had further exposed what he already knew.

He was no Warrior.

Sure, he was a decent enough Scout, and he could function as a fair archer while holding his own in hand-to-hand combat. But against creatures like orcs, he was woefully outmatched. It was a reminder of his place in the world.

Perhaps one day he could rise above that position, but that day had yet to come.

He could run, though, and with his Fleet-Footed enhancement, he could move incredibly quickly through rough terrain. The only person he'd ever found who could rival him was his newest ally, which, as far as he was concerned, didn't really count. The human was clearly an outlier, so comparing himself to Elijah wasn't a fair exercise.

Just when Kurik was on the verge of veering toward one of his traps, he heard a commotion behind him. Then, suddenly, there was only one orc following. Knowing what that meant, he kept running until, suddenly, the noise repeated. It was followed by silence.

"You're clear," came a quiet voice.

Kurik slowed to a stop, then turned around to see Elijah standing over a fallen orc. The creature had had its entire torso ripped open, and its head flopped to the side, its neck nearly severed.

"I was fine," Kurik insisted.

"I know. Just helping where I can," the man said. He made for a curious sight, with his odd collection of equipment and curios. Kurik knew enough to recognize that many of them were magical in nature, though he couldn't even begin to guess their purpose. However, he was well aware that anyone with that many magical items was either rich or dangerous.

Elijah was probably both, at least in relation to the rest of Earth.

"Did it work?" Kurik asked.

Elijah stepped forward into the light and shrugged. "Sort of, I guess," he said. "I got a few of them, but not as many as I would have liked."

"What happened?"

"They have a couple of spellcasters," Elijah stated. "Stopped my spells from doing too much damage. I wasn't expecting that."

"They're more advanced than we thought."

"It looks that way," said the man. He ran a hand through his curly blond hair. "You should go tell Ramik and the others. Take the rest of your squad, too. We're not going to win the fight like this."

"You think we need to come up with another strategy?"

"I do."

"What are you going to do?"

"I'll stay out here and slow them down."

"By yourself?"

"I'll be careful," Elijah said. "In the meantime, you need to make sure everyone's ready for what's coming because this isn't something we can stop before it gets to Ironshore. There's going to be a fight there, one way or another."

"I think that was always the case," Kurik admitted with a sigh. There was little chance of stopping the horde before it reached the budding settlement. Everyone had known that from the very beginning, but some had hoped that they could use Elijah's power to avoid that inevitable eventuality.

"You're not wrong," Elijah said. "You should go. I'm going to keep hunting."

Kurik nodded, and without another word, headed to the rendezvous point to reconnect with his people. As he did, he hoped that Elijah could work a miracle because he expected that that was what it was going to take if they were going to survive.

As soon as Kurik was gone, Elijah shifted back into his draconid form and went on the hunt. The past day had been exhausting in a way he hadn't experienced since the last tower, but in a lot of ways, it was much worse.

First of all, the orcs were far more attentive than the ogres had ever been, and if Elijah wasn't extremely careful about how he moved among them, they would detect his presence. Fortunately, he'd gotten plenty of practice doing just that, so for the most part, he was fine. Yet, he'd still gotten into trouble a couple of times, and he'd barely made it out of those instances alive.

Second, while the orcs were disturbingly humanoid in appearance—aside from their tusks, immense size, and gray skin—they were just as obviously monsters. They had some semblance of a society, but it was a hollow thing, as if they were merely imitating something they had seen.

Or, as Kurik had suggested, acting upon instincts they didn't understand.

As a result, they seemed sapient at first glance, but they weren't. However, even that hint was enough to make killing them a difficult thing. Elijah had pushed the resultant guilt aside, but it was much harder to do so than he'd expected.

Not that it was going to stop him from doing what was necessary, but it definitely didn't help his mindset.

And finally, there was the issue of their advancement. He'd grown used to being able to use Swarm and Calamity whenever he wanted, and the first time he'd done so against the orcs had gone off without a hitch. He'd killed a couple dozen of them, even gaining a level in the process. Yet, when he'd tried to do so a second time, one of the orcs had risen up and cast something to reduce the effect of the spells.

Another had cast some sort of red globe of liquid in his direction. He'd avoided it, but the fact that it had found him so quickly did not bode well for his chances of using his spells in the future.

Which had been his primary strategy, so since then, Elijah had been forced to rethink things. He'd also sent Kurik and his Scouts back to Ironshore to help with the preparations.

Though he didn't see how they could win.

In the meantime, though, Elijah intended to keep fighting as best he could, and if the battle was hopeless, perhaps he could level enough to gain a new spell or ability that would make the difference they needed to survive.

That made Elijah's goals clear.

So, without any further ado, he set off through the underbrush, passing beneath the trees as he headed toward the location where he'd last seen the orcs.

Soon enough, he found their camp. It was still dark, so they had yet to begin their march, but Elijah had already witnessed their routine, so he knew what to expect. Still, he watched from the shadows, waiting for an opportunity. As he did, he studied the camp. There were hundreds of tents, dozens of fires, and thousands of gray-skinned orcs. How the tribe had expanded so rapidly Elijah had no idea.

Perhaps he'd only seen a small portion back at that abandoned Walmart.

Or maybe they reproduced that quickly.

Whatever the case, there were far more than Elijah could handle alone. In truth, even if he hadn't killed Ironshore's security force, the chances of repelling the invasion seemed incredibly slim—unless they could figure out some way to even the odds. Being on the defense would help. So would the fact that the orcs were barely thinking monsters.

But that wasn't going to be enough.

A few minutes after Elijah had begun his vigil, a trio of orcs broke away from the camp and tromped off into the woods. It was only then that Elijah realized something that had eluded him until that very moment.

Orcs had to eat.

That was an unavoidable fact of life. He'd seen them hunting, cooking, and eating by their fires. Yet, he'd not recognized the opportunity that held. Still, before he established a plan, he wanted to confirm his suspicions. So, he followed the trio into the woods, and sure enough, twenty minutes later, he saw them take down a wild hog the size of a hippopotamus. The three orcs expertly dressed the animal, then hauled the meat back to the camp before setting off for another hunting expedition.

That's when Elijah struck, hitting the first one with an attack that utilized Predator Strike. He ripped through the creature with little difficulty, then bounded away into the underbrush. As soon as he was out of sight of the orcs, he skittered up a tree. By that point, the remaining two hunters were alert, but because they never bothered to look up, they had no idea where he was. Elijah dropped out of combat a few moments later, then adopted Guise of the Unseen before repeating the process.

Two more attacks, and the trio of hunters were dead. But that had never been the point. He'd only killed them because it was a good opportunity to thin the horde. With the numbers arrayed against Elijah and Ironshore, he couldn't afford to let such a chance go to waste. However, he didn't linger after finishing them off. Instead, he took off across the landscape with as much speed as he could muster, and soon enough, he found Kurik and his squad of Scouts.

Before he approached, he shifted back into his human form and called out, "It's me. Don't attack."

Then, he stepped out of the trees.

Kurik said, "Thought you were stayin' out here to hunt."

"I was. I did," Elijah said excitedly. "But I figured something out."

"Yeah? What's that?"

Elijah told him, then elaborated on his plan.

"You think we can do that? There are only ten of us here," Kurik said. "Twenty more back in Ironshore."

"You're Scouts and Hunters, right? This is what you do," Elijah stated. "I think this is our best option."

Kurik shrugged. "Better than any idea I got. Best we get to it, then."

70

HUNTERS HUNTING

Wearing Shape of the Predator like a cloak, Elijah crept forward, his body low to the ground as he stalked the stag. It was an enormous deer, at least the size of a full-grown moose, which meant that it was a perfect target for his plan. However, the creature was powerful—he'd known that from the moment he set eyes on it—so he needed to take care in his approach. One wrong move, and he would end up with a set of sharp antlers in his chest.

It had already happened once during an earlier hunt, and he didn't want to repeat that experience. He would survive, at least long enough to heal himself, but that would cost him hours of hunting. And considering the overall goal, that just wasn't an acceptable price to pay. So, over the past two days, he had learned caution, and in a way he'd rarely employed during his previous exploits.

In those instances, he'd always known that, even if he did make a mistake and was injured, he could just heal himself. And while that was still true, the time factor meant that any delay could prove a failure that could, in turn, doom the entirety of Ironshore. Elijah couldn't stomach that, so he'd pushed himself to heights of stealthy hunting he'd not thought possible.

But it was too slow.

Soon, he knew the time to institute his plan would pass, and they would have to implement the next phase. Still, the more animals he and the other hunters killed, the less food there would be for the orcs. It didn't really fall in line with his protector-of-nature image, but he'd pushed that sort of thing aside in favor of survival. So, the goal was to cut down the animal population to the extent that the orcs would no longer have enough to sustain themselves. Sure, it wouldn't kill them. Elijah was certain of that. But it would weaken them, at least to some degree, and he hoped that would prove the difference in the inevitable battle to come.

With that in mind, he silently slipped through the underbrush. Cloaked in Guise of the Unseen, he should have been undetectable for the stag. Yet, when he came within a few feet, the thing skittishly pranced away. However, by that point, Elijah was already close enough to pounce.

He leaped high into the air, landing on the beast's broad back. Digging his claws into its hide for balance, he struck like a crocodile, latching his powerful jaws on the stag's neck. He squeezed, ripping through the animal's flesh and feeling its bones crack beneath his mighty bite. It went limp, having never gotten the chance to resist, and it fell to the ground in a heap. Elijah sprang away, shifting back into his human form before his feet hit the ground.

It was at that moment that the orc struck.

Elijah had no idea the monster was even there, which meant that it had been using the stealth ability some of their hunters and scouts possessed. Still, it never should have happened. He'd been too focused on the task at hand.

Or too exhausted, after three days of constant hunting.

Whatever the case, Elijah never had the opportunity to dodge the creature's thrusting spear. Its flint tip bit deep into his side before ripping a gaping wound in his flesh. He staggered away, but the orc followed close on his heels. Elijah whipped around, spraying the ground with blood as he smashed his staff against the pursuing orc's tusked face.

Under the weight of the blow, the monster stumbled, and Elijah followed that attack up by sweeping his staff toward the orc's ankles. It tripped, tumbling to the ground. Before it had the chance to react, Elijah cast Snaring Roots, and thick, thorny vines snaked up from the ground to wrap around the monster's flailing extremities.

With a couple of moments to spare, he cast Healing Rain before shifting into his lamellar-ape form. The second the spell completed, he transformed, his arms lengthening and scales sprouting across his increasingly muscular body. Finally, he loped forward, raising his clenched fists high into the sky before bringing them down with thunderous force. That brought a whimper of pain from the monster, but it was far from defeated. So, Elijah continued pummeling the creature until he felt bones break beneath his momentous blows. Finally, the thing went quiet and ceased drawing breath.

Elijah didn't stop there, though. Instead, he reached down, grabbed the orc's head in his giant claws, and twisted. Its neck broke, but in his fury, Elijah didn't care. Instead, he wrenched it back and forth until the thick muscles in its neck tore. Once that happened, it only took a couple more twists before the thing's entire head ripped free.

He wanted to roar triumphantly, but even with the bestial fury raging through him, Elijah knew better than to invite further orcish attention. So, he settled for tossing the head aside and beating his chest in victory. However, he only indulged his inner beast for a few moments before the urgency of the situation caught up to him. Usually, where there was one orc, there would be more soon to follow.

So, he shifted back to his human form and examined his injury. Because the flint blade of the orc's spear hadn't been particularly sharp, the wound was jagged and anything but surgical. Still, it hadn't hit anything vital—aside from nicking his intestine, which had already mended from Healing Rain—so he only took the time to pulse Touch of Nature a couple of times before turning his attention to the stag he'd killed.

He unslung the pack on his back, then opened it. The satchel was a special loan from the hunters, and it was one of the reasons they'd been able to implement his plan so flawlessly. Like his normal pack, it was much larger than it appeared from the outside, and it could accommodate the meat from four deer the size of the one he'd just killed. It would also keep that meat fresh. However, it could only be used for that very specific purpose. If he were to put anything but fresh meat inside, it would quickly break down. So, it was incredibly useful for a very specific purpose, but absolutely useless for anything that exceeded that function.

In any case, the pack was nearly full, which meant that as soon as he processed his kill, Elijah would need to return to the forward camp and exchange it for an empty one. After that, he would return to the forest and continue his hunting efforts while someone else took the meat back to Ironshore. It had been going on for a few days by that point, so they had the process down to a science.

But before he could do that, Elijah needed to skin the animal and process the carcass. So, he set to it, using one of the knives he'd taken from the mercenaries who'd invaded his island what felt like a lifetime ago. Once, it might've taken him hours to accomplish the task, yet with so much practice and the indefatigable endurance of a man who was well past the human limits, he accomplished the task in about thirty minutes.

After that, he gathered the pack, which was incredibly heavy because of how much meat he'd stored away, shouldered the hide, and took off across the forest. Even in his human form, he was more than capable of moving quickly and quietly, and besides, he'd been spending quite a lot of time in his bestial forms. Doing that was dangerous, as he'd found in the jungles outside of the Primordial Maze.

About an hour later, he finally arrived at the forward camp, where he was confronted with a blue-haired gnome who was part of Kurik's squad. "Rasana," he acknowledged with a nod.

She grinned. "What do you have for me this time?" she asked, pushing her spectacles up her nose. They weren't for correcting her vision. Instead, they helped her see tracks more easily.

He shook his head, then said, "Just meat. Two deer, a hog, and a couple of giant turkeys."

The two turkeys were closer to dinosaurs than any bird he'd ever seen, and it had taken quite a bit of effort to take the pair of seven-foot-tall birds down. Still, they'd had quite a lot of meat on them, which he supposed would be helpful for the town. More importantly, killing the beasts would deny the orcs any sustenance.

"The pickin's are gettin' pretty slim out there," came Kurik's voice. Elijah turned to see the lead Scout approaching from the right. He carried a large satchel, as well, though he clearly struggled beneath its immense weight. That was the other detriment of the hunting sacks, as they were called. They could hold plenty, but they did nothing to alleviate the weight of whatever was put inside. As such, most of the Hunters and Scouts couldn't get the most out of them like Elijah could. "Think we might need to start pullin' back."

Elijah sighed. He'd seen much the same thing, but he knew they'd missed quite a lot of animals. There just wasn't enough time to truly hunt every denizen of the forest. Yet, they'd gotten the easy prey, which meant that the orcs would have to work that much harder to meet their consumptive needs. That was a small solace in an otherwise desperate situation.

As he and Kurik stepped into the camp, Elijah asked, "Phase two?"

"Probably the best chance we'll get. The others are still workin' on clearing the animals from here to Ironshore. We'll work backward from here, and by the time we get to the city, we'll be as ready as we're gonna get," Kurik answered.

"How should I contribute?" Elijah asked.

The plan was simple. Over the next few days, Kurik's Scouts would riddle the forest with traps. Some, like the dwarven leader himself, had abilities related to those traps. As a result, some of the orcs would die. Others would be injured. But no matter what, the traps would slow them down.

Kurik shook his head, saying, "Can you hit them with that big spell again?"

"No. Those shamans in there are too dangerous," he answered. "If I use Calamity or Swarm when they're paying attention, I'll have the whole horde after me in . . . Wait . . ."

"What?"

"I just had another idea."

"Well, we ain't got all day," Kurik responded. "Spit it out."

"Alright, so what if I do that and lead them back the other way?" Elijah said. "That could give you some extra time to lay traps. And the more we can delay them, the better prepared Ironshore will be, right?"

"Think you can do that without gettin' caught?"

Elijah shrugged. "I think so. Probably. I can move pretty quickly when I want to."

"Then do it," Kurik advised. "The more time we have, the better."

Elijah nodded, then said, "I need a few minutes of rest, though. Any food here?"

"Not much. We've been sendin' everything back home. 'Sides, we can't really have a fire out here. But here," he said, leading Elijah to a barrel. Inside were a bunch of wild edibles, including mushrooms and berries. "Should be enough to keep you goin'."

Elijah grabbed a handful, then sat on one of the nearby fallen logs. Kurik joined him as he ate. "This takes me back," he sighed. "Living in the woods, eating mushrooms. It's like I'm stuck right after the world changed."

"Surprised you survived all by your lonesome," Kurik remarked. Elijah had shared a little of his story with the dwarf, but he hadn't told him everything. "Most people wouldn't've."

"I wasn't alone. Not at first," Elijah said, referring to the panther. "Not completely, at least."

"I reckon it's always hard on the natives when the World Tree touches a new planet. Least there's not a lot of reason for the truly powerful to stick their noses into the situation," Kurik said. "Most of us are runnin' from somethin'. Lookin' for a new life, you know? If any of us had any choice, we wouldn't be here."

"Not sure how to take that," Elijah admitted.

"Don't take it no way. New worlds, they're hard. Dangerous. And most of us won't get the chance to see our families or friends again for years. Decades, if ever. Teleporting off-world is expensive."

"How expensive?"

"Platinums. Plural."

"Oh," Elijah said. So far, he'd only amassed seventeen gold etherium, and from what he remembered, it would take a million of those to equal a single platinum etherium coin. There were guides in the Branch's Knowledge Base that cost as much, but the vast majority were far cheaper. That had led him to believe that he was fairly well off. Now, he knew that wasn't the case.

"Even teleportation within the world's network is prohibitively expensive. Hundreds of gold for the closest locations, and a lot more for ones farther away," Kurik explained. "Not that it matters. The world's too new to have any connections right now. But it'll come. Just wait. In a couple of decades, it won't even be uncommon."

"Right," Elijah said. He'd seen the teleportation option at the various Branches he'd visited, but they'd all been grayed out, so he hadn't thought much more about it.

After a few more minutes, during which the pair went silent as they ate their meager meal, Elijah pushed himself to his feet and said, "I guess I need to get going if I'm going to get this thing done."

With that, he headed out, shifting into the draconid form as soon as he was out of sight. Without using Guise of the Unseen—or worrying about being detected—Elijah could move incredibly quickly across even the most difficult terrain, so it only took him a few hours to reach the orcish horde.

When he arrived, he took a few minutes to observe the enemy. They were on the move, though their progress less resembled an army on the march than a mass of individuals that happened to be going in the same direction. To Elijah, it reminded him of the crowds that came at the end of football games when a hundred thousand people all tried to leave the stadium at once.

There was nothing organized about it, though Elijah did give them a wide berth. At the same time, he used Guise of the Unseen, just to ensure that he remained undetected as he circled around to the back side. Once he reached that position, he shifted into his human form, knelt behind the thick brush, leveled his staff at the tail end of the horde, and used Swarm. Before the mass of insects even manifested, he was casting Calamity.

And the moment the spell left his staff, he shifted back into his draconid form and took off into the forest. A moment later, a blob of red energy splashed down on the spot he'd just vacated. Even from more than twenty feet away, Elijah could feel the sizzling power of the spell, which only reaffirmed his caution. If he hadn't already expected it, that manifestation of ethera would have hit him.

And he didn't want to know what it did.

As he raced through the forest, the tromp of hundreds of orcish feet followed. Elijah stayed ahead of them, but he was careful to let himself be seen more than once. And when he thought the pursuers were far enough away from the main horde, he turned and cast Swarm again.

This time, the red ball came even more quickly, which meant that he couldn't follow it up with Calamity. But that was fine. He wasn't trying to kill anything. Instead, he only wanted to further separate the group and, eventually, slow down the entire horde.

So, he kept going for miles more, narrowly staying ahead of his pursuers. Yet, after more than an hour, Elijah saw an opportunity when, at last, his conjured insects made it past whatever defenses the shaman had erected. He only realized it when he got an influx of experience that signaled a few deaths. More followed soon after, suggesting that, at last, he'd run the shaman out of ethera.

That meant the creature was vulnerable.

And Elijah aimed to take advantage of that. So, he raced ahead, quickly outpacing the subhorde, and the moment he felt Essence of the Wolf kick in, he used Guise of the Unseen. Once he'd rendered himself undetectable, Elijah doubled back, and when he saw the shape of the group of orcs who'd chased him around the forest, a reptilian grin spread across his draconid face.

The orcs who were still standing were clearly on their last legs. Most could barely manage a stumble, no doubt because of Swarm's afflictions, and Elijah suspected that, left alone, they would soon succumb. However, the shaman—identifiable by a large feathery cloak and a skull-topped staff—was busy trying to prevent that. Elijah had no idea what spells it was casting, but he could feel the swirl of ethera and see the effects. Each time the shaman cast a spell, one of the orcs straightened to its full height, reenergized and healed.

Elijah couldn't let that stand.

There were nearly twenty of them left, which was a testament to Elijah's efforts so far. But he didn't care about killing a few dozen regular orcs. He wanted to take out the shaman. So, the way was clear. He needed to continue to drain the creature's ethera by forcing it to continuously heal.

With that in mind, Elijah found another bush, where he crouched and leveled his staff before casting Calamity. Clouds gathered, and thunder rolled while the wind whipped into a frenzy. In seconds, it had reached the height of its fury, sending violent bolts of lightning crashing down and blades of wind slicing through the group of orcs. Meanwhile, the earth rumbled and shook, splitting open and throwing them off-balance. The shaman tried to counter by erecting a shield that looked like a giant red bubble, but it popped after only a second.

And Elijah recognized the sag of the creature's shoulders for what it meant. It was spent, and its charges paid the price. The Calamity tore through the already-damaged orcs, killing quite a few and injuring even more.

That's when Elijah struck from afar, aiming his staff at the shaman and letting loose with Storm's Fury. In all the commotion, none of the monsters even noticed the extra bolt of lightning that slammed into the shaman's chest, sending it flying backward into a tree. Elijah heard the impact even from almost a hundred feet away.

He cast Swarm, then conjured Healing Rain, positioning it above the orcs. Then, he shifted into the lamellar-ape form before rushing forward. He fell upon the monsters with all the furious Strength he could muster, slicing through flesh and breaking bones with wild abandon.

It felt good to finally let loose.

And with Shape of the Guardian active, he could truly appreciate the melee for what it represented. The orcs tried to resist, but after the deluge of damage he'd already brought to bear, they were weak and powerless to fight back. As a result, it ended in glorious slaughter, and when he finally reached the still stunned shaman, he fell upon the feather-cloaked monster without mercy.

It was more of an execution than a fight, and by the time Elijah had finished, he'd earned enough experience to push him to level fifty. Not only did that place him in the top five of Earth's power rankings, but it also awarded him another ability:

Ability: Brand of the Stalker	Sear a brand on an enemy, preventing all forms of stealth and increasing your damage against them by fourteen (14) percent.

"Nice," Elijah said after he'd shifted back into his human form. But it was difficult to feel too excited about his accomplishment. Sure, he'd killed a good number of orcs, but it was barely anything next to the full weight of the horde.

Still, he'd proved the viability of the strategy, so after taking a few minutes to settle himself—and finding that he now had room for another enhancement—he used Essence of the Lion and took off across the wilderness to repeat his actions.

He couldn't kill them all at once, but if he kept chipping away at them, he would accomplish both of his goals. One, it would inevitably slow the horde to a crawl. And two, he'd gain a few more levels while whittling away at the orcs' numbers. Perhaps he could even deprive them of shamans altogether.

Only time would tell, so he bent his will toward the task at hand.

71

EQUIPPING AN ARMY

Searing heat buffeted Carmen as she stepped into her newly expanded forge. Inside, there were seven apprentices working, and that wasn't even considering the number of people who'd been tasked with smelting the freshly mined cold-iron ore. After exterminating the last of the critters, Silverado's miners had found thick veins of the stuff, and ever since then, they'd been steadily pulling it from the earth.

And it was just as potent a resource as Carmen had expected.

She crossed the forge, making her way to a pile of ingots waiting to be worked. She retrieved one, then used Tradesman's Appraisal, resulting in a notification flashing before her inner eye:

Cold-Iron Ingot
Overall Grade: Simple (Medium)
Enchantment Grade: N/A

It was already better than the metal she'd used to create Destroyer, and that had been the product of weeks' worth of work and quite a lot of scavenging. It was no wonder Roman had been so adamant that the mine be tapped. Carmen spent the next few minutes searching for the perfect ingots. Most were on the low end of Simple grade, but there were a couple that were in the middle, like the one she'd inspected. Those were her targets, and after a few more minutes, she found ten such ingots.

Then, she carried them to her personal forge, which was separate from her apprentices'. Normally, she didn't mind working among them, but sometimes, she needed full concentration. As such, she'd had the separate area built to her exacting specifications, which included her own smelter as well as a forge that could handle the intense heat of a fire fueled by ethera-soaked coal.

She was certain that there were better fuels out there, but she'd yet to find any. Perhaps when she did, she'd be able to take the next step in her progression as a Blacksmith.

But that was a worry for another day. For now, she was only concerned with completing the project before her. So, she took the first two ingots and used

Meld Metals to merge them into one. Once she had, she used Refine Material. The results were mixed because the designated smelting crew all had the same technique available to them. As such, the ingots had already been subjected to multiple instances of that, as well as Decontaminate. Still, her technique was a little more powerful than theirs, so she managed to eke a little use out of it.

In truth, it probably wasn't worth the ethera, but Carmen had ever been a perfectionist, and so, she intended to take every step possible to ensure the product was the peak of what she could achieve.

Especially given its purpose.

So, once she'd prepared those two merged ingots, she thrust them into the flames and started working on the rest of her materials. And by the time she'd finished, the metal was hot enough for her to work. So, using Summon Tool, she manifested a pair of tongs and dragged the molten metal ingots out of the fire. Once she'd slapped it onto an anvil, she conjured a hammer and started pounding the metal into submission.

She only got a dozen good blows in before she had to shove it back into the forge. That was one of the problems with cold iron. As its name suggested, it was resistant to fire, and it dissipated heat remarkably quickly. Because of that, a smith who wanted to work with the metal needed to be incredibly cognizant of hammering cold metal, which would result in stress fractures that would, in turn, lower the grade of the item.

Carmen had no intention of letting that happen.

So, over the next few hours, she diligently worked, spending more time letting the forge heat the metal than she actually spent hammering. However, for a crafter, patience was a virtue. It was even more important to maintain focus when the natural inclination was to let her mind wander. Staying on task was an especially difficult thing, what with everything going on.

After meeting with the rebel leaders, Carmen had agreed to provide high-quality armor and weapons to them and their allies. She wasn't sure about working with the roaming war band led by Laramie, but she had been assured that they were better than Roman. She hadn't needed much convincing, given the personal enmity she held for the man. If Carmen was honest with herself—which was a rare thing—she would have admitted that she didn't truly care about the fate of Easton. Instead, the only thing that concerned her was taking revenge on Roman. And as a Blacksmith, the best way she could do that was by providing powerful equipment to the fighters who could give her the opportunity to take her vengeance.

Those thoughts flitted along the surface of Carmen's mind as she worked. If she could have stopped them from doing so, she would have, but that was almost impossible. As a result, her product probably suffered, at least a little. Still, the slow pace of the work did give her the opportunity to use one of her latest techniques:

Ability: Ethereal Fortification	Infuse a single blow with ethera, injecting an in-progress item with additional power.

It did precisely what the description said it would, and each time she struck the metal with it active, it sent a jolt of ethera into the material. However, it came with two issues. First, it was slow to activate, which meant that she had to work with a steady and deliberate pace. As such, using it with cold iron, whose rapid cooling meant that she had a very short amount of time to work with, slowed the work down considerably. The second issue was that it used an incredible amount of ethera, which served to highlight some of the issues with her attribute allocation. She was heavy on Strength and Constitution, but light on Ethera and Regeneration. The less said about her low Dexterity, the better.

Still, each level she attained served as a course correction due to the automatic allocation that came with her class. So, if she wanted to be better, she knew the way. In the meantime, though, she struggled to maintain enough ethera to consistently use her abilities, which slowed her down even more.

Even so, Carmen was nothing if not patient, and she persisted through her own limitations. After nearly seven hours, she finally held up the product she had created. It was a breastplate, sized to fit Colt. The man was her second-in-command, and yet, he wore no armor aside from that ridiculous coat of his.

And it wasn't even Crude grade.

No, if he was going to be effective, he needed better armor. Carmen aimed to satisfy that need. So, after setting the unfinished breastplate aside, she grabbed another ingot and continued the process. Over the next two days, during which she fielded a few questions from her apprentices who'd been tasked with forging the equipment for the rebels, she also managed to hammer an entire set of armor into shape. A breastplate, two bracers, and a pair of greaves. It wasn't ideal, and if she'd had her way, she would have outfitted him in a full set of armor that covered his entire body. However, Colt had made it abundantly clear that he wanted no such thing. So, this was a compromise.

The metal itself was deep blue, with hints of pearlescent white. Hopefully, he would like that color.

In any case, now that the base structure was done, Carmen needed to start with the embellishments. So, she used another new technique:

Ability: Ethereal Etching	Use ethera to carve embellishments into metal. No tools required.

With that ability, she didn't need any tools to create ethera-infused embellishments on the armor. However, that was not the extent of what she had planned. Instead, she intended to adjust things a little more fully, using Shape.

Ability: Shape	Reshape a material with raw ethera.

With that, she could make minor adjustments to the armor that would have otherwise required quite a bit more hammering or a grinder. However, using the two in conjunction was extremely ethera thirsty, which meant that she was in for a long haul. Still, she persisted, using her two techniques as often as she was able. And gradually, the armor took its final shape.

She wasn't going for anything truly eye-catching. Just a mostly plain breast-plate, with etched greaves and bracers. Still, there was beauty in subtle sim-plicity, and what's more, Carmen knew that Colt's taste trended toward the unassuming.

Eventually, she finished, though she didn't dare use Tradesman's Appraisal yet. Just because the armor was forged, it didn't mean the project was complete. So, she gathered the individual pieces and headed away from the forge. When she left the building, she couldn't help but blink as the sunlight of a new day assailed her eyes. Yet, she didn't wait around to let her sight adjust, instead heading to the neighboring building that housed Silverado's overworked Leatherworkers.

There, she found the man she was looking for.

"You finish it?" she asked.

"I did," the Leatherworker said. He wasn't particularly skilled, and he hadn't even reached level twenty yet. However, he was the best Silverado had to offer, so Carmen reasoned that beggars couldn't be choosers.

After he retrieved the piece in question, she inspected it. When she was satisfied, she told him what she wanted. It was just one piece of the puzzle, so she wasn't terribly concerned with the quality of his work. Yet, she knew the end product would be better if she let a real Leatherworker do it rather than try to make it work on her own. So, after explaining everything, she left the armor with him.

With that done, she had a few hours to kill. So, she strode toward the train-ing yard where she expected to find Miguel. Sure enough, he was there, prac-ticing the sword with Colt. The two had a good relationship, which Carmen appreciated. A young boy needed all the positive role models he could get, and Colt satisfied that requirement quite well.

For a long time, she leaned against the fence that encircled the train-ing ground, just watching her son go through his drills. Some of it she understood, but her approach to battle had always been more of a charge-in-and-hit-things-really-hard sort of method. So, the subtleties of sword fighting had never appealed to her.

But watching Miguel, she could certainly see the draw.

When he saw her, he gave her a subdued wave, but he knew better than to interrupt his lessons. So, that was all Carmen was going to get for now.

After a couple of hours, she returned to the Leatherworker and inspected his work. It was adequate, so she handed him a handful of copper etherium for his trouble. He tried to protest being paid, saying that he didn't need payment, but Carmen knew just how much a few extra copper could help. So, she didn't mind.

In any case, she quickly returned to the forge with the item, then, after taking a few minutes to center herself, used Bind to make the Leatherworker's efforts permanent. After that, she started the enchantment process.

She still couldn't do anything more than a Minor Enchantment, but she had learned a few extra methods over the past months. As such, she could imbue the item with a few extra attribute points. She still hadn't gotten the hang of adding an ability, and she suspected that would be the case until she managed to upgrade her Minor Enchantment technique. But that was fine. It would still be better than what anyone else in Easton wore.

The process took many more hours—so many, in fact, that Carmen grew dizzy from lack of food, which interrupted her efforts for a few hours—but in the end, she accomplished precisely what she'd set out to do and created an item set in the middle of the Simple grade.

> **Congratulations! You have created a unique item set, Warden's Armor.**
> **Overall Grade: Simple (Middle)**
> **Enchantment Grade: F**

The bracers had been seamlessly integrated into a new leather duster, which had been made from the hides of the highest-level terrestrial molaks. The Leatherworker had enchanted it for durability, though he was incapable of doing any more than that. Carmen hadn't expected the breastplate or greaves to be included in the set, but she was more than happy with the results.

Hopefully, it would be enough to protect the strongest fighter she had. Because she had a feeling that hard times were coming.

72

THE IMPORTANCE OF DITCHES

Elijah sat on the edge of the ditch, his legs dangling nearly ten feet above the deepest portion. It was filled with sharpened stakes, many of which glistened with ethera from various skills. After his initial success with the divide-and-conquer strategy, he'd managed to use it one more time before the orcs—or, rather, the shamans—wised up and refused to follow him into the wilderness. They still sent a few bands of orcs after him, but he quickly discovered that they weren't nearly as vulnerable to his spells as they'd once been.

It was only a day later when he saw them performing some sort of ritual that he discovered the reason. Obviously, they'd enacted some sort of defense against him. It wasn't really surprising; they'd long proved that they were capable of mitigating his spells. Yet, this was the first time that they'd developed a strategy to do so without the shamans being present. And Elijah didn't like what that represented because it verified everything he'd already learned about orcs.

They were evolving more with every passing day. If he and his allies didn't do something soon, the creatures would grow too powerful to combat. So, he'd retreated to the area around Ironshore, where he hoped to contribute to the preparations of their collective defense. When he'd arrived, he had discovered that they had piled quite a lot of dirt into an edifice that surrounded the town, and they'd built some siege engines, as well. The Alchemist, Biggle, had even lent his expertise to brewing a few dozen barrels of some sort of toxic concoction that he claimed would "make those orc-y bastards think twice about coming to Ironshore."

Elijah wasn't so sure of that because, if there was one thing he'd confirmed, it was that orcs were single-minded in their pursuit of dominance. They'd already swept through the area like a plague, consuming anything they hadn't destroyed. So, Elijah knew there was little chance of them giving up. Nothing short of total annihilation would stop the orcs.

Which meant that the weight on his shoulders wasn't limited to the coming conflict. There was every chance that if he and the other defenders of Ironshore failed, the orcs would rampage across the region and eventually grow too powerful to stop. If the situation got to that point, Earth would almost assuredly be doomed.

And the only thing standing in the way of that was a few ditches, Elijah, and some noncombatants who'd been thrust into a situation they were ill prepared to confront.

He sighed, reaching into his pack and retrieving a jug of water. He drank deeply from it, then set it on the ground. A moment later, the sound of soft footsteps announced the arrival of Kurik.

"Want a drink?" Elijah asked, holding up the jug.

"Water?" asked Kurik.

"Yeah."

"I'll pass," the dwarf said, settling in beside Elijah. He went on: "Should be here in a day or two. We're not sure if they'll stop outside of our range and amass before coming for us."

"Probably," Elijah guessed. "They're getting smarter."

"Orcs do that."

"Have you thought about what's going to happen if we're unsuccessful?" Elijah asked, glancing toward the dwarf. Kurik looked as exhausted as Elijah felt, with large bags beneath his eyes.

"I'll disappear into the wilderness. You should do the same."

"If I'm still alive, I'll be fighting."

"Why?" asked Kurik. "You don't owe nothin' to us. We attacked you in your home. By all rights, you ought to've killed each and every one of us."

"Cabbot was different," Elijah reasoned. "And honestly, he probably wouldn't have tried what he did if he knew what I could do. Definitely not if he knew the orcs were coming."

"If he knew that, he'd've got Mommy and Daddy Eason to pay his way back home," Kurik responded. "They paid most of the fee to get them Ritualists here. Like it wasn't nothin', too. I bet that idiot didn't even know they was subsidizin' his little dragon-kidnappin' plot."

"Maybe," Elijah agreed half-heartedly. He never really knew Cabbot, so he couldn't speak to that. "But you're asking me why I'm doing this? Three reasons."

"Yeah? What are they?"

"First, I'm not the kind of guy to abandon people when they need help. I know that probably makes me a sucker, and I'm sure someone will eventually take advantage of me," he explained. "But if that happens, that's on them. Someone else's dishonesty won't stop me from doing what I think is right."

"Noble words. Maybe you'll change your tune when somebody crosses your lines."

Elijah shrugged, looking out over the array of ditches. There were twelve of them, each just as deep as the last. Hopefully, that would slow the orcs down.

"Maybe," he acknowledged. "But the second reason is a little more personal. I want to protect my home. I like my island, and I can't imagine the orcs leaving me alone if they take Ironshore. So, protecting the city is a roundabout way of protecting myself."

"And the third reason?"

"This is my planet," Elijah said. "If we don't stop them here, those orcs are going to spread. That's what they do, right? They're like a virus. And I've got people out there I care about. Not anyplace close, but they're out there. And if I don't do what I can right now, there's a good chance that they'll find themselves on the wrong end of that horde sometime in the near future. The orcs are vulnerable now. Beatable. That means I've got to take my shot, here and now, because there's a high probability that humanity will never get another chance."

For a few moments, Kurik didn't speak. Then, he took a deep breath before saying, "Nobility and selfishness. I can get behind that."

"Anyone who says they're doing something for purely altruistic reasons is lying," Elijah said. "There's always a little self-interest in there."

"You ain't wrong," Kurik agreed.

Then, the two fell into an easy silence until, a few minutes later, Kurik said, "That sure is a lot of ditches."

"Yeah. A friend of mine from college was on track to being a historian," Elijah said. "Specialized in ancient warfare. And every time we saw a movie or talked about a book that dealt with war or sieges, he would always criticize the tactics on display. His favorite thing to say was that the best and most effective defense is a ditch. If you've already got one ditch, then build another. You can fancy it up with stakes and walls or water, but the bottom line is that ditches are where it's at when it comes to defense."

"Sounds like a smart fella," Kurik said. "'Cept the parts of that I didn't understand at all, of course."

The pair shared a laugh, but then Elijah pushed himself to his feet before saying, "I'm going to get a shower and a real meal. You interested? Might be the last time we'll get the chance."

Kurik shook his head and glanced back at Ironshore. "Got a complicated relationship with cities. Don't do so good with people, if you catch my meaning."

"Yeah. I can understand that. But if you change your mind, you'll know where to find me."

"If I didn't, I'm sure I could just follow the angry glares. Some folks still ain't forgiven you for killin' their so-called security force," Kurik stated.

Elijah shrugged. "Can't blame them for that, I guess. Anyway, I'll see you later."

"Sure."

After that, Elijah ambled toward Ironshore. When he entered the city proper, he was once again confronted by the same resentful glares that had greeted him every other time that he'd visited the city. There was fear there, as well, but it was muted, probably because they were growing accustomed to his presence. Eventually, that would assuredly come to a head.

When that inevitability came to pass, Elijah would have to make an example of someone, which was something he didn't want to have to do.

In any case, they weren't quite there yet, so he traversed the small city without issue. He passed by a few familiar locations, like the barbershop, Mari's boutique, and the central building housing the Branch. In the distance, he saw the mines, as well, though he hadn't visited them since rescuing Sara the dragon.

For a moment, Elijah considered using Ancestral Circle to teleport back to his Grove so he could spend the night there. However, he chose not to for one simple reason: He had no idea if he'd have time to row his way back to the mainland if the orcs attacked. No—it was better to remain in town, even if it meant being a little less comfortable.

"Elijah!" came a shout from behind. He turned to see Ramik jogging in his direction. The prim and proper goblin was dressed in the same Victorian style he always was. That wasn't a precise description, considering that there were some subtle but glaring differences, yet it was close enough that Elijah felt comfortable with that descriptor. In any case, he stopped so that Ramik could catch up. The goblin doffed his bowler and asked, "Can I interest you in a meal? I have a reservation at the Stuck Pig. I remember how much you enjoyed that last time, and I thought you might like another visit."

Elijah looked down at his travel-stained clothes and said, "You know what? Sure. But I'd prefer to get cleaned up a bit first. Give me about an hour?"

"Certainly!" said the excited goblin.

"Any suggestions on a hotel? Somewhere with a shower?"

"Oh—a man of your means will want the Imperium."

"Sounds expensive," Elijah groused.

"It is. Yet, there is no finer accommodation in the city. Indeed, it is the only true hotel in town. We don't get many visitors. Or any, in point of fact. So, there hasn't been much use for the place, if I'm honest. However, that's sure to change as the world begins to open up," Ramik insisted.

Elijah shrugged. It wasn't as if he was short on money, so he said, "Sure. So long as it has a shower and a soft bed, I'll be happy."

"Oh, you will be quite satisfied. Allow me to lead the way."

After a nod from Elijah, Ramik led him through the city and to a large three-story building with elegant architecture that put Elijah in mind of the Palace of Versailles, though on a much smaller scale. It also featured a sizable bronze dome, but the general theme was close enough that it made Elijah wonder about the similarities between the newcomers' cultures and those native to Earth.

As such questions crossed through a couple of facets of Elijah's Mind, he followed Ramik into the Imperium. And when he stepped inside, he couldn't contain a slight gasp. To call the decor rich would have been an understatement. Inlaid marble, gold trim, and elaborately carved moldings abounded, and the floor tiles were arranged in an artful and dizzyingly complex geometric design.

A goblin in a tuxedo greeted them. Aside from a brief glance at Elijah's bare feet, he gave no indication that he was put off by the sheer shabbiness on display before him.

"Welcome to the Imperium," the goblin intoned. "My name is Dakar, and I am the chief proprietor of this branch of the Imperium, the finest hotel in the universe. Please, may I ask what I can do for you?"

"My friend wishes a room," Ramik said. "Money is no object."

"Uh . . . It's some object," Elijah remarked.

"Trust me, my friend—you won't regret spending a few etherium on this," Ramik stated.

Elijah shrugged. He didn't really know what else to spend his money on, so he said, "Sure. Whatever. Fair warning, though—it's got a ways to go if it's going to compete with my tree house."

"I am certain that the Imperium will compare quite favorably to any . . . tree house," said Dakar.

And it did.

Elijah spent the next hour being pampered in a way he never thought possible. Not only was he afforded the opportunity to finally take a shower, but the apartment he rented for the night was twice as large as his tree house. On top of that, it was just as richly decorated as the rest of the hotel. That meant that it looked like it was fit for a literal king.

On top of that, Elijah was also subjected to a massage administered by a skilled dwarven woman. So, when he finally returned to the lobby an hour or so later, he felt more refreshed than he had in months.

The following meal was just as enjoyable, albeit in a different way. There was something so communal about eating a meal in good company. It seemed like such a simple thing, and though the food was good, it shouldn't have relaxed him like it did. However, by the time Elijah finished with the Stuck Pig—where he ate what felt like his weight in smoked meats and sides he couldn't identify— he felt flush with contentment.

A more cynical person would have expected something to interrupt that happiness, but nothing happened, and Elijah ended up settling into his huge bed and falling asleep with some degree of optimism in his heart.

He almost managed to forget about the orcish horde knocking on the proverbial door.

But not quite.

73

AN UNSCRUPULOUS MAN

Trace was bored out of his mind, and the worst part about it was that he didn't think there was any end to it in sight. It was his own fault, really. He knew it, too. He should have just killed the bitch and let the chips fall where they may. It was still on the table, as far as he was concerned, though if he went down that road, he'd have to talk fast to keep Roman from gutting him.

And he would, too.

That cold bastard would slaughter his own children if he thought it would further his goals. Trace had seen it play out in the tower, when he'd watched the man decapitate a woman he'd called his closest friend. And for what? So he could solidify his rule? It was madness of a sort Trace wanted nothing to do with. Yet, he'd stuck around in Easton, largely because, so long as he acted according to Roman's will, he got to do whatever he wanted, whenever he wanted.

And since the world had ended, that was all he cared about.

There had been a time, and not so long ago, that he'd have put his life on the line for family and friends. In fact, he'd done just that right after the world had changed. He was good at it, too, and for a while, he had been successful. But then Marly had died, killed by some sort of humanoid tree monster that had taken Trace nearly an hour to hack apart.

She was the first, but she'd been far from the last. One by one, everyone he'd ever loved had been taken from him until he was the only one left. That's when he broke, when he had chosen to give up on the idea of being a hero. Of protecting people. Of looking out for anything but his own best interests.

Since then, he'd descended down a spiral of hedonism, theft, and murder, only surfacing when his benefactor gave him a task. Nearby, two of his girls—cute little slips of femininity—waited, watching for his signal. He couldn't see them, much to his dismay. Like him, they were equipped with potent stealth skills, so no one that wasn't at least ten levels their senior would be capable of detecting them. Unlike him, though, they were both gorgeous. It was practically a crime, covering that up with a skill. They were also oh so pliable.

Trace had taken advantage of that last trait on more than one occasion. They were broken, too. But instead of throwing caution to the wind and truly committing to the pursuit of pleasure in all its varied forms, they'd simply given up. Most of the time, they didn't even say anything—which was fine by him. The last thing he wanted was to waste time listening to a teenage girl's inane chatter.

However, they'd also been trained well, so the pair were effective enough that he would have kept them around, even if they didn't satisfy his other, much more depraved requirements.

In any case, Trace didn't have to worry about them, so he kept his attention squarely on the two figures in the middle of what looked like a paddock. The area was surrounded by a low fence, and it featured hard-packed dirt that spoke of many hours of trampling feet. The two people within its bounds were interesting enough that Trace barely noticed their surroundings, though.

One was a boy with dark hair and a tan complexion, while the other was a tall, slim man who looked like he'd stepped off the set of an old cowboy movie. However, instead of a six-shooter, he wielded a katana with a gleaming blade and a worn hilt. Next to him, the boy looked even smaller than he truly was. But given his parentage, Miguel Rodriguez was bound to end up on the short side.

Of course, Trace recognized the cowboy, as well, and in truth, he had nothing against Colt Marsters. By all accounts, the man did his job and kept to himself. The only thing that annoyed Trace about him was his propensity to play the hero. The man had never met a dangerous situation he wouldn't throw himself against, which Trace found naive, performative, and a little sad. It was as if the man was trying to prove to everyone how competent and heroic he was.

It made Trace a little nauseous.

The pair clashed, their practice blades clacking as they went through a series of measured drills. For his part, Trace found the entire thing pointless. He'd never practiced his bladework, but he'd done just fine for himself. After all, it wasn't so difficult to understand that the pointy end went into the other man. That was one lesson Trace had learned well, and he'd put it into practice more times than he could count.

Still, he could at least appreciate the dedication involved, especially considering he'd seen Marsters in action. Even if he was nauseatingly heroic, the cowboy certainly knew his way around a fight, and he'd proved his prowess on enough occasions that nobody who wanted to live would underestimate him.

Trace looked past the two faux combatants and into the town beyond. All the buildings were made of rough-hewn timber, giving them the appearance of log cabins. It cast the entire settlement in a rustic light that put Trace in mind of the vacations he'd once taken with his family. Those had been good times, and he remembered them fondly. Yet, it also came with the same heart-wrenching pain that accompanied any memory of the past. So, he quickly shoved it aside.

His true target was in the largest building, probably forging armor for the enemies of Easton. Trace didn't care so much about a petty rebellion because he knew precisely how unsuccessful any attempt would be. Roman wasn't untouchable—not quite—but so long as he stayed inside those walls, he might as well have been. Trace had found himself the target of the man's ire on enough occasions that he no longer held any interest in challenging him.

In any case, armor or not, anyone who chose to attack Easton was going to get a rude awakening. So, Trace wasn't entirely certain why he was even there. He could have assassinated her on the road. Or in her sleep. And he already knew where to find the war band with whom the rebels had made an alliance. Watching Carmen was pointless.

Yet, he was there, doing as he'd been told, like a kept dog.

It was infuriating.

So, it wasn't surprising that his mind quickly turned to a different plan to deal with the uppity Blacksmith and her little band of rebels. After all, if he had something she desperately wanted to keep safe, then it wouldn't be difficult to keep her in line. And Trace remembered his own children well enough to recognize the lengths a mother would go to keep harm from befalling her children.

It took him a while to work himself up to it, but after a couple of hours, Trace had convinced himself that Roman would appreciate his initiative. He may even give him some sort of reward.

No—the plan that had taken root in his mind was a good one. He just needed to make it work, and he'd get whatever he wanted out of Roman. So, he knocked on the tree he'd been hiding behind, which was the signal for the two girls.

After that, he retreated twenty yards into the woods to a prearranged location and canceled Concealment. A moment later, the pair of girls removed their own camouflaging capabilities. They were similar in appearance, though one had black hair while the other was blonde. One day, Trace wanted to get a brunette and a redhead to complete the set.

With a slight smirk, he told them his plan, and to their credit, they didn't argue. They'd long since learned that he wouldn't react well to any questions. In any case, they listened, and when he'd finished, all three adopted their stealth abilities before setting off for the training grounds. As they had been for hours, Colt and the boy continued to practice.

Trace nimbly climbed over the fence, then padded across the training rounds until he was in perfect position. Then, he drew the Stiletto of Sundering from the sheath at his waist and struck, using Armor Pierce.

The blade sliced through the thin protection of the man's shirt—his duster hung over the fence in the other direction—piercing Colt's kidney. The cowboy reacted instantly, lashing out with a backhand that took Trace in the cheek and sent him spinning to the ground. Immediately, he embraced Vanish, hiding himself from view. As he did so, he turned his tumble into a dive, and it was just in time, too, because, only a moment later, the ground erupted into a cloud of dirt and dust as a dozen invisible blades tore through the earth.

Trace looked back to see that Colt had stumbled. The Stiletto of Sundering had done its job, robbing the man of his attributes.

Even as Colt tried to get himself under control, the two girls struck. One high, and the other low.

Their blades bit into the man, but he wasn't considered one of Easton's best combatants for nothing. In the blink of an eye, his sword flashed out, and the blonde girl's head went flying through the air while her body crumpled to the ground. Colt paid no attention to his injuries. Instead, before the other girl could react, he kicked her in the chest, sending her falling backward toward the ground.

She never made it.

Not in one piece, at least.

Colt once again flicked his sword, activating an ability, and she fell to the ground in pieces.

Just like that, Trace was all alone and facing a furious Colt Marsters.

He considered running. He was good at that. Yet, the blood pooling on the ground told Trace that Colt wasn't in the best shape. So, when he saw how wobbly Colt was, he decided to stick it out, circling around and looking for an opening. He didn't dare snatch the child, who stupidly hadn't run away, even when Colt shouted for him to do just that. Instead, Miguel stood his ground, holding his practice sword like it would do any good.

To keep him around, Trace used Intimidate on Miguel. Most of the time, it wouldn't work on people, but the kid didn't even have an archetype yet, so he was entirely unprotected. As a result, he dropped his useless weapon, widened his eyes, and went stiff as all rational thought fled before the face of unmitigated terror.

Meanwhile, Trace darted in, stabbing Colt in the stomach. However, the moment his blade made contact, the wounded cowboy reacted with a lightning-fast slash that nearly took Trace's head off. As it was, he bounded away just in time, picking up a gash on his cheek instead.

But Trace knew he'd been caught out in the open—a fact that was confirmed by a twinge from his Danger Sense—so he immediately activated Riposte. It was perfect timing because Colt used his bread-and-butter attack a second later.

Ability: Riposte	For one and a half (1.5) seconds, block any attack and return it to its origin at fifty (50) percent power.

It was the single most important ability Trace had, but it was also an extremely limited one. As such, he'd trained himself to use it at the most opportune moment. In this case, it sent Colt's attack right back at him. The man never even saw it coming.

Unfortunately, even as it ripped the cowboy to shreds, Trace knew it wouldn't be enough to kill him. It was enough to send him toppling to the ground in a puddle of his own blood, though. Trace stalked forward, tossing his Stiletto of Sundering from one hand to the next as he prepared to finish the job.

Yet, the sudden banging of a door and a shout from within the mining town alerted him that he didn't have the time. So, he ran forward, grabbing the kid and throwing him over a shoulder. As he did so, he used Stun to knock him out. Normally, it would only last an instant, which he usually used to give himself an edge in a fight. But with someone who hadn't even gotten his archetype, the ability was a lot more effective. The kid went out like a light, and Trace sprinted away from the training ground.

After leaping over the fence, he used Light Step to increase his foot speed, leaving any pursuit behind. And just like that, he'd accomplished his goal. Now, he only needed to return to Easton and hand the kid over to Roman, and Carmen would fall into line.

74

THE HORDE ARRIVES

Elijah awoke to the gentle sound of a flute. As his eyes fluttered open, he glanced around the enormous and garishly appointed room, but he couldn't find the origin of the music. Yet, even so, he found it enormously soothing, as if it was capable of washing all his cares away.

Of course, it only took a moment for him to remember the urgency of Ironshore's situation, and when he did, that dense brick of anxiety that had plagued him for the past couple of weeks returned to the pit of his stomach. Tension tightened his muscles, ruining the restful night of sleep he'd just enjoyed.

For a long few minutes, Elijah wished he could just let unconsciousness return and carry him away into blissfully ignorant sleep. Yet, he knew he couldn't do that. Not only did he have responsibilities to tend to, but any possibility of rest had disappeared the moment reality had reasserted itself. Even if he'd wanted to go back to sleep, he couldn't have managed it.

So, with some regret, he threw his blankets aside and pushed himself upright. As he stretched, he noticed that the flute music had ceased, and in the back of his mind, he wondered if he was finally cracking under the pressure. After everything he'd been through, Elijah couldn't help but think it was only a matter of time before his sanity slipped.

Sighing, he glanced toward the window. It was a huge, arched thing that stretched from the richly tiled floors to the molding near the ceiling, and ethera danced along the panes. He shook his head, ignoring the oddity as he looked out over the town. Despite being just past dawn, people were already up and about, moving with no small degree of urgency.

And Elijah couldn't blame them, either.

Every report he'd read suggested that the orcs were soon to arrive. Perhaps it would be today, or maybe it would be tomorrow. But there was no doubt that they were coming, and soon. The people of Ironshore might not have been classed as combatants, but they intended to be ready to defend their new homes.

What other choice did they have?

None of them could afford the fee to teleport to another world, and fleeing into the wilderness was almost as dangerous as facing the orcs. It was especially so because the orcs certainly wouldn't stop at Ironshore. They would keep going, sweeping across the land until there was nothing left.

With that fate before them, the idea of risking everything to cut the threat off before it could grow out of control was an attractive one. Still, some had already fled. Elijah had seen them leave during the night, and though he held no true grudge against them, he couldn't help but think of those people as cowards. They'd been called to defend their homes, and they'd responded by running away.

As understandable as their response was, those were the actions of cowards.

Elijah pushed those thoughts out of his mind. He had no right to judge them. Certainly, he had the ability to resist. He could fight back. But what was a Cobbler supposed to do against a horde of orcs? What of a Cook? Or a Fisherman? They simply weren't equipped to confront the threat, and so, they'd taken the only path available to them.

Then again, they could still help, and that help could well prove the difference in the coming battle.

Elijah's own actions stood in stark contrast to theirs. He was no resident of Ironshore, but he hadn't truly hesitated to come when called. Sure, part of that was motivated by self-interest, but even so, he'd shown up. That the same couldn't be said for every person who called Ironshore home was enough to turn Elijah's anxiety to simmering anger. He wondered if, when he and the city's other defenders defeated the orcs, the deserters would be welcomed back.

Maybe.

But he suspected not. For his part, Elijah had no idea what he would do if he was in charge, and he was glad that was not a decision he'd be forced to make.

Whatever the case, he pushed himself to his feet and stretched. The bed had been comfortable, but after sleeping outside so often, it had been a little too soft. Still, he wasn't going to complain. After that, he headed to the bathroom, where he took care of his business—the presence of a toilet, even one with an odd design, was definitely an improvement over living outdoors—and washed his face. With that done, he donned his clothing and equipment before checking himself in the mirror.

He had changed so much over the past few years, but in a lot of ways, not at all. His hair was much longer than it had ever been before Earth had been touched by the World Tree, and his beard a bit scragglier. Yet, he looked younger and, if he was honest with himself, slightly more handsome than he had even before his cancer diagnosis.

Somewhat marring that effect were the scars that still hadn't faded. His right arm still bore the mark of his torturous time in the whale's physics-defying stomach, and the curious crack-like evidence of his ill-advised misuse of Ancestral Circle remained on his chest and neck. Even so, he wasn't the disfigured abomination those features might have suggested. Instead, he felt they were just interesting rather than off-putting.

But he could at least acknowledge that he was a little biased on that account. Certainly, Delilah hadn't minded, which he thought should have counted for something. Of course, given her insatiable enthusiasm, he didn't think she would have minded if he had been missing whole limbs.

As he thought of her, he couldn't help but grin.

It had been a long three years, and that night had been quite the stress reliever.

Though it wasn't long before Elijah shook his head. He couldn't afford to just sit around and reminisce about a woman he would probably never see again. It had been fun and, in a lot of ways, necessary, but it was over. It was never going to be more than a one-night thing.

Besides, he had other things he needed to focus on, like the impending orc invasion. So, he straightened his shirt, ran his fingers through his hair, then left the bathroom behind. On his way out, he grabbed his staff and pack before leaving the ridiculously opulent room behind. As he strode down the hall, his feet slapped on the cold tile, the sound punctuated by the clack of his staff against the same. Soon, he reached the sweeping stairs that led down to the lobby, and after that short descent, he was greeted by the hotel's goblin manager, Dakar.

"I trust everything was to your liking, sir?" ventured the short, green-skinned fellow.

"It was," Elijah said. "You guys do breakfast around here? Or should I go elsewhere?"

"Alas, but no," said Dakar with an apologetic shake of his head. "I'm afraid our Cooks fled in the night. I hope you won't hold that against the Imperium."

Elijah shrugged. "Not your fault," he said. Then, he reached into his pocket and retrieved his folio. "What do I owe you?"

Dakar answered, "Nine silver."

Elijah nearly choked, but he'd already been told it was expensive. So, he paid the fee and headed in search of some breakfast. To his distress, most of the city's buildings had been boarded up and were closed for business. So, he ended up wandering toward the southern side of town, where the defenses were the thickest. There, he found Kurik supervising yet more ditch digging.

"Get a good night's rest?" he asked the dwarven Scout.

"Rest? What rest?" groused Kurik, running a hand through his coarse and spiky hair. "Ain't nobody got time to rest with an orc horde on our doorstep. We ain't all fancy like you, stayin' at the Imperium."

"It was a bit much," Elijah said with a laugh. "Even the toilet was gold."

"A gold shitter? Ain't that a sight to see," Kurik laughed.

Elijah doffed his pack, then reached inside. He grabbed a handful of berries and, after popping one in his mouth, asked, "Want one?"

Kurik took the offered berry, and when he ate it, his eyes lit up. "What in all of Ignis was that?"

"Like it?"

"Course I like it! Where'd you get those?"

Elijah shrugged, popping another into his mouth. One was more than enough to sate his hunger, but he wanted to make a point. As he chewed, he said, "Here and there. You know how it is. You're out adventuring, you find a bush full of pseudo natural treasures. May as well pick a few, right?"

"I hate you," the dwarf muttered.

"So you don't want another?" asked Elijah. He'd gone back to his island a couple of days before, specifically to gather some of the miraculous berries. His reasoning was that they made for perfect travel rations, but in reality, he was just tired of eating dried and peppery meat.

"Gods damned right I want some more."

Elijah acted as if he wasn't certain about making good on the offer, but then knocked it off when the dwarf started looking a bit antsy. After that, he grabbed another handful and handed it over. To his credit, Kurik made sure all his men got a berry before eating his second one.

After that, Elijah took a swig from one of his jugs of water and asked, "So, you think they'll be here today?"

"I'm sure of it," Kurik stated, staring off across the field. There were nearly a dozen ditches between him and the tree line, each one lined with sharpened stakes. Most had been modified with various abilities, as well. But to Elijah, it seemed a pitiful defense for what he knew was coming. As if he could read Elijah's mind, Kurik said, "Ain't no shame in runnin'. You don't owe us nothin'."

"I'm good" was all he said in response. Kurik knew better than to push, and the two fell silent. And before long, Elijah went to help the Scouts as they continued to dig trenches and festoon them with stakes. Like that, the hours passed until, at last, someone raised the alarm. The clear sound of a ringing bell swept across the would-be battlefield, letting everyone know that, finally, the orcs had arrived.

Kurik asked him, "You ready for this?"

"Not really," Elijah admitted. Over the past couple of years, he'd fought quite a bit, but he'd never been in a real battle. And he knew enough to recognize how different the two situations were.

"Me, neither," admitted Kurik.

"Is anyone ever?"

Kurik shook his head, saying, "Probably not. But—"

It was at that moment that the first orcs stepped out from the tree line. They were just as huge, muscular, and savage looking as ever, which softened the psychological blow of what Elijah knew was about to happen. The orcs had overwhelming numbers on their side, but Elijah knew they were going to need those and more.

The orcs kept piling out from within the forest as they amassed just out-side of the city's defensive perimeter. There were thousands of them, and each one started howling for blood the moment they caught sight of the city and its defenders.

Elijah glanced to his side, and he saw that the townspeople had all come the moment the alarm had been raised. Not only did he see hundreds of people he didn't recognize—goblins in three-piece suits, dwarves wearing the heavy clothing of miners and wielding picks, as well as gnomes with oversize weap-ons—but there were plenty he did know. Mari, the Tailor, wielding a giant club. The trio of Barbers, armed with shears. Ramik with an elegant rapier, and Carisa, who was armed with a pair of hand axes. Even Dakar, the proprietor of the swanky Imperium, had shown up, though he didn't appear to be armed.

But rather than find it comforting, Elijah couldn't help but wonder how many of them would die before the day was done.

He only had a few more moments to contemplate the mortality of his allies before the orcs let out a collective roar, jerking his attention back to the upcom-ing battle. The gray-skinned monsters surged as one, accelerating into a sprint before leaping clear over the first ditch. Then the next. And the next after that. However, they didn't all make it, and because of the nature of such a crowd, the ones in the back couldn't maintain the momentum necessary to complete the leap.

They ended up impaled on the stakes, and their cries of pain were even louder than the enraged shouts of their comrades. Elijah ignored them all, his knuckles whitening as he tightened his grip on the Staff of Natural Harmony. He could feel the familiar carved roots digging into his palm as the orcs raced across the battlefield. Every ditch claimed a few more casualties, and that num-ber climbed as the rest of the orcish army flooded out of the trees.

Then, when the orcs were only a few dozen feet away, Elijah raised his staff and cast Swarm. The now-familiar nimbus of red energy bloomed into being as one of the shamans—unseen amid the horde—blocked the manifested insects from reaching the orcs. Yet, that was never Elijah's goal.

Next, he cast Calamity.

A natural disaster of myriad proportions erupted among the orcs. Slicing winds, rumbling earth, and sizzling lightning tore through them. But they were once again protected by the shaman.

However, Elijah had been watching, and he pinpointed the origin of that red-tinted Ethera. That's when he saw the shaman.

Elijah cast Brand of the Stalker. The spell, which was usable in any of his forms, cut through the chaos as well as the shaman's attempt at a block, and it slammed into the creature's chest. The instant it landed, Elijah knew precisely where the monster was. He could have closed his eyes, and it wouldn't have made a bit of difference.

He raised his staff high into the air, and the rest of the defenders cut loose with any ranged abilities they had at their disposal. For some, that meant loosing a barrage of arrows. For others, there were spells and skills. Fireballs and ice spikes, earthen spears and balls of roiling electricity fell among the horde, scorching, freezing, and impaling. Yet, on the swell of slavering savages came.

Elijah didn't waste his ethera on any more ranged attacks. Instead, he cast Healing Rain, then checked that his various enhancements were active. For this sort of battle, he'd chosen Essence of the Boar, Essence of the Lion, Aura of Renewal, and Shield of Brambles. As always, One with Nature and Essence of the Wolf were active, as well.

However, he'd made certain that his various enhancements weren't limited to himself. Instead, he'd spent much of the morning making certain that each and every person he could see was augmented by appropriate spells. Hopefully, it would be enough to keep some of them alive.

For now, though, as the orcs charged through Calamity and a hundred other spells and skills, he shifted into his lamellar-ape form. It was the first time that most of the townspeople had seen it, and even in the chaos of an impending clash, the sight drew quite a few gasps. One overzealous—or frightened—person even hit him with a weak fireball. Elijah ignored it.

Instead, he planted his feet, roared, and beat his chest as he prepared to meet the orcs' charge.

75

THE BATTLE OF IRONSHORE

The smell of charred flesh and the screams of dying orcs filled the air as Elijah let the rage of the lamellar ape rush through him. All around him, gnomes, dwarves, goblins, and a scattered few elves screamed their various battle cries as the orcish horde bore down on them, leaping the final ditch before ramming into the defenders.

For his part, Elijah threw himself into a trio of clustered orcs, his claws sweeping out to swat them aside. Another roar escaped his maw as he turned that into a shoulder tackle that bore his enormous and muscular target to the ground. He got one pummeling blow in before a flint-headed spear dug into his side. It did no good because he'd activated Iron Scales, preventing any penetration.

The orc on the other end of the spear got the worst of the exchange as a wicked thorn from Shield of Brambles pierced its torso. Elijah paid it no heed, vaulting to his feet and leaping into the mass of orcs. With his overly long arms, he grabbed one around the ankle and swung the monster around like an impromptu weapon. He only got a few good hits in before he spun around like an Olympic hammer tosser, then threw the orc over the heads of its fellows.

That got the attention of the horde, and they collapsed onto him like a wave of dull, gray muscle. They bit and clawed, stabbed and slashed, but Elijah kept Iron Scales active, and at great cost to his stamina. Yet, he had no choice. So long as they were focused on him, the orcs couldn't target his allies.

And the Ironshore defenders used that distraction to great effect, raining destruction onto the throng of attackers. It took the form of a wide variety of spells, skills, and projectiles, but the end results were clear—mass casualties. Most didn't die outright. The orcs were far too hardy for that. However, in a battle like the one before them, a grievous injury was just as good as a kill shot. Whatever took the orcs out of the battle, even for a few minutes, was a win.

Elijah couldn't afford to pay much attention to his allies. Instead, every facet of his Quartz Mind was trained on his surroundings. One paid attention to his mundane senses, while another was focused on One with Nature. The rest he employed to drive his reactions and counterattacks. The result was that, to his enemies, he likely seemed like he had eyes in the back of his head coupled with precognition.

He didn't dodge blows, though.

Instead, he merely shifted to protect his most vital areas. The hide of the lamellar ape was as thick as armor, and even without Iron Scales sending his defenses through the roof, he had more than enough Constitution to protect him. He was especially difficult to harm if he never took a solid blow, so that was what he endeavored to ensure, and to some degree of success.

He still took plenty of hits that would have felled someone with lesser defenses. But ever since he'd attained the Shape of the Guardian spell, he'd trained himself to fight appropriately to the form's strengths and weaknesses. He still hadn't mastered it, but against the comparatively crude orcs, it was enough.

Yet, the sheer weight of numbers was an issue.

There weren't merely hundreds of them. Instead, there were thousands, and it felt like every time Elijah took one out, another pair took its place. Fortunately, his inflated attributes served him well, and he managed to maintain his position at the center of the line, where he anchored the defenses.

Every now and again, he caught sight of the region behind the orcs, and he saw that they'd formed gruesome body bridges across the various ditches. The orcs who'd been incapable of leaping over the obstacles, either due to injury or simple weakness, had simply piled up, creating an avenue for even more orcs to overcome the trenches. Still, the defenses had served their purpose by slowing the orcs, claiming a few lives, and preventing the defenders from being overwhelmed straightaway.

The battle had become a brutal melee where, aside from Elijah and a few of the Scouts, the defenders were more than outmatched. Fortunately, they were better equipped and stood atop a berm that had been constructed from the piled dirt that had once filled the trenches. It was only a few feet high, but it was enough to give them the advantage of positioning to couple with the benefit of superior equipment. It was barely sufficient to keep the defenders' casualties to a minimum—for the time being.

Yet Elijah knew it couldn't last, especially when a trio of red balls of energy splashed down in the middle of the defensive line. Before he could react, a half dozen gnomes and goblins went down screaming, and even if they might've recovered, they never had the chance because the orcs pounced on the opening.

Chaos ensued.

Elijah leaped backward, using his long arms to great effect as he pummeled the orcs in order to reestablish the defensive line. But by that point, ten defenders had died, and there were more of those red balls on the way.

And Elijah knew their origins.

The shamans needed to be dealt with, but he hesitated to leave the defenders. So far, he was the only reason they'd maintained their line. But that wouldn't last long if he left the shamans to their own devices. So, without any more deliberation, he leaped forward, crashing into an orc and shouldering it aside. It attempted an attack, but he used Iron Scales to avoid any damage.

Then, he was among the orcs, swinging his arms like battering rams as he waded through the sea of gray flesh. After a few seconds, Iron Scales ran its course, but he didn't renew it. He had a long way to go, and he knew his endurance was finite. So, he put his head down and forged ahead, leaping over the first trench and landing among the surging sea of gray flesh. There were so many orcs that he was immediately surrounded, and the creatures wasted no time before trying to fill him full of holes.

But Elijah's high attributes weren't just for show, and with the benefit of the Haste effect he got from his Sash of the Whirlwind, he was capable of avoiding the worst of the attacks. Slowly, he battered his way through. It helped that the single-minded orcs weren't willing to give up on their true goal, which was to conquer the town. As a result, they only attempted to attack him in passing instead of bearing down on him with the full weight of their effort. If they had, he never would have gotten much farther than that first trench.

However, with the combination of his high Constitution, Haste, and the orc's borderline indifference to his progress, he finally reached his destination. The Brand of the Stalker burned bright in his awareness, marking the shaman's location. In the sea of orcs, that was important because he would have otherwise never found the creature.

He barreled through the last few orcs and launched himself through the air at the shaman. It never even saw him coming before he crashed into the creature, bearing it to the ground. It hit with a grunt, and to its credit, it started to cast some sort of spell, but Elijah already had the upper hand.

The creature had no chance to recover before he grabbed its head in both of his clawed hands and twisted. Even amid the chaotic roar of battle, he heard the sound of snapping vertebrae. But he wasn't content with that. Instead, he let out a bestial yell as he wrenched the monster's head back and forth until, at last, it tore free.

That's when a red ball of liquid agony hit him in the back.

A scream of torment ripped its way from his mouth as he fell forward, slamming face-first into the ground. Orcs descended upon him, stabbing him mercilessly, but he couldn't spare any attention for that. Instead, there was only one thing on Elijah's mind—the sheer, burning torment boring into his scaled back.

On instinct, he activated Iron Scales, and though it blocked the spear strikes from the orcish warriors, it did nothing to alleviate the immense pain rampaging through his body. He flopped around on the ground, desperately trying to regain control of himself, but it was no use. His muscles seized in a full-body cramp as untenable pain swept through him.

Then, another ball splashed into him.

Elijah's vision went white with agony.

Another came down, though he was in so much pain that he scarcely felt the difference. He couldn't think. He could barely breathe. Yet, utilizing the full force of his Quartz Mind, Elijah shoved the torment into its own facet. It spilled over into another. And another after that. But finally, it was contained, leaving the others to work on the problem.

He couldn't move.

His back was in ruins.

And he felt positive that, in only moments, he was going to die.

With One with Nature, he could feel the location of the other two shamans. They were behind him and to the left, flanked on either side by a pair of enormous orcs that must've been the most evolved warriors in the horde. But Elijah wasn't worried about them. He'd killed bigger and stronger.

What did worry him were the pair of shamans.

He felt the ambient ethera swirl as they raised their skull-topped staves toward the sky, swirling them in some unknowable ritual. Elijah knew that another pair of attacks were incoming.

He had no choice.

He used Guardian's Renewal.

As his body mended, banishing the pain and healing his shredded back, Elijah regained control of his body. It was just in time, too, because the pair of shamans finished their spells. Twin balls of red agony tore across the space between them and Elijah, but by that point, he had already sprung to his feet and launched himself at the two orcish spellcasters.

Their eyes widened in surprise, and the two guards attempted to intercept him. But with his high Strength, coupled with Haste, the monsters had no chance of stopping him. He hit the first shaman like a runaway train, launching it through the air and into a surging line of orcish warriors.

Elijah skidded to a stop, gripping the ground with one clawed hand to arrest his momentum as he pivoted and lashed out. To its credit, the shaman managed to dodge backward just enough to avoid a lethal blow that would have ripped its throat out, but it could do nothing to keep Elijah from grabbing its staff and ripping it away.

That's when he took it in two hands and swung it like a golf club, connecting with the shaman's chin and launching it into a backflip. But Elijah wasn't finished. He turned that swing into a low backhand that sent one of the guards sprawling across the ground. That gave him just enough space to pounce on the fallen shaman and crush its skull beneath a heavy, stomping foot.

One facet of his Quartz Mind let him know that the other shaman had recovered, sending another ball of red energy screaming in his direction. But having seen it coming, Elijah had no trouble dodging the relatively slow-moving projectile. He darted to the side, then loped forward. The shaman tried to block his descending claw, yet it underestimated his immense strength. As a result, the staff broke, and Elijah's claws ripped through its face, sending a spray of blood splattering against the ground.

It howled in pain and rage as it stumbled backward, but Elijah didn't let it put any distance between them. Instead, he refused to allow that, grabbing the monster's shoulder and dragging him close. Then, he followed his instincts and struck.

Not with his hands.

Nor his feet.

Instead, he snapped out like a crocodile, clamping his jaws around the orc's head and crushing it like a melon. The taste of blood and brains filled Elijah's mouth as he flung the dead orc at one of the pursuing guards. The corpse functioned as a perfect distraction to mask Elijah's charge, which took the enormous orc in the midsection. His claw dug deep into the monster's torso until he felt bone.

Then, he latched on to the creature's spine and ripped.

It did not go well for the massive orc, as more than a few vertebrae came free. It flopped to the ground, paralyzed by Elijah's unconventional attack. Meanwhile, armed with a new bony weapon, he threw himself at the remaining guard. And miraculously, the monster turned and ran.

That strategy earned it another few seconds of life as Elijah tore across the battlefield in a pursuit that ended when he tackled it to the ground and pummeled it into submission.

He let out a roar of victory, losing himself in the heady sensation of success. Yet, that lasted only a few seconds until he saw the sea of gray flesh and tusks all around him. The battle was yet to be won.

He intended to change that. So, after checking his surroundings, he shifted into his human form, and the sudden cessation of his bestial rage nearly overwhelmed him. However, he'd experienced it often enough that he quickly adjusted. Then, he cast Swarm, Healing Rain, and targeting a few hundred feet away, Calamity.

Then, before the spells even took hold, he rapidly cast Shape of the Guardian, retaking the form of the lamellar ape. The rage returned, but it was accompanied by a sense of immense satisfaction as he saw his spells crash into the horde, unfettered by the now-dead shamans' protective shield.

Seeing that, Elijah threw himself back into battle, knowing that he had a long fight ahead of him. But in his mind, the odds had just tipped in the defenders' favor.

76

THE WARLORD

With three orcs clinging to his exhausted body, Elijah struggled to stay upright as the monsters bit and clawed, stabbed and scratched. Roaring, he tried to dislodge them, but the creatures were nothing if not tenacious, so his efforts were for naught. Still, he managed to grab hold of one with his free arm and rip it away. A second later, it was sailing through the air to collide with another of its fellows.

When it did, a handful of arrows fell upon that area, piercing through their durable bodies. At that sight, Elijah received a surge of energy and kicked out, sending another one of the orcs tumbling across the blood-soaked earth to bowl over another pair. But the moment he'd freed himself from that set of grasping hands, another orc leaped to the fore to take the dislodged creature's place.

And then another after that.

Before Elijah could bring his sluggish reflexes to bear, two more orcs had latched on to him. So, when a sixth and final monster hit him with a shoulder tackle, sending him staggering backward and into one of the ditches he'd so laboriously helped to dig. For a second, he felt weightless, but then he slammed into the ground. Fortunately, he maintained just enough of his wits to activate Iron Scales before he landed. Otherwise, he would have been impaled by the sharpened stakes that had already claimed the lives of so many orcs.

As it was, his scales were only nicked, but the orcs couldn't claim such good fortune. Two of them were crushed beneath his massive weight, while two others were completely pierced through by the sharpened stakes. That left only the two that had been clinging to his front, and in a daze, Elijah dealt with them the same way he'd killed so many others.

With either hand, he gripped a different monster's head, then squeezed. They screamed in protest, clawing at his wrists, but they could do no good. No—they were powerless to resist his immense Strength, and after only a few more seconds, their skulls shattered. Even as their brains oozed between Elijah's claws, he couldn't help but wonder at how perfectly sized the orc's heads were to fit in his guardian form's hands.

But then a wave of nausea hit him, reminding him that he wasn't out of the woods. Not only was there a battle still raging all around him, but even the tiny scratches he'd gotten from the stakes were enough to send the poison rampaging through his body. His muscles had already started to lock up, and he knew it wouldn't be long before it affected his heart.

It wasn't enough to kill him outright. Not with his high Constitution. However, in his already-depleted condition, it would be even more effective than normal. And in the ongoing battle, any decline in his abilities would probably end with him dead. So, with every ounce of willpower he possessed, Elijah forced himself to his feet and threw the orcish corpses aside. He tried not to notice the sheer carnage all around him, but even a glance was enough to horrify him.

Elijah had never seen so many bodies in one place. Blood and guts abounded, and gray corpses were piled high. It was a miracle that he'd found an uncovered stake in the trench. All the rest of them had already claimed more than one life, and they wore their trophies with however much pride a stake could display.

Which was none.

But Elijah's mind wasn't in any place to make that distinction. Already, his thoughts had grown just as sluggish as his heartbeat, and he knew he needed to get to safety, and soon. So, with his waning willpower pushing him forward, he climbed the steep slope of the trench, surfacing on the other side. Then, he loped in the direction of the defensive line, bowling orcs over with every passing moment.

He didn't stop to attack any of them. He could barely keep his mind on the singular task of making it to the relative safety of the defensive line. If he let himself get distracted, he would never survive.

So it happened that around thirty seconds later, and with the poison already beginning to shut down his organs, he made it. The moment he got there, the dwarves and gnomes in the area parted, allowing him passage. They'd done it before during the battle, and Elijah suspected that they would have to do it again before it was all over.

As he passed through, he shifted into his human form and stumbled to his knees. Then, he cast Healing Rain before pulsing Touch of Nature over and over again until, at last, the poison dissipated.

Then, he promptly vomited.

It was like that, on his hands and knees and with a trail of vomit connecting his lower lip to the suddenly muddy earth, that Kurik found him.

Elijah looked up and said, "I think that was one of yours."

"Stop gettin' stuck with 'em, and you won't have to deal with it anymore," the dwarven Scout said. Like Elijah, he looked worse for wear, with more than a few rips in his leather armor and a couple of chips in the blade of his axe. The dwarf himself didn't look injured, but Elijah could see dark bags beneath his eyes, and his hair was missing in a jagged line that suggested he'd recently been healed. "You aight?"

"Yeah. I'm healed. Just took a lot of ethera, and I had to get rid of the excess poison," Elijah said, nodding at the puddle of vomit. After another moment, he rocked back on his heels and unslung his pack. Then, he retrieved a jug of water, which he used to swish the taste out of his mouth. Spitting, he asked, "How is the battle going?"

"Better than expected," Kurik answered. "Probably thanks to you."

Elijah shrugged. "More like the ditches and your traps," he said. Indeed, they'd been far more effective than even he had anticipated, and the traps had claimed hundreds of orcish lives. He glanced up at the sky and saw that the sun had risen to its zenith. Had it already been an entire day? He remembered fighting into the night, and dawn felt like it had come only minutes before. However, time was difficult to gauge in the middle of a battle, and it was doubly so when he was so exhausted. "How many more are there?"

"A few thousand, at least."

"So many?" Elijah asked, incredulous. He felt like he'd killed that many on his own, and he'd reaped the benefits, too. He was already level fifty-three, and he expected that he wasn't far from getting another level. Soon, he'd gain a new ability at level fifty-five.

"Yeah," said Kurik as he ran his hand through his wild hair. "They just keep comin'. Good news is that our Scouts say the end of the line is near. Won't be long 'fore they start gettin' desperate. They'll start going into a frenzy, then. And any big 'uns they got are gonna come out, then."

"I already killed the shamans."

"Bound to be some higher-level ones in there, too. Can't underestimate those."

Elijah shook his head, then grabbed a bit of dried meat from his pack. He offered some to the dwarf, who took it. As he chewed on the tough rations, he said, "May as well get back to it, then."

Before he could rise, Kurik put his hand on Elijah's shoulder, and he said, "Stay. Rest for a few more minutes. Just keep that rain going, yeah? We'll set up triage right here for the time being."

"I'm more useful out there," Elijah pointed out. He'd seen the difference from when he was out there taking all the attention in his lamellar-ape form and when he'd retreated. And it wasn't a pretty sight, with the orcs pushing the rest of the defenders to their limits. They'd held each time, but only just.

However, Elijah was so exhausted that even he had to admit he couldn't simply hop back into battle. So, he nodded, then made sure that Healing Rain remained in effect before sitting back down. Soon enough, Kurik had brought a few of the wounded to within the area of effect of Healing Rain, though Elijah had already sunk within himself, dragging as much ethera into the nine vortices of his Quartz Mind, pushing the flow into his Soul, and letting it settle into his Dragon Core.

It wasn't real rest, but it was better than nothing. And after half an hour, he stood and refreshed Healing Rain before leaving the wounded behind. They would be tended to by Ironshore's other Healers who could treat the wounded much more efficiently. Once he reached the defensive line, he looked out at the battlefield.

In most places, he couldn't even see the ground, the carpet of gray corpses was so dense. The orcs were pressing the defenders, but the front lines had employed long spears to keep them at bay while the ranged attackers brought their spells, skills, and projectiles to bear. It wasn't perfect, and there were more than a few instances where the orcs broke through. Yet, it was effective enough that Elijah felt free to use his spells.

Specifically, he cast Swarm. Once. Twice. Three times, each subsequent instance targeted on a different portion of the remaining horde. It drained his ethera rapidly, but his Quartz Mind was already hard at work refilling his Core. In seconds, the entire battlefield was subjected to an immense swarm of stinging insects that descended upon the orcs with ruthless fury. They bit and stung, often unseen and ignored, delivering their deadly payload of afflictions.

Meanwhile, Elijah used Calamity the moment his ethera allowed it, and a disaster followed, ripping into the orcs with nature's wrath. Elijah cast it again after only a few seconds, draining his ethera down to the dregs. But it was worth it, judging by the sheer number of orcs that fell before his spellcasting might.

He watched for a few long minutes as the horde's progress slowed to a crawl. That gave him enough time to continue regenerating his ethera. It was a good thing, too, because, not long after, an orc that was at least nine feet tall stepped onto the field.

Immediately, Elijah knew it was the orc's chief. Not because of the elaborate leopard-skin wrap or the enormous slab of metal it wielded as a sword. Rather, he knew because of the thing's aura, which swept out from its position, enveloping the orcish horde and sending them into a fury. They didn't care if they were injured. And any brief respite Elijah's spells had gained quickly dissipated before their rage. Glowing red with ethereal magic, they rushed forward with renewed vigor, and when they clashed with the line of defenders, spears snapped, and they fell upon the people of Ironshore with the ferocity of rabid animals.

It didn't take a genius to figure out the causal effect.

Nor did it take Elijah long to choose a course of action. So, he sighted in on the orc warlord and used Brand of the Stalker. The second it landed, he shifted into his guardian form and bounded forward, barreling through the horde of enraged orcs along the way. He could see the afflictions eating away at them, and more than a few sported grievous injuries. However, the famous endurance of orcs was on full display, and whatever the warlord had done had robbed them of even the most basic survival instincts. They didn't attempt to avoid Elijah's or the defenders' attacks. Instead, they just fell upon their chosen enemies, trading blow for blow.

And they were winning.

Elijah knew he needed to reach the warlord and neutralize it before the battle was lost. So, he leaped over trenches and swept the orcs aside as he used his immense Strength to cover as much ground as possible. Then, finally, he fell upon the massive orc, hitting with all the weight and rage he could muster.

And for the first time since the battle had begun, he was rebuffed. He bounced off the orc like he'd hit a brick wall, then staggered backward, dizzy and dazed. Elijah barely regained his wits in time to dive aside and avoid the orc's descending slab of a blade. It hit the ground, cleaving an orcish corpse in two and spraying blood, dirt, and entrails in every direction.

It recovered quickly, though, aiming a front kick at Elijah's chest. It connected, sending Elijah stumbling back. That kick, which felt like it had broken a couple of ribs, was evidence that Elijah was in over his head.

Yet, he had no choice but to keep going. More than a thousand people were depending on him. So were Nerthus and his Grove. And in a way, the rest of the world. He couldn't give up. He couldn't consider failure. So, with renewed resolve, he launched himself back into the fight.

77

BLIND

Bring her back," growled Carmen, staring down at the woman in the chair. She couldn't have been more than twenty years old, and once upon a time, she'd been quite lovely. And she would be again once Keith was done with her. She glanced at the Healer, seeing hesitation on his face. "Now."

"I'm not comfortable with this," he said, wringing his hands. He'd already brought the woman back from near death a half dozen times, and as far as Carmen was concerned, he would do so a half dozen more before they were done. And a hundred more after that. It would keep going until she gave Carmen what she wanted.

"I don't care. Do it."

"Carmen . . ."

All it took was a scathing glance before he went silent. Then, he used his healing spell—Carmen had no idea what it was called—and the mostly dead woman gasped in surprise. Keith kept channeling the spell until she was back to perfect health.

"Please . . . I didn't . . . I had no idea . . . I didn't want to—"

Carmen didn't care about the woman's excuses. She'd never even asked for a name. All she knew was that after that despicable excuse for a human being had taken Miguel, they'd lost him in the woods. However, their search had yielded some results when they'd found two women trying to hide nearby. They'd been cloaked in some sort of skill meant to camouflage them, but all it took was the direct attention of one of Silverado's Scouts to strip them of the effect. Laid bare, they'd quickly surrendered.

Since then, they'd learned the error of that course of action.

One was already dead, the result of Carmen letting her temper take over and push her much too far. And she'd come close on more than one occasion with the other, which was the woman sitting right in front of her. That was where Keith had come in.

Carmen had beaten the woman near to death so many times that her knuckles had cracked and broken under her own Strength. And yet, the ally of that monster had refused to reveal anything. It would have been admirable if Carmen wasn't so furious—with herself as much as with the Outlaw who'd kidnapped her son. And with Roman, who'd doubtless ordered it.

With the world itself.

So, she took it out on the helpless prisoner she'd tied to a chair.

At first, it had been an attempt to get information, but it had quickly devolved into something much worse. Something far more primal. Once, she'd have looked down on anyone who used such methods, on those who would let their emotions get the better of them when confronted by evil. Now, she embodied that wrath more than she'd have ever thought possible.

It wasn't surprising.

Alyssa's death had changed her, and in more ways than she wanted to contemplate. Before, she'd looked at the world with a fair amount of optimism. But now? That seemed like such an alien viewpoint that she couldn't understand how anyone could see the world through such rose-colored glasses. And when she'd seen Trace fleeing through the woods with her son thrown over his shoulder, Carmen had snapped.

It had almost cost Colt his life. He'd been so thoroughly injured that it took Keith and the town's other Healer nearly six hours to save him. Even then, he wasn't entirely whole. Meanwhile, Carmen had stomped through the woods in a vain attempt to catch a man whose very existence screamed of an ability to hide. He was a rodent. A pest that needed to be exterminated. Yet, like all pests, he was incredibly difficult to pin down.

So, when the two accomplices had been found, Carmen hadn't wasted any time before employing the worst of the worst interrogation tactics, and to almost no effect. Sure, she'd discovered some pertinent information, like the fact that Trace was the head of some sort of secret police in Easton. Or that he'd been sent—along with what sounded like a harem of young and beautiful apprentices—to spy on Carmen. What was unclear was whether or not he'd chosen to kidnap Miguel on his own or if it had been part of the plan.

"Where did he go?" she asked, pulling back her fist. She hit the woman again, breaking the delicate bones in her face. "Where is he keeping my son?"

"I . . . I don't . . . know," she muttered, spitting blood with every syllable. "I didn't even know . . ."

Carmen hit her again.

And again after that.

It was the same answer, over and over again. So, she kept going until, at last, someone grabbed her arm. Then, when that wasn't enough, a second person joined in. And a third. In all, it took four people to restrain her, and even they were barely capable of the job.

Colt, injured and pale, screamed, "We know where he went! You don't have to do this!"

That cut through her fury. "What?" she spat, her eyes wild. "Where?"

"We found a trail," Colt stated. "Heading toward Easton. That's where he's going. I'm sure of it."

"Kill her, then," Carmen growled.

"No, ma'am."

"What did you just say?" she demanded, still struggling against the people restraining her. She glared at the tall, slim man. "Do you know what she did? Do you understand—"

"She didn't do anything," Colt said, his voice calm. "The one responsible is Trace. This girl is a victim, same as anyone else. You know that."

"I don't," Carmen responded. "I won't . . . I can't . . ."

She tried to pull away once again, but much of her fury had dissipated. Instead, it was replaced by hopelessness. "He can't be gone. I . . . I can't . . . I . . . I . . ."

She collapsed into sobs. Colt stepped forward, saying something Carmen didn't hear. Then, she was suddenly free. But she didn't launch herself at the bound woman, as she would have just moments before. Instead, she collapsed to her knees. Colt knelt beside her, wincing in pain as he put his arm around her shoulders.

"It'll be okay. If they was gonna do somethin' to him, they already would've," he said. "We have allies in Easton. We can use them to make Roman give 'im back."

Carmen barely heard him. Instead, she wept as she tried to process the chain of events that had led her to such dire straits. If she hadn't flown off the handle and killed Verin, things might have turned out differently. Yet, she knew that would never have been possible. The moment the Healer had revealed her part in Alyssa's death, her fate was sealed.

Finally, Carmen wiped the tears from her eyes, sniffed loudly, then said, "Then we need to go. Now. Get one of the trucks ready."

"What about her?" asked Colt.

Carmen glared at the injured woman. "Heal her," she told Keith. "But we're not letting her go. Now, let's move."

Everyone in the room did just that, and Colt helped her to her feet. "You okay?" he asked.

"No," Carmen answered. Then, she said, "Put on your armor. You're going to need it."

"Yes, ma'am," the cowboy said before heading toward the door.

"And Colt?" she said. He turned back to face her. "Thanks."

"Yes, ma'am," he repeated.

From there the small town erupted into a whirlwind of activity as Carmen and her most loyal followers assembled. The civilians within the town were vulnerable, but the remaining combatants were more than capable of guarding them against all but the worst threats. That, Carmen reasoned, would have to do. After all, as much as she wanted to protect the people who had put their trust in her, she cared about her son infinitely more.

Soon, she found herself leading a small caravan of trucks through the wilderness toward Easton. Fortunately, the road had been cleared, which allowed the electric trucks to make much better time than normal. However, there was no chance that they would catch Trace. By the time they'd figured out which direction he was traveling—which seemed obvious in retrospect—he had almost a day as a head start. Still, Carmen and her people didn't waste any time, and over the next couple of days, they managed to reach the region surrounding Easton.

But when they arrived at the gate, Carmen was met with an issue.

"Wait right here, ma'am," said the man, who was dressed in the blue-and-white uniform of Easton's guards. The gate itself was massive, and though Carmen had seen it before, she found it extremely imposing. More troubling was the fact that she counted twenty Guards nearby, which was more than normal. On top of that, they were more than enough to overwhelm Carmen's people.

The Guard disappeared into the gatehouse. The wall to which it was attached was nearly a hundred feet high and half as thick, but more distressingly, it pulsed with enough ethera to give Carmen pause. There was far more at play than simple bricks and mortar.

"Don't like this one bit," said Colt, who sat in the passenger's seat. Three more combatants were in the bed of the truck, and just as many occupied the following vehicle. "Feels like an ambush."

Almost as soon as those words left Colt's mouth, a trio of high-level Guards came out of the gatehouse. The moment they locked eyes on Carmen, she knew they hadn't come to talk. That supposition was supported by the fact that one of them drew his sword.

Carmen shouted, "Go!"

It was the signal Colt had been waiting for, but he was still too late. The second the truck surged forward, the portcullis of the gate fell. It clanged to the ground before the truck's tires even got any traction. Seeing that, Colt did what they'd discussed on the way to the city, and after spinning out for a brief moment, he whipped the truck around and fled. The other vehicle followed.

Arrows and various spells fell upon them, but the Guards' aim was inferior to the task of hitting a moving target, so both trucks escaped with only minor damage. Carmen swore as they tore off through the woods, going off road to avoid pursuit. After thirty minutes, Colt said, "I think we lost 'em. Where to?"

"I think you know."

"The rebels aren't ready," Colt said. "And only about a third of the war band has any gear."

"He has Miguel. We can't wait."

"Ma'am, I don't think—"

"I'm not asking you to come with me," Carmen stated. "I'm just telling you what I'm going to do. It has to be now, and for more than just Miguel. It won't be long before word gets back to Roman. He probably already knows what's going on. So, we need to strike now before he has a chance to prepare. You know that's the only play here."

"Let me sneak in," Colt said. "I can—"

"You can't sneak into the palace. You're a Samurai, remember? Not a ninja."

Colt ground his teeth, clearly frustrated. Carmen could agree on that front. However, she also knew there wasn't much either of them could do about it. They only had one chance to get Miguel back, and that meant they needed to put everything on the line.

"You could send someone in to talk to him. Negotiate," Colt suggested.

"You think he'd listen?" Carmen asked. "The only way to deal with somebody like Roman is from a position of strength. He doesn't understand anything else. Besides, he needs to die. I'll do whatever it takes to make that happen."

"We'll get Miggy back," Colt insisted.

"I know. Or I'll tear Easton down to get him," she said. However, in the back of her mind, Carmen knew that wasn't feasible. She had power, but it wasn't the sort of strength she would need to take on a whole city. Even in a one-on-one fight, without all the support that came with running a city, she would come up short against someone like Roman.

But that was why she'd made allies. Now, it was time for them to live up to their side of the bargain. So, she directed Colt to move on. He didn't need directions because he knew as well as anyone where to find the war band. Everyone did, even Roman and his people. Yet, they maintained a tentative peace because neither side wanted to give up their advantage by pushing an attack. For Roman, that meant he and his forces remained in Easton where they could defend from a position of strength. Meanwhile, the war band—which was called the Crimson Eagles—stayed just close enough to the city to pose a credible threat.

By any measure, it was a cold war.

Carmen intended to apply some heat.

With that in mind, they soon arrived at their destination, which was an old mall that had been converted into a veritable fortress. The alterations weren't pretty—not like Easton—but they were functional, with rough walls and towers made of timber. Guarding the compound were hundreds of combatants, each with a raw and ragged look about them.

Carmen understood it. These people had been fighting since the very beginning, and without much in the way of safety. But they weren't the villains Roman and Easton's council made them out to be. Instead, they were composed of castoffs and undesirables as well as the people who'd vowed to protect them.

Quite a few had been turned away from Easton at one point or another because they didn't have useful classes. Most of the fighters were the men and women who refused to abandon family and friends who'd been denied entry.

There were also a few bandits in there. A couple of people who only wanted to murder, pillage, and raid. Though Carmen had been assured that those were kept on tight leashes, their presence was still a point of contention. However, with what was on the line, she wasn't nearly as concerned as she might've once been.

"Something is wrong," Carmen muttered.

"What?" Colt asked. "I don't—"

Just then, a flight of arrows erupted from the surrounding woods. Some hit the trucks with the power of gunshots, but most targeted the tires. Colt slammed the truck in reverse, but it was no use because, only a moment later, someone leaped out from behind a rock. He was an enormous man, wielding a giant hammer that he sent on a collision course with the truck's front end.

The head of the weapon hit with resounding force, tearing through the hood and destroying the engine. At the same time, a bunch of men and women wearing the armor Carmen and her people had created descended on the other truck with merciless fury. Carmen's people tried to fight back, but against such a focused and sudden assault, they were powerless.

Colt leaped from the truck, drawing his sword at the same time. He lashed out, slicing the giant, hammer-wielding man to pieces with Blade Storm, but a second later, someone tackled him to the ground. Meanwhile, Carmen dove free of the truck, summoning her blacksmithing hammer. But before she could bring it to bear, she had someone clinging to both of her arms.

In a second, they had forced her arms behind her back and shoved her to the ground.

Furious, Carmen looked up to see Laramie, the man who stood at the head of the war band, looking down on her. He was a tall and muscular man with dark skin who favored armor that made him look like he'd stepped out of a *Mad Max* movie. But he had clear, intelligent eyes that belied the barbaric appearance of his armor.

"What are you doing?!" she demanded, struggling to free herself. It was useless. Whatever they'd used to bind her arms was stronger than steel. "We're in this together!"

He loomed over her, saying, "We were. But things change, Carmen. We got a better offer." He squatted down. "I hate Roman. I want to see him dead for all the things he did. But I've got people to feed. Civilians to protect. And he can give us that. You can't."

"You asshole! He took my son!"

"He took a lot of sons. Daughters, too," the leader of the war band said. "But the reality of survival doesn't care about that. I'd hoped you would understand, even if you didn't want to accept it."

Then, he pushed himself to his feet and called for the prisoners to be taken away. That included Carmen, and though she struggled, she was incapable of escape. Instead, she and Colt were half dragged, half escorted into the mall before someone shoved the both of them into a makeshift dungeon that had once been some long-closed clothing store.

"I'm sorry," Colt said. "I keep failing you."

Carmen didn't respond. Instead, she turned her attention to their surroundings. The former store had been stripped of everything but a few mannequins, and the entrance was guarded by a roll-down cage. Moreover, both she and Colt—the only two survivors—were bound so tightly that neither could properly move.

That's when the reality of her situation hit her. Her capture had probably sealed her son's fate. If he wasn't dead, he soon would be. And she wouldn't be far behind him. Colt hadn't been the only one to fail.

"There's a lot of that going around," she muttered.

78

TEAMWORK

The warlord roared, and the orcish horde responded to its call, clambering to cross the trench-strewn battlefield on their way to destroy Ironshore. The defenders attempted to fend them off with their long spears and copious use of their various abilities, but the frenzied orcs had no sense of self-preservation. As a result, they crashed into the defenses with reckless fury, nearly breaking the line with the sheer weight of their charge.

Meanwhile, Elijah picked himself up just in time to avoid the warlord's descending blade. He leaped backward, clearing nearly twenty feet in a single bound, but the warlord followed, screaming with fury that was only matched by his followers' collective rage. Elijah batted the flat of the weapon, sending it just off course. As it hit the ground, he lashed out with a hand clad in the Claws of Gluttony, ripping a chunk of flesh free. It was a superficial wound—barely more than a scratch—but the orcish warlord screamed like he'd just taken a mortal injury.

In a sudden move that took Elijah by surprise, it lowered its shoulder and hit him with a charge that knocked him from his feet. He hit the ground on his back, then rolled to a stop a few feet later to see the warlord's blade once again descending in a quest to split him in two. Using the Haste of his Sash of the Whirlwind to great advantage, he again slapped the flat of the blade. This time, however, it wasn't enough to send the blade completely off course, and it hit his shoulder, carving a massive slab of flesh free.

As the meat flopped to the ground, Elijah let out a roar and leaped at the monster's legs. He didn't attack with his claws. Instead, he snapped out with his powerful jaws, and when they closed around the monster's calf, he heard cracking bones. Then, channeling his inner alligator, he rolled, and the monster lost its balance, falling atop Elijah in a heap.

With every point of Strength he had at his disposal, Elijah shoved the monster away. But when he tried to find his feet, he realized that the orcish warlord had latched on to his ankle. He yanked, trying to free it, but it was no use. Its grip was like iron. The only solace was that, in such close proximity, it couldn't bring its massive slab of a sword to bear. Yet, its own two hands were plenty to do all sorts of damage. It demonstrated that fact when it wrenched Elijah's ankle to the side, breaking delicate bones.

Howling in pain, he jerked free, but by that point, the damage had been done. Elijah stumbled to all fours, which quickly turned into a three-legged retreat. The orc followed, screaming bloody murder as it limped in pursuit.

But to Elijah's horror, the thing had the same famous durability of all orcs, and it was far better suited to dealing with a gimpy leg. So, it caught him after only a few seconds. As it reached for his thick tail, Elijah made a choice that he hoped wouldn't come back to bite him.

He shifted into his human form, casting Healing Rain the moment it became available. At the same time, he reversed course and dove between the giant creature's legs. The moment he rolled to a stop, he pulsed Touch of Nature, sending regenerative ethera toward his ruined ankle.

The orc whipped around, mistakenly trying to pivot on its own injured leg and paying the price. When it put weight on the limb, it stumbled slightly, giving Elijah the opportunity to put a few more feet worth of distance between himself and the monster. Then, he pulsed Touch of Nature again, healing his injury enough that he could put weight on that leg. One more, and it was entirely healed.

And it was just in time, too, because the orcish warlord recovered extremely quickly. It launched itself at him, drawing a machete-sized dagger from its hide belt. Even as it descended, Elijah was casting another spell.

Swarm completed just before the orc reached him, and Elijah aimed a baseball-style swing at the creature's already-injured leg. He put every ounce of power he could summon behind it, and he was rewarded with the loud sound of cracking bone.

Or that was what he thought, right up until he looked down at his staff and saw only a jagged wooden stake. He was so surprised that he didn't even see the orc's backhanded blow before it hit him in the stomach, sending his much lighter body flying across the battlefield. He hit the ground almost thirty feet later, collided with a screaming orc, and nearly rolled into one of the trenches.

For a moment, his head swam with what he expected was a concussion, but a reflexive cast of Touch of Nature banished the wooziness. Then, he used it again to heal himself only to discover that he wasn't grievously injured. He thanked his smaller body for that. If he'd been anchored by a lot more mass, he wouldn't have been launched across the field, which had served to dissipate some of the force.

Regardless, he knew he was in a rough state.

His store of ethera was getting much lower, and he knew he couldn't continue the fight like he had so far. His guardian form had no advantages over the massive orc, and his human form was practically useless without ethera. So, Elijah reasoned that he only had one chance of winning the battle. Using a similar tactic to what he'd employed against the ogre champion back in the tower, he shifted into his draconid form after using one last Touch of Nature.

Then, he turned and ran.

The orcish warlord followed, barreling through its own people as it chased him. Meanwhile, Elijah bounded from one enemy to the other, using his superior speed and motor control to dodge any attacks they sent his way. At the same time, his claws flashed every time he passed an orc, severing tendons and ripping through muscles. More importantly, though, he infected them with Contagion.

That was only a side effect of his flight, though. Leading the orc away was the primary goal, and the monster, as single-minded as it was, never suspected that it was being manipulated. Elijah leaped over trenches and wove between the orcs comprising the horde, and though he experienced more than one close call, he narrowly avoided any attacks they sent his way.

For a long few minutes, he utilized every facet of his Quartz Mind to keep track of the chaotic battlefield. But then, the warlord seemed to recognize that it was being led on a merry chase, and it turned back to its original purpose. That was precisely what Elijah had been waiting on, and he leaped, hit an orc to reverse course, and rocketed toward the warlord's back. He leaped upon it, using Venom Strike before savaging the monster a half dozen times, then bounding away.

It reacted with all the fury Elijah would have expected and abandoned its march toward Ironshore so it could chase Elijah's retreating form. The cycle repeated a few more times over the next hour, and every second felt like he was balanced on the edge of a knife. One tiny mistake, and he'd have gotten pummeled by the warlord or its minions. Yet, Elijah had been through multiple crucibles since Earth had been touched by the World Tree, and through those experiences, he'd been forged into the sort of person who could walk that tightrope and expect to maintain his footing.

That was true right up until he made a fatal mistake.

He'd just dashed in for yet another hit-and-run attack on the warlord, but the monster surprised him with a sudden reversal. It might have been dense, but it had finally recognized its situation for what it was. And rather than perpetuating its own doom, it chose to turn the tables on Elijah.

He was in midair when the monster whipped around and clamped its fingers around his neck. He squirmed, scratching and clawing at the creature's arm. It was under the effect of dozens of instances of Contagion as well as the afflictions of Swarm and Venom Strike, and yet, it looked only a little worse for wear. By comparison, the surrounding orcs almost all looked like they were dead on their feet.

But Elijah wasn't worried about them.

Indeed, he wasn't worried about anything but his own life. Panicked, he let his draconid form fall away and immediately initiated a transformation into a lamellar ape. Before it could truly begin, though, the orcish warlord slammed him into the ground. Elijah felt his body crumple. Bones broke, and his organs felt like they ruptured. Yet, the monster wasn't finished. Instead, it lifted him in both hands and slammed him against the ground again. He'd just completed his transformation, though it felt like it did little good. Even though he managed to use Iron Scales, the ability did nothing to alleviate the damage that had already been done.

He hit the ground again with thunderous impact. He kicked out blindly, connecting with the monster's thighs and digging deep grooves in the warlord's gray flesh. Yet, it did little good as the creature once again raised him high into the air. Elijah's mind whirled with strategies to avoid what he knew was coming. Iron Scales protected him a little, but even the ten percent of the damage that made it through was enough to push him closer to his body giving out.

His situation was desperate, and despite using every facet of his Mind to search for an answer, he found no solutions. In that moment, Elijah was certain he was going to die.

Iron Scales gave out, and the monster let out a victorious roar as it slammed Elijah into the ground.

The killing blow didn't come, though. Instead, a dense bubble of blue energy bloomed into being around Elijah, softening the blow. The orcish warlord looked down on him with mingled confusion and surprise, which allowed Elijah to wriggle free. As he did, he activated Rage. Instantly, his body was flooded with renewed Strength, sending his physical attributes skyrocketing well past his normal limits.

And when he hit the ground after having freed himself from the warlord's grip, Elijah used that additional power to great effect. He grabbed hold of the monster's ankle and yanked with all his might. The creature, weakened by various afflictions and blood loss from the Claws of Gluttony's Anticoagulant effect, was incapable of remaining upright. It tipped over, hitting the turf hard.

Elijah knew that wasn't enough to even the slow the monster down, much less put it out of commission. However, he did have an idea. So, ignoring the pain of his injuries, Elijah thrust himself to his feet and dragged the struggling orc a few yards to the nearest trench.

Because he recognized where on the battlefield he'd ended up. After all, it wasn't that long ago that he'd fallen afoul of the stakes at the bottom of that very ditch. With all the Strength granted by his lamellar-ape form, combined with his natural attributes and the effects of Rage, Elijah heaved the orc over the edge. In midair, it flailed for a few seconds before slamming into the bare stakes.

Of course, the monster tried to pull itself free, but Elijah wasn't going to allow that. As Rage dissipated, he switched to his human form. Rather than heal himself, which he desperately needed, Elijah cast Snaring Roots. Thick vines erupted from the ground, holding the monster in place. Then, he cast Storm's Fury. Lightning descended from on high, smashing into the prone warlord.

Without the enhancement of the ruined Staff of Natural Fury, the spell did little damage. Yet, that was never the point. Instead, Elijah had cast Storm's Fury with one intention: to stun the creature. And in that endeavor, it was successful. As the orc ripped itself free of the vines, Elijah cast Snaring Roots again, keeping it in place. But to his horror, the warlord wasn't succumbing to the poison on the stakes as quickly as Elijah had expected.

And he didn't have the ethera to keep going much longer.

Indeed, if he didn't heal himself soon, he was going to die. He could feel fluid building in his lungs, and his insides hurt like never before.

In that moment, Elijah made a decision to end it, one way or another.

So, after pulsing Touch of Nature a single time to keep himself alive, he initiated a transformation back into his lamellar-ape form, draining the last of his ethera. Before he'd completed the change, the orc ripped free of the vines, and it started to extract itself from the stakes.

That's when Elijah fell upon it, raining a series of vicious blows onto the vulnerable monster. He pummeled the creature with every ounce of fury he could muster, and yet, he couldn't do so without taking plenty of hits himself. It was like two heavyweight boxers trading blows in the twelfth round of a championship fight. Neither was in any condition to continue, and yet, they both persisted well past the point of no return, hammering one another with heavy blows that could shake the world.

Elijah knew what his decision entailed. He wasn't going to make it. Even if he managed to take the monster out, the damage was too severe. Without a full Core of ethera, he couldn't heal himself quickly enough to recover.

But he was okay with the choice he'd made.

Running had been an option, and he'd considered it. Yet, that was just delaying the inevitable. The monster had been vulnerable, and if he hadn't pounced when he had, it would have recovered and laid waste to the remaining defenders as well as Ironshore. From there, the horde would sweep across the world.

And though he hadn't seen them in a long time, Elijah had people he cared about out there. Not only were Alyssa, Carmen, and Miguel somewhere out in the world, but he'd had friends back in Hawaii, too. Not to mention the friends he'd made in Ironshore. Isaak and Delilah back in Argos. Or Jess and Essex in Norcastle. Nerthus and his Grove. There were a lot of reasons he couldn't allow the orcs to live.

Elijah channeled that while pummeling the warlord, and it gave him a burst of energy that, in turn, allowed him to, at last, finish the thing off with a massive blow that broke the creature's neck. He only had a brief moment to realize that he'd won before the weight of injuries swept over him.

Dizziness assailed every facet of his Mind, but he managed to climb free of the trench before, at last, collapsing. He crawled forward a few feet, but that was the extent of his ability. Faintly, he heard familiar voices, and he suddenly realized that he'd shifted back to his human form. Someone shoved something into his mouth, and miraculously, he felt a brief surge of healing. More importantly, a drop of additional ethera hit his Core a second later.

Something else hit his tongue, and he felt something tart and familiar. His eyes focused, and he realized that Kurik was standing over him and holding a handful of Elijah's Grove berries.

"Open up, ya moron," the dwarf growled. "Not lettin' you die after all that."

Elijah's jaw fell open, and Kurik shoved another couple of berries into his mouth. That was enough to clear his head, at least a little, and though he had a host of questions, he knew he needed to cast Touch of Nature or he wouldn't survive much longer. So, he did, and soothing energy washed over him, mending his injuries. It was only a drop in the proverbial bucket, but it was enough to return him to complete awareness.

He jerked, croaking, "What happened? The orcs."

"Dead," Kurik said. "When you finished the big 'un off, they lost that enhancement. Wasn't long after that that your afflictions took 'em down. With a little help from us, o' course."

"Oh . . . so . . . it's over?" Elijah asked.

"Everything but the cleanup," Kurik said.

Elijah finally relaxed with a sigh of relief that sent an arc of pain tearing across his torso. "Good," he muttered. "Oh . . . Kurik?"

"Yeah?"

"I need that orc's brains. The big one. Save those for me," he said. "That's very important."

Then, without further conversation, he let himself finally relax. That led to his consciousness slipping away. Before he went out completely, he heard Kurik say, "Brains? Never heard that 'un before."

79

HUMANITY

Trace had screwed up.

He knew it, too. Pacing back and forth, he periodically glanced at the boy who'd caused him so much trouble. Miguel was bound, hand and foot, like a trussed pig—a necessity, after everything that had happened. Over the past few days, Trace had been forced to take a host of precautions against the troublesome child's persistent escape attempts. The moment Stun had worn off, the child had started kicking and screaming, necessitating that Trace chain the ability, over and over, while he fled toward Easton and what he'd hoped was safety.

Usually, Stun was a fairly cheap ability, costing only a touch of ethera and a bit of stamina. Yet, having to use it once every minute for days had taken its toll, so once Trace had reached Easton, he'd quickly found one of his safe houses and tied the kid up. Surely, it wasn't comfortable for the little demon of a child, but it allowed Trace some much-needed rest. At some point, he'd slipped into an exhausted sleep, which had cost him almost six hours.

And perhaps his life.

When he'd awoken, he had quickly discovered that Easton had devolved into riotous chaos. Everywhere he'd looked, there were hundreds—perhaps even thousands—of malcontents protesting and causing violent mischief. More than once during his first scouting expedition, he'd seen Guards being overwhelmed and beaten to death by rebels.

Trace knew it was all pointless. While Roman might not hold every part of the city in quite as tight of a grip as others, that was by choice. He simply didn't care about the poorer parts of Easton, and so, the presence of his Guards was minimal. But the moment the rebellion reached the core of the city, they would be dealt with appropriately.

It would be a slaughter of epic proportions, too.

Trace had seen the planned responses. He'd helped create some of them. Yet, just because the integrity of the city wasn't in question, that didn't mean much for his situation. Because crossing through the riots was still extraordinarily dangerous, and with much of his capability in stealth nullified by having to carry a child along, he knew it wouldn't end well for him.

Because he was well-known in the seedier parts of the city, and after every-thing he'd done, he was not exactly well-liked. Part of that was because of his actions as the head of Roman's secret police, but Trace could admit—at least to himself—that it was mostly due to his own less-than-reputable proclivities. After all, his girls had come from somewhere, and many of them had friends and family who didn't look upon Trace terribly kindly.

And a riot was a perfect opportunity for some of them to exact revenge.

So, he'd spent the past few days holed up in his safe house, only climbing out of the basement to steal provisions. Fortunately, the place was secluded, and the riots never came close enough to risk discovery. Still, despite his relative safety, he was more than ready to head to the palace, present his prize, and get his reward.

So, it was with some degree of excitement that, after pacing for a few more hours, he left the basement and went to scout the situation. And to his surprise, he found that the riots had been put down. Yet, the damage was extensive, with more than a few buildings having been destroyed by spreading fires. Trace also saw plenty of bodies, as well, though those were in the process of being col-lected by the city's dedicated corpsemongers.

Even Trace wasn't certain what those people did with the bodies they col-lected. Each time he'd attempted to infiltrate their underground lair—because of course that was where they would set up shop—he'd been discovered via unknown means. It was one of Easton's burgeoning mysteries, and a reason that Trace intended to leave the city behind once he'd extracted all the benefits he could from Roman.

With that in mind, Trace went back to the safe house and gathered the boy, tossing him over his shoulder. At first, he used Cloak of Skullduggery to mask his presence, but he quickly recognized that it was neither effective nor use-ful. There weren't enough people around to care about his nefarious-looking actions, and even if there were, they were occupied with cleanup efforts.

A few Guards recognized him, though, so he felt confident that they would come to his aid if anyone accosted him.

As he traversed the city, he saw more evidence of the riots of the past few nights. Whole buildings had been brought down, and one of the plazas looked like it had seen a bloody battle. Some of the city's downtrodden maintenance workers were busy trying to clean up all the gore, but they had their work cut out for them. It was further evidence of just how far some of them had fallen. Trace knew for a fact that some of those workers had once held positions of authority and wealth, back in the old world. There were a couple of politicians and former CEOs among them. Yet, they'd made the wrong choice regarding archetypes, and they'd paid the price for that singular bad decision.

Easton was no place for Scholars, especially when their specialties weren't in the few areas Roman had deemed useful.

Even Trace recognized that it was a regressive policy to push those Scholars into manual labor. But he was in no position to change any of it. Not that he would have tried, anyway. As far as he was concerned, the bunch of formerly rich and uppity politicians, CEOs, lawyers, and the like had gotten what they deserved. Maybe they could now appreciate what it was like to live on the bottom rungs of society that Trace knew so well.

He remembered his old life well enough to take some sense of justice from that.

As Trace drew closer to the city's core, the evidence of fighting grew more pronounced until every successive block grew bloodier. Then, suddenly, it ceased. That wasn't surprising, given that the number of Guards had grown right alongside the violent aftermath. A few times, Trace saw Guards looting curiously well-provisioned corpses. More than once, he used Appraisal to determine that the most popular items were Simple grade. If all the dissidents had been armed and armored with equipment like that, the results might've been a little different. Yet, there were only a scattered few such instances that Trace could see, which meant that the effects were minimal.

Still, the only times Trace saw any significant number of Guards' corpses were around such well-armed bodies, suggesting that they'd put up quite the fight. That just underscored how important good equipment really was.

Not that Trace needed to be reminded of that, after he'd used his Stiletto of Sundering to such great effect. It had allowed Roman to kill Alyssa—that uppity bitch—and it had been at least as effective in every fight Trace had fought since then. It was a valuable piece of equipment, and he expected that he'd get years of use out of it before he moved on to something better.

More importantly, it was the linchpin of any plans he'd made to deal with people like Roman. Eventually, they'd come to an impasse—it had come close to happening a few times already—and when that time came, Trace intended to come out on top. Despite the disparity in power, especially in Easton, Trace liked his chances.

Regardless, he put those thoughts aside as he entered the vicinity of the palace. Once there, he dropped any pretense at stealth and was greeted with a mixture of revulsion, respect, and curiosity by the palace Guards. The structure itself was a display of brutal opulence. Roman's Architects had done a phenomenal job of creating a beautiful, yet overbearing building that was dominated by straight lines, sharp angles, and Gothic flourishes that gave it a very distinct appearance.

Trace saw it as needless posturing, but he supposed that Roman had his reasons for commissioning such a building. The rest of the city would soon follow suit, he knew. That was how Roman thought. Everything had to be in its place and conform to the collective. Otherwise, it would drive the man mad.

After entering the palace, Trace made his way through the familiar halls until he reached the wing containing Roman's office. There was a throne room, as well, though that was only for official duties, like hearing the petitions of the useless council. They held no real power, except to suggest things or request Roman's intervention. Ultimately, every major decision was made by the big man himself.

As he swaggered up to the Guards on duty, he said, "Special delivery for the big guy. You want to sign for it?"

At that, the kid squirmed a little more, so Trace reapplied Stun. He went blessedly limp, giving Trace a little peace. The Guards looked at one another, then decided to pass the burden on to someone else. So, one of them disappeared through the doors, presumably to let Roman know what was going on. Meanwhile, Trace tried to make conversation with the remaining Guard, asking, "So, a bit of a scuffle out in the city, huh? What happened?"

"Rebel scum," the man spat, his hand on the hilt of the sword at his waist. "Don't know what they expected to accomplish. They never had a chance, the poor idiots."

"Seems like they did a lot of damage," Trace said.

The Guard shrugged. "Burning down their own homes and businesses. Really smart," he responded. "Like I said, I don't know what they expected that to do, except make their own lives harder. Guess there's a reason they are who they are, right? If they were smart or competent, they wouldn't have anything to bitch about. It's like I was telling my wife—they're just a bunch of useless malcontents who are upset with the way the world works. It's not enough that they're only alive because of the safety and security we provide. No—they want all the benefits without any of the work."

Trace listened as the man went on about how the poor and less useful deserved everything they got, so he was grateful when the other guard returned and waved Trace through. He nodded at the pair of sentries and swaggered through the door and into a long hall. There were other Guards posted at regular intervals, but they didn't move a muscle as he traversed the opulent corridor.

Soon, he found himself at the door to Roman's office. He knocked and immediately received the go-ahead to enter. When he did, he saw the man himself sitting behind a massive wooden desk. The walls were decorated with various trophies from Roman's kills. None of them had been truly impressive prey, and Trace suspected they were more for ambience than to commemorate any significant events. Yet, they did that job well, and when Trace looked at those monstrous heads, a chill went up his spine.

He tossed the kid onto the sofa that stood against the wall—it was upholstered in leather and looked extremely comfortable—and said, "So, I might've took a bit of initiative with the whole Carmen problem."

Roman's eyes flicked to the child, but he didn't give any other reaction until he asked, "Is that who I think it is?"

"If you think it's that bitch's brat, then yeah. I think I killed her second, too," he said, plopping down in one of the chairs on his side of Roman's desk. He added, "You're welcome on that one."

"I told you to watch her. Not to kill anyone."

"Yeah," he said, drawing a small knife from his belt. He picked at his fingernails. "I like to go above and beyond the call of duty. One of my many positive traits. So, here's what I'm thinking—you let the rebel bitch know that—"

In the blink of an eye, Roman was across the desk. If Trace hadn't been so exhausted, he might have responded. Yet, given where they were as well as Roman's advantage in levels, he would have still been overmatched. Still, he did manage to jab the small knife into Roman's shoulder as the taller man slammed him into the ground.

"What the—"

Trace didn't get a chance to finish his sentence before Roman's fist found his face. He tried to activate his abilities, but it was useless. Roman punched him again, growling, "I told you to watch!"

He smashed his fist into Trace's face again.

"Not to kidnap a child!"

Again, he punched Trace. By that point, his mind had gone fuzzy, and though his abilities were suddenly available, he was in no mindset to consciously use them. Especially when Roman hit him again. And again.

Along the way, Roman kept growling about crossing lines, but Trace couldn't understand any of it.

But one thing he did understand was when Roman yanked a dagger from his belt and rammed it into Trace's chest. Over and over again, he stabbed the Outlaw until Trace managed to croak, "W-why . . ."

"You disgust me," Roman said, straightening his back. He pushed a lock of stray hair from his bloody face before adding, "Every man has a line. You just crossed mine."

Then, he reached forward, grabbed Trace by the hair, and sliced the Outlaw's throat. Even as he bled out, Trace's mind whirled with questions. He didn't truly understand what he'd done wrong.

Which was precisely the problem, he belatedly realized right before everything went dark.

80

BOUND FATE

A new day dawned on a field strewn with corpses. Having recovered overnight, Elijah stood on the earthen bulwark where Ironshore's defenders had made their last stand. It was little more than a slight rise next to a trench, but from a symbolic—as well as a literal—perspective, it had been incredibly important. To Elijah, it looked like an island amid a sea of gray bodies.

"How many, do ya think?" came Kurik's familiar and gruff voice.

Elijah turned his head to see the broad-shouldered dwarf standing only a few feet behind him. He'd also been injured in the battle, though not nearly as grievously as Elijah, who'd only been a hair's breadth from death. The only reason he'd survived was due to Kurik's quick thinking with Elijah's Grove berries, which had given him a surge of vitality as well as ethera. In turn, that had given him the fuel he needed to enable his own recovery.

Still, Elijah knew how close he'd come, and he was also well aware that Kurik had saved his life. That wasn't something he would soon forget. Nor would he quickly move on from the sacrifices endured by the people of Ironshore. They'd been challenged by the orcish horde, and they'd risen to the occasion, emerging victorious. That meant something to Elijah, and he respected them all the more because they'd refused to give up.

He could empathize with that kind of attitude.

"At least ten thousand," Elijah said, looking at the carpet of corpses. It was difficult to gauge just how many orcs had assailed the small city. Yet, one thing was certain—it had been more than they'd expected. "Do you think there are more out there?"

"Probably. It's a big world."

Elijah shook his head. "Did you ask around about that shield?" he asked. In the immediate aftermath of the battle, Elijah had been in no position to remember things properly. However, since his recovery, he'd recalled that someone had used a spell to shield him from the orcish warlord's onslaught. Likely, that had saved his life. So, he'd asked Kurik to find out who he should thank for that intervention.

"Oh. That," said the dwarf.

"What?"

"I found out, though it's not the happy endin' you might want for," Kurik answered. "You remember Calix?"

"I do," Elijah answered. Indeed, he'd seen the little goblin who was the lone survivor of the ill-fated expedition to his island on more than one occasion. However, he hadn't really spoken to her, largely because of the fear he had seen in her eyes.

"It was her," Kurik explained. "Took a spear to the gut for her trouble, too. Didn't make it."

"Shit," Elijah muttered, hanging his head. It wasn't as if he'd really known the goblin. And his choice to let her live had been the result of a whim rather than an attempt at mercy. Yet, he didn't know how to react to the knowledge that she had not only saved his live, but she'd died in the process.

"Wasn't for you," Kurik stated. "She knew you were the only one who could save us, so the girl made the only reasonable choice she could."

"I suppose."

That statement, while probably true, still didn't help with Elijah's roiling emotions.

"Got any more of them berries?" Kurik asked.

"Oh," Elijah said. "Sure."

Then, he unshouldered his pack, reached inside, and handed Kurik a handful. The dwarf ate them appreciatively, then said, "They ain't the best taste, and they're a mite too much for me. But damn if they ain't reinvigorating."

"They are that," Elijah stated. Then, he asked, "What are they going to do with all the corpses?"

"Burn 'em, I suppose. Why?"

Elijah shrugged. "They're not useful?"

"Not anymore. 'Cept the brains you asked for. We got to those in time. Most of the rest went bad too quick to harvest," Kurik answered. "Not that anybody was lookin' forward to using it, course. They look too close to people, see. Puts everyone off, even if we all know they're just monsters like any other."

"I can see that," Elijah said. There was a clay vessel filled with the brains in question inside his bag, but he'd yet to really look at them. "Doesn't really feel like we won."

"But we did," Kurik said. "And most of us got the levels to prove it. This little battle probably single-handedly ensured that Ironshore'll survive for years to come. Most of these people are used to levelin' from craftin' and such. That's slow, but it's steady. Killin' that many orcs was enough to push most of 'em to the next ability or technique threshold. That's big."

"You get anything good?" asked Elijah.

"I did."

"Want to share?"

"Nope."

Elijah sighed. "Fair enough," he said.

After that, the two remained silent for a few minutes until Elijah said, "Thanks again for saving my life. I'll pay you back. I promise."

"You saved my home," Kurik said. "That's payback enough."

"Still . . ."

"Don't worry 'bout it," the dwarf insisted. "Friends don't keep score, right?"

Elijah nodded. Until that moment, he hadn't really considered the idea that he and Kurik were friends, but in retrospect, it was obvious. After spending so much time together in the wilderness, he felt more comfortable around the dwarf than he had with anyone since the world had ended. Perhaps even more than anyone from his old life, except Alyssa. Because there was something about going to war with someone that forged a much more meaningful bond. Next to that, his previous friendships felt shallow.

"You should come to my island," Elijah said. "I think you'd like it."

"Last folks who went to your island ended up pretty dead."

"That's not true. Ramik and Carisa have visited twice."

"They didn't go no farther than the beach," Kurik stated. "That don't count."

"This is different. You're invited," Elijah countered. "But no worries if you're not comfortable with it."

"Oh, I'll come. I just wanted to ruffle your feathers a bit's all," the dwarf said with a chuckle. "But for now, I got work to do. Me and some of the other scouts are goin' to make sure there ain't no more orcs out there. You want to come?"

Elijah shook his head. "Not unless you need me," he answered. He'd had enough orc slaughter for two lifetimes, and he wasn't eager to revisit that situation. He would if necessary, but so long as there was a choice, he knew which side of the fence he'd land on. "Besides, I need to talk to Ramik about something."

"Alright then," Kurik said. He extended a hand, which Elijah grasped. "See you soon, then."

"See you soon."

With that, Kurik started to pick his way across the battlefield. Only then did it occur to Elijah that the dwarf had likely volunteered to search for any orcish stragglers in an effort to avoid the cleanup.

Smiling wryly, Elijah turned and descended the berm and started back to the city. As he did, he checked his gains from the battle. First, he noted that he'd gained level fifty-five, as denoted by his updated status:

Name	Elijah Hart
Level	55
Archetype	Druid

Class	Animist		
Specialization	N/A		
Alignment	N/A		
Strength	56		
Dexterity	55		
Constitution	56		
Ethera	64		
Regeneration	58		
Attunement	Nature		
Cultivation Stage: Cultivator			
Body	Core	Mind	Soul
Wood	Hatchling	Quartz	Neophyte

His attributes, even without the benefit of his many enhancements—or buffs, as the people in Argos and Norcastle called them—had become truly impressive. And he knew that with every level, they would become more so. He'd already proved that, from a physical standpoint, he could stand against some incredibly powerful monsters, and he couldn't help but wonder what the future would hold in that department.

However, he was far more interested in the next notification he'd received:

Congratulations! You have achieved the requirements for the evolution of the spell Ancestral Circle. Please choose a path:		
Roots of the World Tree	Protection of the World Tree	Blessing of the World Tree
By creating additional circles, you may spread your roots to new locations.	By expanding your circle, you may enhance the protection afforded by your Grove.	Through a nurturing touch, you may increase the power of your Grove.

It was the first time he'd been afforded the opportunity to evolve one of his spells or abilities, and it was far more involved than he'd expected. So far, he'd simply been awarded spells at specific intervals, but now, it seemed like his progression would require more input in the future.

For the time being, though, he had a decision to make. Based on the descriptions, which seemed a little inadequate, the choices came down to whether or not he wanted to spread his influence or empower his Grove, either via enhancing the protection it afforded or what sounded like increasing the ethera density.

Before he made a decision, he needed to talk to Nerthus to see if the tree spirit could offer any insight. He'd already checked the available guides at the Branch of the World Tree, and he'd found nothing that seemed like it would explain anything. There was precious little concerning Druids at all, and what little existed was incredibly expensive. Of course, it didn't help that none of it was organized in any way that Elijah could understand, so searching for applicable information was a pain.

Apparently, there were classes that specialized in such things, but Ironshore wasn't large or important enough to warrant such people.

In any case, Nerthus offered the best chance of solid information, so he embraced the teleportation portion of Ancestral Circle, and a moment later, he disappeared only to rematerialize in his Grove. Once there, he called out for Nerthus. When he appeared, Elijah let him know what had happened in the battle with the orcs, then broached the subject of his evolutionary path.

"Interesting," said Nerthus as he paced back and forth. As he scratched his chin, Elijah couldn't help but notice that the tree spirit's mannerisms—and speech patterns—had become quite a bit more human of late. He wondered if that was his influence or if it was a normal development for tree spirits. "The first will almost assuredly let you create a teleportation network. The second will allow you to establish a defensive perimeter that will protect the island from would-be invaders. And the third will increase the ethereal density of the Grove."

"Are you sure?" Elijah asked.

"Reasonably so," Nerthus said. Then, he admitted, "However, I should point out that these are guesses. The reality could very well be quite different from what I've inferred from those descriptions. That is unlikely, given the straightforward language used."

"The choice is obvious, then."

"Is it? All three seem very useful," Nerthus stated. "Though there are some caveats to that sentiment."

"Oh? It seems to me that we should increase the ethereal density," Elijah said. His reasoning was simple—according to everything he'd read, advancing his cultivation required incredibly dense ethera. If his Grove could naturally provide that, then he would be halfway to reaching the next stages of his development.

"That is a mistake," Nerthus stated.

"Really? I was thinking that my cultivation—"

"It would be useful, but the timing is troubling," Nerthus said. "Unless I am wrong in my assessment, the increase in density will be multiplicative based on current levels. That means that it would be far more useful to wait until Earth's ethereal density settles. That will be years from now."

That made sense. If he were to do it now, then he'd be giving up long-term benefits for a short-term boost in power. From Nerthus's perspective, that probably seemed like an incredibly poor choice. However, Elijah also knew that that presupposed that he would survive long enough to take advantage of those long-term benefits, which was not guaranteed. Getting the boost that increasing his cultivation stage would provide would no doubt go a long way to ensuring his survival.

"What about the defense one?" Elijah asked, still mulling over the other option.

"Very helpful," Nerthus admitted. "It would have helped with the orcish invasion, certainly. The city on the shore would not benefit, but it might have been enough to let the Grove endure."

That seemed straightforward enough, though Elijah wasn't sure what form that defense might take. So, he asked, "And the other one?"

"Mobility will be very important. Teleportation is extremely expensive," Nerthus stated. "Prohibitively so. If you can move around the world without having to pay that, you will be able to afford many things you otherwise would not."

"So, I could theoretically have a teleportation point that would let me cross the world in an instant?" Elijah asked.

"Assuredly."

"Interesting."

"It should also be noted that you will not evolve the spell immediately. These things require the completion of a quest," Nerthus said. "The more powerful the spell, the more time-consuming the quest. You will also likely be afforded the opportunity to choose the other two options at some point in the future."

"So, it makes sense to take the most immediately impactful."

"Likely, with the aforementioned caveats."

That made Elijah's decision, so he made his choice.

Congratulations! You have chosen to evolve Ancestral Circle into Roots of the World Tree. Complete the following quest to finalize the evolution:

Accomplish two feats of Strength (Complete)

Conquer one tower (Complete)

Build a dolmen (Incomplete)

"Oh. Nice," Elijah said. "Two steps already finished. Only one to go. Apparently, I need to build a dolmen."

From what Elijah remembered, a dolmen was something like Stonehenge. Which meant that he had his work cut out for him. He explained everything to Nerthus, who told him that those dolmens would likely constitute the teleportation points. So, he wouldn't be able to just build the dolmen anywhere he wanted. Instead, he needed to find a proper location first. And he had some ideas about where he wanted to put it.

So, with that taken care of, Elijah collected his things, making sure to stock up on berries, and headed to his rowboat collection—which was dwindling with each time he teleported back to his island—and paddled across the strait and into Ironshore. Once he reached the dock, he set off for the city's governmental building, where he hoped to find Ramik.

Along the way, Elijah noticed two things. First, the residents of the city were incredibly busy in the aftermath of the battle. Some had been tasked with cleaning up the battlefield, while others were repairing damage wreaked by a few orcs who'd broken through the line and descended upon the city. Still others were organizing supplies for the survivors. It was a nice reminder that, when disaster struck, people tended to band together. That those people were gnomes, dwarves, and goblins—as well as a few elves—was immaterial, and it warmed Elijah's heart to see everyone working toward the greater good. Hopefully, that would last.

The second thing he saw was more of an absence than anything else. Gone were the dirty looks and angry glances he'd endured before. There was still fear there, but they didn't seem to hate him. That was progress, at least as far as Elijah was concerned.

Eventually, Elijah reached the governmental headquarters and found Ramik, who looked as busy as anyone else Elijah had seen during his trek through the city. Still, the goblin was quick to greet him, asking, "What can I do for you?"

"I came for my payment," Elijah said.

"Oh. That. What can we give you? Our etherium—"

"I don't want money," Elijah interrupted. "I want cooperation. A friendship, maybe. At least an alliance."

"I . . . I think we can do that," Ramik stated.

"So, here's what I'm thinking I want . . ."

After Elijah explained his plan, and Ramik agreed enthusiastically, he went in search of a perfect location. So it happened that the next day—after Elijah had spent another night in the Imperium—he found himself standing in the center of Ironshore. Ramik had held up his end of the bargain, clearing the large plaza and ripping up the flagstones that had once covered the ground.

Elijah stood in the center, alongside Ramik and Carisa, and looked at the gathered townspeople. Almost everyone was there, though there were some exceptions—most notably, that some familiar faces were missing. Two of the three Barbers had perished in the fight, as had Calix and a couple of the Guards who'd once escorted Elijah through town. Some, like the Tailor Mari, bore visible scars, but most just looked exhausted.

Ramik spoke, his voice loud and clear, "People of Ironshore! We have endured a powerful calamity, and we have survived, not least because of the actions of our friend and ally, Elijah Hart. His benevolence does not end there, though. As a Druid, he has chosen to bless our city by planting a very special tree. Henceforth, this square shall be known as Druid's Park, and any who deface it shall be severely punished."

Elijah remained silent, though his gaze was enough to make some of the townspeople flinch. Hopefully, that would be enough to dissuade anyone who might harm the tree he intended to plant. If not, then there were more direct methods available.

With that, Elijah retrieved the seed he'd taken from the ancestral tree, then planted it in the hole he'd already dug. After covering it, he summoned Healing Rain, then sat cross-legged next to where he'd planted the seed. Closing his eyes, he flared Nature's Bounty.

Like that, days passed, and Elijah healed in ways he didn't think possible. Because of One with Nature, he was aware of people coming to take advantage of the rejuvenating properties of Healing Rain. That brought a smile to his face. After all, he'd always liked healing people.

On the fifth day, Elijah felt the seed sprout. And on the sixth, it had become a tiny seedling. That was when Elijah finally opened his eyes and took a deep breath. Already, the park had begun to flourish, with grass having sprouted. There were other small plants, as well, but most importantly, the tree had taken root. Now, it didn't need his guidance, though he fully intended to usher it into the sapling stage.

So, after eating a few berries, Elijah closed his eyes and continued the cycle.

81

THE DEAL

Carmen struggled against her bonds, though it was no good. She'd tried to use her various techniques to escape, but they were all meant to bind things together, rather than to tear things apart. Her lone ability meant for that kind of thing was only useful on metal, so in her current situation, she had nothing. Perhaps one of her future abilities would fill that void.

If there was a future.

She was well aware of how dire her situation was, which made that a dubious prospect. After she and Colt had been captured, they'd been thrust into a cage—which had taken the form of an old clothing store—where they'd rotted for the past few days. It was only recently that they'd been released from that prison, though freedom wasn't precisely what it was cracked up to be. One of their captors had put bags over their heads, then guided them outside before tossing them into what seemed like the bed of a pickup truck.

That was where she still was, being jostled as the truck sped across what felt like the world's bumpiest road. Not that she was that concerned with comfort at the moment. For three days, she'd beaten herself up over her mistakes. The first was when she'd tried to ally herself with the rebels, but in her anger and desperation, she had made plenty since then, as well. It had all culminated in the kidnapping of her son as well as the deaths of the people who'd followed her.

The only survivor was Colt, and he wasn't doing so well. More than once, he'd tried to escape, and they'd beaten him bloody. If that was the extent of it, Carmen wouldn't have been so worried about him, but they'd also taken his sword hand, lopping it off at the wrist, then having a Healer stop the bleeding.

Even then, Colt had never stopped struggling for escape. Neither had Carmen, but they'd treated her much more gently. So, she at least had all her limbs—which was no comfort, considering the worry she held for not only her own fate, but for her son's, as well. There was no telling what Trace had done to the boy.

Eventually, the truck pulled to a stop, and Carmen heard a muffled conversation that suggested they'd arrived in Easton. That wasn't surprising. After all, Laramie and his war band had clearly made a deal with Roman. But rather than fury, Carmen just felt exhausted. If there was one thing she'd discovered, it was that she wasn't cut out for leadership. She wanted to be, but she simply didn't have the temperament. She was too selfish. Too volatile.

Those thoughts occupied Carmen's mind as the truck entered the city. She knew from experience that vehicles weren't allowed far past the gates, so she wasn't surprised when they came to a stop only a few minutes later. Then, one of Laramie's goons grabbed her and threw her over a shoulder. Presumably, Colt received similar treatment, and like that, they were taken through the city.

More muffled conversation followed them along the way, but Carmen couldn't hear well enough to understand any of it. However, she did smell plenty of smoke as well as the unmistakable odor of blood and death. Something had happened in the city, she reasoned. Something terrible.

It seemed that that was all the new world had to offer.

Eventually, the smells faded, and the murmurs took on a much more aggressive tone. Carmen wasn't certain whether that was for her or for her barbaric captors, but she didn't think it mattered so much. The people of Easton weren't important. Only the man at the top.

Still, it felt like an eternity before the cool and conditioned air of what Carmen assumed was Roman's ridiculous palace assailed her, but it wasn't long after that when she was unceremoniously dumped onto a tile floor. Someone ripped the black hood from her head, and she blinked in the glaring light.

That's when she saw him.

"Miggy!" she shouted, struggling to go to her son. It was no good, though. With her hands and feet bound, she couldn't do anything more than flop over. For his part, Miguel raced to her side and buried his head in her shoulder, muttering one apology after another. She soothed him by saying, "It's okay. You didn't do anything wrong."

"He's a good kid," came the voice of the man who'd been standing behind Miguel. Carmen looked up to see Roman staring down at her, his gaze intense and predatory. "I'm sorry for what happened. If it makes any difference, the man who took your son is dead."

"Fuck you," Carmen growled. "I know what you did."

"I figured as much," Roman said. "You likely care nothing for apologies, but I am sorry. If there had been any other way, I would have taken it."

Then, he gestured toward Miguel, and one of his lackeys stepped forward to drag her son away. Carmen started to protest, but when Roman insisted that he wouldn't be harmed, she let it go, telling Miguel that everything would be okay. She didn't need to be told that Roman held all the cards. They were completely at his mercy, and Carmen knew precisely how thin that could be. So, she chose to subdue her fury and play along.

Once Miguel was out of the room, she said, "What do you want? Why am I still alive?"

"Straight to the point."

"Oh, I'm sorry. Did you want to enjoy a beer together? Reminisce about old times? Like when you killed my fucking wife?"

"Fair," Roman sighed. Then, he glanced at another lackey, saying, "Stand her up and put her in a chair. We can do that much, at least."

After that, the Guard—another man in blue and white—dragged her to her feet before shoving her onto a leather couch. That's when Carmen took in her surroundings, and what she saw was a grotesquerie of ridiculous trophies. Stuffed heads of monsters Roman had presumably killed, skulls, and a few weapons adorned the walls, giving it the air of a man who was trying far too hard to appear strong and deadly.

But Carmen didn't need convincing. She knew that Roman was a snake in a person suit, and though she didn't respect him as a man, she was more than wary of his lethality.

Shifting, she asked, "So, now that we're comfortable, what do you want?"

Roman, who was leaning against the edge of a monstrous slab of a desk, said, "I want your services. You make me a weapon to the best of your abilities. I'll provide the materials. All I care about is the product."

"Or what? You'll kill me?"

"No."

"No?"

"I'm not a monster, Carmen. I don't kill people unnecessarily. And the fact of the matter is that you are powerless now. The rebels have pitched their fit, and they have been punished accordingly. Their leaders are dead. Laramie has agreed to a truce. And everyone loyal to you has been captured or killed. You are no longer a threat to me, so I see no reason to kill you. After this, I intend to let you go. We'll call it banishment. You will no longer be welcome in Easton. But I won't kill you. And I certainly won't do anything to your son. You have my word on it. No matter what else happens here, he'll be safe."

"Is this where you take him hostage or something?" Carmen asked, noting the ambiguous wording.

"Of course not. What do I want with a child? He'll go with you."

"I refuse."

"You haven't heard the rest of it," Roman said. "You do want your people to survive, don't you? What about your friend there? He's a powerful fighter. Shame about his hand, but your captors had to take precautions."

Carmen glanced at Colt, who hadn't moved since she'd had her hood removed. He was still breathing, but he was clearly unconscious. "So, you're going to kill a bunch of other people if I don't build you a weapon. Is that it?"

"It is."

"What kind of weapon? I don't know how to make a proper bow."

"A longsword," Roman answered. "The specifications will be forthcoming once you agree."

There really wasn't much of a choice. Even if he was lying, Carmen could never refuse, if only because of the possibility that Roman would make good on his promise. If he didn't, then Carmen was no better or worse off for having tried. Certainly, she didn't want to give him anything that would make him more powerful, but given the options before her, she didn't see as she could make any other decision.

So, Carmen said, "Fine. I'll do it."

"Really? Just like that?" Roman asked.

"There's not much choice, is there? You're going to kill a bunch of people if I don't. If you think I'm going to make any other decision, you obviously don't know me."

"Perhaps," he allowed. "Maybe I never did."

After that anticlimactic exchange, Roman called for a Healer to take care of Colt. Then, he had someone show Carmen to a forge in the lower reaches of the palace. There, she was given access to a pile of cold-iron ingots and enough ethereal coal to run the forge for a month. She didn't think she'd need that long, though.

As she started working, she considered trying to build a flaw into the weapon or giving it less than her best effort. However, she ultimately chose not to for a couple of reasons. The first was that she wasn't certain how to do the former, and the second was that she was afraid that giving Roman an inferior product would result in the execution of the people she hoped to save. That would have negated the whole decision, so when she embarked on the quest to forge the weapon, she did so with every ounce of skill she possessed.

So, after using Decontaminate and Refine Material on the metal billets, she stacked them atop one another until she had a dozen layers. Then, she shoved the result into the forge so they would weld together. Normally, she would've used Bind to shorten the process, but with the ethereal coal—and so much of it that she didn't have to ration it—she could afford to do it the old-fashioned way. That, in turn, meant that the resulting billet would have been exposed to more ethera, and theoretically, it would have a higher ceiling in terms of quality.

After completing the forge weld, Carmen started in on shaping the piece. The specifications she'd received were simple. Just a typical longsword with a cruciform hilt and a two-inch-wide blade forty-two inches long. Completing the design was a fuller that ran along the length of the blade.

Shaping the piece took quite some time, due to the curious trait of cold iron causing heat to dissipate very quickly, but Carmen was used to working with it. So, she persisted until, what felt like a day later, she completed the blade. However, that didn't mean the project was done. Instead, it was only the beginning.

The next step was to create the cross guard, which required much the same technique, yet with a different aim. This time, after forging a bar in the right length, she used a drift to hammer a hole in the center. Once that was done,

Carmen used Summon Tool to manifest a file so she could shape the hole into a slot that would fit the blade's tang.

It was an arduous and tedious process, but she found the monotonous work soothing. Eventually, Carmen managed to complete the cross guard before slipping it into place. It was close to a perfect fit, and she used Bind to weld the pair together. Just like that, she had a sword, though a crudely shaped and dull one without a proper hilt.

After ensuring that everything fit together properly, Carmen used the forge's grinder to refine the blade into its final shape. Sparks flew as she removed the unneeded metal until, hours later, she was left with a perfectly crafted sword blade. Even the cross guard followed the specifications exactly.

Next came the heat treatment. So, Carmen shoved the entire blade into the forge, then waited for it to reach the proper temperature before summoning a pair of tongs and removing the metal from the forge. Moving quickly, she dropped the blade into a barrel of heated oil. Flames shot toward the ceiling, but because of Resist Fire, Carmen ignored them. Instead, she listened for any tinging sounds that might indicate that the blade had cracked.

She heard nothing, and when she removed the blade, she saw that it was entirely straight. That was a relief because Carmen knew how easily such a long blade could warp.

After that, Carmen created a handle from a block of wood, then fitted it onto the tang. Using Bind, she then attached a pommel and wrapped the handle in soft leather that she then adhered to the wood using her ability.

That completed the sword, though Carmen still needed to add the embellishments as well as the enchantment. For the first embellishment, Carmen spent quite some time filing the likeness of a dragon's head onto the pommel. The second came when she embedded a pair of onyx gemstones on either end of the cross guard.

To her, it looked a little ostentatious, but she was working from Roman's specifications. So, Carmen reasoned that if he wanted the weapon to look like some edgy teenager's idea of a perfect sword, then that was what he would get. The stakes were too high for her to place artistic integrity over the lives of her people.

Once that was finished, she used Bind to ensure the onyx gemstones would never move.

Sighing, she looked at the weapon. She still hadn't sharpened the blade, but it was already beautiful, with a Damascus pattern dancing along the blue-white steel. She hated that it was going to such a monster.

To complete the project, Carmen started in on the enchantment. On the surface, it was a simple task. She simply needed to carve a couple of symbols onto the weapon while using her Minor Enchantment technique. Yet, it required significant concentration as well as a steady flow of ethera. So, after taking a few deep breaths, Carmen got to work, bending her entire mind to the task. It took a lot longer than she would have preferred, but she wasn't one to cut corners. So, after etching one side of the blade, she flipped it over and used a different symbol on the other.

The enchantments themselves weren't complex. One was intended for durability, the other for sharpness. Yet, they were elegant in their own way, and when Carmen finished, she received the notification she'd sought for all those long hours:

> **Congratulations! You have created a unique item, False Dragon's Fang.**
> **Overall Grade: Simple (Peak)**
> **Enchantment Grade: F**

She let out a long, slow sigh. It was the highest-graded item she'd ever created, which came with mixed emotions. On the one hand, Carmen was proud of herself for the accomplishment. It was the culmination of long hours' worth of work as well as years of training and practice. However, at the same time, she hated that it was going to someone like Roman, who would doubtless use it for detestable purposes.

She took solace in the name, at least. While Carmen wasn't certain why the System had labeled it false, she felt it was appropriate, given Alyssa's class. To her, it said that Roman's entire position was a charade. That he was a fake. That gave her some comfort, though it was still a bitter pill to swallow, considering how everything had gone of late.

There was a lesson there, and one that Carmen had only just begun to embrace. The first part was that she was no leader. She didn't want to be responsible for anyone but herself and Miguel. But the second bit was that she needed to keep her priorities straight. Sure, imagining vengeance on Roman was an enticing thought, and she still longed to plunge the False Dragon's Fang's blade into the man's heart. Yet, she knew her priorities should be to protect Miguel and the people she'd already put in danger. So, with some regret, she sheathed her desire for vengeance while doing the same for the blade she had just created.

Once that was done, she left the forge to find a pair of blue-and-white clad Guards standing outside. They escorted her to Roman's office, where she presented the blade. He was impressed, though Carmen saw a slight tick of anger on the man's face when he was told the weapon's name.

But miraculously, Roman was as good as his word, and soon enough, Carmen found herself standing between Miguel and Colt in front of Easton's gates. Fifteen people were to her rear, and each person had been given a small pack of supplies. It was only enough for a few days' survival, but it was more than Carmen had expected.

Nobody had been allowed to take weapons or armor.

"I hate that it ended this way," Roman stated from behind them. Carmen looked back to see that the man was wearing the armor she'd made for Colt. He had the False Dragon's Fang in a scabbard at his hip.

"Me, too," Carmen said. Though, she was certain that they meant very different things. For his part, he probably regretted that she wasn't working for Easton anymore. But for Carmen's, she wished it would have ended with Roman dead at her feet. She had other priorities now, though, so she pushed those thoughts aside and told her people, "Come on. We need to get moving."

Then, without another word, she set off into the wilderness, her son's hand clutched tightly in her own.

82

HUNTER

Thor Gunderson knelt atop the hill, staring across the valley at the creature. The monster was huge, but then again, most of his prey had been of late. It was the only way to get any sort of challenge. The animal was a little bigger than an African elephant, with a long shaggy coat of soft fur that hung down to its ankles. Its head was similarly elephant-like, with a long tapered trunk, great floppy ears, and a pair of massive tusks that Thor had seen disembowel lesser creatures.

But unlike an elephant, this monster was no quadruped. Instead, it stood on two feet like a man. It was intelligent, too, having shown the ability to utilize crude tools. At present, it wielded a giant tree trunk like a club.

For his part, Thor carried a much less impressive weapon. At least on the surface, it appeared that way. But he didn't need to look at his spear to know it was far from ordinary. The haft of the spear was made of bone, and it had been carved with fanciful designs that made it look like scrimshaw. The blade was like black glass, sharper than anything else Thor had ever seen, with bloodred tassels tied just below its base.

Thor himself was far more overtly exceptional. Standing at almost seven feet tall, he had once been a champion powerlifter. After the world had been transformed, he'd utilized his massive strength to his advantage, and in the years since, he'd used that brief head start to keep himself ahead of everyone else.

Or perhaps it was his taste for a great hunt that made him special. Since the very beginning, there had been no peak he didn't try to climb, no monster—bestial or otherwise—he didn't want to hunt. He'd spent the intervening years stalking and killing one powerful creature after another, and he'd reaped the rewards of success, climbing the power ladder until he'd found himself in the top five.

Yet he'd so far been unable to bridge the gap, even after using his talents to help various groups conquer multiple towers. He'd fought in rifts. He'd slaughtered Voxx. And he'd even worked a stint as a bounty hunter. Still, the top of the ladder remained as distant as ever, and Thor's frustration had continued to mount.

The result was that he'd pushed himself into progressively more dangerous hunts, stalking prey that he should never have considered fighting. He'd even ventured into the deadly Frozen Wastes, where he'd hunted ice mammoths. He'd only skirted the edges—anything else would have killed even him—but he'd expected the lethality of the situation to work in his favor.

And it had.

Still, the gap between him and the people at the peak had remained just as wide as ever. Each time he gained a level, so did they. Sometimes, more than one. It was maddening.

Yet, Thor persisted. He knew they would slip up. Those ahead of him would make mistakes and end up dead. Or worse, their pace of improvement would slow. And then, he would pass them by. It was only a matter of time. So, with that in mind, Thor tracked his target with a steady gaze, waiting for the opportune moment to move in.

Meanwhile, the monster, which he'd identified as a tiyeto, meandered around, periodically snatching leaves from nearby trees. It was mostly carnivorous, but the creature would also eat flora if it was hungry enough. Thor decided to make his move, descending the slope on silent feet.

Before Earth had been touched by the World Tree, Thor hadn't been much of a hunter. He'd been a few times growing up, but his training schedule hadn't left much time for anything else. However, soon after the world had changed, he'd discovered the joy of stalking and killing prey. The more dangerous, the better.

Gradually, he covered the distance to the tiyeto, only stopping when he was a little more than ten feet away. Then, he forced ethera into his most important ability, Bite of the Hunter, and his spear erupted into green light. Just before the blade pierced the tiyeto's chest, the monster reacted, darting to the side. It only moved a few inches before Thor's attack landed, ripping through its shoulder and sending chunks of meat and bone flying.

But it was enough to save the monster from a one-shot kill.

Annoyed, Thor landed with a roll that a man of his size never should've been capable of, then found his feet a moment before the tiyeto's counterattack found him. He leaped backward, barely avoiding the monster's sweeping tusks, then darted forward, using the butt of his spear to knock the natural weapons aside. Then, he dipped low, twirled his spear like a quarterstaff, then stabbed the monster through the trunk.

Or that was what he'd intended.

Instead, the blade skipped off the creature's tough skin, barely leaving a scratch. That was the issue with hunting monsters that were a higher level than him. Without powerful abilities like Bite of the Hunter, his weapon was incapable of piercing through their defenses. Still, it wasn't Thor's first hunt, and he had a few more tricks up his sleeve. However, he had to be alive to play those cards, so the moment his attack failed, he used Survival of the Fittest to briefly enhance his physical attributes. The surge of Strength and Dexterity allowed

Thor to dodge the tiyeto's next attack, which came in the form of a sweeping tree trunk.

Then, he used Fury of the Stalker, and his spear took on a red sheen.

Enraged, the tiyeto trumpeted its anger before it leaped at him. Thor didn't immediately react. Instead, he waited patiently. However, when the monster's club descended, it found no resistance until slamming into the ground and sending an eruption of dirt and leaves into the air. That's when Thor, having used Mirror Trap, attacked it from behind. This time, his spear, enhanced by Fury of the Stalker, bit deep into the monster's torso, ripping through its organs and sending an explosion of ethera to do even more damage.

The creature let out another trumpet of rage, but it quickly turned into agony. And, finally, despair.

Thor stabbed it again, this time in the small of its back. Its legs went limp, and it fell to the ground. The once-mighty monster flopped around, swinging its club ineffectually as Thor watched from just out of range. It was pitiful how easily it had fallen. Only thirty seconds, and it was all but dead.

He stood there for a long while, gazing upon the creature as it bled out. Finally, he tired of the show and stepped in, raking his spear across the tiyeto's throat. It finally died thirty seconds later, giving Thor an influx of experience that pushed him to level sixty.

Then, he let out a roar of exultation as he thrust his spear to the sky. Once he did, he looked at the power rankings:

Planetary Power Rankings (Earth)

Oscar Ramirez—Level 61
Sadie Song—Level 60
Thor Gunderson—Level 60
Hu Shui—Level 58
Niko Song—Level 57
Elijah Hart—Level 55
Anupriya Pandey—Level 53
Ram Khandu—Level 52
Gunnar Lindstrom—Level 49

. . .

. . .

. . .

"Number three," he said to himself. By all accounts, it had been an impressive climb, but to him, it was still inadequate. The only result that would satisfy him was to reach the very top and stay there. Anything less was failure. But Thor also knew that success was not built by a single action. It was a winding road, and one comprised by many steps. He'd just taken a big one, and as a result, he had come close to achieving his goals.

Part of that was the next notification he received, which confirmed that he'd gained another new ability:

Ability: Ancestor's Torpor	Summon an ancestral spirit that saps the Strength and Dexterity of your enemy. Duration based on Ethera attribute. Current cooldown: Nineteen (19) seconds.

That had the potential to be a strong ability, though Thor would not make any determinations on its viability until he had the chance to test it out. Still, he'd yet to be disappointed in the skills, spells, or abilities he'd received so far, and he was fairly certain this would follow that same pattern.

"Impressive skill, young one," came a voice from behind him.

Thor wheeled around, identified his target, and leaped. His spear passed through the small creature's head, though he met no resistance whatsoever. He crashed into the ground, his spear sliding into the loamy turf. Expecting an attack, he dove forward, ripping the spear from the ground, and whipped around.

The enemy had not moved.

"Honestly, that's how you react? I didn't even— Oh, you're attacking again."

Indeed, Thor had just thrust his spear through the seemingly insubstantial little man, and it was just as effective as the last attack. Which was to say, not at all. A few more fruitless attacks, and Thor finally pulled back, breathing hard.

"What is going on?" he demanded. "Are you a ghost?"

"That is an interesting question," the little man said. He was no taller than three feet, and he was built like a child. However, he bore a thick red beard and a truly impressive mustache. Coupled with the wrinkled face, bushy eyebrows, and bald head, he looked like a tiny old man. "I'm not dead, but this is a projection of my spirit. Sadly, it's the only way I can visit your wonderfully wild planet."

"I don't understand."

"Of course you don't," the little man said, shaking his head. "I am not of Earth. You have met off-worlders before, yes?"

Thor nodded.

"Not very verbose, are you? Oh well. I'm not here for conversation," he said. "My name is Eason Edmund, clan patriarch of . . . You know what? You don't know what any of that means, do you? Of course not. You're an unlearned and uninformed barbarian— Oh, you're attacking again."

Thor certainly didn't enjoy being called a barbarian, so he'd done what he always did when he didn't like something—attack. It did no more good than his previous attempts to teach the little man some manners.

"If you're done?" said Eason Edmund with a sigh. Thor backed away, still wary. "Good. I am here with an opportunity."

He waved a hand, and a notification bloomed into being before Thor's inner eye:

A powerful entity has offered you a Task:
Objective:
Hunt the Druid (Elijah Hart)
Reward:
Blessing of the Gnome Eason Edmund
Do you accept?

"Blessing? What does that mean?" asked Thor.

"Oh, you can read. Good," Eason Edmund said. "The blessing will give you two options. Either a spell that mimics one of my own abilities or the advancement of your Core."

"And all I have to do is hunt someone?" Thor asked. He recognized the name from the seventh spot on the power rankings.

"Yes."

"Why?" asked Thor.

"Call it family pride," Eason Edmund said. "He took something from me and mine. Now, we weren't exactly using it. Cast it aside, really. But it was still ours. So, he will be punished."

"When you tell me to hunt him, do you mean . . ."

"Oh. Right. That wording is a bit ambiguous. You are the punishment. Kill him. Get a reward. That is the deal. Do you accept?"

Thor didn't need to think about it before he nodded and affirmed it in his System notifications.

"Good. Very good. I can't risk telling you where he is, but you should find him in that direction." The little creature pointed off to the southwest. "That is all the help I can give you, so I hope you are as good of a hunter as I think you are," Eason Edmund said.

"I am the best hunter in the world," Thor said. Then, without another word, he set off through the woods.

Somewhere behind him, a little gnome grinned broadly.

ABOUT THE AUTHOR

Nicholas Searcy is the author of Death: Genesis, Mistrunner, and Path of Dragons, originally released on Royal Road. He enjoys writing, reading, spending time with family, sports, and, of course, a good cup of coffee.

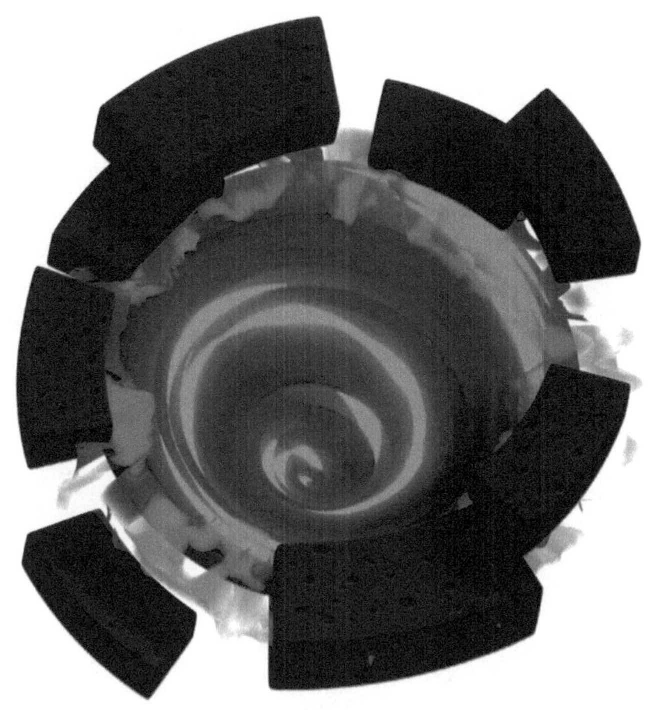

RESPAWN YOUR CURIOSITY

follow us on our socials

podiumentertainment.com

@podiumentertainment

/podiumentertainment

@podium_ent

@podiumentertainment

www.ingramcontent.com/pod-product-compliance
Lightning Source LLC
Chambersburg PA
CBHW031056130726
47906CB00008B/389